Contents

PART I. BOYS TOGETHER..6
    I. 6
    II. 7
    III. 10
    IV. 12
    V. 15
    VI. 18
    VII. 21
    VIII. 23
    IX. 24
    X. 26
    XI. 27
PART II. BOY AND GIRL...28
    I. 28
    II. 31
    III. 33
    IV. 35
    V. 36
    VI. 39
    VII. 40
    VIII. 41
    IX. 42
    X. 43
    XI. 44
    XII. 47
    XIII. 48
    XIV. 49
    XV. 50
    XVI. 51
    XVII. 52
    XVIII. 53
    XIX. 54
    XX. 55
    XXI. 56
    XXII. 57
    XXIII. 59
    XXIV. 63
PART III. MAN AND WOMAN 64
    I. 64
    II. 65
    III. 67
    IV. 68
    V. 69
    VI. 70

VII...71
VIII...74
IX...74
X...79
XI...81
XII..83
XIII...85
XIV...86
XV..87
XVI...88
XVII..89
XVIII...91
XIX...92
XX..93
XXI...94
XXII..96
XXIII...97
XXIV...99
XXV...100
PART IV. MAN AND WIFE...102
I...102
II..103
III...105
IV...106
V..107
VI...107
VII..108
VIII...109
IX...111
X..113
XI...115
    Philip turned pale. "What is it?" he asked.................................115
XII..118
XIII...119
XIV...121
XV..123
XVI...125
XVII..126
XVIII...128
XIX...130
PART V. MAN AND MAN..134
I...134
II..135
III...137
IV...139
V..141
VI...142
VII..144
VIII...147

IX. 148
X. 150
XI. 151
XII. 152
XIII. 153
XIV. 155
XV. 156
XVI. 156
XVII. 159
XVIII. 160
XIX. 162
XX. 164
XXI. 164
XXII. 166
XXIII. 168
XXIV. 169
PART VI. MAN AND GOD. 170
I. 170
II. 171
III. 172
IV. 174
V. 176
VI. 177
VII. 178
VIII. 181
   The Deemster in the half-lit Court-house was passing sentence. 181
IX. 182
X. 184
XI. 187
XII. 188
XIII. 191
XIV. 193
XV. 196
XVI. 196
XVII. 197
XVIII. 198
XIX. 201
XX. 202
XXI. 202
XXII. 205
XXIII. 207

PART I. BOYS TOGETHER.

I.

Old Deemster Christian of Ballawhaine was a hard man—hard on the outside, at all events. They called him Iron Christian, and people said, "Don't turn that iron hand against you." Yet his character was stamped with nobleness as well as strength. He was not a man of icy nature, but he loved to gather icicles about him. There was fire enough underneath, at which he warmed his old heart when alone, but he liked the air to be congealed about his face. He was a man of a closed soul. One had to wrench open the dark chamber where he kept his feelings; but the man who had done that had uncovered his nakedness, and he cut him off for ever. That was how it happened with his son, the father of Philip.

He had two sons; the elder was an impetuous creature, a fiery spirit, one of the masterful souls who want the restraint of the curb if they are not to hurry headlong into the abyss. Old Deemster Christian had called this boy Thomas Wilson, after the serene saint who had once been Bishop of Man. He was intended, however, for the law, not for the Church. The office of Deemster never has been and never can be hereditary; yet the Christians of Ballawhaine had been Deemsters through six generations, and old Iron Christian expected that Thomas Wilson Christian would succeed him. But there was enough uncertainty about the succession to make merit of more value than precedent in the selection, and so the old man had brought up his son to the English bar, and afterwards called him to practise in the Manx one. The young fellow had not altogether rewarded his father's endeavours. During his residence in England, he had acquired certain modern doctrines which were highly obnoxious to the old Deemster. New views on property, new ideas about woman and marriage, new theories concerning religion (always re-christened superstition), the usual barnacles of young vessels fresh from unknown waters; but the old man was no shipwright in harbour who has learnt the art of removing them without injury to the hull. The Deemster knew these notions when he met with them in the English newspapers. There was something awesome in their effect on his stay-at-home imagination, as of vices confusing and difficult to true men that walk steadily; but, above all, very far off, over the mountains and across the sea, like distant cities of Sodom, only waiting for Sodom's doom. And yet, lo! here they were in a twinkling, shunted and shot into his own house and his own stackyard.

"I suppose now," he said, with a knowing look, "you think Jack as good as his master?"

"No, sir," said his son gravely; "generally much better."

Iron Christian altered his will. To his elder son he left only a life-interest in Ballawhaine. "That boy will be doing something," he said, and thus he guarded against consequences. He could not help it; he was ashamed, but he could not conquer his shame—the fiery old man began to nurse a grievance against his son.

The two sons of the Deemster were like the inside and outside of a bowl, and that bowl was the Deemster himself. If Thomas Wilson the elder had his father's inside fire and softness, Peter, the younger, had his father's outside ice and iron. Peter was little and almost misshapen, with a pair of shoulders that seemed to be trying to meet over a hollow chest and limbs that splayed away into vacancy. And if Nature had been grudging with him, his father was not more kind. He had been brought up to no profession, and his expectations were limited to a yearly charge out of his brother's property. His talk was bitter, his voice cold, he laughed little, and had never been known to cry. He had many things against him.

Besides these sons, Deemster Christian had a girl in his household, but to his own consciousness the fact was only a kind of peradventure. She was his niece, the child of his only brother, who had died in early manhood. Her name was Ann Charlotte de la Tremouille, called after the lady of Rushen, for the family of Christian had their share of the heroic that is in all men. She had fine eyes, a weak mouth, and great timidity. Gentle airs floated always about her, and a sort of nervous brightness twinkled over her, as of a glen with the sun flickering through. Her mother died when she was a child of twelve, and in the house of her uncle and her cousins she had been brought up among men and boys.

One day Peter drew the Deemster aside and told him (with expressions of shame, interlarded with praises of his own acuteness) a story of his brother. It was about a girl. Her name was Mona Crellin; she lived on the hill at Ballure House, half a mile south of Ramsey, and was daughter of a man called Billy Ballure, a retired sea-captain, and hail-fellow-well-met with all the jovial spirits of the town.

There was much noise and outcry, and old Iron sent for his son.

6

"What's this I hear?" he cried, looking him down. "A woman? So that's what your fine learning comes to, eh? Take care, sir! take care! No son of mine shall disgrace himself. The day he does that he will be put to the door."

Thomas held himself in with a great effort.

"Disgrace?" he said. "What disgrace, sir, if you please?"

"What disgrace, sir?" repeated the Deemster, mocking his son in a mincing treble. Then he roared, "Behaving dishonourably to a poor girl—that what's disgrace, sir! Isn't it enough? eh? eh?"

"More than enough," said the young man. "But who is doing it? I'm not."

"Then you're doing worse. *Did* I say worse? Of course I said worse. Worse, sir, worse! Do you hear me? Worse! You are trapsing around Ballure, and letting that poor girl take notions. I'll have no more of it. Is this what I sent you to England for? Aren't you ashamed of yourself? Keep your place, sir; keep your place. A poor girl's a poor girl, and a Deemster's a Deemster."

"Yes, sir," said Thomas, suddenly firing up, "and a man's a man. As for the shame, I need be ashamed of nothing that is not shameful; and the best proof I can give you that I mean no dishonour by the girl is that I intend to marry her."

"What? You intend to—what? Did I hear——"

The old Deemster turned his good ear towards his son's face, and the young man repeated his threat. Never fear! No poor girl should be misled by him. He was above all foolish conventions.

Old Iron Christian was dumbfounded. He gasped, he stared, he stammered, and then fell on his son with hot reproaches.

"What? Your wife? Wife? That trollop!—that minx! that—and daughter of that sot, too, that old rip, that rowdy blatherskite—that—— And my own son is to lift his hand to cut his throat! Yes, sir, cut his throat——And I am to stand by! No, no! I say no, sir, no!"

The young man made some further protest, but it was lost in his father's clamour.

"You will, though? You will? Then your hat is your house, sir. Take to it—take to it!"

"No need to tell me twice, father."

"Away then—away to your woman—your jade! God, keep my hands off him!"

The old man lifted his clenched fist, but his son had flung out of the room. It was not the Deemster only who feared he might lay hands on his own flesh and blood.

"Stop! come back, you dog! Listen! I've not done yet. Stop! you hotheaded rascal, stop! Can't you hear a man out then? Come back! Thomas Wilson, come back, sir! Thomas! Thomas! Tom! Where is he? Where's the boy?"

Old Iron Christian had made after his son bareheaded down to the road, shouting his name in a broken roar, but the young man was gone. Then he went back slowly, his grey hair playing in the wind. He was all iron outside, but all father within.

That day the Deemster altered his will a second time, and his elder son was disinherited.

II.

Peter succeeded in due course to the estate of Ballawhaine, but he was not a lawyer, and the line of the Deemsters Christian was broken.

Meantime Thomas Wilson Christian had been married to Mona Crellin without delay. He loved her, but he had been afraid of her ignorance, afraid also (notwithstanding his principles) of the difference in their social rank, and had half intended to give her up when his father's reproaches had come to fire his anger and to spur his courage. As soon as she became his wife he realised the price he had paid for her. Happiness could not come of such a beginning. He had broken every tie in making the one which brought him down. The rich disowned him, and the poor lost respect for him.

"It's positively indecent," said one. "It's potatoes marrying herrings," said another. It was little better than hunger marrying thirst.

In the general downfall of his fame his profession failed him. He lost heart and ambition. His philosophy did not stand him in good stead, for it had no value in the market to which he brought it. Thus, day by day, he sank deeper into the ooze of a wrecked and wasted life.

The wife did not turn out well. She was a fretful person, with a good face, a bad shape, a vacant mind, and a great deal of vanity. She had liked her husband a little as a lover, but when she saw that her marriage brought her nobody's envy, she fell into a long fit of the vapours. Eventually she made herself believe that she was an ill-used person. She never ceased to complain of her fate. Everybody treated her as if she had laid plans for her husband's ruin.

The husband continued to love her, but little by little he grew to despise her also. When he made his first plunge, he had prided himself on indulging an heroic impulse. He was not going to deliver a good woman to dishonour because she seemed to be an obstacle to his success. But she had never realised his sacrifice. She did not appear to understand that he might have been a great man in the island, but that love and honour had held him back. Her ignorance was pitiful, and he was ashamed of it. In earning the contempt of others he had not saved himself from self-contempt.

The old sailor died suddenly in a fit of drunkenness at a fair, and husband and wife came into possession of his house and property at Ballure. This did not improve the relations between them. The woman perceived that their positions were reversed. She was the bread-bringer now. One day, at a slight that her husband's people had put upon her in the street, she reminded him, in order to re-establish her wounded vanity, that but for her and hers he would not have so much as a roof to cover him.

7

Yet the man continued to love her in spite of all. And she was not at first a degraded being. At times she was bright and cheerful, and, except in the worst spells of her vapours, she was a brisk and busy woman. The house was sweet and homely. There was only one thing to drive him away from it, but that was the greatest thing of all. Nevertheless they had their cheerful hours together.

A child was born, a boy, and they called him Philip. He was the beginning of the end between them; the iron stay that held them together and yet apart. The father remembered his misfortunes in the presence of his son, and the mother was stung afresh by the recollection of disappointed hopes. The boy was the true heir of Ballawhaine, but the inheritance was lost to him by his father's fault and he had nothing.

Philip grew to be a winsome lad. There was something sweet and amiable and big-hearted, and even almost great, in him. One day the father sat in the garden by the mighty fuchsia-tree that grows on the lawn, watching his little fair-haired son play at marbles on the path with two big lads whom he had enticed out of the road, and another more familiar playmate—the little barefooted boy Peter, from the cottage by the water-trough. At first Philip lost, and with grunts of satisfaction the big ones promptly pocketed their gains. Then Philip won, and little curly Peter was stripped naked, and his lip began to fall. At that Philip paused, held his head aside, and considered, and then said quite briskly, "Peter hadn't a fair chance that time—here, let's give him another go."

The father's throat swelled, and he went indoors to the mother and said, "I think—perhaps I'm to blame—but somehow I think our boy isn't like other boys. What do you say? Foolish? May be so, may be so! No difference? Well, no—no!"

But deep down in the secret place of his heart, Thomas Wilson Christian, broken man, uprooted tree, wrecked craft in the mud and slime, began to cherish a fond idea. The son would regain all that his father had lost! He had gifts, and he should be brought up to the law; a large nature, and he should be helped to develop it; a fine face which all must love, a sense of justice, and a great wealth of the power of radiating happiness. Deemster? Why not? Ballawhaine? Who could tell? The biggest, noblest, greatest of all Manxmen! God knows!

Only—only he must be taught to fly from his father's dangers. Love? Then let him love where he can also respect—but never outside his own sphere. The island was too little for that. To love and to despise was to suffer the torments of the damned.

Nourishing these dreams, the poor man began to be tortured by every caress the mother gave her son, and irritated by every word she spoke to him. Her grammar was good enough for himself, and the exuberant caresses of her maudlin moods were even sometimes pleasant, but the boy must be degraded by neither.

The woman did not reach to these high thoughts, but she was not slow to interpret the casual byplay in which they found expression. Her husband was taiching her son to dis-respeck her. She wouldn't have thought it of him—she wouldn't really. But it was always the way when a plain practical woman married on the quality. Imperence and dis-respeck—that's the capers! Imperence and disrespeck from the ones that's doing nothing and beholden to you for everything. It was shocking! It was disthressing!

In such outbursts would her jealousy taunt him with his poverty, revile him for his idleness, and square accounts with him for the manifest preference of the boy. He could bear them with patience when they were alone, but in Philip's presence they were as gall and wormwood, and whips and scorpions.

"Go, my lad, go," he would sometimes whimper, and hustle the boy out of the way.

"No," the woman would cry, "stop and see the man your father is."

And the father would mutter, "He might see the woman his mother is as well."

But when she had pinned them together, and the boy had to hear her out, the man would drop his forehead on the table and break into groans and tears. Then the woman would change quite suddenly, and put her arms about him and kiss him and weep over him. He could defend himself from neither her insults nor her embraces. In spite of everything he loved her. That was where the bitterness of the evil lay. But for the love he bore her, he might have got her off his back and been his own man once more. He would make peace with her and kiss her again, and they would both kiss the boy, and be tender, and even cheerful.

Philip was still a child, but he saw the relations of his parents, and in his own way he understood everything. He loved his father best, but he did not hate his mother. She was nearly always affectionate, though often jealous of the father's greater love and care for him, and sometimes irritable from that cause alone. But the frequent broils between them were like blows that left scars on his body. He slept in a cot in the same room, and he would cover up his head in the bedclothes at night with a feeling of fear and physical pain.

A man cannot fight against himself for long. That deadly enemy is certain to slay. When Philip was six years old his father lay sick of his last sickness. The wife had fallen into habits of intemperance by this time, and stage by stage she had descended to the condition of an utterly degraded woman. There was something to excuse her. She had been disappointed in the great stakes of life; she had earned disgrace where she had looked for admiration. She was vain, and could not bear misfortune; and she had no deep well of love from which to drink when the fount of her pride ran dry. If her husband had indulged her with a little pity, everything might have gone along more easily. But he had only loved her and been ashamed. And now that he lay near to his death, the love began to ebb and the shame to deepen into dread.

He slept little at night, and as often as he closed his eyes certain voices of mocking and reproach seemed to be constantly humming in his ears.

"Your son!" they would cry. "What is to become of him? Your dreams! Your great dreams! Deemster! Ballawhaine! God knows what! You are leaving the boy; who is to bring him up? His mother? Think of it!"

At last a ray of pale sunshine broke on the sleepless wrestler with the night, and he became almost happy. "I'll speak to the boy," he thought. "I will tell him my own history, concealing nothing. Yes, I will tell him of my own father also, God rest him, the stern old man—severe, yet just."

An opportunity soon befell. It was late at night—very late. The woman was sleeping off a bout of intemperance somewhere below; and the boy, with the innocence and ignorance of his years in all that the solemn time foreboded, was bustling about the room with mighty eagerness, because he knew that he ought to be in bed.

"I'm staying up to intend on you, father," said the boy.

The father answered with a sigh.

"Don't you asturb yourself, father. I'll intend on you."

The father's sigh deepened to a moan.

"If you want anything 'aticular, just call me; d'ye see, father?"

And away went the boy like a gleam of light. Presently he came back, leaping like the dawn. He was carrying, insecurely, a jug of poppy-head and camomile, which had been prescribed as a lotion.

"Poppy heads, father! Poppy-heads is good, I can tell ye."

"Why arn't you in bed, child?" said the father. "You must be tired."

"No, I'm not tired, father. I was just feeling a bit of tired, and then I took a smell of poppy-heads and away went the tiredness to Jericho. They *is* good."

The little white head was glinting off again when the father called it back.

"Come here, my boy." The child went up to the bedside, and the father ran his fingers lovingly through the long fair hair.

"Do you think, Philip, that twenty, thirty, forty years hence, when you are a man—aye, a big man, little one—do you think you will remember what I shall say to you now?"

"Why, yes, father, if it's anything 'aticular, and if it isn't you can amind me of it, can't you, father?"

The father shook his head. "I shall not be here then, my boy. I am going away——"

"Going away, father? May I come too?"

"Ah! I wish you could, little one. Yes, truly I almost wish you could."

"Then you'll let me go with you, father! Oh, I *am* glad, father." And the boy began to caper and dance, to go down on all fours, and leap about the floor like a frog.

The father fell back on his pillow with a heaving breast. Vain! vain! What was the use of speaking? The child's outlook was life; his own was death; they had no common ground; they spoke different tongues. And, after all, how could he suffer the sweet innocence of the child's soul to look down into the stained and scarred chamber of his ruined heart?

"You don't understand me, Philip. I mean that I am going—to die. Yes, darling, and, only that I am leaving you behind, I should be glad to go. My life has been wasted, Philip. In the time to come, when men speak of your father, you will be ashamed. Perhaps you will not remember then that whatever he was he was a good father to you, for at least he loved you dearly. Well, I must needs bow to the will of God, but if I could only hope that you would live to restore my name when I am gone.... Philip, are you—don't cry, my darling. There, there, kiss me. We'll say no more about it then. Perhaps it's not true, although father tolded you? Well, perhaps not. And now undress and slip into bed before mother comes. See, there's your night-dress at the foot of the crib. Wants some buttons, does it? Never mind—in with you—that's a boy."

Impossible, impossible! And perhaps unnecessary. Who should say? Young as the child was, he might never forget what he had seen and heard. Some day it must have its meaning for him. Thus the father comforted himself. Those jangling quarrels which had often scorched his brain like iron—the memory of their abject scenes came to him then, with a sort of bleeding solace!

Meanwhile, with little catching sobs, which he struggled to repress, the boy lay down in his crib. When half-way gone towards the mists of the land of sleep, he started up suddenly, and called "Good night, father," and his father answered him "Good night."

Towards three o'clock the next morning there was great commotion in the house. The servant was scurrying up and downstairs, and the mistress, wringing her hands, was tramping to and fro in the sick-room, crying in a tone of astonishment, as if the thought had stolen upon her unawares, "Why, he's going! How didn't somebody tell me before?"

The eyes of the sinking man were on the crib. "Philip," he faltered. They lifted the boy out of his bed, and brought him in his night-dress to his father's side; and the father twisted about and took him into his arms, still half asleep and yawning. Then the mother, recovering from the stupidity of her surprise, broke into paroxysms of weeping, and fell over her husband's breast and kissed and kissed him.

For once her kisses had no response. The man was dying miserably, for he was thinking of her and of the boy. Sometimes he babbled over Philip in a soft, inarticulate gurgle; sometimes he looked up at his wife's face with a stony stare, and then he clung the closer to the boy, as if he would never let him go. The dark hour came, and still he held the boy in his arms. They had to release the child at last from his father's dying grip.

The dead of the night was gone by this time, and the day was at the point of dawn; the sparrows in the eaves were twittering, and the tide, which was at its lowest ebb, was heaving on the sand far out in the bay with the sound as of a rookery awakening. Philip remembered afterwards that his mother cried so much that he was afraid, and that when he had been dressed she took him downstairs, where they all ate breakfast together, with the sun shining through the blinds.

The mother did not live to overshadow her son's life. Sinking yet lower in habits of intemperance, she stayed indoors from week-end to week-end, seated herself like a weeping willow by the fireside, and drank and drank. Her excesses led to delusions. She saw ghosts perpetually. To avoid such of them as haunted the death-room of her husband, she had a bed made up on a couch in the parlour, and one morning she was found face downwards stretched out beside it on the floor.

Then Philip's father's cousin, always called his Aunty Nan, came to Ballure House to bring him up. His father had been her favourite cousin, and, in spite of all that had happened, he had been her lifelong hero also. A deep and secret tenderness, too timid to be quite aware of itself, had been lying in ambush in her heart through all the years of his miserable life with Mona. At the death of the old Deemster, her other cousin, Peter, had married and cast her off. But she was always one of those woodland herbs which are said to give out their sweetest fragrance after they have been trodden on and crushed. Philip's father had been her hero, her lost one and her love, and Philip was his father's son.

9

III.

Little curly Pete, with the broad, bare feet, the tousled black head, the jacket half way up his back like a waistcoat with sleeves, and the hole in his trousers where the tail of his shirt should have been, was Peter Quilliam, and he was the natural son of Peter Christian. In the days when that punctilious worthy set himself to observe the doings of his elder brother at Ballure, he found it convenient to make an outwork of the hedge in front of the thatched house that stood nearest. Two persons lived in the cottage, father and daughter—Tom Quilliam, usually called Black Tom, and Bridget Quilliam, getting the name of Bridget Black Tom.

The man was a short, gross creature, with an enormous head and a big, open mouth, showing broken teeth that were black with the juice of tobacco. The girl was by common judgment and report a gawk—a great, slow-eyed, comely-looking, comfortable, easy-going gawk. Black Tom was a thatcher, and with his hair poking its way through the holes in his straw hat, he tramped the island in pursuit of his calling. This kept him from home for days together, and in that fact Peter Christian, while shadowing the morality of his brother, found his own opportunity.

When the child was born, neither the thatcher nor his daughter attempted to father it. Peter Christian paid twenty pounds to the one and eighty to the other in Manx pound-notes, the boys daubed their door to show that the house was dishonoured, and that was the end of everything.

The girl went through her "censures" silently, or with only one comment. She had borrowed the sheet in which she appeared in church from Miss Christian of Ballawhaine, and when she took it back, the good soul of the sweet lady thought to improve the occasion.

"I was wondering, Bridget," she said gravely, "what you were thinking of when you stood with Bella and Liza before the congregation last Sunday morning"—two other Magda-lenes had done penance by Bridget's side.

"'Deed, mistress," said the girl, "I was thinkin' there wasn't a sheet at one of them to match mine for whiteness. I'd 'a been ashamed to be seen in the like of theirs."

Bridget may have been a gawk, but she did two things which were not gawkish. Putting the eighty greasy notes into the foot of an old stocking, she sewed them up in the ticking of her bed, and then christened her baby Peter. The money was for the child if she should not live to rear him, and the name was her way of saying that a man's son was his son in spite of law or devil.

After that she kept both herself and her child by day labour in the fields, weeding and sowing potatoes, and following at the tail of the reapers, for sixpence a day dry days, and fourpence all weathers. She might have badgered the heir of Ballawhaine, but she never did so. That person came into his inheritance, got himself elected member for Ramsey in the House of Keys, married Nessy Taubman, daughter of the rich brewer, and became the father of another son. Such were the doings in the big house down in the valley, while up in the thatched cottage behind the water-trough, on potatoes and herrings and barley bonnag, lived Bridget and her little Pete.

Pete's earliest recollections were of a boy who lived at the beautiful white house with the big fuchsia, by the turn of the road over the bridge that crossed the glen. This was Philip Christian, half a year older than himself, although several inches shorter, with long yellow hair and rosy cheeks, and dressed in a velvet suit of knickerbockers. Pete worshipped him in his simple way, hung about him, fetched and carried for him, and looked up to him as a marvel of wisdom and goodness and pluck.

His first memory of Philip was of sleeping with him, snuggled up by his side in the dark, hushed and still in a narrow bed with iron ends to it, and of leaping up in the morning and laughing. Philip's father—a tall, white gentleman, who never laughed at all, and only smiled sometimes—had found him in the road in the evening waiting for his mother to come home from the fields, that he might light the fire in the cottage, and running about in the meantime to keep himself warm, and not too hungry.

His second memory was of Philip guiding him round the drawing-room (over thick carpets, on which his bare feet made no noise), and showing him the pictures on the walls, and telling him what they meant. One (an engraving of St. John, with a death's-head and a crucifix) was, according to this grim and veracious guide, a picture of a brigand who killed his victims, and always skinned their skulls with a cross-handled dagger. After that his memories of Philip and himself were as two gleams of sunshine which mingle and become one.

Philip was a great reader of noble histories. He found them, frayed and tattered, at the bottom of a trunk that had tin corners and two padlocks, and stood in the room looking towards the harbour where his mother's father, the old sailor, had slept. One of them was his special favourite, and he used to read it aloud to Pete. It told of the doings of the Carrasdhoo men. They were a bold band of desperadoes, the terror of all the island. Sometimes they worked in the fields at ploughing, and reaping, and stacking, the same as common practical men; and sometimes they lived in houses, just like the house by the water-trough. But when the wind was rising in the nor-nor-west, and there was a taste of the brine on your lips, they would be up, and say, "The sea's calling us—we must be going." Then they would live in rocky caves of the coast where nobody could reach them, and there would be fires lit at night in tar-barrels, and shouting, and singing, and carousing; and after that there would be ships' rudders, and figure heads, and masts coming up with the tide, and sometimes dead bodies on the beach of sailors they had drowned—only foreign ones though—hundreds and tons of them. But that was long ago, the Carrasdhoo men were dead, and the glory of their day was departed.

One quiet evening, after an awesome reading of this brave history, Philip, sitting on his haunches at the gable, with Pete like another white frog beside him, said quite suddenly, "Hush! What's that?"

"I wonder," said Pete.

There was never a sound in the air above the rustle of a leaf, and Pete's imagination could carry him no further.

"Pete," said Philip, with awful gravity, "the sea's calling me."

"And me," said Pete solemnly.

Early that night the two lads were down at the most desolate part of Port Mooar, in a cave under the scraggy black rocks of Gobny-Garvain, kindling a fire of gorse and turf inside the remains of a broken barrel.

"See that tremendous sharp rock below low water?" said Philip.

"Don't I, though?" said Pete.

There was never a rock the size of a currycomb between them and the line of the sky.

"That's what we call a reef," said Philip. "Wait a bit and you'll see the ships go splitting on top of it like—like——"

"Like a tay-pot," said Pete.

"We'll save the women, though," said Philip. "Shall we save the women, Pete? We always do."

"Aw, yes, the women—and the boys," said Pete thoughtfully.

Philip had his doubts about the boys, but he would not quarrel. It was nearly dark, and growing very cold. The lads croodled down by the crackling blaze, and tried to forget that they had forgotten tea-time.

"We never has to mind a bit of hungry," said Philip stoutly.

"Never a ha'p'orth," said Pete.

"Only when the job's done we have hams and flitches and things for supper."

"Aw, yes, ateing and drinking to the full."

"Rum, Pete, we always drinks rum."

"We has to," said Pete.

"None of your tea," said Philip.

"Coorse not, none of your ould grannie's two-penny tay," said Pete.

It was quite dark by this time, and the tide was rising rapidly. There was not a star in the sky, and not a light on the sea except the revolving light of the lightship far a Way. The boys crept closer together and began to think of home. Philip remembered Aunty Nan. When he had stolen away on hands and knees under the parlour window she had been sewing at his new check night-shirt. A night-shirt for a Carrasdhoo man had seemed to be ridiculous then; but where was Aunty Nannie now? Pete remembered his mother—she would be racing round the houses and crying; and he had visions of Black Tom—he would be racing round also and swearing.

"Shouldn't we sing something, Phil?" said Pete, with a gurgle in his throat.

"Sing!" said Philip, with as much scorn as he could summon, "and give them warning we're watching for them! Well, you *are* a pretty, Mr. Pete! But just you wait till the ships goes wrecking on the rocks—I mean the reefs—and the dead men's coming up like corks—hundreds and ninety and dozens of them; my jove! yes, then you'll hear me singing."

The darkness deepened, and the voice of the sea began to moan through the back of the cave, the gorse crackled no longer, and the turf burned in a dull red glow. Night with its awfulness had come down, and the boys were cut off from everything.

"They don't seem to be coming—not yet," said Philip, in a husky whisper.

"Maybe it's the same as fishing," said Pete; "sometimes you catch and sometimes you don't."

"That's it," said Philip eagerly, "generally you don't—and then you both haves to go home and come again," he added nervously.

But neither of the boys stirred. Outside the glow of the fire the blackness looked terrible. Pete nuzzled up to Philip's side, and, being untroubled by imaginative fears, soon began to feel drowsy. The sound of his measured breathing startled Philip with the terror of loneliness.

"Honour bright, Mr. Pete," he faltered, nudging the head on his shoulder, and trying to keep his voice from shaking; "*you* call yourself a second mate, and leaving all the work to me!"

The second mate was penitent, but in less than half a minute more he was committing the same offence again. "It isn't no use," he said, "I'm that sleepy you never seen."

"Then let's both take the watch below i'stead," said Philip, and they proceeded to stretch themselves out by the fire together.

"Just lave it to me," said Pete; "I'll hear them if they come in the night. I'll always does. I'm sleeping that light it's shocking. Why, sometimes I hear Black Tom when he comes home tipsy. I've done it times."

"We'll have carpets to lie on to-morrow, not stones," said Philip, wriggling on a rough one; "rolls of carpets—kidaminstrel ones."

They settled themselves side by side as close to each other as they could creep, and tried not to hear the surging and sighing of the sea. Then came a tremulous whimper:

"Pete!"

"What's that?"

"Don't you never say your prayers when you take the watch below?"

"Sometimes we does, when mother isn't too tired, and the ould man's middling drunk and quiet."

"Then don't you like to then?"

"Aw, yes, though, I'm liking it scandalous."

The wreckers agreed to say their prayers, and got up again and said them, knee to knee, with their two little faces to the fire, and then stretched themselves out afresh.

"Pete, where's your hand?"

"Here you are, Phil."

In another minute, under the solemn darkness of the night, broken only by the smouldering fire, amid the thunderous quake of the cavern after every beat of the waves on the beach, the Carrasdhoo men were asleep.

Sometime in the dark reaches before the dawn Pete leapt up with a start "What's that?" he cried, in a voice of fear.

But Philip was still in the mists of sleep, and, feeling the cold, he only whimpered, "Cover me up, Pete."

"Phil!" cried Pete, in an affrighted whisper.

"Cover me up," drawled Philip.

"I thought it was Black Tom," said Pete.

There was some confused bellowing outside the cave.

"My goodness grayshers!" came in a terrible voice, "it's them, though, the pair of them! Impozzible! who says it's impozzible? It's themselves I'm telling you, ma'm. Guy heng! The woman's mad, putting a scream out of herself like yonder. Safe? Coorse they're safe, bad luck to the young wastrels! You're for putting up a prayer for your own one. Eh? Well, I'm for hommering mine. The dirts? Weaned only yesterday, and fetching a dacent man out of his bed to find them. A fire at them, too! Well, it was the fire that found them. Pull the boat up, boys."

Philip was half awake by this time. "They've come," he whispered. "The ships is come, they're on the reef. Oh, dear me! Best go and meet them. P'raps they won't kill us if—if we—Oh, dear me!"

Then the wreckers, hand in hand, quaking and whimpering, stepped out to the mouth of the cave. At the next moment Philip found himself snatched up into the arms of Aunty Nan, who kissed him and cried over him, and rammed a great chunk of sweet cake into his cheek. Pete was faring differently. Under the leathern belt of Black Tom, who was thrashing him for both of them, he was howling like the sea in a storm.

Thus the Carrasdhoo men came home by the light of early morning—Pete skipping before the belt and bellowing; and Philip holding a piece of the cake at his teeth to comfort him.

IV.

Philip left home for school at King William's by Castletown, and then Pete had a hard upbringing. His mother was tender enough, and there were good souls like Aunty Nan to show pity to both of them. But life went like a springless bogey, nevertheless. Sin itself is often easier than simpleness to pardon and condone. It takes a soft heart to feel tenderly towards a soft head.

Poor Pete's head seemed soft enough and to spare. No power and no persuasion could teach him to read and write. He went to school at the old schoolhouse by the church in Maughold village. The schoolmaster was a little man called John Thomas Corlett, pert and proud, with the sharp nose of a pike and the gait of a bantam. John Thomas was also a tailor. On a cowhouse door laid across two school forms he sat cross-legged among his cloth, his "maidens," and his smoothing irons, with his boys and girls, class by class, in a big half circle round about him.

The great little man had one standing ground of daily assault on the dusty jacket of poor Pete, and that was that the lad came late to school. Every morning Pete's welcome from the tailor-schoolmaster was a volley of expletives, and a swipe of the cane across his shoulders. "The craythur! The dunce! The durt! I'm taiching him, and taiching him, and he won't be taicht."

The soul of the schoolmaster had just two human weaknesses. One of these was a weakness for drink, and as a little vessel he could not take much without being full. Then he always taught the Church catechism and swore at his boys in Manx.

"Peter Quilliam," he cried one day, "who brought you out of the land of Egypt and the house of bondage?"

"'Deed, master," said Pete, "I never was in no such places, for I never had the money nor the clothes for it, and that's how stories are getting about."

The second of the schoolmaster's frailties was love of his daughter, a child of four, a cripple, whom he had lamed in her infancy, by letting her fall as he tossed her in his arms while in drink. The constant terror of his mind was lest some further accident should befall her. Between class and class he would go to a window, from which, when he had thrown up its lower sash, dim with the scratches of names, he could see one end of his own white cottage, and the little pathway, between lines of gilvers, coming down from the porch.

Pete had seen the little one hobbling along this path on her lame leg, and giggling with a heart of glee when she had eluded the eyes of her mother and escaped into the road. One day it chanced, after the heavy spring rains had swollen every watercourse, that he came upon the little curly poll, tumbling and tossing like a bell-buoy in a gale, down the flood of the river that runs to the sea at Port Mooar. Pete rescued the child and took her home, and then, as if he had done nothing unusual, he went on to school, dripping water from his legs at every step.

When John Thomas saw him coming, in bare feet, triddle-traddle, triddle-traddle, up the school-house floor, his indignation at the boy for being later than usual rose to fiery wrath for being drenched as well. Waiting for no explanation, concluding that Pete had been fishing for crabs among the stones of Port Lewaigue, he burst into a loud volley of his accustomed expletives, and timed and punctuated them by a thwack of the cane between every word.

"The waistrel! (thwack). The dirt! (thwack). I'm taiching him (thwack), and taiching him (thwack), and he won't be taicht!" (Thwack, thwack, thwack.)

Pete said never a word. Boiling his stinging shoulders under his jacket, and ramming his smarting hands, like wet eels, into his breeches' pockets, he took his place in silence at the bottom of the class.

But a girl, a little dark thing in a red frock, stepped out from her place beside the boy, shot up like a gleam to the schoolmaster as he returned to his seat among the cloth and needles, dealt him a smart slap across the face, and then burst into a lit of hysterical crying. Her name was Katherine Cregeen. She was the daughter of Cæsar the Cornaa miller, the founder of Ballajora Chapel, and a mighty man among the Methodists.

Katherine went unpunished, but that was the end of Pete's schooling. His learning was not too heavy for a big lad's head to carry—a bit of reading if it was all in print, and no writing at all except half-a-dozen capital letters. It was not a formidable equipment for the battle of life, but Bridget would not hear of more.

She herself, meanwhile, had annexed that character which was always the first and easiest to attach itself to a woman with a child but no visible father for it—the character of a witch. That name for his mother was Pete's earliest recollection of the high-road, and when the consciousness of its meaning came to him, he did not rebel, but sullenly acquiesced, for he had been born to it and knew nothing to the contrary. If the boys quarrelled with him at play, the first word was "your mother's a butch." Then he cried at the reproach, or perhaps fought like a vengeance at the insult, but he never dreamt of disbelieving the fact or of loving his mother any the less.

Bridget was accused of the evil eye. Cattle sickened in the fields, and when there was no proof that she had looked over the gate, the idea was suggested that she crossed them as a hare. One day a neighbour's dog started a hare in a meadow where some cows were grazing. This was observed by a gang of boys playing at hockey in the road. Instantly there was a shout and a whoop, and the boys with their sticks were in full chase after the yelping dog, crying, "The butch! The butch! It's Bridget Tom! Corlett's dogs are hunting Bridget Black Tom! Kill her, Laddie! Kill her, Sailor! Jump, dog, jump!"

One of the boys playing at hockey was Pete. When his play-fellows ran after the dogs in their fanatic thirst, he ran too, but with a storm of other feelings. Outstripping all of them, very close at the heels of the dogs, kicking some, striking others with the hockey-stick, while the tears poured down his cheeks, he cried at the top of his voice to the hare leaping in front, "Run, mammy, run! clink (dodge), mammy, clink! Aw, mammy, mammy, run faster, run for your life, run!"

The hare dodged aside, shot into a thicket, and escaped its pursuers just as Corlett, the farmer, who had heard the outcry, came racing up with a gun. Then Pete swept his coat-sleeve across his gleaming eyes and leapt off home. When he got there, he found his mother sitting on the bink by the door knitting quietly. He threw himself into her arms and stroked her cheek with his hand.

"Oh, mammy, bogh," he cried, "how well you run! If you never run in your life you run then."

"Is the boy mad?" said Bridget.

But Pete went on stroking her cheek and crying between sobs of joy, "I heard Corlett shouting to the house for a gun and a fourpenny bit, and I thought I was never going to see mammy no more. But you did clink, mammy! You did, though!"

The next time Katherine Cregeen saw Peter Quilliam, he was sitting on the ridge of rock at the mouth of Ballure Glen, playing doleful strains on a home-made whistle, and looking the picture of desolation and despair. His mother was lying near to death. He had left Mrs. Cregeen, Kath-erine's mother, a good soul getting the name of Grannie, to watch and tend her while he came out to comfort his simple heart in this lone spot between the land and the sea.

Katherine's eyes filled at sight of him, and when, without looking up or speaking, he went on to play his crazy tunes, something took the girl by the throat and she broke down utterly.

"Never mind, Pete. No—I don't mean that—but don't cry, Pete."

Pete was not crying at all, but only playing away on his whistle and gazing out to sea with a look of dumb vacancy. Katherine knelt beside him, put her arms around his neck, and cried for both of them.

Somebody hailed him from the hedge by the water-trough, and he rose, took off his cap, smoothed his hair with his hand, and walked towards the house without a word.

Bridget was dying of pleurisy, brought on by a long day's work at hoeing turnips in a soaking rain. Dr. Mylechreest had poulticed her lungs with mustard and linseed, but all to no purpose. "It's feeling the same as the sun on your back at harvest," she murmured, yet the poultices brought no heat to her frozen chest.

Cæsar Cregeen was at her side; John the Clerk, too, called John the Widow; Kelly, the rural postman, who went by the name of Kelly the Thief; as well as Black Tom, her father. Cæsar was discoursing of sinners and their latter end. John was remembering how at his election to the clerkship he had rashly promised to bury the poor for nothing; Kelly was thinking he would be the first to carry the news to Christian Balla-whaine; and Black Tom was varying the exercise of pounding rock-sugar for his bees with that of breaking his playful wit on the dying woman.

"No use; I'm laving you; I'm going on my long journey," said Bridget, while Granny used a shovel as a fan to relieve her gusty breathing.

"Got anything in your pocket for the road, woman?" said the thatcher.

"It's not houses of bricks and mortal I'm for calling at now," she answered.

"Dear heart! Put up a bit of a prayer," whispered Grannie to her husband; and Cæsar took a pinch of snuff out of his waistcoat pocket, and fell to "wrastling with the Lord."

Bridget seemed to be comforted. "I see the jasper gates," she panted, fixing her hazy eyes on the scraas under the thatch, from which broken spiders' webs hung down like rats' tails.

13

Then she called for Pete. She had something to give him. It was the stocking foot with the eighty greasy Manx banknotes which his father, Peter Christian, had paid her fifteen years before. Pete lit the candle and steadied it while Grannie cut the stocking from the wall side of the bed-ticking.

Black Tom dropped the sugar-pounder and exposed his broken teeth in his surprise at so much wealth; John the Widow blinked; and Kelly the Thief poked his head forward until the peak of his postman's cap fell on to the bridge of his nose.

A sea-fog lay over the land that morning, and when it lifted Bridget's soul went up as well.

"Poor thing! Poor thing!" said Grannie. "The ways were cold for her—cold, cold!"

"A dacent lass," said John the Clerk; "and oughtn't to be buried with the common trash, seeing she's left money."

"A hard-working woman, too, and on her feet for ever; but 'lowanced in her intellecks, for all," said Kelly.

And Cæsar cried, "A brand plucked from the burning! Lord, give me more of the like at the judgment."

When all was over, and tears both hot and cold were wiped away—Pete shed none of them—the neighbours who had stood with the lad in the churchyard on Maughold Head returned to the cottage by the water-trough to decide what was to be done with his eighty good bank-notes. "It's a fortune," said one. "Let him put it with Mr. Dumbell," said another. "Get the boy a trade first—he's a big lump now, sixteen for spring," said a third. "A draper, eh?" said a fourth. "May I presume? My nephew, Bobbie Clucas, of Ramsey, now?" "A dacent man, very," said John the Widow; "but if I'm not ambitious, there's my son-in-law, John Cowley. The lad's cut to a dot for a grocer, and what more nicer than having your own shop and your own name over the door, if you plaze—' Peter Quilliam, tay and sugar merchant!'—they're telling me John will be riding in his carriage and pair soon."

"Chut! your grannie and your carriage and pairs," shouted a rasping voice at last. It was Black Tom. "Who says the fortune is belonging to the lad at all? It's mine, and if there's law in the land I'll have it."

Meanwhile, Pete, with the dull thud in his ears of earth falling on a coffin, had made his way down to Ballawhaine. He had never been there before, and he felt confused, but he did not tremble. Half-way up the carriage-drive he passed a sandy-haired youth of his own age, a slim dandy who hummed a tune and looked at him carelessly over his shoulder. Pete knew him—he was Boss, the boys called him Dross, son and heir of Christian Ballawhaine.

At the big house Pete asked for the master. The English footman, in scarlet knee-breeches, left him to wait in the stone hall. The place was very quiet and rather cold, but all as clean as a gull's wing. There was a dark table in the middle and a high-backed chair against the wall. Two oil pictures faced each other from opposite sides. One was of an old man without a beard, but with a high forehead, framed around with short grey hair. The other was of a woman with a tired look and a baby on her lap. Under this there was a little black picture that seemed to Pete to be the likeness of a fancy tombstone. And the print on it, so far as Pete could spell it out, was that of a tombstone too, "In loving memory of Verbena, beloved wife of Peter Chr—"

The Ballawhaine came crunching the sand on the hall-floor. He looked old, and had now a pent-house of bristly eyebrows of a different colour from his hair. Pete had often seen him on the road riding by.

"Well, my lad, what can I do for *you?*" he said. He spoke in a jerky voice, as if he thought to overawe the boy.

Pete fumbled his stocking cap. "Mothers dead," he answered vacantly.

The Ballawhaine knew that already. Kelly the Thief had run hot-foot to inform him. He thought Pete had come to claim maintenance now that his mother was gone.

"So she's been telling you the same old story?" he said briskly.

At that Pete's face stiffened all at once. "She's been telling me that you're my father, sir."

The Ballawhaine tried to laugh. "Indeed!" he replied; "it's a wise child, now, that knows its own father."

"I'm not rightly knowing what you mane, sir," said Pete.

Then the Ballawhaine fell to slandering the poor woman in her grave, declaring that she could not know who was the father of her child, and protesting that no son of hers should ever see the colour of money of his. Saying this with a snarl, he brought down his right hand with a thump on to the table. There was a big hairy mole near the joint of the first finger.

"Aisy, sir, if you plaze," said Pete; "she was telling me you gave her this."

He turned up the corner of his jersey, tugged out of his pocket, from behind his flaps, the eighty Manx bank-notes, and held them in his right hand on the table. There was a mole at the joint of Pete's first finger also.

The Ballawhaine saw it. He drew back his hand and slid it behind him. Then in another voice he said, "Well, my lad, isn't it enough? What are you wanting with more?"

"I'm not wanting more," said Pete; "I'm not wanting this. Take it back," and he put down the roll of notes between them.

The Ballawhaine sank into the chair, took a handkerchief out of his tails with the hand that had been lurking there, and began to mop his forehead. "Eh? How? What d'ye mean, boy?" he stammered.

"I mane," said Pete, "that if I kept that money there is people would say my mother was a bad woman, and you bought her and paid her—I'm hearing the like at some of them."

He took a step nearer. "And I mane, too, that you did wrong by my mother long ago, and now that she's dead you're blackening her; and you're a bad heart, and a low tongue, and if I was only a man, and didn't *know* you were my father, I'd break every bone in your skin."

Then Pete twisted about and shouted into the dark part of the hall, "Come along, there, my ould cockatoo! It's time to be putting me to the door."

The English footman in the scarlet breeches had been peeping from under the stairs.

14

That was Pete's first and last interview with his father. Peter Christian Ballawhaine was a terror in the Keys by this time, but he had trembled before his son like a whipped cur.

V.

Katherine Cregeen, Pete's champion at school, had been his companion at home as well. She was two years younger than Pete. Her hair was a black as a gipsy's, and her face as brown as a berry. In summer she liked best to wear a red frock without sleeves, no boots and no stockings, no collar and no bonnet, not even a sun-bonnet. From constant exposure to the sun and rain her arms and legs were as ruddy as her cheeks, and covered with a soft silken down. So often did you see her teeth that you would have said she was always laughing. Her laugh was a little saucy trill given out with head aside and eyes aslant, like that of a squirrel when he is at a safe height above your head, and has a nut in his open jaws.

Pete had seen her first at school, and there he had tried to draw the eyes of the maiden upon himself by methods known only to heroes, to savages, and to boys. He had prowled around her in the playground with the wild vigour of a young colt, tossing his head, swinging his arms, screwing his body, kicking up his legs, walking on his hands, lunging out at every lad that was twice as big as himself, and then bringing himself down at length with a whoop and a crash on his hindmost parts just in front of where she stood. For these tremendous efforts to show what a fellow he could be if he tried, he had won no applause from the boys, and Katherine herself had given no sign, though Pete had watched her out of the corners of his eyes. But in other scenes the children came together.

After Philip had gone to King William's, Pete and Katherine had become bosom friends. Instead of going home after school to cool his heels in the road until his mother came from the fields, he found it neighbourly to go up to Ballajora and round by the network of paths to Cornaa. That was a long detour, but Cæsar's mill stood there. It nestled down in the low bed of the river that runs through the glen called Ballaglass.

Song-birds built about it in the spring of the year, and Cæsar's little human songster sang there always.

When Pete went that way home, what times the girl had of it! Wading up the river, clambering over the stones, playing female Blondin on the fallen tree-trunks that spanned the chasm, slipping, falling, holding on any way up (legs or arms) by the rotten branches below, then calling for Pete's help in a voice between a laugh and a cry, flinging chips into the foaming back-wash of the mill-wheel, and chasing them down stream, racing among the gorse, and then lying full length like a lamb, without a thought of shame, while Pete took the thorns out of her bleeding feet. She was a wild duck in the glen where she lived, and Pete was a great lumbering tame duck waddling behind her.

But the glorious, happy, make-believe days too soon came to an end. The swinging cane of the great John Thomas Corlett, and the rod of a yet more relentless tyrant, darkened the sunshine of both the children. Pete was banished from school, and Catherine's father removed from Cornaa.

When Cæsar had taken a wife, he had married Betsy, the daughter of the owner of the inn at Sulby. After that he had "got religion," and he held that persons in the household of faith were not to drink, or to buy or to sell drink. But Grannie's father died and left his house, "The Manx Fairy," and his farm, Glenmooar, to her and her husband. About the same time the miller at Sulby also died, and the best mill in the island cried out for a tenant. Cæsar took the mill and the farm, and Grannie took the inn, being brought up to such profanities and no way bound by principle. From that time forward, Cæsar pinned all envious cavillers with the text which says, "Not that which goeth into the mouth of a man defileth him, but that which cometh out."

Nevertheless, Cæsar's principles grew more and more puritanical year by year. There were no half measures with Cæsar. Either a man was a saved soul, or he was in the very belly of hell, though the pit might not have shut its mouth on him. If a man was saved he knew it, and if he felt the manifestations of the Spirit he could live without sin. His cardinal principles were three—instantaneous regeneration, assurance, and sinless perfection. He always said—he had said it a thousand times—that he was converted in Douglas marketplace, a piece off the west door of ould St. Matthew's, at five-and-twenty minutes past six on a Sabbath evening in July, when he was two-and-twenty for harvest.

While at Cornaa, Cæsar had been a "local" on the preachers' plan, a class leader, and a chapel steward; but at Sulby he outgrew the Union and set up a "body" of his own. He called them "The Christians," a title that was at once a name, a challenge, and a protest. They worshipped in the long barn over Cæsar's mill, and held strong views on conduct. A saved soul must not wear gold or costly apparel, or give way to softness or bodily indulgence, or go to fairs for sake of sport, or appear in the show-tents of play-actors, or sing songs, or read books, or take any diversion that did not tend to the knowledge of God. As for carnal transgression, if any were guilty of it, they were to be cut off from the body of believers, for the souls of the righteous must be delivered.

"The religion that's going among the Primitives these days is just Popery," said Cæsar. "Let's go back to the warm ould Methodism and put out the Romans."

When Pete turned his face from Ballawhaine, he thought first of Cæsar and his mill. It would be more exact to say he thought of Katherine and Grannie. He was homeless as well as penniless. The cottage by the water-trough was no longer possible to him, now that the mother was gone who had stood between his threatened shoulders and Black Tom. Philip was at home for a few weeks only in the year, and Ballure had lost its attraction. So Pete made his way to Sulby, offered himself to Cæsar for service at the mill, and was taken on straightway at eighteenpence a week and his board.

It was a curious household he entered into. First there was Cæsar himself, in a moleskin waistcoat with sleeves open three buttons up, knee-breeches usually unlaced, stockings of undyed wool, and slippers with the tongues hanging out—a grim soul, with whiskers like a hoop about his face, and a shaven upper lip as heavy as a moustache, for, when religion like Cæsar's lays hold of a man, it takes him first by the mouth. Then Grannie, a comfortable body in a cap, with an outlook on life that was all motherhood, a simple, tender, peaceable soul, agreeing with everybody and everything, and seeming to say nothing but "Poor thing! Poor thing!" and "Dear heart! Dear heart!" Then there was Nancy Cain, getting the name of Nancy Joe, the servant in name but the mistress in fact, a niece of Grannie's, a bit of a Pagan, an early riser, a tireless worker, with a plain face, a rooted disbelief in all men, a good heart, an ugly tongue, and a vixenish temper. Last of all, there was Katherine, now grown to be a great girl, with her gipsy hair done up in a red ribbon and wearing a black pinafore bordered with white braid.

Pete got on steadily at the mill. He began by lighting the kiln fire and cleaning out the pit-wheel, and then on to the opening the flood-gates in the morning and regulating the action of the water-wheel according to the work of the day. In two years' time he was a sound miller, safe to trust with rough stuff for cattle or fine flour for white loaf-bread. Cæsar trusted him. He would take evangelising journeys to Peel or Douglas and leave Pete in charge.

That led to the end of the beginning. Pete could grind the farmers' corn, but he could not make their reckonings. He kept his counts in chalk on the back of the mill-house door, a down line for every stone weight up to eight stones, and a line across for every hundredweight. Then, once a day, while the father was abroad, Katherine came over from the inn to the desk at the little window of the mill, and turned Pete's lines into ledger accounts. These financial councils were full of delicious discomfiture. Pete always enjoyed them—after they were over.

"John Robert—Molleycarane—did you say Molleycarane, Pete? Oh, Mylecharane—Myle-c-h-a-r-a-i-n-e, Molleycarane; ten stones—did you say ten? Oh, eight—e-i-g-h-t—no, eight; oatmeal, Pete? Oh, barley-male—meal, I mean—m-e-a-l."

In the middle of the night Pete remembered all these entries. They were very precious to his memory after Katherine had spoken them. They sang in his heart the same as song-birds then. They were like hymns and tunes and pieces of poetry.

Cæsar returned home from a preaching tour with a great and sudden thought. He had been calling on strangers to flee from the wrath to come, and yet there were those of his own house whose faces were not turned Zionwards. That evening he held an all-night prayer-meeting for the conversion of Katherine and Pete. Through six long hours he called on God in lusty tones, until his throat cracked and his forehead streamed. The young were thoughtless, they had the root of evil in them, they flew into frivolity from contrariness. Draw the harrow over their souls, plough the fallows of their hearts, grind the chaff out of their household, let not the sweet apple and the crabs grow on the same bough together, give them a Melliah, let not a sheaf be forgotten, grant them the soul of this girl for a harvest-home, and of this boy for a last stook.

Cæsar was dissatisfied with the results. He was used to groaning and trembling and fainting fits.

"Don't you feel the love?" he cried. "I do—here, under the watch-pocket of my waistcoat."

Towards midnight Katherine began to fail. "Chain the devil,", cried Cæsar. "Once I was down in the pit with the devil myself, but now I'm up in the loft, seeing angels through the thatch. Can't you feel the workings of the Spirit?"

As the clock was warning to strike two Katherine thought she could, and from that day forward she led the singing of the women in the choir among "The Christians."

Pete remained among the unregenerate; but nevertheless "The Christians" saw him constantly. He sat on the back form and kept his eyes fixed on the "singing seat." Observing his regularity, Cæsar laid a hand on his head and told him the Spirit was working in his soul at last. Sometimes Pete thought it was, and that was when he shut his eyes and listened to Katherine's voice floating up, up, up, like an angel's, into the sky. But sometimes he knew it was not; and that was when he caught himself in the middle of Cæsar's mightiest prayers crooking his neck past the pitching bald pate of Johnny Niplightly, the constable, that he might get a glimpse of the top of Katherine's bonnet when her eyes were down.

Pete fell into a melancholy, and once more took to music as a comforter. It was not a home-made whistle now, but a fiddle bought out of his wages. On this he played in the cowhouse on winter evenings, and from the top of the midden outside in summer. When Cæsar heard of it his wrath was fearful. What was a fiddler? He was a servant of corruption, holding a candle to disorderly walkers and happy sinners on their way into the devil's pinfold. And what for was fiddles? Fiddles was for play-actors and theaytres. "And theaytres is *there*," said Cæsar, indicating with his foot one flag on the kitchen-floor, "and hell flames is *there*," he added, rolling his toe over to the joint of the next one.

Grannie began to plead. What was a fiddle if you played the right tunes on it? Didn't they read in the ould Book of King David himself playing on harps and timbrels and such things? And what was harps but fiddles in a way of spak-ing? Then warn't they all looking to be playing harps in heaven? 'Deed, yes, though the Lord would have to be teaching her how to play hers!

Cæsar was shaken. "Well, of course, certainly," he said, "if there's a power in fiddling to bring souls out of bondage, and if there's going to be fiddling and the like in Abraham's bosom—why, then, of course—well, why not?—let's have the lad's fiddle up at 'The Christians.'"

Nothing could have suited Pete so well. From that time forward he went out no more at nights to the cowhouse, but stayed indoors to practise hymns with Katherine. Oh, the terrible rapture of those nightly "practices!" They brought people to the inn to hear them, and so Cæsar found them good for profit both ways.

There was something in Cæsar's definition, nevertheless. It was found that among the saints there were certain weaker brethren who did not want a hymn to their ale. One of these was Johnny Niplightly, the rural constable, who was the complement of Katherine in the choir, being leader of the singing among the men. He was a tall man with a long nose, which seemed to have a perpetual cold. Making his rounds one night, he turned in at "The Manx Fairy," when Cæsar and Grannie were both from home, and Nancy Joe was in charge, and Pete and Katherine were practising a revival chorus.

"Where's Cæsar, dough?" he snuffled.

"At Peel, buying the stock," snapped Nancy.

"Dank de Lord! I mean—where's Grannie?"

"Nursing Mistress Quiggin."

Niplightly eased the strap of his beaver, liberated his lips, took a deep draught of ale, and then turned to Pete, with apologetic smiles, and suggested a change in the music.

At that Katherine leapt up as light as laughter. "A dance," she cried, "a dance!"

"Good sakes alive?" said Nancy Joe. "Listen to the girl? Is it the moon, Kitty, or what is it that's doing on you?"

"Shut your eyes, Nancy," said Katherine, "just for once, now won't you?"

"You can do what you like with me, with your coaxing and woaxing," said Nancy. "Enjoy yourself to the full, girl, but don't make a noise above the singing of the kettle."

Pete tuned his strings, and Katherine pinned up the tail of her skirt, and threw herself into position.

At the sound of the livelier preludings there came thronging out of the road into the parlour certain fellows of the baser sort, and behind them came one who was not of that denomination—a fair young man with a fine face under an Alpine hat. Heeding nothing of this audience, the girl gave a little rakish toss of her head and called on Pete to strike up.

Then Pete plunged into one of the profaner tunes which he had practised in the days of the cowhouse, and off went Katherine with a whoop. The boys stood back for her, bending down on their haunches as at a fight of gamecocks, and encouraging her with shouts of applause.

"Beautiful! Look at that now! Fine, though, fine! Clane done, aw, clane! Done to a dot! There's leaping for you, boys! Guy heng, did you ever see the like? Hommer the floor, girl—higher a piece! higher, then! Whoop, did ye ever see such a nate pair of ankles?"

"Hould your dirty tongue, you gobmouthed omathaun!" cried Nancy Joe. She had tried to keep her eyes away, but could not. "My goodness grayshers!" she cried. "Did you ever see the like, though? Screwing like the windmill on the schoolhouse! Well, well, Kitty, woman! Aw, Kirry, Kirry! Wherever did she get it, then? Goodsakes, the girl's twisting herself into knots!"

Pete was pulling away at the fiddle with both hands, like a bottom sawyer, his eyes dancing, his lips quivering, the whole soul of the lad lifted out of himself in an instant.

"Hould on still, Kate, hould on, girl!" he shouted. "Ma-chree! Machree! The darling's dancing like a drumstick!"

"Faster!" cried Kate. "Faster!"

The red ribbon had fallen from her head, and the wavy black hair was tumbling about her face. She was holding up her skirt with one hand, and the other arm was akimbo at her waist. Guggling, chuckling, crowing, panting, boiling, and bubbling with the animal life which all her days had been suppressed, and famished and starved into moans and groans, she was carried away by her own fire, gave herself up to it, and danced on the flags of the kitchen which had served Cæsar for his practical typology, like a creature intoxicated with new breath.

Meantime Cæsar himself, coming home in his chapel hat (his tall black beaver) from Peel, where he had been buying the year's stock of herrings at the boat's side, had overtaken, on the road, the venerable parson of his parish, Parson Quiggin of Lezayre. Drawing up the gig with a "Woa!" he had invited the old clergyman to a lift by his side on the gig's seat, which was cushioned with a sack of hay. The parson had accepted the invitation, and with a preliminary "Aisy! Your legs a taste higher, sir, just to keep the pickle off your trousers," a "Gee up!" and a touch of the whip, they were away together, with the light of the gig-lamp on the hind-quarters of the mare, as they bobbed and screwed like a mill-race under the splash-hoard.

It was Cæsar's chance, and he took it. Having pinned one of the heads of the Church, he gave him his views on the Romans, and on the general encroachment of Popery. The parson listened complacently. He was a tolerant old soul, with a round face, expressive of perpetual happiness, though he was always blinking his little eyes and declaring, with the Preacher, that all earthly things were vain. Hence he was nicknamed Old Vanity of Vanities.

The gig had swept past Sulby Chapel when Cæsar began to ask for the parson's opinion of certain texts.

"And may I presume, Pazon Quiggin, what d'ye think of the text—'Praise the Lord. O my soul, and all that is within me praise His Holy Name?'"

"A very good text after meat, Mr. Cregeen," said the parson, blinking his little eyes in the dark.

It was Cæsar's favourite text, and his fire was kindled at the parson's praise. "Man alive," he cried, his hot breath tickling the parson's neck, "I've praiched on that text, pazon, till it's wet me through to the waistcoat."

They were near to "The Manx Fairy" by this time.

"And talking of praise," said Cæsar, "I hear them there at their practices. Asking pardon now—it's proud I'd be, sir—perhaps you'd not be thinking mane to come in and hear the way we do 'Crown Him!'"

"So the saints use the fiddle," said the parson, as the gig drew up at the porch of the inn.

Half a minute afterwards the door of the parlour flew open with a bang, and Cæsar stood and glared on the threshold with the parson's ruddy face behind him. There was a moment's silence. The uplifted toe of Katherine trailed back to the ground, the fiddle of Pete slithered to his farther side, and the smacking lips of Niplightly transfixed themselves agape. Then the voice of the parson was heard to say, "Vanity, vanity, all is vanity!" and suddenly Cæsar, still on the threshold, went down on his knees to pray.

Cæsar's prayer was only a short one. His mortified pride called for quicker solace. Rising to his feet with as much dignity as he could command under the twinkling eyes of the parson, he stuttered, "The capers! Making a dacent house into a theaytre! Respectable person, too—one of the first that's going! So," facing the spectators, "just help yourselves home the pack of you! As for these ones," turning on Kate, Pete, and the constable, "there'll be no more of your practices. I'll do without the music of three saints like you. In future I'll have three sinners to raise my singing. These polices, too!" he said with a withering smile. (Niplightly was worming his way out at the back of Parson Quiggin.)

"Who began it?" shouted Cæsar, looking at Katherine.

From the moment that Cæsar dropped on his knees at the door, Pete had been well-nigh choked by an impulse to laugh aloud. But now he bit his lip and said, "I did!"

"Behould ye now, as imperent as a goat!" said Cæsar, working his eyebrows vigorously. "You've mistaken your profession, boy. It's a play-actorer they ought to be making of you. You're wasting your time with a plain, respectable man like me. You must lave me. Away to the loft for your chiss, boy! And just give sheet, my lad, and don't lay till you've fetched up at another lodgings."

Pete, with his eye on the parson's face, could control himself no longer, and he laughed so loud that the room rang.

"Right's the word, ould Nebucannezzar," he cried, and heaved up to his feet. "So long, Kitty, woman! S'long! We'll finish it another night though, and then the ould man himself will be houlding the candle."

Outside in the road somebody touched him on the shoulder. It was the young man in the Alpine hat.

"My gough! What? Phil!" cried Pete, and he laid hold of him with both hands at once.

"I've just finished at King William's and bought a boat," said Philip, "and I came up to ask you to join me—congers and cods, you know—good fun anyway. Are you willing?"

"Willing!" cried Pete. "Am I jumping for joy?"

And away they went down the road, swinging their legs together with a lively step.

"That's a nice girl, though—Kitty, Kate, what do you call her?" said Phil.

"Were you in then? So you saw her dancing?" said Pete eagerly. "Aw, yes, nice," he said warmly, "nice uncommon," he added absently, and then with a touch of sadness, "shocking nice!"

Presently they heard the pattering of light feet in the darkness behind them, and a voice like a broken cry calling "Pete!"

It was Kate. She came up panting and catching her breath in hiccoughs, took Pete's face in both her hands, drew it down to her own face, kissed it on the mouth, and was gone again without a word.

VI.

Philip had not been a success at school; he had narrowly escaped being a failure. During his earlier years he had shown industry without gifts; during his later years he had shown gifts without industry. His childish saying became his by-word, and half in sport, half in earnest, with a smile on his lips, and a shuddering sense of fascination, he would say when the wind freshened, "The sea's calling me, I must be off." The blood of the old sea-dog, his mother's father, was strong in him. Idleness led to disaster, and disaster to some disgrace. He was indifferent to both while at school, but shame found him out at home.

"You'll be sixteen for spring," said Auntie Nan, "and what would your poor father say if he were alive? He thought worlds of his boy, and always said what a man he would be some day."

That was the shaft that found Philip. The one passion that burned in his heart like a fire was reverence for the name and the will of his dead father. The big hopes of the broken man had sometimes come as a torture to the boy when the blood of the old salt was rioting within him. But now they came as a spur.

Philip went back to school and worked like a slave. There were only three terms left, and it was too late for high honours, but the boy did wonders. He came out well, and the masters were astonished. "After all," they said, "there's no denying it, the boy Christian must have the gift of genius. There's nothing he might not do."

If Phil had much of the blood of Captain Billy, Pete had much of the blood of Black Tom. After leaving the mill at Sulby, Pete made his home in the cabin of the smack. What he was to eat, and how he was to be clothed, and where he was to be lodged when the cold nights came, never troubled his mind for an instant. He had fine times with his partner. The terms of their partnership were simple. Phil took the fun and made Pete take the fish. They were a pair of happy-go-lucky lads, and they looked to the future with cheerful faces.

There was one shadow over their content, and that was the ghost of a gleam of sunshine. It made daylight between them, though, day by day as they ran together like two that run a race. The prize was Katherine Cregeen. Pete talked of her till Phil's heart awoke and trembled; but Phil hardly knew it was so, and Pete never once suspected it. Neither confessed to the other, and the shifts of both to hide the secret of each were boyish and beautiful.

There is a river famous for trout that rises in Sulby glen and flows into Ramsey harbour. One of the little attempts of the two lads to deceive each other was to make believe that it was their duty to fish this river with the rod, and so wander away singly up the banks of the stream until they came to "The Manx Fairy," and then drop in casually to quench the thirst of so much angling. Towards the dusk of evening Philip, in a tall silk hat over a jacket and knickerbockers, would come upon Pete by the Sulby bridge, washed, combed, and in a collar. Then there would be looks of great surprise on both sides. "What, Phil! Is it yourself, though? Just thought I'd see if the trouts were biting to-night. Dear me, this is Sulby too! And bless my soul, 'The Fairy' again I Well, a drop of drink will do no harm. Shall we put a sight on them inside, eh?" After that prelude they would go into the house together.

This little comedy was acted every night for weeks. It was acted on Hollantide Eve six months after Pete had been turned out by Cæsar. Grannie was sitting by the glass partition, knitting at intervals, serving at the counter occasionally and scoring up on a black board that was a mass of chalk hieroglyphics. Cæsar himself in ponderous spectacles and with a big book in his hands was sitting in the kitchen behind with his back to the glass, so as to make the lamp of the business serve also for his studies. On a bench in the bar sat Black Tom, smoking, spitting, scraping his feet on the sanded floor, and looking like a gigantic spider with enormous bald head. At his side was a thin man with a face pitted by smallpox, and a forehead covered with strange protuberances. This was Jonaique Jelly, barber, clock-mender, and Manx patriot. The postman was there, too, Kelly the Thief, a tiny creature with twinkling ferret eyes, and a face that had a settled look of age, as of one born old, being wrinkled in squares like the pointing of a cobble wall.

At sight of Pete, Grannie made way, and he pushed through to the kitchen, where he seated himself in a seat in the fireplace just in front of the peat closet, and under the fish hanging to smoke. At sight of Phil she dropped her needles, smoothed her front hair, rose in spite of protest, and wiped down a chair by the ingle. Cæsar eyed Pete in silence from between the top rim of his spectacles and the bottom edge of the big book; but as Philip entered he lowered the book and welcomed him. Nancy Joe was coming and going in her clogs like a rip-rap let loose between the dairy and a pot of potatoes in their jackets which swung from the slowrie, the hook over the fire. A moment later Kate came flitting through the half-lit kitchen, her black eyes dancing and her mouth rippling in smiles. She courtesied to Philip, grimaced at Pete, and disappeared.

Then from the other side of the glass partition came the husky voice of the postman, saying, "Well, I must be taking the road, gentlemen. There's Manx ones starting for Kim-berley by the early sailing to-morrow morning."

And then came the voice of the barber in a hoarse falsetto: "Kimberley! That's the place for good men I'm always saying. There's Billy the Red back home with a fortune. And ould Corlett—look at ould Corlett, the Ballabeg! Five years away at the diggings, and left a house worth twenty pounds per year per annum, not to spoke of other hereditaments."

After that the rasping voice of Black Tom, in a tone of irony and contempt: "Of coorse, aw, yes, of coorse, there's goold on the cushags there, they're telling me. But I thought you were a man that's all for the island, Mr. Jelly."

"Lave me alone for that," said the voice of the barber. "Manx-land for the Manx-man—that's the text I'm houlding to. But what's it saying, 'Custom must be indulged with custom, or custom will die?' And with these English scouring over it like puffins on the Calf, it isn't much that's left of the ould island but the name. The best of the Manx boys are going away foreign, same as these ones."

"Well, I've letters for them to the packet-office anyway," said the postman.

"Who are they, Mr. Kelly?" called Philip, through the doorway.

"Some of the Quarks ones from Glen Rushen, sir, and the Gills boys from Castletown over. Good-night all, goodnight!"

The door closed behind the postman, and Black Tom growled, "Slips of lads—I know them."

"Smart though, smart uncommon," said the barber; "that's the only sort they're wanting out yonder."

There was a contemptuous snort. "So? You'd better go to Kimberley yourself, then."

"Turn the clock back a piece and I'll start before you've time to curl your hair," said the barber.

Black Tom was lifting his pot. "That's the one thing," said he, "the Almighty Himself" (gulp, gulp) "can't do."

"Which?" tittered the barber.

"Both," said Black Tom, scratching his big head, as bald as a bladder.

Cæsar flashed about with his face to the glass partition. "You're like the rest of the infidels, sir," said he, "only spaking to contradick yourself—calling God the Almighty, and telling in the same breath of something He can't do."

Meanwhile an encounter of another sort was going on at the ingle. Kate had re-appeared with a table fork which she used at intervals to test the boiling of the potatoes. At each approach to the fire she passed close to where Pete sat, never looking at Phil above the level of his boots. And as often as she bent over the pot, Pete put his arm round her waist, being so near and so tempting. For thus pestering her she beat her foot like a goat, and screwed on a look of anger which broke down in a stifled laugh; but she always took care to come again to Pete's side rather than to Phil's, until at last the nudging and shoving ended in a pinch and a little squeal, and a quick cry of "What's that?" from Cæsar.

Kate vanished like a flash, the dim room began to frown again, and Phil to draw his breath heavily, when the girl came back as suddenly bringing an apple and a length of string. Mounting a chair, she fixed one end of the string to the lath of the ceiling by the peck, the parchment oatcake pan, and the other end she tied to the stalk of the apple.

"What's the jeel now?" said Pete.

"Fancy! Don't you know? Not heard f'Hop-tu-naa'? It's Hollantide Eve, man," said Kate.

Then setting the string going like a pendulum, she stood back a pace with hands clasped behind her, and snapped at the apple as it swung, sometimes catching it, sometimes missing it, sometimes marking it, sometimes biting it, her body bending and rising with its waggle, and nod, and bob, her mouth opening and closing, her white teeth gleaming, and her whole face bubbling over with delight. At every touch the speed increased, and the laughter grew louder as the apple went faster. Everybody, except the miller, joined in the fun. Phil cried out on the girl to look to her teeth, but Pete egged her on to test the strength of them.

"Snap at it, Kitty!" cried Pete. "Aw, lost! Lost again! Ow! One in the cheek! No matter! Done!"

And Black Tom and Mr. Jelly stood up to watch through the doorway. "My goodness grayshers!" cried one. "What a mouthful!" said the other. "Share it, Kitty, woman; aw, share and share alike, you know."

But then came the thunderous tones of Cæsar. "Drop it, drop it! Such practices is nothing but Popery."

"Popery!" cried Black Tom from over the counter. "Chut! nonsense, man! The like of it was going before St. Patrick was born."

Kate was puffing and panting and taking down the pendulum.

"What does it mean then, Tom?" she said; "it's you for knowing things."

"Mane? It manes fairies!"

"Fairies!"

Black Tom sat down with a complacent air, and his rasping voice came from the other side of the glass. "In the ould times gone by, girl, before Manxmen got too big for their breeches, they'd be off to bed by ten o'clock on Hollantide Eve to lave room for the little people that's outside to come in. And the big woman of the house would be filling the crocks for the fairies to drink, and the big man himself would be raking the ashes so they might bake their cakes, and a girl, same as you, would be going to bed backwards——"

"I know! I know!" cried Kate, near to the ceiling, and clapping her hands. "She eats a roasted apple, and goes to bed thirsty, and then dreams that somebody brings her a drink of water, and that's the one that's to be her husband, eh?"

"You've got it, girl."

Cæsar had been listening with his eyes turned sideways off his book, and now he cried, "Then drop it, I'm telling you. It's nothing but instruments of Satan, and the ones that's telling it are just flying in the face of faith from superstition and contrariety. It isn't dacent in a Christian public-house, and I'm for having no more of it."

Grannie paused in her knitting, fixed her cap with one of her needles and said, "Dear heart, father! Tom meant no harm." Then, glancing at the clock and rising, "But it's time to shut up the house, anyway. Good night, Tom! Good night all! Good night!"

Phil and Pete rose also. Pete went to the door and pretended to look out, then came back to Kate's side and whispered, "Come, give them the slip—there's somebody outside that's waiting for you."

"Let them wait," said the girl, but she laughed, and Pete knew she would come. Then he turned to Philip, "A word in your ear, Phil," he said, and took him by the arm and drew him out of the house and round to the yard of the stable.

"Well, good night, Grannie," said Mr. Jelly, going out behind them. "But if I were as young as your grandson there, Mr. Quilliam, I would be making a start for somewhere."

"Grandson!" grunted Tom, heaving up, "I've got no grandson, or he wouldn't be laving me to smoke a dry pipe. But he's making an Almighty of this Phil Christian—that's it."

After they were gone, Grannie began counting the till and saying, "As for fairies—one, two, three—it may be, as Cæsar says—four—five—the like isn't in, but it's safer to be civil to them anyway."

"Aw, yes," said Nancy Joe, "a crock of fresh water and a few good words going to bed on Hollantide Eve does no harm at all, at all."

Outside in the stable-yard the feet of Black Tom and Jonaique Jelly were heard going off on the road. The late moon was hanging low, red as an evening sun, over the hill to the south-east. Pete was puffing and blowing as if he had been running a race. "Quick, boy, quick!" he was whispering, "Kate's coming. A word in your ear first. Will you do me a turn, Phil?"

"What is it?" said Philip.

"Spake to the ould man for me while I spake to the girl!"

"What about?" said Philip.

But Pete could hear, nothing except his own voice. "The ould angel herself, she's all right, but the ould man's hard. Spake for me, Phil; you've got the fine English tongue at you."

"But what about?" Philip said again.

"Say I may be a bit of a rip, but I'm not such a bad sort anyway. Make me out a taste, Phil, and praise me up. Say I'll be as good as goold; yes, will I though. Tell him he has only to say yes, and I'll be that studdy and willing and hardworking and persevering you never seen."

"But, Pete, Pete, Pete, whatever am I to say all this about?"

Pete's puffing and panting ceased. "What about? Why, about the girl for sure."

"The girl!" said Philip.

"What else?" said Pete.

"Kate? Am I to speak for you to the father for Kate?"

Philip's voice seemed to come up from the bottom depths of his throat.

"Are you thinking hard of the job, Phil?"

There was a moment's silence. The blood had rushed to Philip's face, which was full of strange matter, but the darkness concealed it.

"I didn't say that," he faltered.

Pete mistook Philip's hesitation for a silent commentary on his own unworthiness. "I know I'm only a sort of a waistrel," he said, "but, Phil, the way I'm loving that girl it's shocking. I can never take rest for thinking of her. No, I'm not sleeping at night nor working reg'lar in the day neither. Everything is telling of her, and everything is shouting her name. It's 'Kate' in the sea, and 'Kate' in the river, and the trees and the gorse. 'Kate,' 'Kate,' 'Kate,' it's Kate constant, and I can't stand much more of it. I'm loving the girl scandalous, that's the truth, Phil."

Pete paused, but Philip gave no sign.

"It's hard to praise me, that's sarten sure," said Pete, "but I've known her since she was a little small thing in pinafores, and I was a slip of a big boy, and went into trousers, and we played Blondin in the glen together."

Still Philip did not speak. He was gripping the stable-wall with his trembling fingers, and struggling for composure. Pete scraped the paving-stones at his feet, and mumbled again in a voice that was near to breaking. "Spake for me, Phil. It's you to do it. You've the way of saying things, and making them out to look something. It would be clane ruined in a jiffy if I did it for myself. Spake for me, boy, now won't you, now?"

Still Philip was silent. He was doing his best to swallow a lump in his throat. His heart had begun to know itself. In the light of Pete's confession he had read his own secret. To give the girl up was one thing; it was another to plead for her for Pete. But Pete's trouble touched him. The lump at his throat went down, and the fingers on the wall slacked away. "I'll do it," he said, only his voice was like a sob.

20

Then he tried to go off hastily that he might hide the emotion that came over him like a flood that had broken its dam. But Pete gripped him by the shoulder, and peered into his face in the dark. "You will, though," said Pete, with a little shout of joy; "then it's as good as done; God bless you, old fellow."

Philip began to roll about. "Tut, it's nothing," he said, with a stout heart, and then he laughed a laugh with a cry in it. He could have said no more without breaking down; but just then a flash of light fell on them from the house, and a hushed voice cried, "Pete!"

"It's herself," whispered Pete. "She's coming! She's here!"

Philip turned, and saw Kate in the doorway of the dairy, the sweet young figure framed like a silhouette by the light behind.

"I'm going!" said Philip, and he edged up to the house as the girl stepped out.

Pete followed him a step or two in approaching Kate. "Whist, man!" he whispered. "Tell the old geezer I'll be going to chapel reglar early tides and late shifts, and Sunday-school constant. And, whist! tell him I'm larning myself to play on the harmonia."

Then Philip slithered softly through the dairy door, and shut it after him, leaving Kate and Pete together.

VII.

The kitchen of "The Manx Fairy" was now savoury with the odour of herrings roasting in their own brine, and musical with the crackling and frizzling of the oil as it dropped into the fire.

"It's a long way back to Ballure, Mrs. Cregeen," said Philip, popping his head in at the door jamb. "May I stay to a bite of supper?"

"Aw, stay and welcome," said Cæsar, putting down the big book, and Nancy Joe said the same, dropping her high-pitched voice perceptibly, and Grannie said, also, "Right welcome, sir, if you'll not be thinking mane to take pot luck with us. Potatoes and herrings, Mr. Christian; just a Manxman's supper. Lift the pot off the slowrie, Nancy."

"Well, and isn't he a Manxman himself, mother?" said Cæsar.

"Of course I am, Mr. Cregeen," said Philip, laughing noisily. "If I'm not, who should be, eh?'"

"And Manxman or no Manxman, what for should he turn up his nose at herrings same as these?" said Nancy Joe. She was dishing up a bowlful. "Where'll he get the like of them? Not in England over, I'll go bail."

"Indeed, no, Nancy," said Philip, still laughing needlessly.

"And if they had them there, the poor, useless creatures would be lost to cook them."

"'Deed, would they, Nancy," said Grannie. She was rolling the potatoes into a heap on to the bare table. "And we've much to be thankful for, with potatoes and herrings three times a day; but we shouldn't be thinking proud of our-selves for that."

"Ask the gentleman to draw up, mother," said Cæsar.

"Draw up, sir, draw up. Here's your bowl of butter-milk. A knife and fork, Nancy. We're no people for knife and fork to a herring, sir. And a plate for Mr. Christian, woman; a gentleman usually likes a plate. Now ate, sir, ate and welcome—but where's your friend, though?"

"Pete! oh! he's not far off." Saying this, Philip interrupted his laughter to distribute sage winks between Nancy Joe and Grannie.

Cæsar looked around with a potato half peeled in his fingers. "And the girl—where's Kate?" he asked.

"She's not far off neither," said Philip, still winking vigorously. "But don't trouble about them, Mr. Cregeen. They'll want no supper. They're feeding on sweeter things than herrings even." Saying this he swallowed a gulp with another laugh.

Cæsar lifted his head with a pinch of his herring between finger and thumb half way to his open mouth. "Were you spaking, sir?" he said.

At that Philip laughed immoderately. It was a relief to drown with laughter the riot going on within.

"Aw, dear, what's agate of the boy?" thought Grannie.

"Is it a dog bite that's working on him?" thought Nancy.

"Speaking!" cried Philip, "of course I'm speaking. I've come in to do it, Mr. Cregeen—I've come in to speak for Pete. He's fond of your daughter, Cæsar, and wants your good-will to marry her."

"Lord-a-massy!" cried Nancy Joe.

"Dear heart alive!" muttered Grannie.

"Peter Quilliam!" said Cæsar, "did you say Peter?"

"I did, Mr. Cregeen, Peter Quilliam," said Philip stoutly, "my friend Pete, a rough fellow, perhaps, and without much education, but the best-hearted lad in the island. Come now, Cæsar, say the word, sir, and make the young people happy."

He almost foundered over that last word, but Cæsar kept him up with a searching look.

"Why, I picked him out of the streets, as you might say," said Cæsar.

"So you did, Mr. Cregeen, so you did. I always thought you were a discerning man, Cæsar. What do you say, Grannie? It's Cæsar for knowing a deserving lad when he sees one, eh?"

He gave another round of his cunning winks, and Grannie replied, "Aw, well, it's nothing against either of them anyway."

Cæsar was gitting as straight as a crowbar and as grim as a gannet. "And when he left me, he gave me imperence and disrespeck."

"But the lad meant no harm, father," said Grannie; "and hadn't you told him to take to the road?"

"Let every bird hatch its own eggs, mother; it'll become you better," said Cæsar. "Yes, sir, the lip of Satan and the imperence of sin."

"Pete!" cried Philip, in a tone of incredulity; "why, he hasn't a thought about you that isn't out of the Prayer-book."

Cæsar snorted. "No? Then maybe that's where he's going for his curses."

"No curses at all," said Nancy Joe, from the side of the table, "but a right good lad though, and you've never had another that's been a patch on him."

Cæsar screwed round to her and said severely, "Where there's geese there's dirt, and where there's women there's talking." Then turning back to Philip, he said in a tone of mock deference, "And may I presume, sir—a little question—being a thing like that's general understood—what's his fortune?"

Philip fell back in his chair. "Fortune? Well, I didn't think that you now——"

"No?" said Cæsar. "We're not children of Israel in the wilderness getting manna dropped from heaven twice a day. If it's only potatoes and herrings itself, we're wanting it three times, you see."

Do what he would to crush it, Philip could not help feeling a sense of relief. Fate was interfering; the girl was not for Pete. For the first moment since he returned to the kitchen he breathed freely and fully. But then came the prick of conscience: he had come to plead for Pete, and he must be loyal; he must not yield; he must exhaust all his resources of argument and persuasion. The wild idea occurred to him to take Cæsar by force of the Bible.

"But think what the old book says, Mr. Cregeen, 'take no thought for the morrow'——"

"That's what Johnny Niplightly said, Mr. Christian, when he lit my kiln overnight and burnt my oats before morning.".

"'But consider the lilies'——"

"I have considered them, sir; but I'm foiling still and mother has to spin."

"And isn't Pete able to toil, too," said Philip boldly. "Nobody better in the island; there's not a lazy bone in his body, and he'll earn his living anywhere."

"What *is* his living, sir?" said Cæsar.

Philip halted for an answer, and then said, "Well, he's only with me in the boat at present, Mr. Cregeen."

"And what's he getting? His meat and drink and a bit of pence, eh? And you'll be selling up some day, it's like, and going away to England over, and then where is he? Let the girl marry a mother-naked man at once."

"But you're wanting help yourself, father," said Grannie. "Yes, you are though, and time for chapel too and aisément in your old days———"

"Give the lad my mill as well as my daughter, is that it, eh?" said Cæsar. "No, I'm not such a goose as yonder, either. I could get heirs, sir, heirs, bless ye—fifty acres and better, not to spoke of the bas'es. But I can do without them. The Lord's blest me with enough. I'm not for daubing grease on the tail of the fat pig."

"Just so, Cæsar," said Philip, "just so; you can afford to take a poor man for your son-in-law, and there's Pete——"

"I'd be badly in want of a bird, though, to give a groat for an owl," said Cæsar.

"The lad means well, anyway," said Grannie; "and he was that good to his mother, poor thing—it was wonderful."

"I knew the woman," said Cæsar; "I broke a sod of her grave myself. A brand plucked from the burning, but not a straight walker in this life. And what is the lad himself? A monument of sin without a name. A bastard, what else? And that's not the port I'm sailing for."

Down to this point Philip had been torn by conflicting feelings. He was no match for Cæsar in worldly logic, or at fencing with texts of Scripture. The devil had been whispering at his ear, "Let it alone, you'd better." But his time had come at length to conquer both himself and Cæsar. Rising to his feet at Cæsar's last word, he cried in a voice of wrath, "What? You call yourself a Christian man, and punish the child for the sin of the parent! No name, indeed! Let me tell you, Mr. Cæsar Cregeen, it's possible to have one name in heaven that's worse than none at all on earth, and that's the name of a hypocrite."

So saying he threw back his chair, and was making for the door, when Cæsar rose and said softly, "Come into the bar and have something." Then, looking back at Philip's plate, he forced a laugh, and said, "But you've turned over your herring, sir—that's bad luck." And, putting a hand on Philip's shoulder, he added, in a lower tone, "No disrespeck to you, sir; and no harm to the lad, but take my word for it, Mr. Christian, if there's an amble in the mare it'll be in the colt."

Philip went off without another word. The moon was rising and whitening as he stepped from the door. Outside the porch a figure flitted past him in the uncertain shadows with a merry trill of mischievous laughter. He found Pete in the road, puffing and blowing as before, but from a different cause.

"The living devil's in the girl for sartin," said Pete; "I can't get my answer out of her either way." He had been chasing her for his answer, and she had escaped him through a gate. "But what luck with the ould man, Phil?"

Then Phil told him of the failure of his mission—told him plainly and fully but tenderly, softening the hard sayings but revealing the whole truth. As he did so he was conscious that he was not feeling like one who brings bad news. He knew that his mouth in the darkness was screwed up into an ugly smile, and, do what he would; he could not make it straight and sorrowful.

The happy laughter died off Pete's, lips, and he listened at first in silence, and afterwards with low growls. When Phil showed him how his poverty was his calamity he said, "Ay, ay, I'm only a wooden-spoon man." When Phil told him how Cæsar had ripped up their old dead quarrel he muttered, "I'm on the ebby tide, Phil, that's it." And when Phil hinted at what Cæsar had said of his mother and of the impediment of his own birth, a growl came up from the very depths of him, and he scraped the stones under his feet and said, "He shall repent it yet; yes, shall he."

"Come, don't take it so much to heart—it's miserable to bring you such bad news," said Phil; but he knew the sickly smile was on his lips still, and he hated himself for the sound of his own voice.

Pete found no hollow ring in it. "God bless you, Phil," he said; "you've done the best for me, I know that. My pocket's as low as my heart, and it isn't fair to the girl, or I shouldn't be asking the ould man's lave anyway."

He stood a moment in silence, crunching the wooden laths of the garden fence like matchwood in his fingers, and then said, with sudden resolution, "I know what I'll do."

"What's that?" said Philip.. "I'll go abroad; I'll go to Kimberley."

"Never!"

"Yes, will I though, and quick too. You heard what the men were saying in the evening—there's Manx ones going by the boat in the morning? Well, I'll go with them."

"And you talk of being low in your pocket," said Phil. "Why, it will take all you've got, man."

"And more, too," said Pete, "but you'll lend me the lave of the passage-money. That's getting into debt, but no matter. When a man falls into the water he needn't mind the rain. I'll make good money out yonder."

A light had appeared at the window of an upper room, and Pete shook his clenched fist at it and cried, "Good-bye, Master Cregeen. I'll put worlds between us. You were my master once, but nobody made you my master for ever—neither you nor no man."

All this time Philip knew that hell was in his heart. The hand that had let him loose when his anger got the better of him with Cæsar was clutching at him again. Some evil voice at his ear was whispering, "Let him go; lend him the money."

"Come on, Pete," he faltered, "and don't talk nonsense!"

But Pete heard nothing. He had taken a few steps forward, as far as to the stable-yard, and was watching the light in the house. It was moving from window to window of the dark wall. "She's taking the father's candle," he muttered. "She's there," he said softly. "No, she has gone. She's coming back though." He lifted the stocking cap from his head and fumbled it in his hands. "God bless her," he murmured. He sank to his knees on the ground. "And take care of her while I'm away."

The moon had come up in her whiteness behind, and all was quiet and solemn around. Philip fell back and turned away his face.

VIII.

When Cæsar came in after seeing Philip to the door, he said, "Not a word of this to the girl. You that are women are like pigs—we've got to pull the way we don't want you."

On that Kate herself came in, blushing a good deal, and fussing about with great vigour. "Are you talking of the piggies, father?" she said artfully. "How tiresome they are, to be sure! They came out into the yard when the moon rose and I had such work to get them back."

Cæsar snorted a little, and gave the signal for bed. "Fairies indeed!" he said, in a tone of vast contempt, going to the corner to wind the clock. "Just wakeness of faith," he said over the clank of the chain as the weights rose; "and no trust in God neither," he added, and then the clock struck ten.

Grannie had lit two candles—one for herself and her husband, the other for Nancy Joe. Nancy had slyly filled three earthenware crocks with water from the well, and had set them on the table, mumbling something about the kettle and the morning. And Cæsar himself, pretending not to see anything, and muttering dark words about waste, went from the clock to the hearth, and raked out the hot ashes to a flat surface, on which you might have laid a girdle for baking cakes.

"Good-night, Nancy," called Grannie, from half-way up the stairs, and Cæsar, with his head down, followed grumbling. Nancy went off next, and then Kate was left alone. She had to put out the lamp and wait for her father's candle.

When the lamp was gone the girl was in the dark, save for the dim light of the smouldering fire. She began to tremble and to laugh in a whisper. Her eyes danced in the red glow of the dying turf. She slipped off her shoes and went to a closet in the wall. There she picked an apple out of a barrel, and brought it to the fire and roasted it. Then, down on her knees before the hearth, she took took two pinches of the apple and swallowed them. After that and a little shudder she rose again, and turned about to go to bed, backwards, slowly, tremblingly, with measured steps, feeling her way past the furniture, having a shock when she touched anything, and laughing to herself, nervously, when she remembered what it was.

At the door of her father's room and Grannie's she called, with a quaver in her voice, and a sleepy grunt came out to her. She reached one hand through the door, which was ajar, and took the burning candle. Then she blew out the light with a trembling puff, that had to be twice repeated, and made for her own bedroom, still going backwards.

It was a sweet little chamber over the dairy, smelling of new milk and ripe apples, and very dainty in dimity and muslin. Two tiny windows looked out from it, one on to the stable-yard and the other on to the orchard. The late moon came through the orchard window, over the heads of the dwarf trees, and the little white place was lit up from the floor to the sloping thatch.

Kate went backwards as far as to the bed, and sat down on it She fancied she heard a step in the yard, but the yard window was at her back, and she would not look behind. She listened, but heard nothing more except a see-sawing noise from the stable, where the mare was running her rope in the manger ring. Nothing but this and the cheep-cheep of a mouse that was gnawing the wood somewhere in the floor.

"Will he come?" she asked herself.

She rose and loosened her gown, and as it fell to her feet she laughed.

"Which will it be, I wonder—which?" she whispered.

The moonlight had crept up to the foot of the bed, and now lay on it like a broad blue sword speckled as with rust by the patchwork counterpane.

She freed her hair from its red ribbon, and it fell in a shower about her face. All around her seemed hushed and awful. She shuddered again, and with a back ward hand drew down the sheets. Then she took a long, deep breath, like a sigh that is half a smile, and lay down to sleep.

IX.

Somewhere towards the dawn, in the vague shadow-land between a dream and the awakening, Kate thought she was startled by a handful of rice thrown at her carriage on her marriage morning. The rattle came again, and then she knew it was from gravel dashed at her bedroom window. As she recognised the sound, a voice came as through a cavern, crying, "Kate!" She was fully awake by this time. "Then it's to be Pete," she thought. "It's bound to be Pete, it's like," she told herself. "It's himself outside, anyway."

It was Pete indeed. He was standing in the thin darkness under the window, calling the girl's name out of the back of his throat, and whistling to her in a sort of whisper. Presently he heard a movement inside the room, and he said over his shoulder, "She's coming."

There was the click of a latch and the slithering of a sash, and then out through the little dark frame came a head like a picture, with a face all laughter, crowned by a cataract of streaming black hair, and rounded off at the throat by a shadowy hint of the white frills of a night-dress.

"Kate," said Pete again.

She pretended to have come to the window merely to look out, and, like a true woman, she made a little start at the sound of his voice, and a little cry of dismay at the idea that he was so close beneath and had taken her unawares. Then she peered down into the gloom and said, in a tone of wondrous surprise, "It must be Pete, surely."

"And so it is, Kate," said Pete, "and he couldn't take rest without spaking to you once again."

"Ah!" she said, looking back and covering her eyes, and thinking of Black Tom and the fairies. But suddenly the mischief of her sex came dancing into her blood, and she could not help but plague the lad. "Have you lost your way, Pete?" she asked, with an air of innocence.

"Not my way, but myself, woman," said Pete.

"Lost yourself! Have the lad's wits gone moon-raking, I wonder? Are you witched then, Pete?" she inquired, with vast solemnity.

"Aw, witched enough. Kate——"

"Poor fellow!" sighed Kate. "Did she strike you unknown and sudden?"

"Unknown it was, Kirry, and sudden, too. Listen, though——"

"Aw dear, aw dear! Was it old Mrs. Cowley of the Curragh? Did she turn into a hare? Is it bitten you've been, Pete?"

"Aw, yes, bitten enough. But, Kate——"

"Then it was a dog, it's like. Is it flying from the water you are, Pete?"

"No, but flying *to* the water, woman. Kate, I say——"

"Is it burning they're doing for it?"

"Burning and freezing both. Will you hear me, though? I'm going away—hundreds and thousands of miles away."

Then from the window came a tone of great awe, uttered with face turned upward as if to the last remaining star.

"Poor boy! Poor boy! it's bitten he is, for sure."

"Then it's yourself that's bitten me. Kirry——"

There was a little crow of gaiety. "Me? Am I the witch? You called me a fairy in the road this evening."

"A fairy you are, girl, and a witch too; but listen, now——"

"You said I was an angel, though, at the cowhouse gable; and an angel doesn't bite."

Then she barked like a dog, and laughed a shrill laugh like a witch, and barked again.

But Pete could bear no more. "Go on, then; go on with your capers! Go on!" he cried, in a voice of reproach. "It's not a heart that's at you at all, girl, but only a stone. You see a man going away from the island——"

"From the island?" Kate gasped.

"Middling down in the mouth, too, and plagued out of his life between the ruck of you," continued Pete; "but God forgive you all, you can't help it."

"Did you say you were going out of the island, Pete?"

"Coorse I did; but what's the odds? Africa, Kimberley, the Lord knows where——"

"Kimberley! Not Kimberley, Pete!"

"Kimberley or Timbuctoo, what's it matter to the like of you? A man's coming up in the morning to bid you good-bye before an early sailing, and you're thinking of nothing but your capers and divilments."

"It's you to know what a girl's thinking, isn't it, Mr. Pete? And why are you flying in my face for a word?"

"Flying? I'm not flying. It's driven I am."

"Driven, Pete?"

"Driven away by them that's thinking I'm not fit for you. Well, that's true enough, but they shan't be telling me twice."

"They? Who are they, Pete?"

"What's the odds? Flinging my mother at me, too—poor little mother! And putting the bastard on me, it's like. A respectable man's girl isn't going begging that she need marry a lad without a name."

There was a sudden ejaculation from the window-sash. "Who dared to say that?"

"No matter."

"Whoever they are, you can tell them, if it's me they mean, that, name or no name, when I want to marry I'll marry the man I like."

"If I thought that now, Kitty——"

"As for you, Mr. Pete, that's so ready with your cross words, you can go to your Kimberley. Yes, go, and welcome; and what's more—what's more——"

But the voice of anger, in the half light overhead, broke down suddenly into an inarticulate gurgle.

"Why, what's this?" said Pete in a flurry. "You're not crying though, Kate? Whatever am I saying to you, Kitty, woman? Here, here—bash me on the head for a blockhead and an omathaun."

And Pete was clambering up the wall by the side of the dairy window.

"Get down, then," whispered Kate.

Her wrath was gone in a moment, and Pete, being nearer to her now, could see tears of laughter dancing in her eyes.

"Get down, Pete, or I'll shut the window, I will—yes, I will." And, to show how much she was in earnest in getting out of his reach, she shut up the higher sash and opened the lower one.

"Darling!" cried Pete.

"Hush! What's that?" Kate whispered, and drew back on her knees.

"Is the door of the pig-sty open again?" said Pete.

Kate drew a breath of relief. "It's only somebody snoring," she said.

"The ould man," said Pete. "That's all serene! A good ould sheepdog, that snaps more than, he bites, but he's best when he's sleeping—more safer, anyway."

"What's the good of going away, Pete?" said Kate. "You'd have to make a fortune to satisfy father."

"Others have done it, Kitty—why shouldn't I? Manx ones too—silver kings and diamond kings, and the Lord knows what. No fear of me! When I come back it's a queen you'll be, woman—my queen, anyway, with pigs and cattle and a girl to wash and do for you."

"So that's how you'd bribe a poor girl is it? But you'd have to turn religious, or father would never consent."

"When I come home again, Kitty, I'll be that religious you never seen. I'll be just rolling in it. You'll hear me spaking like the Book of Genesis and Abraham, and his sons, and his cousins; I'll be coming up at night making love to you at the cowhouse door like the Acts of the Apostles."

"Well, that will be some sort of courting, anyway. But who says I'll be wanting it? Who says I'm willing for you to go away at all with the notion that I must be bound to marry you when you come back?"

"I do," said Pete stoutly.

"Oh, indeed, sir."

"Listen. I'll be working like a nigger out yonder, and making my pile, and banking it up, and never seeing nothing but the goold and the girls——"

"My goodness! What do you say?"

"Aw, never fear! I'm a one-woman man, Kate; but loving one is giving me eyes for all. And you'll be waiting for me constant, and never giving a skute of your little eye to them drapers and druggists from Ramsey——"

"Not one of them? Not Jamesie Corrin, even—he's a nice boy, is Jamesie."

"That dandy-divil with the collar? Hould your capers, woman!"

"Nor young Ballawhaine—Ross Christian, you know?"

"Ross Christian be—well, no; but, honour bright, you'll be saying, 'Peter's coming; I must be thrue!'"

"So I've got my orders, sir, eh? It's all settled then, is it? Hadn't you better fix the wedding-day and take out the banns, now that your hand is in? I have got nothing to do with it, seemingly. Nobody asks me."

"Whist, woman!" cried Pete. "Don't you hear it?"

A cuckoo was passing over the house and calling.

"It's over the thatch, Kate. 'Cuckoo! Cuckoo! Cuckoo!' Three times! Bravo! Three times is a good Amen. Omen is it? Have it as you like, love."

The stars had paled out by this time, and the dawn was coming up like a grey vapour from the sea.

25

"Ugh! the air feels late; I must be going in," said Kate.

"Only a bit of a draught from the mountains—it's not morning yet," said Pete.

A bird called from out of the mist somewhat far away.

"It is, though. That's the throstle up the glen," said Kate.

Another bird answered from the eaves of the house.

"And what's that?" said Pete. "Was it yourself, Kitty? How straight your voice is like the throstle's!"

She hung her head at the sweet praise, but answered tartly, "How people will be talking!"

A dead white light came sweeping over the front of the house, and the trees and the hedges, all quiet until then, began to shudder. Kate shuddered too, and drew the frills closer about her throat. "I'm going, Pete," she whispered.

"Not yet. It's only a taste of the salt from the sea," said Pete. "The moon's not out many minutes."

"Why, you goose, it's been gone these two hours. This isn't Jupiter, where it's moonlight always."

"Always moonlight in Jubiter, is it?" said Pete. "My goodness! What coorting there must be there!"

A cock crowed from under the hen-roost, the dog barked indoors, and the mare began to stamp in her stall.

"When do you sail, Pete?"

"First tide—seven o'clock."

"Time to be off, then. Good-bye!"

"Hould hard—a word first."

"Not a word. I'm going back to bed. See, there's the sun coming up over the mountains."

"Only a touch of red on the tip of ould Cronky's nose. Listen! Just to keep them dandy-divils from plaguing you, I'll tell Phil to have an eye on you while I'm away."

"Mr. Christian?"

"Call him Philip, Kate. He's as free as free. No pride at all. Let him take care of you till I come back."

"I'm shutting the window, Pete!"

"Wait! Something else. Bend down so the ould man won't hear."

"I can't reach—what is it?"

"Your hand, then; I'll tell it to your hand."

She hesitated a moment, and then dropped her hand over the window-sill, and he clutched at it and kissed it, and pushed back the white sleeve and ran up the arm with his lips as far as he could climb.

"Another, my girl; take your time, one more—half a one, then."

She drew her arm back until her hand got up to his hand, and then she said, "What's this? The mole on your finger still, Pete? You called me a witch—now see me charm it away. Listen!—'Ping, ping, prash, Cur yn cadley-jiargan ass my chass.'"

She was uttering the Manx charm in a mock-solemn ululation when a bough snapped in the orchard, and she cried, "What's that?"

"It's Philip. He's waiting under the apple-tree," said Pete.

"My goodness me!" said Kate, and down went the window-sash.

A moment later it rose again, and there was the beautiful young face in its frame as before, but with the rosy light of the dawn on it.

"Has he been there all the while?" she whispered.

"What matter? It's only Phil."

"Good-bye! Good luck!" and then the window went down for good.

"Time to go," said Philip, still in his tall silk hat and his knickerbockers. He had been standing alone among the dead brown fern, the withering gorse, and the hanging brambles, gripping the apple-tree and swallowing the cry that was bubbling up to his throat, but forcing himself to look upon Pete's happiness, which was his own calamity, though it was tearing his heart out, and he could hardly bear it.

The birds were singing by this time, and Pete, going back, sang and whistled with the best of them.

X.

In the mists of morning, Grannie had awakened in her bed with the turfy scraas of the thatch just visible above her, and the window-blind like a hazy moon floating on the wall at her side. And, fixing her nightcap, she had sighed and said, "I can't close my eyes for dreaming that the poor lad has come to his end untimeously."

Cæsar yawned, and asked, "What lad?"

"Young Pete, of course," said Grannie.

Cæsar *umpht* and grunted.

"We were poor ourselves when we began, father."

Grannie felt the glare of the old man's eye on her in the darkness. "'Deed, we were; but people forget things. We had to borrow to buy our big overshot wheel; we had, though. And when ould Parson Harrison sent us the first boll of oats, we couldn't grind it for want of——"

Cæsar tugged at the counterpane and said, "Will you lie quiet, woman, and let a hard-working man sleep?"

"Then don't be the young man's destruction, Cæsar."

Cæsar made a contemptuous snort, and pulled the bedclothes about his head.

"Aw, 'deed, father, but the girl might do worse. A fine, strapping lad. And, dear heart, the cheerful face *at* him! It's taking joy to look at—like drawing water from a well! And the laugh *at* the boy, too—that joyful, it's as good to hear in the morning as six pigs at a lit——"

"Then marry the lad yourself, woman, and have done with it," cried Cæsar, and, so saying, he kicked out his leg, turned over to the wall, and began to snore with great vigour.

XI.

The tide was up in Ramsey Harbour, and rolling heavily on the shore before a fresh sea-breeze with a cold taste of the salt in it. A steamer lying by the quay was getting up steam; trucks were running on her gangways, the clanking crane over her hold was working, and there was much shouting of name, and ordering and protesting, and general tumult. On the after-deck stood the emigrants for Kimberley, the Quarks from Glen Rushen, and some of the young Gills from Castletown—stalwart lads, bearing themselves bravely in the midst of a circle of their friends, who talked and laughed to make them forget they were on the point of going.

Pete and Phil came up the quay, and were received by a shout of incredulity from Quayle, the harbour-master. "What, are you going, too, Mr. Philip?" Philip answered him "No," and passed on to the ship.

Pete was still in his stocking cap and Wellington boots, but he had a monkey-jacket over his blue guernsey. Except for a parcel in a red print handkerchief, this was all his kit and luggage. He felt a little lost amid all the bustle, and looked helpless and unhappy. The busy preparations on land and shipboard had another effect on Philip. He sniffed the breeze off the bay and laughed, and said, "The sea's calling me, Pete; I've half a mind to go with you."

Pete answered with a watery smile. His high spirits were failing him at last. Five years were a long time to be away, if one built all one's hopes on coming back. So many things might happen, so many chances might befall. Pete had no heart for laughter.

Philip had small mind for it, either, after the first rush of the salt in his blood was over. He felt at some moments as if hell itself were inside of him. What troubled him most was that he could not, for the life of him, be sorry that Pete was leaving the island. Once or twice since they left Sulby he had been startled by the thought that he hated Pete. He knew that his lip curled down hard at sight of Pete's solemn face. But Pete never suspected this, and the innocent tenderness of the rough fellow was every moment beating it down with blows that cut like ice and burnt like fire.

They were standing by the forecastle head, and talking above the loud throbbing of the funnel.

"Good-bye, Phil; you've been wonderful good to me—better nor anybody in the world. I've not been much of a chum for the like of you, either—you that's college bred and ought to be the first gentry in the island if everybody had his own. But you shan't be ashamed for me, neither—no you shan't, so help me God! I won't be long away, Phil—maybe five years, maybe less, and when I come back you'll be the first Manxman living. No? But you will, though; you will, I'm telling you. No nonsense at all, man. Lave it to me to know."

Philip's frosty blue eyes began to melt.

"And if I come back rich, I'll be your ould friend again as much as a common man may; and if I come back poor and disappointed and done for, I'll not claim you to disgrace you; and if I never come back at all, I'll be saying to myself in my dark hour somewhere, 'He'll spake up for you at home, boy; *he'll* not forget you.'"

Philip could hear no more for the puffing of the steam and the clanking of the chains.

"Chut! the talk a man will put out when he's thinking of ould times gone by!"

The first bell rang on the bridge, and the harbour-master shouted, "All ashore, there!"

"Phil, there's one turn more I'll ask of you, and, if it's the last, it's the biggest."

"What is it?"

"There's Kate, you know. Keep an eye on the girl while I'm away. Take a slieu round now and then, and put a sight on her. She'll not give a skute at the heirs the ould man's telling of; but them young drapers and druggists, they'll plague the life out of the girl. Bate them off, Phil. They're not worth a fudge with their fists. But don't use no violence. Just duck the dandy-divils in the harbour—that'll do."

"No harm shall come to her while you are away."

"Swear to it, Phil. Your word's your bond, I know that; but give me your hand and swear to it—it'll be more surer."

Philip gave his hand and his oath, and then tried to turn away, for he knew that his face was reddening.

"Wait! There's another while your hand's in, Phil. Swear that nothing and nobody shall ever come between us two."

"You know nothing ever will."

"But swear to it, Phil. There's bad tongues going, and it'll make me more aisier. Whatever they do, whatever they say, friends and brothers to the last?"

Philip felt a buzzing in his head, and he was so dizzy that he could hardly stand, but he took the second oath also. Then the bell rang again, and there was a great hubbub. Gangways were drawn up, ropes were let go, the captain called to the shore from the bridge, and the blustering harbour-master called to the bridge from the shore.

"Go and stand on the end of the pier, Phil—just aback of the lighthouse—and I'll put myself at the stern. I want a friend's face to be the last thing I see when I'm going away from the old home."?

Philip could bear no more. The hate in his heart was mastered. It was under his feet. His flushed face was wet.

The throbbing of the funnels ceased, and all that could be heard was the running of the tide in the harbour and the wash of the waves on the shore. Across the sea the sun came up boldly, "like a guest expected," and down its dancing water-path the steamer moved away. Over the land old Bar-rule rose up like a sea king with hoar-frost on his forehead, and the smoke began to lift from the chimneys of the town at his feet.

"Good-bye, little island, good-bye! I'll not forget you. I'm getting kicked out of you, but you've been a good ould mother to me, and, God help me, I'll come back to you yet. So long, little Mona, s'long? I'm laving you, but I'm a Manxman still."

Pete had meant to take off his stocking cap as they passed the lighthouse, and to dash the tears from his eyes like a man. But all that Philip could see from the end of the pier was a figure huddled up at the stern on a coil of rope.

PART II. BOY AND GIRL.

I.

Auntie Nan had grown uneasy because Philip was not yet started in life. During the spell of his partnership with Pete she had protested and he had coaxed, she had scolded and he had laughed. But when Pete was gone she remembered her old device, and began to play on Philip through the memory of his father.

One day the air was full of the sea freshness of a beautiful Manx November. Philip sniffed it from the porch after breakfast and then gathered up his tackle for cod.

"The boat again, Philip?" said Auntie Nan. "Then promise me to be back for tea."

Philip gave his promise and kept it. When he returned after his day's fishing the old lady was waiting for him in the little blue room which she called her own. The sweet place was more than usually dainty and comfortable that day. A bright fire was burning, and everything seemed to be arranged so carefully and nattily. The table was laid with cups and saucers, the kettle was singing on the jockey-bar, and Auntie Nan herself, in a cap of black lace and a dress of russet silk with flounces, was fluttering about with an odour of lavender and the light gaiety of a bird.

"Why, what's the meaning of this?" said Philip.

And the sweet old thing answered, half nervously, half jokingly, "You don't know? What a child it is, to be sure! So you don't remember what day it is?"

"What day? The fifth of Nov—oh, my birthday! I had clean forgotten it, Auntie."

"Yes, and you are one-and-twenty for tea-time. That's why I asked you to be home."

She poured out the tea, settled herself with her feet on the fender, allowed the cat to establish itself on her skirt, and then, with a nervous smile and a slight depression of the heart, she began on her task.

"How the years roll on, Philip! It's twenty years since I gave you my first birthday present I wasn't here when you were born, dear. Grandfather had forbidden me. Poor grandfather! But how I longed to come and wash, and dress, and nurse my boy's boy, and call myself an auntie aloud! Oh, dear me, the day I first saw you! Shall I ever forget it? Grandfather and I were at Cowley, the draper's, when a beautiful young person stepped in with a baby. A little too gay, poor thing, and that was how I knew her."

"My mother?"

"Yes, dear, and grandfather was standing with his back to the street. I grow hot to this day when I remember, but she didn't seem afraid. She nodded and smiled and lifted the muslin veil from the baby's face, and said 'Who's he like, Miss Christian?' It was wonderful. You were asleep, and it was the same for all the world as if your father had slept back to be a baby. I was trembling fit to drop and couldn't answer, and then your mother saw grandfather, and before I could stop her she had touched him on the shoulder. He stood with his bad ear towards us, and his sight was failing, too, but seeing the form of a lady beside him, he swept round, and bowed low, and smiled and raised his hat, as his way was with all women. Then your mother held the baby up and said quite gaily, 'Is it one of the Ballures he is, Dempster, or one of the Ballawhaines?' Dear heart when I think of it! Grandfather straightened himself up, turned about, and was out on the street in an instant."

"Poor father!" said Philip.

Auntie Nan's eyes brightened.

"I was going to tell you of your first birthday, dearest. Grandfather had gone then—poor grandfather!—and I had knitted you a little soft cap of white wool, with a tassel and a pink bow. Your mother's father was living still—Capt'n Billy, as they called him—and when I put the cap on your little head, he cried out, 'A sailor every inch of him!' And sure enough, though I had never thought it, a sailor's cap it was. And Capt'n Billy put you on his knee, and looked at you sideways, and slapped his thigh, and blew a cloud of smoke from his long pipe and cried again, 'This boy is for a sailor, I'm telling you.' You fell asleep in the old man's arms, and I carried you to your cot upstairs. Your father followed me into the bedroom, and your mother was there already dusting the big shells on the mantelpiece. Poor Tom! I see him yet. He dropped his long white hand over the cot-rail, pushed back the little cap and the yellow curls from your forehead, and said proudly, 'Ah, no, this head wasn't built for a sailor!' He meant no harm, but—Oh, dear, Oh, dear!—your mother heard him, and thought he was belittling her and hers. 'These qualities!' she cried, and slashed the duster and flounced out of the room, and one of the shells fell with a clank into the fender. Your father turned his face to the window. I could have cried for shame that he should be ashamed before me. But looking out on the sea,—the bay was very loud that day, I remember—he said in his deep voice, that was like a mellow bell, and trembled ratherly, 'It's not for nothing, Nannie, that the child has the forehead of Napoleon. Only let God spare him and he'll be something some day, when his father, with his broken heart and his broken brain, is dead and gone, and the daisies cover him.'"

Auntie Nan carried her point. That night Philip laid up his boat for the winter, and next morning he set his face towards Ballawhaine with the object of enlisting Uncle Peter's help in starting upon the profession of the law. Auntie Nan went with him. She had urged him to the step by the twofold plea that the Ballawhaine was his only male relative of mature years, and that he had lately sent his own son Ross to study for the bar in England.

Both were nervous and uncertain on the way down; Auntie Nan talked incessantly from under her poke-bonnet, thinking to keep up Philip's courage. But when they came to the big gate and looked up at the turrets through the trees, her memory went back with deep tenderness to the days when the house had been her home, and she began to cry in silence. Philip himself was not unmoved. This had been the birthplace and birthright of his father.

The English footman, in buff and scarlet, ushered them into the drawing-room with the formality proper to strangers.

To their surprise they found Ross there. He was sitting at the piano strumming a music-hall ditty. As the door opened be shuffled to his feet, shook hands distantly with Auntie Nan, and nodded his head to Philip.

The young man was by this time a sapling well fed from the old tree. Taller than his father by many inches, broader, heavier, and larger in all ways, with the slow eyes of a seal and something of a seal's face as well. But with his father's sprawling legs and his father's levity and irony of manner and of voice—a Manxman disguised out of all recognition of race, and apeing the fashionable follies of the hour in London.

Auntie Nan settled her umbrella, smoothed her gloves and her white front hair, and inquired meekly if he was well.

"Not very fit," he drawled; "shouldn't be here if I were. But father worried my life out until I came back to recruit."

"Perhaps," said Auntie Nan, looking simple and sympathetic, "perhaps you've been longing for home. It must be a great trial to a young man to live in London for the first time. That's where a young woman has the advantage—she needn't leave home, at all events. Then your lodgings, perhaps they are not in the best part either."

"I used to have chambers in an Inn of Court——"

Auntie Nan looked concerned. "I don't think I should like Philip to live long at an inn," she said.

"But now I'm in rooms in the Hay market."

Auntie Nan looked relieved.

"That must be better," she said. "Noisy in the mornings, perhaps, but your evenings will be quiet for study, I should think."

"Precisely," said Boss, with a snigger, touching the piano again, and Philip, sitting near the door, felt the palm of his hand itch for the whole breadth of his cousin's cheek.

Uncle Peter came in hurriedly, with short, nervous steps. His hair as well as his eyebrows was now white, his eye was hollow, his cheeks were thin, his mouth was restless, and he had lost some of his upper teeth, he coughed frequently, he was shabbily dressed, and had the look of a dying man.

"Ah! it's you, Anne! and Philip, too. Good morning, Philip. Give the piano a rest, Ross—that's a good lad. Well, Miss Christian, well!"

"Philip came of age yesterday, Peter," said Auntie Nan in a timid voice.

"Indeed!" said the Ballawhaine, "then Ross is twenty next month. A little more than a year and a month between them."

He scrutinised the old lady's face for a moment without speaking, and then said, "Well?"

"He would like to go to London to study for the bar," faltered Auntie Nan.

"Why not the church at home?"

"The church would have been my own choice, Peter, but his father——"

The Ballawhaine crossed his leg over his knee. "His father was always a man of a high stomach, ma'am," he said. Then facing towards Philip, "Your idea would be to return to the island."

"Yes," said Philip.

"Practice as an advocate, and push your way to insular preferment?"

29

"My father seemed to wish it, sir," said Philip.

The Ballawhaine turned back to Auntie Nan. "Well, Miss Christian?"

Auntie Nan fumbled the handle of her umbrella and began—"We were thinking, Peter—you see we know so little—now if his father had been living——"

The Ballawhaine coughed, scratched with his nail on his cheek, and said, "You wish me to put him with a barrister in chambers, is that it?"

With a nervous smile and a little laugh of relief Auntie Nan signified assent.

"You are aware that a step like that costs money. How much have you got to spend on it?"

"I'm afraid, Peter——"

"You thought I might find the expenses, eh?"

"It's so good of you to see it in the right way, Peter."

The Ballawhaine made a wry face. "Listen," he said dryly. "Ross has just gone to study for the English bar."

"Yes," said Auntie Nan eagerly, "and it was partly that——"

"Indeed!" said the Ballawhaine, raising his eyebrows. "I calculate that his course in London will cost me, one thing with another, more than a thousand pounds."

Auntie Nan lifted her gloved hands in amazement.

"That sum I am prepared to spend in order that my son, as an English barrister, may have a better chance——"

"Do you know, we were thinking of that ourselves, Peter?" said Auntie Nan.

"A better chance," the Ballawhaine continued, "of the few places open in the island than if he were brought up at the Manx bar only, which would cost me less than half as much."

"Oh! but the money will come back to you, both for Ross and Philip," said Auntie Nan.

The Ballawhaine coughed impatiently. "You don't read me," he said irritably. "These places are few, and Manx advocates are as thick as flies in a glue-pot. For every office there must be fifty applicants, but training counts for something, and influence for something, and family for something."

Auntie Nan began to be penetrated as by a chill.

"These," said the Ballawhaine, "I bring to bear for Ross, that he may distance all competitors. Do you read me now?"

"Read you, Peter?" said Auntie Nan.

The Ballawhaine fixed his hollow eye upon her, and said, "What do you ask me to do? You come here and ask me to provide, prepare, and equip a rival to my own son."

Auntie Nan had grasped his meaning at last.

"But gracious me, Peter," she said, "Philip is your own nephew, your own brother's son."

The Ballawhaine rubbed the side of his nose with his lean forefinger, and said, "Near is my shirt, but nearer is my skin."

Auntie Nan fixed her timid eyes upon him, and they grew brave in their gathering indignation. "His father is dead, and he is poor and friendless," she said.

"We've had differences on that subject before, mistress," he answered.

"And yet you begrudge him the little that would start him in life."

"My own has earlier claim, ma'am."

"Saving your presence, sir, let me tell you that every penny of the money you are spending on Ross would have been Philip's this day if things had gone different."

The Ballawhaine bit his lip. "Must I, for my sins, be compelled to put an end to this interview?"

He rose to go to the door. Philip rose also.

"Do you mean it?" said Auntie Nan. "Would you dare to turn me out of the house?"

"Come, Auntie, what's the use?" said Philip.

The Ballawhaine was drumming on the edge of the open door. "You are right, young man," he said, "a woman's hysteria is of *no* use."

"That will do, sir," said Philip in a firm voice.

The Ballawhaine put his hand familiarly on Philip's shoulder. "Try Bishop Wilson's theological college, my friend; its cheap and——"

"Take your hand from him, Peter Christian," cried Auntie Nan. Her eyes flashed, her cheeks were aflame, her little gloved hands were clenched. "You made war between his father and your father, and when I would have made peace you prevented me. Your father is dead, and your brother is dead, and both died in hate that might have died in love, only for the lies you told and the deceit you practised. But they have gone where the mask falls from all faces, and they have met before this, eye to eye, and hand to hand. Yes, and they are looking down on you now, Peter Christian, and they know you at last for what you are and always have been—a deceiver and a thief."

By an involuntary impulse the Ballawhaine turned his eyes upward to the ceiling while she spoke, as if he had expected to see the ghosts of his father and his brother threatening him.

"Is the woman mad at all?" he cried; and the timid old lady, lifted out of herself by the flame of her anger, blazed at him again with a tongue of fire.

"You have done wrong, Peter Christian, much wrong; you've done wrong all your days, and whatever your motive, God will find it out, and on that secret place he will bring your punishment. If it was only greed, you've got your wages; but no good will they bring to you, for another will spend them, and you will see them wasted like water from the ragged rock. And if it was hate as well, you will live till it comes back on your own head like burning coal. I know it, I feel it," she cried, sweeping into the hall, "and sorry I am to say it before your own son, who ought to honour and respect his father, but can't; no, he can't and never will, or else he has a heart to match your own in wickedness, and no bowels of compassion at him either."

"Come, Auntie, come," said Philip, putting his arm about the old lady's waist. But she swerved round again to where the Ballawhaine came slinking behind him.

"Turn me out of the house, will you?" she cried. "The place where I lived fifteen years, and as mistress, too, until your evil deeds made you master. Many a good cry I've had that it's only a woman I am, and can do nothing on my own head. But I would rather be a woman that hasn't a roof to cover her than a man that can't warm to his own flesh and blood. Don't think I begrudge you your house, Peter Christian, though it was my old home, and I love it, for all I'm shown no respect in it I would have you to know, sir, that it isn't our houses we live in after all, but our hearts—our hearts, Peter Christian—do you hear me?—our hearts, and yours is full of darkness and dirt—and always will be, always will be."

"Come, come, Auntie, come," cried Philip again, and the sweet old thing, too gentle to hurt a fly, turned on him also with the fury of a wild-cat.

"Go along yourself with your 'come' and 'come' and 'come.' Say less and do more."

With that final outburst she swept down the steps and along the path, leaving Philip three paces behind, and the Ballawhaine with a terrified look under the stuffed cormorant in the fanlight above the open door.

The fiery mood lasted her half way home, and then broke down in a torrent of tears.

"Oh dear! oh dear!" she cried. "I've been too hasty. After all, he is your only relative. What shall I do now? Oh, what shall I do now?"

Philip was walking steadily half a step behind, and he had never once spoken since they left Ballawhaine.

"Pack my bag to-night, Auntie," said he with the voice of a man; "I shall start for Douglas by the coach to-morrow morning."

He sought out the best known of the Manx advocates, a college friend of his father's, and said to him, "I've sixty pounds a year, sir, from my mother's father, and my aunt has enough of her own to live on. Can I afford to pay your premium?"

The lawyer looked at him attentively for a moment, and answered, "No, you can't," and Philip's face began to fall.

"But I'll take you the five years for nothing, Mr. Christian," the wise man added, "and if you suit me, I'll give you wages after two."

II.

Philip did not forget the task wherewith Pete had charged him. It is a familiar duty in the Isle of Man, and he who discharges it is known by a familiar name. They call him the *Dooiney Molla*—literally, the "man-praiser;" and his primary function is that of an informal, unmercenary, purely friendly and philanthropic matchmaker, introduced by the young man to persuade the parents of the young woman that he is a splendid fellow, with substantial possessions or magnificent prospects, and entirely fit to marry her. But he has a secondary function, less frequent, though scarcely less familiar; and it is that of lover by proxy, or intended husband by deputy, with duties of moral guardianship over the girl while the man himself is off "at the herrings," or away "at the mackerel," or abroad on wider voyages.

This second task, having gone through the first with dubious success, Philip discharged with conscientious zeal. The effects were peculiar. Their earliest manifestations were, as was most proper, on Philip and Kate themselves. Philip grew to be grave and wondrous solemn, for assuming the tone of guardian lifted his manners above all levity. Kate became suddenly very quiet and meek, very watchful and modest, soft of voice and most apt to blush. The girl who had hectored it over Pete and played little mistress over everybody else, grew to be like a dove under the eye of Philip. A kind of awe fell on her whenever he was near. She found it sweet to listen to his words of wisdom when he discoursed, and sweeter still to obey his will when he gave commands. The little wistful head was always turning in his direction; his voice was like joy-bells in her ears; his parting how under his lifted hat remained with her as a dream until the following day. She hardly knew what great change had been wrought in her, and her people at home were puzzled.

"Is it not very well you are, Kirry, woman?" said Grannie.

"Well enough, mother; why not?" said Kate.

"Is it the toothache that's plaguing you?"

"No."

"Then maybe it's the new hat in the window at Miss Clu-cas's?"

"Hould your tongue, woman," whispered Cæsar behind the back of his hand. "It's the Spirit that's working on the girl. Give it lave, mother; give it lave."

"Give it fiddlesticks," said Nancy Joe. "Give it brimstone and treacle and a cupful of wormwood and camomile."

When Philip and Kate were together, their talk was all of Pete. It was "Pete likes this," and "Pete hates that," and "Pete always says so and so." That was their way of keeping up the recollection of Pete's existence; and the uses they put poor Pete to were many and peculiar.

31

One night "The Manx Fairy" was merry and noisy with a "Scaltha," a Christmas supper given by the captain of a fishing-boat to the crew that he meant to engage for the season. Wives, sweethearts, and friends were there, and the customs and superstitions of the hour were honoured.

"Isn't it the funniest thing in the world, Philip?" giggled Kate from the back of the door, and a moment afterwards she was standing alone with him in the lobby, looking demurely down at his boots.

"I suppose I ought to apologise."

"Why so?"

"For calling you that."

"Pete calls me Philip. Why shouldn't you?"

The furtive eyes rose to the buttons of his waistcoat. "Well, no; there can't be much harm in calling you what Pete calls you, can there? But then—"

"Well?"

"He calls me Kate."

"Do you think he would like me to do so?"

"I'm sure he would."

"Shall we, then?"

"I wonder!"

"Just for Pete's sake?"

"Just."

"Kate!"

"Philip!"

They didn't know what they felt. It was something exquisite, something delicious; so sweet, so tender, they could only laugh as if some one had tickled them.

"Of course, we need not do it except when we are quite by ourselves," said Kate.

"Oh no, of course not, only when we are quite alone," said Philip.

Thus they threw dust into each other's eyes, and walked hand in hand on the edge of a precipice.

The last day of the old year after Pete's departure found Philip attending to his duty.

"Are you going to put the new year in anywhere, Philip?" said Kate, from the door of the porch.

"I should be the first-foot here, only I'm no use as a qualtagh," said Philip.

"Why not?"

"I'm a fair man, and would bring you no luck, you know."

"Ah!"

There was silence for a moment, and then Kate cried "*I* know."

"Yes?"

"Come for Pete—he's dark enough, anyway."

Philip was much impressed. "That's a good idea," he said gravely. "Being qualtagh for Pete is a good idea. His first New Year from home, too, poor fellow!"

"Exactly," said Kate.

"Shall I, then?"

"I'll expect you at the very stroke of twelve."

Philip was going off. "And, Philip!"

"Yes?"

Then a low voice, so soft, so sweet, so merry, came from the doorway into the dark, "I'll be standing at the door of the dairy."

Philip began to feel alarm, and resolved to take for the future a lighter view of his duties. He would visit "The Manx Fairy" less frequently. As soon as the Christmas holidays were over he would devote himself to his studies, and come back to Sulby no more for half a year. But the Manx Christmas is long. It begins on the 24th of December, and only ends for good on the 6th of January. In the country places, which still preserve the old traditions, the culminating day is Twelfth Day. It is then that they "cut off the fiddler's head," and play valentines, which they call the "Goggans." The girls set a row of mugs on the hearth in front of the fire, put something into each of them as a symbol of a trade, and troop out to the stairs. Then the boys change the order of the mugs, and the girls come back blindfold, one by one, to select their goggans. According to the goggans they lay hands on, so will be the trades of their husbands.

At this game, played at "The Manx Fairy" on the last night of Philip's holiday, Csesar being abroad on an evangelising errand, Kate was expected to draw water, but she drew a quill.

"A pen! A pen!" cried the boys. "Who says the girl is to marry a sailor? The ship isn't built that's to drown her husband."

"Good-night all," said Philip.

"Good-night, Mr. Christian, good-night, sir," said the boys.

Kate slipped after him to the door. "Going so early, Philip?"

"I've to be back at Douglas to-morrow morning," said Philip.

"I suppose we shan't see you very soon?"

"No, I must set to work in earnest now."

"A fortnight—a month may be?"

"Yes, and six months—I intend to do nothing else for half a year."

"That's a long time, isn't it, Philip?"

"Not so long as I've wasted."

"Wasted? So you call it wasted? Of course, it's nothing to me—but there's your aunt——"

"A man can't always be dangling about women," said Philip.

Kate began to laugh.

"What are you laughing at?"

"I'm so glad I'm a girl," said Kate.

"Well, so am I," said Philip.

"Are you?"

It came at his face like a flash of lightning, and Philip stammered, "I mean—that is—you know—what about Pete?"

"Oh, is that all? Well, good-night, if you must go. Shall I bring you the lantern? No need? Starlight, is it? You can see your way to the gate quite plainly? Very well, if you don't want showing. Good-night!"

The last words, in an injured tone, were half lost behind the closing door.

But the heart of a girl is a dark forest, and Kate had determined that, work or no work, so long a spell as six months Philip should not be away.

III.

One morning in the late spring there came to Douglas a startling and most appalling piece of news—-Ross Christian was constantly seen at "The Manx Fairy." On the evening of that day Philip reappeared at Sulby. He had come down in high wrath, inventing righteous speeches by the way on plighted troths and broken pledges. Ross was there in lacquered boots, light kid gloves, frock coat, and pepper and salt trousers, leaning with elbow on the counter, that he might talk to Kate, who was serving. Philip had never before seen her at that task, and his indignation was extreme. He was more than ever sure that Grannie was a simpleton and Cæsar a brazen hypocrite.

Kate nodded gaily to him as he entered, and then continued her conversation with Ross. There was a look in her eyes that was new to him, and it caused him to change his purpose. He would not be indignant, he would be cynical, he would be nasty, he would wait his opportunity and put in with some cutting remark. So, at Cæsar's invitation and Grannie's welcome, he pushed through the bar-room to the kitchen, exchanged salutations, and then sat down to watch and to listen.

The conversation beyond the glass partition was eager and enthusiastic. Ross was fluent and Kate was vivacious.

"My friend Monty?"

"Yes; who is Monty?"

"He's the centre of the Fancy."

"The Fancy!"

"Ornaments of the Ring, you know. Come now, surely you know the Ring, my dear. His rooms in St. James's Street are full of them every night. All sorts, you know—featherweights, and heavy-weights, and greyhounds. And the faces! My goodness, you should see them. Such worn-out old images. Knowledge boxes all awry, mouths crooked, and noses that have had the upper-cut. But good men all; good to take their gruel, you know. Monty will have nothing else about him. He was Tom Spring's packer. Never heard of Tom Spring? Tom of Bedford, the incorruptible, you know, only he fought cross that day. Monty lost a thousand, and Tom keeps a public in Holborn now with pictures of the Fancy round the walls."

Then Kate, with a laugh, said something which Philip did not catch, because Cæsar was rustling the newspaper he was reading.

"Ladies come?" said Ross. "Girls at Monty's suppers? Rather! what should you think? Cleopatra—but you ought to be there. I must be getting off myself very soon. There's a supper coming off next week at Handsome Honey's. Who's Honey? Proprietor of a night-house in the Haymarket. Night-house? You come and see, my dear."

Cæsar dropped the newspaper and looked across at Philip. The gaze was long and embarrassing, and, for want of better conversation, Philip asked Cæsar if he was thinking.

"Aw, thinking, thinking, and thinking again, sir," said Cæsar. Then, drawing his chair nearer to Philip's, he added, in a half whisper, "I'm getting a bit of a skute into something, though. See yonder? They're calling his father a miser. The man's racking his tenants and starving his land. But I believe enough the young brass lagh (a weed) is choking the ould grain."

Cæsar, as he spoke, tipped his thumb over his shoulder in the direction of Ross, and, seeing this, Ross interrupted his conversation with Kate to address himself to her father.

"So you've been reading the paper, Mr. Cregeen?"

"Aw, reading and reading," said Cæsar grumpily. Then in another tone, "You're home again from London, sir? Great doings yonder, they're telling me. Battles, sir, great battles."

Ross elevated his eyebrows. "Have you heard of them then?" he asked.

"Aw, heard enough," said Cæsar, "meetings, and conferences, and conventions, and I don't know what."

"Oh, oh, I see," said Ross, with a look at Kate.

"They're doing without hell in England now-a-days—that's a quare thing, sir. Conditional immorality they're calling it—the singlerest thing I know. Taking hell away drops the tailboard out of a man's religion, eh?"

The time for closing came, and Philip had waited in vain. Only one cut had come his way, and that had not been his own. As he rose to go, Kate had said, "We didn't expect to see you again for six months, Mr. Christian."

"So it seems," said Philip, and Kate laughed a little, and that was all the work of his evening, and the whole result of his errand.

Cæsar was waiting for him in the porch. His face was white, and it twitched visibly. It was plain to see that the natural man was fighting in Cæsar. "Mr. Christian, sir," said he, "are you the gentleman that came here to speak to me for Peter Quilliam?"

"I am," said Philip.

"Then do you remember the ould Manx saying, 'Perhaps the last dog may be catching the hare?'"

"Leave it to me, Mr. Cregeen," said Philip through his teeth.

Half a minute afterwards he was swinging down the dark road homewards, by the side of Ross, who was drawling along with his cold voice.

"So you've started on your light-weight handicap, Philip. Father was monstrous unreasonable that day. Seemed to think I was coming back here to put my shoulder out for your high bailiffships and bum-bailiffships and heaven knows what. You're welcome to the lot for me, Philip. That girl's wonderful, though. It's positively miraculous, too; she's the living picture of a girl of my friend Montague's. Eyes, hair, that nervous movement of the mouth—everything. Old man looked glum enough, though. Poor little woman. I suppose she's past praying for. The old hypocrite will hold her like a dove in the claws of a buzzard hawk till she throws herself away on some Manx omathaun. It's the way with half these pretty creatures—they're wasted."

Philip's blood was boiling. "Do you call it being wasted when a good girl is married to an honest man?" he asked.

"I do; because a girl like this can never marry the right man. The man who is worthy of her cannot marry her, and the man who marries her isn't worthy of her. It's like this, Philip. She's young, she's pretty, perhaps beautiful, has manners and taste, and some refinement. The man of her own class is clumsy and ignorant, and stupid and poor. She doesn't want him, and the man she does want the man she's fit for—daren't marry her; it would be social suicide."

"And so," said Philip bitterly, "to save the man above from social suicide, the girl beneath must choose moral death—is that it?"

Ross laughed. "Do you know I thought old Jeremiah was at you in the corner there, Philip. But look at it straight. Here's a girl like that. Two things are open to her—two only. Say she marries your Manx fellow, what follows? A thatched cottage three fields back from the mountain road, two rooms, a cowhouse, a crock, a dresser, a press, a form, a three-legged stool, an armchair, and a clock with a dirty face, hanging on a nail in the wall. Milking, weeding, digging, ninepence a day, and a can of buttermilk, with a lump of butter thrown in. Potatoes, herrings, and barley bonnag. Year one, a baby, a boy; year two, another baby, a girl; year three, twins; year four, barefooted children squalling, dirty house, man grumbling, woman distracted, measles, hooping-cough; a journey at the tail of a cart to the bottom of the valley, and the awful words 'I am the——'"

"Hush man!" said Philip. They were passing Lezayre churchyard. When they had left it behind, he added, with a grim curl of the lip, which was lost in the darkness, "Well, that's one side. What's the other?"

"Life," said Ross. "Short and sweet, perhaps. Everything she wants, everything she can wish for—five years, four years, three years—what matter?"

"And then?"

"Every one for himself and God for us all, my boy. She's as happy as the day while it lasts, lifts her head like a rosebud in the sun——"

"Then drops it, I suppose, like a rose-leaf in the mud." Ross laughed again. "Yes, it's a fact, old Jeremiah *has* been at you, Philip. Poor little Kitty——"

"Keep the girl's name out of it, if you please."

Ross gave a long whistle. "I was only saying the poor little woman——"

"It's damnable, and I'll have no more of it."

"There's no duty on speech, I hope, in your precious Isle of Man."

"There is, though," said Philip, "a duty of decency and honour, and to name that girl, foolish as she is, in the same breath with your women—But here, listen to me. Best tell you now, so there may be no mistake and no excuse. Miss Cregeen is to be married to a friend of mine. I needn't say who he is—he comes close enough to you at all events. When he's at home, he's able to take care of his own affairs; but while he's abroad I've got to see that no harm comes to his promised wife. I mean to do it, too. Do you understand me, Ross? I mean to do it. Good night!"

They were at the gate of Ballawhaine by this time, and Ross went through it giggling.

IV.

The following evening found Philip at "The Manx Fairy" again. Ross was there as usual, and he was laughing and talking in a low tone with Kate. This made Philip squirm on his chair, but Kate's behaviour tortured him. Her enjoyment of the man's jests was almost uproarious. She was signalling to him and peering up at him gaily. Her conduct disgusted Philip. It seemed to him an aggravation of her offence that as often as he caught the look of her face there was a roguish twinkle in the eye on his side, and a deliberate cast in his direction. This open disregard of the sanctity of a pledged word, this barefaced indifference to the presence of him who stood to represent it, was positively indecent. This was what women were! Deceit was bred in their bones.

It added to Philip's gathering wrath that Cæsar, who sat in shirt-sleeves making up his milling accounts from slates ciphered with crosses, and triangles, and circles, and half circles, was lifting his eyes from time to time to look first at them and then at him, with an expression of contempt.

At a burst of fresh laughter and a shot of the bright eyes, Philip surged up to his feet, thrust himself between Ross and Kate, turned his back on him and his face to her, and said in a peremptory voice, "Come into the parlour instantly—I have something to say to you."

"Oh, indeed!" said Kate.

But she came, looking mischievous and yet demure, with her head down but her eyes peering under their long upper lashes.

"Why don't you send this fellow about his business?" said Philip.

Kate looked up in blank surprise. "What fellow?" she said.

"What fellow?" said Philip, "why, this one that is shillyshallying with you night after night."

"You can never mean your own cousin, Philip?" said Kate.

"More's the pity if he is my cousin, but he's no fit company for you."

"I'm sure the gentleman is polite enough."

"So's the devil himself."

"He can behave and keep his temper, anyway."

"Then it's the only thing he can keep. He can't keep his character or his credit or his honor, and you should not encourage him."

Kate's under lip began to show the inner half. "Who says I encourage him?"

"I do."

"What right have you?"

"Haven't I seen you with my own eyes?"

Kate grew defiant. "Well, and what if you have?"

"Then you are a jade and a coquette."

The word hissed out like steam from a kettle. Kate saw it coming and took it full in the face. She felt an impulse to scream with laughter, so she seized her opportunity and cried.

Philip's temper began to ebb. "That man would be a poor bargain, Kate, if he were twenty times the heir of Ballawhaine. Can't you gather from his conversation what his life and companions are? Of course it's nothing to me, Kate——"

"No, it's nothing to you," whimpered Kate, from behind both hands.

"I've no right——"

"Of course not; you've no right," said Kate, and she stole a look sideways.

"Only——"

Philip did not see the glance that came from the corner of Kate's eye.

"When a girl forgets a manly fellow, who happens to be abroad, for the first rascal that comes along with his dirty lands—"

Down went the hands with an impatient fling. "What are his lands to me?"

"Then it's my duty as a friend——"

"Duty indeed! Just what every old busybody says."

Philip gripped her wrist. "Listen to me. If you don't send this man packing——"

"You are hurting me. Let go my arm."

Philip flung it aside and said, "What do I care?"

"Then why do you call me a coquette?"

"Do as you like."

"So I will. Philip! Philip! Phil! He's gone."

It was twenty miles by coach and rail from Douglas to Sulby, but Philip was back at "The Manx Fairy" the next evening also. He found a saddle-horse linked to the gate-post and Ross inside the house with a riding-whip in his hand, beating the leg of his riding-breeches.

35

When Philip appeared, Kate began to look alarmed, and Ross to look ugly. Cæsar, who was taking his tea in the ingle, was having an unpleasant passage with Grannie in side-breaths by the fire.

"Bad, bad, a notorious bad liver and dirty with the tongue," said Cæsar.

"Chut, father!" said Grannie. "The young man's civil enough, and girls will be girls. What's a word or a look or a laugh when you're young and have a face that's fit for anything."

"Better her face should be pitted with smallpox than bring her to the pit of hell," said Cæsar. "All flesh is grass: the grass withereth, the flower fadeth."

Nancy Joe came from the dairy at that moment. "Gracious me I did you see that now?" she said. "I wonder at Kitty. But it's the way of the men, smiling and smiling and maning nothing."

"Hm! They mane a dale," growled Cæsar.

Ross had recovered from his uneasiness at Philip's entrance, and was engaged in some narration whereof the only words that reached the kitchen were *I know* and *I know* repeated frequently.

"You seem to know a dale, sir," shouted Cæsar; "do you know what it is to be saved?"

There was silence for a moment, and then Ross, polishing his massive signet ring on his corduroy waistcoat, said, "Is that the old gentleman's complaint, I wonder?"

"My husband is a local preacher and always strong for salvation," said Grannie by way of peace.

"Is that all?" said Ross. "I thought perhaps he had taken more wine than the sacrament."

"You're my cross, woman," muttered Cæsar, "but no cross no crown."

"Lave women's matters alone, father; it'll become you better," said Grannie.

"Laugh as you like, Mistress Cregeen; there's One above, there's One above."

Ross had resumed his conversation with Kate, who was looking frightened. And listening with all his ears, Philip caught the substance of what was said.

"I'm due back by this time. There's the supper at Handsome Honey's, not to speak of the everlasting examinations. But somehow I can't tear myself away. Why not? Can't you guess? No? Not a notion? I would go to-morrow—Kitty, a word in your ear——"

"I believe in my heart that man is for kissing her," said Cæsar. "If he does, then by—he's done it! Hould, sir."

Cæsar had risen to his feet, and in a moment the house was in an uproar. Ross lifted his head like a cock. "Were you speaking to me, mister?" he asked.

"I was, and don't demane yourself like that again," said Cæsar.

"Like what?" said Ross.

"Paying coort to a girl that isn't fit for you."

Ross lifted his hat, "Do you mean this young lady?"

"No young lady at all, sir, but the daughter of a plain, respectable man that isn't going to see her fooled. Your hat to your head, sir. You'll be wanting it for the road."

"Father!" cried Kate, in a voice of fear.

Cæsar turned his rough shoulder and said, "Go to your room, ma'am, and keep it for a week."

"You may go," said Ross. "I'll spare the old simpleton for your sake, Kate."

"You'll spare me, sir?" cried Cæsar. "I've seen the day—but thank the Lord for restraining grace! Spare me? If you had said as much five-and-twenty years ago, sir, your head would have gone ringing against the wall."

"I'll spare you no more, then," said Ross. "Take that—and that."

Amid screams from the women, two sounding blows fell on Cæsar's face. At the next instant Philip was standing between the two men.

"Come this way," he said, addressing Ross.

"If I like," Ross answered.

"This way, I tell you," said Philip.

Ross snapped his fingers. "As you please," he said, and then followed Philip out of the house.

Kate had run upstairs in terror, but five minutes afterwards she was on the road, with a face full of distress, and a shawl over head and shoulders. At the bridge she met Kelly, the postman.

"Which way have they gone," she panted, "the young Ballawhaine and Philip Christian?"

"I saw them heading down to the Curragh," said Kelly, and Kate in the shawl, flew like a bird over the ground in that direction.

V.

The two young men went on without a word. Philip walked with long strides three paces in front, with head thrown back, pallid face and contracted features, mouth firmly shut, arms stiff by his side, and difficult and audible breathing. Ross slouched behind with an air of elaborate carelessness, his horse beside him, the reins over its head and round his arm, the riding-whip under his other arm-pit, and both his hands deep in the breeches pockets. There was no road the way they went, but only a cart track, interrupted here and there by a gate, and bordered by square turf pits half full of water.

The days were long and the light was not yet failing. Beyond the gorse, the willows, the reeds, the rushes and the sally bushes of the flat land, the sun was setting over a streak of gold on the sea. They had left behind them the smell of burning turf, of crackling sticks, of fish, and of the cowhouse, and were come into the atmosphere of flowering gorse and damp scraa soil and brine.

"Far enough, aren't we?" shouted Ross, but Philip pushed on. He drew up at last in an open space, where the gorse had been burnt away and its black remains desolated the surface and killed the odours of life. There was not a house near, not a landmark in sight, except a windmill on the sea's verge, and the ugly tower of a church, like the funnel of a steamship between sea and sky.

"We're alone at last," he said hoarsely.

"We are," said Ross, interrupting the whistling of a tune, "and now that you've got me here, perhaps you'll be good enough to tell me what we've come for."

Philip made no more answer than to strip himself of his coat and waistcoat.

"You're never going to make a serious business of this stupid affair?" said Ross, leaning against the horse and slapping the sole of one foot with the whip.

"Take off your coat," said Philip in a thick voice.

"Can I help it if a pretty girl——" began Ross.

"Will you strip?" cried Philip.

Ross laughed. "Ah! now I remember our talk of the other night. But you don't mean to say," he said, flipping at the flies at the horse's head, "that because the little woman is forgetting the curmudgeon that's abroad——"

Philip strode up to him with clenched hands and quivering lips and said, "Will you fight?"

Ross laughed again, but the blood was in his face, and he said tauntingly, "I wouldn't distress myself, man. Daresay I'll be done with the girl before the fellow——"

"You're a scoundrel," cried Philip, "and if you won't stand up to me——"

Ross flung away his whip. "If I must, I must," he said, and then threw the horse's reins round the charred arm of a half-destroyed gorse tree.

A minute afterwards the young men stood face to face.

"Stop," said Ross, "let me tell you first; it's only fair. Since I went up to London I've learnt a thing or two. I've stood up before men that can strip a picture; I've been opposite talent and I can peck a bit, but I've never heard that you can stop a blow."

"Are you ready?" cried Philip.

"As you will. You shall have one round, you'll want no more."

The young men looked badly matched. Ross, in riding-breeches and shirt, with red bullet head and sprawling feet, arms like an oak and veins like willow boughs. Philip in shirt and knickerbockers, with long fair hair, quivering face, and delicate figure. It was strength and some skill against nerve alone.

Like a rush of wind Philip came on, striking right and left, and was driven back by a left-hand body-blow.

"There, you've got it," said Ross, smiling benignly. "Didn't I tell you? That's old Bristol Bull to begin with."

Philip rushed on again, and came back with a smashing blow that cut his nether lip.

"You've got a second," said Ross. "Have you had enough?"

Philip did not hear, but sprang fiercely at Ross once more. The next instant he was on the ground. Then Ross took on a manner of utter contempt. "I can't keep on flipping at you all night."

"Mock me when you've beaten me," said Philip, and he was on his feet again, somewhat blown, but fresh as to spirit and doggedly resolute.

"Toe the scratch, then," said Ross. "I must say you're good at your gruel."

Philip flung himself on his man a third time, and fell more heavily than before, under a flush hit that seemed to bury itself in his chest.

"I can't go on fighting a man that's as good for nothing as my old grandmother," said Ross.

But his contempt was abating; he was growing uneasy; Philip was before him as fierce as ever.

"Fight your equal," he cried.

"I'll fight you," growled Philip.

"You're not fit. Give it up. And look, the dark is falling."

"There's enough daylight yet. Come on."

"Nobody is here to shame you."

"Come on, I say."

Philip did not wait, but sprang on his man like a tiger. Ross met his blow, dodged, feinted; they gripped, swinging to and fro; there was a struggle, and Philip fell again with a dull thud against the ground.

"Will you stop now?" said Ross.

"No, no, no," cried Philip, leaping to his feet.

"I'll eat you up. I'm a glutton, I can tell you." But his voice trembled, and Philip, blind with passion, laughed.

"You'll be hurt," said Ross.

"What of that?" said Philip.

"You'll be killed."

"I'm willing."

Ross tried to laugh mockingly, but the hoarse gurgle choked in his throat. He began to tremble. "This man doesn't know when he's mauled," he muttered, and after a loud curse he stood up afresh, with a craven and shifty look. His blows fell like scorching missiles, but Philip took them like a rock scoured with shingle, raining blood like water, but standing firm.

"What's the use?" cried Ross; "drop it."

"I'll drop myself first," said Philip.

"If you won't give it up, I will," said Ross.

"You shan't," said Philip.

"Take your victory if you like."

"I won't."

"Say you've licked me."

"I'll do it first," said Philip.

Ross laughed long and riotously, but he was trembling like a whipped cur. With a blob of foam on his lips he came up, collecting all his strength, and struck Philip a blow on the forehead that fell with the sound of a hammer on a coffin.

"Are you done?" he snuffled.

"No, by God," cried Philip, black as ink with the burnt gorse from the ground, except where the blood ran red on him.

"This man means to kill me," mumbled Ross. He looked round shiftily, and said, "I mean no harm by the girl."

"You're a liar!" cried Philip.

With a glance of deep malignity, Ross closed with Philip again. It was now a struggle of right with wrong as well as nerve with strength. The sun had set under the sea, the sally bushes were shivering in the twilight, a flight of rooks were screaming overhead. Blows were no more heard. Ross gripped Philip in a venomous embrace, and dragged him on to one knee. Philip rose, Ross doubled round his waist, pushing him backward, and fell heavily on his breast, shouting with the growl of a beast, "You'll fight me, will you? Get up, get up!"

Philip did not rise, and Ross began dragging and lunging at him with brutal ferocity, when suddenly, where he bent double, a blow fell on his ear from behind, another and another, a hand gripped his shirt collar and choked him, and a voice cried, "Let go, you brute, let go, let go."

Ross dropped Philip and swung himself round to return the attack.

It was the girl. "Oh, it's you, is it?" he panted. She was like a fury. "You brute, you beast, you toad," she cried, and then threw herself over Philip.

He was unconscious. She lifted his head on to her lap, and, lost to all shame, to all caution, to all thought but one thought, she kissed him on the cheek, on the lips, on the eyes, on the forehead, crying, "Philip! oh, Philip, Philip!"

Ross was shuddering beside them. "Let me look at him," he faltered, but Kate fired back with a glance like an arrow, and said, screaming like a sea-gull, "If you touch him again I'll strangle you."

Ross caught a glimpse of Philip's face, and he was terrified. Going to a turf pit, he dipped both hands in the dub, and brought some water. "Take this," he said, "for Heaven's sake let me bathe his head."

He dashed the water on the pallid forehead, and then withdrew his eyes, while the girl coaxed Philip back to consciousness with fresh kisses and pleading words.

"Is he breathing? Feel his heart. Any pulsation? Oh, God!" said Ross, "it wasn't my fault." He looked round with wild eyes; he meditated flight.

"Is he better yet?"

"What's it to you, you coward?" said Kate, with a burning glance. She went on with her work: "Come then, dear, come, come now."

Philip opened his eyes in a vacant stare, and rose on his elbow. Then Kate fell back from him immediately, and began to cry quietly, being all woman now, and her moral courage gone again in an instant.

But the moral courage of Mr. Ross came back as quickly. He began to sneer and to laugh lightly, picked up his riding-whip and strode over to his horse.

"Are you hurt?" asked Kate, in a low tone.

"Is it Kate?" said Philip.

At the sound of his voice, in that low whisper, Kate's tears came streaming down.

"I hope youll forgive me," she said. "I should have taken your warning."

She wiped his face with the loose sleeve of her dress, and then he struggled to his feet.

"Lean on me, Philip."

"No, no, I can walk."

"Do take my arm."

"Oh no, Kate, I'm strong enough."

"Just to please me."

"Well—very well."

Ross looked on with jealous rage. His horse, frightened by the fight, had twirled round and round till the reins were twisted into a knot about the gorse stump, and as he liberated the beast he flogged it back till it flew around him. Then he vaulted to the saddle, tugged at the curb, and the horse reared. "Down," he cried with an oath, and lashed brutally at the horse's head.

Meantime Kate, going past him with Philip on her arm, was saying softly, "Are you feeling better, Philip?"

And Ross, looking on in sulky meditation, sent a harsh laugh out of his hot throat, and said, "Oh, you can make your mind easy about *him*, if your other man fights for you like that you'll do. Thought you'd have three of them, did you? Or perhaps you only wanted me for your decoy? Why don't you kiss him now, when he can know it? But he's a beauty to take care of you for somebody else. Fighting for the other one, eh? Stuff and humbug! Take him home, and the curse of Judas on the brace of you."

So saying, he burst into wild, derisive laughter, flogged his horse on the ears and the nose, shouted "Down, you brute, down!" and shot off at a gallop across the open Curragh.

Philip and Kate stood where he had left them till he had disappeared in the mist rising off the marshy land, and the hud of his horse's hoofs could be no more heard. Their heads were down, and though their arms were locked, their faces were turned half aside. There was silence for some time. The girl's eyelids quivered; her look was anxious and helpless. Then Philip said, "Let us go home," and they began to walk together.

Not another word did they speak. Neither looked into the other's eyes. Their entwined arms slackened a little in a passionless asundering, yet both felt that they must hold tight or they would fall. It was almost as if Ross's parting taunt had uncovered their hearts to each other, and revealed to themselves their secret. They were like other children of the garden of Eden, driven out and stripped naked.

At the bridge they met Cæsar, Grannie, Nancy Joe, and half the inhabitants of Sulby, abroad with lanterns in search of them.

"They're here," cried Cæsar. "You've chastised him, then! You'd bait his head off, I'll go bail. And I believe enough you'll be forgiven, sir. Yonder blow was almost bitterer than flesh can bear. Before my days of grace—but, praise the Lord for His restraining hand, the very minute my anger was up He crippled me in the hip with rheumatics. But what's this?" holding the lantern over his head; "there's blood on your face, sir?"

"A scratch—it's nothing," said Philip.

"It's the women that's in every mischief," said Cæsar.

"Lord bless me, aren't the women as good as the men?" said Nancy.

"H'm," said Cæsar. "We're told that man was made a little lower than the angels, but about women we're just left to our own conclusions."

"Scripture has nothing to do with Ross Christian, father," said Grannie.

"The Lord forbid it," said Cæsar. "What can you get from a cat but his skin? And doesn't the man come from Christian Ballawhaine!"

"If it comes to that, though, haven't we all come from Adam?" said Grannie.

"Yes; and from Eve too, more's the pity," said Cæsar.

VI.

For some time thereafter Philip went no more to Sulby. He had a sufficient excuse. His profession made demand of all his energies. When he was not at work in Douglas he was expected to be at home with his aunt at Ballure. But neither absence nor the lapse of years served to lift him out of the reach of temptation. He had one besetting provocation to remembrance—one duty which forbade him to forget Kate—his pledge to Pete, his office as *Dooiney Molla*. Had he not vowed to keep guard over the girl? He must do it. The trust was a sacred one.

Philip found a way out of his difficulty. The post was an impersonal and incorruptible go-between, so he wrote frequently. Sometimes he had news to send, for, to avoid the espionage of Cæsar, intelligence of Pete came through him; occasionally he had love-letters to enclose; now and then he had presents to pass on. When such necessity did not arise, he found it agreeable to keep up the current of correspondence. At Christmas he sent Christmas cards, on Midsummer Day a bunch of moss roses, and even on St. Valentine's Day a valentine. All this was in discharge of his duty, and everything he did was done in the name of Pete. He persuaded himself that he sank his own self absolutely. Having denied his eyes the very sight of the girl's face, he stood erect in the belief that he was a true and loyal friend.

Kate was less afraid and less ashamed. She took the presents from Pete and wore them for Philip. In her secret heart she thought no shame of this. The years gave her a larger flow of life, and made out of the bewitching girl a splendid woman, brought up to the full estate of maidenly beauty.

This change wrought by time on her bodily form caused the past to seem to her a very long way off. Something had occurred that made her a different being. She was like the elder sister of that laughing girl who had known Pete. To think of that little sister as having a kind of control over her was impossible. Kate never did think of it.

39

Nevertheless, she held her tongue. Her people were taken in by the episode of Ross Christian. According to their view, Kate loved the man and still longed for him, and that was why she never talked of Pete. Philip was disgusted with her unfaithfulness to his friend, and that was the reason of his absence. She never talked of Philip either, but they, on their part, talked of him perpetually, and fed her secret passion with his praises. Thus for three years these two were like two prisoners in neighbouring cells, very close and yet very far apart, able to hear each other's voices, yet never to see each other's faces, yearning to come together and to touch, but unable to do so because of the wall that stood between.

Since the fight, Cæsar had removed her from all duties of the inn, and one day in the spring she was in the gable house peeling rushes to make tallow candles when Kelly, the postman, passed by the porch, where Nancy Joe was cleaning the candle-irons.

"Heard the newses, Nancy?" said Kelly. "Mr. Philip Christian is let off two years' time and called to the bar."

Nancy looked grave. "I'm sure the young gentleman is that quiet and studdy," she said. "What are they doing on him?"

"Only making him a full advocate, woman," said Kelly.

"You don't say?" said Nancy.

"He passed his examination before the Govenar's man yesterday."

"Aw, there now!"

"I took the letter to Ballure this evening."

"It's like you would, Mr. Kelly. That's the boy for you. I'm always saying it. 'Deed I am, though, but there's ones here that won't have it at all, at all."

"Miss Kate, you mane? We know the raison. He's lumps in her porridge, woman. Good-day to you, Nancy."

"Yes, it's doing a nice day enough, Mr. Kelly," said Nancy, and the postman passed on.

Kate came gliding out with a brush in her hand. "What was the postman saying?"

"That—Mr.—Philip—Christian—has been passing—for an advocate," said Nancy deliberately.

Kate's eyes glistened, and her lips quivered with delight; but she only said, with an air of indifference, "Was that all his news, then?"

"All? D'ye say all?" said Nancy, digging away at the candle-irons. "Listen to the girl! And him that good to her while her promist man's away!"

Kate shelled her rush, and said, with a sigh and a sly look, "I'm afraid you think a deal too much of him, Nancy."

"Then I'll be making mends," said Nancy, "for some that's thinking a dale too little."

"I'm quite at a loss to know what you see in him," said Kate.

"Now, you don't say!" said Nancy with scorching irony. Then, banging her irons, she added, "I'm not much of a woman for a man myself. They're only poor helpless creatures anyway, and I don't approve of them. But if I was for putting up with one of the sort, he wouldn't have legs and arms like a dolly, and a face like curds and whey, and coat and trousers that loud you can hear them coming up the street."

With this parting shot at Ross Christian, Nancy flung into the house, thinking she had given Kate a dressing that she would never forget. Kate was radiant. Such abuse was honey on her lips, such scoldings were joy-bells in her ears. She took silent delight in provoking these attacks. They served her turn both ways, bringing her delicious joy at the praise of Philip, and at the same time preserving her secret.

VII.

Latter that day Cæsar came in from the mill with the startling intelligence that Philip was riding up on the highroad.

"Goodness mercy!" cried Nancy, and she fled away to wash her face. Grannie with a turn of the hand settled her cap, and smoothed her grey hair under it. Kate herself had disappeared like a flash of light; but as Philip dismounted at the gate, looking taller, and older, and paler, and more serious, but raising his cap from his fair head and smiling a smile like sunshine, she was coming leisurely out of the porch with a bewitching hat over her wavy black hair and a hand-basket over her arm.

Then there was a little start of surprise and recognition, a short catch of quick breath and nervous salutations.

"I'm going round to the nests," she said. "I suppose you'll step in to see mother."

"Time enough for that," said Philip. "May I help you with the eggs first? Besides, I've something to tell you."

"Is it that you're 'admitted?'" said Kate.

"That's nothing," said Philip. "Only the A B C, you know. Getting ready to begin, so to speak."

They walked round to the stackyard, and he tied up his horse and gave it hay. Then, while they poked about for eggs on hands and knees among the straw, under the stacks and between the bushes, she said she hoped he would have success, and he answered that success was more than a hope to him now—it was a sort of superstition. She did not understand this, but looked up at him from all fours with brightening eyes, and said, "What a glorious thing it is to be a man!"

"Is it?" said Philip. "And yet I remember somebody who said she wasn't sorry to be a girl."

"Did I?" said Kate. "But that was long ago. And I remember somebody else who pretended he was glad I was."

"That was long ago too," said Philip, and both laughed nervously.

"What strange things girls are—and boys!" said Kate with a matronly sigh, burying her face in a nest where a hen was clucking and two downy chicks were peeping from her wing.

They went through to the orchard, where the trees were breaking into eager blossoms.

"I've another letter for you from Pete," said Philip.

"So?" said Kate.

"Here it is," said Philip.

"Won't you read it?" said Kate.

"But it's yours; surely a girl doesn't want anybody else——"

"Ah! but you're different, though; you know everything—and besides—read it aloud, Philip."

With her basket of eggs on one arm, and the other hand on the outstretched arm of an apple-tree, she waited while he read:

"Dearest Kitty,—How's yourself, darling, and how's Philip, and how's Grannie? I'm getting on tremendous. They're calling me Captain now—Capt'n Pete. Sort of overseer at the Diamond Mines outside Kimberley. Regular gentleman's life and no mistake. Nothing to do but sit under a monstrous big umbrella, with a paper in your fist, like a chairman, while twenty Kaffirs do the work. Just a bit of a tussle now and then to keep you from dropping off. When a Kaffir turns up a diamond, you grab it, and mark it on the time-sheet against his name. They've got their own outlandish ones, but we always christen them ourselves—Sixpence, Seven Waistcoats, Shoulder-of-Mutton, Twopenny Trotter—anything you like. When a Kaffir strikes a diamond, he gets a commission, and so does his overseer. I'm afraid I'm going to be getting terrible rich soon. Tell the old man I'll be buying that har-monia yet. They are a knowing lot, though, and if they can get up a dust to smuggle a stone when you're not looking, they will. Then they sell it to the blackleg Boers, and you've got to raise your voice like an advocate to get it back somehow. But the Boers can't do no harm to you with their fists at all—it's playing. They're a dirty lot, wonderful straight like some of the lazy Manx ones, especially Black Tom. When they see us down at the river washing, they say, 'What dirty people the English must be if they have to wash themselves three times a day—we only do it once a week.' When a Kaffir steals a stone we usually court-martial him, but I don't hold with it, as the floggers on the compound can't be trusted; so I always lick my own niggers, being more kinder, and if anybody does anything against me, they lynch him."

Kate made a little patient sigh and turned away her head, while Philip, in a halting voice, went on—

"Darling Kitty, I am longing mortal for a sight of your sweet face. When the night comes, and I'll be lying in the huts—boards on the ground, and good canvas, and everything comfortable—says I to the boys, 'Shut your faces, men, and let a poor chap sleep;' but they never twig the darkness of my meaning. I'll only be wanting a bit of quiet for thinking of.... with the stars atwinkling down.... She's looking at that one.... Shine on my angel...."

"Really, Kate," faltered Philip, "I can't——"

"Give it to me, then," said Kate.

She was tugging with her trembling hand at the arm of the apple-tree, and the white blossom was raining over her from the rowels of the thin boughs overhead, like silver fish falling from the herring-net. Taking the letter, she glanced over the close—

"darlin Kirry how is the mackral this saison and is the millin doing middling and I wonder is the hens all layin and is the grace gone out of the mares leg yet and how is the owl man and is he still playin hang with the texes. Theer is a big chap heer that is strait like him he hath swallowed the owl Book and cant help bring it up agen but dear Kirry no more at present i axpect to be Home sune bogh, to see u all tho I dont no azactly With luv your luving swateart peat."

When she had finished the letter, she turned it over in her fingers, and gave another patient little sigh. "You didn't read it as it was spelled, Philip," she said.

"What odds if the spelling is uncertain when the love is as sure as that?" said Philip.

"Did he write it himself, think you?" said Kate.

"He signed it, anyway, and no doubt indited it too; but perhaps one of the Gills boys held the pen."

She coloured a little, slipped the letter down her dress into her pocket, and looked ashamed.

VIII.

This shame at Pete's letter tormented Philip, and he stayed away again. His absence stimulated Kate and made Philip himself ashamed. She was vexed with him that he did not see that all this matter of Pete was foolishness. It was absurd to think of a girl marrying a man whom she had known when he was a boy. But Philip was trying to keep the bond sacred, and so she made her terms with it. She used Pete as a link to hold Philip.

After the lapse of some months, in which Philip had not been seen at Sulby, she wrote him a letter. It was to say how anxious she had been at the length of time since she had last heard from Pete, and to ask if he had any news to relieve her fears. The poor little lie was written in a trembling hand which shook honestly enough, but from the torment of other feelings.

Philip answered the letter in person. Something had been speaking to him day and night, like the humming of a top, finding him pretexts on which to go; but now he had to make excuses for staying so long away. It was evening. Kate was milking, and he went out to her in the cowhouse.

"We began to think we were to see no more of you," she said, over the rattle of the milk in the pail.

"I've—I've been ill," said Philip.

The rattle died to a thin hiss. "Very ill?" she asked.

"Well, no—not seriously," he answered.

"I never once thought of that," she said. "Something ought to have told me. I've been reproaching you, too."

Philip felt shame of his subterfuge, but yet more ashamed of the truth; so he leaned against the door and watched in silence. The smell of hay floated down from the loft, and the odour of the cow's breath came in gusts as she turned her face about. Kate sat on the milking-stool close by the ewer, and her head, on which she wore a sun-bonnet, she leaned against the cow's side.

"No news of Pete, then? No?" she said.

"No," said Philip.

Kate dug her head deeper in the cow, and muttered, "Dear Pete! So simple, so natural."

"He is," said Philip.

"So good-hearted, too."

"Yes."

"And such a manly fellow—any girl might like him," said Kate.

"Indeed, yes," said Philip.

There was silence again, and two pigs which had been snoring on the manure heap outside began to snort their way home. Kate turned her head so that the crown of the sun-bonnet was toward Phillip, and said—

"Oh, dear! Can there be anything so terrible as marrying somebody you don't care for?"

"Nothing so bad," said Philip.

The mouth of the sun-bonnet came round. "Yes, there's one thing worse, Philip."

"No?"

"Not having married somebody you do," said Kate, and the milk rattled like hail.

In the straw behind. Kate there was a tailless Manx cat with three tailed kittens, and Philip began to play with them. Being back to back with Kate, he could keep his countenance.

"This old Horney is terrible for switching," said Kate, over her shoulder. "Don't you think you could hold her tail?"

That brought them face to face again. "It's so sweet to have some one to talk to about Pete," said Kate.

"Yes?"

"I don't know how I could bear his long absence but for that."

"Are you longing so much, Kate?"

"Oh, no, not longing—not to say longing. Only you can't think what it is to be... have you never been yourself, Philip?"

"What?" "Hold it tight... in love? No?"

"Well," said Philip, speaking at the crown of the sun-bonnet. "Ha! ha! well, not properly perhaps—I don't—I can hardly say, Kate."

"There! You've let it go, after all, and she's covered me with the milk! But I'm finished, anyway."

Kate was suddenly radiant. She kissed Horney, and hugged her calf in the adjoining stall; and as they crossed the haggard, Philip carrying the pail, she scattered great handfuls of oats to a cock and his two hens as they cackled their way to roost.

"You'll be sure to come again soon, Philip, eh? It's so sweet to have some one to remind me of——" but Pete's name choked her now. "Not that I'm likely to forget him—now is that likely? But it's such a weary time to be left alone, and a girl gets longing. Did I now? Give me the milk, then. Did I say I wasn't? Well, you can't expect a girl to be *always* reasonable."

"Good-bye, Kate."

"Yes, you had better go now—good-bye."

Philip went away in pain, yet in delight, with a delicious thrill, and a sense of stifling hypocrisy. He had felt like a fool. Kate must have thought him one. But better she should think him a fool than a traitor. It was all his fault. Only for him the girl would have been walled round by her love for Pete. He would come no more.

IX.

Philip held to his resolution for three months, and grew thin and pale. Then another letter came from Pete—a letter for himself, and he wondered what to do with it. To send it by post, pretending to be ill again, would be hypocrisy he could not support. He took it.

The family were all at home. Nancy had just finished a noisy churning, and Kate was in the dairy, weighing the butter into pounds and stamping it. Philip read the letter in a loud voice to the old people in the kitchen, and the soft thumping and watery swishing ceased in the damp place adjoining. Pete was in high feather. He had made a mortal lot of money lately, and was for coming home quickly. Couldn't say exactly when, for some rascally blackleg Boers, who had been corrupting his Kaffirs and slipped up country with a pile of stones, had first to be followed and caught. The job wouldn't take long though, and they might expect to see him back within a twelvemonth, with enough in his pocket to drive away the devil and the coroner anyway.

"Bould fellow!" said Cæsar.

"Aw, deed on Pete!" said Grannie.

"Now, if it wasn't for that Ross——" said Nancy.

Philip went into the dairy, where Kate was now skimming the cream of the last night's milking. He was sorry there was nothing but a message for her this time. Had she answered Pete's former letters? No, she had not.

"I must be writing soon, I suppose," she said, blowing the yellow surface. "But I wish—*puff*—I could have something to tell him—*puff, puff*—about you."

"About me, Kate?"

"Something sweet, I mean "—*puff, puff, puff*.

She shot a sly look upward. "Aren't you sure yet? Can't say still? Not properly? No?"

Philip pretended not to understand. Kate's laugh echoed in the empty cream tins. "How you want people to say things!"

"No, really——" began Philip.

"I've always heard that the girls of Douglas are so beautiful. You must see so many now. Oh, it would be delicious to write a long story to Pete. Where you met—in church, naturally. What she's like—fair, of course. And—and all about it, you know."

"That's a story you will never tell to Pete, Kate," said Philip.

"No, never," said Kate quite as light, and this being just what she wished to hear, she added mournfully. "Don't say that, though. You can't think what pleasure you are denying me, and yourself, too. Take some poor girl to your heart, Philip. You don't know how happy it will make you."

"Are *you* so happy, then, Kate?"

Kate laughed merrily. "Why, what do *you* think?"

"Dear old Pete—how happy *he* should be," said Philip.

Kate began to hate the very name of Pete. She grew angry with Philip also. Why couldn't he guess? Concealment was eating her heart out. The next time she saw Philip, he passed her in the market-place on the market-day, as she stood by the tipped-up gig, selling her butter. There was a chatter of girls all round as he bowed and went on. This vexed her, and she sold out at a penny a pound less, got the horse from the "Saddle," and drove home early.

On the way to Sulby she overtook Philip and drew up. He was walking to Kirk Michael to visit the old Deemster, who was ill. Would he not take a lift? He hesitated, half declined, and then got into the gig. As she settled herself comfortably after this change, he trod on the edge of her dress. At that he drew quickly away as if he had trodden on her foot.

She laughed, but she was vexed; and when he got down at "The Manx Fairy," saying he might call on his way back in the evening, she had no doubt Grannie would be glad to see him.

The girls of the market-place were standing by the mill-pond, work done, and arms crossed under their aprons, twittering like the pairing birds about them in the trees, when Philip returned home by Sulby. He saw Kate coming down the glen road, driving two heifers with a cushag for switch and flashing its gold at them in the horizontal gleams of sunset. She had recovered her good-humour, and was swinging along, singing merry snatches as she came—all life, all girlish blood and beauty.

She pretended not to see him until they were abreast, and the heifers were going into the yard. Then she said, "I've written and told him."

"What?" said Philip.

"That you say you are a confirmed old bachelor."

"That *I* say so?"

"Yes; and that *I* say you are so distant with a girl that I don't believe you have a heart at all."

"You don't?"

"No; and that he couldn't have left anybody better to look after me all these years, because you haven't eyes or ears or a thought for any living creature except himself."

"You've never written that to Pete?" said Philip.

"Haven't I, though?" said Kate, and she tripped off on tiptoe.

He tripped after her. She ran into the yard. He ran also. She opened the gate of the orchard, slipped through, and made for the door of the dairy, and there he caught her by the waist.

"Never, you rogue! Say no, say no!" he panted.

"No," she whispered, turning up her lips for a kiss.

X.

Grannie saw nothing of Philip that night. He went home tingling with pleasure, and yet overwhelmed with shame. Sometimes he told himself that he was no better than a Judas, and sometimes that Pete might never come back. The second thought rose oftenest. It crossed his mind like a ghostly gleam. He half wished to believe it. When he counted up the odds against Pete's return, his pulse beat quick. Then he hated himself. He was in torment. But under his distracted heart there was a little chick of frightened joy, like a young cuckoo hatched in a wagtail's nest.

After many days, in which no further news had come from Pete, Kate received this brief letter from Philip:

"I am coming to see you this evening. Have something of grave importance to tell you."

It was afternoon, and Kate ran upstairs, hurried on her best frock, and came down to help Nancy to gather apples in the orchard. Black Tom was there, new thatching the back of the house, and Cæsar was making sugganes (straw rope) for him with a twister. There was a soft feel of autumn in the air, pigeons were cooing in the ledges of the mill-house gable, and everything was luminous and tranquil. Kate had climbed to the fork of a tree, and was throwing apples into Nancy's apron, when the orchard gate clicked, and she uttered a little cry of joy unawares as Philip entered. To cover this, she pretended to be falling, and he ran to help her.

"Oh, it's nothing," she said. "I thought the bough was breaking. So it's you!" Then, in a clear voice, "Is your apron full, Nancy? Yes? Bring another basket, then; the white one with the handles. Did you come Laxey way by the coach? Bode over, eh? Nancy, do you really think we'll have sugar enough for all these Keswicks?"

"Good evenin', Mr. Christian, sir," said Cæsar. And Black Tom, from the ladder on the roof, nodded his wide straw brim.

"Thatching afresh, Mr. Cregeen?"

"Covering it up, sir; covering it up. May the Lord cover our sins up likewise, or how shall we cover ourselves from His avenging wrath?"

"How vexing!" said Kate, from the tree. "Half of them get bruised, and will be good for nothing but preserving. They drop at the first touch—so ripe, you see."

"May we all be ripe for the great gathering, and good for preserving, too," said Cæsar. "Look at that big one, now—knotted like a blacksmith's muscles, but it'll go rotten as fast as the least lil one of the lot. It's taiching us a lesson, sir, that we all do fall—big mountains as aisy as lil cocks. This world is changeable."

Philip was not listening, but looking up at Kate, with a face of half-frightened tenderness.

"Do you know," she said, "I was afraid you must be ill again—your apron, Nancy—that was foolish, wasn't it?"

"No; I have been well enough," said Philip.

Kate looked at him. "Is it somebody else?" she said. "I got your letter."

"Can I help?" said Philip. "What is it? I'm sure there's something," said Kate.

"Set your foot here," he said.

"Let me down, I feel giddy."

"Slowly, then. Hold by this one. Give me your hand."

Their fingers touched, and communicated fire.

"Why don't you tell me?" she said, with a passionate tightening of his hand. "It's bad news, isn't it? Are you going away?"

"Somebody who went away will never come back," he answered.

"Is it—Pete?"

"Poor Pete is gone," said Philip.

Her throat fluttered. "Gone?"

"He is dead," said Philip.

She tottered, but drew herself up quickly. "Stop!" she said. "Let me make sure. Is there no mistake? Is it true?"

"Too true."

"I can bear the truth now—but afterwards—to-night—tomorrow—in the morning it might kill me if——"

"Pete is dead, Kate; he died at Kimberley."

"Philip!"

She burst into a wild fit of hysterical weeping, and buried her face his his breast.

He put his arms about her, thinking to soothe her. "There! be brave! Hold yourself firm. It's a terrible blow. I was too sudden. My poor girl. My brave girl!"

She clung to him like a terrified child; the tears came from under her eyelids tightly closed; the flood-gates of four years' reserve went down in a moment, and she kissed him on the lips.

And, throbbing with bliss and a blessed relief from four years hypocrisy and treason, he kissed her back, and they smiled through their tears.

Poor Pete! Poor Pete! Poor Pete!

XI.

At the sound of Kate's crying, Cæsar had thrown away the twister and come close to listen, and Black Tom had dropped from the thatch. Nancy ran back with the basket, and Grannie came hurrying from the house.

Cæsar lifted both hands solemnly. "Now, you that are women, control yourselves," said he, "and listen while I spake. Peter Quilliam's dead in Kimberley."

"Goodness mercy!" cried Grannie.

"Lord alive!" cried Nancy.

And the two women went indoors, threw their aprons over their heads, and rocked themselves in their seats.

"Aw boy veen! boy veen!"

Kate came tottering in, ghostly white, and the women fell to comforting her, thereby making more tumult with their soothing moans than Kate with her crying.

"Chut'! Put a good face on it, woman," said Black Tom. "A whippa of a girl like you will be getting another soon, and singing, 'Hail, Smiling Morn!' with the best."

"Shame on you, man. Are you as drunk as Mackillya?" cried Nancy. "Your own grandson, too!"

"Never another for Kate, anyway," wept Grannie. "Aw boy veen, aw boy veen!"

"Maybe he had another himself, who knows?" said Black Tom. "Out of sight out of mind, and these sailor lads have a rag on lots of bushes."

Kate was helped to her room upstairs, Philip sat down in the kitchen, the news spread like a curragh fire, and the barroom was full in five minutes. In the midst of all stood Cæsar, solemn and expansive.

"He turned his herring yonder night when he left goodbye to the four of us," he said. "My father did the same the night he was lost running rum for Whitehaven, and I've never seen a man do it and live."

"It's forgot at you father," wept Grannie. "It was Mr. Philip that turned it. Aw boy veen! boy veen!"

"How could that be, mother?" said Cæsar. "Mr. Philip isn't dead."

But Grannie heard no more. She was busy with the consolations of half-a-dozen women who were gathered around her. "I dreamt it the night he sailed. I heard a cry, most terrible, I did. 'Father,' says I, 'what's that?' It was the same as if I had seen the poor boy coming to his end un-timeously. And I didn't get a wink on the night."

"Well, he has gone to the rest that remaineth," said Cæsar. "The grass perisheth, and the worm devoureth, and well all be in heaven with him soon."

"God forbid, father; don't talk of such dreadful things," said Grannie, napping her apron. "Do you say his mother, ma'am? Is she in life? No, but under the sod, I don't know the years. Information of the lungs, poor thing."

"I've known him since I was a slip of a boy," said one. "It was whip-top time—no, it was peg-top time——"

"I saw him the morning he sailed," said another. "I was standing *so*——"

"Mr. Christian saw him last," moaned Grannie, and the people in the bar-room peered through at Philip with awe.

"I felt like a father for the lad myself," said Cæsar, "he was always my white-headed boy, and I stuck to him with life. He desarved it, too. Maybe his birth was a bit mischancy, but what's the ould saying, 'Don't tell me what I was, tell me what I am.' And Pete was that civil with the tongue—a civiller young man never was."

Black Tom *tsht* and spat. "Why, you were shouting out of mercy at the lad, and knocking him about like putty. He wouldn't get lave to live with you, and that's why he went away."

"You're bad to forget, Thomas—I've always noticed it," said Cæsar.

"You'll be putting the bell about, and praiching his funeral, eh, Cæsar?" said somebody.

"'Deed, yes, man, Sabbath first," said Cæsar.

"That's impossible, father," said Grannie. "How's the girl to have her black ready?"

"Sunday week, then, or Sunday fortnight, or the Sunday after the Melliah (harvest-home)," said Cæsar; "the crops are waiting for saving, but a dead man is past it. Oh, I'll be faithful, I'll give it them straight, it's a time for spaking like a dying man to dying men; I'll take a tex' that'll be a lesson and a warning, 'Ho, every one that thirsteth——"

Black Tom *tsht* and spat again. "I wouldn't, Cæsar; they'll think you're going to trate them," he muttered.

Philip was asked for particulars, and he brought out a letter. Jonaique Jelly, John the Clerk, and Johnny the Constable had come in by this time. "Read it, Jonaique," said Cæsar.

"A clane pipe first," said Black Tom. "Aren't you smook-ing on it, Cæsar? And isn't there a croppa of rum anywhere? No! Not so much as a plate of crackers and a drop of tay going? Is it to be a totaller's funeral then?"

"This is no time for feasting to the refreshment of our carnal bodies," said Cæsar severely. "It's a time for praise and prayer."

"I'll pud up a word or dwo," said the Constable meekly.

"Masther Niplightly," said Cæsar, "don't be too ready to show your gift. It's vanity. I'll engage in prayer myself." And Cæsar offered praise for all departed in faith and fear.

"Cæsar is nod a man of a liberal spirit, bud he is powerful in prayer, dough," whispered the Constable.

"He isn't a prodigal son, if that's what you mane," said Black Tom. "Never seen him shouting after anybody with a pint, anyway."

"Now for the letter, Jonaique," said Cæsar.

It was from one of the Gills' boys who had sailed with Pete, and hitherto served as his letter-writer.

45

"'Respected Sir,'" read Jonaique, "'with pain and sorrow I write these few lines, to tell you of poor Peter Quilliam——'"

"Aw boy veen, boy veen!" broke in Grannie.

"'Knowing you were his friend in the old island, and the one he talked of mostly, except the girl——'"

"Boy ve——"

"Hush, woman."

"'He made good money out here, at the diamond mines——'"

"Never a yellow sovereign he sent to me, then," said Black Tom, "nor the full of your fist of ha'pence either. What's the use of getting grand-childers?"

Cæsar waved his hand. "Go on, Jonaique. It's bad when the deceitfulness of riches is getting the better of a man."

"Where was I? Oh, 'good money ——' 'Yet he was never for taking joy in it——'"

"More money, more cares," muttered Cæsar.

"'But talking and talking, and scheming for ever, for coming home.'"

"Ah! home is a full cup," moaned Grannie. "It was a show the way that lad was fond of it. 'Give me a plate of mate, bolstered with cabbage, and what do I care for their buns and sarves, Grannie,' says he. Aw, boy veen, boy bogh!"

"What does the nightingale care for a golden cage when he can get a twig?" said Cæsar.

"Is the boy's chest home yet?" asked John the Clerk.

"There's something about it here," said Jonaique, "if people would only let a man get on."

"It's mine," said Black Tom.

"We'll think of that by-and-bye," said Cæsar, waving his hand to Jonaique.

"'He had packed his chest for going, when four blacklegs, who had been hanging round the compound, tempting and plaguing the Kaffirs, made off with a bag of stones. Desperate gang, too; so nobody was running to be sent after them. But poor Peter, being always a bit bull-necked, was up to the office in a jiffy, and Might he go? And off in chase in the everin' with the twenty Kaffirs of his own company to help him—not much of a lot neither, and suspected of dealing diamonds with the blacklegs times; but Peter always swore their love for him was getting thicker and stronger every day like sour cream. "The captain's love has been their theme, and shall be till they die," said Peter.'"

"He drank up the Word like a thirsty land the rain," said Cæsar. "Peter Quilliam and I had mortal joy of each other. 'Good-bye, father,' says he, and he was shaking me by the hand ter'ble. But go on, Jonaique."

"'That was four months ago, and a fortnight since eight of his Kaffirs came back.'"

"Aw dear!" "Well, well!" "Lord-a-massy!" "Hush!"

"'They overtook the blacklegs far up country, and Peter tackled them. But they had Winchester repeaters, and Peter's boys didn't know the muzzle of a gun from the neck of a gin-bottle. So the big man of the gang cocked his piece at Peter, and shouted at him like a high bailiff, "You'd better go back the way you came." "Not immajetly," said Peter, and stretched him. Then there was smoke like a smithy on hooping-day, and "To your heels, boys," shouted Peter. And if the boys couldn't equal Peter with their hands, they could bate him with their toes, and the last they heard of him he was racing behind them with the shots of the blacklegs behind him, and shouting mortal, "Oh, oh! All up! I'm done! Home and tell, boys! Oh, oh."'"

"Rejoice not against me, O mine enemy. When I fall I shall arise. Selah," said Cæsar.

Amid the tumult of moans which followed the reading, Philip, sitting with head on his hand by the ingle, grew hot and cold with the thought that after all there was no actual certainty that Pete was dead. Nobody had seen him die, nobody had buried him; the story of the returned Kaffirs might be a lie to cover their desertion of Pete, their betrayal of him, or their secret league with the thieving Boers. At one awful moment Philip asked himself how he had ever believed the letter. Perhaps he had *wanted* to believe it.

Nancy Joe touched him on the shoulder. "Kate is waiting for a word with you alone, sir," she said, and Philip crossed the kitchen into the little parlour beyond, chill with china and bowls of sea-eggs and stuffed sea-birds.

"He's feeling it bad," said Nancy.

"Never been the same since Pete went to the Cape," said Cæsar.

"I don't know for sure what good lads are going to it for," moaned Grannie. "And calling it Good Hope of all names! Died of a bullet in his head, too, aw dear, aw dear! Discussion of the brain it's like. And look at them black-heads too, as naked as my hand, I'll go bail. I hate the nasty dirts! Cæsar may talk of one flesh and brethren and all to that, but for my part I'm not used of black brothers, and as for black angels in heaven, it's ridiculous."

"When you're all done talking I'll finish the letter," said Jonaique.

"They can't help it, Mr. Jelly, the women can't help it," said Cæsar.

"'Respected Sir, I must now close, but we are strapping up the chest of the deceased, just as he left it, and sending it to catch the steamer, the *Johannesburg*, leaving Cape Town Wednesday fortnight——'"

"Hm! Johannesburg. I'll meet her at the quay—it's my duty to meet her," said Cæsar.

"And I'll board her in the bay," shouted Black Tom.

"Thomas Quilliam," said Cæsar, "it's borne in on my spirit that the devil of greed is let loose on you."

"Cæsar Cregeen, don't make a nose of wax of me," bawled Tom, "and don't think because you're praiching a bit that religion is going to die with you. Your head's swelling tre-menjous, and-you won't be able to sleep soon without somebody to tickle your feet. You'll be forgiving sins next, and taking money for absolution, and these ones will be making a pope of you and paying you pence. Pope Cæsar, the publican, in his chapel hat and white choker! But that chiss is mine, and if there's law in the land I'll have it."

With that Black Tom swept out of the house, and Cæsar wiped his eyes.

"No use smoothing a thistle, Mr. Cregeen," said Jonaique soothingly.

"I've a conscience void of offence." said Cæsar. "I can only follow the spirit's leading. But when Belial——"

He was interrupted by a most mournful cry of "Look here! Aw, look, then, look!"

Nancy was coming out of the back-kitchen with something between the tips of her fingers. It was a pair of old shoes, covered with dirt and cobwebs.

"These were his wearing boots," she said, and she put them on the counter.

"Dear heart, yes, the very ones," said Grannie. "Poor boy, they'd move a heart of stone to see them. Something to remember him by, anyway. Many a mile his feet walked in them; but they're resting now in Abraham's bosom."

Then Cæsar's voice rose loud over the doleful tones around the counter. "'Vital Spark of Heavenly Flame'—raise it, Mr. Niplightly. Pity we haven't Peter and his fiddle here—he played with life."

"I can'd sing to-day, having a cold, bud I'll whisle id," said the Constable.

"Pitch it in altoes, then," said Cæsar. "I'm a bit of a base myself, but not near so base as Peter."

Meanwhile a little drama of serious interest was going on upstairs. There sat Kate before the looking-glass, with flushed cheeks and quivering mouth. The low drone of many voices came to her through the floor. Then a dull silence and one voice, and Nancy Joe coming and going between the kitchen and bedroom.

"What are they doing now, Nancy?" said Kate.

"First one's praying, and then another's praying," said Nancy. "Lord-a-massy, thinks I, it'll be my turn next, and what'll I say?"

"Where's Mr. Christian?"

"Gone into the parlour. I whispered him you wanted him alone."

"You never said that, Nancy," said Kate, at Nancy's reflection in the glass.

"Well, it popped out," said Nancy.

Kate went down, with a look of softened sorrow, and Philip, without lifting his eyes, began bemoaning Pete. They would never know his like—so simple, so true, so brave; never, never.

He was fighting against his shame at first seeing the girl after that kiss, which seemed to him now like treason at the mouth of a grave.

But, with the magic of a woman's art, Kate consoled him. He had one great comfort—he had been a loyal friend; such fidelity, such constancy, such affection, forgetting the difference of place, of education—everything.

Philip looked up at last, and there was the lovely face with its beaming eyes. He turned to go, and she said, softly, "How we shall miss you!"

"Why so?" said Philip.

"We can't expect to see you so often now—now that you've not the same reason for coming."

"I'll be here on Sunday," said Philip.

"Then you don't intend to desert us yet—not just yet, Philip?"

"Never!" said Philip.

"Well, good-night! Not that way—not by the porch. Good-night!"

As Philip went down the road in the darkness, he heard the words of the hymn that was being sung inside:

"Thy glory why didst Thou enshrine In such a clod of earth as mine, And wrap Thee in my clay."

XII.

At that moment day was breaking over the plains of the Transvaal. The bare Veldt was opening out as the darkness receded, depth on depth, like the surface of an unbroken sea. Not a bush, not a path, only a few log-houses at long distances and wooden beacons like gibbets to define the Boer farms. No sound in the transparent air, no cloud in the unveiling sky; just the night creeping off in silence as if in fear of awakening the sleeping morning.

Across the soulless immensity a covered waggon toiled along with four horses rattling their link chains, and a lad sideways on the shaft dangling his legs, twiddling the rope reins and whistling. Inside the waggon, under a little window with its bit of muslin curtain, a man lay in the agony of a bullet-wound in his side, and an old Boer and a woman stood beside him. He was lying hard on the place of his pain and rambling in delirium.

"See, boys? Don't you see them?"

"See what, my lad?" said the Boer simply, and he looked through the waggon window.

"There's the head-gear of the mines. Look! the iron roofs are glittering. And yonder's the mine tailings. We'll be back in a jiffy. A taste of the whip, boys, and away!"

Untouched by visions, the old Boer could see nothing.

"What does he see, wife, think you?"

"What can he see, stupid, with his face in the pillow like that?"

With the rushing of blood in his ears the sick man called out again:

"Listen! Don't you hear it? That's the noise of the batteries. Whip up, and away! Away!" and he tore at the fringe of the blanket covering him with his unconscious fingers.

"Poor boy! he's eager to get to the coast But will he live to cover another morgen, think you?"

"God knows, Jan—God only knows."

And the Veldt was very wide, and the sea and its ships were far away, and over the weary stretch of grass, and rock, and sand, there was nothing on the horizon between desolate land and dominating sky but a waste looking like a chaos of purple and green, where no bird ever sang and no man ever lived, and God Himself was not.

XIII.

"She loves me! She loves me! She loves me!" The words sang in Philip's ears like a sweet tune half the way back to Ballure. Then he began to pluck at the brambles by the wayside, to wound his hand by snatching at the gorse, and to despise himself for being glad when he should have been in grief. Still, he was sure of it; there was no making any less of it. She loved him, he was free to love her, there need be no hypocrisy and no self-denial; so he wiped the blood from his fingers, and crept into the blue room of Auntie Nan.

The old lady, in a dainty cap with flying streamers, was sitting by the fireside spinning. She had heard the news of Pete as Philip passed through to Sulby, and was now wondering if it was not her duty to acquaint Uncle Peter. The sweet and natty old gentlewoman, brought up in the odour of gentility, was thinking on the lines of poor Bridget, Black Tom when dying under the bare scraas, that a man's son was his son in spite of law or devil.

She decided against telling the Ballawhaine by remembering an incident in the life of his father. It was about Philip's father, too; so Philip stretched his legs from the sofa towards the hearth, and listened to the old Auntie's voice over the whirr of her wheel, with another voice—a younger voice, an unheard voice—breaking: in at the back of his ears when the wheel stopped, and a sweet undersong inside of him always, saying, "Be sensible; there is no disloyalty; Pete is dead. Poor Pete! Poor old Pete!"

"Though he had cast your father off, Philip, for threatening to make your mother his wife, he never believed there was a parson on the island would dare to marry them against his wish."

"No, really?"

"No; and when Uncle Peter came in at dinner-time a week after and said, 'It's all over,' he said, 'No, sir, no,' and threw down his spoon in the plate, and the hot broth splashed on my hand, I remember. But Peter said, 'It's past praying for, sir,' and then grandfather cried, 'No, I tell you no.' 'But I tell you yes, sir,' said Peter. 'Maughold Church yesterday morning before service.' Then grandfather lost himself, and called Peter 'Liar,' and cried that your father couldn't do it. 'And, besides, he's my own son after all, and would not,' said grandfather. But I could see that he believed what Uncle Peter had told him, and, when Peter began to cry, he said, 'Forgive me, my boy; I'm your father for all, and I've a right to your forgiveness.' All the same, he wouldn't be satisfied until he had seen the register, and I had to go with him to the church."

"Poor old grandfather!"

"The vicar in those days was a little dotty man named Kissack, and it was the joy of his life to be always crushing and stifling somebody, because somebody was always depriving him of his rights or something."

"I remember him—the Cockatoo. His favourite text was, 'Jesus said, then follow Me,' only the people declared he always wanted to go first."

"Shocking, Philip. It was evening when we drove up to Maughold, and the little parson was by the Cross, ordering somebody with a cane. 'I am told you married my son yesterday; is it true?' said grandfather. 'Quite true,' said the vicar. 'By banns or special license?' grandfather asked. 'License, of course,' the vicar answered."

"Curt enough, any way."

"'Show me the register,' said grandfather, and his face twitched and his voice was thick. 'Can't you believe me?' said the vicar. 'The register,' said grandfather. Then the vicar turned the key in the church door and strutted up the aisle, humming something. I tried to keep grandfather back even then. 'What's the use?' I said, for I knew he was only fighting against belief. But, hat in hand, he followed to the Communion rail, and there the vicar laid the open book before him. Oh, Philip, shall I ever forget it? How it all comes back—the little dim church, the smell of damp and of velvet under the holland covers of the pulpit, and the empty place echoing. And grandfather fixed his glasses and leaned over the register, but he could see nothing—only blurr, blurr, blurr."

"'*You* look at it, child,' he said, over his shoulder. But I daren't face it; so he rubbed his glasses and leaned over the book again. Oh dear! he was like one who looks down the list of the slain for the name he prays he may not find. But the name was there, too surely: 'Thomas Wilson Christian... to Mona Crellin... signed Wm. Crellin and something Kissack.'"

Philip's breath came hot and fast.

"The little vicar was swinging his cane to and fro on the other side of the rail and smiling, and grandfather raised his eyes to him and said, 'Do you know what you've done, sir? You've robbed me of my first-born son and ruined him.' 'Nonsense, sir,' said the vicar. 'Your son was of age, and his wife had the sanction of her father. Was I to go round by Ballawhaine for permission to do my duty as a clergyman?' 'Duty!' cried grandfather. 'When a young man marries, he marries for heaven or for hell. Your duty as a clergyman!' he cried, till his voice rang in the roof. 'If a son of yours had his hand at his throat, would you call it my duty as Deemster to hand him a knife.' 'Silence, sir,' said the vicar. Remember where you stand, or, Deemster though you are, you shall repent it.' 'Arrest me for brawling, will you?' cried grandfather, and he snatched the cane out of the vicar's hand and struck him across the breast. 'Arrest me now,' he said, and then tottered and stumbled out of the church by my arm and the doors of the empty pews."

Philip went to bed that night with burning brow and throbbing throat. He had made a startling discovery. He was standing where his father had stood before him; he was doing what his father had done; he was in danger of his father's fate! Where was his head that he had never thought of this before?

It was hard—it was terrible. Now that he was free to love the girl, he realised what it meant to love her. Nevertheless he was young, and he rebelled, he fought, he would not deliberate, The girl conquered in his heart that night, and he lay down to sleep.

But next morning he told himself, with a shudder, that it was lucky he had gone no farther. One step more and all the evil of his father's life might have been repeated in his own. There had been nothing said, nothing done. He would go to Sulby no more.

XIV.

That mood lasted until mid-day, and then a scout of the line of love began to creep into his heart in disguise. He reminded himself that he had promised to go on Sunday, and that it would be unseemly to break off the acquaintance too suddenly, lest the simple folks should think he had borne with them throughout four years merely for the sake of Pete. But after Sunday he would take a new turn.

He found Kate dressed as she had never been before. Instead of the loose red bodice and the sun-bonnet, the apron and the kilted petticoat, she wore a close-fitting dark green frock with a lace collar. The change was simple, but it made all the difference. She was not more beautiful, but she was more like a lady.

It was Sunday evening, and the "Fairy" was closed. Cæsar and Grannie were at the preaching-house, Nancy Joe was cooking crowdie for supper, and Kate and Philip talked. The girl was quieter than Philip had ever known her—more modest, more apt to blush, and with the old audacity of word and look quite gone. They talked of success in life, and she said—

"How I should like to fight my way in the world as you are doing! But a woman can do nothing to raise herself. Isn't it hard? Whatever the place where she was born in, she must remain there all her days. She can see her brothers rise, and her friends perhaps, but she must remain below. Isn't it a pity? It isn't that she wants to be rich or great. No, not that; only she doesn't want to be left behind by the people she likes. She must be, though, and just because she's a woman. I'm sure it's so in the Isle of Man, anyway. Isn't it cruel?"

"But aren't you forgetting something?" said Philip.

"Yes?"

"If a woman can't rise of herself because the doors of life are locked to her, it is always possible for a man to raise her."

"Some one who loves her, you mean, and so lifts her to his own level, and takes her up with him as he goes up?"

"Why not?" said Philip.

Kate's eyes beamed like sunshine. "That is lovely," she said in a low voice. "Do you know, I never thought of that before! If it were my case, I should like that best of all. Side by side with him, and he doing all? Oh, that is beautiful!"

And she gazed up with a timid joy at the inventive being who had thought of this as at something supernatural.

Cæsar and Grannie came back, both in fearful outbursts of Sunday clothes. Nevertheless Cæsar's eyes, after the first salutation with Philip, fixed themselves on Kate's unfamliar costume.

"Such worldly attire!" he muttered, following the girl round the kitchen and blowing up his black gloves. "This caring for the miserable body that will one day be lowered into the grave! What does the Book say?—put my tall hat on the clane laff, Nancy. 'Let it not be the outward adorning of putting on of apparel, but let it be the hidden man of the heart.'"

"But sakes alive, father," said Grannie, loosening a bonnet like a diver's helmet, "if it comes to that, what is Jeremiah saying, 'Can a maid forget her ornaments?'"

"It's like she can if she hasn't any to remember," said Cæsar. "But maybe the prophet Jeremiah didn't know the mothers that's in now."

"Chut, man! Girls are like birds, and the breed comes out in the feathers," said Grannie.

"Where's she getting it then? Not from me at all," said Cæsar.

"Deed, no, man," laughed Grannie, "considering the smart she is and the rasonable good-looking."

"Hould your tongue, woman; it'll become you better," said Cæsar.

Philip rose to go. "You're time enough yet, sir," cried Cæsar. "I was for telling you of a job."

Some of the fishermen of Ramsey had been over on Saturday. Their season was a failure, and they were loud in their protests against the trawlers who were destroying the spawn. Cæsar had suggested a conference at his house on the following Saturday of Ramsey men and Peel men, and recommended Philip as an advocate to advise with them as to the best means to put a stop to the enemies of the herring. Philip promised to be there, and then went home to Auntie Nan.

He told himself on the way that Kate was completely above her surroundings, and capable of becoming as absolute a lady as ever lived on the island, without a sign of her origin in look or speech, except perhaps the rising inflexion in her voice which made the talk of the true Manxwoman the sweetest thing in the world to listen to.

Auntie Nan was sitting by the lamp, reading her chapter before going to bed.

"Auntie," said Philip, "don't you think the tragedy in the life of father was accidental? Due, I mean, to the particular characters of grandfather and poor mother? Now, if the one had been less proud, less exclusive, or the other more capable of rising with her husband——"

"The tragedy was deeper than that, dear; let me tell you a story," said Auntie Nan, laying down her book. "Three days after your father left Ballawhaine, old Maggie, the housemaid, came to my side at supper and whispered that some one was wanting me in the garden. It was Thomas. Oh dear! it was terrible to see him there, that ought to have been the heir of everything, standing like a stranger in the dark beyond the kitchen-door."

"Poor father!" said Philip.

"'Whist, girl, come out of the light,' he whispered. 'There's a purse with twenty pounds odd in my desk upstairs; get it, Nan, here's the key.' I knew what he wanted the money for, but I couldn't help it; I got him the purse and put ten pounds more of my own in it. 'Must you do it?' I said. 'I must,' he answered. 'Your father says everybody will despise you for this marriage,' I said. 'Better they should than I should despise myself,' said he. 'But he calls it moral suicide,' I said. 'That's not so bad as moral murder,' he replied. 'He knows the island,' I urged, 'and so do you, Tom, and so do I, and nobody can hold up his head in a little place like this after a marriage like that.' 'All the worse for the place,' said he, 'if it stains a man's honour for acting honourably.'"

"Father was an upright man," interrupted Philip. "There's no question about it, my father was a gentleman."

"'She must be a sweet, good girl, and worthy of you, or you wouldn't marry her,' said I to father; 'but are you sure that you will be happy and make her happy?' We shall have each other, and it is our own affair,' said father."

"Precisely," said Philip.

"'But if there is a difference between you now,' I said, 'will it be less when you are the great man we hope to see you some day?' 'A man is not always thinking of success,' he answered.

"My father was a great man already, Auntie," burst out Philip.

"He was shaken and I was ashamed, but I could not help it, I went on. 'Has the marriage gone too far?' I asked. 'It has never been mentioned between us,' said he. 'Your father is old, and can't live long,' I pleaded. 'He wants me to behave like a scoundrel,' he answered. 'Why that, if the girl has no right to you yet?' I said, and he was silent. Then I crept up and looked in at the window. 'See,' I whispered, 'he's in the library. We'll take him by surprise. Come!' It was not to be. There was a smell of tobacco on the air and the thud of a step on the grass. 'Who's that?' I said. 'Who should it be,' cried father, 'but the same spy again. I'll shake the life out of him yet as a terrier would a rat. No use, girl,' he shouted hoarsely, facing towards the darkness, 'they're driving me to destruction.' 'Hush!' I said, and covered his mouth with my hands, and his breath was hot, like fire. But it was useless. He was married three days afterwards."

Philip resolved to see Kate no more. He must go to Sulby on Saturday to meet the fishermen, but that would be a business visit; he need not prolong it into a friendly one. All the week through he felt as if his heart would break; but he resolved to conquer his feelings. He pitied himself somewhat, and that helped him to rise above his error.

XV.

On Saturday night he was early at Sulby. The bat-room was thronged with fishermen in guernseys, sea-boots, and sou'-westers. They were all on their feet together, twisting about like great congers on the quay, drinking a little and smoking a great deal, thumping the table, and all talking at once. "How've you done, Billy?"—"Enough to keep away the divil and the coroner, and that's about all."—"Where's Tom Dug?"—"Gone to Austrilla."—"Is Jimmy over to-day?"—"He's away to Cleveland."—"Gough, bless me, every Manx boy seems to be going foreign."—"That's where we'll all be after long and last, if we don't stop these southside trawlers."

Philip went in and was received with goodwill and rough courtesy, but no man abated a jot of his freedom of action or liberty of speech, and the thumping and shouting were as loud as before. "Appeal to the Receiver-General."—"Chut! an ould woman with a face winking at you like a roast potato."—"Will we go to the Bishop, then?"—"A whitewashed Methodist with a soul the size of a dried pea."—"The Governor is the proper person," said Philip above the hubbub, "and he is to visit Peel Castle next Saturday afternoon about the restorations. Let every Manx fisherman who thinks the trawl-boats are enemies of the fish be there that day. Then lay your complaint before the man whose duty it is to inquire into all such grievances; and if you want a spokesman, I'm ready to speak for you."—"Bravo!"—"That's the ticket!"

Then the meeting was at an end; the men went on with stories of the week's fishing, stories of smugglers, stories of the Swaddlers (the Wesleyans), stories of the totalers (teetotallers), and Philip made for the door. When he got there, he began to reflect that, being in the house, he ought to leave good-night with Cæsar and Grannie. Hardly decent not to do so. No use hurting people's feelings. Might as well be civil. Cost nothing anyway. Thus an overpowering compulsion in the disguise of courtesy drew him again into Kate's company; but to-morrow he would take a new turn.

"Proud to see you, Mr. Philip," said Cæsar.

"The water's playing in the kettle; make Mr. Philip a cup of tay, Nancy," said Grannie. Cæsar was sitting back to the partition, pretending to read out of a big Bible on his knees, but listening with both ears and open mouth to the profane stories being told in the bar-room. Kate was not in the kitchen, but an open book, face downwards, lay on the chair by the turf closet.

"What's this?" said Philip. "A French exercise-book! Whoever can it belong to here?"

"Aw, Kirry, of coorse," said Grannie, "and sticking that close to it of an everin that you haven't a chance to put a word on her."

"Vanity, sir, vanity, all vanity," said Cæsar; and again he listened hard.

Philip's eyes began to blink. "Teaching herself French, is she? Has she been doing it long, Grannie?"

"Long enough, sir, three years or better, since poor Pete went away maybe; and at the books for ever, grammars and tex' books, and I don't know what."

Cæsar, with his ear at the glass, made an impatient gesture for silence, but Grannie continued, "I don't know what for people should be larning themselves foreign languages at all. For my part, there isn't one of them bates the Manx itself for plainness. And aren't we reading, when the Lord wanted to bring confusion on Noah and his disobedient sons and grandsons at going up the Tower of Babel, he made them spake different tongues?"

"Good thing too," snapped Cæsar, "if every poor man was bound to carry his wife up with him."

Philip's eyes were streaming, and, unobserved, he put the lesson-book to his lips. He had guessed its secret. The girl was making herself worthy of him. God bless, her!

Kate came downstairs in the dark dress and white collar of Sunday night. She saw Philip putting down the book, lowered her head and blushed, took up the volume, and smuggled it out of sight. Then Cæsar's curiosity conquered his propriety and he ventured into the bar-room, Grannie came and went between the counter and the fishermen, Nancy clicked about from dairy to door, and Kate and Philip were left alone.

"You were wrong the other night," she said. "I have been thinking it over, and you were quite, quite wrong."

"So?"

"If a man marries a woman beneath him, he stoops to her, and to stoop to her is to pity her, and to pity her is to be ashamed of her, and to be ashamed of would kill her. So you are wrong."

"Yes?" said Philip.

"Yes," said Kate, "but do you know what it ought to be? The *woman* ought to marry beneath herself, and the man *above* himself; then as much as the woman descends, the man rises, and so——-don't you see?"

She faltered and stopped, and Philip said, "Aren't you talking nonsense,' Kate?"

"Indeed, sir!"

Kate pretended to be angry at the rebuff, and pouted her lips, but her eyes were beaming.

"There is neither above nor below where there is real liking," said Philip. "If you like any one, and she is necessary to your life, that is the sign of your natural equality. It is God's sign, and all the rest is only man's book-keeping."

"You mean," said Kate, trying to keep a grave mouth, "you mean that if a woman belongs to some one she can like, and some one belongs to her, that is being equal, and everything else is nothing? Eh?"

"Why not?" said Philip.

It was music to her, but she wagged her head solemnly and said, "I'm sure you're wrong, Philip. I am, though. Yes, indeed I am. But it's no use arguing. Not against you. Only——"

The glorious choir of love-birds in her bosom were singing so loud that she could say no more, and the irresistible one had his way. After a while, she stuffed something into the fire.

"What's that?" said Philip.

"Oh, nothing," she answered brightly.

It was the French exercise-book.

XVI.

Philip went home rebelling against his father's fate. It was accidental; it was inevitable only in the Isle of Man. But perdition to the place where a man could not marry the woman he loved if she chanced to be born in the manger instead of the stable loft. Perdition to the land where a man could not live unless he was a skunk or a cur. Thank God the world was wide.

That night he said to Auntie Nan, "Auntie, why didn't father go away when he found the tide setting so strongly against him?"

"He always meant to, but he never could," said Auntie Nan. "A woman isn't like a man, ready to pitch her tent here to-day and there to-morrow. We're more like cats, dear, and cling to the places we're used to, if they're only ruins of tumbling stones. Your mother wasn't happy in the Isle of Man, but she wouldn't leave it. Your father wouldn't go without her, and then there was the child. He was here for weal or woe, for life or death. When he married his wife he made the chain that bound him to the island as to a rock."

"It wouldn't be like that with Kate," thought Philip. But did Auntie know anything? Had somebody told her? Was she warning him? On Sunday night, on the way home from church, she talked of his father again.

"He came to see at last that it wasn't altogether his own affair either," she said. "It was the night he died. Your mother had been unwell and father had sent for me. It was a dark night, and late, very late, and they brought me down the hill from Lewaige Cottage with a lantern. Father was sinking, but he *would* get out of bed. We were alone together then, he and I, except for you, and you were asleep in your cot by the window. He made straight for it, and struggled down on his knees at its side by help of the curtains. 'Listen,' he said, trying to whisper, though he could not, for his poor throat was making noises. You were catching your breath, as if sobbing in your sleep. 'Poor little boy, he's dreaming,' said I; 'let me turn him on his side.' 'It's not that,' said father; 'he went to sleep in trouble.'"

"I remember it, Auntie," said Philip. "Perhaps he had been trying to tell me something."

"'My boy, my son, forgive me, I have sinned against you,' he said, and he tried to reach over the cot rail and put his lips to your forehead, but his poor head shook like palsy and bobbed down into your little face. I remember you rubbed your nose with your little fist, but you did not waken. Then I helped him back to bed, and the table with the medicine glasses jingled by the trembling of his other hand. 'It's dark, all, all dark, Nannie,' he said, 'sure some angel will bring me light,' and I was so simple I thought he meant the lamp, for it was dying down, and I lit a candle."

Philip went about his work that week as if the spirit of his father were hovering over him, warning him when awake in words of love and pleading, crying to him in his sleep in tones of anger and command, "Stand back; you are at the edge of the precipice."

Nevertheless his soul rose in rebellion against this league as of the past and the dead. It was founded in vanity, in the desire for glory and success. Only let a man renounce the world and all that the world can give, and he can be true to himself, to his heart's impulse, to his honour, and to his love. He would deliberate no longer. He despised himself for deliberating. If was the world against Kate, let the world go to perdition.

XVII.

On Saturday afternoon he was at Peel. It was a beautiful day; the sun was shining, and the bay was blue and flat and quiet. The tide was down, the harbour was empty of water, but full of smacks with hanging sails and hammocks of nets and lines of mollags (bladders) up to the mast heads. A flight of seagulls were fishing in the mud, and swirling through the brown wings of the boats and crying. A flag floated over the ruins of the castle, the church-bells were ringing, and the harbour-masters were abroad in best blue and gold buttons.

On the tilting-ground of the castle the fishermen had gathered, sixteen hundred strong. There were trawlers among them, Manx, Irish, and English, prowling through the crowd, and scooping up the odds and ends of gossip as their boats on the bottom scraped up the little fish. Occasionally they were observed by the herring-fishers, and then there were high words and free fights. "Taking a creep round from Port le Murrey are you, Dan?"—"Thought I'd put a sight on Peel to-day."—"Bad for your complexion, though; might turn it red, I'm thinking."—"Strek me with blood will you? I'd just like you to strek me, begough. I'd put a Union Jack on your face as big as a griddle."

The Governor came, an elderly man, with a formidable air, an aquiline nose, and cheeks pitted with small-pox. Philip introduced the fishermen and told their grievance. Trawling destroyed immature fish, and so contributed to the failure of the fisheries. They asked for power to stop it in the bays of the island, and within three miles of the coast.

"Then draft me a bill with that object, Mr. Christian," said the Governor, and the meeting ended with cheers for His Excellency, shouts for Philip, and mutterings of contempt from the trawlers. "Didn't think there was a man on the island could spake like it."—"But hasn't your fancy-man been rubbing his back agen the college?"—"I'd take lil tacks home if I was yourself, Dan."—"Drink much more and it'll be two feet deep inside of you."

Philip was hurrying away under the crumbling portcullis, when a deputation of the fishermen approached him. "What are we owing you, Mr. Christian?" asked their spokesman.

"Nothing," answered Philip.

"We thank you, sir, and you'll be hearing from us again. Meanwhile, a word if you plaze, sir?"

"What is it, men?" said Philip.

"When a young man can spake like yonder, it's a gift, sir, and he's houlding it in trust for something. The ould island's wanting a big man ter'ble bad, and it hasn't seen the like since the days of your own grandfather. Good everin, and thank you—good everin!"

With that the rough fellows dismissed him at the ferry steps, and he hastened to the market-place, where he had left his horse. On putting up, he had seen Cæsar's gig tipped up in the stable-yard. It was now gone, and, without asking questions, he mounted and made towards Ramsey.

He took the old road by the cliffs, and as he cantered and galloped, he hummed, and whistled, and sang, and slashed the trees to keep himself from thinking. At the crest of the hill he sighted the gig in front, and at Port Lady he came up with it. Kate was driving and Cæsar was nodding and dozing.

"You've been having a great day, Mr. Christian," said Cæsar. "Wish I could say the same for myself; but the heart of man is decaitful, sir, and desperately wicked. I'm not one to clap people in the castle and keep them from sea for debts of drink, and they're taking a mane advantage. Not a penny did I get to-day, sir, and many a yellow sovereign owing to me. If I was like some—now there's that Tom Raby, Glen Meay. He saw Dan the Spy coming from the total meeting last night. 'Taken the pledge, Dan?' says he. 'Yes, I have,' says Dan. 'I'm plazed to hear it,' says he; 'come in and I'll give you a good glass of rum for it.' And Dan took the rum for taking the pledge, and there he was as drunk as Mackilley in the castle this morning."

Philip listened as he rode, and a half-melancholy, half-mocking expression played on his face. He was thinking of his grandfather, old Iron Christian, brought into relation with his mother's father, Capt. Billy Ballure, of the dainty gentility of Auntie Nan and the unctuous vulgarity of the father of Kate.

Cæsar grumbled himself to sleep at last, and then Philip was alone with the girl, and riding on her side of the gig. She was quiet at first, but a joyous smile lit up her face.

"I was in the castle, too," she said, with a look of pride.

The sun went down over the waters behind them, and cast their brown shadows on the road in front; the twilight deepened, the night came down, the moon rose in their faces, and the stars appeared. They could hear the tramp of the horses' hoofs, the roll of the gig wheels, the wash and boom of the sea on their left, and the cry Of the sea-fowl somewhere beneath. The lovelinese and warmth of the autumn night stole over Kate, and she began to keep up a flow of merry chatter.

"I can tell all the sounds of the fields in the darkness. By the moonlight? No; but with my eyes shut, if you like. Now try me."

She closed her eyes and went on: "Do you hear that—that patter like soft rain? That's oats nearly ripe for harvest. Do you hear that, then—that pit-a-pat, like sheep going by on the street? That's wheat, just ready. And there—that whiss, whiss, whiss? That's barley."

She opened her eyes: "Don't you think I'm very clever?"

Philip felt an impulse to lean over the wheel and put his arms about the girl's neck.

"Take care," she cried merrily; "your horse is shying."

He gazed at her face, lit up in the white moonlight. "How bright and happy you seem, Kate!" he said with a shiver; and then he laid one hand on the gig rail.

Her eyelids quivered, her mouth twitched, and she answered gaily, "Why not? Aren't you? You ought to be, you know. How glorious to succeed! It means so much—new things to see, new houses to visit, new pleasures, new friends——"

Her joyous tones broke down in a nervous laugh at that last word, and he replied, in a faltering voice, "That may be true of the big world over yonder, Kate, but it isn't so in a little island like ours. To succeed here is like going up the tower of Castle Rushen with some one locking the doors on the stone steps behind you. At every storey the room becomes less, until at the top you have only space to stand alone. Then, if you should ever come down again, there's but one way for you—over the battlements with a crash."

She looked up at him with startled eyes, and his own were large and full of trouble. They were going through Kirk Michael by the house of the Deemster, who was ill, and both drew rein and went slowly. Some acacias in the garden slashed their broadswords in the night air, and a windmill behind stood out against the moon like a gigantic bat. The black shadow of the horses stepped beside them.

"Are you feeling lonely to-night, Philip?"

"I'm feeling——"

"Yes?"

"I'm feeling as if the dead and the living, the living and the dead—oh, Kate, Kate, I don't know what I'm feeling."

She put her hand caressingly on the top of his hand. "Never mind, dear," she said softly; "I'll stand by you. You shan't be *alone*."

XVIII.

It was midday, then, on the tropic seas, and the horizon was closing in with clouds as of blood and vapours of stifling heat. A steamship was rolling in a heavy swell, under winds that were as hot as gusts from an open furnace. Under its decks a man lay in an atmosphere of fever and the sickening odour of bandages and stale air. Above the throb of the engines and the rattle of the rudder chain he heard a step going by his open door, and he called in a feeble voice that was cheerful and almost merry, but yet the voice of a homesick boy—

"How many days from home, engineer?"

"Not more than twenty now."

"Put on steam, mate; put it on. Wish I could be skipping below and stoking up for you like mad."

As the ship rolled, the green reflection of the water and the red light of the sky shot alternately through the porthole and lit up the berth like firelight flashing in a dead house.

"Ask the boys if they'll carry me on deck, sir—just for a breath of fresh air."

The sailors came and carried him. "You can do anything for a chap like that."

The big sun was straight overhead, weighing down on their shoulders, and there was no shelter anywhere, for the shadows were under foot.

"Slip out the sails, lads, and let's fly along. Wish I could tumble up the rigging myself and look out from the yards same as a gull, but I'm only an ould parrot chained down to my stick."

They left him, and he gazed out on the circle of water and the vapour shaking over it like a veil. The palpitating air was making the circle smaller every minute, but the world seem cruelly large for all that. He was looking beyond the visible things; he was listening deeper than the wash of the waves; he was dreaming, dreaming. Apparitions were floating in the heat-clouds over him. Home! Its voices whispered at his ear, its face peered into his eyes. But the hot winds came up and danced round him; the air, the sea, the sky, the whole world, the utter universe seemed afire; his eyes rolled upwards to his brow; he almost choked and fainted.

"Carry him below, poor fellow! He's got a good heart to think he'll ever see home again. He'll never see it."

Half-way down the companion-ladder he opened his eyes with a look of despair. Would God let him die after all?

XIX.

Kate began to feel that Philip was slipping away from her. He loved her, she was sure of that, but something was dragging them apart Her great enemy was Philip's success. This was rapid and constant. She wanted to rejoice in it; she struggled to feel glad and happy, and even proud. But that was impossible. It was ungenerous, it was mean, but she could not help it—she resented every fresh mark of Philip's advancement.

The world that was carrying Philip up was carrying him away. She would be left far below. It would be presumptuous to lift her eyes to him. Visions came to her of Philip in other scenes than her scenes, among ladies in drawing-rooms, beautiful, educated, clever, able to talk of many things beyond her knowledge. Then she looked at herself, and felt vexed with her hands, made coarse by the work of the farm; at her father, and felt ashamed of the moleskin clothes he wore in the mill; at her home, and flushed deep at the thought of the bar-room.

It was small and pitiful, she knew that, and she shuddered under the sense of being a meaner-hearted girl than she had ever thought. If she could do something of herself to counteract the difference made by Philip's success, if she could raise herself a little, she would be content to keep behind, to let him go first, to see him forge ahead of her, and of everybody, being only in sight and within reach. But she could do nothing except writhe and rebel against the network of female custom, or tear herself in the thorny thicket of female morals.

Harvest had begun; half the crop of Glenmooar had been saved, a third was in stook, and then a wet day had come and stopped all work in the fields. On this wet day, in the preaching-room of the mill, amid forms and desks, with the cranch of the stones from below, the wash of the wheel from outside, and the rush of the uncrushed corn from above, Cæsar sat rolling sugganes for the stackyard, with Kate working the twister, and going backward before him, and half his neighbours sheltering from the rain and looking on.

"Thought I'd have a sight up and tell you," said Kelly, the postman.

"What's the news, Mr. Kelly?" said Cæsar.

"The ould Dempster's dying," said Kelly.

"You don't say?" said everybody.

"Well, as good as dying at ten minutes wanting eight o'clock this morning," said the postman.

"The drink's been too heavy for the man," said John, the clerk.

"Wine is a serpent, and strong drink a mocker," said Cæsar.

"Who'll be the new Dempster, Mr. Niplightly," said Jonaique.

"Hm!" snuffled the constable, easing his helmet, "dat's a serious matter, Mr. Jelly. We'll dake our time—well dake our time."

"Chut! There's only one man for it," said Cæsar.

"Perhaps yes, perhaps no," said the constable.

"Do you mane the young Ballawhaine, Mr. Cregeen?" said the postman.

"Do I mane fiddlesticks!" said Cæsar.

"Well, the man's father is at the Govenar reg'lar, they're telling me," said Kelly, "and Ross is this, and Ross is that—"

"Every dog praises his own tail," said Cæsar.

"I'm not denying it, the man isn't fit—he has sold himself to the devil, that's a fact——"

"No, he hasn't," said Cæsar, "the devil gets the like for nothing."

"But he's a Christian for all, and the Christians have been Dempsters time out of time——"

"Is he the only Christian that's in, then, eh?" said Cæsar. "Go on, Kate; twist away."

"Is it Mr. Philip? Aw, I'm saying nothing against Mr. Philip," said the postman.

"You wouldn't get lave in this house, anyway," said Cæsar.

"Aw, a right gentleman and no pride at all," said the postman. "As free and free with a poor man, and no making aisy either. I've nothing agen him myself. No, but a bit young for a Dempster, isn't he? Just a taste young, as the man said, eh?"

"Older than the young Ballawhaine, anyway," said John, the clerk.

"Aw, make him Dempster, then. I'm raising no objection," said Mr. Kelly.

"Go on, girl. Does that twister want oiling? Feed it, woman, feed it," said Cæsar.

"His father should have been Dempster before him," said John, the clerk. "Would have been too, only he went crooked when he married on yonder woman. She's through though, and what more natural——"

The rope stopped again, and Kate's voice, hard and thick, came from the farther end of it. "His mother being dead, eh?"

"It was the mother that done for the father, anyway," said the clerk.

"Consequently," said Kate, "he is to praise God that his mother is gone!"

"That girl wants a doctor," muttered Jonaique.

"The man couldn't drag the woman up after him," began the clerk. "It's always the way——"

"Just that," said Kate, with bitter irony.

"Of coorse, I'm not for saying it was the woman's fault entirely——"

"Don't apologise for her," said Kate. "She's gone and forgotten, and that being so, her son has now a chance of being Deemster."

"So he has," shouted Cæsar, "and not second Dempster only, but first Dempster itself in time, and go on with the twister."

Kate laughed loudly, and cried, "Why don't you keep it up when your hand's in? First Deemster Christian, and then Sir Philip Christian, and then Lord Christian, and then——But you're talking nonsense, and you're a pack of tattlers. There's no thought of making Philip Christian a Deemster, and no hope of it and no chance of it, and I trust there never will be."

So saying, she flung the twister on the floor and rushed out of the mill, sobbing hysterically.

"Dr. Clucas is wonderful for females and young girls," said Jonaique.

"It's that Ross again," muttered Cæsar.

"And he'll have her yet," said Kelly, the postman.

"I'd see her dead first," said Cæsar. "It would be the jaws of hell and the mouth of Satan."

That she who loved Philip to distraction should be the first to abuse and defame him was agony near to madness, for Kate knew where she stood. It was not merely that Philip's success was separating them, not merely that the conventions of life, its usages, its manners, and its customs were putting worlds between them. The pathos of the girl's position was no accidental thing. It was a deeper, older matter; it was the same to-day as it had been yesterday and would be to-morrow; it began in the garden of Eden and would go on till the last woman died——it was the natural inferiority of woman in relation to man.

She had the same passions as Philip, and was moved by the same love. But she was not free. Philip alone was free. She had to wait on Philip's will, on Philip's word. She saw Philip slipping away from her, but she could not snatch at him before he was gone; she could not speak first; she could not say, "I love you; stay with me!" She was a woman, only a woman! How wretched to be a woman! How cruel!

But ah! the dear delicious thought! It came stealing up into her heart when the red riot was nearly killing her. What a glorious thing it was to be a woman after all! What a powerful thing! What a lovely and beloved thing! To rule the king, being the slave, was sweeter than to be the king himself. That was woman's place. It was where heaven itself had put her from the beginning until now. What weapons had it given her! Beauty! Charm! Love! The joy of it! To be the weak and overcome the strong! To be nothing in the battle of life, and yet conqueror of all the world!

Kate vowed that, come what would, Philip should never leave her.

XX.

On the day when the last of the harvest is saved in the Isle of Man, the farmer gives a supper to his farm-people, and to the neighbours who have helped him to cut and house it. This supper, attended by simple and beautiful ceremonies, is called the Melliah. The parson may be asked to it, and if there is a friend of position and free manners, he also is invited. Cæsar's Melliah fell within a week of the rope-making in the mill, and partly to punish Kate, partly to honour himself, he asked Philip to be present.

"He'll come," thought Kate with secret joy, "I'm sure he'll come;" and in this certainty, when the day of Melliah came, she went up to her room to dress for it. She was to win Philip that day or lose him for ever. It was to be her trial day—she knew that. She was to fight as for her life, and gain or lose everything. It was to be a battle royal between all the conventions of life, all the network of female custom, all the inferiority of a woman's position as God himself had suffered it to be, and one poor girl.

She began to cry, but struggling with her sadness, she dashed the tears from her glistening eyes. What was there to cry about? Philip *wanted* to love her, and he should, he must.

It was a glorious day, and not yet more than two o'clock. Nancy had washed up the dinner things, the fire-irons were polished, the boots and spare whips were put up on, the lath, the old hats like lines of heads on a city gate were hung round the kitchen walls, the hearthrug was down, the turf was piled up on the fire, the kettle was singing from the slowrie, and the whole house was taking its afternoon nap.

Kate's bedroom looked over the orchard and across the stackyard up the glen. She could see the barley stack growing in the haggard; the laden cart coming down the glen road with the driver three decks up over the mare, now half smothered and looking suddenly little, like a snail under the gigantic load; and beyond the long meadow and the Bishop's bridge, the busy fields dotted with the yellow stooks and their black shadows like a castle's studded doors.

When she had thrown off her blue-black dress to wash her arms and shoulders and neck were bare. She caught sight of herself in the glass, and laughed with delight. The years had brought her a fuller flow of life. She was beautiful, and she knew it. And Philip knew it too, but he should know it to day as he had never known it before. She folded her arms in their roundness over her bosom in its fulness and walked up and down the little room over the sheep-skin rugs, under the turfy scraas, glowing in the joy of blooming health and conscious loveliness. Then she began to dress.

She took from a drawer two pairs of stockings, one black and the other red, and weighed their merits with moral gravity—which? The red had it, and then came the turn of the boots. There was a grand new pair, with countless buttons, two toecaps like two flowers, and an upward curve like the arm of a glove. She tried them on, bent back and forward, but relinquished them with a sigh in favour of plain shoes cut under the ankles and tied with tape.

Her hair was a graver matter. Its tangled curls had never satisfied her. She tried all means to bring them into subjection; but the roll on top was ridiculous, and the roll behind was formal. She attempted long waves over the temples. It was impossible. With a lash-comb she dragged her hair back to its natural lawlessness, and when it fell on her forehead and over her ears and around her white neck in little knowing rings that came and went, and peeped out and slid back, like kittens at hide-and-seek, she laughed and was content.

From a recess covered by a shawl running on a string she took down her bodice. It was a pink blouse, loose over the breast, like hills of red sand on the shore, and loose, too, over the arms, but tight at the wrist. When she put it on it lit up her head like a gleam from the sunset, and her eyes danced with delight.

The skirt was a print, with a faint pink flower, the sash was a band of cotton of the colour of the bodice, and then came the solemn problems of the throat. It was round, and full, and soft, and like a tower. She would have loved to leave it bare, but dared not. Out of a drawer under the looking-glass she took a string of pearls. They were a present from Kimberley, and they hung over her fingers a moment and then slipped back. A white silk handkerchief, with a watermark, was chosen instead. She tied it in a sailor's knot, with the ends flying loose, and the triangular corner lying down her back.

Last of all, she took out of a box a broad white straw hat, like an oyster shell, with a silver-grey ribbon, and a sweeping ostrich feather.. She looked at it a moment, blew on it, plucked at its ribbon, lifted it over her head, held it at poise there, dropped it gently on to her hair, stood back from the glass to see it, and finally tore it off and sent it skimming on to the bed.

The substitute was her everyday sun-bonnet, which had been lying on the floor by the press. It was also of pale pink, with spots on its print like little shells on a big scallop. When she had tossed it over her black curls, leaving the strings to fall on her bosom, she could not help but laugh aloud.

After all, she was dressed exactly the same as on other days of life, except Sunday, only smarter, perhaps, and fresher maybe.

The sun-bonnet was right though, and she began to play with it. It was so full of play; it lent itself to so many moods. It could speak; it could say anything. She poked it to a point, as girls do when the sun is hot, by closing its mouth over the tip of her nose, leaving only a slumberous dark cave visible, through which her black eyes gleamed and her eyelashes shone. She tied the strings under her chin, and tipped the bonnet back on to her neck, as girls will when the breeze is cool, leaving her hair uncovered, her mouth twitching merrily, and her head like a nymph-head in an aureole. She took it off and tossed it on her arm, the strings still knotted, swinging it like a basket, then wafting it like a fan, and walking as she did so to and fro in the room, the floor creaking, her print frock crinkling, and she herself laughing with the thrill of passion vibrating and of imagined things to come.

Then she went downstairs with a firm and buoyant step, her fresh lithe figure aglow with young blood and bounding health.

At the gate of the "haggard" she met Nancy Joe coming out of the washhouse.

"Lord save us alive!" exclaimed Nancy. "If I ever wanted to be a man until this day!"

Kate kissed and hugged her, then fled away to the Melliah field.

XXI.

Philip, in Douglas, had received the following communication from Government House:—

"His Excellency will be obliged to Mr. Philip Christian if he will not leave the island for the present without acquainting him of his destination."

The message was a simple one: it said little, and involved and foreshadowed nothing, but it threw Philip into a condition of great excitement. To relieve his restlessness by giving way to it, he went out to walk. It was the end of the tourist season, and the *Ben-my-Chree* was leaving the harbour. Newsboys, burrowing among the crowds on the pier to sell a Manx evening paper, were crying, "Illness of the Deemster—serious reports."

Philip's hair seemed to rise from his head. The two things came together in his mind. With an effort to smudge out the connection he turned back to his lodgings, looking at everything that his eyes fell on in the rattling streets, speaking to everybody he knew, but seeing nothing and hearing nobody. The beast of life had laid its claws on him.

Back in his rooms, he took out of his pocket a packet which Auntie Nan had put in his hand when he was leaving Ramsey. It was a bundle of his father's old letters to his sister cousin, written from London in the days when he was studying law and life was like the opening dawn. "The ink is yellow now," said Auntie Nan; "it was black then, and the hand that wrote them is cold. But the blood runs red in them yet. Read them, Philip," she said with a meaning look, and then he was sure she knew of Sulby.

Philip read his father's letters until it was far into the night, and he had gone through every line of them. They were as bright as sunshine, as free as air, easy, playful, forcible, full of picture, but, above all, egotistical, proud with the pride of intellectuality, and vain with the certainty of success. It was this egotism that fascinated Philip. He sniffed it up as a colt sniffs the sharp wind. There was no need to make allowances for it. The castles which his father had been building in the air were only as hovels to the golden palaces which his son's eager spirit was that night picturing. Philip devoured the letters. It was almost as if he had written them himself in some other state of being. The message from Government House lay on a table at his right, and sometimes he put his open hand over it as he sat close under the lamp on a table at his left and read on:—

... "Heard old Broom in the House last night, and today I lunched with him at Tabley's. They call him an orator and the king of conversationalists. He speaks like a pump, and talks like a bottle running water. No conviction, no sincerity, no appeal. Civil enough to me though, and when he heard that father was a Deemster, he told me the title meant Doomster, and then asked me if I knew the meaning of 'House of Keys,' and said it had its origin in the ancient Irish custom of locking the muniment chests with twenty-four keys, whereof each counsellor kept one. When he had left us Tabley asked if he wasn't a wonderful man, and if he didn't know something of everything, and I said, 'Yes, except the things of which I knew a little, and of them he knew nothing.'... My pen runs, runs. But, Nannie, my little Nannie, if this is what London calls a great man, I'll kick the ball like a toy before me yet."

... "So you are wondering where I am living—in man-sion or attic! Behold me then in Brick Court, Temple, second floor. Goldsmith wrote the 'Vicar' on the third, but I've not got up to that yet. His rooms were those immediately above me. I seem to see him coming down past my door in that wonderful plum-coloured coat. And sitting here at night I think of him—the sudden fear, the solitary death, then these stairs thronged with his pensioners, the mighty Burke pushing through, Reynolds with his ear-trumpet, and big 'blinking Sam,' and last of all the unknown grave, God knows where, by the chapel wall. Poor little Oliver! They say it was a women that was 'in' at the end. No more of the like now, no more debts, no more vain 'talk like poor Poll:' the light's out—all still and dark."

... "How's my little Nannie? Does she still keep a menagerie for sick dogs and lost cats? And how's the parson-gull with the broken wing, and does he still strut like Parson Kis-sack in his surplice? I was at Westminster Hall yesterday. It was the great trial of Mitchell, M. P., who forged his father's will. Stevens defended—bad, bad, bad, smirking all the while with small facetiæ. But Denman's summing up—oh! oh! such insight, such acuteness! It was wonderful. I had a seat in the gallery. The grand old hall was a thrilling scene—the dense throng, the upturned faces, the counsel, the judges, the officers of court, and then the windows, the statues, the echo of history that made every stone and rafter live—Oh, Nan, Nan, listen to me! If I live I'll sit on the bench there some day—I will, so help me God!"

When Philip had finished his father's letters, he was on the heights, and poor Kate was left far below, out of reach and out of sight. Hitherto his ambitions had been little more than the pale shadow of his father's hopes, but now they were his own realities.

XXII.

Next morning the letter came from Cæsar inviting him to the Melliah, and then he thought of Kate more tenderly. She would suffer, she would cry—it would make his heart bleed to see her; but must he for a few tears put by the aims of a lifetime? If only Pete had been alive! If only Pete were yet to come home! He grew hot and ashamed when he remembered the time, so lately past, when the prayer of his secret heart would have been different. It was so easy now to hate himself for such evil impulses.

Philip decided to go to the Melliah. It would give him the chance he wanted of breaking off the friendship finally. More than friendship there had never been, except secretly, and that could not count. He knew he was deceiving himself; he felt an uneasy sense of loss of honour and a sharp pang of tender love as often as Kate's face rose up before him.

On the day of the Melliah he set off early, riding by way of St. John's that he might inquire at Kirk Michael about the Deemster.. He found the great man's house a desolate place. The gate was padlocked, and he had to clamber over it; the acacias slashed above him going down the path, and the fallen leaves encumbered his feet At the door, which was shut, he rang, and before it was opened to him an old woman put her untidy head out of a little window at the side.

"It's scandalous the doings that's here, sir," she whispered. "The Dempster's gone into 'sterics with the drink, and the lil farmer fellow, Billiam Cowley, is over and giving him as much as he wants, and driving everybody away."

"Can I speak to him?" said Philip.

"Billiam? It isn't fit. He'll blackguard you mortal, and the Dempster himself is past it. Just sitting with the brandy and drinking and drinking, and ateing nothing; but that dirt brought up on the Curragh shouting for beefstakes morning and night, and having his dinner laid on a beautiful new white sheet as clane as a bed."

From the ambush of a screen before an open door, Philip looked into the room where the Deemster was killing himself. The window shutters were up to keep out the daylight; candles were burning in the necks of bottles on the mantelpiece; a fire smouldered in a grate littered with paper and ashes; a coarse-featured man was eating ravenously at the table, a chop-bone in his fingers, and veins like cords moving on his low forehead—and the Deemster himself, judge of his island since the death of Iron Christian, was propped up in a chair, with a smoking glass on a stool beside him, and a monkey perched on his shoulder. "Turn them out, neck and crop, Dempster; the women

57

are all for robbing a man," said the fellow; and a husky, eaten-out voice replied to him with a grunt and a laugh, "H'm! That's only what you're doing yourself, then, you rascal, and if I'd let the right one in long ago you wouldn't be here now—nor I neither, would I, Jacko?" The tail of the monkey flapped on the Deemster's breast, and Philip crept away with a shiver.

The sun was shining brightly outside the house, and the air was fresh and sweet. Remounting his horse, which was neighing and stamping at the gate, Philip rode hard to bring back a sense of warmth. At the "Fairy" he alighted and put up, and saw Grannie, who was laying tables in the mill.

"I'm busy as Trap's wife," she said, "and if you were the Govenar itself you wouldn't get lave to spake to me now. Put a sight on himself on the field yonder, the second meadow past the Bishop's bridge, and come back with the boys to supper."

Philip found the Melliah field. Two-score workers, men, women, and children, a cart and a pair of horses were scattered over it. Where the corn had been cut the day before the stubble had been woven overnight into a white carpet of cobwebs, which neither sun nor step of man had yet dispelled. There were the smell of the straw, the cawing of the rooks in the glen, the hissing to the breeze of the barley still standing, the swish of the scythe and the gling of the sickle, the bending and rising of the shearers, the swaying of the binders dragging the sheaves, the gluck of the wheels of the cart, the merry head of a child peeping out of a stook like a young bird out of the broken egg, and a girl in scarlet, whom Philip recognised, standing at the farthest hedge, and waving the corn band with which she was tieing to some one below.

Philip vaulted into the field, and was instantly seized by every woman working in it, except Kate, tied up with the straw ropes, and only liberated on paying the toll of an intruder.

"But I've come to work," he protested, and Cæsar who, was plotting the last rigs of the harvest, paired him with Kate and gave him a sickle. "He's a David, he'll smite down his thousands/," said Cæsar. Then cocking his eye up the field, "the Ballabeg for leader," he cried, "he's a plate-ribbed man. And let ould Maggie take the butt along with him. Jemmy the Red for the after-rig, and Robbie to follow Mollie with the cart Now ding-dong, boys, bend your backs and down with it."

Kate had not looked up when Philip came into the field, but she had seen him come, and she gave a little start when he took his place in his shirt-sleeves beside her. He used some conventional phrases which she scarcely answered, and then nothing was heard but the sounds of the sickle and the corn. She worked steadily for some time, and he looked up at her at intervals with her round bare arms and supple waist and firm-set foot and tight red stocking. Two butterflies tumbling in the air played around her sun bonnet and a lady-clock settled on her wrist.

Time was called for rest as Nancy Joe came through the gate bringing a basket with bottles and a can.

"The belly's a malefactor that forgets former kindness," said Cæsar; "ate and drink."

Then the men formed a group about the ale, the older women drank tea, the children making bands were given butter-milk, and the younger women with babes went cooing and clucking to the hedge where the little ones lay nuzzled up and unattended, some asleep in shawls, some awake on their backs and grabbing at the wondrous forests of marguerites towering up beside them, and all crying with one voice at sight of the breast, which the mothers were as glad to give as they to take.

The rooks cawed in the glen, there was a hot hum of bees, and a company of starlings passed overhead, glittering in the sunlight like the scales of a herring.

"They're taiching us a lesson," said Cæsar. "They're going together over the sea; but there's someones on earth would sooner go to heaven itself solitary, and take joy if they found themselves all alone and the cock of the walk there."

Kate and Philip stood and talked where they had been shearing quietly, simply, without apparent interest, and meanwhile the workers discussed them.

First the men: "He works his siggle like a man though."—"A stout boy anyway; give him practice and he'd shear many a man in bed." Then the women: "She's looking as bright as a pewter pot, and she's all so pretty as the Govenar's daughter too."—"Got a good heart, though. Only last week she had word of Pete, and look at the scarlet perricut." Finally both men and women: "Lave her alone, mother; it's that Ross that's wasting the woman."—"Well, if I was a man I'd know my tack."—"Wouldn't trust. It comes with Cæsar anyway; the Lord prospers him; she'll have her pickings. Nothing bates religion in this world. It's like going to the shop with an ould Manx shilling—you get your pen'orth of taffy and twelve pence out."—"Lend's a hand with the jough then, boy. None left? Aw, Cæsar's wonderful religious, but there's never much lavings of ale with him."

Cæsar was striding through the stooks past Philip and Kate.

"Will it thrash well, Mr. Cregeen?" said Philip.

"Eight bolls to the acre maybe, but no straw to spake of, sir," said Cæsar. "Now, boys, let the weft rest on the last end, finish your work."

The workers fell to again, and the sickle of the leader sang round his head as he hacked and blew and sent off his breath in spits until the green grass springing up behind him left only a triangular corner of yellow corn. Fore-rig and the after-rig took a tussle together, and presently nothing was standing of all the harvest of Glenmooar but one small shaft of ears a yard wide or less. Then the leaders stopped, and all the shearers of the field came up and cast down their sickles into the soil in a close circle, making a sheaf of crescent moons.

"Now for the Melliah," said Cæsar. "Who's to be Queen?"

There was a cry for Kate, and she sailed forward buoyantly, fresh still, warm with her work, and looking like the afterglow from the sunset in the lengthening shadows from the west.

"Strike them from their legs, Kirry," cried Nancy Joe, and Kate drew up one of the sickles, swept her left arm over the standing corn, and at a single stroke of her right brought the last ears to the ground.

Then there was a great shout. "Hurrah for the Mel-liah!" It rang through the glen and echoed in the mountains. Grannie heard it in the valley, and said to herself, "Cæsar's Melliah's took."

"Well, we've gathered the ripe corn, praise His name," said Cæsar, "but what shall be done at the great gathering for unripe Christians?"

58

Kate lifted her last sheaf and tied it about with a piece of blue ribbon, and Philip plucked the cushag (the ragwort) from the hedge, and gave it her to put in the band.

This being done; the Queen of the Melliah stepped back, feeling Philip's eyes following her, while the oldest woman shearer came forward.

"I've a crown-piece, here that's being lying in my pocket long enough, Joney," said Cæsar with an expansive air, and he gave the woman her accustomed dole.

She was a timid, shrinking creature, having a face walled with wrinkles, and wearing a short blue petticoat, showing heavy dull boots like a man's, and thick black stockings.

Then the young fellows went racing over the field, vaulting the stooks, stretching a straw rope for the girls to jump over, heightening and tightening it to trip them up, and slacking and twirling it to make them skip. And the girls were falling with a laugh, and leaping up again and flying off like the dust, tearing their frocks and dropping their sun-bonnets as if the barley grains they had been reaping had got into their blood.

In the midst of this maddening frolic, while Cæsar and the others were kneeling behind the barley stack, Kate snatched Philip's hat from his head and shot like a gleam into the depths of the glen.

Philip dragged up his coat by one of its arms and fled after her.

XXIII.

Sulby Glen is winding, soft, rich, sweet, and exquisitely beautiful. A thin thread of blue water, laughing, babbling, brawling, whooping, leaping, gliding, and stealing down from the mountains; great boulders worn smooth and ploughed hollow by the wash of ages; wet moss and lichen on the channel walls; deep, cool dubbs; tiny reefs; little cascades of boiling foam; lines of trees like sentinels on either side, making the light dim through the overshadowing leafage; gaunt trunks torn up by winds and thrown across the stream with their heads to the feet of their fellows; the golden fuschia here, the green trammon there; now and again a poor old tholthan, a roofless house, with grass growing on its kitchen floor; and over all the sun peering down with a hundred eyes into the dark and slumberous gloom, and the breeze singing somewhere up in the tree-tops to the voice of the river below.

Kate had run out on the stem of one of the fallen trees, and there Philip found her, over the middle of the stream, laughing, dancing, waving his hat in one hand, and making sweeping bows to her reflection in the water below.

"Come back," he cried. "You terrible girl, you'll fall. Sit down there—don't torment me, sit down."

After a curtsey to him she turned her attention to her skirts, wound them about her ankles, sat on the trunk, and dangled her shapely feet half an inch over the surface of the stream.

Then Philip had time to observe that the other end of the tree did not reach the opposite bank, but dipped short into the water. So he barricaded his end by sitting on it, and said triumphantly: "My hat, if you please."

Kate looked and gave a little cry of alarm and then a chuckle, and then she said—

"You thought you'd caught me, didn't you? You can't, though," and she dropped on to a boulder from which she might have skipped ashore.

"I can't, can't I?" said Philip; and he twisted a smaller boulder on his side, so that Kate was surrounded by water and cut off from the bank. "My hat now, madam," he said with majestic despotism. 10

She would not deliver it, so he pretended to leave her where she was. "Good-bye, then; good evening," he cried over the laughter of the stream, and turned away a step bareheaded.

A moment later his confidence was dashed. When he turned his head back Kate had whipped off her shoes and stockings, and was ramming the one inside the other.

"What are you doing?" cried Philip.

"Catch this—and this," she said, flinging the shoes across to him. Then clapping his straw hat on the crown of her sun-bonnet, she tucked up her skirts with both hands and waded ashore.

"What a clever boy you are! You thought you'd caught me again, didn't you?" she said.

"I've caught your shoes, anyway," said Philip, "and until you give me my hat I'll stick to them."

She was on the shingle, but in her bare feet, and could not make a step.

"My shoes, please?" she pleaded.

"My hat first," he answered.

"Take it."

"No; you must give it me."

"Never! I'll sit here all night first," said Kate.

"I'm willing," said Philip.

They were sitting thus, the one bare-headed, the other with bare feet, and on the same stone, as if seats in the glen were scarce, when there came the sound of a hymn from the field they had left, and then it was agreed by way of mutual penalty that Kate should put on Philip's hat on condition that Philip should be required to put on Kate's shoes.

At the next moment Philip, suddenly sobered, was reproaching himself fiercely. What was he doing? He had come to tell Kate that he should come no more, and this was how he had begun! Yesterday he was in Douglas reading his father's letters, and here he was to-day, forgetting himself, his aims in life, his duties, his obligations—everything. "Philip," he thought, "you are as weak as water. Give up your plans; you are not fit for them; abandon your hopes—they are too high for you."

"How solemn we are all at once!" said Kate.

The hymn (a most doleful strain, dragged out to death on every note) was still coming from the Melliah field, and she added, slyly, shyly, with a mixture of boldness and nervousness, "Do you think this world is so very bad, then?"

"Well—aw—no," he faltered, and looking up he met her eye, and they both laughed.

"It's all nonsense, isn't it?" she said, and they began to walk down the glen.

"But where are we going?"

"Oh, we'll come out this way just as well."

The scutch grass, the long rat-tail, and the golden cushag were swishing against his riding-breeches and her print dress. "I must tell her now," he thought. In the narrow places she went first, and he followed with a lagging step, trying to begin. "Better prepare her," he thought. But he could think of no commonplace leading up to what he wished to say.

Presently, through a tangle of wild fuchsia, there was a smell of burning turf in the air and the sound of milking into a pail, and then a voice came up surprisingly as from the ground, saying:

"Aisy on the thatch, Miss Cregeen, ma'am."

It was old Joney, the shearer, milking her goat, and Kate had stepped on to the roof of her house without knowing it, for the little place was low and opened from the water's edge and leaned against the bank.

Philip made some conventional inquiries, and she answered that she had been thirty years there, and had one son living with her, and he was an imbecile.

"There was once a flock at me, and I was as young as you are then, miss, and all as happy; but they're laving me one by one, except this one, and he isn't wise, poor boy."

Philip tried to steel his heart. "It is cruel," he thought, "it will hurt her; but what must be, must be." She began to sing and went carolling down the glen, keeping two paces in front of him. He followed like an assassin meditating the moment to strike. "He is going to say something," she thought, and then she sang louder.

"Kate," he called huskily.

But she only clapped her hands, and cried in a voice of delight, "The echo! Here's the echo! Let's shout to it."

Her kindling features banished his purpose for the time, and he delivered himself to her play. Then she called up the gill, "Ec—ho! Ec—ho!" and listened, but there was no response, and she said, "It won't answer to its own name. What shall I call?"

"Oh, anything," said Philip.

"Phil—ip! Phil—ip!" she called, and then said pettishly, "No, Philip won't hear me either." She laughed. "He's always so stupid though, and perhaps he's asleep."

"More this way," said Philip. "Try now."

"You try."

Philip took up the call. "Kate!" he shouted, and back came the answer, *Ate!* "Kate—y!"—*Ate—y.*

"Ah! how quick! Katey's a good girl. Hark how she answers you," said Kate.

They walked a few steps, and Kate called again, "Philip!" There was no answer. "Philip is stubborn; he won't have anything to do with me," said Kate.

Then Philip called a second time, "Katey!" And back came the echo as before. "Well, that's too bad. Katey is—yes, she's actually *following* you!"

Philip's courage oozed out of him. "Not yet," he thought. *Traa-dy-liooar*—time enough. "After supper, when everybody is going! Outside the mill, in the half light of candles within and darkness without! It will sound so ordinary then, 'Good-bye! Haven't you heard the news? Auntie Nan is reconciled at last to leaving Ballure and joining me in Douglas.' That's it; so simple, so commonplace."

The light was now coming between the trees on the closing west in long swords of sunset red. They could hear the jolting of the laden cart on its way down the glen. The birds were fairly rioting overhead, and all sorts of joyous sounds filled the air. Underfoot there were long ferns and gorse, which caught at her crinkling dress sometimes, and then he liberated her and they laughed. A trailing bough of deadly nightshade was hanging from the broken head of an old ash stump, whose wasted feet were overgrown by two scarlet-tipped toadstools, and she plucked a long tendril of it and wound it about her head, tipping her sun-bonnet back, and letting the red berries droop over her dark hair to her face. Then she began to sing,

> O were I monarch o' the globe,
> Wi' thee to reign, wi' thee to reign.

Radiant gleams shot out of her black pupils, and flashes of love like lightning passed from her eye to his.

Then he tried to moralise. "Ah!" he said, out of the gravity of his wisdom, "if one could only go on for ever like this, living from minute to minute! But that's the difference between a man and a woman. A woman lives in the world of her own heart. If she has interests, they centre there. But a man has his interests outside his affections. He is compelled to deny himself, to let the sweetest things go by."

Kate began to laugh, and Philip ended by laughing too.

"Look!" she cried, "only look."

On the top of the bank above them a goat was skirmishing. He was a ridiculous fellow; sometimes cropping with saucy jerks, then kicking up his heels, as if an invisible imp had pinched him, then wagging his rump and laughing in his nostrils.

"As I was saying," said Philip, "a man has to put by the pleasures of life. Now here's myself, for example. I am bound, do you know, by a kind of duty—a sort of vow made to the dead, I might say————"

"I'm sure he's going to say something," thought Kate. The voice of his heart was speaking louder and quicker than his halting tongue. She saw that a blow was coming, and looked about for the means to ward it off.

"The fairy's dubb!" she cried suddenly, and darted from his side to the water's edge.

It was a little round pool, black as ink, lying quiet and apparently motionless under a noisy place where the waters swirled and churned over black moss, and the stream ran into the dark. Philip had no choice but to follow her.

"Cut me a willow! Your penknife! Quick, sir, quick! Not that old branch—a sapling. There, that's it. Now you shall hear me tell my own fortune."

"An ordeal is it?" said Philip.

"Hush! Be quiet, still, or little Phonodoree wont listen. Hush, now hush!"

With solemn airs, but a certain sparkle in her eyes, she went down on her knees by the pool, stretched her round arm over the water, passed the willow bough slowly across its surface, and recited her incantation:

    Willow bough, willow bough, which of the four,
    Sink, circle, or swim, or come floating ashore?
    Which is the fortune you keep for my life,
    Old maid or young mistress or widow or wife?

With the last word she flung the willow bough on to the pool, and sat back on her heels to watch it as it moved slowly with the motion of the water.

"Bravo!" cried Philip.

"Be quiet. It's swimming. No, it's coming ashore."

"It's wife, Kate. No, it's widow. No, it's——"

"Do be serious. Oh, dear! it's going—yes, it's going round. Not that either. No, it has—yes, it has——oh!"

"Sunk!" said Philip, laughing and clapping his hands. "You're doomed to be an old maid, Kate. Phonodoree says so."

"Cruel Brownie! I'm vexed that I bothered with him," said Kate, dropping her lip. Then nodding to her reflection in the water where the willow bough had disappeared, she said, "Poor little Katey! He might have given you something else. Anything but that dear, eh?"

"What," laughed Philip, "crying? Because Phonodoree—never!"

Kate leapt up with averted face. "What nonsense you are talking!" she said.

"There are tears in your eyes, though," said Philip.

"No wonder, either. You're so ridiculous. And if I'm meant for an old maid, you're meant for an old bachelor—and quite right too!"

"Oh, it is, is it?"

"Yes, indeed. You've got no more heart than a mushroom, for you're all head and legs, and you're going to be just as bald some day."

"I am, am I, mistress?"

"If I were you, Philip, I should hire myself out for a scarecrow, and then having nothing under your clothes wouldn't so much matter."

"It wouldn't, wouldn't it?" said Philip.

She was shying off at a half circle; he was beating round her.

"But you're nearly as old as Methuselah already, and what you'll be when you're a man——"

"Lookout!"

She made him an arch curtsey and leapt round a tree, and cried from the other side, "I know. A squeaking old croaker, with the usual old song, 'Deed yes, friends, this world is a vale of sin and misery.' The men's the misery and the women's the sin——"

"You rogue, you!" cried Philip.

He made after her, and she fled, still speaking, "What do you think a girl wants with a——Oh! Oh! Oo!"

Her tirade ended suddenly. She had plunged into a bed of the prickly gorse, and was feeling in twenty places at once what it was to wear low shoes and thin stockings.

"With a Samson, eh?" cried Philip, striding on in his riding breeches, and lifting the captured creature in his arms. "Why, to carry her, you torment, to carry her through the gorse like this."

"Ah!" she said, turning her face over his shoulder, and tickling his neck with her breath.

Her hair caught in a tree, and fell in a dark shower over his breast. He set her on her feet; they took hands, and went carolling down the glen together:

"The brightest jewel in my crown, Wad be my queen, wad be my queen."

The daylight lingered as if loth to leave them. There was the fluttering of wings overhead, and sometimes the last piping of birds. The wind wandered away, and left their voices sovereign of all the air.

Then there came a distant shout; the cheer of the farm people on reaching home with the Melliah.. It awakened Philip as from a fit of intoxication.

"This is madness," he thought. "What am I doing?" "He is going to speak now," she told herself.

Her gaiety shaded off into melancholy, and her melancholy burst into wild gaiety again. The night had come down, the moon had risen, the stars had appeared. She crept closer to Philip's side, and began to tell him the story of a witch. They were near to the house the witch had lived in. There it was—that roofless cottage—that tholthan under the deep trees like a dungeon.

"Have you never heard of her, Philip? No? The one they called the Deemster's lady?"

"What Deemster?" said Philip.

"This one, Deemster Mylrea, who is said to be dying."

"He is dying; he is killing himself; I saw him to-day,' said Philip.

"'Well, she was the blacksmith's daughter, and he left her, and she went mad and cursed him, and said she was his wife though they hadn't been to church, and he should never marry anybody else. Then her father turned her out, and she came up here all alone, and there was a baby, and they were saying she killed it, and everybody was afraid of her. And all the time her boy was making himself a great, great man until he got to be Deemster. But he never married, never, though times and times people were putting this lady on him and then that; but when they told the witch, she only laughed and said, 'Let him, he'll get lave enough!' At last she was old and going on two sticks, and like to die any day, and then he crept out of his big house unknown to any one and stole up here to the woman's cottage. And when she saw the old man she said, 'So you've come at last, boy; but you've been keeping me long, bogh, you've been keeping me long.' And then she died. Wasn't that strange?"

Her dark eyes looked up at him and her mouth quivered.

"Was it witchcraft, then?" said Philip.

"Oh, no; it was only because he was her husband. That was the hold she had of him. He was tempted away by a big house and a big name, but he *had* to come back to her. And it's the same with a woman. Once a girl is the wife of somebody, she *must* cling to him, and if she is ever false she must return. Something compels her. That's if she's really his wife—really, truly. How beautiful, isn't it? Isn't it beautiful?"

"Do you think that, Kate? Do you think a man, like a woman, would cling the closer?"

"He couldn't help himself, Philip."

Philip tried to say it was only a girl's morality, but her confidence shamed him. She slipped her moist fingers into his hand again. They were close by the deserted tholthan, and she was creeping nearer and nearer to his side. A bat swirled above their heads and she made a faint cry. Then a cat shot from under a gooseberry bush, and she gave a little scream. She was breathing irregularly. He could smell the perfume of her fallen hair. He was in agony of pain and delight. His heart was leaping in his bosom; his eyes were burning.

"She's right," he thought. "Love is best. It is everything. It is the crown of life. Shall I give it up for the Dead Sea fruit of worldly success? Think of the Deemster! Wifeless, childless, living solitary, dying alone, unregretled, unmourned. What is the wickedness you are plotting? Your father is dead, you can do him neither good nor harm. This girl is alive. She loves you. Love her. Let the canting hypocrites prate as they will."

She had disengaged her hand, and was creeping away from him in the half darkness, treading softly and going off like a gleam.

"Kate!" he called.

He heard her laughter, he heard the drowsy hum of the gill, he could smell the warm odour of the gorse bushes.

"But this is madness," he thought. "This is the fever of an hour. Yield now and I am ruined for life. The girl has come between me and my aims, my vows, my work—everything. She has tempted me, and I am as weak as water."

"Kate!"

She did not answer.

"Come here this moment, Kate. I have something to say to you."

"Bite!" she said, coming back and holding an apple to his lips. She had plucked it in the overgrown garden.

"Listen! I'm leaving Ramsey for good—don't intend to practise in the northern courts any longer—settling in Douglas—best work lies there, you see—worst of it is—we shan't meet again soon—not very soon, you know—not for years, perhaps——"

He began by stammering, and went on stuttering, blurting out his words, and trembling at the sound of his own voice.

"Philip, you must not go!" she cried. "I'm sorry, Kate, very sorry. Shall always remember so tenderly—not to say fondly—the happy boy and girl days together."

"Philip, Philip, you must not go—you cannot go—you shall not go!"

He could see her bosom heaving under her loose red bodice. She took hold of his arm and dragged at it.

"Won't you spare me? Will you shame me to death? Must I tell you? If you won't speak, I will. You cannot leave me, Philip, because—because—what do I care?—because I love you!"

"Don't say that, Kate!"

"I love you, Philip—I love you—I love you!"

"Would to God I had never been born!"

"But I will show you how sweet it is to be alive. Take me, take me—I am yours!"

Her upturned face seemed to flash. He staggered like one seized with giddiness. It was a thing of terror to behold her. Still he struggled. "Though apart, we shall remember each other, Kate."

"I don't want to remember. I want to have you with me."

"Our hearts will always be together."

"Come to me then, Philip, come to me!"

"The purest part of our hearts—our souls——"

"But I want *you!* Will you drive a girl to shame herself again? I want *you*, Philip! I want your eyes that I may see them every day; and your hair, that I may feel it with my hands; and your lips—can I help it?—yes, and your lips, that I may kiss and kiss them!"

"Kate! Kate! Turn your eyes away. Don't look at me like that!" She was fighting for her life. It was to be now or never.

"If you won't come to me, I'll go to you!" she cried; and then she sprang upon him, and all grew confused, the berries of the nightshade whipped his forehead, and the moon and the stars went out.

"My love! My darling! My girl!"

"You won't go now?" she sobbed.

"God forgive me, I cannot."

"Kiss me. I feel your heart beating. You are mine—mine—mine! Say you won't go now!"

"God forgive us both!"

"Kiss me again, Philip! Don't despise me that I love you better than myself!"

She was weeping, she was laughing, her heart was throbbing up to her throat. At the next moment she had broken from his embrace and was gone.

"Kate! Kate!"

Her voice came from the tholthan.

"Philip!"

When a good woman falls from honour, is it merely that she is a victim of momentary intoxication, of stress of passion, of the fever of instinct? No. It is mainly that she is a slave of the sweetest, tenderest, most spiritual and pathetic of all human fallacies—the fallacy that by giving herself to the man she loves she attaches him to herself for ever. This is the real betrayer of nearly all good women that are betrayed. It lies at the root of tens of thousands of the cases that make up the merciless story of man's sin and woman's weakness. Alas! it is only the woman who clings the closer. The impulse of the man is to draw apart. He must conquer it or she is lost. Such is the old cruel difference and inequality of man and woman as nature made them—the old trick, the old tragedy.

XXIV.

Old Mannanin, the magician, according to his wont, had surrounded his island with mist that day, and, in the helpless void of things unrevealed, a steamship bound for Liverpool came with engines slacked some points north of her course, blowing her fog-horn over the breathless sea with that unearthly yell which must surely be the sound whereby the devil summons his legions out of chaos.

Presently something dropping through the dense air settled for a moment on the damp rope of the companion ladder, and one of the passengers recognised it.

"My gough! It's a bird, a sparrow," he cried.

At the same moment there was a rustle of wind, the mist lifted, and a great round shoulder rose through the white gauze, as if it had been the ghost of a mountain.

"That's the Isle of Man," the passenger shouted, and there was a cry of incredulity. "It's the Calf, I'm telling you, boys. Lave it to me to know." And instantly the engines were reversed.

The passenger, a stalwart fellow, with a look as of pallor under a tawny tan, walked the deck in a fever of excitement, sometimes shouting in a cracked voice, sometimes laughing huskily, and at last breaking down in a hoarse gurgle like a sob.

"Can't you put me ashore, capt'n?"

"Sorry I can't, sir, we've lost time already."

There was a dog with him, a little, misshappen, ugly creature, and he lifted it up in his arms and hugged it, and called it by blusterous swear names, with noises of inarticulate affection. Then he went down to his berth in the second cabin and opened a little box of letters, and took them out one by one, and leaned up to the port to read them. He had read them before, and he knew them by heart, but he traced the lines with his broad forefinger, and spelled the words one by one. And as he did so he laughed aloud, and then cried to himself, and then laughed once more. "She is well and happy, and looking lovely, and, if she does not write, don't think she is forgetting you."

"God bless her. And God bless him, too. God bless them both!"

He went up on deck again, for he could not rest in one place long. There was a breeze now, and he filled his lungs and blew and blew. The island was dying down over the sea in a pale light of silver grey. An engineman and a stoker were leaning over the bulwark to cool themselves.

"Happy enough now, sir, eh?"

"Happy as a sand-boy, mate, only mortal hungry. Tiffin you say? Aw, the heart has its hunger same as anything else, and mine has been on short commons these five years and better. See that island there, lying like a salmon gull atop of the water? Looks as if she might dip under it, doesn't she? That's my home, my native land, as the man says, and only three weeks ago I wasn't looking to see the thundering ould thing again; but God is good, you see, and I am middling fit for all. I'm a Manxman myself, mate, and I've got a lil Manx woman that's waiting for me yonder. It's only an ould shirt I'm bringing her to patch, as the saying is, but she'll be that joyful you never seen. It's bad to take a woman by surprise, though—these nervous creatures—'sterics, you see—I'll send her a tally graph from the Stage. My sakes! the joy she'll be taking of that boy, too! He'll be getting sixpence for himself and a drink of butter-milk. It's always the way of these poor lil things—can't stand no good news at all—people coming home and the like—not much worth, these women—crying reglar—can't help it. Well, you see, they're tender-hearteder than us, and when anybody's been five years... Be gough, we're making way, though! The island's going under, for sure. Or is it my eyes that isn't so clear since my bit of a bullet-wound! Aw, God is good, tremen-jous!"

The breaking voice stopped suddenly, and the engine-men turned about, but the passenger was stumbling down the cabin stairs.

"If ever a man came back from the dead it's that one," said both men together.

PART III. MAN AND WOMAN

I.

Philip was vanquished, and he knew it, but he was not daunted, he was not distressed. To have resisted the self-abandonment of Kate's love would have been monstrous. Therefore, he had done no wrong, and there was nothing to be ashamed of. But when he reached Ballure he did not dash into Auntie Nan's room, according to his wont, though a light was burning there, and he could hear the plop and click of thread and needle; he crept upstairs to his own, and sat down to write a letter. It was the first of his love letters.

"I shall count the days, the hours, and the minutes until we meet again, my darling, and I shall be constantly asking what time it is. And seeing we must be so much apart, let us contrive a means of being together, nevertheless. Listen!—I whisper the secret in your ear. To-morrow night and every night eat your supper at eight o'clock exactly; I will do the same, and so we shall be supping in each other's company, my little wife, though twenty miles divide us. If any body asks me to supper, I will refuse in order that I may sup with you. 'I am promised to a friend,' I'll say, and then I'll sit down in my rooms alone, but you will be with me."

Tingling with delight, he wrote this letter to Kate, though less than an hour parted from her, and went out to post it. He was going upstairs again, steadily, on tiptoe, his head half aside and his face over his shoulder, when Auntie Nan's voice came from the blue room—"Philip!"

He returned with a sheepish look, and a sense, never felt before, of being naked, so to speak. But Auntie Nan did not look at him. She was working a lamb on a sampler, and she reached over the frame to take something out of a drawer and hand it to him. It was a medallion of a young child—a boy, with long fair curls like a girl's, and a face like sunshine.

"Was it father, Auntie?"

"Yes; a French painter who came ashore with Thurlot painted it for grandfather."

Philip laid it on the table. He was more than ever sure that Auntie Nan had heard something. Such were her tender ways of warning him. He could not be vexed.

"I'm sleepy to-night, Auntie, and you look tired too. You've been waiting up for me again. Now, you really must not. Besides, it limits one's freedom."

"That's nothing, Philip. You said you would come home after calling on the poor Deemster, and so——"

"He's in a bad way, Auntie. Drink—delirium—such a wreck. Well, good night!"

"Did you read the letters, dear?"

"Oh, yes. Father's letters. Yes, I read them. Good night."

"Aren't they beautiful? Haven't they the very breath of ambition and enthusiasm? But poor father! How soon the brightness melted away! He never repined, though. Oh, no, never. Indeed, he used to laugh and joke at our dreams and our castles in the air. 'You must do it all yourself, Nannie; you shall have all the cakes and ale.' Yes, when he was a dying man he would joke like that. But sometimes he would grow serious, and then he would say, 'Give little Philip some for all. He'll deserve it more than me. Oh, God,' he would say, 'let me think to myself when I'm *there*, you've missed the good things of life, but your son has got them; you are here, but he is on the heights; lie still, thou poor aspiring heart, lie still in thy grave and rest.'"

Philip felt like a bird struggling in the meshes of a net.

"My father was a poet, Auntie, trying to be a man of the world. That was the real mischief in his life, if you think of it."

Auntie Nan looked up with her needle at poise above the sampler, and said in a nervous voice, "The real mischief of your father's life, Philip, was love—what they call love. But love is not that. Love is peace and virtue, and right living, and that is only madness and frenzy, and when people wake up from it they wake up as from a nightmare. Men talk of it as a holy thing—it is unholy. Books are written in praise of it—I would have such books burnt. When anybody falls to it, he is like a blind man who has lost his guide, tottering straight to the precipice. Women fall to it too. Yes, good women as well as good men; I have seen them tempted——"

Philip was certain of it now. Some one had been prying upon him at Sulby. He was angry, and his anger spent itself on Auntie Nan in a torrent of words. "You are wrong, Aunt Anne, quite wrong. Love is the one lovely thing in life. It is beauty, it is poetry. Call it passion if you will—what would the world be like without it? A place where every human heart would be an island standing alone; a place without children, without joy, without merriment, without laughter. No, no; Heaven has given us love, and we are wrong when we try to put it away. We cannot put it away, and when we make the attempt we are punished for our pride and arrogance. It ought to be enough for us to let heaven decide whether we are to be great men or little men, and to decide for ourselves whether we are to be good men and happy men. And the greatest happiness of life is love. Heaven would have to work a miracle to enable us to live without it. But Heaven does not work such a miracle, because the greatest miracle of heaven is love itself."

The needle hand of Auntie Nan was trembling above her sampler, and her lips were twitching.

"You are a young man yet, Philip," she faltered, "but I am an old lady now, dear, and I have seen the fruits of the intoxication you call passion. Oh, have I not, have I not? It wrecks lives, ruins prospects, breaks up homes, sets father against son, and brother against brother———"

Philip would give her no chance. He was tramping across the room, and he burst out with, "You are wrong again, Auntie. You are always wrong in these matters, because you are always thinking from the particular to the general—you are always thinking of my father. What you have been calling my father's fall was really his fate. He deserved it. If he had been fit for the high destiny he aspired to—if he had been fit to be a judge, he would not have fallen. That he did fall is proof enough that he was not fit. God did not intend it. My father's aspirations were not the call of a stern vocation, they were mere poetic ambition. If he had ever by great ill-fortune lived to be made Deemster, he would have found himself out, and the island would have found him out, and you yourself would have found him out, and all the world would have been undeceived. As a poet he might have been a great man, but as a Deemster he must have been a mockery, a hypocrite, an impostor, and a sham."

Auntie Nan rose to her feet with a look of fright on her sweet old face, and something dropped with a clank on to the floor.

"Oh, Philip, Philip, if I thought you could ever repeat the error——"

But Philip gave her no time to finish. Tossing his disordered hair from his forehead, he swung out of the room.

Being alone, he began to collect himself. Was it, in sober fact, he who had spoken like that? Of his father too? To Auntie Nan as well? He saw how it was; he had been speaking of his father, but he had been thinking of himself; he had been struggling to justify himself, to reconcile, strengthen, and fortify himself. But in doing so he had been breaking an idol, a life-long idol, his own idol and Auntie Nan's.

He stumbled downstairs in a rush of remorse, and burst again into the room crying in a broken voice, "Auntie! Auntie!"

But the room was empty; the lamp was turned down; the sampler was pushed aside. Something crunched under his foot, and he stooped and picked it up. It was the medallion, and it was cracked across. The accident terrified him. His skin seemed to creep. He felt as if he had trodden on his father's face. Putting the broken picture into his pocket, he turned about like a guilty man and crept silently to bed in the darkness.

But the morning brought him solace for the pains of the night—it brought him a letter from Kate.

"The Melliah is over at long, long last, and I am allowed to be alone with my thoughts. They sang 'Keerie fu Snaighty' after you left, and 'The King can only love his wife, And I can do the sa-a-me, And I can do the same.' But there is really nothing to tell you, for nothing happened of the slightest consequence. Good night! I am going to bed after I have posted this letter at the bridge. Two hours hence you will appear to me in sleep, unless I lie that long awake to think of you. I generally do. Good-bye, my dear lord and master! You will let me know what you think best to be done. Your difficulties alarm me terribly. You see, dear, we two are about to do something so much out of the common. Good night! I lift my head that you may give me another kiss on the eyes, and here are two for yours."

Then there were empty brackets [ ], which Kate had put her lips to, expecting Philip to do the same.

II.

Philip was going into his chambers in Douglas that morning when he came upon a messenger from Government House in stately intercourse with his servant. His Excellency begged him to step up to Onchan immediately, and to remain for lunch.

The Governor's carriage was at the door, and Philip got into it. He was not excited; he remembered his agitation at the Governor's former message and smiled. On leaving his own rooms he had not forgotten to order supper for eight o'clock precisely.

He found the Governor polite and expansive as usual. He was sitting in a room hung round with ponderous portraits of former Governors, most of them in frills and ruffles, and one vast picture of King George.

"You will have heard," he said, "that our northern Deemster is dead."

65

"Is he so?" said Philip. "I saw him at one o'clock yesterday."

"He died at two?" said the Governor.

"Poor man, poor man!" said Philip.

That was all. Not a tremble of the eyelid, not a quiver of the lip.

"You are aware that the office is a Crown appointment?" said the Governor. "Applications are made, you know, to the Home Office, but it is probable that my advice may be asked by the Secretary in his selection. I may, perhaps, be of use to a candidate."

Philip gave no sign, and the Governor shifted his leg and continued with a smile, "Certainly that appears to be the impression of your brother advocates, Mr. Christian; they are about me already, like wasps at a glue-pot. I will not question but you'll soon be one of them."

Philip made a gesture of protestation, and the Governor waved his hand and smiled again. "Oh, I shan't blame you; young men are ambitious. It is natural that they should wish to advance themselves in life. In your case, too, if I may say so, there is the further spur of a desire to recover the position your family once held, and lately lost through the mistake or misfortune of your father."

Philip bowed gravely, but said nothing.

"That, no doubt," said the Governor, "would be a fact in your favour. The great fact against you would be that you are still so young. Let me see, is it eight-and twenty?"

"Twenty-six," said Philip.

"No more? Only six-and-twenty? And then, successful as your career has been thus far—perhaps I should say distinguished or even brilliant—you are still unsettled in life."

Philip asked if his Excellency meant that he was still unmarried.

"And if I do," the Governor replied, with pretended severity, "and if I do, don't smile too broadly, young man. You ought to know by this time that the personal equation counts for something in this old-fashioned island of yours. Now, the late Deemster was an example which it would be perilous to repeat. If it were repeated, I know who would hear of the blunder every day of his life, and it wouldn't be the Home Secretary either. Deemster Mylrea was called upon to punish the crimes of drink, and he was himself a drunkard; to try the offences of sensuality, and he was himself a sensualist."

Philip could not help it—he gave a little crack of laughter.

"To be sure," said the Governor hastily, "you are in no danger of his excesses; but you will not be a safe candidate to recommend until you have placed yourself to all appearances out of the reach of them. 'Beware of these Christians,' said the great Derby to his son; and pardon me if I revive the warning to a Christian himself."

The colour came strong into Philip's face. Even at that moment he felt angry at so coarse a version of his father's fault.

"You mean," said he, "that we are apt to marry unwisely."

"I do that," said the Governor.

"There's no telling," said Philip, with a faint crack of his fingers; and the Governor frowned a little—the pock-marks seemed to spread.

"Of course, all this is outside my duty, Mr. Christian—I needn't tell you that; but I feel an interest in you, and I've done you some services already, though naturally a young man will think he has done everything for himself. Ah!" he said, rising from his seat at the sound of a gong, "luncheon is ready. Let us join the ladies." Then, with one hand on Philip's shoulder familiarly, "only a word more, Mr. Christian. Send in your application immediately, and—take the advice of an old fiddler—marry as soon afterwards as may be. But with your prospects it would be a sin not to walk carefully. If she's English, so much the better; but if she's Manx—take care."

Philip lunched with the Governor's wife, who told him she remembered his grandfather; also with his unmarried daughter, who said she had heard him speak for the fishermen at Peel. An official "At home," the last of the summer, was to be held in the garden that afternoon, and Philip was invited to remain. He did so, and thereby witnessed the assaults of the wasps at the glue-pot. They buzzed about the Governor, they buzzed about his wife, they buzzed about his dog and about a tame deer, which took grapes from the hands of the guests.

An elderly gentleman, sitting alone in a carriage, drove up to the lawn. It was Peter Christian Ballawhaine, looking feebler, whiter, and more splay-footed than before. Philip stepped up to his uncle and offered his arm to alight by. But the Ballawhaine brushed it aside and pushed through to the Governor, to whom he talked incessantly for some minutes of his son Ross, saying he had sent for him and would like to present him to his Excellency.

If Philip lacked enjoyment of the scene, if his face lacked heart and happiness, it was not the fault of his host. "Will you not take Lady So-and-so to have tea?" the Governor would say; and presently Philip found himself in a circle of official wifedom, whose husbands had been made Knights by the Queen, and themselves made Ladies by—God knows whom. The talk was of the late Deemster.

"Such a life! It's a mercy he lasted so long!"

"A pity, you mean, my dear, not to be hard on him either."

"Poor thing! He ought to have married. Such a man wants a wife to look after him. Don't you think so, Mr. Christian?"

"Why," said a white-haired dame, "have you never heard of his great romance?"

"Ah! tell us of that. Who was the lady?"

"The lady——" there was a pause; the white-haired dame coughed, smiled, closed her little ferret eyes, dropped her voice, and said with mock gravity, "The lady was the blacksmith's daughter, dearest." And then there was a merry trill of laughter.

Philip felt sick, bowed to his hosts, and left. As he was going off, his uncle intercepted him, holding out both hands.

"How's this, Philip? You never come to Ballawhaine now. I see! Oh, I see! Too busy with the women to remember an old man. They're all talking of you. Putting the comather on them, eh? I know, I know; don't tell me."

III.

Philip's way home lay through the town, but he made a circuit of the country, across Onchan, so heartsick was he, so utterly choked with bitter feelings. He felt as if all the angels and devils together must be making a mock at him. The thing he had worked for through five heavy years, the end he had aimed at, the goal he had fought for, was his already—his for the stretching out of his hand. Yet now that it was his, he could not have it. Oh, the mockery of his fate! Oh, the irony of his life! It was shrieking, it was frantic!

Then his bolder spirit seemed to say, "What is all this childish fuming about? Fortune comes to you with both hands full. Be bold, and you may have both the wish of your soul and the desire of your heart—both the Deemster-ship and Kate."

It was impossible to believe that. If he married Kate, the Governor would not recommend him as Deemster. Had he not admitted that he stood in some fear of the public opinion of the island? And was it not conceivable that, besides the unselfish interest which the Governor had shown in him, there was even a personal one that would operate more powerfully than fear of the old-fashioned Manx conventions to prevent any recommendation of the husband of the wrong woman? At one moment a vague memory rose before Philip, as he crossed the fields, of the lunch at Government House, of the Governor's wife and daughter, of their courtesy and boundless graciousness. At the next moment he had drawn up sharply, with pangs of self-contempt, hating himself, loathing himself, swearing at himself for a mean-souled ingrate, as he kicked up the grass and the turf beneath it But the idea had taken root. He could not help it; the Governor's interest went for nothing in his reckoning.

"What a fool you are, Philip," something seemed to whisper out of the darkest corner of his conscience; "take the Deemstership first, and marry Kate afterwards." But it was impossible to think of that either. Say it could be done by any arts of cunning or duplicity, what then? Then there were the high walls of custom and prejudice to surmount. Philip remembered the garden-party, and saw that they could never be surmounted. The Deemster who slapped the conventions in the face would suffer for it. He would be taboo to half the life of the island—in public an official, in private a recluse. An icy picture rose before his mind's eye of the woman who would be his wife in her relations with the ladies he had just left. She might be their superior in education, certainly in all true manners, and in natural grace and beauty, in sweetness and charm, their mistress beyond a dream of comparison. But they would never forget that she was the daughter of a country innkeeper, and every little cobble in the rickety pyramid, even from the daughter of the innkeeper in the town, would look down on her as from a throne.

He could see them leaving their cards at his door and driving hurriedly off. They must do that much. It was the bitter pill which the Deemster's doings made them swallow. Then he could see his wife sitting alone, a miserable woman, despised envied, isolated, shut off from her own class by her marriage with the Deemster, and from his class by the Deemster's marriage with her. Again, he could see himself too powerful to offend, too dangerous to ignore, going out on his duties without cheer, and returning to his wife without company. Finally, he remembered his father and his mother, and he could not help but picture himself sitting at home with Kate five years after their marriage, when the first happiness of each other's society had faded, had staled, had turned to the wretchedness of starvation in its state of siege. Or perhaps going out for walks with her, just themselves, always themselves only, they two together, this evening, last evening, and to-morrow evening; through the streets crowded by visitors, down the harbour where the fishermen congregate, across the bridge and over the head between sea and sky; people bowing to them respectfully, rigidly, freezingly; people nudging and whispering and looking their way. Oh, God, what end could come of such an abject life but that, beginning by being unhappy, they should descend to being bad as well?

"What a fuss you are making of things," said the voice again, but more loudly. "This hubbub only means that you can't have your cake and eat it. Very well, take Kate, and let the Deemstership go to perdition."

There was not much comfort in that counsel, for it made no reckoning with the certainty that, if marriage with Kate would prevent him from being Deemster, it would prevent him from being anything in the Isle of Man. As it had happened with his father, so it would happen with him—there would be no standing ground in the island for the man who had deliberately put himself outside the pale.

"Don't worry me with silly efforts to draw a line so straight. If you can't have Kate and the Deemstership together, and if you can't have Kate without the Deemstership, there is only one thing left—the Deemstership without Kate. You must take the office and forego the girl. It is your duty, your necessity."

This was how Philip put it to himself at length, and the daylight had gone by that time, and he was walking in the dark. But the voice which had been pleading on his side now protested on hers.

"Don't prate of duty and necessity. You mean self-love and self-interest. Man, be honest. Because this woman is an obstacle in your career, you would sacrifice her. It is boundless, pitiless selfishness. Suppose you abandon her, dare you think of her without shame! She loves you, she trusts you, and she has given you proof of her love and trust. Hold your tongue. Don't dare to whisper that nobody knows it but you and heir—that you will be silent, that she will have no temptation to speak. She loves you. She has given you all. God bless her!"

Affectionate pity swept down the selfish man in him. As the lights of the town appeared on his path, he was saying to himself boldly, "Since either way there is trouble, I'll do as I said last night—I'll leave Heaven to decide whether I'm to be a great man or a little man, and decide for myself whether I'm to be a true man or a happy man. I'll take my heart in my hand and go right forward."

In this temper he returned to his chambers. The rooms fronted to Athol Street, but backed on to the churchyard of St. George's. They were quiet, and not overlooked. His lamp was lit. The servant was laying the cloth.

"Lay covers for two, Jemmy," said Philip. Then he began to hum something.

Presently, in feeling for his keys, his fingers touched an unfamiliar substance in his pocket. He remembered what it was. It was the cracked medallion of his father. He could not bear to look at it. Unlocking a chest, he buried it at the bottom under a pile of winter clothing.

This recalled a possession yet more painful, and going to a desk, he drew out the packet of his father's letters and proceeded to hide them away with the medallion. As he did so his hand trembled, his limbs shook, he felt giddy, and he thought the voice that had tormented him with conflicting taunts was ringing in his ears again. "Bury him deep! Bury your father out of all sight and all remembrance. Bury his love of you, his hopes of you, his expectations and dreams of you. Bury and forget him for ever."

Philip hesitated a moment, and then banged down the lid of the chest, and relocked it as his servant returned to the room. The man was a solemn, dignified, and reticent person, who had been groom to the late Bishop. His gravity he had acquired from his horses, his dignity from his master; but his reticence he had created for himself, being a thing beyond nature in creature or man. His proper name was Cottier; he had always been known as Jemy-Lord.

"Company not arrived, sir," he said. "Wait or serve?"

"What is the time?" said Philip.

"Struck eight; but clock two minutes soon."

"Serve the supper at once," said Philip.

When the dishes had been brought in and the man dismissed, Philip, taking his place at the table, drew from his button-hole a flower which he had picked out of his water-bowl at lunch, and, first putting it to his lips, he tossed it on to the empty place before the chair which had been drawn up opposite. Then he sat down to eat.

He ate little; and, do what he would, he could not keep his mind from wandering. He thought of his aunt, and how hurt she had been the previous night; of his uncle, and how he had snubbed and then slavered over him; of the Governor, and how strange the interest he had shown in him; and finally, he thought of Pete, and how lately he was dead, and how soon forgotten.

In the midst of these memories, all sad and some bitter, suddenly he remembered again that he was supping with Kate. Then he struggled to be bright and even a little gay. He knew that she would be taking her supper at Sulby at that moment, thinking of him and making believe that he was with her. So he tried to think that she was with him, sitting in the chair opposite, looking across the table between the white cloth and the blue lamp-shade, out of her beaming eyes, with her rings of dark hair dancing on her forehead, and her ripe mouth twitching merrily. Then the air of the room seemed to be filled with a sweet presence. He could have fancied there was a perfume of lace and dainty things. "Sweetheart!" He laughed—he hardly knew if it was himself that had spoken. It was dear, delicious fooling.

But his eyes fell on the chest wherein he had buried the letters and the medallion, and his mind wandered again. He thought of his father, of his grandfather, of his lost inheritance, and how nearly he had reclaimed the better part of it, and then once more of Pete, crying aloud at last in the coil of his trouble, "Oh, if Pete had only lived!"

His voice startled and his words horrified him. To wipe out both in the first moment of recovered consciousness, he filled his glass to the brim, and lifted it up, rising at the same time, looking across the table, and saying in a soft whisper, "Your health, darling, your health!"

The bell rang from the street door, and he stood listening with the wine-glass in his hand. When he knew anything more, a voice at his elbow was saying out of a palpitating gloom, "The gentleman can't come, seemingly; he has sent a telegram."

It was Jem-y-Lord holding a telegram in his hand.

Philip tore open the envelope and read—

"Coming home by Ramsey boat to-morrow well and hearty tell Kirry Peat."

IV.

Somewhere in the dead and vacant dawn Philip went to bed, worn out by a night-long perambulation of the dark streets. He slept a heavy sleep of four deep hours, with oppressive dreams of common things swelling to enormous size about him.

When Jem-y-Lord took the tea to his master's bedroom in the morning, the tray was almost banged out of his hands by the clashing back of the door, after he had pushed it open with his knee. The window was half up, and a cold sea-breeze was blowing into the room; yet the grate and hearth showed that a fire had been kindled in the night, and his master was still sleeping.

Jem set down his tray, lifted a decanter that stood on the table, held it to the light, snorted like an old horse, nodded to himself knowingly, and closed the window.

Philip awoke with the noise, and looked around in a bewildered way. He was feeling vaguely that something had happened, when the man said—

"The horse will be round soon, sir."

"What horse?" said Philip.

"The horse you ride, sir," said Jem, and, with an indulgent smile, he added, "the one I ordered from Shimmen's when I posted the letter."

"What letter?"

"The letter you gave me to post before I went to bed."

All was jumbled and confused in Philip's mind. He was obliged to make an effort to remember. Just then the newsboys went shouting down the street beyond the churchyard: "Special edition—Death of the Deemster."

Then everything came back. He had written to Kate, asking her to meet him at Port Mooar at two o'clock that day. It was then, and in that lonesome place, that he had decided to break the news to her. He must tell all; he had determined upon his course.

Without appetite he ate his breakfast. As he did so he heard voices from a stable-yard in the street. He lifted his head and looked out mechanically. A four-wheeled dogcart was coming down the archway behind a mettlesome young horse with silver-mounted harness. The man driving it was a gorgeous person in a light Melton overcoat. One of his spatted feet was on the break, and he had a big cigar between his teeth. It was Ross Christian.

The last time Philip had seen the man he had fought him for the honour of Kate. It was like whips and scorpions to think of that now. Ashamed, abased, degraded in his own eyes, he turned away his head.

V.

In the middle of the night following the Melliah, Kate, turning in bed, kissed her hand because it had held the hand of Philip. When she awoke in the morning she felt a great happiness. Opening her eyes and half raising herself in bed, she looked around. There were the pink curtains hanging like a tent above her, there were the scraas of the thatched roof, with the cracking whitewash snipping down on the counterpane, there were the press and the wash-hand table, the sheep-skin on the floor, and the sun coming through the orchard window. But everything was transfigured, everything beautiful, everything mysterious. She was like one who had gone to sleep on the sea, with only the unattainable horizon round about, and awakened in harbour in a strange land that was warm and lovely and full of sunshine. She closed her eyes again, so that nothing might disturb the contemplation of the mystery. She folded her round arms as a pillow behind her head, her limbs dropped back of their own weight, and her mouth broke into a happy smile. Oh, miracle of miracles! The whole world was changed.

She heard the clatter of pattens in the room below; it was Nancy churning in the dairy. She heard shouts from beyond the orchard—it was her father stacking in the haggard; she heard her mother talking in the bar, and the mill-wheel swishing in the pond. It seemed almost wonderful that the machinery of ordinary life could be working away the same as ever.

Could she be the same herself? She reached over for a hand-glass to look at her face. As she took it off the table, it slipped from the tips of her fingers, and, falling face downwards, it broke. She had a momentary pang at that accident as at a bad omen, but just then Nancy came up with a letter. It was the letter which Philip had written at Ballure. When she was alone again she read it. Then she put it in her bosom. It seemed to be haunted by the odour of the gorse, the odour of the glen, of the tholthan, of Philip, and of all delights.

A faint ghost of shame came to frighten her. Had she sinned against her sex? Was it disgraceful that she had wooed and not waited to be won? With all his love of her, would Philip be ashamed of her also? Her face grew hot. She knew that she was blushing, and she covered up her head as if her lover were there to see. Such fears did not last long. Her joy was too bold to be afraid of tangible things. So overwhelming was her happiness that her only fear was lest she might awake at some moment and find that she was asleep now, and everything had been a dream.

That was Friday, and towards noon word came from Kirk Michael that the Deemster had died on the afternoon of the day before.

"Then they ought to put Philip Christian in his place," she said promptly; "I'm sure no one deserves it better."

They had been talking in low tones in the kitchen with their backs to her, but faced about with looks of astonishment.

"Sakes alive, Kirry," cried Nancy, "is it yourself it was? What were you saying a week ago?"

"Well, do you expect a girl to be saying the one thing always?" laughed Kate.

"Aw, no," said Cæsar. "A woman's opinions isn't usually as stiff as the tail of a fighting Tom cat. They're more coming and going, of a rule."

Next day, Saturday, she received Philip's second letter, the letter written at Douglas after the supper and the arrival of Pete's telegram. It was written crosswise, in a hasty hand, on a half-sheet of note-paper, and was like a postscript, without signature or superscription:—.

"Most urgent. Must see you immediately. Meet me at Port Mooar at two o'clock to-morrow. We can talk there without interruption. Be brave, my dear. There are serious matters to discuss and arrange."

The message was curt, and even cold, but it brought her no disquiet. Marriage! That was the only vision it conjured up. The death of the Deemster had hastened things—that was the meaning of the urgency. Port Mooar was near to Ballure—that was why she had to go so far. They would have to face gossip, perhaps backbiting, perhaps even abuse—that was the reason she had to be brave. Why and how the Deemster's death should affect her marriage with Philip was a matter she did not puzzle out. She had vague memories of girls marrying in delightful haste and sailing away with their husbands, and being gone before you had time to think they were to go. But this new fact of her life was only a part of the great mystery, and was not to be explained by everyday ideas and occurrences.

Kate ran up to dress, and came down like a bud bursting into flower. She had dressed more carefully than ever. Philip had great expectations; he must not be disappointed. Making the excuse of shopping, she was setting off towards Ramsey, when her father shouted from the stable that he was for driving the same way. The mare was harnessed to the gig, and they got up together.

Cæsar had made inquiries and calculations. He had learned that the *Johannesburg*, from Cape Town, arrived in Liverpool the day before; and he concluded that Pete's effects would come by the *Peveril*, the weekly steamer to Ramsay, on Saturday morning. The *Peveril* left Liverpool at eight; she would be due at three. Cæsar meant to be on the quay at two.

"It's my duty as a parent, Kate," said he. "What more natural but there's something for yourself? It's my duty as a pastor, too, for there's Manx ones going that's in danger of the devil of covetousness, and it's doing the Lord's work to put them out of the reach of temptation. You may exhort with them till you're black in the face, but it's throwing good money in the mud. Just *chuck!* No ring at all; no way responsive!"

Kate was silent, and Cæsar added familiarly, "Of course, it's my right too, for when a man's birth is *that* way, there's no heirship by blood, and possession is nine points of the law. That's so, Kate. You needn't be looking so hard. It's truth enough, girl. I've had advocate's opinion."

Kate had looked, but had not listened. The matter of her father's talk was too trivial, it's interest was too remote. As they drove, she kept glancing seaward and asking what time it was.

"Aw, time enough yet, woman," said Cæsar. "No need to be unaisy at all. She'll not be round the Head for an hour anyway. Will you come along with me to the quay, then? No? Well, better not, maybe."

At the door of a draper's she got down from the gig, and told her father not to wait for her on going home. Cæsar moistened his forefinger and held it in the air a moment.

"Then don't be late," said he, "there's weather coming."

A few minutes afterwards she was walking rapidly up Ballure. Passing Ballure House, she found herself treading softly. It was like holy ground. She did not look across; she gave no sign; there was only a tremor of the eyelids, a quiver of the mouth, and a tightening of the hand that held her purse, as, with head down, she passed on. Going by the water-trough, she saw the bullet-head of Black Tom looking seaward over the hedge through a telescope encased in torn and faded cloth. Though the man was repugnant to her, she saluted him cheerfully.

"Fine day, Mr. Quilliam."

"It *was* doing a fine day, ma'am, but the bees is coming home," said Tom.

He glowered at her as at a scout of the enemy, but she did not mind that. She was very happy. The sun was still shining. On reaching the top of the brow, she began to skip and run where the road descends by Folieu. Thus, with a light heart and a light step, thinking ill of no one, in love with all the world, she went hurrying to her doom.

The sea below lay very calm and blue. Nothing was to be seen on the water but a line of black smoke from the funnel of a steamship which had not yet risen above the horizon.

VI.

Philip put up his horse at the Hibernian, a mile farther on the high-road, and the tongue of the landlady, Mistress Looney went like a mill-race while he ate his dinner. She had known three generations of his family, and was full of stories of his grandfather, of his father, and of himself in his childhood. Full of facetiæ, too, about his looks, which were "rasonable promising," and about the girls of Douglas, who were "neither good nor middling." She was also full of sage counsel, advising marriage with a warm girl having "nice things at her—nice lands and pigs and things"—as a ready way to square the "bobbery" of thirty years ago at Ballawhaine.

Philip left his plate half full, and rose from the table to go down to Port Mooar.

"But, boy veen, you've destroyed nothing,", cried the landlady. And then coaxingly, as if he had been a child, "You'll be ateing bits for me, now, come, come! No more at all? Aw, it's failing you are, Mr. Philip! Going for a walk is it? Take your topcoat then, for the clover is closing."

He took the road that Pete had haunted as a boy on returning home from school in the days when Kate lived at Cornaa, going through the network of paths by the mill, and over the brow by Ballajora. The new miller was pulling down the thatched cottage in which Kate had been born to put up a slate house. They had built a porch for shelter to the chapel, and carved the figure of a slaughtered lamb on a stone in the gable. Another lamb—a living lamb—was being killed by the butcher of Ballajora as Philip went by the shambles. The helpless creature, with its inverted head swung downwards from the block, looked at him with its piteous eyes, and gave forth that distressful cry which is the last wild appeal of the stricken animal when it sees death near, and has ceased to fight for life.

The air was quiet, and the sea was calm, but across the Channel a leaden sky seemed to hover over the English mountains, though they were still light and apparently in sunshine. As Philip reached Port Mooar, a cart was coming out of it with a load of sea-wrack for the land, and a lobster-fisher on the beach was shipping his gear for sea.

"Quiet day," said Philip in passing.

"I'm not much liking the look of it, though," said the fisherman. "Mortal thick surf coming up for the wind that's in." But he slipped his boat, pulled up sail, and rode away.

Philip looked at his watch and then walked down the beach. Coming to a cave, he entered it. The sea-wrack was banked up in the darkness behind, and between two stones at the mouth there were the remains of a recent fire. Suddenly he remembered the cave. It was the cave of the Carasdhoo men. He éould hear the voice of Pete in its rumbling depths; he could hear and see himself. "Shall we save the women, Pete?—we always do." "Aw, yes, the women—and the boys." The tenderness of that memory was too much for Philip. He came out of the cave, and walked back over the shore.

70

"She will come by the church," he thought, and he climbed the cliffs to look out. A line of fir-trees grew there, a comb of little misshapen ghoul-like things, stunted by the winds that swept over the seas in winter. In a fork of one of these a bird's nest of last year was still hanging; but it was now empty, songless, joyless, and dead.

"She's here." he told himself, and he drew his breath noisily. A white figure had turned the road by the sundial, and was coming on with the step of a greyhound.

The black clouds above the English mountains were heeling down on the land. There was a storm on the other coast, though the sky over the island was still fine. The steamship had risen above the horizon, and was heading towards the bay.

VII.

She met him on the hill slope with a cry of joy, and kissed him. It came into his mind to draw away, but he could not, and he kissed her back. Then she linked her arm in his, and they turned down the beach.

"I'm glad you've come," he began.

"Did you ever dream I wouldn't?" she said. Her face was a smile, her voice was an eager whisper.

"I have something to say to you, Kate—it is something serious."

"Is it so?" she said. "So very serious?"

She was laughing and blushing together. Didn't she know what he was going to say? Didn't she guess what this serious something must be? To prolong the delicious suspense before hearing it, she pretended to be absorbed in the things about her. She looked aside at the sea, and up at the banks, and down at the little dubbs of salt water as she skipped across them, crying out at sight of the sea-holly, the anemone, and the sea-mouse shining like fire, but still holding to Philip's arm and bounding and throbbing on it.

"You must be quiet, dear, and listen," he said.

"Oh, I'll be good—so very good," she said. "But look! only look at the white horses out yonder—far out beyond the steamer. Davy's putting on the coppers for the parson, eh?"

She caught the grave expression of Philip's face, and drew herself up with pretended severity, saying, "Be quiet, Katey. Behave yourself. Philip wants to talk to you—seriously—very seriously."

Then, leaning forward with head aside to look up into his face, she said, "Well, sir, why don't you begin? Perhaps you think I'll cry out. I won't—I promise you I won't."

But she grew uneasy at the settled gravity of his face, and the joy gradually died off her own. When Philip spoke, his voice was like a cracked echo of itself.

"You remember what you said, Kate, when I brought you that last letter from Kimberley—that if next morning you found it was a mistake———"

"*Is* it a mistake?" she asked.

"Becalm, Kate."

"I am quite calm, dear. I remember I said it would kill me. But I was very foolish. I should not say so now. Is Pete alive?"

She spoke without a tremor, and he answered in a husky whisper, "Yes."

Then, in a breaking voice, he said, "We were very foolish Kate—jumping so hastily to a conclusion was very foolish-it was worse than foolish, it was wicked. I half doubted the letter at the time, but, God forgive me, I *wanted* to believe it, and so———"

"I am glad Pete is living," she said quietly.

He was aghast at her calmness. The irregular lines in his face showed the disordered state of his soul, but she walked by his side without the quiver of an eyelid, or a tinge of colour more than usual. Had she understood?

"Look!" he said, and he drew Pete's telegram from his pocket and gave it to her.

She opened it easily, and he watched her while she read it, prepared for a cry, and ready to put his arms about her if she fell. But there was not a movement save the motion of her fingers, not a sound except the crinking of the thin paper. He turned his head away. The sun was shining; there was a steely light on the firs, and here and there a white breaker was rising like a sea-bird out of the blue surface of the sea.

"Well?" she said.

"Kate, you astonish me," said Philip. "This comes on us like a thundercloud, and you seem not to realise it."

She put her arms about his neck, and the paper rustled on his shoulder. "My darling," she said, "do you love me still?"

"You know I love you, but———"

"Then there is no thundercloud in heaven for me now," she said.

The simple grandeur of the girl's love shamed him. Its trust, its confidence, its indifference to all the evil chance of life if only he loved her still, this had been beyond him. But he disengaged her arms and said, "We must not live in a fool's paradise, Kate. You promised yourself to Pete———"

71

"But, Philip," she said, "that was when I was a child. It was only a half promise then, and I didn't know what I was doing. I didn't know what love was. All that came later, dearest, much later—you know when."

"To Pete it is the same thing, Kate," said Philip. "He is coming home to claim you——"

She stopped him by getting in front of him and saying, with face down, smoothing his sleeve as she spoke, "You are a man, Philip, and you cannot understand. How can you, and how can I tell you? When a girl is not a woman, but only a child, she is a different person. She can't love anybody then—not really—not to say love, and the promises she makes can't count. It was not I that promised myself to Pete—if I did promise. It was my little sister—the little sister that was me long, long ago, but is now gone—put to sleep inside me somewhere. Is that *very* foolish, darling?"

"But think of Pete," said Philip; "think of him going away for love of you, living five years abroad, toiling, slaving, saving, encountering privations, perhaps perils, and all for you, all for love of you. Then think of him coming home with his heart full of you, buoyed up with the hope of you, thirsting, starving, and yearning for you, and finding you lost to him, dead to him, worse than dead—it will kill him, Kate."

She was unmoved by the picture. "I am very sorry, but I do not love him," she said quietly. "I am sorry—what else can a girl be when she does not love a young man?"

"He left me to take care of you, too, and you see—you see by the telegram—he is coming home with faith in my loyalty. How can I tell him that I have broken my trust? How can I meet him and explain——"

"I know, Philip. Say we heard he was dead and——"

"No, it would be too wretched. It's only three weeks since the letter came—and it would not be true, Kate—it would revolt me."

She lifted her eyes in a fond look of shame-faced love, and said again, "*I* know, then—lay the blame on me, Philip. What do I care? Say it was all my fault, and I made you love me. *I* shan't care for anybody's talk. And it's true, isn't it? Partly true, eh?"

"If I talked to Pete of temptation I should despise myself," said Philip; and then she threw her head up and said proudly—

"Very well, tell the truth itself—the simple truth, Philip. Say we tried to be faithful and loyal, and all that, and could not, because we loved each other, and there was no help for it."

"If I tell him the truth, I shall die of shame," said Philip. "Oh, there is no way out of this miserable tangle. Whether I cover myself with deceit, or strip myself of evasion, I shall stain my soul for ever. I shall become a base man, and year by year sink lower and lower in the mire of lies and deceit."

She listened with her eyes fixed on his quivering face, and her eyelids fluttered, and her fond looks began to be afraid.

"Say that we married," he continued; "we should never forget that you had broken your promise and I my trust. That memory would haunt us as long as we lived. We should never know one moment's happiness or one moment's peace. Pete would be a broken-hearted man, perhaps a wreck, perhaps—who knows?—dead of his own hand. He would be the ghost between us always."

"And do you think I should be afraid of that?" she said. "Indeed, no. If you were with me, Philip, and loved me still, I should not care for all the spirits of heaven itself."

Her face was as pale as death now, but her great eyes were shining.

"Our love would fail us, Kate," said Philip. "The sense of our guilt would kill it. How could we go on loving each other with a thing like that about us all day and all night—sitting at our table—listening to our talk—standing by our bed? Oh, merciful God!"

The terror of his vision mastered him, and he covered his face with both hands. She drew them down again and held them in a tight lock in her fingers. But the stony light of his eyes was more fearful to look upon, and she said in a troubled voice, "Do you mean, Philip, that we—could—not marry—now?"

He did not answer, and she repeated the question, looking up into his face like a criminal waiting for his sentence—her head bent forward and her mouth open.

"We cannot," he muttered. "God help us, we dare not," he said; and then he tried to show her again how their marriage was impossible, now that Pete had come, without treason and shame and misery. But his words frayed off into silence. He caught the look of her eyes, and it was like the piteous look of the lamb under the hands of the butcher.

"Is that what you came to tell me?" she asked.

His reply died in his throat. She divined rather than heard it.

Her doom had fallen on her, but she did not cry out. She did not yet realise in all its fulness what had happened. It was like a bullet-wound in battle; first a sense of air, almost of relief, then a pang, and then overwhelming agony.

They had been walking again, but she slid in front of him as she had done before. Her arms crept up his breast with a caressing touch, and linked themselves behind his neck.

"This is only a jest, dearest," she said, "some test of my love, perhaps. You wished to make sure of me—quite, quite sure—now that Pete is alive and coming home. But, you see, I want only one to love me, only one, dear. Come, now, confess. Don't be afraid to say you have been playing with me. I shan't be angry with you. Come, speak to me."

He could not utter a word, and she let her arms fall from his neck; and they walked on side by side, both staring out to sea. The English mountains were black by this time. A tempest was raging on the other shore, though the air on this side was as soft as human breath. .

Presently she stopped, her feet scraped the gravel, and she exclaimed in a husky tone, "I know what it is. It is not Pete. I am in your way. That's it. You can't get on with me about you. I am not fit for you. The distance between us is too great."

He struggled to deny it, but he could not. It was part of the truth. He knew too well how near to being the whole truth it was. Pete had come at the last moment to cover up his conscience, but Kate was stripping it naked and showing him the skeleton.

"It's all very well for you," she cried, "but where am I? Why didn't you leave me alone? Why did you encourage me? Yes, indeed, encourage me! Didn't you say, though a woman couldn't raise herself in life, a man could lift her up if he only loved her? And didn't you tell me there was neither below nor above where there was true liking, and that if a woman belonged to some one, and some one belonged to her, it was God's sign that they were equal, and everything else was nothing—pride was nothing and position was nothing and the whole world was nothing? But now I know different. The world is between us. It always has been between us, and you can never belong to me. You will go on and rise up, and I will be left behind."

Then she broke into frightful laughter. "Oh, I have been a fool! How I dreamt of being happy! I knew I was only a poor ignorant thing, but I saw myself lifted up by the one I loved. And now I am to be left alone. Oh, it is awful! Why did you deceive me? Yes, deceive me! Isn't that deceiving me? You deceived me when you led me to think that you loved me more than all the world. You don't I It is the world itself you love, and Pete is only your excuse."

As she spoke she clutched at his arms, his hands, his breast, and at her own throat, as if something was strangling her. He did not answer her reproaches, for he knew well what they were. They were the bitter cry of her great love, her great misery, and her great jealousy of the world—the merciless and mysterious power that was luring him away. After awhile his silence touched her, and she came up to him, full of remorse, and said, "No, no, Philip, you have nothing to reproach yourself with. You did not deceive me at all. I deceived myself. It was my own fault. I led you on—I know that. And yet I've been saying these cruel things. You'll forgive me, though, will you not? A girl can't help it sometimes, Philip. Are you crying? You are not crying, are you? Kiss me, Philip, and forgive me. You can do that, can't you?"

She asked like a child, with her face up and her lips apart. He was about to yield, and was reaching forward to touch her forehead, when suddenly the child became the woman, and she leapt upon his breast, and held him fervently, her blood surging, her bosom exulting, her eyes flaming, and her passionate voice crying, "Philip, you are mine. No, I will not release you. I don't care about your plans—you shall give them up. I don't care about your trust—you shall break it. I don't care about Pete coming—let him come. The world can do without you—I cannot. You are mine, Philip, and I am yours, and nobody else's, and never will be. You *must* come back to me, sooner or later, if you go away. I know it, I feel it, it's in my heart. But I'll never let you go. I can't, I can't. Haven't I a right to you? Yes, I have a right. Don't you remember?... Can you ever forget?... My *husband!*"

The last word came muffled from his breast, where she had buried her head in the convulsions of her trembling at the moment when her modesty went down in the fierce battle with a higher pain. But the plea which seemed to give her the right to cling the closer made the man to draw apart. It was the old deep tragedy of human love—the ancient inequality in the bond of man and woman. What she had thought her conquest had been her vanquishment. He could not help, it—her last word had killed everything.

"Oh, God," he groaned, "that is the worst of all."

"Philip," she cried, "what do you mean?"

"I mean that neither can I marry you, nor can you marry Pete. You would carry to him your love of me, and bit by bit he would find it out, and it would kill him. It would kill you, too, for you have called me your husband, and you could never, never, never forget it."

"I don't want to marry Pete," she said. "If I'm not to marry you, I don't want to marry any one. But do you mean that I must not marry at all—that I never can now that——"

The word failed her, and his answer came thick and indistinct—"Yes."

"And you, Philip? What about yourself?"

"As there is no other man for you, Kate," he said, "so there is no other woman for me. We must go through the world alone."

"Is this my punishment?"

"It is the punishment of both, Kate, the punishment of both alike."

Kate stopped her breathing. Her clenched hands slackened away from his neck, and she stepped back from him, shuddering with remorse, and despair, and shame. She saw herself now for the first time a fallen woman. Never before had her sin touched her soul. It was at that moment she fell.

They had come up to the cave by this time, and she sat on the stone at the mouth of it in a great outburst of weeping. It tore his heart to hear her. The voice of her weeping was like the distressful cry of the slaughtered lamb. He had to wrestle with himself not to take her in his arms and comfort her. The fit of tears spent itself at length, and after a time she drew a great breath and was quiet. Then she lifted her face, and the last gleam of the autumn sun smote her colourless lips and swollen eyes. When she spoke again, it was like one speaking in her sleep, or under the spell of somebody who had magnetised her.

"It is wrong of me to think so much of myself, as if that were everything. I ought to feel sorry for you too. You must be driven to it, or you could never be so cruel."

With his face to the sea, he mumbled something about Pete, and she caught up the name and said, "Yes, and Pete too. As you think it would be wrong to Pete, I will not hold to you. Oh, it will be wrong to me as well! But I will not give you the pain of turning a deaf ear to my troubles any more."

She was struggling with a pitiless hope that perhaps she might regain him after all. "If I give him up," she thought, "he will love me for it;" and then, with a sad ring in her voice, she said, "You will go on and be a great man now, for you'll not have me to hold you back."

"For pity's sake, say no more of that," he said, but she paid no heed.

"I used to think it a wonderful thing to be loved by a great man. I don't now. It is terrible. If I could only have you to myself! If you could only be nothing to anybody else! You would be everything to me, and what should I care then?"

Between torture and love he had almost broken down at that, but he gripped his breast and turned half aside, for his eyes were streaming. She came up to him and touched with the tips of her fingers the hand that hung by his side, and said in a voice like a child's, "Fancy! this is the end of everything, and when we part now we are to meet no more. Not the same way at all—not as we have met. You will be like anybody else to me, and I will be like anybody else to you. Miss Cregeen, that will be my name and you will be Mr. Christian. When you see me you'll say to yourself, 'Yes, poor thing; long ago, when she was a girl, I made her love me. Nobody ever loved me like that.' And fancy! when you pass me in the street, you will not even look my way. You won't, will you? No—no, it will be better not. Goodbye!"

Her simple tenderness almost stifled him. He had to hold his under lip with his teeth to keep back the cry that was bursting from his tongue. At last he could bear it no longer, and he broke out, "Would to God we had never loved each other! Would to God we had never met!"

But she answered with the same childish sweetness, "Don't say that, Philip. We have had some happy hours together. I would rather be parted from you like this, though it is so hard, so cruel, than never to have met you at all. Isn't it something for me to think of, that the truest, cleverest, noblest man in all the world has loved me?... Good-bye!... Good-bye!"

His heart bled, his heart cried, but he uttered no sound. They were side by side. She let his hand slip from the tips of her fingers, and drew silently away. At three paces apart she paused, but he gave no sign. She climbed the low brow of the hill slowly, very slowly, trying to command her throat, which was fluttering, and looking back through her tears as she went. Philip heard the shingle slip under her feet while she toiled up the cliff, and when she reached the top the soft thud on the turf seemed to beat on his heart. She stood there a moment against the sky, waiting for a sound from the shore, a cry, a word, the lifting of a hand, a sob, a sigh, her own name, "Kate," and she was ready to fly back even then, wounded and humiliated as she was, a poor torn bird that had been struggling in the lime. But no; he was silent and motionless, and she disappeared behind the hill. He saw her go, and all the light of heaven went with her.

VIII.

It was so far back home, so much farther than it had been to come. The course is short and easy going out to sea when the tide is with you, and the water is smooth, and the sun is shining, but long and hard coming back to harbour, when the waves have risen, and the sky is low, and the wind is on your bow.

So far, so very far. She thought everybody looked at her, and knew her for what she was—a broken, forsaken, fallen woman. And she was so tired too; she wondered if her limbs would carry her.

When Philip was left alone, the sky seemed to be lying on his shoulders. The English mountains were grey and ghostly now, and the storm, which had spent itself on the other coast, seemed to hang over the island. There were breakers where the long dead sea had been, and the petrel outside was scudding close to the white curves, and uttering its dismal note.

So heavy and confused had the storm and wreck of the last hour left him, that he did not at first observe by the backward tail of smoke that the steamer had passed round the Head, and that the cart he had met at the mouth of the port had come back empty to the cave for another load of sea-wrack. The lobster-fisher, too, had beached his boat near by, and was shouting through the hollow air, wherein every noise seemed to echo with a sepulchral quake, "The block was going whistling at the mast-head. We'll have a squall I was thinking, so in I came."

That night Philip dreamt a dream. He was sitting on a dais with a wooden canopy above him, the English coat of arms behind, and a great book in front; his hands shook as he turned the leaves; he felt his leg hang heavily; people bowed low to him, and dropped their voices in his presence; he was the Deemster, and he was old. A young woman stood in the dock, dripping water from her hair, and she had covered her face with her hands. In the witness-box a young man was standing, and his head was down. The man had delivered the woman to dishonour; she had attempted her life in her shame and her despair. And looking on the man, the Deemster thought he spoke in a stern voice, saying, "Witness, I am compelled to punish her, but oh to heaven that I could punish you in her place! What have you to say for yourself?" "I have nothing to say for myself," the young man answered, and he lifted his head and the old Deemster saw his face. Then Philip awoke with a smothered scream, for the young man's face had been his own.

IX.

When Cæsar got to the quay, he looked about with watchful eyes, as if fearing he might find somebody there before him. The coast was clear, and he gave a grunt of relief. After fixing the horse-cloth, and settling the mare in a nose-bag, he began to walk up and down the fore part of the harbour, still keeping an eager look-out. As time went on he grew comfortable, exchanged salutations with the harbour-master, and even whistled a little to while away the time.

"Quiet day, Mr. Quayle."

"Quiet enough yet, Mr. Cregeen; but what's it saying? 'The greater the calm the nearer the south wind.'"

By the time that Cæsar, from the end of the pier, saw the smoke of the steamer coming round Kirk Maughold Head, he was in a spiritual, almost a mournful, mood. He was feeling how melancholy was the task of going to meet the few possessions, the clothes and such like, which were all that remained of a dear friend departed. It was the duty of somebody, though, and Cæsar drew a long breath of resignation.

The steamer came up to the quay, and there was much bustle and confusion. Cæsar waited, with one hand on the mare's neck, until the worst of it was over. Then he went aboard, and said in a solemn voice to the sailor at the foot of the gangway, "Anything here the property of Mr. Peter Quilliam?"

"That's his luggage," said the sailor, pointing to a leather trunk of moderate size among similar trunks at the mouth of the hatchway.

"H'm!" said Cæsar, eyeing it sideways, and thinking how small it was. Then, reflecting that perhaps valuable papers were all it was thought worth while to send home, he added cheerfully, "I'll take it with me."

Somewhat to Cæsar's surprise, the sailor raised no difficulties, but just as he was regarding the trunk with that faith which is the substance of things hoped for, a big, ugly hand laid hold of it, and began to rock it about like a pebble.

It was Black Tom, smoking with perspiration.

"Aisy, man, aisy," said Cæsar, with lofty dignity. "I've the gig on the quay."

"And I've a stiff cart on the market," said Black Tom.

"I'm wanting no assistance," said Cæsar; "you needn't trouble yourself."

"Don't mention it, Cæsar," said Black Tom, and he turned the trunk on end and bent his back to lift it.

But Cæsar put a heavy hand on top and said, "Gough bless me, man, but I am sorry for thee. Mammon hath entered into thy heart, Tom."

"He have just popped out of thine, then," said Black Tom, swirling the trunk on one of its corners.

But Cæsar held on, and said, "I don't know in the world why you should let the devil of covetousness get the better of you."

"I don't mane to—let go the chiss," said Black Tom, and in another minute he had it on his shoulder.

"Now, I believe in my heart," said Cæsar, "I would be forgiven a little violence," and he took the trunk by both hands to bring it down again.

"Let go the chiss, or I'll strek thee into the harbour," bawled Black Tom under his load.

"The Philistines be upon thee, Samson," cried Cæsar, and with that there was a struggle.

In the midst of the uproar, while the men were shouting into each other's faces, and the trunk was rocking between them shoulder high, a sunburnt man, with a thick beard and a formidable voice, a stalwart fellow in a pilot jacket and wide-brimmed hat, came hurrying up the cabin-stairs, and a dog came running behind him. A moment later he had parted the two men, and the trunk was lying at his feet.

Black Tom fell back a step, lifted his straw hat, scratched his bald crown, and muttered in a voice of awe. "Holy sailor!"

Cæsar's face was livid, and his eyes went up toward his forehead. "Lord have mercy upon me," he mumbled; "have mercy on my soul, O Lord."

"Don't be afraid," said the stranger. "I'm a living man and not a ghost."

"The man himself," said Black Tom.

"Peter Quilliam alive and hearty," said Cæsar.

"I am," said Pete. "And now, what's the bobbery between the pair of you? Shuperintending the beaching of my trunk, eh?"

But having recovered from his terror at the idea that Pete was a spirit, Cæsar began to take him to task for being a living man. "How's this?" said he. "Answer me, young man, I've praiched your funeral."

"You'll have to do it again, Mr. Cregeen, for I'm not gone yet," said Pete.

"No, but worth ten dead men still," said Black Tom. "And my goodness, boy, the smart and stout you're looking, anyway. Been thatching a bit on the chin, eh? Foreign parts has made a man of you, Peter. The straight you're like the family, too! You'll be coming up to the trough with me—the ould home, you know. I'll be whipping the chiss ashore in a jiffy, only Cæsar's that eager to help, it's wonderful. No, you'll not then?"

Pete was shaking his head as he went up the gangway, and seeing this, Cæsar said severely—

"Lave the gentleman alone, Mr. Quilliam. He knows his own business best."

"So do you, Mr. Collecting Box," said Black Tom. "But your head's as empty as a mollag, and as full of wind as well. It's a regular ould human mollag you are, anyway, floating other people's nets and taking all that's coming to them."

They were ashore by this time; one of the quay porters was putting the trunk into the gig, and Cæsar was removing the horse-cloth and the nose-bag.

"Get up, Mr. Peter, and don't listen to him," said Cæsar. "If my industry and integrity have been blessed with increase under Providence——"

"Lave Providence out of it, you grasping ould Ebenezer, Zachariah, Amen," bawled Black Tom.

"You've been flying in the face of Providence all your life, Tom," said Cæsar, taking his seat beside Pete.

"You haven't though, you miser," said Black Tom; "you'd sell your soul for sixpence, and you'd raffle your ugly ould body if you could get anybody to take tickets."

"Go home, Thomas," said Cæsar, twiddling the reins, "go home and try for the future to be a better man."

But that was too much for Black Tom. "Better man, is it? Come down on the quay and up with your fiss, and I'll show you which of us is the better man."

A moment later Cæsar and Pete were rattling over the cobbles of the market-place, with the dog racing behind. Pete was full of questions.

"And how's yourself, Mr. Cregeen?"

"I'm in, sir, I'm in, sir, praise the Lord."

"And Grannie?"

"Like myself, sir, not getting a dale younger, but caring little for spiritual things, though."

"Going west, is she, poor ould angel? There ought to be a good piece of daylight at her yet, for all. And—and Nancy Joe?"

"A happy sinner still," said Cæsar. "I suppose, sir, you'd be making good money out yonder now? We were hearing the like, anyway."

"Money!" said Pete. "Well, yes. Enough to keep off the divil and the coroner. But how's—how's——"

"There now! For life, eh?" said Cæsar.

75

"Yes, for life; but that's nothing," said Pete; "how's——"

"Wonderful!" cried Cæsar; "five years too! Boy veen, the light was nearly took out of my eyes when I saw you."

"But Kate? How's Kate? How's the girl, herself?" said Pete nervously.

"Smart uncommon," said Cæsar.

"God bless her!" cried Pete, with a shout that was heard across the street.

"We'll pick her up at Crellin's, it's like," said Cæsar.

"What? Crellin's round the corner—Crellin the draper's I Woa! Let me down! The mare's tired, father;" and Pete was over the wheel at a bound.

He came out of the shop saying Kate had left word that her father was not to wait for her—she would perhaps be home before him. Amid a crowd of the "mob beg" children of the streets, to whom he showered coppers to be scrambled for, Pete got up again to Cæsar's side, and they set off for Sulby. The wind had risen suddenly, and was hooting down the narrow streets coming up from the harbour.

"And Philip? How's Philip?" shouted Pete.

"Mr. Christian? Well and hearty, and doing wonders, sir."

"I knew it," cried Pete, with a resounding laugh.

"Going like a flood, and sweeping everything before him," said Cæsar.

"The rising day with him, is it?" said Pete. "I always said he'd be the first man in the island, and he's not going to deceave me neither."

"The young man's been over putting a sight on us times and times—he was up at my Melliah only a week come Wednesday," said Cæsar.

"Man alive!" cried Pete; "him and me are same as brothers."

"Then it wasn't true what they were writing in the letter, sir—that your black boys left you for dead?"

"They did that, bad luck to them," said Pete; "but I was thinking it no sin to disappoint them, though."

"Well, well! lying began with the world, and with the world it will end," said Cæsar.

As they passed Ballywhaine, Pete shouted into Cæsar's ear, above the wind that was roaring in the trees, and scattering the ripening leaves in clouds, "And how's Dross?"

"That wastrel? Aw, tearing away, tearing away," said Cæsar.

"Floating on the top of the tide, is he?" shouted Pete.

"Maybe so, but the devil is fishing where yonder fellow's swimming," answered Cæsar.

"And the ould man—the Ballawhaine—still above the sod?" bawled Pete behind his hand.

"Yes, but failing, failing, failing," shouted Cæsar. "The world's getting too heavy for the man. Debts here, and debts there, and debts everywhere."

"Not much water in the harbour then, eh?" cried Pete.

"No, but down on the rocks already, if it's only myself that knows it," shouted Cæsar.

When they had turned the Sulby Bridge, and come in sight of "The Manx Fairy," Pete's excitement grew wild, and he leaped up from his seat and shouted above the wind like a man possessed.

"My gough, the very place! You've been thatching, though—yes, you have. The street! Holy sailor, there it is! Brownie at you still? Her heifer, is it? Get up, Molly! A taste of the whip'll do the mare no harm, sir. My sakes, here's ould Flora hobbling out to meet us. Got the rheumatics, has she? Set me down, Cæsar. Here we are, man. Lord alive, the smell of the cowhouse. That warm and damp, it's grand! What, don't you know me, Flo? Got your temper still, if you've lost your teeth? My sakes, the haggard! The same spot again! It's turf they're burning inside! And, my gracious, that's herrings roasting in their brine! Where's Grannie, though? Let's put a sight in, Cæsar. Well, well, aw well, aw well!"

Thus Pete came home, laughing, shouting, bawling, and bellowing above the tumult of the wind, which had risen by this time to the strength of a gale.

"Mother," cried Cæsar, going in at the porch, "gentleman here from foreign parts to put a word on you."

"I never had nobody there belonging to me," began Grannie.

"No, then, nobody?" said Cæsar.

"One that was going to be, maybe, if he'd lived, poor boy——"

"Grannie!" shouted Pete, and he burst into the bar-room.

"Goodness me!" cried Grannie; "it's his own voice anyway."

"It's himself," shouted Pete, and the old soul was in his arms in an instant.

"Aw dear! Aw dear!" she panted. "Pete it is for sure. Let me sit down, though."

"Did you think it was his ghost, then, mother!" said Cæsar with an indulgent air.

"'Deed no," said Grannie. "The lad wouldn't come back to plague nobody, thinks I."

"Still, and for all the uprisement of Peter, it bates everything," said Cæsar. "It's a sort of a resurrection. I thought I'd have a sight up to the packet for his chiss, poor fellow, and, behould ye, who should I meet in the two eyes but the man himself!"

"Aw, dear! It's wonderful I it's terrible! I'm silly with the joy," said Grannie.

"It was lies in the letter the Manx ones were writing," said Cæsar.

"Letters and writings are all lies," said Grannie. "As long as I live I'll take no more of them, and if that Kelly, the postman, comes here again, I'll take the bellows to him."

"So you thought I was gone for good, Grannie?" said Pete. "Well, I thought so too. 'Will I die?' I says to myself times and times; but I bethought me at last there wasn't no sense in a good man like me laving his bones out on the bare Veldt yonder; so, you see, I spread my wings and came home again."

"It's the Lord's doings—it's marvellous in our eyes," said Cæsar; and Grannie, who had recovered herself and was bustling about, cried—

"Let me have a right look at him, then. Goodness me, the whisker! And as soft as Manx carding from the mill, too. I like him best when he takes off his hat. Well, I'm proud to see you, boy. 'Deed, but I wouldn't have known you, though. 'Who's the gentleman in the gig with father?' thinks I. And I'd have said it was the Dempster himself, if he hadn't been dead and in his coffin."

"That'll do, that'll do," roared Pete. "That's Grannie putting the fun on me."

"It's no use talking, but I can't keep quiet; no I can't," cried Grannie, and with that she whipped up a bowl from the kitchen dresser and fell furiously to peeling the potatoes that were there for supper.

"But where's Kate?" said Pete.

"Aw, yes, where is she? Kate! Kate!" called Grannie, leaning her head toward the stairs, and Nancy Joe, who had been standing silent until now, said——

"Didn't she go to Ramsey with the gig, woman?"

"Aw, the foolish I am! Of course she did," said Grannie; "but why hasn't she come back with father?"

"She left word at Crellin's not to wait," said Cæsar.

"She'll be gone to Miss Clucas's to try on," said Nancy.

"Wouldn't trust now," said Grannie. "She's having two new dresses done, Pete. Aw, girls are ter'ble. Well, can you blame them either?"

"She shall have two-and-twenty if she likes, God bless her," said Pete.

"Goodness me!" said Nancy, "is the man for buying frocks for a Mormon?"

"But you'll be empty, boy. Put the crow down and the griddle on, Nancy," said Grannie. "We'll have cakes. Cakes? Coorse I said cakes. Get me the cloth and I'll lay it myself. The cloth, I'm saying, woman. Did you never hear of a tablecloth? Where is it? Aw, dear knows where it is now! It's in the parlour; no, it's in the chest on the landing; no, it's under the sheets of my own bed. Fetch it, bogh."

"Will I bring you a handful of gorse, mother?" said Cæsar.

"Coorse you will, and not stand chattering there. But I'm laving you dry, Pete. Is it ale you'll have, or a drop of hard stuff? You'll wait for Kate? Now I like that. There's some life at these totallers. 'Steady abroad?' How dare you, Nancy Joe? You're a deal too clever. Of course he's been steady abroad—steady as a gun."

"But Kate," said Pete, tramping the sanded floor, "is she changed at all?"

"Aw, she's a woman now, boy," said Grannie.

"Bless my soul!" said Pete.

"She was looking a bit white and narvous one while there, but she's sprung out of it fresh and bright, same as the ling on the mountains. Well, that's the way with young women."

"I know," said Pete. "Just the break of the morning with the darlings."

"But she's the best-looking girl on the island now, Pete," said Nancy Joe.

"I'll go bail on it," cried Pete.

"Big and fine and rosy, and fit for anything."

"Bless my heart!"

"You should have seen her at the Melliah; it was a trate."

"God bless me!"

"Sun-bonnet and pink frock and tight red stockings, and straight as a standard rase."

"Hould your tongue, woman," shouted Pete. "I'll see herself first, and I'm dying to do it."

Cæsar came back with the gorse; Nancy fed the fire and Grannie stirred the oatmeal and water. And while the cakes were baking, Pete tramped the kitchen and examined everything and recognised old friends with a roar.

"Bless me! the same place still. There's the clock on the shelf, with the scratch on its face and the big finger broke at the joint, and the lath—and the peck—and the whip—you've had it new corded, though——"

"'Sakes, how the boy remembers!" cried Grannie.

"And the white rumpy" (the cat had leapt on to the dresser out of the reach of Pete's dog, and from that elevation was eyeing him steadfastly), "and the slowrie—and the kettle—and the poker—my gracious, the very poker——"

"Now, did you ever!" cried Grannie with amazement.

"And—yes—no—it is, though—I'll swear it before the Dempster—that's," said Pete, picking up a three-legged stool, "that's the very stool she was sitting on herself in the fire-seat in front of the turf closet. Let me sit there now for the sake of ould times gone by."

He put the stool in the fireplace and sat on it, shouting as he did so between a laugh and a cry, "Aw, Grannie, bogh—Grannie, bogh! to think there's been half world between us since I was sitting here before!"

And Grannie herself, breaking down, said, "Wouldn't you like the tongs, boy? Give the boy the tongs, woman, just to say he's at home."

Pete plucked the tongs out of Nancy's hands, and began feeding the fire with the gorse. "Aw, Grannie, have I ever been away?" he cried, laughing, and his wet eyes gleaming.

"Nancy Joe, have you no nose at all?" cried Grannie. "The cake's burning to a cinder."

"Let it burn, mother," shouted Pete. "It's the way she was doing herself when she was young and forgetting. Shillings a-piece for all that's wasted. Aw, the smell of it's sweet!"

So saying he piled the gorse on the fire, ramming it under the griddle and choking it behind the crow. And while the oatcake crackled and sparched and went black, he sniffed up the burning odour, and laughed and cried in the midst of the smoke that went swirling up the chimney.

And meanwhile, Grannie herself, with the tears rolling down her cheeks, was flapping her apron before her face and saying, "He'll make me die of laughing, he will, though—yes, he will!" But behind the apron she was blubbering to Nancy, "It's coming home, woman, that's it—it's just coming home again, poor boy!"

By this time word of Pete's return had gone round Sulby? and the bar-room was soon thronged with men and women, who looked through the glass partition into the kitchen at the bronzed and bearded man who sat smoking by the fire, with his dog curled up at his feet. "There'll be a wedding soon," said one. "The girl's in luck," said another. "Success to the fine girl she always was, and lucky they kept her from the poor toot that was beating about on her port bow."—"The young Ballawhaine, eh?"—"Who else?"

Presently the dog went out to them, and, in default of its master, became a centre of excited interest. It was an old creature, with a settled look of age, and a gravity of expression that seemed to say he had got over the follies of youth, and was now reserved and determined to keep the peace. His back was curved in as if a cart-wheel had gone over his spine, he had gigantic ears, a stump of a tail, a coat thin and prickly like the bristles of a pig, but white and spotted with brown.

"Lord save us! a queer dog, though—what's his breed at all?" said one; and then a resounding voice came from the kitchen doorway, saying—

"A sort of a Manxman crossed with a bat. Got no tail to speak of, but there's plenty of ears at him. A handy sort of a dog, only a bit spoiled in his childhood. Not fit for much company anyway, and no more notion of dacent behaviour than my ould shoe. Down, Dempster, down."

It was Pete. He was greeted with loud welcomes, and soon filled the room all round with the steaming odour of spirits and water.

"You've the Manx tongue at you still, Mr. Quilliam," said Jonaique; "and you're calling the dog Dempster; what's that for at all?"

"For sake of the ould island, Mr. Jelly, and for the straight he's like Dempster Mylrea when he's a bit crooked," said Pete.

"The old man's dead, sir," said John the Clerk.

"You don't say?" said Pete.

"Yes, though; the sun went down on him a Wednesday. The drink, sir, the drink! I've been cutting a sod of his grave to-day."

"And who's to be Dempster now?" asked Pete. "Who are they putting in for it?"

"Well," said John the Clerk, "they're talking and talking, and some's saying this one and others that one; but the most is saying your ould friend Philip Christian."

"I knew it—I always said it," shouted Pete; "best man in the island, bar none. Oh, he'll not deceave me."

The wind was roaring in the chimney, and the light was beginning to fail. Pete became restless, and walked to and fro, peering out at intervals by the window that looked on to the road. At this there was some pushing and nudging and indulgent whispering.

"It's the girl! Aw, be aisy with the like! Five years apart, be aisy!"

"The meadow's white with the gulls sitting together like parrots; what's that a sign of, father?" said Pete.

"Just a slant of rain maybe, and a puff of wind," said Cæsar.

"But," said Pete, looking up at the sky, "the long cat tail was going off at a slant awhile ago, and now the thick skate yonder is hanging mortal low."

"Take your time, sir," said Cæsar. "No need to send round the Cross Vustha (fiery cross) yet. The girl will be home immadiently."

"It'll be dark at her, though," said Pete.

The company tried to draw him into conversation about the ways of life in the countries he had visited, but he answered absently and jerkily, and kept going to the door.

"Suppose there'll be Dempsters enough where you're coming from?" said Jonaique.

"Sort of Dempsters, yes. Called one of them Ould Necessity, because it knows no law. He rigged up the statute books atop of his stool for a high sate, and when he wanted them he couldn't find them high or low. Not the first judge that's sat on the law, though.... It's coming, Cæsar, d'ye hear it? That's the rain on the street."

"Aisy, man, aisy, man," said Cæsar. "New dresses isn't rigged up in no time. There'll be chapels now, eh? Chapels and conferences, and proper religious instruction?"

"Divil a chapel, sir, only a rickety barn, belonging to some-ones they're calling the Sky Pilots to. Wanted the ould miser that runs it to build them a new tabernacle, but he wouldn't part till a lump of plaster fell on his bald head at a love-feast, and then he planked down a hundred pound, and they all shouted, 'Hit him again, Lord—you might!'... D'ye hear that, then? That's the water coming down from the gill. I can't stand no more of it, Grannie."

Grannie was at the door, struggling to hold it against the wind, while she looked out into the gathering darkness. "'Deed, but I'm getting afraid of it myself," she said, "and dear heart knows where Kirry can be at this time of night." "I'm off to find her," said Pete, and, catching up his hat and whistling to the dog, in a moment he was gone.

X.

The door was hard to close behind him, for it was now blowing a gale from the north-east. Cæsar slipped through the dairy to see if the outbuildings were safe, and came back with a satisfied look. The stable and cow-house were barred, the barns were shut up, the mill-wheel was on the brake, the kiln fire was burning gently, and all was snug and tight. Grannie was wringing her hands as he returned, crying "Kate! Oh, Kate!" and he reproved her for want of trust in Providence.

People were now coming in rapidly with terrible stories of damage done by the storm. It was reported that the Chicken Rock Lighthouse was blown down, that the tide had risen to twenty-five feet in Ramsey and torn up the streets, and that a Peel fisherman had been struck by his mainsail into the sea and drowned.

More came into the house at every minute, and among them were all the lonesome and helpless ones within a radius of a mile—Blind Jane, who charmed blood, but could not charm the wind; Shemiah, the prophet, with beard down to his waist and a staff up to his shoulder; and old Juan Vessy, who "lived on the houses" in the way of a tramp. The people who had been there already were afraid to go out, and Grannie, still wringing her hands and crying "Kate, Kate," called everybody into the kitchen to gather about the fire. There they bemoaned their boys on the sea, told stories of former storms, and quarrelled about the years of wrecks and the sources of the winds that caused them.

The gale increased to fearful violence, and sometimes the wind sounded like sheets flapping against the walls, sometimes like the deep boom of the waves that roll on themselves in mid-ocean and never know a shore. It began to groan in the chimney as if it were a wild beast struggling to escape, and then the smoke came down in whorls and filled the kitchen. They had to put out the fire to keep themselves from suffocation, and to sit back from the fireplace to protect themselves from cold. The door of the porch flew open, and they barricaded it with long-handled brushes; the windows rattled in their frames, and they blocked them up with the tops of the tables. In spite of all efforts to shut out the wind, the house was like a basket, and it quaked like a ship at sea. "I never heard the like on the water itself, and I'm used of the sea, too," said one. The others groaned and mumbled prayers.

Kelly the Thief, who had come in unopposed by Grannie, was on his knees in one corner with his face to the wall, calling on the Lord to remember that he had seen things in letters—stamps and such—but had never touched them. John the Clerk was saying that he had to bury the Deemster; Jonaique, the barber, that he had been sent for to "cut" the Bishop; and Claudius Kewley, the farmer, that he had three fields of barley still uncut and a stack of oats unthatched. "Oh, Lord," cried Claudius, "let me not die till I've got nothing to do!"

Cæsar stood like a strong man amidst their moans and groans, their bowings of the head and clappings of the hands, and, when he heard the farmer, his look was severe.

"Cloddy," said he, "how do you dare to doubt the providence of God?"

"Aisy to talk, Mr. Cregeen," the farmer whined, "but you've got your own harvest saved," and then Cæsar had no resource but to punish the man in prayer. "The Lord had sent His storm to reprove some that were making too sure of His mercies; but there was grace in the gale, only they wouldn't be patient and trust to God's providence; there was milk in the breast, only the wayward child wouldn't take time to find the teat. Lord, lead them to true stillness——"

In the midst of Cæsar's prayer there was a sudden roar outside, and he leapt abruptly to his feet with a look of vexation. "I believe in my heart that's the mill-wheel broken loose," said he, "and if it is, the corn on the kiln will be going like a whirlingig."

"Trust in God's providence, Cæsar," cried the farmer.

"So I will," said Cæsar, catching up his hat, "but I'll put out my kiln fire first."

When Pete stepped out of the porch, he felt himself smitten as by an invisible wing, and he gasped like a fish with too much air. A quick pain in the side at that moment reminded him of his bullet-wound, but his heels had heart in them, and he set off to run. The night had fallen, but a green rent was torn in the leaden sky, and through this the full moon appeared.

When he got to Ramsey the tide was up to the old cross, slates were flying like kites, and the harbour sounded like a battlefield with its thunderous roar of rigging. He made for the dressmaker's, and heard that Kate had not been there for six hours. At the draper's he learned that at two o'clock in the afternoon she had been seen going up Ballure. The sound rocket was fired as he pushed through the town. A schooner riding to an anchor in the bay was flying her ensign for help. The sea was terrific—a slaty grey, streaked with white foam like quartz veins; but the men who had been idling on the quay when the water was calm were now struggling, chafing, and fighting to go out on it, for the blood of the old Vikings was in them.

Going by the water-trough, Pete called on Black Tom, who was civil and conciliatory until he heard his errand, then growled with disappointment, but nevertheless answered his question. Yes, he had seen the young woman. She went up early in the "everin," and left him good-day. Giving this grateful news, Black Tom could not deny himself a word of bitterness to poison the pleasure. "And when you are finding her," said he, "you'll be doing well to take her in tow, for I'm thinking there's some that's for throwing her a rope."

"Who d'ye mane?" said Pete.

"I lave it with you," said Black Tom; and Pete pulled the door after him.

On the breast of the hill there was the meeting of two roads, one of them leading up to the "Hibernian," the other going down to Port Mooar. To resolve the difficulty of choice, Pete inquired at a cottage standing some paces beyond, and as Kate had not been seen to pass up the higher road, he determined to take the lower one. But he gathered no tidings by the way, for Billy by the mill knew nothing, and the woman by the sundial had gone to bed. At length he dipped into Port Mooar, and came to a little cottage like a child's Noah's ark, with its tiny porch and red light inside, looking out on the white breakers that were racing along the beach. It was the cottage of the lobster-fisher. Pete inquired if he had seen Kate. He answered no; he had seen nobody that day but Mr. Christian. Which of the Christians? Mr. Philip Christian.

The news carried only one message to Pete's mind. It seemed to explain something which had begun to perplex him—why Philip had not met him at the quay, and why Kate had not heard of his coming. Clearly Philip was at present at Ballure. He had not yet received the telegram addressed to Douglas.

Pete turned back. Surely Kate had called somewhere. She would be at home by this time. He tried to run, but the wind was now in his face. It was veering northwards every minute, and rising to the force of a hurricane. He tied his handkerchief over his head and under his chin to hold on his hat. His hair whipped his ears like rods. Sometimes he was swept into the hedge; often he was brought to his knees. Still he toiled along through sheets of spray that glistened with the colours of a rainbow, and ran over the ground like driven rain. His eyes smarted, and the taste on his lips was salt.

The moon was now riding at the full through a wild flecked sky, and Pete could clearly see, as he returned towards the bay, a crowd of human figures on the cliffs above Port Lewaige. Quaking with undefined fears, he pushed on until he had joined them. The schooner, abandoned by her crew, had parted her cable, and was rolling like a blinded porpoise towards the rocks. She fell on them with the groan of a living creature, and, the instant her head was down, the white lions of the sea leapt over her with a howl, the water swirled through her bulwarks and filled her hatches, her rudder was unshipped, her sails were torn from their gaskets, and the floating home wherein men had sailed, and sung, and slept, and laughed, and jested, was a broken wreck in the heavy wallowings of the waves.

Kate had not returned when Pete got back to Sulby, but the excitement of her absence was eclipsed for the time by the turmoil of Cæsar's trouble. Standing in the dark on the top of the midden, he was shouting to the dairy door in a voice of thunder, which went off at the end of his beard like the puling of a cat. The mill-wheel was going same as a "whirlingig"—was there nobody to "hould the brake?" The stable roof was stripped, and the mare was tearing herself to pieces in a roaring "pit of hell"—was there never a shoulder for the door? The cow-house thatch was flapping like a sail—was there nothing in the world but a woman (Nancy Joe) to help a man to throw a ladder and a stone over it?

Only when Cæsar had been pacified was there silence to speak of Kate. "I picked up news of her coming back by Claughbane," said Pete, "and traced her as near home as the 'Ginger.' She can't be far away. Where is she?"

Those who were cool enough fell to conjecture. Grannie had no resource but groans. Nancy was moaning by her side. The rest were full of their own troubles. Blind Jane was bewailing her affliction.

"You can all see," she cried, "but I'm not knowing the harm that's coming on me."

"Hush, woman, hush," said Pete; "we're all same as yourself half our lives—we're all blind at night."

In the midst of the tumult a knock came to the door, and Pete made a plunge towards the porch.

"Wait," cried Cæsar. "Nobody else comes here to-night except the girl herself. Another wind like the last and we'll have the roof off the house too."

Then he called to the new-comer, with his face to the porch door, and the answer came back to him in a wail like the wind itself.

"Who's there?"

It was Joney from the glen.

"We're like herrings in a barrel—we can't let you in."

She wasn't wanting to come in. But her roof was going stripping, and half her house was felled, and she couldn't get her son (the idiot boy) to leave his bed. He would perish; he would die; he was all the family she had left to her—wouldn't the master come and save him?

"Impossible!" shouted Cæsar. "We've our own missing this fearful night, Joney, and the Lord will protect His children."

Was it Kate? She had seen her in the glen——

"Let me get at that door," said Pete.

"But the house will come down," cried Cæsar.

"Let it come," said Pete.

Pete shut the door of the bar-room, and then the wind was heard to swirl through the porch.

"When did you see her, Joney, and where?" said the voice of Pete; and the voice of Joney answered him—

"Goings by my own house at the start of the storm this everin."

"I'll come with you—go on," said Pete, and Grannie shouted across the bar—

"Take Cæsar's topcoat over your monkey-jacket."

"I've sail enough already for a wind like this, mother," cried the voice of Pete, and then the swirling sound in the porch went off with a long-drawn whirr, and Cæsar came back alone to the kitchen.

Pete's wound ached again, but he pressed his hand on the place of it and struggled up the glen, dragging Joney behind him. They came to her house at last. One half of the thatch lay over the other half; the rafters were bare like the ribs of the wreck; the oat-cake peck was rattling on the lath; the meal-barrel in the corner was stripped of its lid, and the meal was whirling into the air like a waterspout; the dresser was stripped, the broken crockery lay on the uncovered floor, and the iron slowrie hanging over the place of the fire was swinging and striking against the wall, and ringing like a knell. And in the midst of this scene of desolation the idiot boy was placidly sleeping on his naked bed, and over it the moon was scudding through a tattered sky.

The night wore on, and the company in the kitchen listened long, and sometimes heard sounds as of voices crying in the wind, but Pete did not return. Then they fell to groaning again, to praying aloud without fear, and to confessing their undiscovered sins without shame.

"I'm searched terrible—I can see through me," cried Kelly, the postman.

Some were chiefly troubled lest death should fall on them while they were in a public-house.

"I keep none," cried Cæsar.

"But you wouldn't let us open the door," whined the farmer.

If the door had been wide enough for a Bishop, not a soul would have stirred. For the first time within anyone's recollection, Nancy Joe was on her knees.

"O Lord," she prayed, "Thou knowest well I don't often bother Thee. But save Kate, Lord; oh, save and prasarve my little Kirry! It's twenty years and better since I asked anything of Thee before and if Thou wilt only take away this wind, I'll promise not to say another prayer for twenty years more."

"Say it in Manx, woman," moaned Grannie. "I always say my prayers in Manx as well, and the Lord can listen to the one He knows best."

"There's prayer as well as praise in singing," cried Cæsar; and they began to sing, all down on their knees, their eyes tightly closed, and their hands clasped before their faces. They sang of heaven and its peaceful plains, its blue lakes and sunny skies, its golden cities and emerald gates, its temples and its tabernacles, where "congregations ne'er break up and Sabbaths never end." It was some comfort to drown with the wild discord of their own voices the fearful noises of the tempest. When they finished the hymn, they began on it again, keeping it up without a break, sweeping the dying note of the last word into the rising pitch of the first one. In the midst of their singing, they thought a fiercer gust than ever was beating on the door, and, to smother the fear of it, they sang yet louder. The gust came a second time, and Cæsar cried—

"Again, brothers," and away they went with another wild whoop through the hymn.

It came a third time, and Cæsar cried—

"Once more, beloved," and they raced madly through the hymn again.

Then the door burst open as before a tremendous kick, and Pete, fierce and wild-eyed, and green with the drift of the salt foam caked thick on his face, stepped over the threshold with the unconscious body of Kate in his arms and the idiot boy peering over his shoulder.

"Thank the Lord for an answer to prayer," cried Cæsar. "Where did you find her?"

"In the tholthan up the glen," said Pete. "Up in the witch's tholthan."

XI.

On the second morning afterwards the air was quiet and full of the odour of seaweed; the sky was round as the inside of a shell, and pale pink like the shadow of flame; the water was smooth and silent; the hills had lost the memory of the storm, and land and sea lay like a sleeping child.

In this broad and steady morning Kate came back to consciousness. She had slid out of delirium into sleep as a boat slides out of the open sea into harbour, and when she awoke there was a voice in her ears that seemed to be calling to her from the quay. It was a familiar voice, and yet it was unfamiliar; it was like the voice of a friend heard for the first time after a voyage. It seemed to come from a long way off, and yet to be knocking at the very door of her heart. She kept her eyes closed for a moment and listened; then she opened them and looked again.

The light was clouded and yet dazzling, as if glazed muslin were shaking before her eyes. Grannie was sitting by her bedside, knitting in silence.

"Why are you sitting there, mother?" she asked.

Grannie dropped her needles and caught at her apron. "Dear heart alive, the child's herself again!" she said.

"Has anything happened?" said Kate. "What time is it?"

"Monday morning, bogh, thank the Lord for all His mercies!" cried Grannie.

The familiar voice came again. It came from the direction of the stairs. "Who's that?" said Kate, whispering fearfully.

"Pete himself, Kirry. Aw well! Aw dear!"

"Pete!" cried Kate in terror.

"Aw, no, woman, but a living man come back again. No fear of him, bogh! Not dead at all, but worth twenty dead men yet, and he brought you safe out of the storm."

"The storm?"

"Yes, the storm, woman. There warn such a storm on the island I don't know the years. He found you in the tholthan up the glen. Lost your way in the wind, it's like, and no wonder. But let me call father. Father! father! Chut! the man's as deaf as little Tom Hommy. Father!" called Grannie, bustling about at the stair-head in a half-demented way.

There was some commotion below, and the voice on the stairs was saying, "*This* way? No, *sir*. That way, if *you* plaze."

"D'ye hear him, Kirry?" cried Grannie, putting her head back into the room. "That's the man himself. Sitting on the bottom step same as an ould bulldog, and keeping watch that nobody bothers you. The good-naturedst bulldog breathing, though, and he hasn't had a wink on the night. Saved your life, darling. He did; yes, he did, praise God."

At mention of the tholthan, Kate had remembered everything. She dropped back on the pillow, and cried, in a voice of pain, "Why couldn't he leave me to die?"

Grannie chuckled knowingly at that, and wiped her eyes with the corner of her apron. "The bogh is herself, for sure. When they're wishing themselves dead they're always mending father! But I'll go down instead. Lie still, bogh, lie still!"

The voice of Grannie went muffled down the stairs with many "Aw dears, aw dears!" and then crackled from below through the floor and the unceiled joists, saying sharply but with a tremor, too, "Nancy Joe, why aren't you taking a cup of something upstairs, woman?"

"Goodness me, Mistress Cregeen, is it true for all?" said Nancy.

"Why, of course it's true. Do you think a poor child is going fasting for ever?"

"What's that?" shouted the familiar voice again. "Was it herself you were spaking to in the dairy loft, Grannie?"

"Who else, man?" said Grannie, and then there was a general tumult.

"Aw, the joy! Aw, the delight! Gough bless me, Grannie, I was thinking she was for spaking no more."

"Out of the way," cried Nancy, as if pushing past somebody to whip the kettle on to the fire. "These men creatures have no more rising in their hearts than bread without balm."

"You're balm enough yourself, Nancy, for a quiet husband. But lend me a hould of the bellows there—I'll blow up like blazes."

Cæsar came into the house on the top of this commotion, grumbling as he stepped over the porch, "The wind has taken half the stacks of my haggard, mother."

"No matter, sir," shouted Pete. "The best of your Melliah is saved upstairs."

"Is she herself?" said Cæsar. "Praise His name!"

And over the furious puffing and panting and quacking of the bellows and the cracking and roaring of the fire, the voice of Pete came in gusts through the floor, crying, "I'll go mad with the joy! I will; yes, I will, and nobody shall stop me neither."

The house, which seemed to have been holding its breath since the storm, now broke into a ripple of laughter. It began in the kitchen, it ran up the stairs, it crept through the chinks in the floor, it went over the roof. But Kate lay on her pillow and moaned, and turned her face to the wall.

Presently Nancy Joe appeared in the bedroom, making herself tidy at the doorway with a turn of the hand over her hair. "Mercy on me!" she cried, clapping her hands at the first sight of Kate's face, "who was the born blockhead that said the girl's wedding was as like to be in the churchyard as in the church?"

"That's me," said a deep voice from the middle of the stairs, and then Nancy clashed the door back and poured Pete into Kate in a broadside.

"It was Pete that done it, though," she said. "You can't expect much sense of the like, but still and for all he saved your life, Kitty. Dr. Mylechreest says so. 'If the girl had been lying out another hour,' says he——And, my goodness, the fond of you that man is; it's wonderful! Twisting and turning all day yesterday on the bottom step yonder same as a live conger on the quay, but looking as soft about the eyes as if he'd been a week out of the water. And now! my sakes, now! D'ye hear him, Kirry? He's fit to burst the bellows. No use, though—he's a shocking fine young fellow—he's all that.... But just listen!"

There was a fissing sound from below, and a sense of burning. "What do I always say? You can never trust a man to have sense enough to take it off. That's the kettle on the boil."

Nancy went flopping downstairs, where with furious words she rated Pete, who laughed immoderately. Cæsar came next. He had taken off his boots and was walking lightly in his stockings; but Kate felt his approach by his asthmatic breathing. As he stepped in at the door he cried, in the high pitch of the preacher, "Praise the Lord, O my soul, and all that is within me praise His holy name!" Then he fell to the praise of Pete as well.

"He brought you out of the jaws of death and the mouth of Satan. It was a sign, Katherine, and we can't do better than follow the Spirit's leading. He saved your life, woman, and that's giving him the right to have and to hould it. Well, I've only one child in this life, but, if it's the Lord's will, I'm willing. He was always my white-headed boy, and he has made his independent fortune in a matter of five years' time."

The church bell began to toll, and Kate started up and listened.

"Only the Dempster's funeral, Kitty," said Cæsar. "They were for burying him to-morrow, but men that drink don't keep. They'll be putting him in the family vault at Lezayre with his father, the staunch ould Rechabite. Many a good cow has a bad calf, you see, and that's bad news for a man's children; but many a good calf is from a bad cow, and that's good news for the man himself. It's been the way with Peter anyway, for the Lord has delivered him and prospered him, and I'm hearing on the best authority he has five thousand golden sovereigns sent home to Mr. Dumbell's bank at Douglas."

Grannie came up with a basin of beef-tea, and Cæsar was hustled out of the room.

"Come now, bogh; take a spoonful, and I'll lave you to yourself," said Grannie.

"Yes, leave me to myself," said Kate, sipping wearily; and then Grannie went off with the basin in her hand.

"Has she taken it?" said some one below.

"Look at that, if you plaze," said Grannie in a jubilant tone; and Kate knew that the empty basin was being shown around.

Kate lay back on the pillow, listened to the tolling of the bell, and shuddered. She thought it a ghostly thing that the first voice she had heard on coming as from another world had been the voice of Pete, and the first name dinned into her ears had been Pete's name. The procession of the Deemster's funeral passed the house, and she closed her eyes and seemed to see it—the coffin on the open cart, the men on horseback riding beside it, and then the horses tied up to posts and gates about the churchyard, and the crowd of men of all conditions at the grave-side. In her mind's eye, Kate was searching through that crowd for somebody. Was *he* there? Had he heard what had happened to her?

She fell into a doze, and was awakened by a horse's step on the road, and the voices of two men talking as they came nearer.

"Man alive, the joy I'm taking to see you! The tallygraph? Coorse not. Knew I'd find you at the funeral, though." It was Pete.

"But I meant to come over after it." It was Philip, and Kate's heart stood still.

The voices were smothered for a moment (as the buzzing is when the bees enter the hive), and then began with as sharper ring from the rooms below.

"How's she now, Mrs. Cregeen?" said the voice of Philip.

"Better, sir—much better," answered Grannie.

"No return of the unconsciousness?"

"Aw, no," said Grannie.

"Was she"—Kate thought the voice faltered—"was she delirious?"

"Not rambling at all," replied Grannie.

"Thank God," said Philip, and Kate felt a long breath of relief go through the air.

"I didn't hear of it until this morning," said Philip. "The postman told me at breakfast-time, and I called on Dr. Mylechreest coming out. If I had known——I didn't sleep much last night, anyway; but if I had ever imagined——"

"You're right good to the girl, sir," said Grannie, and then Kate, listening intently, caught a quavering sound of protestation.

"'Deed you are, though, and always have been," said Grannie, "and I'm saying it before Pete here, that ought to know and doesn't."

"Don't I, though?" came in the other voice—the resounding voice—the voice full of laughter and tears together. "But I do that, Grannie, same as if I'd been here and seen it. Lave it to me to know Phil Christian. I've summered and wintered the man, haven't I? He's timber that doesn't start, mother, blow high, blow low."

Kate heard another broken sound as of painful protest, and then with a sickening sense she covered up her head that she might hear no more.

XII.

She was weak and over-wrought, and she fell asleep as she lay covered. While she slept a babel of meaningless voices kept clashing in her ears, and her own voice haunted her perpetually. When she awoke it was broad morning again, and the house was full of the smell of boiling stock-fish. By that she knew it was another day, and the hour of early breakfast. She heard the click of cups and saucers on the kitchen table, the step of her father coming in from the mill, and then the heartsome voice of Pete talking of the changes in the island since he went away. New houses, promenades, iron piers, breakwaters, lakes, towers—wonderful I extraordinary! tre-menjous!

"But the boys—w here's the Manx boys at all?" said Pete. "Gone like a flight of birds to Austrillya and Cleveland and the Cape, and I don't know where. Not a Manx house now that hasn't one of the boys foreign. And the houses themselves—where's the ould houses and the crofts? Felled, all felled or boarded up. And the boats—where's the boats? Lying rotting at the top of the harbour."

Grannie's step came into the kitchen, and Pete's loud voice drooped to a whisper. "How's herself this morning, mother?"

"Sleeping quiet and nice when I came downstairs," said Grannie.

"Will I be seeing her myself to-day, think you?" asked Pete.

"I don't know in the world, but I'll ask," answered Grannie.

"You're an angel, Grannie," said Pete, "a reg'lar ould archangel."

Kate shuddered with a new fear. It was clear that in the eyes of her people the old relations with Pete were to stand. Everybody expected her to marry Pete; everybody seemed anxious to push the marriage on.

Grannie came up with her breakfast, pulled aside the blind, and opened the window.

"Nancy will tidy the room a taste," she said coaxingly, "and then I shouldn't wonder if you'll be sending for Pete."

Kate raised a cry of alarm.

"Aw, no harm when a girl's poorly," said Grannie, "and her promist man for all."

Kate tried to protest and explain, but courage failed her. She only said, "Not yet, mother. I'm not fit to see him yet."

"Say no more about it. Not to-day at all—to-morrow maybe," said Grannie, and Kate clutched at the word, and answered eagerly—

"Yes, tomorrow, mother; to-morrow maybe."

Before noon Philip had come again. Kate heard his horse's step on the road, trotting hard from the direction of Peel. He drew up at the porch, but did not alight, and Grannie went out to him.

"I'll not come in to-day, Mrs. Cregeen," he said. "Does she continue to improve?"

"As nice as nice, sir," said Grannie.

Kate crept out of bed, stole to the window, hid behind the curtains, and listened intently.

"What a mercy all goes well," he said; Kate could hear the heaving of his breath. "Is Pete about?"

"No, but gone to Ramsey, sir," said Grannie. "It's like you'll meet him if you are going on to Ballure."

"I must be getting back to business," said Philip, and the horse swirled across the road.

"Did you ride from Douglas on purpose, then?" said Grannie, and Philip answered with an audible effort—

"I was anxious. What an escape she has had! I could scarcely sleep last night for thinking of it."

Kate put her hand to her throat to keep back the cry that was bubbling up, and her mother's voice came thick and deep.

"The Lord's blessing. Master Philip——" she began, but the horse's feet stamped out everything as it leapt to a gallop in going off.

Kate listened where she knelt until the last beat of the hoofs had died away in the distance, and then she crept back to bed and covered up her head in the clothes as before, but with a storm of other feelings. "He loves me," she told herself with a thrill of the heart. "He loves me—he loves me still! And he will never, never, never see me married to anybody else."

She felt an immense relief now, and suddenly found strength to think of facing Pete. It even occurred to her to send for him at once, as a first step towards removing the impression that the old relations were to remain. She would be quiet, she would be cold, she would show by her manner that Pete was impossible, she would break the news gently.

Pete came like the light at Nancy's summons. Kate heard him on the stairs whispering with Nancy and breathing heavily. Nancy was hectoring it over him and pulling him about to make him presentable.

"Here," whispered Nancy, "take the redyng comb and lash your hair out, it's all through-others. And listen—you've got to be quiet. Promise me you'll be quiet. She's wake and low and nervous, so no kissing. D'ye hear me now, no kissing."

"Aw, kissing makes no noise to spake of, woman," whispered Pete; and then he was in the room.

Kate saw him come, a towering dark figure between her and the door. He did not speak at first, but slid down to the chair at the foot of the bed, modestly, meekly, reverently, as if he had entered a sanctuary. His hand rested on his knee, and she noticed that the wrist was hairy and tattooed with the three legs of Man.

"Is it you, Pete?" she asked; and then he said in a low tone, almost in a whisper, as if speaking to himself in a hush of awe—

"It's her own voice again! I've heard it in my drames these five years."

He looked helplessly about him for a moment, fixed his watery eyes on Nancy as if he wanted to burst into sobs but dare not for fear of the noise, then turned on his chair and seemed on the point of taking to flight. But just at that instant his dog, which had followed him into the room, planted its forelegs on the counterpane and looked impudently into Kate's face.

"Down, Dempster, down!" cried Pete; and after that, the ice being broken by the sound of his voice, Pete was his own man once more.

"Is that your dog, Pete?" said Kate.

"Aw, no, Kate, but I'm his man," said Pete. "He does what he likes with me, anyway. Caught me out in Kimber-ley and fetched me home."

"Is he old?"

"Old, d'ye say? He's one of the lost ten tribes of dogs, and behaves as if he'd got to inherit the earth."

She felt Pete's big black eyes shining on her.

"My gracious, Kitty, what a woman you're growing, though!" he said.

"Am I so much changed?" she asked.

"Changed, is it?" he cried. "Gough bless me heart! the nice little thing you were when we used to play fishermen together down at Cornaa Harbour—d'ye remember? The ould kipper-box rolling on a block for a boat at sea—do you mind it? Yourself houlding a bit of a broken broomstick in the rope handle for a mast, and me working the potato-dibber on the ground, first port and then starboard, for rudder and wind and oar and tide. 'Mortal dirty weather this, cap'n?' 'Aw, yes, woman, big sea extraordinary'—d'ye mind it, Kirry!"

Kate tried to laugh a little and to say what a long time ago it was since then. But Pete, being started, laughed uproariously, slapped his knee, and rattled on.

"Up at the mill, too—d'ye remember that now? Yourself with the top of a barrel for a flower basket, holding it 'kimbo at your lil hip and shouting, 'Violets! Swate violets! Fresh violets!'" (He mocked her silvery treble in his lusty baritone and roared with laughter.)

"And then me, woman, d'ye mind me?—me, with the pig-stye gate atop of my head for a fish-board, yelling, 'Mackerel! Fine ladies, fresh ladies, and bellies as big as bishops—Mack-er-el!' Aw, Kirry, Kirry! Aw, the dear ould times gone by! Aw, the changes, the changes!... Did I *know* you then? Are you asking me did I know you when I found you in the glen? Did I know I was alive, Kitty? Did I know the wind was howling? Did I know my head was going round like a compass, and my heart thumping a hundred and twenty pound to the square inch? Did I kiss you and kiss you while you were lying there useless, and lift you up and hitch your poor limp arms around my neck, and carry you out of the dirty ould tholthan that was going to be the death of you—the first job I was doing on the island, too, coming back to it.... Lord save us, Kitty, what have I done?"

Kate had dropped back on the pillow, and was sobbing as if her heart would break, and seeing this, Nancy fell on Pete with loud reproaches, took the man by the shoulders and his dog by the neck, and pushed both out of the room.

"Out of it," cried Nancy. "Didn't I tell you to be quiet? You great blethering omathaun, you shall come no more."

Abashed, ashamed, humiliated, and quiet enough now, Pete went slowly down the stairs.

XIII.

Late that night Kate heard Cæsar and her mother talking together as they were going to bed. Cæsar was saying—

"I got him on the track of a good house, and he went off to Ramsey this morning to put a sight on it."

"Dear heart alive, father!" Grannie answered, "Pete isn't home till a week come Saturday."

"The young man is warm on the wedding," said Cæsar, "and he has money, and store is no sore."

"But the girl's not fit for it, 'deed she isn't," said Grannie.

"If she's wake," said Cæsar, "she'll be no worse for saying 'I will,' and when she's said it she'll have time enough to get better."

Kate trembled with fear. The matter of her marriage with Pete was going on without her. A sort of supernatural power seemed to be pushing it along. Nobody asked if she wished it, nobody questioned that she did so. It was taken for granted that the old relations would stand. As soon as she could go about she would be expected to marry Pete. Pete himself would expect it, because he believed he had her promise; her mother would expect it, because she had always thought of it as a thing understood; her father would expect it, because Pete's prosperity had given him a new view of Pete's piety and pedigree; and Nancy Joe would expect it, too, if only because she was still haunted by her old bugbear, the dark shadow of Ross Christian. There was only one way to break down these expectations, and that was to speak out. But how was a girl to speak? What was she to say?

Kate pretended to be ill. Three days longer she lay, like a hunted wolf in its hole, keeping her bed from sheer dread of the consequences of leaving it. The fourth day was Sunday. It was morning, and the church bells were ringing. Cæsar had shouted from his bedroom for some one to tie his bow, then for some one to button his black gloves. He had gone off at length with the footsteps of the people stepping round to chapel. The first hymn had been started, and its doleful notes were trailing through the mill walls. Kate was propped up in bed, and the window of her room was open. Over the droning of the hymn she caught the sound of a horse's hoofs on the road. They stopped at a little distance, and then came on again, with the same two voices as before.

Pete was talking with great eagerness. "Plenty of house, aw plenty, plenty," he was saying. "Elm Cottage they're calling it—the slate one with the ould fir-tree behind the Coort House and by the lane to Claughbane. Dry as a bone and clane as a gull's wing. You could lie with your back to the wall and ate off the floor. Taps inside and water as white as gin. I've been buying the cabin of the 'Mona's Isle' for a summer-house in the garden. Got a figurehead for the porch too, and I'll have an anchor for the gate before I'm done. Aw, I'm bound to have everything nice for her."

There was a short silence, in which nothing was heard but the step of the horse, and then Philip said in a faltering voice, "But isn't this being rather in a hurry, Pete?"

"Short coorting's the best coorting, and ours has been long enough anyway," said Pete. They had drawn up at the porch, and Pete's laugh came in at the window.

"But think how weak she is," said Philip. "She hasn't even-left her bed yet, has she?"

"Well, yes, of coorse, sartenly," said Pete, in a steadier voice, "if the girl isn't fit——"

"It's so sudden, you see," said Philip. "Has she—has she—consented?"

"Not to say consented——" began Pete; and Philip took him up and said quickly, eagerly, hotly—

"She can't—I'm sure she can't."

There was silence again, broken only by the horse's impatient pawing, and then Philip said more calmly, "Let Dr. Mylechreest see her first, at all events."

"I'm not a man for skinning the meadow to the sod, no——" said Pete, in a doleful tone; but Kate heard no more.

She was trembling with a new thought. It was only a shadowy suggestion as yet, and at first she tried to beat it back. But it came again, it forced itself upon her, it mastered her, she could not resist it.

The way to break the fate that was pursuing her was to make *Philip* speak out! The way to stop the marriage with Pete was to compel Philip to marry her! He thought she would never consent to marry Pete—what if he were given to understand that she had consented. That was the way to gain the victory over Philip, the way to punish him!

He would not blame her—he would lay the blame at the door of chance, of fate, of her people. He would think they were forcing this marriage upon her—the mother out of love of Pete, the father out of love of Pete's money, and Nancy out of fear of Ross Christian. He would know that she could not struggle because she could not speak. He would believe she was yielding against her will, in spite of her love, in the teeth of their intention. He would think of her as a victim, as a martyr, as a sacrifice.

It was a deceit—a small deceit; it looked so harmless, too—so innocent, almost humorous, half ridiculous; and she was a woman, and she could not put it away. Love, love, love! It would be her excuse and her forgiveness. She had appealed to Philip himself and in vain. Now she would pretend to go on with her old relations. It was so little to do, and the effects were so certain. In jealousy and in terror Philip would step out of himself and claim her.

She had craft—all hungry things have craft. She had inklings of ambition, a certain love of luxury, and desire to be a lady. To get Philip was to get everything. Love would be satisfied, ambition fulfilled, the aims of refinement reached. Why not risk the great stake?

Nancy came to tidy the room, and Kate said, "Where's Pete all this time, I wonder?"

85

"Sitting in the fire-seat this half-hour," said Nancy. "I don't know in the world what's come over the man. He's rocking and moaning there like a cow licking a dead calf."

"Would he like to come up, think you?"

"Don't ask the man twice if you want him to say no," said Nancy.

Blushing and stammering, and trying to straighten his black curls, Pete came at Nancy's call.

Kate had few qualms. The wound she had received from Philip had left her conscienceless towards Pete. Yet she turned her head a little sideways as she welcomed him.

"Are you better, then, Kirry?" said Pete timidly.

"I'm nearly as well as ever," she answered.

"You are, though?" said Pete. "Then you'll be down soon, it's like, eh?"

"I hope so, Pete—quite soon."

"And fit for anything, now—yes?"

"Oh, yes, fit for anything."

Pete laughed from his heart like a boy. "I'll take a slieu round to Ballure and tell Philip immadiently."

"Philip?" said Kate, with a look of inquiry.

"He was saying this morning you wouldn't be equal to it, Kirry."

"Equal to what, Pete?"

"Getting—going—having—that's to say—well, you know, putting a sight on the parson himself one of these days, that's the fact." And, to cover his confusion, Pete laughed till the scraas of the roof began to snip.

There was a moment's pause, and then Kate said, with a cough and a stammer and her head aside, "Is that so *very* tiring, Pete?"

Pete leapt from his chair and laughed again like a man demented. "D'ye say so, Kitty? The word then, darling—the word in my ear—as soft as soft——"

He was leaning over the bed, but Kate drew away from him, and Nancy pulled him back, saying, "Get off with you, you goosey gander! What for should you bother a poor girl to know if sugar's sweet, and if she's willing to change a sweetheart for a husband?"

It was done. One act—nay, half an act; a word—nay, no word at all, but only silence. The daring venture was afoot.

Grannie came up with Kate's dinner that day, kissed her on both cheeks, felt them hot, wagged her head wisely, and whispered, "I know—you needn't tell *me!*"

XIV.

The last hymn was sung, Cæsar came home from chapel, changed back from his best to his work-day clothes, and then there was talking and laughing in the kitchen amid the jingling of plates and the vigorous rattling of knives and forks.

"Phil must be my best man," said Pete. "He'll be back to Douglas now, but I'll get you to write me a line, Cæsar, and ask him."

"Do you hold with long engagements, Pete?" said Grannie.

"A week," said Pete, with the air of a judge; "not much less anyway—not of a rule, you know."

"You goose," cried Nancy, "it must be three Sundays for the banns."

"Then John the Clerk shall get them going this evening," said Pete. "Nancy had the pull of me there, Grannie. Not being in the habit of getting married, I clane forgot about the banns."

John the Clerk came in the afternoon, and there was some lusty disputation.

"We must have bridesmaids and wedding-cakes, Pete—it's only proper," said Nancy.

"Aw, yes, and tobacco and rum, and everything respectable," said Pete.

"And the parson—mind it's the parson now," said Grannie; "none of their nasty high-bailiffs. I don't know in the world how a dacent woman can rest in her bed——"

"Aw, the parson, of coorse—and the parson's wife, maybe," said Pete.

"I think I can manage it for you for to-morrow fortnight," said John the Clerk impressively, and there was some clapping of hands, quickly suppressed by Cæsar, with mutterings of—

"Popery! clane Popery, sir! Can't a person commit matrimony without a parson bothering a man?"

Then Cæsar squared his elbows across the table and wrote the letter to Philip. Pete never stood sponsor for anything so pious.

"Respected and Honoured Sir,—I write first to thee that it hath been borne in on my mind (strong to believe the Lord hath spoken) to marry on Katherine Cregeen, only beloved daughter of Cæsar Cregeen, a respectable man and a local preacher, in whose house I tarry, being free to use all his means of grace. Wedding to-morrow fortnight at Kirk Christ, Lezayre, eleven o'clock forenoon, and the Lord make it profitable to my soul.—With love and-reverence, thy servant, and I trust the Lord's, Peter Quilliam."

Having written this, Cæsar read it aloud with proper elevation of pitch. Grannie wiped her eyes, and Pete said, "Indited beautiful, sir—only you haven't asked him."

"My pen's getting crosslegs," said Cæsar, "but that'll do for an N.B."

"N. B.—Will you come for my best man?"

Then there was more talk and more laughter. "You're a lucky fellow, Pete," said Pete himself. "My sailor, you are, though. She's as sweet as clover with the bumbees humming over it, and as warm as a gorse bush when the summer's gone."

And then, affection being infectious beyond all maladies known to mortals, Nancy Joe was heard to say, "I believe in my heart I must be having a man myself before long, or I'll be losing the notion."

"D'ye hear that, boys?" shouted Pete. "Don't all spake at once."

"Too late—I've lost it," said Nancy, and there was yet more laughter.

To put an end to this frivolity, Cæsar raised a hymn, and they sang it together with cheerful voices. Then Cæsar prayed appropriately, John the Clerk improvised responses, and Pete went out and sat on the bottom step in the lobby and smoked up the stairs, so that Kate in the bedroom should not feel too lonely.

XV.

Meanwhile Kate, overwhelmed with shame, humiliation, self-reproach, horror of herself, and dread of everything, lay with cheeks ablaze and her head buried in the bedclothes. She had no longer any need to pretend to be sick; she was now sick in reality. Fate had threatened her. She had challenged it. They were gambling together. The stake was her love, her life, her doom.

By the next day she had worked herself into a nervous fever. Dr. Mylechreest came to see her, unbidden of the family. He was one of those tall, bashful men who, in their eagerness to be gone, seem always to have urgent business somewhere else. After a single glance at her and a few muttered syllables, he went off hurriedly, as if some one were waiting for him round the corner. But on going downstairs he met Cæsar, who asked him how he found her.

"Feverish, very; keep her in bed," he answered. "As for this marriage, it must be put off. She's exciting herself, and I won't answer for the consequences. The thing has fallen too suddenly. To tell you the truth—this way, Mr. Cregeen—I am afraid of a malady of the brain."

"Tut, tut, doctor," said Cæsar.

"Very well, if you know better. Good-day! But let the wedding wait. *Traa dy liooar*—time enough, Mr. Cregeen. A right good Manx maxim for once. Put it off—put it off!"

"It's not my putting off, doctor. What can you do with a man that's wanting to be married? You can't bridle a horse with pincers."

But when the doctor was gone, Cæsar said to Grannie, "Cut out the bridesmaids and the wedding-cakes and the fiddles and the foolery, and let the girl be married immadiently."

"Dear heart alive, father, what's all the hurry?" said Grannie.

"And Lord bless my soul, what's all the fuss?" said Cæsar. "First one objecting this, then another objecting that, as if everybody was intarmined to stop the thing. It's going on, I'm telling you; d'ye hear me? There's many a slip—but no matter. What's written with the pen can't be cut out with the axe, so lave it alone, the lot of you."

Kate was in an ecstasy of exultation. The doctor had been sent by Philip. It was Philip who was trying to stop the marriage. He would never be able to bear it; he would claim her soon. It might be to-day, it might be to-morrow, it might be the next day. The odds were with her. Fate was being worsted. Thus she clung to her blind faith that Philip would intervene.

That was Monday, and on Tuesday morning Philip came again. He was very quiet, but the heart has ears, and Kate heard him. Pete's letter had reached him, and she could see his white face. After a few words of commonplace conversation, he drew Pete out of the house. What had he got to say? Was he thinking that Pete must be stopped at all hazards? Was he about to make a clean breast of it? Was he going to tell all? Impossible! He could not; he dared not; it was *her* secret.

Pete came back to the house alone, looking serious and even sad. Kate heard him exchange a few words with her father as they passed through the lobby to the kitchen. Cæsar was saying—

"Stand on your own head, sir, that's my advice to you."

In the intensity of her torment she could not rest. She sent for Pete.

"What about Philip?" she said. "Is he coming? What has he been telling you?"

"Bad news, Kate—very bad," said Pete.

There was a fearful silence for a moment. It was like the awful hush at the instant when the tide turns, and you feel as if something has happened to the world. Then Kate hardened her face and said, "What is it?"

"He's ill, and wants to go away in a week. He can't come to the wedding," said Pete.

"Is that all?" said Kate. Her heart leapt for joy. She could not help it—she laughed. She saw through Philip's excuse. It was only his subterfuge—he thought Pete would not marry without him.

"Aw, but you never seen the like, though, Kirry," said Pete; "he was that white and wake and narvous. Work and worry, that's the size of it. There's nothing done in this world without paying the price of it, and that's as true as gospel. 'The sea's calling me, Pete,' says he, and then he laughed, but it was the same as if a ghost itself was grinning."

In the selfishness of her enfeebled spirit, Kate still rejoiced. Philip was suffering. It was another assurance that he would come to her relief.

"When does he go?" she asked.

"On Tuesday," answered Pete.

"Isn't there a way of getting a Bishop's license to marry in a week?" said Kate.

"But will you, though?" said Pete, with a shout of joy.

"Ask Philip first. No use changing if Philip can't come."

"He shall—he must. I won't take No."

"You may kiss me now," said Kate, and Pete plucked her up into his arms and kissed her.

She was heart-dead to him yet, from the wound that Philip had dealt her, but at the touch of his lips a feeling of horror seemed to cramp all her limbs. With a shudder she crept down in the bed and hid her face, hating herself, loathing herself, wishing herself dead.

He stood a moment by her side, crying like a big boy in his great happiness. "I don't know in the world what she sees in me to be so fond of me, but that's the way with the women always, God bless them!"

She did not lift her face, and he stepped quietly to the door. Half-way through he turned about and raised one arm over his head. "God's rest and God's peace be with you, and may the man that gets you keep a clane heart and a clane hand, and be fit for the good woman he's won for his wife."

At the next minute he went tearing down the stairs, and the kitchen rang with his laughter.

XVI.

Fate scored one. Kate had been telling herself that Philip was tired of her, that he did not love her any longer, that having taken all he could take he desired to be done with her, that he was trying to forget her, and that she was a drag upon him, when suddenly she remembered the tholthan, and bethought herself for the first time of a possible contingency. Why had she not thought of it before? Why had *he* never thought of it? *If* it should come to pass! The prospect did not appal her; it did not overwhelm her with confusion or oppress her with shame; it did not threaten to fall like a thunderbolt; the thought of it came down like an angel's whisper.

She was not afraid. It was only an idea, only a possibility, only a dream of consequences, but at one bound it brought her so much nearer to Philip. It gave her a right to him. How dare he make her suffer so? She would not permit him to leave her. He was her husband, and he must cling to her, come what would. Across the void that had divided them a mysterious power drew them together. She was he, and he was she, and they were one, for—who knows?—who could say?—perhaps Nature herself had willed it.

Thus the first effect of the new thought upon Kate was frenzied exultation. She had only one thing to do now. She had only to go to Philip as Bathsheba went to David. True, she could not say what Bathsheba said. She had no certainty, but her case was no less strong. "Have you never thought of what may possibly occur?" This is what she would say now to Philip. And Philip would say to her, "Dearest, I have never thought of that. Where was my head that I never reflected?" Then, in spite of his plans, in spite of his pledge to Pete, in spite of the world, in spite of himself—yea, in spite of his own soul if it stood between them—he would cling to her; she was sure of it—she could swear to it—he could not resist.

"He will believe whatever I tell him," she thought, and she would say, "Come to me, Philip; I am frightened." In the torture of her palpitating heart she would have rejoiced at that moment if she could have been sure that she was in the position of what the world calls a shameful woman. With that for her claim she could see herself going to Philip and telling him, her head on his breast, whispering sweetly the great secret—the wondrous news. And then the joy, the rapture, the long kiss of love! "Mine, mine, mine! he is mine at last!"

That could not be quite so; she was not so happy as Bathsheba; she was not sure, but her right was the same for all that. Oh, it was joyful, it was delicious!

The little cunning arts of her sex, the small deceits in which she had disguised herself fell away from her now. She said to herself, "I will stop the nonsense about the marriage with Pete." It was mean, it was foolish, it was miserable trifling, it was wicked, it was a waste of life—above all, it was doing a great, great wrong to her love of Philip! How could she ever have thought of it?

Next morning she was up and was dressing when Grannie came into the room with a cup of tea. "I feel so much better," she said "that I think I'll go to Douglas by the coach today, mother."

"Do, bogh," said Grannie cheerfully, "and Pete shall go with you."

"Oh, no; I must be quite alone, mother."

"Aw, aw! A lil errand, maybe! Shopping is it? Presents, eh? Take your tay, then." And Grannie rolled the blind, saying, "A beautiful morning you'll have for it, too. I can see the spire as plain as plain." Then, turning about, "Did you hear the bells this morning, Kitty?"

"Why, what bells, mammy?" said Kate, through a mouthful of bread and butter.

"The bells for Christian Killip. Her old sweetheart took her to church at last. He wouldn't get rest at your father till he did—and her baby two years for Christmas. But what d'ye think, now? Robbie left her at the church door, and he's off by the Ramsey packet for England. Aw, dear, he did, though. 'You can make me marry her,' said he, 'but you can't make me live with her,' he said, and he was away down the road like the dust."

"I don't think I'll go to Douglas to-day, mother," said Kate in a broken voice. "I'm not so very well, after all."

"Aw, the bogh!" said Grannie. "Making too sure of herself, was she? It's the way with them all when they're mending."

With cheerful protestations Grannie helped her back to bed, and then went off with an anxious face to tell Cæsar that she was more ill than ever.

She was ill indeed; but her worst illness was of the heart. "If I go to him and tell him," she thought, "he will marry me—yes. No fear that he will leave me at the church door or elsewhere. He will stay with me. We will be man and wife to the last. The world will know nothing. But *I* will know. As long as I live I will remember that he only sacrificed himself to repair a fault That shall never be—never, never!"

Cæsar came up in great alarm. He seemed to be living in hourly dread that some obstacle would arise at the last moment to stop the marriage. "Chut, woman!" he said play-. fully. "Have a good heart, Kitty. The sun's not going down on you yet at all."

That night there were loud voices from the bar-room. The talk was of the marriage which had taken place in the morning, and of its strange and painful sequel. John the Clerk was saying, "But you'd be hearing of the by-child, it's like?"

"Never a word," said somebody.

"Not heard of it, though? Fetching the child to the wedding to have the bad name taken off it—no? They were standing the lil bogh—it's only three—two is it, Grannie, only two?—well, they were standing the lil thing under its mother's perricut while the sarvice was saying."

"You don't say!"

"Aw, truth enough, sir! It's the ould Manx way of legitimating. The parsons are knowing nothing of it, but I've seen it times."

"John's right," said Mr. Jelly; "and I can tell you more—it was just *that* the man went to church for."

"Wouldn't trust," said John the Clerk. "The woman wasn't getting much of a husband out of it anyway."

"No," said Pete—he had not spoken before—"but the child was getting the name of its father, though."

"That's not mountains of thick porridge, sir," said somebody. "Bobbie's gone. What's the good of a father if he's doing nothing to bring you up?"

"Ask your son if you've got any of the sort," said Pete; "some of you have. Ask me. I know middling well what it is to go through the world without a father's name to my back. If your lad is like myself, he's knowing it early and he's knowing it late. He's knowing it when he's saying his bits of prayers atop of the bed in the gable loft: 'God bless mother—and grandmother,' maybe—there's never no 'father' in his little texes. And he's knowing it when he's growing up to a lump of a lad and going for a trade, and the beast of life is getting the grip of him. Ten to one he comes to be a waistrel then, and, if it's a girl instead, a hundred to nothing she turns out a—well, worse. Only a notion, is it? Just a parzon's lie, eh? Having your father's name is nothing—no? That's what the man says. But ask the *child*, and shut your mouth for a fool."

There was a hush and a hum after that, and Kate, who had reached from the bed to open the door, clutched it with a feverish grasp.

"But Christian Killip is nothing but a trollop, anyway, sir," said Cæsar.

"Every cat is black in the night, father—the girl's in trouble," said Pete. "No, no! If I'd done wrong by a woman, and she was having a child by me, I'd marry her if she'd take me, though I'd come to hate her like sin itself."

Grannie in the kitchen was wiping her eyes at these brave words, but Kate in the bedroom was tossing in a delirium of wrath. "Never, never, never!" she thought.

Oh, yes, Philip would marry her if she imposed herself upon him, if she hinted at a possible contingency. He, too, was a brave man; he also had a lofty soul—he would not shrink. But no, not for the wealth of worlds.

Philip loved her, and his love alone should bring him to her side. No other compulsion should be put upon him, neither the thought of her possible future position, nor of the consequences to another. It was the only justice, the only safety, the only happiness now or in the time to come.

"He shall marry me for *my* sake," she thought, "for my own sake—my own sake only."

Thus in the wild disorder of her soul—the tempest of conflicting passions—her pride barred up the one great way.

XVII.

There was no help for it after all—she must go on as she had begun, with the old scheme, the old chance, the old gambling hazard. Heart-sick and ashamed, waiting for Philip, and listening to every step, she kept her room two days longer. Then Cæsar came and rallied her.

"Gough bless me, but nobody will credit it," he said. "The marriage for Monday, and the bride in bed a Wednesday. People will say it isn't coming off at all."

This alarmed her. It partly explained why Philip did not come. If he thought there was no danger of the marriage, he would be in no hurry to intervene. Next day (Thursday) she struggled up and dressed in a light wrapper, feeling weak and nervous, and looking pale and white like apple-blossom nipped by frost. Pete would have carried her downstairs, but she would not have it. They established her among a pile of cushions before a fire in the parlour, with its bowl of sea-birds' eggs that had the faint, unfamiliar smell—its tables of old china that shook and rang slightly with every step and sound. The kitchen was covered with the litter of dressmakers preparing for the wedding. There were bodices to try on, and decisions to give on points of style. Kate agreed to everything. In a weak and toneless voice she kept on telling them to do as they thought best. Only when she heard that Pete was to pay did she assert her will, and that was to limit the dresses to one.

"Sakes alive now, Kirry," cried Nancy, "that's what I call ruining a good husband—the man was willing to buy frocks for a boarding-school."

Pete came, sat on a stool at her feet, and told stories. They were funny stories of his life abroad, and now and again there came bursts of laughter from the kitchen, where they were straining their necks to catch his words through the doors, which they kept ajar. But Kate hardly listened. She showed signs of impatience sometimes, and made quick glances around when the door opened, as if expecting somebody. On recovering herself at these moments, she found Pete looking up at her with the big, serious, moist eyes of a dog.

He began to tell of the house he had taken, to excuse himself for not consulting her, and to describe the progress of the furnishing.

"I've put it all in the hands of Cannell & Quayle, Kitty," he said, "and they're doing it beautiful. Marble slabs, bless you, like a butcher's counter; carpets as soft as daisies, and looking-glasses as tall as a man."

Kate had not heard him. She was trying to remember all she knew of the courts of the island—where they were held, and on what days. "Have you seen Philip lately?" she asked.

"Not since Monday," said Pete. "He's in Douglas, working like mad to be here on Monday, God bless him!"

"What did he say when he heard we had changed the day?"

"Wanted to get out of it first. 'I'm sailing on Tuesday,' said he."

"Did you tell him that I proposed it?"

"Trust me for not forgetting that at all. 'Aw, then,' says he, 'there's no choice left,' he says."

Kate's pale face became paler, the dark circles about her eyes grew yet more dark. "I think I'll go back to bed, mother," she said in the same toneless voice.

Pete helped her to the foot of the stairs. The big, moist eyes were looking at her constantly. She found it hard to keep an equal countenance.

"But will you be fit for it, darling?" said Pete.

"Why, of course she'll be fit, sir," said Cæsar. "What girl is ever more than middling the week before she's married?"

Next day she persuaded her father to take her to Douglas. She had little errands there that could not be done in Ramsey. The morning was fine but cold. Pete helped her up in the gig, and they drove away. If only she could see Philip, if only Philip could see her, he would know by the look of her face that the marriage was not of her making—that compulsion of some sort was being put on her. She spent four hours going from shop to shop, lingering in the streets, but seeing nothing of Philip. Her step was slow and weary, her features were pinched and starved, but Cæsar could scarcely get her out of the town. At length the daylight began to fail, and then she yielded to his importunities.

"How short the days are now," she said with a sigh, as they ran into the country.

"Yes, they are a cock's stride shorter in September," said Cæsar; "but when a woman once gets shopping, Midsummer day itself won't do—she's wanting the land of the midnight sun."

Pete lifted her out of the gig in darkness at the door of the "Fairy," and, his great arms being about her, he carried her into the house and set her down in the fire-seat. She would have struggled to her feet if she had been able; she felt something like repulsion at his touch; but he looked at her with the mute eloquence of love, and she was ashamed.

The house was full of gossips that night. They talked of the marriage customs of old times. One described the "pay-weddings," where the hat went round, and every guest gave something towards the cost of the breakfast and the expenses of beginning housekeeping—rude forefather of the practice of the modern wedding present. Another pictured the irregular marriages made in public-houses in the days when the island had three breweries and thirty drinking shops to every thousand of its inhabitants. The publican laid two sticks crosswise on the floor, and said to the bride and bridegroom—

"Hop over the sticks and lie crossed on the floor, And you're man and wife for nevermore."

There was some laughter at this, but Kate sat in the fire-seat and sipped her tea in silence, and Pete said quietly, "Nothing to laugh at, though. I remember a girl over Foxal way that was married to a man like that, and then he went off to Kinsale, and got kept for the herring riots—d'ye mind them? She was a strapping girl, though, and when the man was gone the boys came bothering her, first one and then another, and good ones among them too. And honour bright for all, they were for taking her to the parzon about right But no! Did they think she was for committing beggamy? She was married to one man, and wasn't that enough for a dacent girl anyway. And so she wouldn't and she didn't, and last of all her own boy came back, and they lived together man and wife, and what for shouldn't they?"

This question from the man who was on the point of going to church was received with shouts of laughter, through which the voice of Grannie rose in affectionate remonstrance, saying, "Aw, Pete, it's ter'ble to hear you, bogh."

"What's there ter'ble about that, Grannie?" said Pete. "Isn't it the Almighty and not the parzon that makes the marriage?"

"Aw, boy veen, boy veen," cried Grannie, "you was used to be a good man, but you have fell off very bad."

Kate was in a fever of eagerness. She wanted to open her heart to Pete, to beg him to spare her, to tell him that it was impossible that they should ever marry. Pete would see that Philip was her husband by every true law, human and divine. In this mood she lived through much of the following day, Friday, tossing and turning in bed, for the exhaustion of the day in Douglas had confined her to her room again.

In the evening she came downstairs, and was established in the fire-seat as before. There were four or five old women in the kitchen spinning yarn for a set of blankets which Grannie intended for a wedding present. "When the day's work was nearly done, two or three old men, the old husbands of the old women, came to carry their wheels home again. Then, as the wheels whirred for the last of the twist, Pete set the old crones to tell stories of old times.

"Tell us of the days when you were young, Anne," said Pete to an ancient dame of eighty. Her husband of eighty-four sat sucking his pipe by her side.

"Well," said old Anne, stretching her arms to the yarn, "I was as near going foreign, same as yourself, sir, just as near, now, as makes no matter. It was the very day I married this man, and his brother was making a start for Austrillya. Jemmy was my ould sweetheart, only I had given him up because he was always stealing my pocket-handkerchers. But he came that morning and tapped at my window, and 'Will you come, Anne?' says he, and I whipped on my perricut and stole out and down to the quay with him. But my heart was losing me when I saw the white horses on the water, and home I came and went to church with this one instead."

While old Anne told her story her old husband opened his mouth wider and wider, until the pipe-shank dropped out of his toothless gums on to his waistcoat. Then he stretched his left arm and brought down his clenched hand with a bang on to her shoulder.

"And have you been living with me better than sixty years," said he, "and never telling me that before?"

Pete tried to pacify his ancient jealousy, but it was not to be appeased, and he shouldered the wheel and hobbled off, saying, "And I sent out two pound five to put a stone on the man's grave!"

There was loud laughter when the old couple were gone, but Pete said, nevertheless, "A secret's a secret, though, and the ould lady had no right to tell it. It was the dead man's secret too, and she's fouled the ould man's memory. If a person's done wrong, the best thing he can do next is to say darned little about it."

Kate rose and went off to bed. Another door had been barred to her, and she felt sick and faint.

XVIII.

The next day was Saturday. Kate remembered that Philip came to Ballure on Saturdays. She felt sure that he would come to Sulby also. Let him only set eyes on her, and he would divine the trouble that had taken the colour out of her cheeks. Then he would speak to Pete and to her father; he would deliver her; he would take everything upon himself. Thus all day long, like a white-eyed gambler who has staked his last, she waited and listened and watched. At breakfast she said to herself, "He will come this morning." At dinner, "He will come this evening." At supper, "He will come tonight."

But Philip did not come, and she grew hysterical as well as restless. She watched the clock; the minutes passed with feet of lead, but the hours with wings of fire. She was now like a criminal looking for a reprieve. Every time the clock warned to strike, she felt one hour nearer her doom.

The strain was wearing her out. She reproached Philip for leaving her to this cruel uncertainty, and she suffered the pangs of one who tries at the same time to love and to hate. Then she reproached herself with altering the date of the marriage, and excused Philip on the grounds of her haste. She felt like a witch who was burning by her own spell. Hope was failing her, and Will was breaking down as well. Nevertheless, she determined that the wedding should be postponed.

That was on Saturday night. On Sunday morning she had gone one step farther. The last pitiful shred of expectation that Philip would intervene seemed then to be lost, and she had resolved that, come what would, she should not marry at all. No need to appeal to Pete; no necessity to betray the secret of Philip. All she had to do was to say she would not go on with the wedding, and no power on earth should compel her.

With this determination, and a feeling of immense relief, she went downstairs. Cæsar was coming in from the preaching-room, and Pete from the new house at Ramsey. They sat down to dinner. After dinner she would speak out. Cæsar sharpened the carving-knife on the steel, and said, "We've taken the girl Christian Killip back to communion to-day."

"Poor thing," said Grannie, "pity she was ever put out of it, though."

"Maybe so,—maybe no," said Cæsar. "Necessary anyway; one scabby sheep infects the flock."

"And has marriage daubed grace on the poor sheep's sore then, Cæsar?" said Pete.

"She's Mistress Robbie Teare and a dacent woman, sir," said Cæsar, digging into the beef, "and that's all the truck a Christian church has got with it."

Kate did not eat her dinner that day, and neither did she speak out as she had intended. A supernatural power seemed to have come down at the last moment and barred up the one remaining pathway of escape. She was in the track of the storm. The tempest was ready to fall on her. Where could she fly for shelter?

What her father had said of the girl had revealed her life to her in the light of her relation to Philip. The thought of the possible contingency which she had foreseen with so much joy, as so much power, had awakened the consciousness of her moral position. She was a fallen woman! What else was she? And if the contingency befell, what would become of her? In the intensity of her father's pietistic views the very shadow of shame would overwhelm his household, overthrow his sect, and uproot his religious pretensions. Kate trembled at the possibility of such a disaster coming through her. She saw herself being driven from house and home. Where could she fly? And though she fled away, would she not still be the cause of sorrow and disgrace to all whom she left behind—her mother, her father, Pete, everybody?

If she could only tear out the past, at least she could stop this marriage. Or if she had been a man she could stop it, for a man may sin and still look to the future with a firm face. But she was a woman, and a woman's acts may be her own, but their consequences are beyond her. Oh, the misery of being a woman! She asked herself what she could do, and there was no answer. She could not break the web of circumstances. Her situation might be false, it might be dishonourable, but there was no escape from it. There was no gleam of hope anywhere.

Late that night—Sunday night—they were sitting together in the kitchen, Kate in the fire-seat as usual, Pete on the stool by the turf closet, smoking up the chimney, Cæsar reading aloud, Grannie listening, and Nancy cooking the supper, when the porch door burst open and somebody entered. Kate rose to her feet with a startled cry of joy, looked round eagerly, and then sat down again covered with confusion.

It was the girl Christian Killip, a pale, weak, frightened creature, with the mouth and eyes of a hare.

"Is Mr. Quilliam here?" she asked.

"Here's the man himself, Christian," said Grannie. "What do you want with him?"

"Oh, God bless you, sir," said the girl to Pete, "God bless you for ever and ever."

Then turning back to Grannie, she explained in woman's fashion, with many words, that somebody unknown had sent her twenty pounds, for the child, by post, the day before, and she had only now guessed who it must be when John the Clerk had told her what Pete had said a week before.

Pete grunted and glimed, smoked up the chimney, and said, "That'll do, ma'am, that'll do. Don't believe all you hear. John says more than his Amens, anyway."

"I'm axing your pardon, miss," said the girl to Kate, "but I couldn't help coming—I couldn't really—no, I couldn't," and then she began to cry.

"Where's that child?" said Pete, heaving up to his feet with a ferocious look. "What! you mane to say you've left the lil thing alone, asleep? Go back to it then immajent. Good night!"

"Good night, sir, and God bless you, and when you're married to-morrow, God bless your wife as well!"

"That'll do—that'll do," said Pete, backing her to the porch.

"You desarve a good woman, sir, and may the Lord be good to you both."

"Tut! tut!" said Pete, and he tut-tutted her out of the house.

She smoothed her baby's hair more tenderly than ever that night, and kissed it again and again.

Kate could scarcely breathe, she could barely see. Her pride and her will had broken down utterly. This greathearted man loved her. He would lay down his life if need be to save her. To morrow he would marry her. Here, then, was her rock of refuge—this strong man by her side.

She could struggle against fate no longer. It's invisible hand was pushing her on. It's blind power was dragging her. If Philip would not come to claim her she must marry Pete.

And Pete? She meant no harm to Pete. She had not yet thought of things from Pete's point of view. He was like the camel-bag in the desert to the terrified wayfarer when the sand-cloud breaks oyer him. He flies to it. It shelters him. But what of the camel itself, with its head in the storm? Until the storm is over he does not think of that.

XIX.

Meantime Philip himself was in the throes of his own agony. At the news of Kate's illness he was overwhelmed with remorse, and when he inquired if she had been delirious, he was oppressed with a sense of meanness never felt before. At his meeting with Pete he realised for the first time to what depths his duplicity had degraded him. He had prided himself on being a man of honour, and he was suddenly thrown out of the paths in which he could walk honourably.

When the first shock of Kate's disaster was over, he remembered the interview with the Governor. The Deemstership burnt in his mind with a growing fever of desire, but he did not apply for it. He did not even mention it to Auntie Nan. She heard of his prospects from Peter Christian Balla-whaine, who first set foot in her house on this errand of congratulation. The sweet old soul was wildly excited. All the hopes of her life were about to be realised, the visions and the dreams were coming true. Philip was going to regain what his father had lost. Had he made his application yet? No? He would, though; it was his duty.

But Philip could not apply for the Deemstership. To sit down in cold blood and write to the Home Secretary while Kate was lying sick in bed would be too much like asking the devil's wages for sacrificing her. Then came Pete with his talk of the wedding. That did not really alarm him. It was only the last revolution of the old wheel that had been set spinning before Pete went away. Kate would not consent. They had taken her consent for granted. He felt easy, calm, and secure.

Next came his old master, the college friend of his father, now promoted to the position of Clerk of the Polls. He was proud of his pupil, and had learnt that Philip was first favourite with the Governor.

"I always knew it," he said. "I did, ma'am, I did. The first time I set eyes on him, thinks I, 'Here comes the makings of the best lawyer in the island,' and by ——— he's not going to disappoint me either."

The good fellow was a noisy, hearty, robustious creature, a bachelor, and when talking of the late Deemster, he said women were usually the chief obstacles in a man's career. Then he begged Auntie Nan's pardon, but the old lady showed no anger. She agreed that it had been so in some cases. Young men should be careful what stumbling-blocks they set up in the way of their own progress.

Philip listened in silence, and was conscious, through all the unselfish counselling, of a certain cynical bitterness. Still he did not make application for the Deemstership. Then came Cæsar's letter announcing the marriage, and even fixing a date for it. This threw him into a fit of towering indignation. He was certain of undue pressure. They were forcing the girl. It was his duty to stop the marriage. But how? There was one clear course, but that course he could not take. He could not go back on his settled determination that he must not, should not, marry the girl himself. Only one thing was left—to rely on Kate. She would never consent. Not being able to marry *him*, she would marry no man. She would do as he was doing—she would suffer and stand alone.

By this time Philip's love, which, in spite of himself, had grown cool since the Melliah, and in his fierce battle with his worldly aims, suddenly awakened to fresh violence at the approach of another man. But his ambition fought with his love, and he began to ask himself if it made, any difference after all in this matter of Kate whether he took the Deemstership or left it. Kate was recovering; he had nothing to reproach himself with, and it would be folly to sacrifice the ambition of a lifetime to the love of a woman who could never be his, a woman he could never marry. At that he wrote his letter to the Home Secretary. It was a brilliant letter of its kind, simple, natural, strong, and judicious. He had a calm assurance that nothing so good would leave the island, yet he could not bring himself to post it. Some quiverings of the old tenderness came back as he held it in his hand, some visions of Kate, with her twitching lips, her passionate eyes, some whisperings of their smothered love.

Then came Pete again with the decisive blow. Kate *had* consented. There was no longer any room for doubt. His former indignation seemed almost comic, his confidence absurd. Kate was willing to marry Pete, and after all, what right had he to blame her? What right had he to stop the marriage? He had wronged the girl enough already. A good man came and offered her his love. She was going to take it. How should he dare to stop her from marrying another, being unable to marry her himself?

That night he posted his letter to the Home Secretary, and calmed the gnawings of his love with dreams of ambition. He would regain the place of his father; he would revive the traditions of his grandfather; the Christians should resume their ancient standing in the Isle of Man; the last of their race should be a strong man and a just one. No, he would never marry; he would live alone, a quiet life, a peaceful one, slightly tinged with melancholy, yet not altogether unhappy, not without cheer.

Under all other emotions, strengthening and supporting him, was a secret bitterness towards Kate—a certain contempt of her fickleness, her lightness, her shallow love, her readiness to be off with the old love and on with the new. There was a sort of pride in his own higher type of devotion, his sterner passion. Pete invited him to the wedding, but he would not go, he would invent some excuse.

Then came the change of the day to suit his supposed convenience, and also Kate's own invitation. Very well, be it so. Kate was defying him. Her invitation was a challenge. He would take it; he would go to the wedding. And if their eyes should meet, he knew whose eyes must fall.

XX.

Early next day the sleeping morning was awakened by the sound of a horn. It began somewhere in the village, wandered down the glen, crossed the bridge, plodded over the fields, and finally coiled round the house of the bride in thickening groans of discord. This restless spirit in the grey light was meant as herald of the approaching wedding. It came from the husky lungs of Mr. Jonaique Jelly.

Before daylight "The Manx Fairy" was already astir. Somewhere in the early reaches of the dawn the house had its last dusting down at the hands of Nancy Joe. Then Grannie finished, on hearth and griddle, the baking of her cakes. After that, some of the neighbours came and carried off to their own fires the beef, mutton, chickens, and ducks intended for the day's dinner. It was woman's work that was to the fore, and all idle men were hustled out of the way.

Towards nine o'clock breakfast was swallowed standing. Then everybody began to think of dressing. In this matter the men had to be finished off before the women could begin. Already they were heard bellowing for help from unseen regions upstairs. Grannie took Cæsar in hand. Pete was in charge of Nancy Joe.

It was found at the last moment that Pete had forgotten to provide himself with a white shirt. He had nothing to be married in except the flannel one in which he came home from Africa. This would never do. It wasn't proper, it wasn't respectable. There was no choice but to borrow a shirt of Cæsar's. Cæsar's shirt was of ancient pattern, and Pete was shy of taking it. "Take it, or you'll have none," said Nancy, and she pushed him back into his room. When he emerged from it he walked with a stiff neck down the stairs in a collar that reached to his ears at either side, and stood out at his cheeks like the wings of a white bat, with two long sharp points on the level of his eyes, which he seemed to be watching warily to avoid the stab of their ironed starch. At the same moment Cæsar appeared in duck trousers, a flowered waistcoat, a swallow-tail coat, and a tall hat of rough black beaver.

The kitchen was full of men and women by this time, and groups of young fellows were gathered on the road outside, some with horses, saddled and bridled for the bride's race home after the ceremony; others with guns ready loaded for firing as the procession appeared; and others again with lines of print handkerchiefs, which, as substitutes for flags, they were hanging from tree to tree.

At every moment the crowd became greater outside, and the company inside more dense. John the Clerk called on his way to church, and whispered Pete that everything was ready, and they were going to sing a beautiful psalm.

93

"It isn't many a man's wedding I would be taking the same trouble with," said John. "When you are coming down the alley give a sight up, sir, and you'll see me."

"He's only a poor thing," said Mr. Jelly in Pete's ear as John the Clerk went off. "No more music in the man than my ould sow. Did you hear the horn this morning, sir? Never got up so early for a wedding before. I'll be giving you 'the Black and the Grey' going into the church."

Grannie came down in a gigantic bonnet like a half-moon, with her white cap visible beneath it; and Nancy Joe appeared behind her, be-ribboned out of all recognition, and taller by many inches for the turret of feathers and flowers on the head that was usually bare.

Then the church bells began to peal, and Cæsar made a prolonged A—hm! and said in a large way, "Has the carriage arrived?"

"It's coming over by the bridge now," said somebody at the door, and at the next moment a covered wagonette drew up at the porch.

"All ready?" asked Cæsar.

"Stop, sir," said Pete, and then, turning to Nancy Joe, "Is it glad a man should be on his wedding-day, Nancy?"

"Why, of coorse, you goose. What else?" she answered.

"Well, no man can be glad in a shirt like this," said Pete; "I'm going back to take it off."

Two minutes afterwards he reappeared in his flannel one, under his suit of blue pilot, looking simple and natural, and a man every inch of him.

"Now call the bride," said Cæsar.

XXI.

Kate had been kept awake during the dark hours with a sound in her ears that was like the measured ringing of far-off bells. When the daylight came she slept a troubled sleep, and when she awoke she had a sense of stupefaction, as if she had taken a drug, and was not yet recovered from the effects of it. Nancy came bouncing into her room and crying, "It's your wedding-day, Kitty!" She answered by repeating mechanically, "It's your wedding day, Kitty."

There was an expression of serenity on her face; she even smiled a little. A sort of vague gaiety came over her, such as comes to one who has watched long in agony and suspense by the bed of a sick person and the person is dead. Nancy drew the little window curtain aside, stooped down, and looked out and said, "'Happy the bride the sun shines on' they're saying, and look! the sun is shining."

"Oh, but the sun is an old sly-boots," she answered.

They came up to dress her. She kept stumbling against things, and then laughing in a faint way. The dress was the new one, and when they had put it on they stood back from her and shouted with delight. She took up the little broken hand-glass to look at herself. Her great eyes sparkled piteously.

The church bells began to ring her wedding-peal. She had to listen hard to hear it. All sounds seemed to be very far away; everything looked a long way off. She was living in a sort of dead white dawn of thought and feeling.

At last they came to say the coach was ready and everything was waiting for the bride. She repeated their message like a machine, made a slow gesture, and followed them downstairs. When she got near to the bottom, she looked around on the faces below as if expecting to see somebody. Just then her father was saying, "Mr. Christian is to meet us at the church."

She smiled faintly and answered the people's greetings in an indistinct tone. There was some indulgent whispering at sight of her pale face. "Pale but genteel," said some one, and then Nancy reached over and drew the bride's veil down over her face.

At the next minute she was outside the house, standing at the back of the wagonette. The coachman, with his white rosette, was holding the door open on one side, and her father was elevating her hand on the other.

"Am I to go, then?" she asked in a helpless voice.

"Well, what do *you* think?" said Cæsar. "Shall the man slip off and get married to himself, think you?"

There was laughter among the people standing round, and she laughed also and stepped into the coach. Her mother followed her, crinkling in noisy old silk, and Nancy Joe came next, smelling of lavender and hair-oil. Then her father got in, and then Pete, with his great warm presence.

A salute of six guns was fired straight up by the coach-windows. The horses pranced, Nancy screamed, and Grannie started, but Kate gave no sign. People were closing round the coach-door and shouting altogether as at a fair. "Good luck to you, boy. Good luck! Good luck!" Pete was answering in a rolling voice that seemed to be lifting the low roof off, and at the same time flinging money out in handfuls as the horses moved away.

They were going slowly down the road. From somewhere in front came the sound of a clarionet. It was playing "the Black and the Grey." Immediately behind there was the tramp of people walking with an even step, and on either side the rustle of an irregular crowd. The morning was warm and beautiful. Here and there the last of the golden cushag glistened on the hedges with the first of the autumn gorse. They passed two or three houses that had been made roofless by the recent storm, and once or twice they came on a fallen tree-trunk with its thin leaves yellowing on the fading grass.

Kate was floating vaguely through these sights and sounds. It was all like a dream to her—a waking dream in shadow-land. She knew where she was and where she was going. Some glimmering of hope was left yet. She was half expecting a miracle of some sort. Philip would be at the church. Something supernatural would occur.

They drew up sharply, the glass of the windows rattled, and the talk that had been going on in the carriage ceased. "Here we are," cried Cæsar; there were voices outside, and then the others inside stepped down. She saw a hand held out to her and knew whose it was before her eyes had risen to the face. Philip was there. He was helping her to alight.

"Am I to get down too?" she asked in a helpless way.

Cæsar said something that made the people laugh again, and then she smiled like faded sunshine and took the hand of Philip. She held it a moment as if expecting him to say something, but he only raised his hat. His face was white as marble. He will speak yet, she thought.

Over the gateway to the churchyard there was an arch of flowers and evergreens, with an inscription in coloured letters: "God bless the happy pair." The sloping path going down as to a dell was strewn with gilvers and slips of fuchsia.

At the bottom stood the old church mantled in ivy, like a rock of the sea covered by green moss.

Leaning on her father's arm she walked in at the porch. The church was full of people. As they passed under the gallery there was a twittering as of birds. The Sunday-school girls were up there, looking down and talking eagerly. Then the coughing and hemming ceased; there was a sort of deep inspiration; the church seemed to hold its breath for a moment. After that there were broken exclamations, and the coughing and hemming began again. "How pale!"—"Not fit, poor thing." Everybody was pitying her starved features.

"Stand here," said somebody in a soft voice.

"Must I?" she said quite loudly.

All at once she was aware that she was alone before the communion rail, with the parson—old ruddy-faced Parson Quiggin—in his white surplice facing her. Some one came and stood beside her. It was Pete. She did not look at him, but she felt his warm presence again, and was relieved. It was like shelter from the eyes around. After a moment she turned about Philip was one step behind Pete. His head was bent.

Then the service began. The voice of the parson muttered words in a low voice, but she did not listen. She found herself trying to spell out the Manx text printed over the chancel arch: "Bannet T'eshyn Ta Cheet ayns Ennyn y Chearn" ("Blessed is he that cometh in the name of the Lord").

Suddenly the words the parson was speaking leapt into meaning and made her quiver.

".... is commended of Saint Paul to be honourable among all men, and therefore not by any to be enterprised, nor taken in hand unadvisedly, lightly, or wantonly——"

She seemed to know that Philip's eyes were on her. They were on the back of her head, and the veil over her face began to shake.

The voice of the parson was going on again—

"Therefore if any man can show just cause why they may not lawfully be joined together, let him now speak, or else hereafter for ever hold his peace."

She turned half around. Her eyes fell on Philip. His face was colourless, almost fierce; his forehead was deathly white. She was sure that something was about to happen.

Now was the moment for the miracle. It seemed to her as if the whole congregation were beginning to divine what tie there was between him and her. She did not care, for he would soon declare it. He was going to do so now; he raised his head, he was about to speak.

No, there was no miracle. Philip's eyes fell before her eyes, and his head went down. He was only digging at the red baize with one of his feet. She felt tired, so very tired, and oh! so cold. The parson had gone on with his reading. When she caught up with him he was saying—

"—as ye shall, answer at the great day of judgment, when the secrets of all hearts shall be disclosed, that if either of you know any impediment why ye may not lawfully be joined together in matrimony, ye do now confess it."

The parson paused. He had always paused at that point. The pause had no meaning for him, but for Kate how much! Impediment! There was indeed an impediment. Confess? How could she ever confess? The warning terrified her. It seemed to have been made for her alone. She had heard it before, and thought nothing of it. Now it seemed to scorch her very soul. She began to tremble violently.

There was an indistinct murmur which she did not catch. The parson seemed to be speaking to Pete—

"—love her, comfort her, honour and keep her... so long as ye both shall live."

And then came Pete's voice, full and strong from his great chest, but far off, and going by her ear like a voice in a shell—"I will."

After that the parson's words seemed to be falling on her face.

"Wilt thou have this man to thy wedded husband, to live together after God's ordinance in the holy estate of matrimony? Wilt thou obey him and serve him, love, honour, and keep him in sickness and in health; and forsaking all other, keep thee unto him, so long as ye both shall live?"

Kate was far away. She was spelling out the Manx text, "Bannet T'eshyn Ta Cheet," but the letters were dancing in and out of each other, and yellow lights were darting from her eyes. Suddenly she was aware that the parson's voice had stopped. There was blank silence, then an uneasy rustle, and then somebody was saying something in a soft tone.

"Eh?" she said aloud.

The parson's voice came now in a whisper at her breast—"Say, 'I will.'"

"Ah I," she murmured.

"I-will! That's all, my dear. Say it with me, 'I—will.'"

She framed her lips to speak, but the words were half uttered by the parson. The next thing she knew was that a stray hand was holding her hand. She felt more safe now that her poor cold fingers lay in that big warm palm.

It was Pete, and he was speaking again. She did not so much hear him as feel his voice tingling through her veins.

"I, Peter Quilliam, take thee, Katherine Cregeen——'"

But it was all a vague murmur, fraying off into nothing, ending like a wave with a long upward plash of low sound.

The parson was speaking to her again, softly, gently, caressingly, almost as if she were a frightened child. "Don't be afraid, my dear! try to speak after me. Take your time."

Then, aloud, "'I, Katherine Cregeen.'"

Her throat gurgled; she faltered, but she spoke at length in the toneless voice of one who speaks in sleep.

"'I, Katherine Cregeen——'"

"'Take thee, Peter Quilliam——'"

The toneless voice broke—— "take thee, Peter Quilliam——'"

And then all came in a rush, with some of the words distinctly repeated, and some of them droned and dropped—

"—'to my wedded husband, to have and to hold——'"

"—'have and to hold——'"

"—'from this day forward.... till death do us part——'"

"—'death do us part——'"

"—'therefore I give thee my troth——'"

"—'troth——'"

The last word fell like a broken echo, and then there was a rustle in the church, and much audible breathing. Some of the school-girls in the gallery were reaching over the pews with parted lips and dancing eyes.

Pete had taken her left hand, and was putting the ring on her finger. She was conscious of his warm breath and of the words—

"With this ring I thee wed, with my body I thee worship, and with all my worldly goods I thee endow, Amen."

Again she left her cold hand in Pete's warm hand. He was stroking it on the outside with his other one.

It was all a dream. She seemed to rally from it as she moved down the aisle. Ghostly faces were smiling at her out of the air on either side, and the choir in the gallery behind the school-girls were singing the psalm, with John the Clerk's husky voice drawling out the first word of each new verse as his companions were singing the last word of the preceding one—

```
"Thy wife shall be as the fruitful vine upon the walls of thine house;
Thy children like the olive branches round about thy table.
As it was in the beginning, is now, and ever shall be;
World without end, A-men."
```

They were all in the vestry now, standing together in a group. Her mother was wiping her eyes, Pete was laughing, and Nancy Joe was nudging him and saying in an audible whisper, "Kiss her, man—it's only respectable."

The parson was leaning over the table. He spoke to Pete, and then said, "A substantial mark, too. The lady's turn next."

The open book was before her, and the pen was put into her hand. When she laid it down, the parson returned his spectacles to their sheath, and a nervous voice, which thrilled and frightened her, said from behind, "Let me be the first to wish you happiness, Mrs. Quilliam."

It was Philip. She turned towards him, and their eyes met for a moment. But she was only conscious of his prominent nose, his clear-cut chin, his rapid smile like sunshine, disappearing as before a cloud. He said something else—something about a new life and a new beginning—but she could not gather its meaning, her mind would not take it in. At the next moment they were all in the open air.

XXII.

Philip had been in torment—first the torment of an irresistible hatred of Kate. He knew that this hatred was illogical, that it was monstrous; but it supported his pride, it held him safe above self-contempt in being present at the wedding. When the carriage drew up at the church gate, and he helped Kate to alight, he thought she looked up at him as one who says, "You see, things are not so bad after all!" And when she turned her face to him at the beginning of the service, he thought it wore a look of fierce triumph, of victory, of disdain. But as the ceremony proceeded and he observed her absent-ness, her vacancy, her pathetic imbecility, he began to be oppressed by an awful sense of her consciousness of error. Was she taking this step out of pique? Was she thinking to punish him, forgetting the price she would have to pay? Would she awake to-morrow morning with her vexation and vanity gone, face to face with a hideous future—the worst and most terrible that is possible to any woman—that of being married to one man and loving another?

Faugh! Would his own vanity haunt him even there? Shame, shame! He forced himself to do the duty of a best man. In the vestry he approached the bride and muttered the conventional wishes. His heart was devouring itself like a rapid fire, and it was as much as he could do to look into her piteous eyes and speak. Struggle as he might at that moment, he could not put out of his heart a passionate tenderness. This frightened him, and straightway he resolved to see no more of Kate. He must be fair to her, he must be true to himself. But walking behind her up the path strewn with flowers from the church door to the gate, the gnawings of the worm of buried love came on him again, and he felt like a man who was being dragged through the dirt.

XXIII.

Four saddle-horses, each with its rider seated and ready, had been waiting at the churchyard gate, pawing up the gravel. The instant the bride and bridegroom came out of the church the horses set off for Cæsar's house at a furious gallop. Kate and Pete, Cæsar, Grannie, and Nancy, with the addition of Philip and Parson Quiggin, returned in the covered carriage.

At the turn of the road the way was blocked by a group of stalwart girls out of the last of the year's cornfields. With the straw rope of the stackyard stretched across, they demanded toll before the carriage would be allowed to pass. Pete, who sat by the door, put his head out and inquired solemnly if the highway women would take their charge in silver or in kind—half-a-crown apiece or a kiss all round. They laughed, and answered that they saw no objection to taking both. Whereupon Pete, whispering behind his hand that the mistress was looking, tossed into the air a paper bag, which rose like a cannon-ball, broke in the air like a shell, and fell over their white sun-bonnets like a shower.

At the door of "The Manx Fairy" the four riders were waiting with smoking horses. The first to arrive had been rewarded already with a bottle of rum. He had one other ancient privilege. As the coach drove up to the door, he stepped up to the bride with the wedding-cake and broke it over her head. Then there was a scramble for the pieces among the girls who gathered round her, that they might take them to bed and dream of a day to come when they should themselves be as proud and happy.

The wedding-breakfast (a wedding-dinner) was laid in the loft of the mill, the chapel of The Christians. Cæsar sat at the head of the table, with Grannie on one side and Kate on the other. Pete sat next to Kate, and Philip next to Grannie. The parson sat at the foot with Nancy Joe, a lady of consequence, receiving much consideration, at his reverent right hand. Jonaique Jelly sat midway down the table, with a fine scorn on his features, for John the Clerk sat opposite with a fiddle gripped between his knees.

The neighbours brought in the joints of beef and mutton, the chickens and the ducks. Cæsar and the parson carved. Black Tom, who had been invited by way of truce, served out the liquor from an eighteen-gallon cask, and sucked it up himself like the sole of an old shoe. Then Cæsar said grace, and the company fell to. Such noise, such sport, such chaff, such laughter! Everything was a jest—every word had wit in it. "How are you doing, John?"—"Haven't done as well for a month, sir; but what's it saying, two hungry meals make the third a glutton."—"How are *you* doing, Tom?"—"No time to get a right mouthful for myself Cæsar; kept so busy with the drink."—"Aw, there'll be some with their top works hampered soon."—"Got plenty, Jonaique?"—"Plenty, sir, plenty. Enough down here to victual a menagerie. It'll be Sunday every day of the week with the man that's getting the lavings."—"Take a taste of this beef before it goes, Mr. Thomas Quilliam, or do you prefer the mutton?"—"I'm not partic'lar, Mr. Cregeen. Ateing's nothing to me but filling a sack that's empty."

Grannie praised the wedding service—it was lovely—it was beautiful—she didn't think the ould parzon could have made the like; but Cæsar criticised both church and clergy—couldn't see what for the cross on the pulpit and the petticoat on the parson. "Popery, sir, clane Popery," he whispered across Grannie to Philip.

Away went the shanks of mutton, the breasts of birds, and the slabs of beef, and up came an apple-pudding as round as a well-fed salmon, and as long as a twenty-pound cod. There was a shout of welcome. "None of your dynamite pudding that,—as green as grass and as sour as vinegar."

Kate was called on to make the first cut of the monster. A faint colour had returned to her cheeks since she had come home. She was talking a little, and even laughing sometimes, as if the weight on her heart was lightening every moment. She rose at the call, took, with the hand nearest to the dish, the knife that her father held out, and plunged it into the pudding. As she did so, with all eyes upon her, the wedding-ring on her finger flashed in the light and was seen by everybody.

"Look at that, though," cried Black Tom. "There's the wife for a husband, if you plaze. Ashamed of showing it, is she? Not she, the bogh."

Then there was much giggling among the younger women, and cries of "Aw, the poor girl! Going to church has been making her left-handed!"

"Time enough, my beauties," cried Pete; "and mind you're not struck that way yourselves one of these days."

Away went the dishes, and the parson rose to return thanks.

"Never heard that grace but once before, Parson Quiggin," said Pete, "and then"—lighting his pipe—"then it was a burial sarvice."

"A *burial* sarvice!"

A dozen voices echoed the words together, and in a moment the table was quiet.

"Yes, though," said Pete. "It was up at Johannesburg. Two chums settled there, and one married a girl. Nice lil thing, too; some of the Boer girls, you know; but not much ballast at her at all. The husband went up country for the Consolidated Co., and when he came back there was trouble. Chum had been sweethearting the wife a bit!"

"Aw, dear!"—"Aw, well, well!"

"Do? The husband? He went after the chum with a repeater, and took him. Bath-chair sort of a chap—no fight in him at all. 'Mercy!' he cries. 'I can't,' says the husband. 'Forgive him this once,' says the wife. 'It's only once a woman loses herself,' says the man. 'Mercy, mercy!' 'Say your prayers.' 'Mercy, mercy, mercy!' 'Too late!' and the husband shot him dead. The woman dropped in a faint, but the man said, 'He didn't say his prayers, though—I must be doing it for him.' Then down he went on his knees by the body, but the prayers were all forgot at him—all but the bit of a grace, so he said that instead."

Loud breathings on every side followed Pete's story, and Cæsar, leaning over towards Philip, whose face had grown ashy, said, "Terrible, sir, terrible! But still and for all, right enough, though, eh! What's it saying, Better an enemy than a bad friend."

Philip answered absently; his eyes were on the opposite side of the table. There was a sudden rising of the people about Kate.

"Water, there," shouted Pete. "It's a thundering blockhead I am for sure—frightning the life out of people with stories fit for a funeral."

"No, no," said Kate; "I'm not faint Why should you think so?"

"Of coorse, not, bogh," said Nancy, who was behind her in a twinkling. "White is she? Well, what of it, man? It's only becoming on a girl's wedding-day. Take a lil sup, though, woman—there, there!"

Kate drank the water, with the glass jingling against her teeth, and then began to laugh. The parson's ruddy face rose at the end of the table. "Friends," he said, "after that tragic story, let us indulge in a little vanity. Fill up your glasses to the brim, and drink with me to the health of the happy couple. We all know both of them. We know the bride for a good daughter and a sweet girl—one so naturally pure that nobody can ever say an evil word or think an evil thought when she is near. We know the bridegroom for a real Manxman, simple and rugged and true, who says all he thinks and thinks all he says. God has been very good to them. Such virginal and transparent souls have much to be thankful for. It is not for them to struggle with that worst enemy of man, the enemy that is within, the enemy of bad passions. So we can wish them joy on their union with a full heart and a sure hope that, whatever chance befall them on the ways of this world, they will be happy and content."

"Aw, the beautiful advice," said Grannie, wiping her eyes.

"Popery, just Popery," muttered Cæsar. "What about original sin?"

There was a chorus of applause. Kate was still laughing. Philip's head was down.

"And now, friends," continued the parson, "Captain Quilliam has been a successful man abroad, but he has had to come home to do the best piece of work he ever did." (A voice—"Do it yourself, parzon.") "It is true I've never done it myself. Vanity of vanities, love is not for me. It's been the Lord's will to put me here to do the marrying and leave my people to do the loving. But there is a young man present who has all the world before him and everything this life can promise except one thing, and that's the best thing of all—a wife." (Kate's laughter grew boisterous.) "This morning he helped his friend to marry a pure and beautiful maiden. Now let me remind him of the text which says, 'Go thou and do likewise.'"

The toast was drunk standing, with shouts of "Cap'n Pete," and, amid much hammering on the table, stamping on the floor, and other thunderings of applause, Cap'n Pete rolled up to reply. After a moment's pause, in which he distributed sage winks and nods on every side, he said: "I'm not much for public spaking myself. I made my best speech and my shortest in church this morning—*I will*. The parzon has has been telling my *dooiney molla* to do as I have done today. He can't. Begging pardon of the ladies, there's only one woman on the island fit for him, and I've got her." (Kate's laughter grew shrill.) "My wife——"

At this word, uttered with an air of life-long familiarity, twenty clay pipes lost their heads by collision with the table, and Pete was interrupted by roars of laughter.

"Gough bless me, can't a married man mention his wife in company? Well then. Mistress Cap'n Peter Quilliam——"

This mouthful was the signal for another riotous interruption, and a general call for more to drink.

"Won't that do for you neither? I'm not going back on it, though. 'Whom God hath joined together let no man put asunder'—isn't that it, Parzon Quiggin? What's it you're saying—no man but the Dempster? Well, the Dempster's here that is to be—I'll clear him of *that*, anyway."

Kate's laughter became explosive and uncontrollable. Pete nodded sideways to fill up the gap in his eloquence, and then went on. "But if my *dooiney molla* can't marry my wife, there's one thing he can do for her—he can make her house his home in Ramsey when he goes to Douglas for good and comes down here to the coorts once a fortnight."

Kate laughed more immoderately than ever; but Philip, with a look of alarm, half rose from his seat, and said across the table, "There's my aunt at Ballure, Pete."

"She'll be following after you," said Pete.

"There are hotels enough for travellers," said Philip.

"Too many by half, and that's why I asked in public," said Pete.

"I know the brotherly feeling——" began Philip.

"Is it a promise?" demanded Pete.

"If I can't escape your kindness——"

"No, you can't; so there's an end of it."

"It will kill me yet——"

"May you never die till it polishes you off.".

At Philip's submission to Pete's will, there was a general chorus of cheers, through which Kate's shrill laughter rang like a scream. Pete patted the back of her hand, and continued, "And now, young fellows there, let an ould experienced married man give you a bit of advice—he swore away all his worldly goods this morning, so he hasn't much else to give. I've no belief in bachelors myself. They're like a tub without a handle—nothing to lay hould of them by." (Much nudging and whispering about the bottom of the table.) "What's that down yonder? 'The vicar,' you say? Aw, the vicar's a grand man, but he's only a parzon, you see. Mr. Christian, is it? He's got too much work to do to be thinking about women. We're living on the nineteenth century, boys, and it's middling hard feeding for some of us. If the fishing's going to the dogs and the farming going to the deuce, don't be tossing head over tip at the tail of the tourist. If you've got the pumping engine inside of you, in plain English, if you've got the indomable character of the rael Manxman, do as I done—go foreign. Then watch your opportunity. What's Shake-spar saying?" Pete paused. "What's that he's saying, now?" Pete scratched his forehead. "Something about a flood, anyway." Pete stretched his hand out vigorously. "'Lay hould of it at the flood,' says he, 'that's the way to make your fortune.'"

Then Pete melted to sentiment, glanced down at Kate's head, and continued, "And when you come back to the ould island—and there isn't no place like it—you can marry the girl of your heart, God bless her. Work's black, but money's white, and love is as sweet on potatoes and herrings three times a day, as on nothing for dinner, and the same every night of the week for supper. While you're away, you'll be draming of her. 'Is she faithful?' 'Is she thrue?' Coorse she is, and waiting to take you the very minute you come home." Kate was still laughing as if she could not stop. "Look out for the right sort, boys. Plenty of the like in yet. If the young men of these days are more smart and more educated than their fathers, the young women are more handsome and more virtuous than their mothers. So *ben-my-chree*, my hearties, and enough in the locker to drive away the divil and the coroner."

Through the volley of cheers which followed Pete's speech came the voice of Black Tom, thick with drink, "Drive off the crow at the wedding-breakfast."

Everybody rose and looked. A great crow, black as night, had come in at the open door of the mill, calmly, sedately, as if by habit, for the corn that usually lay there.

"It manes divorce," said Black Tom.

"Scare it away," cried some one.

"It's the new wife must do it," said another.

"Where's Kate?" cried Nancy.

But Kate only looked and went on laughing as before.

The crow turned tail and took flight of itself at finding so eager an audience. Then Pete said, "Whose houlding with such ould wife's wonders?"

And Cæsar answered, "Coorse not, or fairies either. I've slept out all night on Cronk-ny-airy-Lhaa—before my days of grace, I mane—and I never seen no fairies."

"It would be a fool of a fairy, though, that would let *you* see him, Cæsar," said Black Tom.

At nine o'clock Cæsar's gig was at the door of "The Manx Fairy" to take the bride and bridegroom home. They had sung "Mylecharane," and "Keerie fu Snaighty," and "Hunting the Wren," and "The Win' that Shook the Barley," and then they had cleared away the tables and danced to the fiddle of John the Clerk and the clarionet of Jonaique Jelly. Kate, with wild eyes and flushed cheeks, had taken part in everything, but always fiercely, violently, almost tempestuously, until people lost enjoyment of her heartiness in fear of her hysteria, and Cæsar whispered Pete to take her away, and brought round the gig to hasten them.

Kate went up for her cloak and hat, and in the interval between her departure and reappearance, Grannie and Nancy Joe, both glorified beings, Nancy with her unaccustomed cap askew, stood in the middle of a group of women, who were deferring, and inquiring, and sympathising.

"I don't know in the world how she has kept up so long," said Grannie.

"And dear heart knows how *I'm* to keep up when she's gone," said Nancy, with her apron to her eyes.

Kate came down ready. Everybody followed her into the road, and all stood round the gig with flashes from the gig-lamps on their faces, while Pete swung her up into the seat, lifting her bodily in his great arms.

"You wouldn't drown yourself to-night for an ould rusty nail, eh, Capt'n?" cried somebody with a laugh.

"You go bail," said Pete, and he leapt up to Kate's side, twiddled the reins, cracked the whip, and they drove away.

XXIV.

Philip had stood at the door of the porch, struggling to command his soul, and employing all his powers to look cheerful and even gay. But as Kate had passed she had looked at him with an imploring look, and then he had seemed to understand everything—that she had made a mistake and that she knew it, that her laughter had been bitterer than tears, that some compulsion had been put upon her, and that she was a wretched and miserable woman. At the next moment she had gone by with an odour of lace and perfume; and then a flood of tenderness, of pity, of mad jealousy had come upon him, and it had been as much as he could do to restrain himself. One instant he held himself in hand, and at the next the wheels of the gig had begun to move, the horse had started, the women had trooped into the house again, and there was nothing before him but the broad back of Cæsar, who was looking into the darkness after the vanishing gig-lamps, and breathing asthmatical breath.

"Therefore shall a man leave his father and his mother and shall cleave unto his wife," said Cæsar. "You're time enough yet, sir; come in, come in."

99

But the man was odious to Philip at that moment, the house was odious, the people and the talk inside were odious, and he slipped away unobserved.

Too late! From the torment of his own thoughts he could not escape—his lost love, his lost happiness, his memories of the past, his dreams of the future. A voice—it was his own voice—seemed to be taunting him constantly: "You were not worthy of her. You did not know her value. She is gone; and what have you got instead!"

The Deemstership! That was of no consequence now. A name, an idle name! Love was the only thing worth having, and it was lost. Without it all the rest was nothing, and he had flung it away. He had been a monster, he had been a fool. The thought of his folly was insupportable; the recollection of his selfishness was stifling; the memory of his calculating deliberations was dragging him again in the dust. Thus, with a sense of crushing shame, he plunged down the dark road, trying not to think of the gig that had gone swinging along in front of him.

He would leave the island. To-morrow he would sail for England. No matter if he lost the chance of promotion. To-morrow, to-morrow! But to-night? How could he live through the hours until morning, with the black thoughts which the darkness generated? How could he sleep? How lie awake? What drug would bring forgetfulness? Kate! Pete! To-night! Oh, God! oh, God!

XXV.

Six strides of the horse into the darkness and Kate's hysteria was gone. She had been lost to herself the whole day-through, and now she possessed herself again. She grew quiet and silent, and even solemn. But Pete rattled on with cheerful talk about the day's doings. At the doors of the houses on the road as they passed, people were standing in the half-light to wave them salutations, and Pete sent back his answers in shouts and laughter. Turning the bridge they saw a little group at the porch of the "Ginger."

"There's company waiting for us yonder," said Pete, giving the mare a touch of the whip.

"Let us get on," said Kate in a nervous whisper.

"Aw, let's be neighbourly, you know," said Pete. "It wouldn't be dacent to disappoint people at all. We'll hawl up for a minute just, and hoof up the time at a gallop. Woa, lass, woa, mare, woa, bogh!"

As the gig drew up at the inn door, a voice out of the porch cried, "Joy to you, Capt'n, and joy to your lady, and long life and prosperity to you both, and may the Lord give you children and health and happiness to rear them, and may you see your children's children, and may they call you blessed."

"Glasses round. Mrs. Kelly," shouted Pete.

"Go on, please," said Kate in a fretful whisper, and she tugged at Pete's sleeve.

The stars came out; the moon gave a peep; the late hay of the Curragh sent a sweet odour through the night. Kate shuddered and Pete covered her shoulders with a rug. Then he began to sing snatches. He sang bits of all the songs that had been sung that night, but kept coming back at intervals to an old Manx ditty which begins—

> "Little red bird of the black turf ground,
>   Where did you sleep last night?"

Thus he sang like a great boy as he went rolling down the dark road, and Kate sat by his side and trembled.

They came to the town, rattled down the Parliament Street, passed the Court-house under the trees, turned the sharp angle by the market-place, and drew up at Elm Cottage in the corner.

"Home at last," cried Pete, and he leapt to the ground.

A dog began to bark inside the house. "D'ye hear him?" said Pete. "That's the master in charge."

The porch door was opened, and a comfortable-looking woman in a widow's cap came out with a lighted candle shaded by her hand.

"And this is your housekeeper, Mrs. Gorry," said Pete.

Kate did not answer. Her eyes had been fixed in a rigid stare on the hind-quarters of the horse, which were steaming in the light of the lamps. Pete lifted her down as he had lifted her up. Then Mrs. Gorry took her by the hand, and saying, "Mind the step, ma'am—this way, ma'am," led her through the gate and along the garden path, and up to the porch. The porch opened on a square hall, furnished as a sitting-room. A fire was burning, a lamp was lit, the table was laid for supper, and the place was warm and cosy.

"*There!* What d'ye say to *that*?" cried Pete, coming behind with the whip in his hand.

Kate looked around; she did not speak; her eyes began to fill.

"Isn't it fit for a Dempster's lady?" said Pete, sweeping the whip-handle round the room like a showman.

Kate could bear no more. She sank into a chair and burst into a fit of tears. Pete's glowing face dropped in an instant.

"Dear heart alive, darling, what is it?" he said. "My poor girl, what's troubling you at all? Tell me, now—tell me, bogh, tell me."

"It's nothing, Pete, nothing. Don't ask me," said Kate. But still she sobbed as if her heart would break.

Pete stood a moment by her side, smoothing her arm with his hand. Then he said, with a crack and a quaver in his great voice, "It *is* hard for a girl, I know that, to lave father and mother and every one and everything that's been sweet and dear to her since she was a child, and to come to the house of her husband and say, 'The past has been very good to me; but still and for all, I'm for trusting the future to you.' It's hard, darling; I know it's hard."

"Oh, leave me! leave me!" cried Kate, still weeping.

Pete brushed his sleeve across his eyes, and said, "Take her upstairs, Mrs. Gorry, while I'm putting up the mare at the 'Saddle.'"

Then he whistled to the dog, which had been watching him from the hearthrug, and went out of the house. The handle of the whip dragged after him along the floor.

Mrs. Gorry, full of trouble, took Kate to her room. Would she not eat her supper? Then salts were good for headache-should she bring a bottle from her box? After many fruitless inquiries and nervous protestations, the good soul bade Kate good-night and left her.

Being alone, Kate broke into yet wilder paroxysms of weeping. The storm-cloud which had been gathering had burst at last. It seemed as if the whole weight of the day had been deferred until then. The piled-up hopes of weeks had waited for that hour, to be cast down in the sight of her own eyes. It was all over. The fight with Fate was done, and the frantic merriment with which she had kept down her sense of the place where the blind struggle had left her made the sick recoil more bitter.

She thought of Philip, and her trouble began to moderate. Somewhere out of the uncrushed part of her womanhood there came one flicker of womanly pride to comfort her. She saw Philip at last from the point of revenge. He loved her; he would never cease to love her. Do what he might to banish the thought of her, she would be with him always; the more surely with him, the more reproachfully and unattainably, because she would be the wife of another man. If he could put her away from him in the daytime, and in the presence of those worldly aims for which he had sacrificed her, when night came he would be able to put her away no more. He would never sleep but he would see her. In every dream he would stretch out his arms to her, but she would not be there, and he would awake with sobs and in torment. There was a real joy in this thought, although it tore her heart so terribly.

She got strength from the cruel comforting, and Mrs. Gorry in the room below, listening intently, heard her crying cease. With her face still shut in both her hands, she was telling herself that she had nothing to reproach herself with; that she could not have acted differently; that she had not really made this marriage; that she had only submitted to it, being swept along by the pitiless tide, which was her father, and Pete, and everybody. She was telling herself, too, that, after all, she had done well. Here she lay in close harbour from the fierce storm which had threatened her. She was safe, she was at peace.

The room lay still. The night was very quiet within those walls. Kate drew down her hands and looked about her. The fire was burning gently, and warming her foot on the sheepskin rug that lay in front of it. A lamp burned low on a table behind her chair. At one side there was a wardrobe of the shape of an old press, but with a tall mirror in the door; on the other side there was the bed, with the pink curtains hanging like a tent. The place had a strange look of familiarity. It seemed as if she had known it all her life. She rose to look around, and then the inner sense leapt to the outer vision, and she saw how it was. The room was a reproduction of her own bedroom at home, only newer and more luxurious. It was almost as if some ghost of herself had been there while she slept—as if her own hand had done everything in a dream of her girlhood wherein common things had become grand.

Kate's eyes began to fill afresh, and she turned to take off her cloak. As she did so, she saw something on the dressing-table with a label attached to it. She took it up. It was a little mirror, a handglass like her own old one, only framed in ivory, and the writing on the label ran—

Insted of The one that is bruk with fond Luv to Kirry.

peat.

Her heart was now beating furiously. A flood of feeling had rushed over her. She dropped the glass as if it stung her fingers. With both hands she covered her face. Everything in the room seemed to be accusing her. Hitherto she had thought only of Philip. Now for the first time she thought of Pete.

She had wronged him—deeply, awfully, beyond atonement or hope of forgiveness. He loved her; he had married her; he had brought her to his home, to this harbour of safety, and she had deceived and betrayed him—she had suffered herself to be married to him while still loving another man.

A sudden faintness seized her. She grew dizzy and almost fell. A more terrible memory had come behind. The thought was like ravens flapping their black wings on her brain. She felt her temples beating against her hands. They seemed to be sucking the life out of her heart.

Just then the voice of Pete came beating up the echoes between the house and the chapel beyond the garden—

"Little red bird of the black turf ground,
        Where did you sleep last night?"

She heard him open the garden gate, clash it back, come up the path with an eager step, shut the door of the house and chain it on the inside. Then she heard his deep voice speaking below.

"Better now, Mrs. Gorry?"

"Aw, better, sir, yes, and quiet enough this ten minutes."

"Give her time, the bogh! Be aisy with the like, be aisy."

Presently she heard him send off Mrs. Gorry for the night, saying he should want no supper, and should be going to bed soon. Then the house became quiet, and the smell of tobacco smoke came floating up the stairs.

Kate's hot breath on her hands grew damp against her face. She felt herself swooning, and she caught hold of the mantelpiece.

"It cannot be," she thought. "He must not come. I will go down to him and say, 'Pete, forgive me, I am really the wife of another.'"

Then she would tell him everything. Yes, she would confess all now. Oh, she would not be afraid. His love was great. He would do what she wished.

101

She made one step towards the door, and was pulled up as by a curb. Pete would say, "Do you mean that you have been using me as a cloak? Do you ask me to live in this house, side by side with you, and let no one suspect that we are apart? Then why did you not ask me yesterday? Why do you ask me to-day, when it is too late to choose?"

No, she could not confess. If confession had been difficult yesterday, it was a thousand times more difficult to-day, and it would be a thousand thousand times more difficult tomorrow.

Kate caught up the cloak she had thrown aside. She must go away. Anywhere, anywhere, no matter where. That was the one thing left to her—the only escape from the wild tangle of dread and pain. Pete was in the hall; there must be a way out at the back; she would find it.

She lowered the lamp, and turned the handle of the door. Then she saw a light moving on the landing, and heard a soft step on the stairs. It was Pete, with a candle, coming up in his stockinged feet. He stopped midway, as if he heard the click of the latch, and then went noiselessly down again.

Kate closed the door. She would not go. If she left the house that night she would cover Pete with suspicion and disgrace. The true secret would never be known; the real offender would never suffer; but the finger of scorn would be raised at the one man who had sheltered and shielded her, and he would die of humiliation and blind self-reproach.

This reflection restrained her for the moment, and when the stress of it was spent she was mastered by a fear that was far more terrible. For good or for all she was now married to Pete, and he had the rights of a husband. He had a right to come to her, and he *would* come. It was inevitable; it had to be. No boy or girl love now, no wooing, no dallying, no denying, but a grim reality of life—a reality that comes to every woman who is married to a man. She was married to Pete. In the eye of the world, in the eye of the law, she was his, and to fly from him was impossible.

She must remain. God himself had willed it As for the shame of her former relation to Philip, it was her own secret. God alone knew of it, and He would keep it safe. It was the dark chamber of her heart which God only could unlock. He would never unlock it until the Day of Judgment, and then Philip would be standing by her side, and she would cast it back upon him, and say, "His, not mine, O God," and the Great Judge of all would judge between them.

But she began to cry again, like a child in the dark. As she threw off her cloak a second time, her dress crinkled, and she looked down at it and remembered that it was her wedding-dress. Then she looked around at the room, and remembered that it was her wedding chamber. She remembered how she had dreamt of coming in her bridal dress to her bridal room—proud, afraid, tingling with love, blushing with joy, whispering to herself, "This is for me—and this—and this. *He* has given it, for he loves me and I love him, and he is mine and I am his, and he is my love and my lord, and he is coming to—"

There was a gentle knocking at the door. It made her flesh creep. The knock came again. It went shrieking through and through her.

"Kirry," whispered a voice from without.

She did not stir.

"It's only Pete."

She neither spoke nor moved.

There was silence for a moment, and then, half nervously, half jovially, half in laughter, half with emotion as if the heart outside was palpitating, the voice came again, "I'm coming in, darling!"

PART IV. MAN AND WIFE.

I.

Next morning Kate said to herself, "My life must begin again from to-day." She had a secret that Pete did not share, but she was not the first woman who had kept something from her husband. When people had secrets which it would hurt others to reveal, they ought to keep them close. Honour demanded that she should be as firm as a rock in blotting Philip from her soul. Remembering the promise which Pete had demanded of Philip at the wedding to make their house his home in Ramsey, and seeing that Philip must come, if only to save appearances, she asked herself if she ought to prevent him. But no! She resolved to conquer the passion that made his presence a danger. There was no safety in separation. In her relation to Philip she was like the convict who is beginning his life again—the only place where he can build up a sure career is precisely there where his crime is known. "Let Philip come," she thought. She made his room ready.

She was married. It was her duty to be a good wife. Pete loved her—his love would make it easy. They were sitting at breakfast in the hall-parlour, and she said, "I should like to be my own housekeeper, Pete."

"And right, too," said Pete. "Be your own woman, darling—not your woman's woman—and have Mrs. Gorry for your housemaid."

To turn her mind from evil thoughts, she set to work immediately, and busied herself with little duties, little economies, little cares, little troubles. But the virtues of housekeeping were just those for which she had not prepared herself. Her first leg of mutton was roasted down to the proportions of a frizzled shank, and her first pudding was baked to the colour and consistency of a badly burnt brick. She did not mend rapidly as a cook, but Pete ate of all that his faultless teeth could grind through, and laid the blame on his appetite when his digestion failed.

She strove by other industries to keep alive a sense of her duty as a wife. Buying rolls of paper at the paperhanger's, she set about papering every closet in the house. The patterns did not join and the paste did not adhere. She initialled in worsted the new blankets sent by Grannie, with a P and a Q and a K intertwined. Than she overhauled the linen; turned out every room twice a week; painted every available wooden fixture with paint which would not dry because she had mixed it herself to save a sixpence a stone and forgotten the turpentine. Pete held up his hands in admiration at all her failures. She had thought it would be easy to be a good wife to a good husband. It was hard—hard for any one, hardest of all for her. There are the ruins of a happy woman in the bosom of every over-indulged wife.

She could not keep to anything long, but every night for a week she gave Pete lessons in reading, writing, and arithmetic. His reading was laborious, his spelling was eccentric, his figuring he did on the tips of his heavy fingers, and his writing he executed with his tongue in his cheek and his ponderous thumb down on the pen nib.

"What letter is that, Pete?" she said, pointing with her knitting needle to the page of a book of poems before them.

Pete looked up in astonishment. "Is it *me* you're asking, Kitty? If *you* don't know, *I* don't know."

"That's a capital M, Pete."

"Is it, now?" said Pete, looking at the letter with a searching eye. "Goodness me, the straight it's like the gate of the long meadow."

"And that's a capital A."

"Sakes alive, the straight it's like the coupling of the cart-house."

"And that's a B."

"Gough bless me, d'ye say so? But the straight it's like the hoof of a bull, though."

"And M A B spells Mab—Queen Mab," said Kate, going on with her knitting.

Pete looked up at her with eyes wide open. "I suppose, now," he said, in a voice of pride, "I suppose you're knowing all the big spells yourself, Kitty?"

"Not all. Sometimes I have to look in the dictionary," said Kate.

She showed him the book and explained its uses.

"And is it taiching you to spell every word, Kitty?" he asked.

"Every ordinary word," said Kate.

"My gough!" said Pete, touching the book with awe.

Next day he pored over the dictionary for an hour, but when he raised his face it wore a look of scepticism and scorn. "This spelling-book isn't taiching you nothing, darling," he said.

"Isn't it, Pete?"

"No, nothing," said Pete. "Here I've been looking for an ordinary word—a *very* ordinary word—and it isn't in."

"What word is it?" said Elate, leaning over his shoulder.

"*Love*," said Pete. "See," pointing his big forefinger, "that's where it ought to be, and where is it?"

"But *love* begins *lo*," said Kate, "and you're looking at *lu*. Here it is—love."

Pete gave a prolonged whistle, then fell back in his chair, looked slowly up and said, "So you must first know how the word begins; is that it, Kitty?"

"Why, yes," said Kate.

"Then it's you that's taiching the spelling-book, darling; so we'll put it back on the shelf."

For a fortnight Kate read and replied to Pete's correspondence. It was plentiful and various. Letters from heirs to lost fortunes offering shares in return for money to buy them out of Chancery; from promoters of companies proposing dancing palaces to meet the needs of English visitors; from parsons begging subscriptions to new organs; from fashionable ladies asking Pete to open bazaars; from preachers inviting him to anniversary tea-meetings, and saying Methodism was proud of him. If anybody wanted money, he kissed the Blarney Stone and applied to Pete. Kate stood between him and the worst of the leeches. The best of them he contrived to deal with himself, secretly and surreptitiously. Sometimes there came acknowledgments of charities of which Kate knew nothing. Then he would shuffle them away and she would try not to see them. "If I stop him altogether, I will spoil him," she thought.

One day the post brought a large envelope with a great seal at the back of it, and Kate drew out a parchment deed and began to read the indorsement—"'Memorandum of loan to Cæsar Cre———'"

"That's nothing," said Pete, snatching the document and stuffing it into his jacket-pocket.

Kate lifted her eyes with a look of pain and shame and humiliation, and that was the end of her secretaryship.

II.

103

A month after their marriage a man came through the gate with the air of one who was doing a degrading thing. The dog, which had been spread out lazily in the sun before the porch, leapt up and barked furiously.

"Who's this coming up the path with his eyes all round him like a scallop?" said Pete.

Kate looked. "It's Ross Christian," she said, with a catch in her breathing.

Ross came up, and Pete met him at the door. His face was puffy and pale, his speech was soft and lisping, yet there lurked about the man an air of levity and irony.

"Your dog doesn't easily make friends, Peter," he said.

"He's like his master, sir; it's against the principles of his life," said Pete.

Ross laughed a little. "Wants to be approached with consideration, does he, Capt'n?"

"You see, he's lived such a long time in the world and seen such a dale," said Pete.

Ross looked up sharply and said in another tone, "I've just dropped in to congratulate you on your return home in safety and health and prosperity, Mr. Quilliam."

"You're welcome, sir," said Pete.

Pete led the way indoors. Ross followed, bowed distantly to Kate, who was unpicking a dress, and took a chair.

"I must not conceal from you, however, that I have another object—in fact, a private matter," said Ross, glancing at Kate.

The dress rustled in Kate's fingers, her scissors dropped on to the table, and she rose to go.

Pete raised his hand. "My wife knows all my business," he said.

Ross gave out another little chirp of laughter. "You'll remember what they say of a secret, Captain—too big for one, right for two, tight for three."

"A man and his wife are one, sir—so that's two altogether," said Pete.

Kate took up the scissors and went on with her work uneasily. Ross twisted on his seat and said, "Well, I feel I *must* tell you, Peter."

"Quilliam, sir," said Pete, charging a pipe; but Ross pretended not to hear.

"Only natural, perhaps, for it—in fact, it's about our father."

"Tongue with me, tongue with thee," thought Pete, lighting up.

"Five years ago he made me an allowance, and sent me up to London to study law. He believes I've been called to the English bar, and, in view of this vacant Deemstership, he wants me admitted to the Manx one."

Pete's pipe stopped in its puffing. "Well?"

"That's impossible," said Ross.

"Things haven't come with you, eh?"

"To tell you the truth, Captain, on first going up I fell into extravagant company. I thought my friends were rich men, and I was never a niggard. There was Monty, the patron of the Fancy"—the scissors in Kate's hand clicked and stopped—and Ross blurted out, "In fact, I've *not* been called, and I've never studied at all."

Ross squirmed in his chair, glancing under his brows at Kate. Pete leaned forward and puffed up the chimney without speaking.

"You see I speak freely, Peter—something compels me. Well, if a man can't reveal his little failings to his own brother, Peter——"

"Don't let's talk about brothers," said Pete. "What am I to do for you?"

"Lend me enough to help me to do what our father thinks I've done already," said Ross, and then he added, hastily, "Oh, I'll give you my note of hand for it."

"They're telling me, sir," said Pete, "your notes of hand are as cheap as cowries."

"Some one has belied me to you, Captain. But for our father's sake—he has set his heart on this Deemstership—there may still be time for it."

"Yes," said Pete, striking his open hand on the table, "and better men to fill it."

Ross glanced at Kate, and a smile that was half a sneer crossed his evil face. "How nice," he said, "when the great friends of the wife are also the great friends of the husband."

"Just so," said Pete, and then Ross laughed a little, and the clicking of Kate's scissors stopped again. "As to you, sir," said Pete, rising, "if it's no disrespect, you're like the cormorant that chokes itself swallowing its fish head-ways up. The gills are sticking in your gizzard, sir, only," touching Ross's shoulder with something between a pat and push, "you shouldn't be coming to your father's son to help you to ram it down."

As Ross went out Cæsar came in. "That wastrel's been wanting something," said Cæsar.

"The tide's down on him," said Pete.

"Always was, and always will be. He was born at low water, and he'll die on the rocks. Borrowing money, eh?" said Cæsar, with a searching glance.

"Trying to," said Pete indifferently.

"Then lend it, sir," said Cæsar promptly. "He's not to trust, but lend it on his heirship. Or lend it the ould man at mortgage on Ballawhaine. He's the besom of fire—it'll come to you, sir, at the father's death, and who has more right?"

The shank of Pete's pipe came down from his mouth as he sat for some moments beating out the ash on the jockey bar. "Something in that, though," he said mechanically. "But there's another has first claim for all. He'd be having the place now if every one had his own. I must be thinking of it—I must be thinking of it."

III.

Philip had left the island on the morning after the marriage. He had gone abroad, and when they heard from him first he was at Cairo. The voyage out had done him good—the long, steady nights going down the Mediterranean—walking the deck alone—the soft air—the far-off lights—thought he was feeling better—calmer anyway. He hoped they were settled in their new home, and well—and happy. Kate had to read the letter aloud. It was like a throb of Philip's heart made faint, feeble, and hardly to be felt by the great distance. Then she had to reply to it on behalf of Pete.

"Tell him to be quick and come out of the land of Egypt and the house of bondage," said Pete. "Say there's no manner of sense of a handsome young man living in a country where there isn't a pretty face to be seen on the sunny side of a blanket. Write that Kirry joins with her love and best respects and she's busy whitewashing, and he'd better have no truck with Pharaoh's daughters."

The next time they heard from Philip he was at Rome. He had suffered from sleeplessness, but was not otherwise unwell. Living in that city was like an existence after death—all the real life was behind you. But it was not unpleasant to walk under the big moon amid the wrecks of the past. He congratulated Mrs. Quilliam on her active occupation—work was the same as suffering—it was strength and power. Kate had to read this letter also. It was like a sob coming over the sea.

"Give him a merry touch to keep up his pecker," said Pete. "Tell him the Romans are ter'ble jealous chaps, and, if he gets into a public house for a cup of tay, he's to mind and not take the girls on his knee—the Romans don't like it."

The last time they heard from Philip he was in London. His old pain had given way; he thought he was nearly well again, but he had come through a sharp fire. The Governor had been very good—kept open the Deemstership by some means—also surrounded him with London friends—he was out every night. Nevertheless, an unseen force was drawing him home—they might see him soon, or it might be later he had been six months away, but he felt that it had not been all waste and interruption—he would return with a new sustaining power.

This letter could not be answered, for it bore no address. It came by the night-mail with the same day's steamer from England. Two hours later Mrs. Gorry ran in from an errand to the town saying—

"I believe in my heart I saw Mr. Philip Christian going by on the road."

"When?" said Pete.

"This minute," she answered.

"Chut! woman," said Pete; "the man's in London. Look, here's his letter"—running his forefinger along the headline—"'London, January 21st—that's yesterday. See!'"

Mrs. Gorry was perplexed. But the next night she was out at the same hour on the same errand, and came flying into the house with a scared look, making the same announcement.

"See for yourself, then," she cried, "he's going up the lane by the garden."

"Nonsense! it's browning you're ateing with your barley," said Pete; and then to Kate, behind his hand, he whispered, "Whisht! It's sights she's seeing, poor thing—and no wonder, with her husband laving her so lately."

But the third night also Mrs. Gorry returned from a similar errand, at the same hour, with the same statement.

"I'm sure of it," she panted. She was now in terror. An idea of the supernatural had taken hold of her.

"The woman manes it," said Pete, and he began to cross-question her. How was Mr. Christian dressed? She hadn't noticed that night, but the first night he had worn a coat like an old Manx cape. Which way was he going? She couldn't be certain which way to-night but the night before he had gone up the lane between the chapel and the garden. Had she seen his face at all? The first time she had seen it, and it was very thin and pale.

"Oh, I wouldn't deceave you, sir," said Mrs. Gorry, and she fell to crying.

"Gough bless me, but this is mortal strange, though," said Pete.

"What time was it exactly, Jane?" asked Kate.

"On the minute of ten every night," answered Mrs. Gorry.

"Is there any difference in time, now," said Pete, "between the Isle of Man and London, Kitty?"

"Nothing to speak of," said Kate.

Pete scratched his head. "I must be putting a sight up on Black Tom. A dirty old trouss, God forgive me, if he is my grandfather, but he knows the Manx yarns about right. If it had been Midsummer day now, and Philip had been in bed somewhere, it might have been his spirit coming home while he was sleeping to where his heart is—they're telling of the like, anyway."

Kate read the mystery after her own manner, and on the following night, at the approach of ten o'clock, she went into the parlour of the hall, whence a window looked out on to the road. The day had been dull and the night was misty. A heavy white hand seemed to have come down on to the face of sea and land. Everything lay still and dead and ghostly. Kate was in the dark room, trembling, but not with fear. Presently a form that was like a shadow passed under a lamp that glimmered opposite. She could see only the outlines of a Spanish cape.

But she listened for the footsteps, and she knew them. They came on and paused, came up and paused again, and then they went past and deadened off and died in the dense night-air.

Kate's eyes were red and swollen when she came back to supper. She had promised herself enjoyment of Philip's sufferings. There was no enjoyment, but only a cry of yearning from the deep place where love calls to love. She tried afresh to make the thought of Philip sink to the lowest depth of her being. It was hard—it was impossible; Pete was for ever strengthening the recollection of him—of his ways, his look, his voice, his laugh. What he said was only the echo of her own thoughts; but it was pain and torment, nevertheless. She felt like crying, "Let me alone—let me alone!"

People in the town began to talk of Mrs. Gorry's mysterious stories.

"Philip will be forced to come now," thought Kate; and he came. Kate was alone. It was afternoon; dinner was over, the hearth was swept, the fire was heaped up, and the rug was down. He entered the porch quietly, tapped lightly at the door, and stepped into the house. He hoped she was well. She answered mechanically. He asked after Pete. She replied vacantly that he had been gone since morning on some fishing business to Peel. It was a commonplace conversation—brief, cold, almost trivial. He spoke softly, and stood in the middle of the floor, swinging his soft hat against his leg. She was standing by the fire, with one hand on the mantelpiece and her head half aside, looking sideways towards his feet; but she noticed that his eyes looked larger than before, and that his voice, though so soft, had a deeper tone. At first she did not remember to ask him to sit, and when she thought of it she could not do so. The poor little words would have been a formal recognition of all that had happened so terribly—that she was mistress in that house, and the wife of Pete.

IV.

They were standing so, in a silence hard to break, harder still to keep up, when Pete himself came back, like a rush of wind, and welcomed Philip with both hands.

"Sit, boy, sit," he cried; "not that one—this aisy one. Mine? Well, if it's mine, it's yours. Not had dinner, have you? Neither have I. Any cold mate left, Kitty? No? Fry us a chop, then, darling."

Kate had recovered herself by this time, and she went out on this errand. While she was away, Pete rattled on like a mill-race—asked about the travels, laughed about the girls, and roared about Mrs. Gorry and her ghost of Philip.

"Been buying a Nickey at Peel to-day, Phil," he said; "good little boat—a reg'lar clipper. Aw, I'm going to start on the herrings myself next sayson sir, and what for shouldn't I? Too many of the Manx ones are giving the fishing the goby. There's life in the ould dog yet, though. Would be, anyway, if them rusty Kays would be doing anything for the industry. They're building piers enough for the trippers, but never a breakwater the size of a tooth-brush for the fishermen. That's reminding me, Phil—the boys are at me to get you to petition the Tynwald Court for better harbours. They're losing many a pound by not getting out all weathers. But if the child doesn't cry, the mother will be giving it no breast. So we mane to squall till they think in Douglas we've got spavined wind or population of the heart, or something. The men are looking to you, Phil. 'That's the boy for us,' says they. 'He's stood our friend before, and he'll do it again,' they're saying."

Philip promised to draw up the petition, and then Mrs. Gorry came in and laid the cloth.

Kate, meanwhile, had been telling herself that she had not done well. Where was the satisfaction she had promised herself on the night of her wedding-day, when she had seen Philip from the height of a great revenge, if she allowed him to think that she also was suffering? She must be bright, she must be gay, she must seem to be happy and in love with her husband.

She returned to the hall-parlour with a smoking dish, and a face all sunshine.

"I'm afraid they're not very good, dear," she said.

"Chut!" said Pete; "we're not particular. Phil and I have roughed it before to-day."

She laughed merrily, and, under pretext of giving orders, disappeared again. But she had not belied the food she had set on the table. The mutton was badly fed, badly killed, badly cut, and, above all, badly cooked. To eat it was an ordeal. Philip tried hard not to let Pete see how he struggled. Pete fought valiantly to conceal his own efforts. The perspiration began to break out on their foreheads. Pete stopped in the midst of some wild talk to glance up at Philip. Philip tore away with knife and fork and answered vaguely. Then Pete looked searchingly around, rose on tiptoe, went stealthily to the kitchen door, came back, caught up a piece of yellow paper from the sideboard, whipped the chops into it from his own plate and then from Philip's, and crammed them into his jacket pocket.

"No good hurting anybody's feelings," said he; and then Kate reappeared smiling.

"Finished already?" she said with an elevation of pitch.

"Ha! ha!" laughed Pete. "Two hungry men, Kate! You'd rather keep us a week than a fortnight, eh?"

Kate stood over the empty dish with a look of surprise. Pete winked furiously at Philip. Philip's eyes wandered about the tablecloth.

"*She* isn't knowing much about a hungry man's appetite, is she, Phil?"

"But," said Kate—"but," she stammered—"what's become of the bones?"

Pete scratched his chin through his beard. "The bones? Oh, the bones? Aw, no, we're not ateing the bones, at all." Then with a rush, as his eyes kindled, "But the dog, you see—coorse we always give the bones to the dog—Dempster's dead on bones."

Dempster was lying at the moment full length under the table, snoring audibly. Mrs. Gorry cleared the cloth, and Kate took up her sewing and turned towards the sideboard.

"Has any one seen my pattern?" she asked.

"Pattern?" said Pete, diving into his jacket-pocket. "D'ye say pattern," he muttered, rummaging at his side. "Is this it?" and out came the yellow paper, crumpled and greasy, which had gone in with the chops. "Bless me, the stupid a man is now—I took it for a pipe-light."

Kate's smile vanished, and she fled out to hide her face. Then Pete whispered to Philip, "Let's take a slieu round to the 'Plough.'"

They were leaving the house on that errand when Kate came back to the hall. "Just taking a lil walk, Kirry," said Pete. "They're telling me it's good wonderful after dinner for a wake digestion of the chest," and he coughed repeatedly and smote his resounding breast.

"Wait a moment and I'll go with you," said Kate.

There was no help for it. Kate's shopping took them in the direction of the "Plough." Old Mrs. Beatty, the innkeeper, was at the door as they passed, and when she saw Pete approaching on the inside of the three, she said aloud—meaning no mischief—"Your bread and cheese and porter are ready, as usual, Capt'n."

V.

The man was killing her. To be his spoiled and adored wife, knowing she was unworthy of his love and tenderness, was not happiness—it was grinding misery, bringing death into her soul. If he had blamed her for her incompetence; if he had scolded her for making his home cheerless; nay, if he had beaten her, she could have borne with life, and taken her outward sufferings for her inward punishment.

She fell into fits of hysteria, sat whole hours listless, with her feet on the fender. Pete's conduct exasperated her. As time went on and developed the sweetness of Pete, the man grew more and more distasteful to her, and she broke into fits of shrewishness. Pete hung his head and reproached himself. She wasn't to mind if he said things—he was only a rough fellow. Then she burst into tears and asked him to forgive her, and he was all cock-a-hoop in a moment, like a dog that is coaxed after it has been beaten.

Her sufferings reached a climax—she became conscious that she was about to become a mother. This affected her with terrible fears. She went back to that thought of a possible contingency which had torn her with conflicting feelings on the eve of her marriage. It was impossible to be sure. The idea might be no more than a morbid fancy, born of her un-happiness, of her secret love for Philip, of her secret repugnance for Pete (the inadequate, the uncouth, the uncongenial) but nevertheless it possessed her with the force of an overpowering conviction, it grew upon her day by day, it sat on her heart like a nightmare—the child that was to be born to her was not the child of her husband.

VI.

In spite of Pete's invitations, Philip came rarely. He was full of excuses—work—fresh studies—the Governor—his aunt. Pete said "Coorse," and "Sartenly," and "Wouldn't trust," until Philip began to be ashamed, and one evening he came, looking stronger than usual, with a more sustaining cheerfulness, and plumped into the house with the words, "I've come at last!"

"To stay the night?" said Pete.

"Well, yes," said Philip.

"That's lucky and unlucky too, for I'm this minute for Peel with two of the boys to fetch round my Nickey by the night-tide. But youll stay and keep the wife company, and I'll be back first tide in the morning. You'll be obliged to him, won't you, Kate?" he cried, pitching his voice over his shoulder; and then, in a whisper, "She's a bit down at whiles, and what wonder, and her so near—but you'll see, you'll see," and he winked and nodded knowingly.

There was no harking back, no sheering off on the score of modesty before Pete's large faith. Kate looked as if she would cry "Mercy, mercy!" but when she saw the same appeal on Philip's face she was stung.

Pete went off, and then Kate and Philip sat down to tea. While tea lasted it was not hard to fill the silences with commonplaces. After it was over she brought him a pipe, and they lapsed into difficult pauses. Philip puffed vigorously and tried to look happy. Kate struggled not to let Philip see that she was ill at ease. Every moment their imagination took a new turn. He began to read a book, and while they sat without speaking she thought it was hardly nice of him to treat her with indifference. When he spoke she thought he was behaving with less politeness than before. He went over to the piano and they sang a part song, "Oh, who will o'er the downs so free?" Their voices went well enough together, but they broke down. The more they tried to forget the past the more they remembered it. He twiddled the backs of his fingertips over the keyboard; she swung on one foot and held to the candle-bracket while they talked of Pete. That name seemed to fortify them against the scouts of passion. Pete was their bulwark. It was the old theme, but played as a tragedy, not as a comedy, now.

"It is delightful to see you settled in this beautiful home," he said.

"*Isn't* it beautiful?" she answered.

"You ought to be very happy."

"Why should I not be happy?" with a little laugh.

"Why, indeed? A home like a nest and a husband that worships you——"

She laughed again because she could not speak. Speech was thin gauze, laughter was rolling smoke; so she laughed and laughed.

"What a fine hearty creature he is!" said Philip.

"Isn't he?" said Kate.

"Education and intellect don't always go together."

"Any wife might love such a husband," said Kate.

"So simple, so natural, so unsuspicious——"

But that was coming to quarters too close, so they fell back on silence. The silence was awful; the power of it was pitiless. If they could have spoken the poorest commonplaces, the spell might have dissolved. Philip thought he would rise, but he could not do so. Kate tried to turn away, but felt herself rooted to the spot. With faces aside, they remained some moments where they were, as if a spirit had passed between them.

Mrs. Gorry came in to lay the supper, and then Kate recovered herself. She got back her power of laughter, and laughed at everything. He was not deceived. "She loves me still," said the voice of his heart. He hated himself for the thought, but it haunted him with a merciless persistence. He remembered the evening of the wedding-day, and the imploring look she gave him on going away with Pete; and he returned to the idea that she had been married under the compulsion of her father, Cæsar, the avaricious hypocrite. He told himself it would be easy to kindle a new fire on the warm hearth. As she laughed and he looked into her beautiful eyes and caught the nervous twitch of her mouth, he felt something of the old thrill, the old passion, the old unconditioned love of her who loved him in spite of all, and merely because she must. But no! Had he spent six months abroad for nothing? He would be strong; he would be loyal. If need be he would save this woman from herself.

At last Kate lit a candle and said, "I must show you to your room."

She talked cheerily going upstairs. On the landing she opened the door of the room above the hall, and went into it, and drew down the blind. She was still full of good spirits, said perhaps he had no night-shirt, so she had left out one of Pete's, hoped he would find it big enough, and laughed again. He took the candle from her at the threshold, and kissed the hand that had held it. She stood a moment quivering like a colt, then she bounded away; there was the clash of a door somewhere beyond, and Kate was in her own room, kneeling before the bed with her face buried in the counterpane to stifle the sobs that might break through the walls.

Under all her lightness, in spite of all her laughter, the old tormenting thought had been with her still. Should she tell him? Could he understand? Would he believe? If he realised the gravity of the awful position in which she was soon to be placed, would he make an effort to extricate her? And if he did not, would not, could not, should not she hate him for ever after? Then the old simple love, the pure passion, came back upon her at the sight of his face, at the touch of his hand, at the sound of his voice? Oh, for what might have been—what might have been!

Pete's Nickey came into harbour with the morning tide, and the three breakfasted together. As Kate moved heavily in front of the fire, Pete crowed, cooed, and scattered wise winks round the table.

"More milk, mammy," he whimpered, and then he imitated all kinds of baby prattle.

After breakfast the men smoked, and Kate took up her sewing. She was occupying herself with the little labours, so pretty, so full of delicate humour and delicious joy, which usually open a new avenue for a woman's tenderness. Philip's eyes fell on her, and she dropped below into her lap the tiny piece of white linen she was working on. Pete saw this, stole to the back of her chair, reached over her shoulder, snatched the white thing out of her fingers, held it outstretched in his ponderous hands, and roared like a smithy bellows. It was a baby's shirt.

"Never mind, darling," he coaxed, as the colour leapt to Kate's face. "Philip must be a sort of a father to the boy some day—a godfather, anyway—so he won't mind seeing his lil shiff. We must be calling him Philip, too. What do you say, Kirry—Philip, is it agreed?"

VII.

As her time drew near, the conviction deepened upon her that she could not be confined in her husband's house. Being there at such a crisis was like living in a volcanic land. One false step, one passionate impulse, and the very earth under her feet would split. "I must go home for awhile, Pete," she said.

"Coorse you must," said Pete. "Nobody like the ould angel when a girl's that way."

Pete took her back to her mother's in the gig, driving very slowly, and lifting her up and down as tenderly as if she had been a child. She breathed freely when she left Elm Cottage, but when she was settled in her own bedroom at "The Manx Fairy" she realised that she had only stepped from misery to misery. So many memories lived like ghosts there—memories of innocent slumbers, and of gleeful awakenings amid the twittering of birds and the rattling of gravel. The old familiar place, the little room with the poor little window looking out on the orchard, the poor little bed with its pink curtains like a tent, the sweet old blankets, the wash-basin, the press, the blind with the same old pattern, the sheepskin rug underfoot, the whitewashed scraas overhead—everything the same, but, O God! how different!

"Let me look at myself in the glass, Nancy," she said, and Nancy gave her the handglass which had been cracked the morning after the Melliah.

She pushed it away peevishly. "What's the use of a thing like that?" she said.

Pete haunted the house day and night. There was no bed for him there, and he was supposed to go home to sleep. But he wandered away in the darkness over the Curragh to the shore, and in the grey of morning he was at the door again, bringing the cold breath of the dawn into the house with the long whisper round the door ajar. "How's she going on now?"

The women bundled him out bodily, and then he hung about the roads like a dog disowned. If he heard a sigh from the dairy loft, he sat down against the gable and groaned. Grannie tried to comfort him. "Don't be taking on so, boy. It'll be all joy soon," said she, "and you'll be having the child to shew for it."

But Pete was bitter and rebellious. "Who's wanting the child anyway?" said he. "It's only herself I'm wanting; and she's laving me; O Lord, she's laving me. God forgive me!" he muttered. "O good God, forgive me!" he groaned: "It isn't fair, though. Lord knows it isn't fair," he mumbled hoarsely.

At last Nancy Joe came out and took him in hand in earnest.

"Look here, Pete," she said. "If you're wanting to kill the woman, and middling quick too, you'll go on the way you're going. But if you don't, you'll be taking to the road, and you won't be coming back till you're wanted."

This settled Pete's restlessness. The fishing had begun early that season, and he went off for a night to the herrings.

Kate waited long, and the women watched her with trembling. "It's a week or two early," said one. "The weather's warm," said another. "The boghee millish! She's a bit soon," said Grannie.

There was less of fear in Kate's own feelings.

"Do women often die?" she asked.

"The proportion is small," said the doctor.

Half an hour afterwards she spoke again.

"Does the child sometimes die?"

"Well, I've known it to happen, but only when the mother has had a shock—lost her husband, for example."

She lay tossing on the bed, wishing for her own death, hoping for the death of the unborn child, dreading its coming lest she should hate and loathe it. At last came the child's first cry—that cry out of silence that had never broken on the air before, but was henceforth to be one of the world's voices for laughter and for weeping, for joy and for sorrow, to her who had borne it into life. Then she called to them to show her the baby, and when they did so, bringing it up with soft cooings and foolish words, she searched the little wrinkled face with a frightened look, then put up her arms to shut out the sight, and cried "Take it away," and turned to the wall. Her vague fear was a certainty now; the child was the child of her sin—she was a bad woman.

Yet there is no shame, no fear, no horror, but the pleading of a new-born babe can drown its clamour. The child cried again, and the cruel battle of love and dread was won for motherhood. The mother heart awoke and swelled. She had got her baby, at all events. It was all she had for all she had suffered; but it was enough, and a dear and precious prize.

"Are you sure it is well?" she asked. "Quite, quite well? Doesn't its little face look as if its mammy had been crying—no?"

"'Deed no," said Grannie, "but as bonny a baby as ever was born."

The women were scurrying up and down, giggling on the landings, laughing on the stairs, and saying *hush* at their own noises as they crept into the room. In a fretful whimper the child was still crying, and Grannie was telling it, with many wags of the head and in a mighty stern voice, that they were going to have none of its complaining now that it *had* come at last; and Kate Herself, with hands clasped together, was saying in a soft murmur like a prayer, "God is very good, and the doctor is good too. God is good to give us doctors."

"Lie quiet, and I'll come back in an hour or two," said Dr. Mylechreest from half-way through the door.

"Dear heart alive, what will the father say?" cried Grannie, and then the whole place broke into that smile of surprise which comes to every house after the twin angels of Life and Death have brooded long over its roof-tree, and are gone at length before the face of a little child.

VIII.

When Pete came up to the quay in the raw sunshine of early morning, John the Clerk, mounted on a barrel, was selling by auction the night's take of the boats.

"I've news for you, Mr. Quilliam," he cried, as Pete's boat, with half sail set, dropped down the harbour. Pete brought to, leapt ashore, and went up to where John, at the end of the jetty, surrounded by a crowd of buyers in little spring-carts, was taking bids for the fish.

"One moment, Capt'n," he cried, across his outstretched arm, at the end whereof was a herring with gills still opening and closing. "Ten maise of this sort for the last lot, well fed, alive and kicking—how much for them? Five shillings? Thank you—and three, Five and three. It's in it yet, boys—only five and three—and six, thank *you*. It'll do no harm at five and six—six shillings? All done at six—*and six?* All done at six and six?" "Seven shillings," shouted somebody with a voice like a foghorn. "They're Annie the Cadger's," said John, dropping to the ground. "And now, Capt'n Quilliam, we'll go and wet the youngster's head."

Pete went up to Sulby like an avalanche, shouting his greetings to everybody on the way. But when he got near to the "Fairy," he wiped his steaming forehead and held his panting breath, and pretended not to have heard the news.

"How's the poor girl now?" he said in a meek voice, trying to look powerfully miserable, and playing his part splendidly for thirty seconds.

Then the women made eyes at each other and looked wondrous knowing, and nodded sideways at Pete, and clucked and chuckled, saying, "Look at him,—he doesn't know anything, does he?" "Coorse not, woman—these men creatures are no use for nothing."

"Out of a man's way," cried Pete, with a roar, and he made a rush for the stairs.

Nancy blocked him at the foot of them with both hands on his shoulders. "You'll be quiet, then," she whispered. "You were always a rasonable man, Pete, and she's wonderful wake—promise you'll be quiet."

"TO be like a mouse," said Pete, and he whipped off his long sea-boots and crept on tiptoe into the room.

There she lay with the morning light on her, and a face as white as the quilt that she was plucking with her long fingers.

"Thank God for a living mother and a living child," said Pete, in a broken gurgle, and then he drew down the bedclothes a very little, and there, too, was the child on the pillow of her other arm.

Then do what he would to be quiet, he could not help but make a shout.

"He's there! Yes, he is! He is, though! Joy! Joy!"

The women were down on him like a flock of geese. "Out of this, sir, if you can't behave better!'

"Excuse me, ladies," said Pete humbly, "I'm not in the habit of babies. A bit excited, you see, Mistress Nancy, ma'am. Couldn't help putting a bull of a roar out, not being used of the like." Then, turning back to the bed, "Aw, Kitty, the beauty it is, though! And the big! As big as my fist already. And the fat! It's as fat as a bluebottle. And the straight! Well, not so *very* straight, neither, but the complexion at him now! Give him to me, Kitty I give him to me, the young rascal. Let me have a hould of him, anyway."

"*Him*, indeed! Listen to the man," said Nancy.

"It's a girl, Pete," said Grannie, lifting the child out of the bed.

"A girl, is it?" said Pete doubtfully. "Well," he said, with a wag of the head, "thank God for a girl." Then, with another and more resolute wag, "Yes, thank God for a living mother and a living child, if it is a girl," and he stretched out his arms to take the baby.

"Aisy, now, Pete—aisy," said Grannie, holding it out to him.

"Is it aisy broke they are, Grannie?" said Pete. A good spirit looked out of his great boyish face. "Come to your ould daddie, you lil sandpiper. Gough bless me, Kitty, the weight of him, though! This child's a quarter of a hundred if he's an ounce. He is, I'll go bail he is. Look at him! Guy heng, Grannie, did ye ever see the like, now! It's absolute perfection. Kitty, I couldn't have had a better one if I'd chiced it. Where's that Tom Hommy now? The bleating little billygoat, he was bragging outrageous about his new baby—saying he wouldn't part with it for two of the best cows in his cow-house. This'll floor him, I'm thinking. What's that you're saying, Mistress Nancy, ma'am? No good for nothing, am I? You were right, Grannie. 'It'll be all joy soon,' you were saying, and haven't we the child to show for it? I put on my stocking inside out on Monday, ma'am. 'I'm in luck,' says I, and so I was. Look at that, now! He's shaking his lil fist at his father. He is, though. This child knows me. Aw, you're clever, Nancy, but—no nonsense at all, Mistress Nancy, ma'am. Nothing will persuade me but this child knows me."

"Do you hear the man?" said Nancy. "*He* and *he*, and *he* and *he!* It's a girl, I'm telling you; a girl—a girl—a girl."

"Well, well, a girl, then—a girl we'll make it," said Pete, with determined resignation.

"He's deceaved," said Grannie. "It was a boy he was wanting, poor fellow!"

But Pete scoffed at the idea. "A boy? Never! No, no—a girl for your life. I'm all for girls myself, eh, Kitty? Always was, and now I've got two of them."

The child began to cry, and Grannie took it back and rocked it, face downwards, across her knees.

"Goodness me, the voice at him!" said Pete. "It's a skipper he's born for—a harbour-master, anyway."

The child slept, and Grannie put it on the pillow turned lengthwise at Kate's side.

"Quiet as a Jenny Wren, now," said Pete. "Look at the bogh smiling in his sleep. Just like a baby mermaid on the egg of a dogfish. But where's the ould man at all? Has he seen it? We must have it in the papers. The *Times?* Yes, and the 'Tiser too. 'The beloved wife of Mr. Capt'n Peter Quilliam, of a boy—a girl,' I mane. Aw, the wonder there'll be all the island over—everybody getting to know. Newspapers are like women—ter'ble bad for keeping sacrets. What'll Philip say? But haven't you a toothful of anything, Grannie? Gin for the ladies, Nancy. Goodness me, the house is handy. What time was it? Wait, don't tell me! It was five o'clock this morning, wasn't it? Yes? Gough bless me, I knew it! High water to the very minute—aw, he'll rise in the world, and die at the top of the tide. How did I know when the child was born, ma'am? As aisy as aisy. We were lying adrift of Cronk ny Irrey Lhaa, looking up for daylight by the fisherman's clock. Only light enough to see the black of your nail, ma'am. All at once I heard a baby's cry on the waters. 'It's the nameless child of Earey Cushin,' sings out one of the boys. 'Up with the clout,' says I. And when we were hauling the nets and down on our knees saying a bit of a prayer, as usual, 'God bless my new-born child,' says I, 'and God bless my child's mother, too,' I says, and God love and protect them always, and keep and presarve myself as well.'" There was a low moaning from the bed.

"Air! Give me air! Open the door!" Kate gasped.

"The room is getting too hot for her," said Grannie.

"Come, there's one too many of us here," said Nancy. "Out of it," and she swept Pete from the bedroom with her apron as if he had been a drove of ducks.

Pete glanced backward from the door, and a cloak that was hanging on the inside of it brushed his face.

"God bless her!" he said in a low tone. "God bless and reward her for going through this for me!"

Then he touched the cloak with his lips and disappeared. A moment later his curly black poll came stealing round the door jamb, half-way down, like the head of a big boy.

"Nancy," in a whisper, "put the tongs over the cradle; it's a pity to tempt the fairies. And, Grannie, I wouldn't lave it alone to go out to the cow-house—the lil people are shocking bad for changing."

Kate, with her face to the wall, listened to him with an aching heart. As Pete went down the doctor returned.

"She's hardly so well," said the doctor. "Better not let her nurse the child. Bring it up by hand. It will be best for both."

So it was arranged that Nancy should be made nurse and go to Elm Cottage, and that Mrs. Gorry should come in her place to Sulby.

Throughout four-and-twenty hours thereafter, Kate tried her utmost to shut her heart to the child. At the end of that time, being left some minutes alone with the little one, she was heard singing to it in a sweet, low tone. Nancy paused with the long brush in her hand in the kitchen, and Granny stopped at her knitting in the bar.

"That's something like, now," said Nancy.

"Poor thing, poor Kirry! What wonder if she was a bit out of her head, the bogh, and her not well since her wedding?"

They crept upstairs together at the unaccustomed sounds, and found Pete, whom they had missed, outside the bedroom door, half doubled up and holding his breath to listen.

"Hush!" said he, less with his tongue than with his mouth, which he pursed out to represent the sound. Then he whispered, "She's filling all the room with music. Listen! It's as good as fairy music in Glentrammon. And it's the little fairy itself that's 'ticing it out of her."

Next day Philip came, and nothing would serve for Pete but that he should go up to see the child.

"It's only Phil," he said, through the doorway, dragging Philip into Kate's room after him, for the familiarity that a great joy permits breaks down conventions. Kate did not look up, and Philip tried to escape.

"He's got good news for himself, too" said Pete. "They're to be making him Dempster a month to-morrow."

Then Kate lifted her eyes to Philip's face, and all the glory of success withered under her gaze. He stumbled downstairs, and hurried away. There was the old persistent thought, "She loves me still," but it was working now, in the presence of the child, with how great a difference! When he looked at the little, downy face, a new feeling took possession of him. Her child—hers—that might have been his also! Had his bargain been worth having? Was any promotion in the world to be set against one throb of Pete's simple joy, one gleam of the auroral radiance that lights up a poor man's home when he is first a father, one moment of divine partnership in the babe that is fresh from God?

Three weeks later, Pete took his wife home in Cæsar's gig. Everything was the same, as when he brought her, save that within the shawls with which she was wrapped about the child now lay with its pink eyelids to the sky, and its fiat white bottle against her breast. It was a beautiful spring morning, and the young sunlight was on the sallies of the Curragh and the gold of the roadside gorse. Pete was as silly as a boy, and he chirped and croaked all the way home like every bird and beast of heaven and earth. When they got to Elm Cottage, he lifted his wife down as tenderly as if she had been the babe she had in her arms. He was strong and she was light, and he half helped, half carried her to the porch door. Nancy was there to take the child out of her hands, and, as she did so, Pete, back at the horse's head, cried, "That's the last bit of furniture the house was waiting for, Nancy. What's a house without a child? Just a room without a clock."

"Clock, indeed," said Nancy; "clocks are stopping, but this one's for going like a mill."

"Don't be tempting the Nightman, Nancy," cried Pete; but he was full of childlike delight.

Kate stepped inside. The fire burned in the hall parlour, the fire-irons shone like glass, there were sprigs of fuchsia-bud in the ornaments on the chimneypiece—everything was warm and cheerful and homelike. She sat down without taking off her hat. "Why can't I be quiet and happy?" she thought. "Why can't I make myself love him and forget?"

But she was like one who traversed a desert under the sea—a vast submerged Sahara. Over her head was all her life, with all her love and all her happiness, and the things around her were only the ghostly shadows cast by them.

IX.

The more Kate realised that she was in the position of a bad woman, the more she struggled to be a good one. She flew to religion as a refuge. There was no belief in her religion, no faith, no creed, no mystical transports, but only fear, and shame, and contrition. It was fervent enough, nevertheless. On Sunday morning she went to The Christians, on Sunday afternoon to church, on Sunday evening to the Wesleyan chapel, and on Wednesday night to the mission-house of the Primitives. Her catholicity did not please her father. He looked into her quivering face, and asked if she had broken any commandment in secret. She turned pale, and answered "No."

Pete followed her wherever she went, and, seeing this, some of the baser sort among the religious people began to follow him. They abused each other badly in their efforts to lay hold of his money-bags. "You'll never go over to yonder lot," said one. "They're holding to election—a soul-destroying doctrine." "A respectable man can't join himself to Cowley's gang," said another. "They're denying original sin, and aren't a ha'p'orth better than infidels."

Pete took the measure of them all, down to the watch-pockets of their waistcoats.

"You remind me," said he, "when you're a-gate on your doctrines, of the Kaffirs out at Kimberley. If one of them found an ould hat in the compound that some white man had thrown away, they'd light a camp-fire after dark, and hould a reg'lar Tynwald Coort on it. There they'd be squatting round on their haunches, with nothing to be seen of them but their eyes and their teeth, and there'd be as many questions as the Catechism. '*Who* found it!' says one. '*Where* did he find it?' says another. 'If *he* hadn't found it, who else would have found it?' That's how they'd be going till two in the morning, and the fire dead out, and the lot of them squealing away same as monkeys in the dark. And all about an ould hat with a hole in it, not worth a ha'penny piece."

"Blasphemy," they cried. "But still and for all, you give to the widow and lend to the Lord—you practise the religion you don't believe in, Cap'n Quilliam."

"There's a pair of us, then." said Pete, "for you believe in the religion you don't practise."

But Cæsar got Pete at last, in spite of his scepticism. The time came for the annual camp-meeting. Kate went off to it, and Pete followed like a big dog at her heels. The company assembled at Sulby Bridge, and marched through the village to a revival chorus. They stopped at a field of Cæsar's in the glen—it was last year's Melliah field—and Cæsar mounted a cart which had been left there to serve as a pulpit. Then they sang again, and, breaking up into many companies, went off into little circles that were like gorse rings on the mountains. After that they reassembled to the strains of another chorus, and gathered afresh about the cart for Cæsar's sermon.

It dealt with the duty of sinless perfection. There were evil men and happy sinners in the island these days, who were telling them it was not good to be faultless in this life, because virtue begot pride, and pride was a deadly sin. There were others who were saying that because a man must repent in order to be saved, to repent he had to sin. Doctrines of the devil—don't listen to them. Could a man in the household of faith live one second without committing sin? Of course he could. One minute? Certainly. One hour? No doubt of it. Then, if a man could live one hour without sin, he could live one day, one week, one month, one year—nay, a whole lifetime.

In getting thus far, Cæsar had worked himself into a perspiration, and he took off his coat, hung it over the cartwheel, and went on in his shirt-sleeves. Let them make no excuses for backsliders. It was a trick of the devil to deal with you, and forget to pay strap (the price). It was an old rule and a good one that, if any were guilty of the sins of the flesh, they should be openly punished in this world, that their sins might not be counted against them in the day of the Lord.

Cæsar threw off his waistcoat and finished with a passionate exhortation, calling upon his hearers to deliver themselves of secret sins. If oratory is to be judged of by its effects, Cæsar's sermon was a great oration. It began amid the silence of his own followers, and the *tschts* and *pshaws* of a little group of his enemies, who lounged on the outside of the crowd to cast ridicule on the "swaddler" and the "publican preacher." But it ended amid loud exclamations of praise and supplications from all his hearers, sighing and groaning, and the bodily clutching of one another by the arm in paroxysms of fear and rapture.

When Cæsar's voice died down like a wave of the sea, somebody leapt up from the grass to pray. And before the first prayer had ended, a second was begun. Meantime the penitents had begun to move inward through the throng, and they fell weeping and moaning on their knees about the cart. Kate was among them, and, when she took her place, Pete still held by her side A strong shuddering passed over her shoulders, and her wet eyes were on the grass. Pete took her hand, and feeling how it trembled, his own eyes also filled. Above their heads Cæsar was towering with fiery eyes and face aflame. In a momentary pause between two prayers, he tossed his voice up in a hymn. The people joined him at the second bar, and then the wailing of the penitents was drowned in a general shout of the revival tune—

```
"If some poor wandering child of Thine
Have spurned to-day the voice divine,
Now, Lord, the gracious work begin,
Let him no more lie down in sin."
```

Kate sobbed aloud—poor vessel of human passions tossed about, tormented by the fire that was consuming her.

As the penitents grew calmer, they rose one by one to give their experience of Satan and salvation. At length Cæsar seized his opportunity and said, "And now Brother Quilliam will give us his experience."

Pete rose from Kate's side with tearful eyes amid a babel of jubilation, most of it facetious. "Be of good cheer, Peter, be not afraid."

"I've not much to tell," said Pete—"only a story of backsliding. Before I earned enough to carry me up country, I worked a month at Cape Town with the boats. My master was a pious old Dutchman getting the name of Jan. One Saturday night a big ship lost her anchor outside, and on Sunday morning forty pounds was offered for finding it. All the boatmen went out except Jan. 'Six days shalt thou labour,' says he, 'but the seventh is the Sabbath.'"

Pete's address was here punctuated by loud cries of thanksgiving.

"All day long he was seeing the boats beating up the bay, so, to keep out of temptation, he was going up to the bedroom and pulling the blind and getting down on his knees and wrastling like mad. And something out of heaven was saying to him, 'It's the Lord's day, Jannie; they'll not get a ha'p'orth.' Neither did they; but when Jan's watch said twelve o'clock midnight the pair of us were going off like rockets. Well, we hadn't been ten minutes on the water before our grapplings had hould of that anchor."

There were loud cries of "Glory!"

"Jan was shouting, 'The Lord has put us atop of it as straight as the lid of a taypot!'"

Great cries of "Hallelujah!"

"But when we came ashore we found Jan's watch was twenty minutes fast, and that was the end of the ould man's religion."

That day the word went round that both Pete and Kate had been converted. Their names were entered in Class, and they received their quarterly tickets.

X.

Next morning Kate set out to church for her churching. Her household duties had lost their interest by this time, and she left Nancy to cook the dinner. Pete had volunteered to take charge of the child. This he began to do by establishing himself with his pipe in an armchair by the cradle, and looking steadfastly down into it until the little one awoke. Then he rocked it, rummaged his memory for a nursery song to quiet it, and smoked and sang together.

> "A frog he would a-wooing go,
> *Kitty alone, Kitty alone,*
> (Puff, puff.)
> A wonderful likely sort of a beau,
> *Kitty alone and I!*"
> *(Puff, puff, puff.)*

The sun was shining in at the doorway, and a man's shadow fell across the cradle-head. It was Philip. Pete put his mouth out into the form of an unspoken "Hush," and Philip sat down in silence, while Pete went on with his smoke and his song.

> "But when her husband rat came home,
> *Kitty alone, Kitty alone,*
> Pray who's been here since I've been gone?
> *Kitty alone and I!*" *(Puff, Puff)*

Pete had got to the middle of the verse about "the worthy gentleman," when the low whine in the cradle lengthened to a long breath and stopped.

"Gone off at last, God bless it," said Pete. "And how's yourself, Philip? And how goes the petition?"

With his head on his hand, Philip was gazing absently into the fire, and he did not hear.

"How goes the petition?" said Pete.

"It was that I came to speak of," said Philip. "Sorry to say it has had no effect but a bad one. It has only drawn attention to the fact that Manx fishermen pay no harbour dues."

"And right too," said Pete. "The harbours are our fathers' harbours, and were freed to us forty years ago."

"Nevertheless," said Philip, "the dues are to be demanded. The Governor has issued an order."

"Then we'll rise against it—every fisherman in the island," said Pete. "And when they're making you Dempster, you'll back us up in the Tynwald Coort."

"Take care, Pete, take care," said Philip.

Then Kate came in from church, and Pete welcomed her with a shout. Philip rose and bowed in silence. The marks of the prayers of the week were on her face, but they had brought her no comfort. She had been constantly promising herself consolation from religion, but every fresh exercise of devotion had seemed to tear open the wound from which she bled to death.

She removed her cloak and stepped to the cradle. The child was sleeping peacefully, but she convinced herself that it must be unwell. Her own hands were cold and moist, and when she touched the child she thought its skin was clammy. Presently her hands became hot and dry, and when she touched the child again she thought its forehead was feverish.

"I'm sure she's ill," she said.

"Chut! love," said Pete; "no more ill than I am."

But, to calm her fears, he went off for the doctor. The doctor was away in the country, and was not likely to be back for hours. Kate's fears increased. Every time she looked at the child she applied to it the symptoms of her own condition.

"My child is dying—I'm sure it is," she cried.

"Nonsense, darling," said Pete. "Only an hour ago it was looking up as imperent as a tomtit."

At last a new terror seized her, and she cried, "My child is dying unbaptized."

"Well, we'll soon mend that, love," said Pete. "I'll be going off for the parson." And he caught up his hat and went out.

He called on Parson Quiggin, who promised to follow immediately. Then he went on to Sulby to fetch Cæsar and Grannie and some others, having no fear for the child's life, but some hope of banishing Kate's melancholy by the merriment of a christening feast.

Meanwhile, Philip and Kate were alone with the little one, save in the intervals of Nancy's coming and going between the hall and the kitchen. She was restless, and full of expectation, starting at every sound and every step. He could see that she had gone whole nights without sleep, and was passing through an existence that was burning itself away.

Do what he would to explain her sufferings as the common results of childbirth, he could not help resolving them in the old flattering solution. She was paying the penalty of having married the wrong man. And she was to blame. Whatever the compulsion put upon her, she ought to have withstood it. There was no situation in life from which it was not possible to escape. Had *he* not found a way out of a situation essentially the same? Thus a certain high pride in his own conduct took possession of him even in the presence of Kate's pain.

But his tenderness fought with his self-righteousness. He looked at her piteous face and his strength almost ebbed away. She looked up into his eyes and affectionate pity almost overwhelmed him. Once or twice she seemed about to say something, but she did not speak, and he said little. Yet it wanted all his resolution not to take her in his arms and comfort her, not to mingle his tears with hers, not to tell her of six months spent in vain in the effort to wipe her out of his heart, not to whisper of cheerless days and of nights made desolate with the repetition of her name. But no, he would be stronger than that. It was not yet too late to walk the path of honour. He would stand no longer between husband and wife.

Pete came back, bringing Grannie and Cæsar. The parson arrived soon after them. Kate was sitting with the child in her lap, and brooding over it like a bird above its nest. The child was still sleeping the sleep of health and innocence, but the mother's eyes were wild.

"Bogh, bogh!" said Grannie, and she kissed her daughter. Kate made no response. Nancy Joe grew red about the eyelids and began to blow her nose.

"Here's the prazon, darling," whispered Pete, and Kate rose to her feet. The company rose with her, and stood in a half-circle before the fire. It was now between daylight and dark, and the firelight flashed in their faces.

"Are the godfather and godmothers present?" the parson asked.

"Mr. Christian will stand godfather, parzon; and Nancy and Grannie will be godmothers."

Nancy took the child out of Kate's arms, and the service for private baptism began with the tremendous words, "Dearly beloved, forasmuch as all men are conceived and born in si——"

The parson stopped. Kate had staggered and almost fallen. Pete put his arm around her to keep her up, and then the service went on.

Presently the parson turned to Philip with a softening voice and an inclination of the head.

"Dost thou, in the name of this child, renounce the devil and all his works, the vain pomp and glory of the world, with all covetous desires of 'the same, and the carnal desires of the flesh, so that thou wilt not follow nor be led by them?"

And Philip answered, in a firm, low voice, "I renounce them all."

The parson took the child from Nancy. "Name this child."

Nancy looked at Kate, but Kate, who was breathing violently, gave no sign.

"Kate," whispered Pete; "Kate, of coorse."

"Katherine," said Nancy, and in that name the child was baptized.

Dr. Mylechreest came in as the service ended. Grannie held little Katherine up to him, and he controlled his face and looked at her.

"There's not much amiss with the child," he said.

"I knew it," shouted Pete.

"But perhaps the mother is a little weak and nervous," he added quietly.

"Coorse she is, the bogh," cried Pete.

"Let her see more company," said the doctor.

"She shall," said Pete.

"If that doesn't do, send her away for awhile."

"I will."

"Fresh scenes, fresh society; out of the island, by preference."

"I'm willing."

"She'll come back another woman."

"I'll put up with the same one," said Pete; and, while the company laughed, he flung open the door, and cried "Come in!" and half a dozen men who had been waiting outside trooped into the hall. They entered with shy looks because of the presence of great people.

"Now for a pull of jough, Nancy," cried Pete.

"Not too much excitement either," said the doctor, and with that warning he departed. The parson went with him. Philip had slipped out first, unawares to anybody. Grannie carried little Katherine to the kitchen, and bathed her before the fire. Kate was propped up with pillows in the armchair in the corner. Then Nancy brought the ale, and Pete welcomed it with a shout. Cæsar looked alarmed and rose to go.

"The drink's your own, sir," said Pete; "stop and taste it."

But Cæsar couldn't stay; it would scarcely be proper.

"You don't christen your first granddaughter every day," said Pete. "Enjoy yourself while you're alive, sir; you'll be a long time dead."

Cæsar disappeared, but the rest of the company took Pete's counsel, and began to make themselves comfortable.

"The last christening I was at was yesterday," said John the Clerk. "It was Christian Killip's little one, before she was married, and it took the water same as any other child."

"The last christening I was at was my own," said Black Tom, "when I was made an in inheriter, but I've never inherited yet."

"That's truth enough," said an asthmatic voice from the backstairs.

"Well, the last christening I was at was at Kimberley," said Pete, "and I was the parzon myself that day. Yes, though, Parzon Pete. And godfather and godmother as well, and the baby was Peter Quilliam, too. Aw, it was no laughing matter at all. There's always a truck of women about a compound, hanging on to the boys like burrs. Dirty little trousses of a rule, but human creatures for all. One of them had a child by somebody, and then she came to die, and couldn't take rest because it hadn't been christened. There wasn't a pazon for fifty miles, anywhere, and it was night-time, too, and the woman was stretched by the camp-fire and sinking. 'What's to be done?' says the men. *I'll* do it,' says I, and I did. One of the fellows got a breakfast can of water out of the river, and I dipped my hand in it. 'What's the name,' says I; but the poor soul was too far gone for spaking. So I gave the child my own name, though I didn't know the mother from Noah's aunt, and the big chaps standing round bareheaded began to blubber like babies. 'I baptize thee, Peter Quilliam, in the name of the Father, and of the

Son, and of the Holy Ghost, Amen.' Then the girl died happy and aisy, and what for shouldn't she? The words were the same, and the water was the same, and if the hand wasn't as clane as usual, maybe Him that's above wouldn't bother about the diff'rance."

Kate got up with a flush on her cheeks. The room had become too close. Pete helped her into the parlour, where a bright fire was burning, then propped and wrapped her up afresh, and, at her own entreaty, returned to his guests. The company had increased by this time, and there were women and girls among them. They went on to sing and to playt and at last to dance.

Kate heard them. Through the closed door between the hall and the parlour their merriment came to her. At intervals Pete put in his head, brimming over with laughter, and cried in a loud whisper, "Did you hear that, Kate? It's rich!"

At length Philip came, too, with his hat in one hand and a cardboard box in the other. "The godfather's present to little Katherine," he said.

Kate opened the lid, and drew out a child's hood in scarlet plush.

"You are very good," she said vacantly.

"Don't let us talk of goodness," he answered; and he turned to go.

"Wait," she faltered. "I have something to say to you. Shut the door."

XI.

Philip turned pale. "What is it?" he asked.

She tried to speak, but at first she could not.

"Are you unhappy, Kate?" he faltered.

"Can't you see?" she answered.

He sat down by the fire, and leaned his face on his hands. "Yes, we have both suffered," he said, in a low tone.

"Why did you let me marry him?"

Philip raised his head. "How could I have hindered you?"

"How? Do you ask me how?" She spoke with some bitterness, but he answered quietly.

"I tried, Kate, but I could do nothing. You seemed determined. Do what I would to prevent, to delay, to stop your marriage altogether, the more you hastened and hurried it. Then I thought to myself, Well, perhaps it is best. She is trying to forget and forgive, and begin again. What right have I to stand in her way? Haven't I wronged her enough already? A good man offers her his love, and she is taking it. Let her do so, if she can, God help her! I may suffer, but I am nothing to her now. Let me go my way."

She put her arms on the table, and hid her face in them. "Oh, I cannot bear it," she said.

He rose to his feet slowly. "If it is my presence here that hurts you, Kate, I will go away. It has been but a painful pleasure to come, and I have been forced to take it. You will acquit me of coming of my own choice, Kate. But I will not torment you. I will go away, and never come again."

She lifted her face, and said in a passionate whisper, "Take me with you."

He shook his head. "That's impossible, Kate. You are married now. Your husband loves you dearly. He is a better man than I am, a thousand, thousand times."

"Do you think I don't know what he is?" she cried, throwing herself back. "That's why I can't live with him. It's killing me. I tell you I can't bear it," she cried, rising to her feet. "Love me! Haven't I tried to make myself love *him*. Haven't I tried to be a good wife! I can't—I can't. He never speaks but he torments me. Nothing can happen but it cuts me through and through. I can't live in this house. The walls are crushing me, the ceiling is falling on me, the air is stifling me. I tell you I shall die if you do not take me out of it. Take me, Philip, take me, take me!"

She caught him by the arm imploringly, but he only dropped his head down between both hands, saying in a deep thick voice, "Hush, Kate, hush! I cannot and I will not. You are mad to think of it."

Then she sank down into the chair again, breathless and inert, and sobbing deep, low sobs. The sound of dancing came from the hall, with cries of "Hooch!" and the voice of Pete shouting—

   "Hit the floor with heel and toe
   'Till heaven help the boords below."

"Yes, I am mad, or soon will be," she said in a hard way. "I thought of that this morning when I crossed the river coming home from church. It would soon be over *there*, I thought. No more trouble, no more dreams, no more waking in the night to hear the breathing of the one beside me, and the voice out of the darkness crying——"

"Kate, what are you saying?" interrupted Philip.

"Oh, you needn't think I'm a bad woman because I ask you take me away from my husband. If I were that, I could brazen it out perhaps, and live on here, and pretend to forget; many a woman does, they say. And I'm not afraid that he will ever find me out either. I have only to close my lips, and he will never know. But *I* shall know, Philip Christian," she said, with a defiant look into his eyes as he raised them.

115

Her reproaches hurt him less than her piteous entreaties, and in a moment she was sobbing again. "Oh, what can God do but let me die! I thought He would when the child came; but He did not, and then—am I a wicked woman, after all?—I prayed that He would take my innocent baby, anyway."

But she dashed the tears away in anger at her weakness, and said, "I'm not a bad woman, Philip Christian; and that's why I won't live here any longer. There is something you have never guessed, and I have never told you; but I must tell you now, for I can keep my secret no longer."

He raised his head with a noise in his ears that was like the flapping of wings in the dark.

"Your secret, Kate?"

"How happy I was," she said. "Perhaps I was to blame—I loved you so, and was so fearful of losing you. Perhaps you thought of all that had passed between us as something that would go back and back as time went on and on. But it has been coming the other way ever since. Yes, and as long as I live and as long as the child lives——"

Her voice quivered like the string of a bow and stopped. He rose to his feet.

"The child, Kate? Did you say the child?"

She did not answer at once, and then she muttered, with her head down, "Didn't I tell you there was something you had never guessed?"

"And is it that?" he said in a fearful whisper.

"Yes."

"You are sure? You are not deceiving yourself? This is not hysteria?"

"No."

"You mean that the child——"

"Yes."

His questions had come in gasps, like short breakers out of a rising sea; her answers had fallen like the minute-gun above it. Then, in the silence, Pete's voice came through the wall. He was singing a rough old ditty—

"It was to Covent Gardens I chanced for to go,
To see some of the prettiest flowers which in the gardens grow."

Nancy came in with a scuttle of coals. "The lil one's asleep," she said, going down on her knees at the fire. She had left the door ajar, and Pete's song was rolling into the room—

"The first was lovely Nancy, so delicate and fair,
The other was a vargin, and she did laurels wear."

"Grannie bathed her, and she's like a lil angel in the cot there," said Nancy. "And, 'Dear heart alive, Grannie,' says I,' the straight she's like her father when she's sleeping.'"

Nancy brushed the hearth and went off. As she closed the door, Pete's voice ebbed out.

Philip's lips trembled, his eyes wandered over the floor, he grew very pale, he tried to speak and could not. All his self-pride was overthrown in a moment The honour in which he had tried to stand erect as in a suit of armour was stripped away. Unwittingly he had been laying up an account with Nature. He had forgotten that a sin has consequences. Nature did not forget. She had kept her own reckoning. He had struggled to believe that after all he was a moral man, a free man; but Nature was a sterner moralist; she had chained him to the past, she had held him to himself.

He was still by the fire with his head down. "Did you know this before you were married to Pete?" he asked, without looking up.

"Hadn't I wronged him enough without that?" she answered.

"But did you think of it as something that might perhaps occur?"

"And if I did, what then?"

"If you had told me, Kate, nothing and nobody should have come between us—no," he said in a decisive voice, "not Pete nor all the world."

"And wasn't it your own duty to remember? Was it for me to come to you and say, 'Philip, something may happen, I am frightened.'"

Was this the compulsion that had driven her into marriage with the wrong man? Was it all hysteria? Could she be sure? In any case she could not think this awful thought and continue to live with her husband.

"You are right," he said, with his head still down. "You cannot live here any longer. This life of deception must end."

"Then you will take me away, Philip?"

"I must, God forgive me, I must. I thought it would be sin. But *that* was long ago. It will be punishment. If I had known before—and I have been coming here time and again—looking on his happiness—but if I had once dreamt—and then only an hour ago—the oath at its baptism—O God!"

Her tears were flowing again, but a sort of serenity had fallen on her now.

"Forgive me," she whispered. "I tried to keep it to myself——"

"You could not keep it; you ought never to have kept it so long; the finger of God Himself ought to have burnt it out of you."

He spoke harshly, and she felt pain; but there was a secret joy as well.

"I am ruining you, Philip," she said, leaning over him.

"We are both drifting to ruin, Katherine," he answered hoarsely. He was an abandoned hulk, with anchorage gone and no hand at the helm—broken, blind, rolling to destruction.

116

"I can offer you nothing, Kate, nothing but a hidden life, a life in the dark. If you come to me you will leave a husband who worships you for one to whom your life can never be joined. You will exchange a life of respect by the side of a good man for a life of humiliation, a life of shame. How can it be otherwise now? It is too late, too late!"

"Don't think of that, Philip. If you love me there can be no humiliation and no shame for me in anything. I love you, dear, I cannot help but love you. Only love me a little, Philip, just a little, dearest, and I will never care—no, I will never, never care whatever happens."

Her passionate devotion swept down all his scruples. His throat thickened, his eyes grew dim. She put one arm tenderly on his shoulder.

"I will follow you wherever you must go," she said. "You are my real husband, Philip, and always have been. We will love one another, and that will make up for everything. There is nothing I will not do to make you forget. If you must go away—far away—no matter where—I will go with you—and the child as well—and if we must be poor, I'll work with you."

But he did not seem to hear her as he crouched with buried face by the fire. And, in the silence, Pete's muffled voice came again through the wall, singing his rugged ditty—

> "I'm not engaged to any young man, I solemnly do swear,
> For I mane to be a vargin and still the laurels wear."

Unconsciously their hands touched and their fingers intertwined.

"It will break his heart," he muttered.

She only grasped his hand the closer, and crouched beside him. They were like two guilty souls at the altar steps, listening to the cheerful bell that swings in the tower for the happy world outside.

The door opened with a bang, and Pete rolled in, heaving with laughter.

"Did you think it was an earth wake, Philip?" he shouted, "or a blackbird a bit tipsy, eh? Bless me, man, it's good of you, though, sitting up in the chimney there same as a good ould jackdaw, keeping the poor wife company when her selfish ould husband is flirting his tail like a stonechat. The company's going now, Kitty. Will they say good-night to you? No? Have it as you like, bogh. You're looking tired, anyway. Dempster, the boys are asking when the ceremony is coming off, and will you come home to Ramsey that night? But, sakes alive, man, your eye is splashed with blood as bad as the egg of a robin."

In his suffering and degradation, Philip felt as if he wished the earth to open and swallow him.

"Bloodshot, is it?" he said. "It's nothing. The ceremony? I'm to take the oath to-morrow at three o'clock at the Special Council in Douglas. Yes, I'll come back to Ballure for the night?"

"Driving, eh?"

"Yes."

"Six o'clock, maybe?"

"Perhaps seven to eight."

"That's all right. Mortal inquisitive the boys are, though. It's in the breed of these Manx ones, you know. Laxey way, now?"

"I'll drive by St. John's," said Philip.

With a look of wondrous wisdom, and a knowing wink at Kate across Philip's back, Pete went out. Then there was much talking in low tones in the hall, and on the paths outside the house.

Philip understood what it meant. He glanced back at the door, leaned over to Kate, and said in a whisper, without looking into her eyes—

"The carriage shall come at half-past seven. It will stand for a moment in the Parsonage Lane, and then drive back to Douglas by way of Laxey."

His face was broken and ugly with shame and humiliation. As she saw this she thought of her confession, and it seemed odious to her now; but there was an immense relief in the feeling that the crisis was over.

Pete was shouting at the porch, "Good-night, all! Goodnight!"

"Good-night!" came back in many voices.

Grannie came in muffled up to the throat. "However am I to get back to Sulby, and your father gone these two hours?" she said.

"Not him," said Pete, coming behind with one eye screwed up and a finger to his nose. "The ould man's been on the back-stairs all night, listening and watching wonderful. His bark's tremenjous, but his bite isn't worth mentioning."

And then a plaintive voice came from the hall, saying, "Are you *never* coming home, mother? I'm worn out waiting for you."

A little patch of youth had blossomed in Grannie since the baby came.

"Good-night, Pete," she cried from the gate, "and many happy returns of the christening-day."

"One was enough for yourself, mother," said Cæsar, and then his voice went rumbling down the street.

Philip had come out into the hall. "You're time enough yet," said Pete. "A glass first? No? I've sent over to the 'Mitre' for your mare. There she is; that's her foot on the path. I must be seeing you off, anyway. Where's that lantern, at all?"

They stepped out. Pete held the light while Philip mounted, and then he guided him, under the deep shadow of the old tree, to the road.

"Fine night for a ride, Phil. Listen! That's the churning of the nightjar going up to Ballure glen. Well, good-night! Good-night, and God bless you, old fellow!"

Kate inside heard the deadened sound of Philip's "Goodnight," the crunch of the mare's hoofs on the gravel and the clink of the bit in her teeth. Then the porch door closed with a hollow vibration like that of a vault, the chain rattled across it, and Pete was back in the room.

"*What* a night we've had of it! And now to bed."

XII.

Kate was up early the next morning, but Pete was stirring before her. As soon as he had heard the news of Philip's appointment he had organised a drum and brass band to honour the day of the ceremony. The brass had been borrowed from Laxey, but the drum had been bought by Pete.

"Let's have a good sizable drum," said he; "something with a voice in it, not a bit of a toot, going off with a pop like bladder-wrack."

The parchment was three feet across, the steel rings round it were like the hoops of a dog-cart, and the black drumsticks, according to Pete, were like the bullet heads of two niggers. Jonaique Jelly played the clarionet, and John the Widow played the trombone, but the drum was the leading instrument. Pete himself played it. He pounded it, boomed it, thundered it. While he did so, his eyes blazed with rapture. A big heroic soul spoke out of the drum for Pete. With the strap over his shoulders, he did not trouble much about the tune. When the heart Leapt inside his breast, down came the nigger heads on to the mighty protuberance in front of it; and surely that was the end and aim of all music.

The band practised in the cabin which Pete had set up for a summer-house in the middle of his garden. They met at daybreak that morning for the last of their rehearsals. And, being up before their morning meal, they were constrained to smoke and drink as well as play. This they did out of a single pipe and a single pot, which each took up from the table in turn as it fell to his part to have a few bars' rest.

While their muffled melody came to the house through the wooden walls and the dense smoke, Kate was cooking breakfast. She did everything carefully, for she was calmer than usual, and felt relieved of the load that had oppressed her. But once she leaned her head on the mantelshelf while stooping over the frying-pan, and looked vacantly into the fire; and once she raised herself up from the table-cloth at the sound of the drum, and pressed her hand hard on her brow.

The child awoke in the bedroom above and cried. Nancy Joe went flip-flapping upstairs, and brought her down with much clucking and cackling. Kate took the child and fed her from a feeding-bottle which had been warming on the oven top. She was very tender with the little one, kissing all its extremities in the way that women have, worrying its legs, and putting its feet into her mouth.

Pete came in, hot and perspiring, and Kate handed the child back to Nancy.

"Hould hard," cried Pete; "don't take her off yet. Give me a hould of her, the lil rogue. My sailor! What a child it is, though! Look at that, now. She's got a grip of my thumb. What a fist, to be sure! It's lying in my hand like a meg. Did you stick a piece of dough on the wall at your last baking, Nancy? Just as well to keep the evil eye off. Coo—oo—oo! She's going it reg'lar, same as the tide of a summer's day. By jing, Kitty, I didn't think there was so much fun in babies."

Kate, seated at the table, was pouring out the tea, and a sudden impulse seized her.

"That's the way," she said. "First the wife is everything; but the child comes, and then good-bye to the mother who brought it."

"No, by gough!" said Pete. "The child is eighteen carat goold for the mother's sake, but the mother is di'monds for sake of the child. If I lost that little one, Kitty, it would be like losing the half of you."

"Losing, indeed!" said Nancy. "Who's talking about losing? Does she look like it, bless her lil heart!"

"Take her into the kitchen, Nancy," said Kate.

"Going to have a rare do to-day," said Pete, over a mouthful. "I'm off for Douglas, to see Philip made Dempster. Coming home with himself by way of St. John's. It's all arranged, woman. Boys to meet the carriage by Kirk Christ Lezayre at seven o'clock smart. Then out I'm getting, laying hould of the drum, the band is striking up, and we're bringing him into Ramsey triumphant. Oh, we'll be doing it grand," said Pete, blowing over the rim of his saucer. "John the Clerk is tremenjous on the trombones, and there's no bating Jonaique with the clar'net—the man is music to his little backbone. The town will be coming out too, and the fishermen shouting like one man. We're bound to let the Governor see we mane it. A friend's a friend, say I, and we're for bucking up for the man that's bucking up for us. And when he goes to the Tynwald Coort there, it'll be lockjaw and the measles with some of them. If the ould Governor's got a tongue like a file, Philip's got a tongue like a scythe—he'll mow them down. 'No harbour-dues,' says he, 'till we've a raisonable hope of harbour improvements. Build your embankments for your trippers in Douglas if you like, but don't ask the fisher-, men to pay for them.'"

Pete wiped his mouth and charged his pipe. "It'll be a rare ould dust, but we're not thinking of ourselves only, though. Aw, no, no. If there wasn't nothing doing we would be giving him a little tune for all, coming home Dempster."

Pete lit up. "My sailor! It'll be a proud man I'll be this day, Kitty. Didn't I always say it? 'He'll be the first Manxman living,' says I times and times, and he's not going to de-ceave me neither."

Kate was in fear lest Pete should look up into her face. Catching sight of a rent in the cloth of his coat, she whipped out her needle and began to stitch it up, bending closely over it.

"What an eye a woman's got now," said Pete. "That was the steel of the drum ragging me sideways when I was a bit excited. Bless me, Kitty, there won't be a rag left at me when I get through this everin'. They're ter'ble on clothes is drums."

He was puffing the smoke through her hair as she knelt below him. "Well, he deserves it all. My sakes, the years I've known him! Him and me have been same as brothers. Yes, have we, ever since I was a slip of a boy in jackets, and we went nesting on Maughold Head together. And getting married hasn't been making no difference. When a man marries he shortens sail usually, and pitches out some ballast, but not me at all. You're taking a chill, Kitty. No? Shuddering any way. Chut! This dress is like paper; you should be having warmer things under it. Don't be going out to-day, darling, but to-night, about twenty-five minutes better than seven, just open the door and listen. We'll be agate of it then like mad, and when you're hearing the drum booming you'll be saying to yourself, 'Pete's there, and going it for all he knows.'"

"Oh, Pete, Pete!" cried Kate, and she dropped back at his feet

"Why, what's this at all?" said Pete.

"You've been very, very good to me, Pete, and if I never see you again you'll think the best of me, will you not?"

She had an impulse to tell all—she could hardly resist it.

He smoothed the black ripples of her hair back from her forehead, and said, tenderly, "She's not so well to-day, that's it. Her eyes are bubbling like the laver." Then aloud, with a laugh, "Never see me again, eh? I'm not willing to share you with heaven yet, though. But I'll have to be doing as the doctor was saying—sending you to England aver. I will now, I will," he said, lifting his big finger threateningly.

She slid backwards to the ground, but at the next moment was landed on Pete's breast. "My poor lil Kirry! Not willing to stay with me, eh? Tut, tut! She'll be as smart as ever, soon."

She drew away from him with shame and self-reproach, mingled with that old feeling of personal repulsion which she could not conquer.

Then the gate of the garden clicked, and Ross Christian came up the path. "He's sticking to me as tight as a limpet," said Pete.

"Mr. Quilliam," said Ross, "I come from my father this time."

"'Deed, man," said Pete.

"He is a little pressed for money."

"And Mr. Peter Christian sends to me?"

"He thought you might like to lend on mortgage."

"On Ballawhaine?"

Ross stammered and stuttered, "Well, yes, certainly, as you say, on Balla——"

"To think, to think," muttered Pete. He gazed vacantly before him for a moment, and then said, sharply, "I've no time to talk of it now, sir. I'm off to Douglas, but if you like to stop awhile and talk of it with Mrs. Quilliam, I'll be hearing everything when I come back. Good-day, Kate. Take care of my wife. Good-day, Nancy; look after my two girls while I'm away. And Kitty, bogh" (whispering), "mind you send to Robbie Clucas, the draper, for some nice warm underclothing. Good-bye! Another! Just one more" (then aloud) "Good-day to you, sir, good-day."

XIII.

"... He, the Spirit Himself, may come
When all the nerve of sense is numb."

Philip had not slept at Ballure. The house was in darkness as he passed. He was riding to Douglas. It is sixteen miles between town and town, six of them over the steep headland of Kirk Maughold. Before he reached the top of the ascent he had been an hour on the road, and the night was near to morning. He had seen no one after leaving Ramsey, except a drunken miner with his bundle on his stick, marching home to a tipsy travesty of some brave song.

His self-righteousness was overthrown; his pride was in the dust. Since he returned home, he had struggled to feel strong and easy in the sense of being an honourable man; but now he was thrown violently out of the path in which he had meant to walk rightly. What he was about to do was necessary, was inevitable, yet in his relation to Kate he was in the position of an immoral man, a betrayer, an adulterer, with a vulgar secret, which he must support by lying and share with servants. And what was the outlook? What would be the end? Here was a situation from which there was no escape. Let there be no false glamour, no disguise, no self-deception. On the eve of his promotion to the dignities and responsibilities of a Judge, he was taking the first step down on the course of the criminal!

The moon was shining at the full. It was low down in the sky, on his right, and casting his shadow on to the road. He walked his horse up the long hill. The even pace, the quiet of the night, the drowsy sounds of unseen stream and far-off murmuring sea overcame him in spite of himself, and he dozed in the saddle. As he reached the hilltop the level step of the horse awoke him, and he knew that he was passing that desolate spot on the border of parish and parish which is known as Tom Alone's.

Opening his eyes, without realising that he had slept, he thought he became aware of another horse and another rider walking by his side. They were on the left of him, going pace for pace, stepping along with him like his shadow. "It *is* my shadow," he thought, and he forced up his head to look. Nothing was there but a whitewashed wall that fenced a sheepfold. The moon had gone under the mountains on the right, and the night would have been dark but for the stars. With an astonishment near to terror, Philip gripped the saddle with his quaking knees, and broke his horse into a trot.

When the hard ride had brought warmth to his blood and a glow to his cheeks, he told himself he had been the victim of fancy. It was nothing; it was a delusion of the sight; a mere shadow cast off by his distempered brain. He was passing at a walking pace through Laxey by this time, and as the horse's feet beat up the echoes of the sleeping town, his heart grew brave.

Next day, at noon, he was talking with his servant, Jem-y-Lord, in his rooms in Athol Street. He had lately become tenant of the entire house. They were in his old chambers on the first floor, looking on to the churchyard.

119

"I may rely on you, Jemmy?"

"You may, Deemster."

His voice was low and husky, his eyes were down, he was fumbling the papers on the table. "Get the carriage, a landau, from Shimmin's, but drive it yourself. Be at Government offices at four—we'll go by St. John's. If there is any attempt at Ramsey to take the horse out of the carriage, resist it. I will alight at the head of the town. Then drive on to the lane between the chapel and Elm Cottage. The moment the lady joins you, start away. Return to Laxey—are the rooms upstairs ready?"

"They will be."

"The two in front of your own, and the little parlour behind this. We shall need no other servants—the lady will be housekeeper."

"I quite understand, Deemster."

Philip turned his face aside and spoke thickly, "And you know what name——"

"I know what name, Deemster."

"You have no objection?"

"None whatever, Deemster."

Phillip drew a long breath. "I am not Deemster yet, Jemmy. Perhaps it might have been... but God knows. You are a good fellow—I shall not forget it."

He made a motion as if to dismiss the man, but Jemmy did not go.

"Beg pardon, your honor—"

"Yes?"

"Your honour has eaten nothing at breakfast—and the bed wasn't slept in last night."

"I was riding late—then I had work to do."

"But I heard your foot on the floor—-it woke me times."

"I may have speeches to make to-day.... Fetch me a glass of water."

Jemmy brought water-bottle and glass. As Philip took the water an icy numbness seemed to seize his arm. "I—well, I—I declare I can't lift—ah! thanks."

The man raised Philip's arm to his mouth; the glass rattled against his teeth while he drank.

"Pardon, your honour. You're looking ten years older lately. The sooner this day is over the better."

"Sleep, Jemmy—I only want sleep. I must have a long, long sleep at Ballure to-night."

He left the house at three minutes to three, carrying his cloak over his arm. It was a hot day at the beginning of June, and when he stepped out at the door the air of the street smote his face like a blast from an open furnace. He reeled and almost fell. The sun's heat was like a load on his head, its dazzling rays made his sight dim, and he had a sound in his ears like running water. As he walked down the street he caught his wandering reflection in the shop windows. "Jemmy was right," he thought. "My worst enemy would not accuse me of looking too young to-day."

There was a small crowd about the entrance to Government offices. Carriages were driving up, discharging their occupants and going on. The Bishop, the Attorney-General, finally the Governor with his wife and daughter passed into the house. In the commotion of these arrivals Philip reached the door unobserved. When he was recognised, there was a sudden hush of voices, and then a low buzz of gossip. He walked through with a firm step, going in alone, all eyes upon him.

The doorway opens on a narrow passage, which is neither wide nor very light, and the sunshine without made the gloom within more grey and uncertain. As Philip stepped over the threshold he was conscious that somebody was coming out. When he had taken two paces more, he drew up sharply with the sense of walking into a mirror. At the next instant he saw that what he had taken for the reflection of his own face in a glass was the actual face of another man.

The man was coming out as he went in. They were approaching each other. At two paces more they were side by side. He looked at the man with creeping horror. The man looked at him with amazement and dread. Thus, eye to eye, they crossed and passed. Then each turned his head over his shoulder and looked after the other, Philip stepping into the gloom, the stranger striding into the light.

At the next moment the narrow doorway was darkened by a ponderous figure rolling through. Then a heavy hand fell on Philip's shoulder, and a hearty voice exclaimed, "Hilloa, Christian; proud to see you, boy! You've outstripped old stick-in-the-mud; but I always knew you would lead me the way though.... Funking a bit, are you? Hands like ice, anyway. Come along—nothing to be nervous about—we're not going to give you the dose of Illiam Dhone—-don't martyr the Christians these days, you know."

Is was Philip's old master, the Clerk of the Rolls. Taking Philip's arm, he was for swinging him along; but Philip, still looking towards the street, said falteringly, "Did you, perhaps, see a man—a young man—going out at the door?"

"When?"

"As you came in."

"Was there?" said the Clerk dubiously; then, as by a sudden light, "Did he wear a round hat and a monkey-jacket?"

"Maybe—I hardly know—I didn't observe."

"That'll be the man. He's been at me half the morning for admission to the Council. Said he'd known you all his life. Bough as a thorn-bush, but somehow I couldn't say no to the fellow at last. He ought to be inside, though."

"It's nothing," thought Philip. "Only another shadow from a tired brain. Jemmy's talk about my altered looks—the reflection in the shop-windows—the sudden gloom after the dazzling sunlight—that's all, that's all. Sleep, I want sleep."

When the Governor took his seat with the first Deemster on his right, and motioned Philip to the chair on his left, an involuntary murmur passed over the chamber at the contrast there presented—the one Deemster very old, with round, russet face, quick, gleaming eyes, and a comfortable, youthful, even merry expression; the other, very young, with long, pallid, powerful face, large eyes, and a tired look of age.

Philip presented his commission received from the Home Secretary, and the oath of office was administered to him. Kissing a stained copy of a leather-bound Testament, he repeated the words after the Governor in a thick croak that seemed to hack the air—

"By this book, and by the holy contents thereof, and by the wonderful works that God hath miraculously wrought in heaven above and on the earth beneath in six days and seven nights, I, Philip Christian, do swear that I will, without respect of favour or friendship, love or hate, loss or gain, consanguinity or affinity, envy or malice, execute the laws of this Isle justly, betwixt our Sovereign Lady the Queen and her subjects within this Isle, and betwixt party and party, as indifferently as the herring backbone doth lie in the midst of the fish."

As Philip pronounced these words, he was conscious of only one face in that assembly. It was not the face of the Governor, of the Bishop, of any dignitary of Church or State—but a rugged, eager, dark face over a black beard in the grip of a great brown hand, with sparkling eyes, parted lips, and a look of boyish pride—it was the face of Pete.

"It only remains for me," said the Governor, "to congratulate your Honour on the high office to which it has pleased Her Majesty to appoint you, and to wish you long life and health to fulfil its duties, with blameless credit to yourself and distinction to your country."

There was some other speaking, and then Philip replied. He spoke clearly, firmly, and well. A reference to his grandfather provoked applause. His modesty and natural manner made a strong impression. "His Excellency is not so far wrong, after all," was the common whisper.

Some further business, and the Council broke up for general gossip. Then, on the pavement outside, while the carriages were coming in line, there were renewed congratulations, invitations, and warnings. The Governor invited Philip to dinner. He excused himself, saying he had promised to dine with his aunt at Ballure. The ladies warned him to spare himself, and recommended a holiday; and then the Clerk of the Rolls, proud as a peacock, strutting here and there and everywhere, and assuming the airs of a guardian, cried, "Can't yet, though, for he holds his first court in Ramsey tomorrow morning.... Put on the cloak, Christian. It will be cold driving. Good men are scarce."

An open landau came up at length, with Jem-y-Lord on the box-seat, and Pete walking by the horse's head, smoothing its neck and tickling its ears.

"Why, you were talking of the young man, Christian, and behold ye, here's the great fellow himself. Well, young chap," slapping Pete on the back, "see your Deemster take the oath, eh?"

"He's my cousin," said Philip.

"Cousin! Is he, then—can he perhaps be—Ah! yes, of course, certainly————" The good man stammered and stopped, remembering the marriage of Philip's father. He opened the carriage door and stood aside for Philip, but Philip said—

"Step in, Pete;" and, with a shamefaced look, Pete rolled into the carriage. Philip took the seat beside him, amid a buzz of voices from the people standing about the door.

"Well, as you like; good day, then, boy, good day," said the Clerk of the Rolls, clashing the door back. The carriage began to move.

"Good day, your Honour," cried several out of the crowd.

Philip raised his hat. The hats of the men went up to him. Some of the girls were wiping their eyes.

XIV.

While Pete and Philip were driving over the road from Douglas, Kate was sitting with the child on her lap before the fire in Elm Cottage. Her eyes were restless, her manner agitated. She looked out at the window from time to time. The setting sun behind the house still held the day with horizontal shafts of light in the spring green of the transparent leaves.

"Wouldn't you like to see the procession to-night, Nancy?" she said.

"Aw, mortal," said Nancy. "But I won't get lave, though. 'Take care of my two girls,' says he——"

"You may go, Nancy; I'll see to baby," said Kate.

"But the man himself, woman; he'll be coming home as hungry as a hunter."

"I'll see to his supper, too," said Kate. "Carry the key with you that you may let yourself in, and be back at half-past seven."

Then Nancy began to fly about the kitchen like sputter-ings out of the frying-pan—filling the kettle, lighting the lamp, and getting together the baby's night-clothes. Kate watched her and glanced at the clock.

"Was the town quiet when you were out for the bacon, Nancy?" she said.

"Quiet enough," said Nancy. "Everybody flying off Le-zayre way already—except what were making for the quay."

"Is the steamer sailing to-night, then?"

"Yes, the *Peveril*; but not water enough to float her till half-past seven, they were saying. Here's the lil one's nightdress, and here's her binder, bless her—just big enough for a bandage for a person's wrist if she sprained it churning."

"Lay them on the fender to air, Nancy—I'll not undress baby yet awhile. And see—it's nearly seven."

"I'll be pinning my shawl on and away like the wind," said Nancy. "The bogh!" she said, with the pin between her teeth. "She's off again. Do you really think, now, the angels in heaven are as sweet and innocent, Kirry? I don't. They can't if they're grown up. And having to climb Jacob's ladder, poor things, they must be. Then, if they're men—but that's ridiculous, anyway."

"The clock is striking, Nancy. No use going when everything's over," said Kate, and the foot with which she rocked the child went faster now that the little one was asleep.

"Sakes alive! Let me tie the strings of my bonnet, woman. Pity you can't come yourself, Kitty. But if they're worth their salt they'll be whipping round this way and giving you a lil tune, anyway."

"Have you got the key, Nancy?"

"Yes, and I'll be back in an hour. And mind you put baby to bed soon, and mind you—and mind you——"

With as many warnings as if she had been mistress and Kate the servant, Nancy backed herself out of the house. It was now dark outside.

Kate rose immediately, put the child in the cradle, and began to lay the table for Pete's supper—the cruet, the plates, the teapot on the hob to warm, and then—by force of habit—two cups and saucers. But sight of the cups awakened her to painful consciousness. She put one of them back in the cupboard, broke the coal on the fire, settled the kettle up to the blaze, fixed the Dutch oven with three rashers of bacon before the bars, then lit a candle, and, with a nervous look around, turned to go upstairs.

In the bedroom she drew on her cloak, pinned her hat and veil with trembling fingers, then took her purse from her pocket and emptied its contents onto the dressing-table.

"Not mine," she thought. And standing before the mirror at that moment, she caught sight of her earrings. "I must take nothing of his," she told herself, and she raised her hands to her ears. Then her heart smote her. "As if Pete would ever think of such things," she thought. "No, not if I took everything he has in the world. And must I be thinking of them?... Yet I cannot—I will not take them with me."

She opened a drawer and hurried everything into it—the money, the earrings, the keeper off her finger, and then she paused at the touch of the wedding-ring. A superstitious instinct restrained her. Yet the ring was the badge of her broken covenant. "With this ring I thee wed———" She tore off the wedding-ring also, and cast it with the rest.

"He will find them," she thought. "There will be nothing else to tell him what has happened. He will come, and I shall be gone. He will call, and there will be no answer. He will look for me, and I shall be lost to him for ever. Not a word left behind. Not a line to say, 'Thank you and good-bye and God bless you, dear Pete, for all your love and goodness to rae.'"

It was cruel—very cruel—yet what could she write? What could she say that had not better be left unsaid? The least syllable—no, the uncertainty would be kinder. Perhaps Pete would think she was dead—perhaps that she had destroyed herself. Even that would not be so bitter as the truth. He would get over it—he would become reconciled. "No," she thought, "I can write nothing—I can leave no message."

She shut the drawer quickly, and picked up the candle. As she did so, the shadow of herself moved about her. It mounted from the floor to the wall, from the wall to the ceiling. When she walked it seemed to be on top of her, hanging over her, pressing down on her, crushing her. She grew cold and sick, and hastened to the door. The room was full of other shadows—the memories of sleepless nights and of painful awakenings. These stared at her from every familiar thing—the watch ticking in its stand on the mantelpiece, the handle of the wardrobe, the pink curtains of the bed, the white pillow beneath them. She felt like a frightened child. With a terrified glance over her shoulder she crept out of the room.

Being downstairs again, she breathed more freely. There was light all about her, and the hall-parlour was bright and warm. The kettle was now singing in the cheerful blaze, the cat was purring on the rug, and there was a smell of bacon slowly frying. She looked at the clock—it was a quarter after seven. "Time to waken baby," she thought.

She took from a chest the child's outdoor clothes—a robe, a pelisse, and a white hood. Her fingers had touched a scarlet hood in a cardboard box, but "not that" she thought, and left it. She spread the clothes about her chair, and then lifted the little one from the cradle to her pillowing arm. The child awoke as she raised it, and made a fretful cry, which she smothered in a gurgling kiss.

"I can love the darling without shame now," she thought. "It's sweet face will reproach me no more."

With soft cooings at the baby's cheek, she was stooping to take the robe that lay at her feet, when her eyes fell on the round place in the cradle where the child had been. That made her think again of Pete. He would come home and find the little nest cold and empty. It would kill him; it would be a second bereavement. Was it not enough that she should go away herself? Must she rob him of the child as well? He loved it; he doted on it. It was the light of his eyes, the joy of his life. To lose it would be a blow like the blow of death.

Yet could a mother leave her child behind her? Impossible! The full tide of motherhood came over her, and its tender selfishness swept down everything. "I cannot," she thought; "come what may, I cannot and I will not leave her." And then she reached her hand for the child's pelisse.

"It would be a kind of atonement, though," she thought. To leave the little one to Pete would be making amends in some sort for the wrong that she was doing him. To deny herself the sight of the child's sweet face day by day and hour by hour—that would be a punishment also, and she deserved to be punished. "Can I leave her?" she thought. "Can I? Oh, what mother could bear it? No, no—never, never! And yet I ought—I must—Oh, this is terrible!"

In the midst of this agony of uncertainty, thinking of Pete and of the wrong she had done him, yet pressing the child to her breast with trembling arms, as if some one were tearing it away, the babe itself settled everything. Making some inarticulate whimper of communication, it nuzzled up to her, its eyes closed, but its head working against her bosom with the instinct of suckling, though it had never sucked.

"I'm only half a mother, after all," she thought.

The highest joys, the deepest rights of motherhood had been denied to her—the child taking from the mother, the mother giving to the child, the child and the mother one—: this had not been hers.

"My little baby can live without me," she thought. "If I leave her, she will never miss me."

She nearly broke down at that thought, and almost let her purpose slip. It was like God's punishment in advance, God's hand directing her—thus to withdraw the child from dependence on herself.

"Yes, I must leave her with Pete," she thought.

She put the child back into the cradle, half dressed as it was, and rocked it until it slept again. Then she hung over the tiny bed as a mother hangs over the little coffin that is soon to be shut up from her eyes for ever. Her tears rained down on the small counterpane. "My sweet baby I my little Katherine! I may never kiss you again—never see you any more'—you may grow up to be a woman and know nothing of your mother!"

The clock ticked loud in the quiet room—it was twenty-five minutes past seven.

"One kiss more, my little darling. If they ever tell you... they'll say because your mother left you... Oh, will she think I did not love her? Hush!"

Through the walls of the house there came the sound of a band playing at a distance. She looked at the clock again—it was nearly half-past seven. Almost at the same moment there was the rumble of carriage-wheels on the road. They stopped in the lane that ran between the chapel and the end of the garden.

Kate rose from her knees and opened the door softly. The house had been as a dungeon to her, and she was flying from it like a prisoner escaping. A shrill whistle pierced the air. The *Peveril* was leaving the quay. Through the streets there was a sound as of water running over stones. It was the scuttling of the feet of the townspeople as they ran to meet the procession.

She stepped out. The garden was dark and quiet as a prison yard; Hardly a leaf stirred, but the moon was breaking through the old fir-tree as she lifted her troubled face to the untroubled sky. She stood and listened. The band was coming nearer. She could hear the thud of the big drum.

Boom! Boom! Boom!

Pete was there. He was helping at Philip's triumph. That was the beat of his great heart made audible.

At this her own heart stopped for a moment. She grew chill at the thought of the brave man who asked no better lot than to love and cherish her, and at the memory of the other upon whose mercy she had cast herself. The band stopped. There was a noise like the breaking of a mighty rocket in the sky. The people were cheering and clapping hands. Then a clearer sound struck her ear. It was the clock inside the house chiming the half-hour.

Nancy would be back soon.

Kate listened intently, inclining her head inwards. If the child had awakened at that instant, if it had stirred and cried, she must have gone back for good. She returned for one moment and flung herself over the cradle again. One spasm more of lingering tenderness. "Good-bye, my little one! I am leaving you with him, darling, because he loves you dearly. You will grow up and be a good, good girl to him always. Good-bye, my pet! My precious, my precious! You will reward him for all he has done for me. You are half of myself, dearest—the innocent half. Yes, you will wipe out your mother's sin. You will be all he thinks I am, but never have been. Farewell, my sweet Katherine, my little, darling baby—good-bye—farewell—good-bye!"

She leapt up and fled out of the house at last, on tiptoe, like a thief, pulling the door after her.

When she heard the click of the lock she felt both wretchedness and exultation—immense agony and immense relief. If little Katherine were to cry now, she could not return to her. The door was closed, the house was shut, the prison was left behind. And behind her, too, were the treachery, the duplicity, and deceit of ten stifling months.

She hurried through the garden to a side-door in the wall leading to the lane. The path was like a wave of the sea to her stumbling feet. Her breathing was short, her sight was weak, her temples were beating audibly. Half across the garden something touched her dress, and she made a faint scream. It was Pete's dog, Dempster. He was looking up at her out of the darkness of the bushes. By the light through the blind of the house she could see his bat's ears and watchful eyes.

Boom! Boom! Boom!

The band had begun again. It was coming nearer. Philip! Philip! He was her only refuge now. All else was a blank.

The side-door had been little used. Its hinges and bolt were rusty and stiff. She broke her nails in opening it. From the other side came the light jingle of a curb chain, and over the wall hovered a white sheet of smoking light.

The carriage was in the lane, and the driver—Philip's servant, Jem-y-Lord—stood with the door open. Kate stumbled on the step and fell into the seat. The door was closed.

Then a new thought smote her. It was about the child, about Philip, about Pete. In leaving the little one behind her, though she had meant it so unselfishly, she had done the one thing that must be big with consequences. It would bring its penalty, its punishment, its retribution. Stop! She would go back even yet. Her face was against the glass; she was struggling with the strap. But the carriage was moving. She heard the rumble of the wheels; it was like a deafening reverberation from the day of doom. Then her senses dwaled away and the carriage drove on.

XV.

Outside Ballure House there was a crowd which covered the garden, the fence, the high-road, and the top of the stone wall opposite. The band had ceased to play, and the people were shouting, clapping hands, and cheering. At the door—which was open—Philip stood bareheaded, and a shaft of the light in the house behind him lit up a hundred of the eager faces gathered in the darkness. He raised his hand for silence, but it was long before he was allowed to speak. Salutations rugged, rough—almost rude—but hearty to the point of homeliness, and affectionate to the length of familiarity, flew at his head from every side. "Good luck to you, boy!"—"Bravo for Ramsey!"—"The Christians for your life!"—"A chip of the ould block—Dempster Christian the Sixth!"—"Hush, man, he's spaking!"—"Go it, Phil!"—"Give it fits, boy!"—"Hush! hush!"

"Fellow-townsmen," said Philip—his voice swung like a quivering bell over a sea,—"you can never know how much your welcome has moved me. I cannot say whether in my heart of hearts I am more proud of it or more ashamed. To be ashamed of it altogether would dishonour *you*, and to be too proud of it would dishonour *me*, I am not worthy of your faith and good-fellowship. Ah!"—he raised his hand to check a murmur of dissent (the crowd was now hushed from end to end)—"let me utter the thought of all. In honouring me you are thinking of others also ('No,' 'Yes'); you are thinking of my people—above all, of one who was laid under the willows yonder, a wrecked, a broken, a disappointed man—my father, God rest him! I will not conceal it from you—his memory has been my guide, his failures have been my lightship, his hopes my beacon, his love my star. For good or for evil, my anchor has been in the depths of his grave. God forbid that I should have lived too long under the grasp of a dead hand. It was my aim to regain what he had lost, and this day has witnessed its partial reclamation. God grant I may not have paid too dear for such success."

There were cries of "No, sir, no."

He smiled faintly and shook his head. "Fellow-countrymen, you believe I am worthy of the name I bear. There is one among you, an old comrade, a tried and trusted friend, whose faith would be a spur if it were not a reproach——"

His voice was breaking, but still it pealed over the sea of heads. "Well, I will try to do my duty—from this hour onwards you shall see me try. Fellow-Manxmen, you will help me for the honour of the place I fill, for the sake of our little island, and—yes, and for my own sake also, I know you will—to be a good man and an upright judge. But"—he faltered, his voice could barely support itself—"but if it should ever appear that your confidence has been misplaced—if in the time to come I should seem to be unworthy of this honour, untrue to the oath I took to-day to do God's justice between man and man, a wrongdoer, not a righter of the wronged, a whited sepulchre where you looked for a tower of refuge—remember, I pray of you, my countrymen, remember, much as you may be suffering then, there will be one who will be suffering more—that one will be myself."

The general impression that night was that the Deemster's speech had not been a proper one. Breaking up with some damp efforts at the earlier enthusiasm, the people complained that they were like men who had come for a jig and were sent home in a wet blanket. There should have been a joke or two, a hearty word of congratulation, a little natural glorification of Ramsey, and a quiet slap at Douglas and Peel and Castletown, a few fireworks, a rip-rap or two, and some general illumination. "But sakes alive! the solemn the young Dempster was! And the melancholy! And the mystarious!"

"Chut!" said Pete. "There's such a dale of comic in you, boys. Wonder in the world to me you're not kidnapped for pantaloonses. Go home for all and wipe your eyes, and remember the words he's been spaking. I'm not going to forget them myself, anyway."

Handing over the big drum to little Jonaique, Pete turned to go into the house. Auntie Nan was in the hall, hopping like a canary about Philip, in a brown silk dress that rustled like withered ferns, hugging him, drawing him down to the level of her face, and kissing him on the forehead. The tears were raining over the autumn sunshine of her wrinkled cheeks, and her voice was cracking between a laugh and a cry.

"My boy! My dear boy! My boy's boy! My own boy's own boy!"

Philip freed himself at length, and went upstairs without turning his head, and then Auntie Nan saw Pete standing in the doorway.

"Is it you, Pete?" she said with an effort. "Won't you come in for a moment? No?"

"A minute only, then—just to wish you joy, Miss Christian, ma'am," said Pete.

"And you, too, Peter. Ah!" she said, with a bird-like turn of the head, "you must be a proud man to-night, Pete."

"Proud isn't the word for it, ma'am—I'm clane beside myself."

"He took a fancy to you when you were only a little barefooted boy, Pete."

"So he did, ma'am."

"And now that he's Deemster itself he owns you still."

"Aw, lave him alone for that, ma'am."

"Did you hear what he said about you in his speech. It isn't everybody in his place would have done that before all, Pete."

"'Deed no, ma'am."

"He's true to his friends, whatever they are."

"True as steel."

The maid was carrying the dishes into the dining-room, and Auntie Nan said in a strained way, "You won't stay to dinner, Pete, will you? Perhaps you want to get home to the mistress. Well, home is best for all of us, isn't it? Martha, I'll tell the Deemster myself that dinner is on the table. Well, good-night, Peter. I'm always so glad to see you."

She was whisking about to go upstairs, but Pete had taken one step into the dining-room, and was gazing round with looks of awe.

"Lord alive, Miss Christian, ma'am, what feelings now-barefooted boy, you say? You're right there, and cold and hungry too, sleeping in the gable-house with the cow, and not getting much but the milk I was staling from her, and a leathering at the ould man for that. Philip fetched me in here one evenin'—that was the start, ma'am. See that pepper-and-salt egg on the string there? It's a Tommy Noddy's. Philip got it nesting up Gob-ny-Garvain. Nearly cost him his life, though. You see, ma'am, Tommy Noddy has only one, and she fights like mad for it. We were up forty fathom and better, atop of a cave, and had two straight rocks below us in the sea, same as an elephant's hoofs, you know, walking out on the blue floor. And Phil was having his lil hand on the ledge where the egg was keeping, when swoop came the big white wings atop of his bare head. If I hadn't had a stick that day, ma'am, it would have been heaven help the pair of us. The next minute Tommy Noddy was going splash down the cliffs, all feathers and blood together, or Philip wouldn't have lived to be Dempster.... Aw, frightened you, have I, ma'am, for all it's so long ago? The heart's a quare thing, now, isn't it? Got no yesterday nor to-morrow neither. Well, good-night, ma'am." Pete was making for the door, when he looked down and said, "What's this, at all? Down, Dempster, down!"

The dog had came trotting into the hall as Pete was going out. He was perking up his big ears and wagging his stump of a tail in front of him.

"My dog, ma'am? Yes, ma'am, and like its master in some ways. Not much of itself at all, but it has the blood in it, though, and maybe it'll come out better in the next generation. Looking for me, are you, Dempster? Let's be taking the road, then."

"Perhaps you're wanted at home, Pete?"

"Wouldn't trust. Good night, ma'am." Auntie Nan hopped upstairs in her rustling dress, relieved and glad in the sweet selfishness of her love to get rid of Pete and have Philip to herself.

XVI.

Pete went off whistling in the darkness, with the dog driving ahead of him. "I'm to blame, though," he thought. "Should have gone home directly."

The town was now quiet, the streets were deserted, and Pete began to run. "She'd be alone, too. That must have been Nancy in the crowd yonder by Mistress Beatty's. 'Lowed her out to see the do, it's like. Ought to be back now, though."

As Pete came near to Elm Cottage, the moon over the tree-tops lit up the panes of the upper windows as with a score of bright lamps. One step more, and the house was dark.

"She'll be waiting for me. Listening, too, I'll go bail."

He was at the gate by this time, and the dog was panting at his feet with its nose close to the lattice.

"Be quiet, dog, be quiet."

Then he raised the latch without a sound, stepped in on tiptoe, and closed the gate as silently behind him.

"I'll have a game with her; I'll take her by surprise."

His eyes began to dance with mischief, like a child's, and he crept along the path with big cat strides, half doubled up, and holding his breath, lest he should laugh aloud.

"The sweet creatures! A man shouldn't frighten them, though," he thought.

When he reached the porch he went down on all fours, and began mewing like a mournful tom-cat near to the bottom of the door. Then he listened with his ear to the jamb. He expected a faint cry of alarm, the raucous voice of Nancy Joe, and the clatter of feet towards the porch. There was not a sound.

"She's upstairs," he thought, and stepped back to look up at the front of the house. There was no light in the rooms above.

"I know what it is. Nancy is not home yet, and Kirry's fallen asleep at the rocking."

He stole up to the window and tried to look into the hall, but the blind was down, and he could not see much through the narrow openings at the sides of it.

"She's sleeping, that's it. The house was quiet and she dropped off, rocking the lil one, that's all."

He scraped a handful of the light gravel and flung a little of it at the window. "That'll remind her of something," he thought, and he laughed under his breath.

Then he listened again with his ear at the sill. There was no noise within. He flung more gravel and waited, thinking he might catch her breathing, but he could hear nothing.

Then rising hurriedly and throwing off his playfulness, he strode to the door and tried to open it. The door was locked. He returned to the window.

"Kate!" he called softly. "Kate! Are you there? Do you hear me? It's Pete. Don't be frightened, Kate, bogh!"

There was no response. He could hear the beat of the sea on the shore. The dog had perched himself on one end of the window sill and was beginning to whine.

"What's this at all? She can't be out. Couldn't take the child anyway. Where's that Nancy? What right had the woman to lave her? She has fainted, being left alone; that's what's going doing."

He tried to open the window, but the latch was shot. Then he tried the other windows, and the back door, and the window above the hall, which he reached from the roof of the porch; but they would not stir. When he returned to the hall window, the white blind was darker. The lamp inside the room was going out.

The moonlight was dripping down on him through the leaves of the trees. He found some matches beside his pipe in his side pocket, struck one, and looked at the sash, then took out his clasp knife to remove the pane under the latch. His hand trembled and shook and burst through the glass with a jerk. It cut his wrist, but he felt the wound no more than if it had been the glass instead of his arm that bled. He thrust his hand through, shot back the latch, then pushed up the sash, and clambered into the room past the blind. The cat, sitting on the ledge inside, rubbed against his hand and purred.

"Kirry! Kate!" he whispered.

The lamp had given up its last gleam with the puff of wind from the window, and, save for the slumbering fire, all was dark within the house. He hardly dared to drop to his feet for fear of treading on something. When he was at last in the middle of the floor he stood with legs apart, struck another match, held the light above his head, and looked down and around, like a man in a cave.

There was nothing. The child, awakened by the draught of the night air, began to cry from the cradle. He took it up and hushed it with baby words of tenderness in a breaking voice. "Hush, bogh, hush! Mammie will come to it, then. Mammie will come for all."

He lit a candle and crept through the house, carrying the light about with him. There was no sign anywhere until he came to the bedroom, when he saw that the hat and cloak of Kate's daily wear had gone. Then he knew that he was a broken-hearted man. With a cry of desolation he stopped in his search and came heavily downstairs.

He had been warding off the moment of despair, but he could do so no longer now. The empty house and the child, the child and the empty house; these allowed of only one interpretation. "She's gone, bogh, she's left us; she wasn't willing to stay with us, God forgive her!"

Sitting on a stool with the little one on his knees, he sobbed while the child cried—two children crying together. Suddenly he leapt up. "I'm not for believing it," he thought. "What woman alive could do the like of it? There isn't a mother breathing that hasn't more bowels. And she used to love the lil one, and me too—and does, and does."

He saw how it was. She was ill, distraught, perhaps even—God help her I—perhaps even mad. Such things happened to women after childbirth—the doctor himself had said as much. In the toils of her bodily trouble, beset by mental terrors, she had fled away from her baby, her husband, and her home, pursued by God knows what phantoms of disease. But she would get better, she would come back.

"Hush, bogh, hush, then," he whimpered tenderly. "Mammie will come home again. Still and for all she'll come back."

There was the click of a key in the lock, and he crept back to the stool. Nancy came in, panting and perspiring.

"Dear heart alive! what a race I've had to get home," she said, puffing the air of the night.

She was throwing off her bonnet and shawl, and talking before looking round.

"Such pushing and scrooging, you never seen the like, Kirry. Aw, my best Sunday bonnet, only wore at me once, look at the crunched it is! But what d'ye think now? Poor Christian Killip's baby is dead for all. Died in the middle of the rejoicings. Aw, dear, yes, and the band going by playing 'The Conquering Hero' the very minute. Poor thing! she was distracted, and no wonder. I ran round to put a sight on the poor soul, and——why, what's going wrong with the lamp, at all? Is that yourself on the stool, Kirry? Pete, is it? Then where's the mistress?"

She plucked up the poker, and dug the fire into a blaze. "What's doing on you, man? You've skinned your knuckles like potato peel. Man, man, what for are you crying, at all?"

Then Pete said in a thick croak, "Hould your bull of a tongue, Nancy, and take the child out of my arms."

She took the baby from him, and he rose to his feet as feeble as an old man.

"Lord save us!" she cried. "The window broke, too. What's happened?"

"Nothing," growled Pete.

"Then what's coming of Kirry? I left her at home when I went out at seven.".

"I'm choking with thirst, woman. Can't you be giving a man a drink of something?"

He found a dish of milk on the table, where the supper had been laid, and he gulped it down at a mouthful.

"She's gone—that's what it is. I see it in your face." Then going to the foot of the stairs, she called, "Kirry! Kate! Katherine Cregeen!"

"Stop that!" shouted Pete, and he drew her back from the stairs.

"Why aren't you spaking, then?" she cried. "If you're man enough to bear the truth, I'm woman enough to hear it."

"Listen to me, Nancy," said Pete, with uplifted fist. "I'm going out for an hour, and till I'm back, stay you here with the child, and say nothing to nobody."

"I knew it!" cried Nancy. "That's what she hurried me out for. Aw, dear! Aw, dear! What for did you lave her with that man this morning?"

"Do you hear me, woman?" said Pete; "say nothing to nobody. My heart's lying heavy enough already. Open your lips, and you'll kill me straight."

Then he went out of the house, staggering, stumbling, bent almost double. His hat lay on the floor; he had gone bareheaded.

He turned towards Sulby. "She's there," he thought "Where else should she be? The poor, wandering lamb wants home."

XVII.

The bar-room of "The Manx Fairy" was full of gossips 'that night, and the puffing of many pipes was suspended at a story that Mr. Jelly was telling.

"Strange enough, I'm thinking. 'Deed, but it's mortal strange. Talk about tale-books—there's nothing in the 'Pilgrim's Progress' itself to equal it. The son of one son coming home Dempster, with processions and bands of music, at the very minute the son of the other son is getting kicked out of the house same as a dog."

"Strange uncommon," said John the Widow, and other voices echoed him.

Jonaique looked round the room, expecting some one to question him. As nobody did so, except with looks of inquiry, he said, "My ould man heard it all. He's been tailor at the big house since the time of Iron Christian himself."

"Truth enough," said Cæsar.

"And he was sewing a suit for the big man in the kitchen when the bad work was going doing upstairs."

"You don't say!"

"'You've robbed me!' says the Ballawhaine."

"Dear heart alive!" cried Grannie. "To his own son, was it?"

"'You've cheated me!' says he, 'you deceaved me, you've embezzled my money and broke my heart!' says he. 'I've spent a fortune on you, and what have you brought me back?' says he. 'This,' says he, 'and this—and this—barefaced forgeries, all of them!' says he."

"The Lord help us!" muttered Cæsar.

"'They're calling me a miser, aren't they?' says he. 'I grind my people to the dust, do I? What for, then? *Whom* for? I've been a good father to you, anyway, and a fool, too, if nobody knows it!' says he."

"Nobody! Did he say nobody, Mr. Jelly?" said Cæsar, screwing up his mouth.

"'If you'd had *my* father to deal with,' says he, 'he'd have turned you out long ago for a liar and a thief.' 'My God, father,' says Ross, struck silly for the minute. 'A thief, d'ye hear me?' says the Ballawhaine; 'a thief that's taken every penny I have in the world, and left me a ruined man.'"

"Did he say that?" said Cæsar.

"He did, though," said Jonaique. "The ould man was listening from the kitchen-stairs, and young Ross snaked out of the house same as a cur."

"And where's he gone to?" said Cæsar.

"Gone to the devil, I'm thinking," said Jonaique.

"Well, he'd be good enough for him with a broken back—pity the ould man didn't break it," said Cæsar. "But where is the wastrel now?"

"Gone to England over with to-night's packet, they're saying."

"Praise God, from whom all blessings flow," said Cæsar.

A grunt came out of the corner from behind a cloud of smoke. "You've your own rasons for saying so, Cæsar," said the husky voice of Black Tom. "People were talking and talking one while there that he'd be 'bezzling somebody's daughter, as well as the ould miser's money."

"Answer a fool according to his folly," muttered Cæsar; and then the door jerked open, and Pete came staggering into the room. Every pipe shank was lowered in an instant, and Grannie's needles ceased to click.

Pete was still bareheaded, his face was ghastly white, and his eyes wandered, but he tried to bear himself as if nothing had happened. Smiling horribly, and nodding all round, as a man does sometimes in battle the moment the bullet strikes him, he turned to Grannie and moved his lips a little as if he thought he was saying something, though he uttered no sound. After that he took out his pipe, and rammed it with his forefinger, then picked a spill from the table, and stooped to the fire for a light.

"Anybody—belonging—me—here?" he said, in a voice like a crow's, coughing as he spoke, the flame dancing over the pipe mouth.

"No, Pete, no," said Grannie. "Who were you looking for, at all?"

"Nobody," he answered. "Nobody partic'lar. Aw, no," he said, and he puffed until his lips quacked, though the pipe gave out no smoke. "Just come in to get fire to my pipe. Must be going now. So long, boys! S'long! Bye-bye, Grannie!"

No one answered him. He nodded round the room again and smiled fearfully, crossed to the door with a jaunty roll, and thus launched out of the house with a pretence of unconcern, the dead pipe hanging upside down in his mouth, and his head aside, as if his hat had been tilted rakishly on his uncovered hair.

When he had gone the company looked into each other's faces in surprise and fear, as if a ghost in broad daylight had passed among them. Then Black Tom broke the silence.

"Men," said he, "that was a d——— lie."

"Si———" began Cæsar, but the protest foundered in his dry throat.

"Something going doing in Ramsey," Black Tom continued. "I believe in my heart I'll follow him."

"I'll be going along with you, Mr. Quilliam," said Jonaique.

"And I," said John the Clerk.

"And I"—"And I," said the others, and in half a minute the room was empty.

"Father," whimpered Grannie, through the glass partition, "hadn't you better saddle the mare and see if any thing's going wrong with Kirry?"

"I was thinking the same myself, mother."

"Come, then, away with you. The Lord have mercy on all of us!"

127

XVIII.

As soon as he was out of earshot Pete began to run. Within half an hour he was back at Elm Cottage. "She'll be home by this time," he told himself, but he dared not learn the truth too suddenly. Creeping up to the hall window, he listened at the broken pane. The child was crying, and Nancy Joe was talking to herself, and sobbing as she bathed the little one.

"Bless its precious heart, it's as beautiful as the angels in heaven. I've bathed her mother on the same knee a hundred times. 'Deed have I, and a thousand times too. Mother, indeed! What sort of mothers are in now at all? She must have a heart-as hard as a stone to lave the like of it. Can't be a drop of nature in her.... Goodness, Nancy, what are saying for all? Kate is it? Your own little Kirry, and you blackening her! Aw, dear!—aw, dear! The bogh!—the bogh!"

Pete could not go in. He crept back to the cabin in the garden and leaned against it to draw his breath and think. Then he noticed that the dog was on the path with its long tongue hanging over its jaw. It stopped its panting to whine woefully, and then it turned towards the darker part of the garden.

"He's telling me something," thought Pete.

A car rattled down the side road at that moment, and the light of its lamp shot through the bushes to his feet.

"The ould gate must be open," he thought.

He looked and saw that it was, and then a new light dawned on him.

"She's gone up to Philip's," he told himself. "She's gone by Claughbane to Ballure to find me."

Five minutes afterwards he was knocking at Ballure House. His breath was coming in gusts, perspiration was standing in beads on his face, and his head was still bare, but he was carrying himself bravely as if nothing were amiss. His knock was answered by the maid, a tall girl of cheerful expression, in a black frock, a white apron, and a snow-white cap. Pete nodded and smiled at her.

"Anybody been here for me? No?" he asked.

"No, sir, n—o, I think not," the girl answered, and as she looked at Pete her face straightened.

There was a rustling within as of autumn leaves, and then a twittering voice cried, "Is it Capt'n Quilliam, Martha?"

"Yes, ma'am."

Some whispered conference took place at the dining-room door, and Auntie Nan came hopping through the hall. But Pete was already moving away in the darkness.

"Shall I call the Deemster, Peter?"

"Aw, no, ma'am, no, not worth bothering him. Good everin', Miss Christian, ma'am, good everin' to you."

Auntie Nan and Martha were standing in the light at the open door when the iron gate of the garden swung to with a click, and Pete swung across the road.

He was making for the lane which goes down to the shore at the foot of Ballure Glen. "No denying it," he thought. "It must be true for all. The trouble in her head has driven her to it. Poor girl, poor darling!"

He had been fighting against an awful idea, and the quagmire of despair had risen to his throat at last. The moon was behind the cliffs, and he groped his way through the shadows at the foot of the rocks like one who looks for something which he dreads to find. He found nothing, and his catchy breathing lengthened to sighs.

"Thank God, not here, anyway!" he muttered.

Then he walked down the shore towards the harbour. The tide was still high, the wash of the waves touched his feet; on the one hand the dark sea, unbroken by a light, on the other the dull town blinking out and dropping asleep.

He reached the end of the stone pier at the mouth of the harbour, and with his back to the seaward side of the lighthouse he stared down into the grey water that surged and moaned under the rounded wall. A black cloud like a skate was floating across the moon, and a startled gannet scuttled from under the pier steps into the moon's misty waterway. There was nothing else to be seen.

He turned back towards the town, following the line of the quay, and glancing down into the harbour when he came to the steps. Still he saw nothing of the thing he looked for. "But it was high water then, and now it's the ebby tide," he told himself.

He had met with nobody on the shore or on the pier, but as he passed the sheds in front of the berth for the steamers he was joined by the harbour-master, who was swinging home for the night, with his coat across his arm. Then he tried to ask the question that was slipping off his tongue, but dared not, and only stammered awkwardly——

"Any news to-night, Mr. Quay le?"

"Is it yourself, Capt'n? If you've none, I've none. It's independent young rovers like you for newses, not poor ould chaps tied to the harbour-post same as a ship's cable. I was hearing you, though. You'd a power of music in the everin' yonder. Fine doings up at Ballure, seemingly."

"Nothing fresh with yourself then, Daniel? No?"

"Except that I am middling sick of these late sailings, and the sooner they're building us a breakwater the better. If the young Deemster will get that for us, he'll do."

They were nearing a lamp at the corner of the marketplace.

"It's like you know the young Ballawhaine crossed with the boat to-night? Something wrong, with the ould man, they're telling me. But boy, veen, what's come of your hat at all?"

"My hat?" said Pete, groping about his head. "Oh, my hat? Blown off on the pier, of coorse."

"'Deed, man! Not much wind either. You'll be for home and the young wife, eh, Capt'n?"

"Must be," said Pete, with an empty laugh. And the harbour-master, who was a bachelor, laughed more heartily, and added——

"You married men are like Adam, you've lost the rib of your liberty, but you've got a warm little woman to your side instead."

"Ha! ha! ha! Goodnight!"

Pete's laugh echoed through the empty market-place.

The harbour-master had seen nothing. Pete drew a long breath, followed the line of the harbour as far as to the bridge at the end of it, and then turned back through the town. He had forgotten again that he was bareheaded, and he walked down Parliament Street with a tremendous step and the air of a man to whom nothing unusual had occurred. People were standing in groups at the corner of every side street, talking eagerly, with the low hissing sound that women make when they are discussing secrets. So absorbed were they that Pete passed some of them unobserved. He caught snatches of their conversation.

"The rascal," said one.

"Clane ruined the ould man, anyway," said another.

"Ross Christian again," thought Pete. But a greater secret swamped everything. Still he heard the people as he passed.

"Sarve her right, though, whatever she gets—she knew what he was."

"Laving the child, too, the unfeeling creature."

Then the sharp voices of the women fell on the dull consciousness of Pete like forks of lightning.

"Whisht, woman! the husband himself," said somebody.

There was a noise of feet like the plash of retiring waves, and Pete noticed that one of the groups had broken into a half circle, facing him as he strode along the street. He nodded cheerfully over both sides, threw back his bare head, and plodded on. But his teeth were set hard, and his breathing was quick and audible.

"I see what they mane," he muttered.

Outside his own house he found a crowd. A saddle-horse, with a cloud of steam rising from her, was standing with the reins over its head, linked to the gate-post. It was Cæsar's mare, Molly. Every eye was on the house, and no one saw Pete as he came up behind.

"Black Tom's saying there's not a doubt of it," said a woman.

"Gone with the young Ballawhaine, eh?" said a man.

"Shame on her, the hussy," said another woman.

Pete ploughed his way through with both arms, smiling and nodding furiously. "If you, plaze, ma'am I If _you_ plaze."

As he pushed on he heard voices behind him. "Poor man, he doesn't know yet."—"I'm taking pity to look at him."

The house-door was open. On the threshold stood a young man with long hair and a long note-book. He was putting questions. "Last seen at seven o'clock—left alone with child—husband out with procession—any other information?"

Nancy Joe, with the child on her lap, was answering querulously from the stool before the fire, and Cæsar, face down, was leaning on the mantelpiece.

Pete took in the situation at a glance. Then he laid his big hand on the young man's shoulder and swung him aside as if he had been turning a swivel.

"What going doing?" he asked.

The young man faltered something. Sorry to intrude—Capt'n Quilliam's trouble.

"What trouble?" said Pete.

"Need I say—the lamented—I mean distressing—in fact, the mysterious disappearance——"

"What disappearance?" said Pete, with an air of amazement.

"Can it be, sir, that you've not yet heard——"

"Heard what? Your tongue's like a turnip-watch in a fob pocket—out with it, man."

"Your wife, Captain——"

"What? My wife disa—— What? So this is the jeel! My wife mysteriously disappear—— Oh, my gough!"

Pete burst into a peal of laughter. He shouted, roared, held his sides, doubled, rocked up and down, and at length flung himself into a chair, threw back his head, heaved out his legs, and shook till the house itself seemed to quake.

"Well, that's good! that's rich! that bates all!" he cried.

The child awoke on Nancy's knee and sent its thin pipe through Pete's terrific bass. Cæsar opened his mouth and gaped, and the young man, now white and afraid, scraped and backed himself to the door, saying—

"Then perhaps it's not true, after all, Capt'n?"

"Of coorse it's not true," said Pete.

"Maybe you know where she's gone."

"Of course I know where's she's gone. I sent her there myself!"

"You did, though?" said Cæsar.

"Yes, did I—to England by the night sailing."

"'Deed, man!" said Cæsar.

"The doctor ordered it. You heard him yourself, grandfather."

"Well, that's true, too," said Cæsar.

The young man closed his long note-book and backed into a throng of women who had come up to the porch. "Of course, if you say so, Capt'n Quilliam——"

"I do say so," shouted Pete; and the reporter disappeared.

The voices of two women came from the gulf of white faces wherein the reporter had been swallowed up. "I'm right glad it's lies they've been telling of her, Capt'n," said the first.

"Of coorse you are, Mistress Kinnish," shouted Pete.

"I could never have believed the like of the same woman, and I always knew the child was brought up by hand," said the other.

"Coorse you couldn't, Mistress Kewley," Pete replied.

But he swung up and kicked the door to in their faces. The strangers being shut out, Cæsar said cautiously—

"Do you mane that, Peter?"

"Molly's smoking at the gate like a brewer's vat, father," said Pete.

"The half hasn't been told you, Peter. Listen to me. It's only proper you should hear it. When you were away at Kim-berley this Ross Christian was bothering the girl terrible."

"She'll be getting cold so long out of the stable," said Pete.

"I rebuked him myself, sir, and he smote me on the brow. Look! Here's the mark of his hand over my temple, and I'll be carrying it to my grave."

"Ross Christian! Ross Christian!" muttered Pete impatiently.

"By the Lord's restraining grace, sir, I refrained myself—but if Mr. Philip hadn't been there that night—I'm not hould-ing with violence, no, resist not evil—but Mr. Philip fought the loose liver with his fist for me; he chastised him, sir; he—"

"D———the man!" cried Pete, leaping to his feet. "What's he to me or my wife either?"

Cæsar went home huffed, angry, and unsatisfied. And then, all being gone and the long strain over, Pete snatched the puling child out of Nancy's arms, and kissed it and wept over it.

"Give her to me, the bogh," he cried, hoarse as a raven, and then sat on the stool before the fire, and rocked the little one and himself together. "If I hadn't something innocent to lay hould of I should be going mad, that I should. Oh, Katherine bogh! Katherine bogh! My little bogh! My I'll bogh millish!"

In the deep hours of the night, after Nancy had grumbled and sobbed herself to sleep by the side of the child, Pete got up from the sofa in the parlour and stole out of the house again.

"She may come up with the morning tide," he told himself. "If she does, what matter about a lie, God forgive me? God help me, what matter about anything?"

If she did not, he would stick to his story, so that when she came back, wherever she had been, she would come home as an honest woman.

"And *will be*, too," he thought. "Yes, will be, too, spite of all their dirty tongues—as sure as the Lord's in heaven."

The dog trotted on in front of him as he turned up towards Ballure.

XIX.

Philip had not eaten much that night at dinner. He had pecked at the wing of a fowl, been restless, absent, preoccupied, and like a man struggling for composure. At intervals he had listened as for a step or a voice, then recovered himself and laughed a little.

Auntie Nan had explained his uneasiness on grounds of natural excitement after the doings of the great day. She had loaded his plate with good things, and chirruped away under the light of the lamp.

"So sweet of you, Philip, not to forget Pete amid all your success. He's really such a good soul. It would break his heart if you neglected him. Simple as a child, certainly, and of course quite uneducated, but——"

"Pete is fit to be the friend of any one, Auntie."

"The friend, yes, but you'll allow not exactly the companion——"

"If he is simple, it is the simplicity of a nature too large for little things."

"The dear fellow! He's not a bit jealous of you, Philip."

"Such feelings are far below him, Auntie."

"He's your first cousin after all, Philip. There's no denying that. As he says, the blood of the Christians is in him."

The conversation took a turn. Auntie Nan fell to talking of the other Peter, uncle Peter Christian of Ballawhaine. This was the day of the big man's humiliation. The son he had doted on was disgraced. She tried, but could not help it; she struggled, but could not resist the impulse—in her secret heart the tender little soul rejoiced.

"Such a pity," she sighed. "So touching when a father—no matter how selfish—is wrecked by love of a thankless son. I'm sorry, indeed I am. But I warned him six years ago. Didn't I, now?"

Philip was far away. He was seeing visions of Pete going home, the deserted house, the empty cradle, the desolate man alone and heart-broken.

They rose from the table and went into the little parlour, Auntie Nan on Philip's arm, proud and happy. She fluttered down to the piano and sang, to cheer him up a little, an old song in a quavering old voice.

> "Of the wandering falcon
>   The cuckoo complains,
> He has torn her warm nest,
>   He has scattered her young."

Suddenly Philip got up stiffly, and said in a husky whisper, "Isn't that his voice?"

"Who's, dear?"

"Pete's."

"Where, dearest?"

"In the hall."

"I hear nobody. Let me look. No, Pete's not here. But how pale you are, Philip. What's amiss?"

"Nothing," said Philip. "I only thought——"

"Take some wine, dear, or some brandy. You've overtired yourself to-day, and no wonder. You must have a long, long rest to-night."

"Yes I'll go to bed at once."

"So soon! Well, perhaps it's best. You want sleep: your eyes show that. Martha! Is everything ready in the Deemster's room? All but the lamp? Take it up, Martha. Philip, you'll drink a little brandy and water first? I'll carry it to your room then; you might need it in the night. Go before me, dear. Yes, yes, you must. Do you think I want you to see how old I am when I'm going upstairs? Ah! I hadn't to climb by the banisters this way when I came first to Bal-lure."

On reaching the landing, Philip was turning to his old room, the bedroom he had occupied from his boyhood up, the bedroom of his mother's father, old Capt'n Billy.

"Not that way to-night, Philip. This way—*there!* What do you say to *that?*"

She pushed open the door of the room opposite, and the glow of the fire within rushed out on them.

"My father's room," said Philip, and he stepped back.

"Oh, I've aired it, and it's not a bit the worse for being so long shut up. See, it's like toast Oo—oo—oo! Not the least sign of my breath. Come!"

"No, Auntie, no."

"Are you afraid of ghosts? There's only one ghost lives here, Philip, the memory of your dear father, and that will never harm you."

"But this place is too sacred. No one has slept here since——"

"That's why, dearest. But now you have justified your father's hopes, and it must be your room for the future. Ah! if he could only see you himself, how proud he would be! Poor father! Perhaps he does. Who knows—perhaps—kiss me, Philip. See what an old silly I am, after all. So happy that I have to cry. But mind now, you've got to sleep in this room every time you come to hold court in Ramsey. I refuse to share you with Elm Cottage any longer. Talk about jealousy! If Pete isn't jealous, I know somebody who is—or soon will be. But Philip—Philip Christian——"

"Yes?"

The sweet old face grew solemn. "The greatest man has his cares and doubts and divisions. That's only natural—out in the open field of life. But don't be ashamed to come here whenever you are in trouble. It's what home is for, Philip. Just a place of peace and shelter from the rough world, when it wounds and hurts you. A quiet spot, dear, with memories of father and mother and innocent childhood—and with an old goose of an auntie, maybe, who thinks of you all day and every day, and is so vain and foolish—and—and who loves you, Philip, better than anybody in the World."

Philip's arms were about the old soul, but he had not heard her. With a terrified glance towards the window, he was saying in a low quick voice, "Isn't that a footstep on the gravel?"

"N—o, no! You're nervous to-night, Philip. Lie and rest. When you're asleep, I'll creep back and look at you."

She left him, and he looked around. Not in all the world could Philip have found a spot so full of terrors. It was like a sepulchre of dead things—his dead father, his dead mother, his dead youth, his dead innocence, his slaughtered friendship, and his outraged conscience.

Over the fireplace hung a portrait of his mother. It was the picture of a comely girl, young and soft, with full ripe lips and bright brown eyes. Philip shuddered as he looked at it. The portrait was like the ghost of himself looking through the veil of a woman's face.

Facing this, and hanging over the side of the bed, was a portrait of his father. The eyes were full of light, the lines of the cheek were round; the mouth seemed to quiver with a tender smile. But Philip could not see it as it was. He saw it with straggling hair, damp and long

131

as reeds, the cheeks pallid and drawn, the eyes like lamps in a mist, the throat bare of the shirt, and the lips kept apart by laboured breathing.

Near the window stood the cot where he had once slept with Pete, and leaped up in the morning and laughed. On every hand, wherever his eye could rest, there rose a phantom of his lost and buried life. And Auntie Nannie's love and pride had brought him to this chamber of torture!

The night was calm enough outside; but it seemed to lie dead within that room, so quiet was it and so still. There was a clock, but it did not go; and there was a cage for a bird, but no bird pecked in it, Philip thought he heard a knocking at the door of the house. Nobody answered it, so he rang for the maid. She came upstairs with a smile.

"Didn't you hear a knock at the front door, Martha?"

"No, sir," said the girl.

"Strange! Very strange! I could have sworn it was the knock of Mr. Quilliam."

"Perhaps it was, sir. Ill go and look."

"No matter. I've a singing in my ears to-night. It must be that."

The girl left him. He threw off his boots and began to creep about the room as if he were doing something in which he feared detection. Every time his eyes fell on the portrait of his father he dropped his head and turned aside. Presently he heard voices in the room below. This time the sound in his ears was no dreaming. He opened the door noiselessly and listened. It was Pete. Martha was answering him. Auntie Nan was calling from the dining-room, and Pete was saying "No, no," in a light way and moving off. The gate of the garden clicked and the front door was closed quietly. Then Philip shut the door of his own room without a sound.

A moment later Auntie Nan re-opened it. She was carrying a lighted candle.

"Such an extraordinary thing, Philip. Martha says you thought you heard Peter knocking, and, do you know, he must have been coming up the hill at that very moment. He was so strange, too, and looked so wild. Asked if anybody had been here inquiring for him; as if anybody should. Wouldn't have me call to you, and went off laughing about nothing. Really, if I hadn't known him for a sober man——"

Philip felt sick-and chill, and-he began to shiver. An irresistible impulse took hold of him. It was like the half-smothered fear which makes guilty men go to sit at the inquests on their murdered victims.

"Something wrong," he said. "Where are my boots?"

"Going to Elm Cottage, Philip? Pity the coachman drove back to Douglas. Hadn't you better send Martha? Besides, it may be only my fancy. Why worry in any case? You're too tender-hearted—indeed you are."

Philip fled downstairs like one who flies from torture. While dragging on his coat in the hall, he began to foresee what was before him. He was to go to Pete, pretending to know nothing; he was to hear Pete's story, and show surprise; he was to comfort Pete—perhaps to help him in his search, for he dared not appear *not* to help—he was to walk by Pete's side, looking for what he knew they should not find. He saw himself crawling along the streets like a snake, and the part he had to play revolted him. He went upstairs again.

"On second thoughts, you must be right, auntie."

"I'm sure I am."

"If not, he'll come again."

"I'm sure he will."

"If there's anything amiss with Pete, he'll come first to me."

"There can be nothing amiss except what I say. Just a glass too much maybe and no great sin either, considering the day, and how proud he is, for your sake, Philip. I believe in my heart that young man couldn't be prouder and happier if he stood in your own shoes instead."

"Good-night, Auntie," said Philip, in a thick gurgle.

"Good-night, dear. I'm going to bed, and mind you go yourself."

Being alone, Philip found himself leaning against the mantelpiece and looking across at his father's picture. He began to contrast his father with himself. He was a success, his father had been a failure. At seven-and-twenty he was Deemster at all events; at thirty his father had died a broken man. He had got what he had worked for; he had recovered the place of his people; and yet how mean a man he was compared to him who had done nothing and lost all.

Failure was all that his father had had to reproach himself with; but he had to accuse himself of dishonour as well. His father's offence had been a fault; his own was a crime. If his father had been willing to betray love and friendship, he might have succeeded. Because he himself had been true to neither, he had not failed. The very excess of his father's virtues had kept him down. Every act of his own selfishness had pushed him up. His father had thought first of love and truth and an upright life, and last of money and rank and applause. The world had renounced his father because his father had first renounced the world. But it had opened its arms to him, and followed him with shouts and cheers, and loaded him with honours. And yet, miserable man, better be down in the ooze and slime of a broken life, better be dead and in the grave—for the dead in his grave must despise him.

An awful picture rose before Philip. It was a picture of himself in the time to come. An old man—great, powerful, perhaps even beloved, maybe worshipped, but heart-dead, tottering on to the grave, and the mockery of a gorgeous funeral, with crowds and drums and solemn music. Then suddenly a great silence, as if the snow had begun to fall, and a great white light, and an awful voice crying, "Who is this that comes with dust for a bleeding heart, and ashes for a living soul?"

Philip screamed aloud at the vision, as piece by piece he put it together. His cry died off with a tingle in the china ornaments of the mantelpiece, and he remembered where he was. Then two gentle taps came to the door of his room. He composed himself a little, snatched up a book, and cried "Come in!"

It was Auntie Nan. She was in her night-dress and night-cap. A candle was in her hand, and the flame was shaking.

"Whatever's to do, my child?" she said.

"Only reading aloud, Auntie. Did I awaken you?"

"But you screamed, Philip."

"Macbeth, Auntie. See, the banquet scene. He has become king, you know, but his conscience——"

He stopped. The little lady looked at him dubiously and made a pull at the string of her night-cap, causing it to fall aside and give a grotesque appearance to her troubled old face.

"Take a little brandy, dear. I left it here on the dressing-table."

"Don't trouble about me, Auntie. Good-night again. There! go back to bed."

Half coaxing, half forcing her, he drew her to the door, and she went out slowly, reluctantly, doubtfully, the wandering strings of her cap trailing on her shoulders, and her bare feet nipping up the bottom of the night-dress behind her.

Philip looked at the book he had snatched up in his haste. What had put that book of all books into his hand? What had brought him to that room of all rooms? And on that night of all nights? What devil out of hell had tempted Auntie Nan to torture him? He would not stay; he would go back to his own bed.

Out on the landing he heard a low voice. It came from Auntie Nan's room. A spear of candle-light shot from her door, which was ajar. He paused and looked in. The white night-dress was by the bedside, the night-cap was buried in the counterpane. A cat had established itself beside it, and was purring softly. Auntie Nan was on her knees. Philip heard his own name——

"God bless my Philip in the great place to which he has been called this day. Give him wisdom and strength and peace!"

Holy woman, with angels hovering over you, who dared to think of devils tempting your innocence and love?

Philip went back to his father's room. He began to reconcile himself to his position. Though he had been extolling his father at his own expense, what had he done but realise his father's hopes. And, after all, he could not have acted differently. At no point could he have behaved otherwise than he had. What had he to accuse himself for? If there had been sin, he had been dragged into it by blind powers which he could not command. And what was true of himself was also true of Kate.

Ah! he could see her now. She was gone where he had sent her. There were tears in her beautiful eyes, but time would wipe them away. The duplicity of her old life was over; the corroding deceit, the daily torment, the hourly infidelity—all were left behind. If there was remorse, it was the fault of destiny; and if she was suffering the pangs of shame, she was a woman, and she would bear it cheerfully for the sake of the man she loved. She was going through everything for him. Heaven bless her! In spite of man and man's law, she was his love, his darling, his wife—yes, his wife—by right of nature and of God; and, come what would, he should cling to her to the last.

Suddenly a thick voice cut through the still air of the night.

"Philip!"

It was Pete at last He was calling up at the window from the path below. Philip groaned and covered his face with his hands.

"Philip!"

With rigid steps Philip walked to the window and threw up the sash. It was starlight, and the branches were bending in the night air.

"Is it you, Pete?"

"Yes, it's me. I was seeing the lamp, so I knew you war'n in bed at all. Studdying a bit, it's like, eh? I thought I wouldn't waken the house, but just shout up and tell you."

"What is it, Pete?" said Philip. His voice shivered like a sail at tacking.

"Nothing much at all. Only the wife's gone to England over by the night's steamer."

"To England?"

"Aw, time for it too, I'm thinking; the wake and narvous she's been lately. You remember what the doctor was saying yonder everin,' when we christened the child? 'Send her out of the island,' says he, 'and she'll be coming home another woman.' Wasn't for going, though. Crying and shouting she wouldn't be laving the lil one. So I had to put out a bit of authority. Of course, a husband's got the right to do that, Philip, eh? Well, I'll be taking the road again. Doing a fine night, isn't it? Make's a man unwilling to go to bed."

Philip trembled and felt sick. He tried to speak, but could utter nothing except an inarticulate noise. As Pete went off, an owl screeched in the glen. Philip drew down the sash, pulled the blind, tugged the curtains across, stumbled into the middle of the floor, and leaned against the bed.

"Such is the beginning of the end," he thought.

The duplicity, the deceit, the daily torment which Kate had left behind, were henceforward to be his own! At one flash, as of lightning, he saw the path before him. It was over cliffs and chasms and quagmires, where his foot might slip at any step.

His head began to reel. He took the brandy bottle from the dressing-table, poured out half a tumbler, and drained it at one draught. As he did so, his eyes above the rim of the glass rested on the portrait of his mother over the fireplace. The face as he saw it then was no longer the face of the winsome bride. It was the living face as he remembered it—bleared, bloated, gross, and drunken. She smiled on him, she beckoned to him.

It was the beginning of the end indeed. He was his mother's son as well as his father's. The father had ruled down to that day, but it was the turn of the mother now. He could not resist her. She was alive in his blood, and he was hers.

Never before had he touched raw spirits, and the brandy mastered him instantly. Feeling dizzy, he made an effort to undress and get into bed. He dragged off his coat and his waistcoat, and threw his braces over his shoulders. Then he stumbled, and he had to lay hold of the bedpost. His hand grew chill and relaxed its hold. Stupor came over him. He slipped, he slid, he fell, and rolled with outstretched arms on to the floor. The fire went out and the lamp died down.

133

Then the sun came up over the sea. It was a beautiful morning. The town awoke; people hailed each other cheerfully in the streets, and joy-bells rang from the big church tower for the first court-day of the new Deemster. But the Deemster himself still lay on the floor, with damp forehead and matted hair, behind the blind of the darkened room.

PART V. MAN AND MAN.

I.

It was Saturday, and the market-place was covered with the carts and stalls of the country people. After some feint of eating breakfast, Pete lit his pipe, called for a basket, and announced his intention of doing the marketing.

"Coming for the mistress, are you, Capt'n?"

"I'm a sort of a grass-widow, ma'am. What's your eggs to-day, Mistress Cowley?"

"Sixteen this morning, sir, and right ones too. They were telling me you've been losing her."

"Give me a shilling's worth, then. Any news over your side, Mag?"

"Two—four—eight—sixteen—it's every appearance we'll be getting a early harvest, Capt'n."

"Is it yourself, Liza? And how's your butter to-day?"

"Bad to bate to-day, sir, and only thirteen pence ha'penny. Is the lil one longing for the mistress, Capt'n?"

"I'll take a couple of pounds, then. What for longing at all when it's going bringing up by hand it is? Put it in a cabbage leaf, Liza."

Thus, with his basket on his arm and his pipe in his mouth, Pete passed from stall to stall, chatting, laughing, bargaining, buying, shouting his salutations over the general hum and hubbub, as he ploughed his way through the crowd, but listening intently watching eagerly, casting out grapples to catch the anchor he had lost, and feeling all the time that if any eye showed sign of knowledge, if any one began with "Capt'n, I can tell you where she is," he must leap on the man like a tiger, and strangle the revelation in his throat.

Next day, Sunday, his friends from Sulby came to quiz and to question. He was lounging in his shirt-sleeves on a deck-chair in his ship's cabin, smoking a long pipe, and pretending to be at ease and at peace with all the world.

"Fine morning, Capt'n," said John the Clerk.

"It *is* doing a fine morning, John," said Pete.

"Fine on the sea, too," said Jonaique.

"Wonderful fine on the sea, Mr. Jelly."

"A nice fair wind, though, if anybody was going by the packet to Liverpool. Was it as good, think you, for the mistress on Friday night, Mr. Quilliam?"

"I'll gallantee," said Pete.

"Plucky, though—I wouldn't have thought it of the same woman—I wouldn't raelly," said Jonaique.

"Alone, too, and landing on the other side so early in the morning," said John the Clerk.

"Smart, uncommon! It isn't every woman would have done it," said Kelly the Postman.

"Aw, we've mighty boys of women deese days—we have dough," snuffled the constable, and then they all laughed together.

Pete watched their wheedling, fawning, and whisking of the tail, and then he said, "Chut! What's there so wonderful about a woman going by herself to Liverpool when she's got somebody waiting at the stage to meet her?"

The laughing faces lengthened suddenly. "And had she, then," said John the Clerk.

Pete puffed furiously, rolled in his seat, laughed like a man with a mouth full of water, and said, "Why, sartenly—my uncle, of coorse."

Jonaique wrinkled his forehead. "Uncle," he said, with a click in his throat.

"Yes, my Uncle Joe," said Pete.

Jonaique looked helplessly across at John the Clerk. John the Clerk puckered up his mouth as if about to whistle, and then said, in a faltering way, "Well, I can't really say I've ever heard tell of your Uncle Joe before, Capt'n."

"No?" said Pete, with a look of astonishment. "Not my Uncle Joseph? The one that left the island forty years ago and started in the coach and cab line? Well, that's curious. Where's he living? Bless me, where's this it is, now? Chut! it's clane forgot at me. But I saw him myself coming home from Kimberley, and since then he's been writing constant. 'Send her across,' says he; 'she'll be her own woman again like winking.' And you never heard tell of him? Not Uncle Joey with the bald head? Well, well! A smart ould man, though. Man alive, the lively he is, too, and the laughable, and the good company. To look at that man's face you'd say the sun was shining reg'lar. Aw, it's fine times she'll be having with Uncle Joe. No woman could be ill with yonder ould man about. He'd break your face with laughing if it was bursting itself with a squinsey. And you never heard tell of my Uncle Joe, of Scotland Road, down Clarence Dock way? To think of that now!"

They went off with looks of perplexity, and Pete turned into the house. "They're trying to catch me; they're wanting to shame my poor lil Kirry. I must keep her name sweet," he thought.

The church bells had begun to ring, and he was telling himself that, heavy though his heart might be, he must behave as usual.

"She'll be going walking to church herself this morning, Nancy," he said, putting on his coat, "so I'll just slip across to chapel."

He was swinging up the path on his return home to dinner, when he heard voices inside the house.

"It's shocking to see the man bittending this and bittending that." It was Nancy; she was laying the table; there was a rattle of knives and forks. "Bittending to ate, but only pecking like a robin; bittending to sleep, but never a wink on the night; bittending to laugh and to joke and wink, and a face at him like a ghose's, and his hair all through-others. Walking about from river to quay, and going on with all that rubbish—it's shocking, ma'am, it's shocking!"

"Hush-a-bye, hush-a-bye!" It was the voice of Grannie, low and quavery; she was rocking the cradle.

"You can't spake to him neither but he's scolding you scandalous. 'I'm not used of being cursed at,' I'm saying, 'and is it myself that has to be tould to respect my own Kitty?' But cry shame on her I must when I look at the lil bogh there, and it so helpless and so beautiful. 'Stericks, you say? Yes, indeed, ma'am, and if I stay here much longer, it's losing myself I will be, too, with his bittending and bittending."

"Lave him to it, Nancy. His poor head's that moidered and mixed it's like a black pudding—there's no saying what's inside of it. But he's good, though; aw, right good he is for all, and the world's cold and cruel. Lave him alone, woman; lave him alone, poor boy."

The child awoke and cried, and, under cover of this commotion and the crowing and cooing of the two women, Pete stepped back to the gate, clashed it hard, swung noisily up the gravel, and rolled into the house with a shout and a laugh.

"Well, well! Grannie, my gough! Who'd have thought of seeing Grannie, now? And how's the ould angel to-day? So you've got the lil one there? Aw, you rogue, you. You're on Grannie's lap, are you? How's Cæsar? And how's Mrs. Gorry doing? Look at that now—did you ever? Opening one eye first to make sure if the world's all right. The child's wise. Coo—oo—oo! Smart with the dinner, Nancy—wonderful hungry the chapel's making a man. Coo—oo! What's she like, now, Grannie?"

"When I set her to my knee like this I can see my own lil Kirry again," said Grannie, looking down ruefully, rocking the child with one knee and doubling over it to kiss it.

"So she's like the mammy, is she?" said Pete, blowing at the baby and tickling its chin with his broad forefinger. "Mammy's gone to the ould uncle's—hasn't she, my lammie?"

At that Grannie fell to rocking herself as well as the child, and to singing a hymn in a quavery voice. Then with a rattle and a rush, throwing off his coat and tramping the floor in his shirt-sleeves, while Nancy dished up the dinner, Pete began to enlarge on Kate's happiness in the place where she had gone.

"Tremenjous grand the ould man's house is—you wouldn't believe. A reg'lar Dempster's palace. The grandeur on it is a show and a pattern. Plenty to ate, plenty to drink, and a boy at the door with white buttons dotting on his brown coat, bless you like—like a turnip-field in winter. Then the man himself; goodness me, the happy that man is—Happy Joe they're calling him. Wouldn't trust but he'll be taking Kate to a theaytre. Well, and why not, if a person's down a bit? A merry touch and go—where's the harm at all? Fact is, Grannie, that's why we couldn't tell you Kate was going. Cæsar would have been objecting. He's fit enough for it—ha, ha, ha!"

Grannie looked up at Pete as he laughed, and the broad rose withered on his face.

"H'm! h'm!" he said, clearing his throat; "I'm bad dreadful wanting a smook." And past the dinner-table, now smoking and ready, he slithered out of the house.

Cæsar was Pete's next visitor. He said nothing of Kate, and neither did Pete mention Uncle Joe. The interview was a brief and grim one. It was a lie that Ross Christian had been sent by his father to ask for a loan, but it was true that Peter Christian was in urgent need of money. He wanted six thousand pounds as mortgage on Ballawhaine. Had Pete got so much to lend? No need for personal intercourse; Cæsar would act as intermediary.

Pete took only a moment for consideration. Yes, he had got the money, and he would lend it. Cæsar looked at Pete; Pete looked at Cæsar. "He's talking all this rubbish," thought Cæsar, "but he knows where the girl has gone to. He knows who's taken her; he manes to kick the rascal out of his own house neck and crop; and right enough, too, and the Lord's own vengeance."

But Pete's thoughts were another matter. "The ould man won't live to redeem it, and the young one will never try—it'll do for Philip some day."

II.

For three days Pete bore himself according to his wont, thinking to silence the evil tongues of the little world about him, and keep sweet and alive the dear name which they were waiting to befoul and destroy. By Tuesday morning the strain had become unbearable. On pretences of business, of pleasure, of God knows what folly and nonsense, he began to scour the island. He visited every parish on the north, passed through every village, climbed every glen, found his way into every out-of-the-way hut, and scraped acquaintance with every old woman living alone. Sometimes he was up in the vague fore-dawn, creeping through the quiet streets like a thief, going silently,

135

stealthily, warily, until he came to the roads, or the fields, or the open Curragh, and could give swing to his step, and breath to his lungs, and voice to the cries that burst from him.

Two long weeks he spent in this wild quest, and meanwhile he was as happy as a boy to all outward seeming—whistling, laughing, chaffing, bawling, talking nonsense, any nonsense, and kicking up his heels like a kid. But wheresoever he went, and howsoever early he started on his errands, he never failed to be back at home at seven o'clock in the evening—washed, combed, in his slippers and shirt-sleeves, smoking a long clay over the garden gate as the postman went by with the letters.

"She'll write," he told himself. "When she's mending a bit she'll aise our mind and write. 'Dear ould Pete, excuse me for not writing afore'—that'll be the way of it. Aw, trust her, trust her."

But day followed day, and no letter came from Kate. Ten evenings running he smoked over the gate, leisurely, largely, almost languidly, but always watching for the peak of the postman's cap as it turned the corner by the Court-house, and following the toes of his foot as they stepped off the curb, to see if they pointed in his direction—and then turning aside with a deep breath and a smothered moan that ended in a rattle of the throat and a pretence at spitting.

The postman saw him as he went by, and his little eyes twinkled treacherously.

"Nothing for you yet, Capt'n," he said at length.

"Chut!" said Pete, with a mighty puff of smoke; "my business isn't done by correspondence, Mr. Kelly."

"Aw, no; but when a man's wife's away——" began the postman.

"Oh, I see," said Pete, with a look of intelligence, and then, with a lofty wave of the hand, "She's like her husband, Mr. Kelly—not bothering much with letters at all."

"You'll be longing for a line, though, Capt'n—that's only natural."

"No news is good news—I can lave it with her."

"Of coorse, that's truth enough, yes! But still and for all, a taste of a letter—it's doing no harm, Capt'n—aisy writ, too, and sweet to get sometimes, you know—shows a woman isn't forgetting a man when she's away."

"Mr. Kelly! Mr. Kelly!" said Pete, with his hand before his face, palm outwards.

"Not necessary? Well, I lave it with you. Good-night, Capt'n."

"Good-night to you, sir," said Pete.

He had laughed and tut-tutted, and lifted his eyebrows and his hands in mock protest and a pretence of indifference, but the postman's talk had cut him to the quick. "People are suspecting," he thought. "They're saying things."

This made him swear, but a thought came behind that made him sweat instead. "Philip will be hearing them. They'll be telling him she doesn't write to me; that I don't know where she is; that she has left me, and that she's a bad woman."

To make Kate stand well with Philip was an aim that had no rival but one in Pete's reckoning—to make Philip stand well with Kate. Out of the shadow-land of his memory of the awful night of his bereavement, a recollection, which had been lying dead until then, came back now in its grave-clothes to torture him. It was what Cæsar had said of Philip's fight with Ross Christian. Philip himself had never mentioned it—that was like him. But when evil tongues told of Ross and hinted at mischief, Philip would know something already; he would be prepared, perhaps he would listen and believe.

Two days longer Pete sat in the agony of this new terror and the dogged impatience of his old hope. "She'll write. She'll not lave me much longer." But she did not write, and on the second night, before returning to the house from the gate, he had made his plan. He must silence scandal at all hazards. However his own heart might bleed with doubts and fears and misgivings, Philip must never cease to think that Kate was good and sweet and true.

"Off to bed, Nancy," he cried, heaving into the hall like a man in drink. "I've work to do to-night, and want the house to myself."

"Goodness me, is it yourself that's talking of bed, then?" said Nancy. "Seven in the everin', too, and the child not an hour out of my hands? And dear knows what work it is if you can't be doing it with good people about you."

"Come, get off, woman; you're looking tired mortal. The lil one's ragging you ter'ble. But what's it saying, Nancy—bed is half bread. Truth enough, too, and the other half is beauty. Get off, now. You're spoiling your complexion dreadful—I'll never be getting that husband for you."

Thus coaxing her, cajoling her, watching her, dodging her, nagging her, driving her, he got her off to bed at last. Being alone, he looked around, listened, shut the doors of the parlour and the kitchen, put the bolt on the door of the stairs, the chain on the door of the porch, took off his boots, and went about on tiptoe. Then he blew out the lamp, filled and trimmed and relit it, going down on the hearthrug to catch the light of the fire. After that he settled the table, drew up the armchair, took from a corner cupboard pens and ink, a blotting pad, a packet of notepaper and envelopes, a stick of sealing wax, a box of matches, a postage stamp, the dictionary, and the exercise-book in which Kate had taught him to write.

As the clock was striking nine, Pete was squaring himself at the table, pen in hand, and his tongue in his left cheek. Half an hour later he was startled, by an interruption.

"Who's there?" he shouted in a ferocious voice, leaping up with a look of terror, like a man caught in a crime. It was only Nancy, who had come creeping down the stairs under pretence of having forgotten the baby's bottle. He made a sort of apologetic growl, handed the flat bottle through an opening like a crack, and ordered her back to bed.

"Goodness sakes!" said Nancy, going upstairs. "Is it coining money the man is? Or is it whisky itself that's doing on him?"

Two hours afterwards Pete fancied he saw a face at the window, and he caught up a stick, unchained the door, and rushed into the garden. It was no one; the town lay asleep; the night was all but airless; only the faintest breeze moved the leaves of the trees; there was no noise anywhere, except the measured beat of the sea in its everlasting coming and going on the shore.

Stepping back into the house, where the fire chirped and the kettle sang and all else was quiet, he resumed his task, and somewhere in the dark hours before the dawn he finished it. The fingers of his right hand were then inky up to the first joint, his collar was open, his neck was bare, his eyes were ablaze, the cords on his face were big and blue, great beads of cold sweat were standing on his forehead, and the carpet around his chair was littered as white as if a snowstorm had fallen on it.

He went down on his knees and gathered up these remnants and burnt them, with the air of a man destroying the evidences of his guilt. Then he put back the ink and the dictionary, the blotting pad and sealing wax, and replaced them with a loaf of bread, a table knife, a bottle of brandy, and a drinking glass. After that he made up the fire with a shovel of slack, that it might burn until morning; removed the lamp from the table to the window recess that it might cast its light into the darkness outside; and unchained the outer door that a wanderer of the night, if any such there were, might enter without knocking.

He did all this in the absent manner of a man who did it nightly. Then unbolting the staircase door, and listening a moment for the breathing of the sleepers overhead, he crept into the dark parlour overlooking the road, and lay down on the sofa to sleep.

It was done! Pete's great scheme was afoot! The mighty secret which he had enshrouded with such awful mystery lay in an envelope in the inside breast-pocket of his monkey-jacket, signed, sealed, stamped, and addressed.

Pete had written a letter to himself.

III.

Next day the crier was crying: "Great meeting—Manx fishermen—on Zigzag at Peel when boats come in to-morrow morning—protest agen harbour taxes."

"The thing itself," thought Pete, with his hand pressed hard on the outside of his breast-pocket. At five o'clock in the afternoon he went down to the harbour, where his Nickey lay by the quay, shouted to the master, "Take an odd man tonight, Mr. Kemish?" then dropped to the deck and helped to fetch the boat into the bay.

They had to haul her out by poles alone the quay wall, for the tide was low, and there was no breakwater. It was still early in the herring season, but the fishing was in full swing. Five hundred boats from all parts were making for the fishing round. It lay off the south-west tail of the island. Before Pete's boat reached it the fleet were sitting together, like a flight of sea-fowl, and the sun was almost gone.

The sun went down that night over the hills of Mourne very angry and red in its setting; the sky to the north-west was dark and sullen; the round line of the sea was bleared and broken, but there was little wind, and the water was quiet.

"Bring to and shoot," cried Pete, and they dropped sail to the landward of the fleet, off the shoulder of the Calf Island, with its two lights making one. The boat was brought head to the wind, with the flowing tide veering against her; the nets were shot over the starboard quarter, and they dropped astern; the bow was swung round to the line of the floating mollags, and boat and nets began to drift together.

Supper was served, the pump was worked, the lights were run up, the small boat was sent round with a flare to fright away the evil spirits, and then the night came down—a dark night, without moon or stars, shutting out the island, though it stood so near, and even the rocks of the Hen and Chicken. The first man for the look-out took up his one hour's watch at the helm, and the rest went below.

Pete's bunk was under the binnacle, and the light of its lamp fell on a stamped envelope which he took out of his breast-pocket from time to time that he might read the inscription. It ran—

        Capn Peatr Quilliam,

        Lm Cottig Ramsey I O Man.

He looked at it lovingly, fondly, yearningly, yet with a certain awe, too, as if it were the casket of some hidden treasure, and he hardly knew what it contained. The dim-lit cabin was quiet, the net boiler sparched drops of hot water at intervals, the fire of the cooking stove slid and fell, the men breathed heavily from unseen beds, and the sea washed as the boat rolled.

"What's she saying, I wonder! I wonder! God bless her!" he mumbled, and then he, too, fell asleep.

Two hours before hauling, they proved the fishing by taking in a "pair" of the net, found good herring, and blew the horn as signal that they were doing well. Then out of the black depths around, wherein no boat could be seen, the lights of other boats came floating silently astern, until the company about them in the darkness was like a little city of the sea and the night.

At the first peep of morning over the round shoulder of the Calf, the little city awoke. There were the clicks of the capstan, and the shouts of the men as the nets came back to the boats, heavy and white with fish. All being aboard, the men went down on the deck, according to their wont, every man on his knee with his face in his cap, and then leapt up with a shout (perhaps an oath), swung to the wind, hoisted the square sails, and made for home. The dark northwest was lowering by this time, and the sea was beginning to jump.

"Breakfast, boys," sang out Pete, with his head above the companion, and all but the helmsman went below. There was a pot full of the drop-fish, and every man ate his warp of herring. It had been a great night's fishing. Some of the boats were full to the mouth, and all had plenty.

"We'll do middling if we get a market," said Pete.

"We've got to get home first," said the master, and at the same moment a sea struck the windward quarter with the force of a sledge-hammer, and the block at the masthead began to sing.

137

"We'll run for Peel this morning, boys," said Pete, smothering his voice in a mouthful.

"Peel?" said the master, shooting out his lip. "They've got no harbour there at all with a cat's paw of a breeze, let alone a northwester."

"I'm for going up to the meeting," said Pete in an incoherent way.

Then they tacked before the rising gale, and went off with the fleet as it swirled like a flight of gulls abreast of the wind. The sea came tumbling down like a shoal of seahogs, and washed the faces of the men as they sat in oilskins on the hatch-head, shaking the herring out of the nets into the hold.

But their work only began when they came into Peel. The tide was down; there was no breakwater; the neck of the harbour was narrow, and four hundred boats were coming to take shelter and to land their cargoes. It was a scene of tumult and confusion—shouting, swearing, and fighting among the men, and crushing and cranching among the boats as they nosed their way to the harbour mouth, threw ropes on to the quay, where fifty ropes were round one post already, or cast anchors up the bank of the castle rock, which was steep and dangerous to lie on.

Pete got landed somehow, but his Nickey with half the fleet turned tail and went round the island. As he leapt ashore, the helpless harbour-master, who had been bellowing over the babel through a cracked trumpet, turned to him and said, "For the Lord's sake, Capt'n Quilliam, if you've got a friend that can lend us a hand, go off to the meeting at seven o'clock."

"I mane to," said Pete, but he had something else to do first. It was the task that had brought him to Peel, and no eye must see him do it. Slowly and slyly, like one who does a doubtful thing and pretends to be doing nothing, he went stealing through the town—behind the old Court-house and up Castle Street, into the market-place, and across it to the line of shops which make the principal thoroughfare.

At one of these shops, a little single-roomed place, with its small shutter still up, but the door half open and a noise of stamping going on inside, he stopped in a lounging way, half twisting on his heel as if idly looking back. It was the Post-Office.

With a stealthy look around, he put a trembling hand into his breast-pocket, drew out the letter, screened it by the flat of his big palm, and posted it. Then he turned hurriedly away, and was gone in a moment, like a man who feared pursuit, down a steep and tortuous alley that led to the shore. The morning was early; the shops were not yet open; only the homes of the fishermen were putting out curling wreaths of smoke; the silent streets echoed to his lightest footstep.

But the shore road was busy enough. Fishermen in sea-boots and sou'westers, with oilskin over one arm and a string of herring in the other hand, were trooping from the harbour up to the Zigzag by the rock called the Creg Malin. It was at the end of the bay, where cliff and beach and sea together form a bag like the cod-end of the trawl net.

"It's not the fishermen at all—it's the farmers they're thinking of," said one.

"You're right," said Pete, "and it's some of ourselves that's to blame for it."

"How's that?" said somebody.

"Aisy enough," said Pete. "When I came home from Kimberly I met an ould fisherman—*you* know the man, Billy—well, *you* do, Dan—Phil Nelly, of Ramsey. 'How's the fishing, Phil?' says I. He gave me a Hm! and a heise of his neck, and 'I'm not fishing no more,' says he. 'The wife's keeping a private hotel,' says he. 'And what are you doing yourself,' says I. 'I'm walking about,' says he, and, gough bless me, if the man wasn't wearing a collar and carrying a stick, and prating about advertising the island, if you plaze."

At the sound of Pete's voice a group of the men gathered about him. "That's not the worst neither," said he. "The other day I tumbled over Tom Hommy—*you* know Tom Hommy, yes, you do, the lil deaf man up Ballure. He was lying in the hedge by the public-house, three sheets in the wind. 'Why aren't you out with the boats, Tom?' says I. 'Wash for should I go owsh wish the boash, when the childer can earn more on the roads?' says the drunken wastrel. 'And is yonder your boys and girls tossing summersaults at the tail of the trippers' car?' says I. 'Yesh,' says he; 'and they'll earn more in a day at their caperings than their father in a week at the herrings.'"

"I believe it enough," said one. "The man's about right," said another; and a querulous voice behind said, "Wonderful the prosperity of the island since the visitors came to it."

"Get out with you, there, for a disgrace to the name of Manxman," sang out Pete over the heads of those that stood between. "With the farming going to the dogs and the fishing going to the divil, d'ye know what the ould island's coming to? It's coming to an island of lodging-house keepers and hackney-car drivers. Not the Isle of Man at all, but the Isle of Manchester."

There was a tremendous shout at this last word. In another minute Pete was lifted shoulder high over the crowd on to the highest turn of the zigzag path, and bidden to go on. There were five hundred faces below him, putting out hot breath in the cool morning air. The sun was shooting over the cliffs a canopy as of smoke above their heads. On the top of the crag the sea-fowl were jabbering, and the white sea itself was climbing on the beach.

"Men," said Pete, "there's not much to say. This morning's work said everything. We'd a right fishing last night, hadn't we? Four hundred boats came up to Peel, and we hadn't less than ten maise apiece. That's—you that's smart at your figguring and ciphering, spake out now—that's four thousand maise isn't it?" (Shouts of "Right.") "Aw, you're quick wonderful. No houlding you at all when it's money that's in. Four thousand maise ready and waiting for the steamers to England—but did we land it? No, nor half of it neither. The other half's gone round to other ports, too late for the day's sailing, and half of that half will be going rotten and getting chucked back into the sea. That's what the Manx fishermen have lost this morning because they haven't harbours to shelter them, and yet they're talking of levying harbour dues."

"Man veen, he's a boy!"—"He's all that"—"Go it, Capt'n. What are we to do?"

"Do?" cried Pete. "I'll tell you what you're to do. This is Friday. Next Thursday is old Midsummer Day. That's Tynwald Coort day. Come to St. John's on Thursday—every man of you come—come in your sea-boots and your jerseys—let the Governor see you mane it. 'Give us raisonable hope of harbour improvement and we'll pay,' says you. 'If you don't, we won't; and if you try to make us, we're two thousand strong, and we'll rise like one man.' Don't be freckened; you've a right to be bould in a good cause. I'll get somebody to spake for you. You know the man I mane. He's stood the fisherman's friend before to-day, and he isn't going taking off his cap to the best man that's setting foot on Tynwald Hill."

It was agreed. Between that day and Tynwald day Pete was to enlist the sympathy of Philip, and to go to Port St. Mary to get the co-operation of the south-side fishermen. The town was astir by this time, the sun was on the beach, and the fishermen trooped off to bed.

IV.

Pete was back in his ship's cabin in the garden the same evening with a heart the heavier because for one short hour it had forgotten its trouble. The flowers were opening, the roses were creeping over the porch, the blackbird was singing at the top of the tree; but his own flower of flowers, his rose of roses, his bird of birds—where was she? Summer was coming, coming, coming—coming with its light, coming with its music, coming with its sweetness—but she came not.

The clock struck seven inside the house, and Pete, pipe in hand, swung over to the gate. No need to-night to watch for the postman's peak, no need to trace his toes.

"A letter for you, Mr. Quilliam."

Hearing these words, Pete, his eyes half shut as if dosing in the sunset, wakened himself with a look of astonishment.

"What? For me, is it? A letter, you say? Aw, I see," taking it and turning it in his hand, "just'a line from the mistress, it's like. Well, well! A letter for me, if you plaze," and he laughed like a man much tickled.

He was in no hurry. He rammed his dead pipe with his finger, lit it again, sucked it, made it quack, drew a long breath, and then said quietly, "Let's see what's her news at all."

He opened the letter leisurely, and read bits of it aloud, as if reading to himself, but holding the postman while he did so in idle talk on the other side of the gate. "And how are you living to-day, Mr. Kelly? Aw, h'm—*getting that much better* it's extraordinary—Yes, a nice everin', very, Mr. Kelly, nice, nice—*that happy and comfortable and Uncle Joe is that good*—heavy bag at you to-night, you say? Aw, heavy, yes, heavy—*love to Grannie and all inquiring friends*—nothing, Mr. Kelly, nothing—just a scribe of a line, thinking a man might be getting unaisy. She needn't, though—she needn't. But chut! It's nothing. Writing a letter is nothing to her at all. Why, she'd be knocking that off, bless you," holding out a half sheet of paper, "in less than an hour and a half. Truth enough, sir." Then, looking at the letter again, "What's this, though? PN. They're always putting a P.N. at the bottom of a letter, Mr. Kelly. P.N.—*I was expecting to be home before, but I wouldn't get away for Uncle Joe taking me to the theaytres.* Ha, ha, ha! A mighty boy is Uncle Joe. But, Mr. Kelly, Mr. Kelly," with a solemn look, "not a word of this to Cæsar?"

The postman had been watching Pete out of the corners of his ferret eyes. "Do you know, Capt'n, what Black Tom is saying?"

"What's that?" said Pete, with a sudden change of tone.

"He's saying there *is* no Uncle Joe."

"No Uncle Joe?" cried Pete, lifting voice and eyebrows together.

The postman signified assent with a nod of his peak.

"Well, that's rich," said Pete, in a low breath, raising his face as if to invoke the astonishment of the sky itself. "No Uncle Joe?" he repeated, in a tone of blank incredulity. "Ask the man if it's in bed he is. Why," and Pete's eyes opened and closed like a doll's, "he'll be saying there's no Auntie Joney next."

The postman looked up inquiringly.

"Never heard of Auntie Joney—Uncle Joe's wife? No? Well, really, really—is it sleeping I am? Not Auntie Joney, the Primitive? Aw, a good ould woman as ever lived. A saint, if ever the like was in, and died a triumphant death, too. No theaytres for her, though. She won't bemane herself. No, but she's going to chapel reg'lar, and getting up in the middle of every night of life to say her prayers. 'Deed she is. So Black Tom says there is no Uncle Joe?"

Pete gave a long whistle, then stopped it sudden with his mouth agape, and said from his throat, "I see."

He put his mouth close to the postman's ear and whispered, "Ever hear Black Tom talk of the fortune he's expecting through the Coort of Chancery?" The postman's peak bobbed downwards. "You have? Tom's thinking to grab it all for himself. Ha, ha! That's it! Ha, ha!"

The postman went off blinking and giggling, and Pete reeled up the path, biting his lip, and muttering, "Keep it up, Pete, keep it up—it's ploughing a hard furrow, though." Then aloud, "A letter from the mistress, Nancy."

Nancy met him in the porch, clearing her fingers, thick with dough.

"There you are," said Pete, flapping the letter on one hand.

"Good sakes alive!" said Nancy. "Did it come by the post, though, Pete?"

"Look at the stamp, woman, and see for yourself," said Pete.

"My goodness me! From Kirry, you say?"

"Let me in, then, and I'll be reading you bits."

Nancy went back to her kneading with looks of bewilderment, and Pete followed her, opening the letter.

139

"She's well enough, Nancy—no need to read that part at all. But see," running his forefinger along the writing "'*Kisses for the baby, and love to Nancy, and tell Grannie not to be fretting?* et setterer, et setterer. See?'"

Nancy looked up at her thumping and thunging, and said, "Did Mr. Kelly give it you?"

"He did that," said Pete, "this minute at the gate. It's his time, isn't it?"

Nancy glanced at the clock. "I suppose it must be right," she said.

"Take it in your hand, woman," said Pete.

Nancy cleaned her hands and took the letter, turned it over and felt it in her fingers as if it had been linen. "And this is from Kirry, is it? It's nice, too. I haven't much schooling, Pete, but I'm asking no better than a letter myself. It's like a peppermint in your frock on Sunday—if you're low you're always knowing it's there, anyway." She looked at it again, and then she said, like one who says a strange thing, "I once had a letter myself—'deed I had, Pete. It was from father. He went down in the *Black Sloop*, trading oranges with the blacks in their own island somewhere. They put into the port of London one day when they were having a funeral there. What's this one they were calling after the big boots—Wellingtons, that's the man. They were writing home all about it—the people, and the chariots, and the fighting horses, and the music in the streets and the Cateedrals—and we were never hearing another word from them again—never. 'To Miss Annie Cain—your affecshunet father, Joe Cain.' I knew it all off—every word—and I kept it ten years in my box under the lavender."

Philip came later. He was looking haggard and tired; his face was pallid and drawn; his eyes were red, quick, and wandering; his hair was neglected and ragged; his step was wavering and uncertain.

"Gough alive, man," cried Pete, "didn't you take oath to do justice between man and man?"

Philip looked up with alarm. "Well?" he said.

"Well," cried Pete, with a frown and a clenched fist, "there's one man you're not doing justice to."

"Who's that?" said Philip with eyes down.

"Yourself," said Pete, and Philip drew a long breath. Pete laughed, protested that Philip must not work so hard, and then plunged into an account of the morning's meeting.

"Tremenjous! Talk of enthusiasm! Man veen, man veen! Didn't I say we'd rise as one man? We will, too. We're going up to Tynwald Coort on Tynwald day, two thousand strong. Tynwald Coort? Yes, and why not? Drum and fife bands, bless you—two of them. Not much music, maybe, but there'll be noise enough. It's all settled. Southside fishermen are coming up Foxal way; north-side men going down by Peel. Meeting under Harry Delany's tree, and going up to the hill on mass (en masse). No bawling, though—no singing out—no disturbing the Coort at all."

"Well, well! What then?" said Philip.

"Then we're wanting you to spake for us, Dempster. Aw, nothing much—nothing to rag you at all. Just tell them flat we won't—that'll do."

"It's a serious matter, Pete. I must think it over."

"Aw, think and think enough, Dempster—but mind you do it, though. The boys are counting on you. 'He's our anchor and he'll hould,' they're saying; But, bother the harbours, anyway," reaching his hand for something on the mantelpiece. "What do you think?"

"Nay," said Philip, with a long breath of weariness and relief.

"Guess, then," said Pete, putting his hand behind him.

Philip shook his head and smiled feebly. Then, with the expression of a boy on his birthday, Pete leaned over Philip, and said in a half-whisper across the top of his head, "I've heard from Kate."

Philip turned ghastly, his lip trembled, and he stammered, "You've—you've—heard from Kate, have you?"

"Look at that," cried Pete, and round came the letter with a triumphant sweep.

Philip's respiration grew difficult and noisy. Slowly, very slowly, he reached out his hand, took the letter, and looked at its superscription.

"Read it—read it," said Pete; "no secrets at all."

With head down and eyebrows hiding his eyes, with trembling hands that tore the envelope, Philip took out the letter and read it in passages—broken, blurred, smudged, as by the smoke of a fo'c'stle lamp.

```
"Deerest peat i am gettin that much better... i am that
happy and comforbel... sometimes i am longing for a sight of
the lil ones swate face... no more at present... ure own
trew wife."
```

"Come to the P. N. yet, Philip?" said Pete. He was on his knees before the fire, lighting his pipe with a red coal.

```
"axpectin to be home sune but... give my luv and bess
respects to the Dempster when you see him he was so good to me
when "were forren the half was never towl you"
```

"She's not laving a man unaisy, you see," said Pete.

Philip could not speak. His throat was choking; his tongue filled his mouth; his eyes were swimming in tears that scorched them. Nancy, who had been up to Sulby with news of the letter, came in at the moment, and Philip raised his head.

"I told my aunt not to expect me to-night, Nancy. Is my room upstairs ready?"

"Aw, yes, always ready, your honour," said Nancy, with a curtsey.

He got up, with head aside, took a candle from Nancy's hand, excused himself to Pete—he was tired, sleepy, had a heavy day to-morrow—said "Good-night," and went upstairs—stumbling and floundering—tore open his bedroom door, and clashed it back like a man flying from an enemy.

Pete thought he had succeeded to admiration, but he looked after Philip, and was not at ease. He had no misgivings. Writing was writing to him, and it was nothing more. But in the deep midnight, Philip, who had not slept, heard a thick voice that was like a sob coming from somewhere downstairs. He opened his door, crept out on to the stairhead, and listened. The house was dark. In some unseen place the voice was saying—

"Lord, forgive me for deceaving Philip. I couldn't help it, though; Thou knows, Thyself, I couldn't. A lie's a dirty thing, Lord. It's like chewing dough—it sticks in your throat and chokes you. But I had to do it to save my poor lost lamb, and if I didn't I should go mad myself—Thou knows I should. So forgive me, Lord, for Kirry's sake. Amen."

The thick voice stopped, the house lay still, then the child awoke in a room beyond, and its thin cry came through the darkness. Philip crept back in terror.

"This is what *she* had to go through! O God! My God!"

V.

Cæsar called next day and took Pete to the office of the High Bailiff, where the business of the mortgage was completed. The deeds of Ballawhaine were then committed to Cæsar's care for custody and safe keeping, and he carried them off to his safe at the mill with a long stride and a face of fierce triumph.

"The ould Ballawhaine is dying," he thought; "and if we kick out the young one some day, it'll only be the Lord's hand on a rascal."

On drawing his big cheque, Pete had realised that, with reckless spending, and more reckless giving, he had less than a hundred pounds to his credit. "No matter," he thought; "Philip will pay me back when he comes in to his own."

Grannie was with Nancy at Elm Cottage when Pete returned home. The child was having its morning bath, and the two women were on their knees at either side of the tub, cackling and crowing like two old hens over one egg.

"Aw, did you *ever*, now, Nancy? 'Deed, no; you never *did* see such a lil angel. Up-a-daisy!"

"Cry I must, Grannie, when I see it looking so beautiful. Warm towels, you say? I'm a girl of this sort—when I get my heart down, I can never get it up again. Fuller's earth, is it? Here, then."

"Boo—loo—loo! the bog millish! Nancy, we must be shortening her soon."

And with that they fell to an earnest council on frocks and petticoats, and other mysteries unread by man. Pete sat and watched and listened. "People will be crying shame on her if they see the Grannie doing everything," he thought.

That night he lounged through the town and examined the shop windows out of the corner of his eye. He was trying to bear himself like a workman enjoying his Saturday night's ramble in clean clothes, but the streets were thronged, and he found himself observed. "Not here," he told himself. "I can buy nothing here. Doesn't do to be asleep at all, and a man isn't always in bed when he's sleeping."

Some hours later, Nancy and the child being upstairs, Pete bethought himself of something that was kept at the bottom of a drawer. Going to the drawer to open it, he found it stiff to his tugging, and it came back with a jerk, which showed it had not lately been disturbed. Pete found what he looked for, and came upon something beside. It was a cardboard box, tied about with a string, which was knotted in a peculiar way. "Kate's knot," thought Pete with a sigh. He slipped it, and opened the lid and took out a baby's hood of scarlet plush. "The very thing," he thought. He held it, mouth open, over his big brown hand, and laughed with delight. "She's been buying it for the child and never using it." His eyes glistened. "The *very* thing," he thought, and then he took down pen and paper to write something to go with it.

This is what he wrote—

"For lil Katerin from her Luvin mother"

Then he held it at arm's length and looked at it. The subscription crossed the whole face of a half-sheet of paper. But the triumphant success of his former effort had made him bold. He could not resist the temptation to write more. So he turned the paper over and wrote on the back—

"tell pa pa not to wurry about me i aspect to be home sune
but dont no ezactly"

His eyes were swimming by the time he got that down, but they brightened again as he remembered something.

"Weve had grate times ear uncle Jo—"

"Must go on milking that ould cow," he thought

"tuk me to sea the prins of Wales yesterda"

He could not help it—he began to take a wild joy in his own inventions.

"flags and banns of musick all day and luminerashuns all
night it was grand we were top of an umnibuss goin down lord
strete and saw him as plane as plane"

141

"Bless me," said Pete, dropping his pen, and rubbing his hands in ravishing contemplation of his own fiction; "the next thing we hear she'll be riding in her carriage and' pair."

He was sobbing a little, for all that, in a low, smothered way, but he could not deny himself one word more—

```
"luv to all enquirin frens and bess respecs to the Dempster
if im not forgot at him."
```

This second forgery of love being finished, he went about the house on tiptoe, found brown paper and twine, put the hood back into the box with his half-sheet peeping from between the frills where the little face would go, and made it up, with his undeft fingers, into an ungainly parcel, which he addressed to himself as before. After that he did his accustomed duty with the lamp and the door, and lay down in the parlour to sleep.

On Monday, at dinner, he broke out peevishly with "Ter'ble botheration, Nancy—I must be going to Port St. Mary about that thundering demonstration."

Then from underneath the sofa in the parlour he rooted up a brown paper parcel, stuffed it under his coat, buttoned it up, and so smuggled it out of the house.

VI.

They set sail early in the afternoon, and ran down the coast under a fair breeze that made the canvas play until the sea hissed. The day was wet and cheerless; a thick mist enshrouded the land, and going by Laxey they could just descry the top arc of the great wheel like a dun-coloured ghost of a rainbow in a grey sky. As they came to Douglas the mist was lifting, but the rain was coming down in a soaking drizzle. A band was playing dance tunes on the iron pier, which shot like a serpent's tongue out of the mouth of the bay. The steamer from England was coming round the head, and her sea-sick passengers were dense as a crowd on her forward deck, the men with print handkerchiefs tied over their caps, the women with their skirts over their drooping feathers. A harp and a violin were scraping lively airs amidships. The town was like a cock with his tail down crowing furiously in the wet.

When they came to Port St. Mary the mist had risen and the rain was gone, but the fishing-town looked black and sullen under a lowering cloud. The tide was down, and many boats lay on the beach and in the shallow water within the rocks.

Pete was put ashore; his Nickey went round the Calf to the herring ground beyond the shoulder; a number of fishermen were waiting for him on the quay, with heavy looks and hands deep in their trousers-pockets.

"No need for much praiching at all," said Pete, pointing to the boats lying aground. "There you are, boys, fifty of you at the least, with no room to warp for the rocks. Yet they're for taxing you for dues for a harbour."

"Go ahead, Capt'n," said one of the fishermen; "there's five hundred men here to back you up through thick and thin."

Pete posted his brown paper parcel as stealthily as he had posted his letter, and left Port St. Mary the same night for Douglas. The roads were thick with coaches, choked full with pleasure-seekers from Port Erin. These cheerful souls were still wearing the clothes which had been drenched through in the morning; their boots were damp and cold; they were chill with the night-air, but they did not repine. They sang and laughed and ate oranges, drew up frequently at wayside houses, and handed round bottles of beer with the corks drawn. In their own way they were bright and cheerful company. Sometimes "Hold the Fort," sung in a brake going ahead, mingled with "Molly and I and the Baby," from lusty throats coming behind. Battling through Castletown, they shouted wild chaff at the redcoats lounging by the Castle, and when the darkness fell they dropped asleep—the men usually on the women's shoulders; and then the horses' hoofs were heard splashing along the muddy road, and every rider cracked his whip over a chorus of stertorous snores.

Douglas was ablaze with light as they dipped down to it from the dark country. Long sinuous tails of light where the busy streets were, running in and out, this way and that, and belching into the wide squares and market-places like the race of a Curragh fire. The sleepers awoke and shook themselves. "Going to the Castle to-night?" said one. "What do you think?" said another, and they all laughed at the foolish question.

"I'll sleep here," thought Pete. "I've not searched Douglas yet."

The driver found him a bed at his mother's house. It was a lodging-house in Church Street, overlooking the churchyard. Finding himself so near to Athol Street, Pete thought he would look at the outside of Philip's chambers. He lit on the house easily, though the street was dark. It was one of a line of houses having brass plates, each with its name, and always the word *Advocate*. Philip's house bore one plate only, a small one, with the name hardly legible in the uncertain light. It ran—*The Deemster Christian*.

Having spelt out this inscription, Pete crept away. That was the last house in the island at which he wished to call. He was almost afraid of being seen in the same town. Philip might think he was in Douglas to look for Kate.

Pete rambled through the narrow thoroughfares of Post-Office Place, Heywood Lane, and Fancy Street, until he came to the sea front. It was now full tide of busy night, and the holiday town seemed to be given over to enjoyment. The steps of the terraces were thronged; itinerant photographers pitched their cameras on the curb-stones; every open window had its dark heads with the light behind; pianos were clashing in the houses, harps were twanging in the street, tinkling tram-cars, like toast-racks, were sweeping the curve of the bay; there was a steady flow of people on the pavement, and from water's edge to cliff top, three parts round like a horse's shoe, the town flashed and fizzed and sparkled and blazed under its thousand lights with the splendour of a forest fire.

Pete called to mind the blinking and groping of the dear old half-lit town to the north; he remembered the dark village at the foot of the lonely hills, with its trout-stream burrowing under the low bridge, and he thought, "She may have tired of it all, poor thing!"

He looked at every woman's face as she went by him, hungering for one glimpse of a face he feared to see. He did not see it, and he wandered like a lost soul through the little gay town until he drifted with the wave that flowed around the bay into the place that was known as the Castle.

It was a dancing palace in a garden, built in the manner of a conservatory, with the ground level for those who came to dance, and the galleries for such as came to see. Seated by the front rail of the gallery, Pete peered down into the faces below. Three thousand young men and young women were dancing, the men in flannels and coloured scarves, the women in light muslins and straw hats. Sometimes the white lights in the glass roof were coloured with red and blue and yellow. The low buzz of the dancers' feet, the clang and clash of the brass instruments, the boom of the big drum, the quake of the glass house itself, and the low rumble of the hollow floor beneath—it was like a battle-field set to music.

"She may have tired, poor thing; God knows she may," thought Pete.

His eyes were growing hazy and his head dizzy, when he became conscious of a waft of perfume behind him, and a soft voice saying at his ear, "Were you looking for anybody, then?"

He turned with a start, and looked at the speaker. It was a young girl with a pretty face, thick with powder. He could not be angry with the little thing; she was so young, and she was smiling.

"Yes," he said, "I *was* looking for somebody;" and then he tried to shake her off.

"Is it Maudie, you mane, dear? Are you the young man from Dublin?"

"Lave me, my girl; lave me," said Pete, patting her hand, and twisting about.

The girl looked at him with a sort of pity, and then close at his neck she said, "A fine boy like you shouldn't be going fretting his heart about the best girl that's in."

He looked at the pretty face again, and the little knowing airs began to break down. "You're a Manx girl, aren't you?"

The smile vanished like a flash. "How do you know that? My tongue doesn't tell you, does it?" And the little thing was ashamed.

Pete took the tight-gloved fingers in his big palm. "So you're my lil countrywoman, then?" he said. "How old are you?"

The painted lips began to tremble. "Sixteen for harvest," she answered.

"My God!" exclaimed Pete.

The darkened eyelids blinked; she was beginning to cry. "It wasn't my fault. He was a visitor with my mother at Ballaugh, and he left me to it."

Pete took a sovereign out of his pocket, and shut it in the girl's hand.

"Go home to-night, my dear," he whispered, and then he clambered out of the place.

"Not there!" cried Pete in his heart; "not there—I swear to God she is not there."

That ended his search. He resolved to go home the same night, and he went back to his lodgings to pay his bill. Turning out of Athol Street, Pete was almost overrun by a splendid equipage, with two men in buff on the box-seat, and one man behind. "The Governor's carriage," said somebody. At the next moment it drew up at Philip's door, its occupant alighted, and then it swung about and moved away. "It was the young Deemster," said a girl to her companion, as she went skipping past.

Pete had seen the tall, dark figure, bent and feeble, as it walked heavily up the steps. "Truth enough," he thought, "there's nothing got in this world without paying the price of it."

It was three in the morning when Pete reached Ramsey, Elm Cottage was dark and silent. He had to knock again and again before awakening Nancy. "Now, if this had been Kate!" he thought, and a new fear took hold of him. His poor darling, his wandering lamb, could she have knocked twice? Where was she to-night? He had been picturing her in happiness and plenty—was she in poverty and distress? All the world was sleeping—was she asleep? His hope was slipping away; his great faith was breaking down. "Lord, do not forsake me! Master, strengthen me! My poor lost love, where is she? What is she? Shall I see her face again?"

Something cold touched his hand. It was the dog. Without a bark he had put his nose into Pete's palm. "What, Dempster, man, Dempster!" The bat's ears were cocked—Pete felt them—the scut of a tail was wagged, and Pete got comfort from the battered old friend that had tramped the world at his heels.

Nancy unchained the door, opened it an inch, held a candle over her head, and peered out. "My goodness, is it the man himself? However did you come home?"

"By John the Flayer's pony," said Pete; and he laughed and made light of his night-long walk.

But next morning, when Nancy came downstairs with the child, Pete was busy with a screwdriver taking the chain off the door. "Ter'ble ould-fashioned, these chains—must be moving with the times, you know."

"Then what are you putting in its place?" said Nancy.

"You'll see, you'll see," said Pete.

At seven that night Pete was smoking over the gate when Kelly the Thief came up with a brown paper parcel. "Parcel for you, Mr. Quilliam," said the postman, with the air of a man who knew something he should not know.

Pete blinked and looked bewildered. "You don't say!" he said.

"Well, if that's your name," began the postman, holding the address for Pete to read.

Pete gave it a searching look. "Cap'n Peatr Quilliam, that's it sartenly, *Lm Cottig*—yes, it must be right," he said, taking the parcel gingerly. Then with a prolonged "O——o!" shutting his eyes and nodding his head, "I know—a bit of a present from the mother to the lil one. Wonderful thoughtful a woman is about a baby when she's a mother, Mr. Kelly."

The postman giggled, threw his finger seaward over one shoulder, and said, "Why aren't you writing back to her, then?"

"What's that?" said Pete sharply, making the parcel creak.

"Why aren't you writing to tell her how the lil one is, I'm saying?"

Pete looked at the postman as if the idea had dropped from heaven. "I must have a head as thick as a mooring-post, Mr. Kelly. Do you know, I never once thought of it. I'm like Goliath when he got little David's stone at his forehead—such a thing never entered my head before."

"Do it for all, Mr. Quilliam," said the postman, moving off.

"I will, I will," said Pete; and then he turned into the house.

"Scissors, Nancy," he shouted, throwing the parcel on the table.

"My sakes, a parcel!" cried Nancy.

"Aisy to tell where it comes from, too. See that knot, woman?" said Pete, with a knowing wink.

"What in the world is it, Pete?" said Nancy.

"I wonder!" said Pete. "Papers enough round it, anyway. A letter? We'll look at that after," he said loftily, and then out came the scarlet hood. "Gough bless mee what's this thing at all?" and he held it up by the crown.

Nancy made a cry of alarm, took the hood out of his hand, and scolded him roundly. "These men, they're fit to spoil an angel's wings."

Then she whipped up the baby out of the cradle, tried the hood on the little round head, and shouted with delight.

"Now I was thinking of that, d'ye know?" she said. "I was, yes, I was; believe me or not, I was. 'Kirry will be sending something for the lil one the next time she writes,' I was thinking, and behould ye—here it is."

"Something spakes to us, Nancy," said Pete. "'Deed it does, though."

The child gurgled and purred, and for all her fine headgear she was absorbed in her bare toes.

"And there's yourself, Pete—going to Peel and to Douglas, and I don't know where—and you've never once thought of the lil one—and knowing we were for shortening her, too."

Pete cast down his head and looked ashamed.

"Well, no—of coorse—I never have—that's truth enough," he faltered.

VII.

Pete went out to buy a sheet of notepaper and an envelope, a pen, and a postage stamp. He had abundance of all theso at home, but that did not serve his turn. Going to as many shops as might be, he dropped hints everywhere of the purpose to which his purchases were to be put. Finally, he went to the barber's in the market-place and said, "Will you write an address for me, Jonaique?"

"Coorse I will," said the barber, sweeping a hand of velvet over one cheek of the postman, who was in the chair, leaving the other cheek in lather while he took up the pen.

"Mistress Peter Quilliam, care of Master Joseph Quilliam, Esquire, Scotland Road, Liverpool" dictated Pete.

"What number, Capt'n?" said Jonaique.

"Number?" said Pete, perplexed. "Bless me, what's this the number is now? Oh," by a sudden inspiration, "five hundred and fifteen."

"Five hundred—d'ye say *five*" said the postman from the half of his mouth that was clear.

"Five," said Pete emphatically. "Aw, they're well up."

"If *you* say so, Capt'n," said the barber, and down went "515."

Pete returned home with the stamped and addressed envelope open in his hands, "Clane the table quick," he shouted; "I must be writing to Kirry. Will I give her your love, Nancy?"

With much hem-ing and ha-ing and clearing of his throat, Pete was settling himself before a sheet of note-paper, when the door opened, and Philip stepped into the house. His face was haggard and emaciated; his eyes burned as with a fire that came up from within.

"I've come to warn you," he said; "you are in great danger. You must stop that demonstration."

"Sit down, sir, sit down," said Pete.

Philip did not seem to hear. He walked to and fro with short, nervous, noiseless steps. "The Governor sent for me last night, and I found him in a frenzy. 'Deemster,' he said, 'they tell me there's to be a disturbance at Tynwald—have you heard of anything?' I said, 'Yes, I had heard of a meeting of fishermen at Peel.' 'They talk of their rights,' said he; 'I'll teach them something of one right they seem to forget—the right of the Governor to shoot down the disturbers of Tynwald, without judge or jury.' 'That's a very old prerogative, your Excellency,' I said; 'it comes down from more lawless days than ours. You will never use it.' 'Will I not?' said he. 'Listen, I'll tell you what I've done already. I've ordered the regiment at Castletown to be on Tynwald Hill on Tynwald day. Every man of these—there are three hundred—

shall have twenty rounds of ball-cartridge. Then, if the vagabonds try to interrupt the Court, I've only to lift my hand—so—and they'll be mown down like grass.' 'You can't mean it,' I said, and I tried to take his big talk lightly. 'Judge for yourself—see,' and he showed me a paper. It was an order for the ambulance waggons to be stationed on the ground, and a request to the doctors of Douglas to be present."

"Then we've made the ould boy see that we mane it," said Pete.

"'If you know any one of the ringleaders, Deemster,' he said, with a look into my face—somebody had been with him—there are tell-tales everywhere——"

"It's the way of the world still," said Pete.

"'Tell him,' said he, 'that I don't want to take the life of any man—I don't want to send any one to penal servitude.'" It was useless to protest. The man was mad, but he was in earnest. His plan was folly—frantic folly—but it was based on a sort of legal right. "So, for the Lord's sake, Pete, stop this thing. Stop it at once, and finally. It's life or death. If ever you thought my word worth anything, you'll do as I bid you, now. God knows where I should be myself if the Governor were to do what he threatens. Stop it, stop it; I haven't slept for thinking of it."

Pete had been sitting at the table, chewing the tip of the pen, and now he lifted to the paleness and wildness of Philip's face a cool, bold smile.

"It's good of you, Phil.... We've a right to be there, though, haven't we?"

"You've a right, certainly, but——"

"Then, by gough, we'll go," said Pete, dropping the pen, and bringing his fist down on the table.

"The penalty will be yours, Pete—yours. You are the man who will suffer—you first—you alone."

Pete smiled again. "No use—I'm incorr'iblê. I'm like Dan-ny-Clae, the sheep-stealer, when he came to die. 'I'm going to eternal judgment—what'll I do?' says Dan. 'Give back all you've stolen,' says the parzon. 'I'll chance it first,' says the ould rascal. It's the other fellow that's for stealing this time; but I'll chance it, Philip. Death it may be, and judgment too, but I'll chance it, boy."

Philip's eyes wandered over the floor. "Then you'll not change your plan for anything I've told you?"

"I will, though," said Pete, "for one thing, anyway. *You* shan't be getting into trouble—I'll be spokesman for the fishermen myself. Oh, I'll spake enough if they get my dander up. I'll just square my arms acrost my chest and I'll say, 'Your Excellency,' I'll say, 'you can't do it, and you shan't do it—*because it isn't* right.' But chut! botheration to all such bobbery! Look here—man alive, look here! She's not forgetting the lil one, you see," and, making a proud sweep of the hand, Pete pointed to the scarlet hood. It had been put to sit across the back of a china dog on the mantelpiece, with Pete's half sheet of paper pinned to the strings.

Philip recognised it. The hood was the present he had made as godfather. His eyes blinked, his mouth twitched, the cords of his forehead moved.

"So she—she sent that," he stammered.

"Listen here," said Pete, and he unpinned the paper and read the message aloud, with flourishes of voice and gesture—"For lil Katherine from her loving mother... papa not to worry... love to all inquiring friends... best respects to the Dempster if Im not forgot at him." Then in an off-hand way he tossed the paper into the fire. "Aw, what's a bit of a letter," he said largely, as it took flame and burned.

Philip's bloodshot eyes seemed to be starting from his head.

"Nancy's right—a man would never have thought of the like of that—now, would he?" said Pete, looking proudly from Philip to the hood, and from the hood back to Philip.

Philip did not answer. Something seemed to be throttling him.

"But when a woman goes away she leaves her eyes behind her, as you might say. 'What'll I be getting for them that's at home?' she's thinking, and up comes a nice warm lil thing for the baby. Aw, the women's good, Philip. They're what they make the sovereigns of, God bless them!"

Philip felt as if he must rush out of the house shrieking. One moment he stood up before Pete, as though he meant to say something, and then he turned to go.

"Not sleeping to-night, no? Have to get back to Douglas? Then maybe you'll write me a letter first?"

Philip nodded his head and returned, his mouth tightly closed, sat down at the table, and took up the pen.

"What is it?" he asked.

"Am I to give you the words, Phil? Yes? Well, if you won't be thinking mane——"

Pete charged His pipe out of his waistcoat pocket, and began to dictate:

"Dear wife.'"

At that Philip gave an involuntary cry.

"Aw, best to begin proper, you know. 'Dear wife,'" said Pete again.

Philip made a call on his resolution, and put the words down. His hand felt cold; his heart felt frozen to the core. Pete lit up, and walked to and fro as he dictated his letter. Nancy sat knitting by the cradle, with one foot on the rocker.

"'Glad to get your welcome letter, darling, and the bonnet for the baby'——"

"'Go on," said Philip, in an impassive voice.

"Got that down, Philip? Aw, you're smart wonderful with the pen, though....

'When she's got it on her lil head you'd laugh tremenjous.

145

> She's straight like a lil John the Baptist in the church
> window'—"

Pete paused; Philip lifted his pen and waited.

"Done already? Man veen, there's no houlding you....

> 'Glad to hear you're so happy and comfortable with Uncle Joe
> and Auntie Joney. Give the pair of them my fond love and
> best respects. We're getting on beautiful, and I'm as happy
> as a sandboy. Sometimes Grannie gets a bit down with
> longing, and so does Nancy, but I tell them you'll be home
> for their funeral sarmon, anyway, and then they're comforted
> wonderful.'"

"Don't be writing his rubbage and lies, your Honour," said Nancy.

"Chut! woman; where's the harm at all? A merry touch to keep a person's spirits up when she's away from home—eh, Philip?" and Pete appealed to him with a nudge at his writing elbow.

Philip gave no sign. With a look of stupor he was staring down at the paper as he wrote. Pete puffed and went on—

> "'Cæsar's at it still, going through the Bible same as a
> trawl-boat, fishing up the little texes. The Dempster's
> putting a sight on us reg'lar, and you're not forgot at him
> neither. 'Deed no, but thinking of you constant, and
> trusting you're the better for laving home——'

... Going too fast, am I? So I'm bating you at last, eh?"

A cold perspiration had broken out on Philip's forehead, and he was looking up with the eyes of a hunted dog.

"Am I to—must I write that?" he said in a helpless way.

"Coorse—go ahead," said Pete, puffing clouds of smoke, and laughing.

Philip wrote it. His hand was now stiff. It sprawled and splashed over the paper.

> "'As for myself, I'm a sort of a grass-widow, and if you
> keep me without a wife much longer they'll be taxing me for
> a bachelor.'"

Pete put his pipe on the mantelpiece, cleared his throat repeatedly, and began to be afflicted with a cough.

> "'Glad to hear you're coming home soon, darling (*cough*).
> Dearest Kirry, I'm missing you mortal (*cough*), worse nor
> at Kimberley (*cough*). When I'm going to bed, 'Where is she
> to-night?' I'm saying. And when I'm getting up, 'Where is
> she now?' I'm thinking. And in the dark midnight I'm asking
> myself, 'Is she asleep, I wonder?' (*Cough, cough*.) Come
> home quick, bogh; but not before you're well at all.'

... Never do to fetch her too soon, you know," he said in a whisper over Philip's shoulder, with another nudge at his elbow.

Philip answered incoherently, and shrank under Pete's touch as if he had been burnt. The coughing continued; the dictating began again.

> '"I'm keeping a warm nest for you here, love. There'll be a
> welcome from everybody, and nobody saying anything but the
> good and the kind. So come home soon, my true lil wife,
> before the foolish ould heart of your husband is losing
> him'——"

Pete coughed violently, and stretched his neck and mouth awry. "This cough I've got in my neck is fit to tear me in pieces," he said. "A spoonful of cold pinjane, Nancy—it's ter'ble good to soften the neck."

Nancy was nodding over the cradle—she had fallen asleep.

Philip had turned white and giddy and sick. For one moment an awful impulse seized him. He wanted to fall on Pete; to lay hold of him, to choke him. The consciousness of his own inferiority, his own duplicity, made him hate Pete. The very sweetness of the man sickened him. He could not help it—the last spark of his self-pride was fighting for its life. Then in shame, in remorse, in horror of himself and dread of everything, he threw down the pen, caught up his hat, shouted "Good night" in a voice like the growl of a beast in terror, and ran out of the house.

Nancy started up from a doze. "Goodness grazhers!" she cried, and the cradle rocked violently under her foot.

"He's that tender-hearted and sympathising," whispered Pete as he closed the door. (*Cough, cough*)... "The letter's finished, though—and here's the envelope."

VIII.

The following evening the Deemster was in his rooms in Athol Street. His hat was on, his cloak was over his arm, he was resting his elbow on the sash of the window and looking vacantly into the churchyard. Jem was behind him, answering at his back. Their voices were low; they scarcely moved.

"All well upstairs?" said Philip.

"Pretty well, your Honour."

"More cheerful and content?"

"Much more, except when your Honour is from home. 'The Deemster's back,' she'll say, and her poor face will be like sunshine on a rainy day."

Philip remained silent for a moment, and then said in a scarcely audible voice—

"Not fretting so much about the child, Jemmy?"

"Just as anxious to hear of it, though. 'Has he been to Ramsey to-day? Did he see her? Is she well?' That's the word constant, sir."

The Deemster was silent again, and Jem was withdrawing with a deep bow. "Jemmy, I'm going to Government House, and may be late. Don't wait up for me."

Jem answered in a half whisper, "Some one waits up for your Honour whether I do or not 'He's at home now,' she'll say, and then creep away to bed."

Philip muttered, thickly and huskily, "The decanter is empty—leave out another bottle." Then he turned to go from the room, keeping his eyes from his servant's face.

He found the Governor as violent as before, and eager to fall on him before he had time to speak.

"They tell me. Deemster, that the leader of this rising is a sort of left-hand relative of yours. Surely you can stop the man."

"I've tried to, your Excellency, and failed," said Philip.

The Governor tossed up his chin. "I'm told the fellow can't even write his own name," he said.

"It's true," said Philip.

"An illiterate and utterly uneducated person."

"All the same, he's the wisest and strongest man on this island," said Philip decisively.

The Governor frowned, and the pockmarks on his forehead seemed to swell. "The wisest and strongest man on this island will have to leave it," he said.

Philip made no answer. He had come to plead, but he saw that it was hopeless. The Governor put his right hand in the breast, of his white waistcoat—he was alone in the dining-room after dinner—and darted at Philip a look of anger and command.

"Deemster," he said, "if, as you say, you cannot stop this low-bred rascal, there's one thing you can do—leave him to himself."

"That is to say," said Philip out of a corner of his mouth, "to you."

"To me be it, and who has more right?" said the Governor hotly.

Philip held himself in hand. He was silent, and his silence was taken for submission. Cracking some nuts and munching them, the Governor began to take another tone.

"I should be sorry, Mr. Christian, if anything came between you and me—very sorry. We've been good friends thus far, and you will allow that you owe me something. Don't you see it yourself—this man is dishonouring me in the eyes of the island? If you have tried your best to keep his neck out of the halter, let the consequences be his own."

"Eh?" said Philip, with his eyes on the floor.

"You have done your duty by the man, I say. Help yourself to a glass of wine."

Still Philip did not speak. The Governor saw his advantage, but little did he guess the pitiless power of it.

"The fellow is your kinsman, Deemster, and I shall not ask you to deal with him. That would be inhuman. If there is no hope of restraining him to-morrow—wise as he is, if he will not listen to saner counsels, I will only beg of you—but this is a matter for the police. You are a high official now. It would be a pity to give you pain. Stay at home—I'll gladly excuse you—you look as if a day's rest would do you good."

Philip drank two glasses of the wine in quick succession. The Governor poured him a third, and went on—

"I don't know what you're feeling for the man may be—it can't be friendship. I'm sure he's a thorn in your flesh. And as long as he's here he will always be."

Philip looked up with inquiry, doubt, and fear.

"Ah! I knew it. Even if this matter goes by, your time will come. You'll quarrel with the fellow yet—you know you will—it's in the nature of things—if he's the man you say."

Philip drank the third glass of wine and rose to go.

147

"Leave him to me—I'll deal with him. You'll be done with him, and a good riddance, too, I reckon. And now come in to the ladies—they'll know you're here."

Philip excused himself and went off with feverish gestures and an excited face.

"The Governor is right," he thought, as he went home over the dark roads. Pete was a thorn in his flesh, and always would be; his enemy, his relentless enemy, notwithstanding his love for him.

The misery of the past month could not be supported any longer. Perpetual fear of discovery, perpetual guard of the tongue, keeping watch and ward on every act of life—to-day, to-morrow, the next day, on and on until life's end in wretchedness or disgrace—it was insupportable, it was impossible, it could not be attempted.

Then came thoughts that were too fearful to take form-too awful to take words. They were like the flapping of unseen wings going by him in the night, but the meaning of them was this: If Pete persists in his purpose, there will be a riot. If any one is injured, Pete will be transported. If any one is killed, Pete will be indicted for his life.

"Well, I have done my duty by him," his heart whimpered. "I have tried to restrain him. I have tried to restrain the Governor. It isn't my fault. What more can I do?"

Philip walked fast. Here was the way of escape from the evil that beset his path. Fate was stretching out her hands to him. When men had done wrong, they did yet more wrong to elude the consequences of their first fault; but there was no need for that in his case.

The hour was late. A strong breeze was blowing off the sea. It flicked his face with salt as he went swinging down the hill into the town. His blood was a-fire. He had a feeling, never felt before, of courage and even ferocity. Something told him that he was not so good a man as he had been, but it was a tingling pleasure to feel that he was a stronger man than before.

Should he tell Kate? No! Let the thing go on; let it end. After it was over she would see where their account lay. Thinking in this way, he laughed aloud.

The town was quiet when he came to it. So absorbed had he been that, though the air was sharp, he had been carrying his cloak over his arm. Now he put it on, and drew the hood close over his head. A dog, a homeless cur, had begun to follow at his heels. He drove it off, but it continued to hang about him. At last it got in front of his feet, and he stumbled over it in one of his large, quick strides. Then he kicked the dog, and it crossed the dark street yelping. He was a worse man, and he knew it.

He let himself into the house with his latch-key, and banged the door behind his back. But no sooner had he breathed the soft, woolly, stagnant air within than a change came over him. His ferocious strength ebbed away, and he began to tremble.

The hall passage and staircase were in darkness. This was by his orders—coming in late, he always forgot to put out the gas. But the lamp of his room was burning on the candle rest at the stairhead, and it cast a long sword of light down the staircase well.

Chilled by some unknown fear, he had set one foot on the first tread when he thought he heard the step of some one coming down the stairs. It was a familiar step. He was sure he knew it. It must be a step he heard daily.

He stopped, and the step seemed to stop also. At that moment there was a shuffling of slippered feet on an upper landing, and Jem-y-Lord called down, "Is it you, your Honour?"

With an effort he answered, "Yes."

"Is anything the matter?" called the man-servant.

"There's somebody coming downstairs, isn't there?" said Philip.

"Somebody coming downstairs?" repeated the man-servant, and the light shifted as if he were lifting the lamp.

"Is it you coming down, Jem?"

"Me coming down? I'm here, holding the lamp, your Honour."

"Another of my fancies," thought Philip; and he laid hold of the handrail, and started afresh. The step came on. He knew it now; it was his own step. "An echo," he told himself. "A dream," he thought, "a mirage of the mind;" and he compelled himself to go up. The step came down. It passed him on the stairs, going by the wall as he went by the rail, with an irresistible down-drive, headlong, heavily.

Then came one of those moments of partial unconsciousness in which the sensation of a sound takes shape. It seemed to Philip that the figure of a man had passed him. He remembered it instantly. It was the same that he had seen in the lobby to the Council Chamber, his own figure, but wrapped in a cloak like the one he was then wearing, and with the hood drawn over the head. The body had been half turned aside, the face had been hidden, and the whole form had expressed contempt, repugnance, and loathing.

"Not well to-night, your Honour?" said the far-off voice of Jem-y-Lord. He was holding the dazzling lamp up to the Deemster's face.

"A little faint—that's all. Go to bed."

Then Philip was alone in his room. "Conscience!" he thought. "Pete may go, but *this* will be with me to the end. Which, O God?—which?"

He poured out half a tumbler from the bottle on the table, and gulped it down at a draught. At the same moment he heard a light foot overhead. It was a woman's foot; it crossed the floor, and then ceased.

IX.

Next morning the Deemster was still sleeping while the sun was shining into his room. He was awakened by a thunderous clamour, which came as from a nail driven into the back of his head. Opening his eyes, he realised that somebody was knocking at his door, and shouting in a robustious bass—

"Christian, I say! Ever going to get up at all?"

It was the Clerk of the Rolls. Under one of his heavy poundings the catch of the door gave way, and he stepped into the room.

"Degenerate Manxman!" he roared. "In bed on Tynwald morning. Pooh! this room smells of dead sleep, dead spirits, and dead everything. Let me get at that window—you pitch your clothes all over the floor. Ah! that's fresher! Headache? I should think so. Get up, then, and I'll drive you to St. John's."

"Don't think I'll go to-day, sir," said Philip in a feeble whimper.

"Not go? Holy saints! Judge of his island and not go to Tynwald! What will the Governor say?"

"He said last night he would excuse my absence."

"Excuse your fiddlesticks! The air will do you good. I've got the carriage below. Listen! it's striking ten by the church. I'll give you fifteen minutes, and step into your breakfast-room and look over the *Times*."

The Clerk rolled out, and then Philip heard his loud voice through the door in conversation with Jem-y-Lord.

"And how's Mrs. Cottier to-day?"

"Middling, sir, thank you, sir."

"You don't let us see too much of her, Jemmy."

"Not been well since coming to Douglas, sir."

Cups and saucers rattled, the newspaper creaked, the Clerk cleared his throat, and there was silence.

Philip rose with a heavy heart, still in the torment of his great temptation. He remembered the vision of the night before, and, broad morning as it was, he trembled. In the Isle of Man such visions are understood to foretell death, and the man who sees them is said to "see his soul." But Philip had no superstitions. He knew what the vision was: he knew what the vision meant.

Jem-y-Lord came in with hot water, and Philip, without looking round, said in a low tone as the door closed, "How now, my lad?"

"Fretting again, your Honour," said the man, in a half whisper. He busied himself in the room a moment, and then added, "Somehow she gets to know things. Yesterday evening now—I was taking down some of the bottles, and I met her on the stairs. Next time I saw her she was crying."

Philip said in a confused way, fumbling the razor. "Tell her I intend to see her after Tynwald."

"I have, your Honour. 'It's not that, Mr. Cottier,' she answered me."

"My wig and gown to-day, Jemmy," said Philip, and he went out in his robes as Deemster.

The day was bright, and the streets were thronged with vehicles. Brakes, wagonettes, omnibuses, private carriages, and cadger's carts all loaded to their utmost, were climbing out of Douglas by way of the road to Peel. The town seemed to shout; the old island rock itself seemed to laugh.

"Bless me, Christian," said the Clerk of the Rolls, looking at his watch, "do you know it's half-past ten? Service begins at eleven. Drive on, coachman. You've eight miles to do in half an hour."

"Can't go any faster with this traffic on the road, sir," said the coachman over his shoulder.

"I got so absorbed in the newspaper," said the Clerk, "that—— Well, if we're late, we're late, that's all."

Philip folded his arms across his breast and hung his head. He was fighting a great battle.

"No idea that the fisherman affair was going to be so serious," said the Clerk. "It seems the Governor has ordered out every soldier and pensioner. If I know my countrymen, they'll not stand much of that."

Philip drew a long breath: there was a cloud of dust; the women in the brakes were laughing.

"I hear a whisper that the ringleader is a friend of yours, Christian—'an irregular relative of a high official,' as the reporter says."

"He is my cousin, sir," said Philip.

"What? The big, curly-pated fellow you took home in the carriage?... I say, coachman, no need to drive *quite* so fast."

Philip's head was still down. The Clerk of the Rolls sat watching him with an anxious face.

"Christian, I am not so sure the Governor wasn't right after all. Is this what's been troubling you for a month? You're the deuce for a secret. If there's anything good to tell, you're up like the sun; but if there's bad news going, an owl is a poll-parrot compared with you for talking."

Philip made some feeble effort to laugh, and to say his head was still aching. They were on the breast of the steep hill going up to Greeba. The road ahead was like a funnel of dust; the road behind was like the tail of a comet.

"Pity a fine lad like that should get into trouble," said the Clerk. "I like the rascal. He got round an old man's heart like a rope round a capstan. One of the big, hearty dogs that make you say, 'By Jove, and I'm a Manxman, too.' He's in the right in this affair, whatever the Governor may say. And the Governor knows it, Christian—that's why he's so anxious to excuse you. He can overawe the Keys; and as for the Council, we're paid our wages, God bless us, and are so many stuffed snipes on his stick. But you—you're different. Then the man is your kinsman, and blood is thicker than water, if it's only—— Why, what's this?"

There was some whooping behind; the line of carriages swirled like a long serpent half a yard near the hedge, and through the grey dust a large covered car shot by at the gallop of a fire-engine. The Clerk-sat bolt upright.

"Now, what in the name of——"

"It's an ambulance waggon," said Philip between his set teeth.

A moment later a second waggon went galloping past, then a third, and finally a fourth.

"Well, upon my—— Ah! good day. Doctor! Good day, good day!"

The Clerk had recognised friends on the waggons, and was returning their salutations. When they were gone, he first looked at Philip, and then shouted, "Coachman, right about face. We're going home again—and chance it."

"We can't be turning here, sir," said the coachman. "The vehicles are coming up like bees going a-swarming. We'll have to go as far as Tynwald, anyway."

"Go on," said Philip in a determined voice.

After a while the Clerk said, "Christian, it isn't worth while getting into trouble over this affair. After all, the Governor is the Governor. Besides, he's been a good friend to you."

Philip was passing through a purgatorial fire, and his old master was feeding it with fuel on every side. They were nearing Tynwald, and could see the flags, the tents, and the crowd as of a vast encampment, and hear the deep hum of a multitude, like the murmur of a distant sea.

X.

Tynwald Hill is the ancient Parliament ground of Man. It is an open green in the midst of the island, with hills on three of its sides, and on the fourth a broad plain dipping to the coast. This green is of the shape of a guitar. Down the middle of the guitar there is a walled enclosure of the shape of a banjo. At the end stands a church. The round drum is the mount, which has four circles, the topmost being some six paces across.

The carriage containing the Deemster and the Clerk of the Bolls had drawn up at the west gate of the church, and a policeman had opened the door. There came the sound of singing from the porch.

"A quarter late," said the Clerk of the Rolls, consulting his watch. "Shall we go in, your Honor?"

"Let us take a turn round the fair instead," said Philip.

The carriage door was shut back, and they began to move over the green. The open part of it was covered with booths, barrows, stands, and show-tents. There were cheap jacks with shoddy watches, phrenologists with two chairs, fat women, dwarfs, wandering minstrels, itinerant hawkers of toffee in tin hat-boxes, and other shiny and slimy creatures with the air and grease of the towns. There were a few oxen and horses also, tethered and lanketted, and kicking up the dust under the dry turf.

The crowd was dense already, and increasing at every moment. As the brakes arrived, they drove up with a swing that sent the people surging on either side. Some brought well-behaved visitors, others brought an eruption of ruffians.

Down the neck of the enclosure, and round the circular end of it, stood a regiment of soldiers with rifles and bayonets. The steps to the mount were laid down with rushes. Two armchairs were on the top, under a canopy hung from a flagstaff that stood in the centre. These chairs were still empty, and the mount and its approaches were kept clear.

The sun was overhead, the heat was great, the odour was oppressive. Now and again the sound of the service within the church mingled with the crack of the toy rifle-ranges and the jabber of the cheap jacks. At length there was another sound—a more portentous sound—the sound of bands playing in the distance. It came from both south and west, from the direction of Peel, and from that of Port St. Mary.

"They're coming," said the Clerk, and Philip's face, when he turned his head to listen, quivered and grew yet more pale.

As the bands approached they ceased to play. Presently a vast procession of men from the west came up in silence to the skirt of the hill, and turned off in the direction from which the men from the south were seen to be coming. They were in jerseys and sea-boots, marching four deep, and carrying nothing in their brawny hands. One stalwart fellow walked firmly at the head of them.. It was Pete.

Philip could support the strain no longer. He got out of the carriage. The Clerk of the Rolls got out also, and followed him as he walked with wavering, irregular steps.

Under a great tree at the junction of three roads, the two companies of fishermen met and fell into a general throng. There was a low wall around the tree-trunk, and, standing on this, Pete's head was clear above the rest.

"Boys," he was saying, "there's three hundred armed soldiers on the hill yonder, with twenty rounds of ball-cartridge apiece. You're going to the Coort because you've a right to go. You're going up peaceable, and, when you're getting there, you're going to mix among the soldiers, three to every man, two on either side and one behind. Then your spokesmen are going to spake out your complaint. If they're listened to, you're wanting no better. But if they're not, and if the word is given to fire on them, then, before there's time to do it, you're going to stretch every man of the three hundred on his back and take his weapon. Don't hurt the soldiers—the poor soldiers are only doing what they're tould. But don't let the soldiers hurt you neither. You're going there for justice. You're not going there to fight. But if anybody fights you, let him never forget the day he done it. Break up every taffy stand in the fair, if you can't find anything better. And if blood is shed, lave the man that orders it to me. And now go up, boys, like men and like Manxmen."

There was no cheering, no shouting, no clapping of hands. Only broken exclamations and a sort of confused murmur. "Come," whispered the Clerk of the Rolls, putting his hand through Philip's quivering arm. "Little does the poor devil think that, if blood is shed, he will be the first to fall." "God in heaven!" muttered Philip.

150

XI.

The crowd on Tynwald had now gathered thick down the neck of the enclosure and dense round the mount. To the strains of the National Anthem, played by the band of the regiment, the Governor had come out of the church. He was in cocked hat and with sword, and the sword of state was carried upright before him. With his Keys, Council, and clergy, he walked to the hill-top. There he took one of the two chairs under the canopy; the other, was taken by the Bishop in his lawn. Their followers came behind, and broke up on the hill into an indiscriminate mass. A number of ladies were admitted to the space on the topmost round. They stood behind the chairs, with their parasols still open.

There are men that the densest crowd will part and make way for. The crowd had parted and made way for Philip. As the court was being "fenced," he appeared with his companion at the foot of the mount. There he was recognised by many, but he scarcely answered their salutations. The Governor made a deferential bow, smiled, and beckoned to him to come up to his side. He went up slowly, pausing at every other step, like a man who was in doubt if he ought to go higher. At length he stood at the Governor's right hand, with all eyes upon him, for the favourite of the great is favoured. He was then the highest figure on the mount, the Governor and the Bishop being seated. The people could see him from end to side of the Tynwald, and he could see the people as they stood closely packed on the green below.

The business of the Court began. It was that of promulgating the laws. Philip's senior colleague, the old Deemster of the happy face, read the titles of the laws in English.

Then the Coroner of the premier sheading began to recite the same titles in Manx. Nobody heard them; hardly anybody listened. The ladies on the mount chatted among themselves, the Keys and the clergy intermingled and talked, the officials of the Council looked at the crowd, and the crowd itself, having nothing to hear, no more to see, indifferent to doings they could not understand, resumed their amusements among the frivolities of the fair.

There were three persons in that assembly of fifteen thousand who were following the course of events with feverish interest. The first of these was the Governor, whose restless eyes were rolling from side to side with almost savage light; the second was the captain of the regiment, who was watching the Governor's face for a signal; the third was Philip, who was looking down at the crowd and seeing something that had meaning for himself alone.

The fishermen came up quietly, three thousand strong. Half a hundred of them lounged around the magazine—the ammunition was at their command. The rest pushed, edged, and elbowed their way through the people until they came to the line of the guard. Wherever there was a red coat, behind it there were three jerseys and stocking-caps, Philip saw it all from his elevation on the mount. His face was deadly pale, his eyelids wavered, his lower lip trembled, his hand twitched; when he was spoken to, he hardly answered; he was like a man holding counsel with himself, and half in fear that everybody could read his hidden thoughts. He was in the last throes of his temptation. The decisive moment was near. It was heavy with the fate of his after life. He thought of Pete and the torture of his company; of Kate and the unending misery of her existence; of himself and the deep duplicity to which he was committed. From all this he could be freed for ever—by what? By doing nothing, having already done his duty? Only let him command himself, and then—relief from an existence enthralled by torment—from constant alarm and watchfulness—peace—sleep—love—Kate!

Somebody was speaking to him over his shoulder. It was nothing—only the quip of a witty fellow, descendant of a Spanish freebooter. Ladies caught his eye, smiled and bowed to him. A little man, whose swarthy face showed African blood, reached up and quoted something about the bounds of freedom wide and wider.

The Coroner had finished, the proceedings were at an end—there was a movement—something had happened—the Governor had half risen from his chair. Twelve men in sea-boots and blue jerseys had passed the line of the guard, and were standing midway across the steps of the mount. One of them was beginning to speak. It was Pete.

"Governor," he said; but the captain of the regiment was abreast of him in a moment, and a score of the soldiers were about his companions at the next breath. The fishermen stood their ground like a wall, and the soldiers fell back. There was hardly any scuffle.

"Governor," said Pete again, touching his cap.

The Governor was twisting in his seat. Looking first at Pete, and then at the captain, he was in the act of lifting his hand when suddenly it was held by another hand at his side, and a low voice whispered at his ear, "No, sir; for God's sake, no!"

It was Philip. The Governor looked at him with amazement. "What do you mean?"

"I mean," said Philip, still whispering over him hotly and impetuously, "that there's only one way back to Government House, but if you lift your hand it will be one too many; I mean that if blood is shed you'll never live to leave this mount; I mean that your three hundred soldiers are only as three hundred rabbits in the claws of three thousand crows."

At the next instant he had left the Governor, and was face to face with the fishermen.

"Fishermen," he cried, lifting both hands before him, "let there be no trouble here to-day, no riot, for God's sake, no bloodshed. Listen to me. I am the grandson of a fisherman; I have been a fisherman myself; I love the fishermen. As long as I live I will stand by you. Your rights shall be my rights, your sins my sins, and where you go I will go too."

Then, swinging back to the Governor, he bowed low, and said in a deferential voice—

"Your Excellency, these men mean no harm; they wish to speak to you; they have a petition to make; they will be loyal and peaceable."

But the Governor, having recovered from his first fear, was now in a flame of anger.

151

"No," he said, with the accent of authority; "this is no time and no place for petitions."

"Forgive me, your Excellency," said Philip, with a deeper bow; "this is the time of all times, the place of all places."

There had been a general surging of the Keys and clergy towards the steps, and now one of them cried out of their group, "Is Tynwald Court to be turned into a bear-garden?" And another said in a cynical voice, "Perhaps your Excellency has taken somebody else's seat."

Philip raised himself to his full height, and answered, with his eyes on the speakers, "We are free-born men on this island, your Excellency. We did not come to Tynwald to learn order from the grandson of a Spanish pirate, or freedom from the son of a black chief."

"Hould hard, boys!" cried Pete, lifting one hand against his followers, as if to keep them quiet. He was boiling with a desire to shout till his throat should crack.

The Governor had exchanged rapid looks and low whispers with the captain. He saw that he was outwitted, that he was helpless, that he was even in personal danger. The captain was biting his leg with vexation that he had not reckoned more seriously with this rising—that he had not drawn up his men in column.

"Your Excellency will hear the fishermen?" said Philip.

"No, no, no," said the Governor. He was at least a brave man, if a vain and foolish one.

There was silence for a moment. Then, standing erect, and making an effort to control himself, Philip said, "May it please your Excellency, you fill a proud position here; you are the ruler of this island under your sovereign lady our Queen. But we, your subjects, your servants, are in a prouder position still. We are Manxmen. This is the Court of our country."

"Hould hard," cried Pete again.

"For a thousand years men with our blood and our names have stood on this hill to hear the voice of the people, and to do justice between man and man. That's what the place was meant for. If it has lost that meaning, root it up—it is a show and a sham."

"Bravo!" cried Pete; he could hold himself in no longer, and his word was taken up with a shout, both on the hill and on the green beneath.

Philip's voice had risen to a shrill cry, but it was low and meek as he added, bowing yet lower while he spoke—

"Your Excellency will hear the fishermen?"

The Governor rolled in his seat. "Go on," he said impatiently.

The men made their petition. Three or four of them spoke briefly and to the point. They had had harbours, their fathers' harbours, which had been freed to them forty years before; don't ask them to pay harbour dues until proper harbours were provided:

The Governor gave his promise. Then he rose, the band struck up "God save the Queen," and the Legislature filed back to the chapel.

Philip went with them. He had fought a great battle, and he had prevailed. Through purging fires the real man had emerged, but he had paid the price of his victory. His eye burned like live coal, his cheek-bones seemed to have upheaved. He walked alone; his ancient colleague had stepped ahead of him. But now and again, as he passed down the long path to the church-door, fishermen and farmers pushed between the rifles of the guards, and said in husky voices, "Let me shake you by the hand, Dempster."

The scene was repeated with added emotion half an hour afterwards, when, the court being adjourned and the Governor gone in ominous silence, Philip came out, white and smiling, and leaning on the arm of his old master, the Clerk of the Rolls. He could scarcely tear himself through the thick-set hedge of people that lined the path to the gate. As he got into the carriage his smile disappeared. Sinking into the seat, he buried himself in the corner and dropped his head on his breast. The people began to cheer.

"Drive on," he cried.

The cheering became loud.

"Drive, drive," he cried.

The people cheered yet louder. They thought that they had seen a grand triumph that day—a man triumphing over the Governor. But there had been a grander triumph which they had not seen—a man triumphing over himself. Only one saw that, and it was God.

XII.

Pete seemed to be beside himself. He laughed until he cried; he cried until he laughed. His resonant voice rang out everywhere.

"Hear him? My gough, it was like a bugle spaking. There's nobody can spake but himself. When the others are toot-tooting, it's just 'Polly, put the kettle on' (mimicking a mincing treble). See the lil Puffin on his throne of turf there? Looked as if Ould Nick had been thrashing peas on his face for a week."

Pete's enthusiasm rose to frenzy, and he began to sweep through the fair, bemoaning his country and pouring mouth-fuls of anathema on his countrymen.

"*Mannin veg villish* (sweet little Isle of Man), with your English Governors and your English Bishops, and boys of your own worth ten of them. *Manninee graihagh* (beloved Manxmen), you're driving them away to be Bishops for others and Governors abroad—and yourselves going to the dogs and the divil, and d——— you."

Pete's prophetic mood dropped to a jovial one. He bought the remaining stock-in-trade of an itinerant toffee-seller, and hammered the lid of the tin hat-box to beat up the children. They followed him like hares hopping in the snow; and he distributed his bounty in inverse relation to size, a short stick to a big lad, a long stick to a little one, and two sticks to a girl. The results were an infantile war. Here, a damsel of ten squaring her fists to fight a hulking fellow of twelve for her sister of six; and there, a mother wiping the eyes of her boy of five, and whispering "Hush, bogh; hush! You shall have the bladder when we kill the pig."

Pete began to drink. "How do, Faddy? Taking joy of you, Juan. Are you in life, Thom! Half a glass of rum will do no harm, boys. Not the drink at all—just the good company, you know."

He hailed the women also, but they were less willing to be treated. "I'd have more respect for my quarterly ticket, sir," said Betsy—she was a Primitive, with her husband on the "Planbeg." "There's a hole in your pocket, Capt'n; stop it up with your fist, man," said Liza—she was a gombeen woman, and when she got a penny in her hand it was a prisoner for life. "Chut! woman," said Pete, "what's the good book say ing? 'Riches have wings;' let the birds fly then," and off he went, reeling and tottering, and laughing his formidable laugh.

Pete grew merry. Rooting up the remains of the fishermen's band, he hired them to accompany him through the fair. They were three little musicians, now exceedingly drunk, and their duty was to play "Hail, Isle of Man," as he went swaggering along in front of them.

> "Hail, Isle of Man,
> Swate ocean lan',
>   I love thy sea-girt border."

"Play up, Jackie."

> "The barley sown,
> Potatoes down,
>   We'll get our boats in order."

Thus he forged through the fair, capering, laughing, shouting protests over his shoulder when the tipsy music failed, pretending to be very drunk, trying to show that he was carrying on, that he was going it, that he hadn't a second thought, but watching everything for all that, studying every face, and listening to the talk of everybody.

"Whips of money at him, Liza—whips of it—millions, they're saying."—"He's spending it like flitters then. The Manx chaps isn't fit for fortunes—no, they aren't. I wonder in the world what sort of wife there's at him. _I_ don't 'low my husband the purse. Three ha'pence is enough to be giving any man at once."—"Wife, you're saying? Don't you know, woman?" Then some whispering.

"Bass, boy—more bass, I tell thee."

> "We then sought nex'
> The soothing sex,
>   Our swatearts at Port Erin."

"Who _is_ the man at all?"—"Why, Capt'n Quilliam from Kimberley."—"'Deed, man! Him that married with some of the Cæsar Glenmooar's ones?"—"She's left him, though, and gone off with a wastrel."—"You don't say?"—"Well, I saw the young woman myself——"

> "At Quiggin's Hall
> There's enough for all,
>   Good beer, and all things proper."

"Hould, boys!"

Pete had drawn up suddenly, and stopped his musicians with a sweep of the arm.

"Were you spaking, Mr. Corteen?"

"Nothing, Capt'n. No need to stare at all. I was only saying I was at the camp-meeting at Sulby, and I saw——"

"Go on, Jackie."

> "A pleasant place,
> With beds of aise,
>   When we are done our supper."

The unhappy man was deceiving himself at least as much as anybody else. After looking for the light of intelligence in every face, waiting for a word, watching for a glance, expecting every moment that some one from south or north, or east or west, would say, "I've seen her;" yet, covering up the burning coal of his anxiety with the ashes of mock merriment, he tried to persuade himself that Kate was not on the island if nobody at Tynwald had seen her; that he had told the truth unwittingly, and that he was as happy as the day was long.

XIII.

A man in a gig came driving a long-horned cow in front of him. Driver, horse, gig, and cow were like animated shapes of dust, but Pete recognised them.

"Is it yourself, Cæsar? So you're for selling ould Horney?"

"Grieved in my heart I am to do it, sir. Many a good glass of milk she has given to me and mine," and Cæsar was ready to weep.

153

"Going falling in fits, isn't she, Cæsar?"

"Hush, man! hush, man!" said Cæsar, looking about. "A good cow, very; but down twice since I left home this morning."

"I'd give a bad sixpence to see Cæsar selling that cow," thought Pete.

Three men were bargaining over a horse. Two were selling, the third (it was Black Tom) was buying.

"Rising five years, sir. Sired by Mahomet. Oh, I've got the papers to prove it," said one of the two.

"What, man? Five?" shouted Black Tom down the horse's open mouth. "She'll never see eight the longest day she lives."

"No use decaiving the man," said the other dealer, speaking in Manx. "She's sixteen—'low she's nine, anyway."

"Fair play, boys; spake English before a poor fellow," said Black Tom, with a snort.

"This brother of mine lows she's seven," said the first of the two.

"You thundering liar," said Black Tom in Manx. "He says she's sixteen."

"Dealing ponies then?" asked Pete.

"Anything, sir; anything. Buying for farmers up Lonan way," said Black Tom.

"Come on," said Pete; "here's Cæsar with a long-horned cow."

They found the good man tethering a white, long-horned cow to the wheel of the tipped-up gig.

"How do, Cæsar? And how much for the long-horn?" said Black Tom.

"Aw, look at the base (beast), Mr. Quilliam. Examine her for yourself," said Cæsar.

"Middling fair ewer, good quarter, five calves—is it five, Cæsar?" said Black Tom, holding one of the long horns.

"Three, sir, and calving again for February."

"No milk fever? No? Kicks a bit at milking? Never? Fits? Ever had fits, Cæsar?" opening wide one of the cow's eyes.

"Have you known me these years for a dacent man, Mr. Quilliam——" began Cæsar in an injured tone.

"Well, what's the figure?"

"Fourteen pound, sir! and she'll take the road before I'll go home with a pound less!"

"Fourteen—what! Ten; I'll give you ten—not a penny more."

"Good day to *you*, Mr. Quilliam," said Cæsar. Then, as if by an afterthought, "You're an ould friend of mine, Thomas; a very ould friend, Tom—I'll split you the diff'rance."

"Break a straw on it," said Black Tom; and the transaction was complete.

"I've had a clane strike here—the base is worth fifteen," chuckled Black Tom in Pete's ear as he drove the cow in to a shed beyond.

"I must be buying another cow in place of poor ould Horney," whispered Cæsar as he dived into the cattle stand.

"Strike up, Jackie," shouted Pete.

> "West of the mine,
> The day being fine.
> The tide against us veering."

Ten minutes later Pete heard a fearful clamour, which drowned the noise that he himself was making. Within the shed the confusion of tongues was terrific.

"What's this at all?" he asked, crushing through with an innocent face.

"The man's cow has fits," cried Black Tom. "I'll have my money back. The ould psalm-singing Tommy Noddy! did he think he was lifting the collection? My money! My twelve goolden pounds!"

If Black Tom had not been as bald as a bladder, he would have torn his hair in his mortification. But Pete pacified him.

"Cæsar is looking for another cow—sell him his own back again. Impozz'ble? Who says it's impozz'ble? Cut off her long horns, and he'll never be knowing her from her grandmother."

Then Pete made up to Cæsar and said, "Tom's got a mailie (hornless) cow to sell, and it's the very thing you're wanting."

"Is she a good mailie?" asked Cæsar.

"Ten quarts either end of the day, Cæsar, and fifteen pounds of butter a week," said Pete.

"Where's the base, sir?" said Cæsar.

They met Black Tom leading a hornless, white cow from the shed to the green.

"Are you coming together, Peter?" he said cheerfully.

Cæsar eyed the cow doubtfully for a moment, and then said briskly, "What's the price of the mailie, Mr. Quilliam?"

"Aw, look at the base first, Mr. Cregeen. Examine her for yourself, sir."

"Yes—yes—well, yes; a middling good base enough. Four calves, Thomas?"

"Two, sir, and calves again for January. Twenty-four quarts of new milk every day of life, and butter fit to burst the churn for you."

"No fever at all? No fits? No?"

"Aw, have you known me these teens of years, Mr. Cregeen——"

"Well, what d'ye say—eleven pounds for the cow, Tom!"

"Thirteen, Cæsar; and if you warn an ould friend——"

"Hould your hand, Mr. Quilliam; I'm not a man when I've got a bargain.... Manx notes or the dust, Thomas? Goold? Here you are, then—one—two—three—four..." (giving the cow another searching glance across his shoulder). "It's wonderful, though, the straight she's like ould Horney... five—six—seven... in colour and size, I mane... eight—nine—ten... and if she warn a mailie cow, now... eleven—twelve—" (the money hanging from his thumb). "Will that be enough, Mr. Quilliam? No? Half a one, then? Aw, you're hard, Tom... thirteen."

Having paid the last pound, Cæsar stood a moment contemplating his purchase, and then said doubtfully, "Well, if I hadn't... Grannie will be saying it's the same base back——" (the cow began to reel). "Yes, and it—no, surely—a mailie for all——" (the cow fell). "It's got the same fits, anyway," cried Cæsar; and then he rushed to the cow's head. "It *is* the same base. The horns are going cutting off at her. My money back! Give me my money back—my thirteen yellow sovereigns—the sweat of my brow!" he cried.

"Aw, no," said Black Tom. "There's no money giving back at all. If the cow was good enough for you to sell, she's good enough for you to buy," and he turned on his heel with a laugh of triumph.

Cæsar was choking with vexation.

"Never mind, sir," said Pete. "If Tom has taken a mane advantage of you, it'll be all set right at the Judgment. You've that satisfaction, anyway."

"Have I? No, I haven't," said Cæsar from between his teeth. "The man's clever. He'll get himself converted before he comes to die, and then there'll not be a word about cutting the horns off my cow."

"Strike up, Jackie," shouted Pete.

> "Hail, Isle of Man,
> Swate ocean làn',
>   I love thy sea-girt border."

XIV.

The sky became overcast, rain began to fall, and there was a rush for the carts. In half an hour Tynwald Hill was empty, and the people were splashing off on every side like the big drops of rain that were pelting down.

Pete hired a brake that was going back to the north, and gathered up his friends from Ramsey. When these were seated, there was a rush of helpless and abandoned ones who were going in the same direction—young mothers with children, old men and old women. Pete hauled them up till the seats and the floor were choked, and the brake could hold no more. He got small thanks. "Such crushing and scrooging! I declare my black merino frock, that I've only had on once, will be teetotal spoilt."—"If they don't start soon I'll be taking the neuralgy dreadful."

They got started at length, and, at the tail of a line of stiff carts, they went rattling over the mountain-road. The harebells nodded their washed faces from the hedge, and the talk was brisk and cheerful.

"Our Thorn's sowl a hafer, and got a good price."—"What for didn't you buy the mare of Corlett Beldroma, Juan?"—"Did I want to be killed as dead as a herring?"—"Kicks, does she? Bate her, man; bate her. A horse is like a woman. If you aren't bating her now and then——"

They stopped at every half-way houses—it was always halfway to somewhere. The men got exceedingly drunk and began to sing. At that the women grew very angry.

"Sakes alive! you're no better than a lot of Cottonies."—"Deed, but they're worse than any Cottonies, ma'am. Some excuse for the like of *them*. In their cotton-mills all the year, and nothing at home but a piece of grass the size of your hand in the backyard, and going hopping on it like a lark in a cage."

The rain came down in torrents, the mountain-path grew steep and desolate, the few houses passed were empty and boarded up, gorse bushes hissed to the rising breeze, geese scuttled and screamed across the untilled land, a solitary black crow flew across the leaden sky, and on the sea outside a tall pillar of smoke went stalking on and on, where the pleasure-steamer carried her freight of tourists round the island. Then songs gave way to sighs, some of the men began to pick quarrels, and some to break into fits of drunken sobbing.

Pete kept them all up. He chaffed and laughed and told funny stories. Choking, stifling, wounded to the heart as he was, still he was carrying on, struggling to convince everybody and himself as well, that nothing was amiss, that he was a jolly fellow, and had not a second thought.

He was glad to get home, nevertheless, where he need play the hypocrite no longer. Going through Sulby, he dropped out of the brake and looked in at the "Fairy." The house was shut. Grannie was sitting up for Cæsar, and listening for the sound of wheels. There was something unusual and mysterious about her. Cruddled over the fire, she was smoking, a long clay in little puffs of blue smoke that could barely be seen. The sweet old soul in her troubles had taken to the pipe as a comforter. Pete could see that something had happened since morning, but she looked at him with damp eyes, and he was afraid to ask questions. He began to talk of the great doings of the day at Tynwald, then of Philip, and finally of Kate, apologising a little wildly for the mother not coming home sooner to the child, but protesting that she had sent the little one no end of presents.

"Presents, bless ye," he began rapturously——

"You don't ate enough, Pete, 'deed you don't," said Grannie.

155

"Ate? Did you say ate?" cried Pete. "If you'd seen me at the fair you'd have said, 'That man's got the inside of a limekiln!' Aw, no, Grannie, I'm not letting my jaws travel far. When I've got anything before me it's—down—same as an ostrich."

Going away in the darkness, he heard Cæsar creaking up in the gig with old Horney, now old Mailie, diving along in front of him.

Nancy was waiting for Pete at Elm Cottage. She tried to bustle him upstairs.

"Come, man, come," she said; "get yourself off to bed and I'll bring your clothes down to the fire."

He had never slept in the bedroom since Kate had left. "Chut! I've lost the habit of beds," he answered. "Always used of the gable loft, you know, and the wind above the thatch."

Not to be thought to behave otherwise than usual, he went upstairs that night. But—

> "Feather beds are saft,
>   Pentit rooms are bonnie,
> But ae kiss o' my dear love
>   Better's far than ony."

The rain was still falling, the sea was loud, the mighty breath of night was shaking the walls of the house and rioting through the town. He was wet and tired, longing for a dry skin and a warm bed and rest.

> "Yet fain wad I rise and rin
>   If I tho't I would meet my dearie."

The long-strained rapture of faith and confidence was breaking down. He saw it breaking. He could deceive himself no more. She was gone, she was lost, she would lie on his breast no more.

"God help me! O, Lord, help me," he cried in his crushed and breaking heart.

XV.

When Kate thought of her husband after she had left him, it was not with any crushing sense of shame. She had injured him, but she had gained nothing by it. On the contrary, she had suffered, she had undergone separation from her child. To soften the hard blow inflicted, she had outraged the tenderest feelings of her heart. As often as she thought of Pete and the deep wrong she had done him, she remembered this sacrifice, she wept over this separation. Thus she reconciled herself to her conduct towards her husband. If she had bought happiness at the cost of Pete's sufferings, her remorse might have been deep; but she had only accepted shame and humiliation and the severance of the dearest of her ties.

When she had said in the rapture of passionate confidence that if she possessed Philip's love there could be no humiliation and no shame, she had not yet dreamt of the creeping degradation of a life in the dark, under a false name, in a false connection: a life under the same roof with Philip, yet not by his side, unacknowledged, unrecognised, hidden and suppressed. Even at the moment of that avowal, somewhere in the secret part of her heart, where lay her love of refinement and her desire to be a lady, she had cherished the hope that Philip would find a way out of the meanness of their relation, that she would come to live openly beside him, she hardly knew how, and she did not care at what cost of scandal, for with Philip as her own she would be proud and happy.

Philip had not found that way out, yet she did not blame him. She had begun to see that the deepest shame of their relation was not hers but his. Since she had lived in Philip's house the man in him had begun to decay. She could not shut her eyes to this rapid demoralisation, and she knew well that it was the consequence of her presence. The deceptions, the subterfuges, the mean shifts forced upon him day by day, by every chance, every accident, were plunging him in ever-deepening degradation. And as she realised this a new fear possessed her, more bitter than any humiliation, more crushing than any shame—the fear that he would cease to love her, the terror that he would come to hate her, as he recognised the depth to which she had dragged him down.

XVI.

Back from Tynwald, Philip was standing in his room. From time to time he walked to the window, which was half open, for the air was close and heavy. A misty rain was falling from an empty sky, and the daylight was beginning to fail. The tombstones below were wet, the treed were dripping, the churchyard was desolate. In a corner under the wall lay the angular wooden lid which is laid by a gravedigger over an open grave. Presently the iron gates swung apart, and a funeral company entered. It consisted of three persons and an uncovered deal coffin. One of the three was the sexton of the church, another was the curate, the third was a policeman. The sexton and the policeman carried the coffin to the church-door, which the curate opened. He then went into the church, and was followed by the other two. A moment later there were three strokes of the church bell. Some minutes after that the funeral company reappeared. It made for the open grave in the corner by the wall. The cover was removed, the coffin was lowered, the policeman half lifted his helmet, and the sexton put a careless hand to his cap. Then the curate opened a book and closed it again. The burial service was at an end. Half an hour longer the sexton worked alone in the drenching rain, shovelling the earth back into the grave.

"Some waif," thought Philip; "some friendless, homeless, nameless waif."

He went noiselessly up the stairs to the floor above, slinking through the house like a shadow. At a door above his own he knocked with a heavy hand, and a woman's voice answered him from within—

"Is any one there?"

"It is!," he said. "I am coming to see you."

Then he opened the door and slipped into the room. It was a room like his own at all points, only lower in the ceiling, and containing a bed. A woman was standing with her back to the window, as if she had just turned about from looking into the churchyard. It was Kate. She had been expecting Philip, and waiting for him, but she seemed to be overwhelmed with confusion. As he crossed the floor to go to her, he staggered, and then she raised her eyes to his face.

"You are ill," she said. "Sit down. Shall I ring for the brandy?"

"No," he answered. "We have had a hard day at Tyn-wald—some trouble—some excitement—I'm tired, that's all."

He sat on the end of the bed, and gazed out on the veil of rain, slanting across the square church tower and the sky.

"I was at Ramsey two days ago," he said; "that's what I came to tell you."

"Ah!" She linked her hands before her, and gazed out also. Then, in a trembling voice, she asked, "Is mother well?"

"Yes; I did not see her, but—yes, she bears up bravely."

"And—and—" the words stuck in her throat, "and Pete?"

"Well, also—in health, at all events."

"You mean that he is broken-hearted?"

With a deep breath he answered, "To listen to him you would think he was cheerful enough."

"And little Katherine?"

"She is well too. I did not see her awake. It was late, and she was in her cradle. So rosy, and fresh, and beautiful!"

"My sweet darling! She was clean too? They take care of her, don't they?"

"More care they could not take."

"My darling baby! Has she grown?"

"Yes; they talk of taking her out of the long clothes soon. Nancy is like a second mother to her."

Kate's foot was beating the floor. "Oh, why can't her own mother——" she began, and then in a faltering voice, "but that cannot be, I suppose.... Do her eyes change? Are they still blue? But she was asleep, you say. My dear baby! Was it very late? Nine o'clock? Just nine? I was thinking of her at that moment. It is true I am always thinking of her, but I remember, because the clock was striking. 'She will be in her little cot now,' I thought, 'bathed and clean, and so pretty in her nightdress, the one with the frill!' My sweet, sweet angel!"

Her speech was confused and broken. "Do you think if I never see her until... Will I know her if... It's useless to think of that, though. Is her hair like... What is the colour of her hair, Philip?"

"Fair, quite fair; as fair as mine was——"

She swirled round, came face to face with him, and cried, "Philip, Philip, why can't I have my darling to myself? She would be well enough here. I could keep her quiet. Oh, she would not disturb you. And I should be so happy with my little Kate for company. The time is long with me sometimes, Philip, and I could play with her all the day. And then at night, when she would be in the cot, I could make her little stock of clothes—her frocks and her little pinafores, and——"

"Impossible, Kate, impossible!" said Philip.

She turned to the window. "Yes," she said, in a choking voice, "I suppose it would even be stealing to fetch her away now. Only think! A mother stealing her own child! O gracious heaven, have I sinned myself so far from my innocent baby! My child, my child! My little Katherine!"

Her bosom heaved, and she said in a hard tone, "I daresay they think I'm a bad mother because I left her to others to nurse her and to love her, to see her every day and all day, to bathe her sweet body, and to comb her yellow hair, to look into her little blue eyes, and to watch all her pretty, pretty ways—Oh, yes, yes." she said, with increasing emotion, "I daresay they think that of me."

"They think nothing but what is good of you, Kate—nothing but what is good and kind."

She looked out on the rain which fell unceasingly, and said in a low voice, "Is Pete still telling the same story—that I am only away for a little while—that I am coming back?"

"He is writing letters to himself now, and saying they come from you."

"From me?"

"Such simple things—all in his own way—full of love and happiness—*I am so happy and comfortable*—it is pitiful. He is like a child—he never suspects anything. You are better and enjoying yourself and looking forward to coming home soon. Sending kisses and presents for the baby, too, and greetings for everybody. There are messages for me also. *Your true and loving wife*—it is terrible."

She covered her face with both hands. "And is he telling everybody?"

"Yes; that's what the letters are meant for. He thinks he is keeping your name sweet and your place clean, so that you may return at any time, and scandal may not touch you."

"Oh, why do you tell me that, Philip? It is dragging me back. And the child is dragging me back also... Does he show the letters to you?"

"Worse than that, Kate—much worse—he makes me answer them. I answered one the other night. Oh, when I think of it! *Dear wife, glad to get your welcome letters.* God knows how I held the pen—I was giddy enough to drop it. He gave you all the news—about your father, and Grannie, and everybody. All in his own bright way—poor old Pete, the cheeriest, sunniest soul alive. *The Dempster is putting a sight on us regular—trusts you are the better for leaving home.* It was awful—awful! *Dearest Kirry, I'm missing you mortal—worse than Kimberley. So come home soon, my true lil wife, to your foolish ould husband, for his heart is losing him.*"

He leapt up, and began to tramp the floor. "But why do I tell you this? I should bear my own burdens."

Her hands had come down from her face, which was full of a great compassion. "And did *you* have to write all that?" she asked.

"Oh, he meant no harm. He had no thought of hurting anybody! He never dreamt that every word was burning and blistering me to the heart of hearts."

His voice deepened, and his face grew hard and ugly. "But it was the same as if some devil out of hell had entered into the man and told him how to torture me—as if the cruellest tyrant on earth had made me take up the pen and write down my own death-warrant. I could have killed him—I could not help it—yes, I felt at that moment as if—— Oh, what am I saying?"

He stopped, sat on the end of the bed again, and held his head between his hands.

She came and sat by his side. "Philip," she said, "I am ruining you. Yes, I am corrupting you. I who would have had you so high and pure—and you so pure-minded—I am bringing you to ruin. Having me here is destroying you, Philip. No one visits you now. You are shutting the door on everybody.... I heard you come in last night, Philip. I hear you every night. Yes, I know everything. Oh, you will end by hating me—I know you will. Why don't you send me away? It will be better to send me away in time, Philip. Besides, it will make no difference. We are in the same house, yet we never meet. Send me away now, before it is too late."

He dropped his hand and felt for her hand; he was trying not to look into her face. "We have both suffered, Kate. We can never hate one another—we have suffered for each other's sake."

She clung tightly to the hand he gave her, and said, "Then you will never forsake me, whatever happens?"

"Never, Kate, never," he answered; and with a smothered cry she threw her arms about his neck.

The rain continued to pour down on the roofs and on the tombs with a monotonous plash. "But what is to be done?" she said.

"God knows," he answered.

"What is to become of us, Philip? Are we never to smile on each other again? We cannot carry a burden like this for ever. To-day, to-morrow, the next day, the next year—is it to go on like this for a lifetime? Is this life? Is there nothing that will end it?"

"Yes, Kate, yes; there is one thing that will end it—one thing only."

"Do you mean—*death?*"

He did not answer. She rose slowly from his side and returned to the window, rested her forehead against the pane, and looked down on the desolate churchyard and the sexton at his work in the rain. Suddenly she broke the silence. "Philip," she said, "I know now what we ought to do. I wonder we have never thought of it before."

"What is it?" he asked.

She was standing in front of him. Her breath came quickly. "Tell Pete that I am dead."

"No, no, no."

She took both his hands. "Yes, yes," she said.

He kept his face away from her. "Kate, what are you saying?"

"What is more natural, Philip? Only think—if you had been anybody else, it would have come to that already. You must have hated me for dragging you down into this mire of deceit, you must have forsaken me, and I must have gone to wreck and ruin. Oh, I see it all—just as if it had really happened. A solitary room somewhere—alone—sinking—dying—unknown, unnamed—forgotten——"

His eyes were wandering about the room. "It will kill him. If his heart can break, it will break it," he said.

"He has lived after a heavier blow than that, Philip. Do you think he is not suffering? For all his bright ways and hopeful talk and the letters and the presents, do you think he is not suffering?"

He liberated his hands, and began to tramp the room as before, but with head down dud hands linked behind him.

"It will be cruel to deceive him," he said.

"No, Philip, but kind. Death is not cruel. The wound it makes will heal. It won't bleed for ever. Once he thinks I am dead he will weep a little perhaps, and then "—she was stifling a sob—"then it will be all over. 'Poor girl,' he will say, 'she was much to blame. I loved her once, and never did her any wrong. But she is gone, and she was the mother of little Katherine—let us forget her faults'——"

He had not heard her; he was standing before the window looking down. "You are right, Kate, I think you must be right."

"I'm sure I am."

"He will suffer, but he will get over it."

"Yes, indeed. And you, Philip—he will torture you no longer. No more letters, no more presents, no more messages——"

"I'll do it—I'll do it to-morrow," he said.

She opened her arms wide, and cried, "Kiss me, Philip, kiss me. We shall live again. Yes, we shall laugh together still—kiss me, kiss me."

"Not yet—when I come back."

"Very well—when you come back."

She sank into a chair, crying with joy, and he went out as he had entered, noiselessly, stealthily, like a shadow.

When a man who is not a criminal is given over to a deep duplicity of life, he will clutch at any lie, wearing the mask of truth, which seems to shield him from shame and pain. He may be a wise man in every other relation, a shrewd man, a far-seeing and even a cunning man, but in this relation—that of his own honour, his own fame, his own safety—he is certain to be a blunderer, a bungler, and a fool. Such is the revenge of Nature, such is God's own vengeance!

XVII.

Philip was walking from Ballure House to Elm Cottage. It was late, and the night was dark and silent—a muggy, dank, and stagnant night, without wind or air, moon or stars. The road was quiet, the trees were still, the sea made only a far-off murmur.

And as he walked he struggled to persuade himself that in what he was about to do he would be doing well. "It will not be wrong to deceive him," he thought. "It will only be for his own good. The suspense would kill him. He would waste away. The sap of the man's soul would dry up. Then why should I hesitate? Besides, it is partly true—true in its own sense, and that is the real sense. She *is* dead—dead to him. She can never return to him; she is lost to him for ever. So it is true after all—it is true."

"It is a lie," said a voice at his ear.

He started. He could have been sure that somebody had spoken. Yet there was nobody by his side. He was alone in the road. "It must have been my own voice," he thought. "I must have been thinking aloud." And then he resumed his walk and his meditation.

"And if it is a lie, is it therefore a crime?" he asked himself. "Sure it is—how very sure!—it was a wise man that said so—a great fault once committed is the first link in a chain. The other links seem to be crimes also, but they are not—they are consequences. *Our* fault was long ago, and even then it was partly the fault of Fate. If the past could be recalled we could not act differently unless our fates were different. And what has followed has been only the consequence. It was the consequence when Kate was married to Pete; it was the consequence when she left him—and *this* is the consequence."

"It is a lie," said the same voice by his side.

He stopped. The darkness was gross around him—he could see nothing.

"Who's there?" he demanded.

There was no answer. He stretched his hand out nervously. There was no one at his side. "It must have been the wind in the trees," he thought; but there could be no wind in the stagnant dampness of that air. "It was like my own voice," he thought. Then he remembered how his man in Douglas had told him that he had contracted a habit of talking to himself of late. "It was my own voice," he thought, and he went on again.

"A lie is a bad foundation to build on—that's certain. The thing that should be cannot rest on the thing that is not. It will topple down; it will come to ruin; it will wreck everything. Still——"

"It is a lie," said the voice again. There could be no mistaking it this time. It was a low, deep whisper. It seemed to be spoken in the very cavity of his ear. It was not his own voice, and yet it struck upon his sense with the sound as of his own. It must be his own voice speaking to himself!

When this idea took hold of him, he was seized with a deadly shuddering. His heart knocked against his ribs, and an icy coldness came over him. "Only the same tormenting dream," he thought. "Before it was a vision; now it is a voice. It is generated by solitude and separation. I must resist it I must be strong. It will drive me into an oppression as of madness. Men do not 'see their souls' until they are bordering on madness from religious mania or crime."

"A lie! a lie!" said the voice.

"This is madness itself. To paint faces on the darkness, to hear voices in the air, is madness. The madman can do no more."

"A lie!" said the voice again. He cast a look over his shoulder. It was the same as if some one had touched him and spoken.

He walked faster. The voice seemed to walk with him. "I will hold myself firm," he thought; "I will not be afraid. Reason does not fail a man until he allows himself to *believe* that it is failing. 'I am going mad,' he thinks; and then he shrieks and is mad indeed. I will not depart from my course. If I do so now, I shall be lost. The horror will master me, and I shall be its slave for ever."

He had turned out of Ballure into the Ramsey Road, and he could see the town lights in the distance. But the voice continued to haunt him persistently, besiegingly, despotically.

"Great God!" he thought, "what is the imaginary devil to the horror of this presence? Your own eye, your own voice, always with you, always following you! No darkness so dense that it can hide the sight, no noise so loud that it can deaden the sound!"

He walked faster. Still the voice seemed to stride by his side, an invisible thing, with deliberate and noiseless step, from which there was no escape.

He drew up suddenly and walked slower. His knees were tottering, he was treading as on waves; yet he went on. "I will not yield. I will master myself. I will do what I intended. I am not mad," he thought.

He was at the gate of Elm Cottage by this time, and, with a strong glow of resolution, he walked boldly to the door and knocked.

159

XVIII.

Pete had not awakened until late that morning. While still in bed he had heard Grannie and Nancy in the room below. The first sound of their voices told him that something was amiss.

"Aw, God bless me, God bless me!" said Nancy, as though with uplifted hands.

"It was Kelly the postman," said Grannie in a doleful tone—the tone in which she had spoken between the puffs of her pipe.

"The dirt!" said Nancy.

"He was up at Cæsar's before breakfast this morning," said Grannie.

"There now!" cried Nancy. "There's men like that, though. Just aiger for mischief. It's sweeter than all their prayers to them.... But where can she be, then? Has she made away with herself, poor thing?"

"That's what I was asking Cæsar," said Grannie. "If she's gone with the young Ballawhaine, what for aren't you going to England over and fetching her home?" says I.

"And what did Cæsar say?"

"'No,' says he, 'not a step,' says he. 'If she's dead,' says he, 'we'll only know it a day the sooner, and if she's in life, it'll be a disgrace to us the longest day we live.'"

"Aw, bolla veen, bolla veen!" said Nancy. "When some men is getting religion there's no more inside at them than a gutted herring, and they're good for nothing but to put up in the chimley to smook."

"It's Black Tom, woman," said Grannie. "Cæsar's freckened mortal of the man's tongue going. 'It's water to his wheel,' he's saying. 'He'll be telling me to set my own house in order, and me a local preacher, too.' But how's the man himself?"

"Pete?" said Nancy. "Aw, tired enough last night, and not down yet.... Hush!... It's his foot on the loft."

"Poor boy! poor boy!" said Grannie.

The child cried, and then somebody began to beat the floor to the measure of a long-drawn hymn. Grannie must have been sitting before the fire with the baby across her knees.

"Something has happened," thought Pete as he drew on his clothes. A moment later something had happened indeed. He had opened a drawer of the dressing-table and found the wedding-ring and the earrings where Kate had left them. There was a commotion in the room below by this time, but Pete did not hear it. He was crying in his heart. "It is coming! I know it! I feel it! God help me! Lord forgive me! Amen! Amen!"

Cæsar, the postman, and the constable, as a deputation from "The Christians," had just entered the house. Black Tom was with them. He was the ferret that had fetched them out of their holes.

"Get thee home, woman," said Cæsar to Grannie, "This is no place for thee. It is the abode of sin and deception."

"It's the home of my child's child, and that's enough for me," said Grannie.

"Get thee back, I tell thee," said Cæsar, "and come thee to this house of shame no more."

"Take her, Nancy," said Grannie, giving up the child. "Shame enough, indeed, I'm thinking, when a woman has to shut her heart to her own flesh and blood if she's not to disrespect her husband," and she went off, weeping.

But Cæsar's emotions were walled in by his pietistical views. "Every one that hath forsaken houses, or brethren, or sisters, or father, or mother, or wife, or children, or land, for My name's sake, shall receive an hundredfold," said Cæsar, with a cast of his eye towards Black Tom.

"Well, if I ever!" said Nancy. "The husband that wanted the like of that from me now.... A hundredfold, indeed! No, not for a hundred hundredfolds, the nasty dirt."

"Don't he turning up your nose, woman, but call your master," said Cæsar.

"It's more than some ones need do, then, and I won't call my master, neither—no, thank you," said Nancy.

"I've something to tell him, and I've come, too, for to do it," said Cæsar.

"The devil came farther than ever you did, and it was only a lie he was bringing for all that," said Nancy.

"Hould your tongue, Nancy Cain," said Cæsar, "and take that Popish thing off the child's head." It was the scarlet hood.

"Pity the money that's wasted on the like wasn't given to the poor."

"I've heard something the same before, Cæsar Cregeen," said Nancy. "It was Judas Iscariot was saying it first, and you're just thieving it from a thief."

"Chut!" cried Cæsar, goaded by the laughter of Black Tom. "I'll call the man myself. Peter Quilliam!" and he made for the staircase door.

"Stand back," cried Nancy, holding the child like a pillow over one of her arms, and lifting the other threateningly.

"Aw, you'll never be raising your hand to the man of God, woman," giggled Black Tom.

"Won't I, though?" said Nancy grimly, "or the man of the devil either," she added, flashing at himself.

"The woman's not to trust, sir," snuffled the constable. "She's only an infidel, anyway. I've heard tell of her saying she didn't believe the whale swallowed Jonah."

"That's the diff'rance between us, then," said Nancy; "for there's some of you Manx ones would believe if Jonah swallowed the whale."

The staircase door opened at the back of Nancy, and Pete stepped into the room. "What's this, friends?" he asked, in a careworn voice.

Cæsar stepped forward with a yellow envelope in his hand. "What's *that*, sir?" he answered.

Pete took the envelope and opened it.

"That's your letter back to you through the dead letter office, isn't it?" said Cæsar.

"Well?" said Pete.

"There's nobody of that name in that place, is there!" said Cæsar.

"Well?" said Pete again.

"Letters from England don't come through Peel, but your first letter had the Peel postmark, hadn't it?"

"Well?"

"Parcels from England don't come through Port St. Mary, but your parcel was stamped in Port St. Mary, wasn't it?"

"Anything else?"

"The handwriting inside the letter wasn't your own handwriting, was it? The address on the outside of the parcel wasn't your own address—no?"

"Is that all?"

"Enough to be going on, I'm thinking."

"What about Uncle Joe?" said Black Tom, with another giggle.

"Your mistress is not in Liverpool. You don't know where she is. She has gone the way of all sinners," said Cæsar.

"Is that what you're coming to tell me?" said Pete.

"No; we're coming to tell you," said Cæsar, "that, as a notorious loose liver, we must be putting her out of class. And we're coming to call on yourself to look to your own salvation. You've deceaved us, Mr. Quilliam. You've grieved the Spirit of the Lord," with another "glime" in the direction of Black Tom; "you've brought contempt on the fellowship that counts you for one of the fold. You've given the light of your countenance to the path of an evildoer, and you've brought down the head of a child of God with sorrow to the grave."

Cæsar was moved by his self-satisfied piety, and began to make' noises in his nostrils. "Let us lay the case before the Lord," he said; and he went down on his knees and prayed—

"Our brother has deceived us, O Lord, but we forgive him freely. Forgive Thou also his trespasses, so that at the last he escape hell-fire. Count not Thy handmaid for a daughter of Belial, wherever she is this day. May it be good for her to be cut off from the body of the righteous. Grant that she feel this mercy in her carnal body before her eternal soul be called to everlasting judgment. Lord, strengthen Thy servant. Let not his natural affections be as the snare of the fowler unto his feet. Though it grieve him sore, even to tears and tribulation, help him to pluck out the gourd that groweth in his own bosom——"

"Dear heart alive!" cried Nancy, clattering her clogs, "it's a wonder in the world the man isn't thinking shame to blacken his own daughter before the Almighty Himself."

"Be merciful, O Lord," continued Cæsar, "to all rank unbelievers, and such as live in heathen darkness in a Christian land, and don't know Saturday from Sunday, and are imper-ent uncommon and bad with the tongue——"

"Stop that now." cried Nancy, "that's meant for me."

Pete had stood through this in silence, but with an angry, miserable face.

"Beg pardon all," he said. "I'm not going for denying to what you say. I'm like the fish at the heel of the trawl-boat—the net's closing in on me and I'm caught. The game's up. I did deceave you. I *did* write those letters myself. I've no Uncle Joe, nor no Auntie Joney neither. My wife's left me. I'm not knowing where she is, or what's becoming of her. I'm done, and I'm for throwing up the sponge."

There were grunts of satisfaction. "But don't you feel the need of pardon, brother," said Cæsar.

"I don't," said Pete. "What I was doing I was doing for the best, and, if I was doing wrong, the Almighty will have to forgive me—that's about all."

Cæsar shot out his lip. Pete raised himself to his full height and looked from face to face, until his eyes settled on the postman.

"But it takes a thief to catch a thief," he said. "Which of you was the thief that catcht me? Maybe I've been only a blundering blockhead, and perhaps you've been clever, and smart uncommon, but I'm thinking there's some of you hasn't been rocked enough for all that."

He held out the yellow envelope. "This letter was sealed when you gave it to me, Mr. Cregeen—how did you know what was inside of it? 'On Her Majesty's Sarvice,' you say. But it isn't dead letters only that's coming with words same as that."

The postman was meddling with his front hair.

"The Lord has His own wayses of doing His work, has He, Cæsar? I never heard tell, though, that opening other people's letters was one of them."

Mr. Kelly's ferret eyes were nearly twinkling themselves out.

Pete threw letter and envelope into the fire. "You've come to tell me you're going to turn my wife out of class. All right! You can turn me out, too, and if the money I gave you is anywhere handy, you can turn that out at the same time and make a clane job."

Black Tom was doubling with suppressed laughter at the corner of the dresser, and Cæsar was writhing under his searching glances.

"You're knowing a dale about the ould Book and I'm not knowing much," said Pete, "but isn't it saying somewhere, 'Let him that's without sin amongst you chuck the first stone?' I'm not worth mentioning for a saint myself, so I lave it with you."

His voice began to break. "You're thinking a dale about the broken law seemingly, but I'm thinking more about the broken heart. There's the like in somewhere, you go bail. The woman that's gone may have done wrong—I'm not saying she didn't, poor thing; but if she comes home again, you may turn her out, but I'll take her back, whatever she is and whatever she's done—so help me God I will—and I'll not wait for the Day of Judgment to ask the Almighty if I'm doing right."

161

Then he sat down with his back to them on a chair before the fire.

"Now you can go home to nurse," said Nancy, wiping her eyes, "and lave me to sweeten the kitchen—it's wanting water enough after dirts like you."

Cæsar also was wiping his eye—the one nearest to Black Tom. "Come," he said with plaintive resignation, "our errand was useless. The Ethiopian cannot change his skin, nor the leopard his spots."

"No, but he can get a topcoat to cover them, though," said Nancy. "Oh, that flea sticks, does it, Cæsar? Don't blame the looking-glass if your face is ugly."

Cæsar pretended not to hear her. "Well," he said, with a sigh discharged at Pete's back, "we'll pray, spite of appearances, that we may all go to heaven together some day."

"No, thank you, not me," said Nancy. "I wouldn't be-mane myself going anywhere with the like of you."

The Job in Cæsar could bear up no longer. "Vain and ungrateful woman," he cried, "who hath eaten of my bread and drunken of my cup——"

"Cursing me, are you?" said Nancy. "Sakes! you must have been found in the bulrushes at Pharaoh's daughter and made a prophet of."

"No use bandying words, sir, wid a single woman dat lives alone wid a single man," said Mr. Niplightly.

Nancy flopped the child from her right arm to her left, and with the back of her hand she slapped the constable across the face. "Take that for the cure of a bad heart," she said, "and tell the Dempster I gave it you."

Then she turned on the postman and Black Tom. "Out of it, you lil thief, your mouth's only a dirty town-well and your tongue's the pump in it. Go home and die, you big black spider—you're ould enough for it and wicked enough, too. Out of it, the lot of you!" she cried, and clashed the door at their backs, and then opened it again for a parting shot. "And if it's true you're on your way to heaven together, just let me know, and I'll see if I can't put up with the other place myself."

XIX.

That evening Pete was sitting with one foot on the cradle rocker, one arm on the table, and the other hand trifling tenderly with the ring and the earrings which he had found in the drawer of the dressing-table, when there was a hurried knock on the door. It had the hollow reverberation of a knock on the lid of a coffin.

"Come in," called Pete.

It was Philip, but it was almost as if Death had entered, so thin and bony were his cheeks, so wild his eyes, so cold his hands.

Pete was prepared for anything. "You've found me out, too, I see you have," he said defiantly. "You needn't tell *me*—it's chasing caught fish."

"Be brave, Pete," said Philip. "It will be a great shock to you."

Pete looked up and his manner changed. "Speak it out, sir. It's a poor man that can't stand——"

"I've come on the saddest errand," said Philip, taking a seat as far away as possible.

"You've found her—you've seen her, sir. Where is she?"

"She is——" began Philip, and then he stopped.

"Go on, mate; I've known trouble before to-day," said Pete.

"Can you bear it?" said Philip. "She is——" and he stopped again.

"She is—where?" said Pete.

"She is dead," said Philip at last.

Pete rose to his feet. Philip rose also, and now poured out his message with the headlong rush of a cataract.

"In fact, it all happened some time ago, Pete, but I couldn't bring myself to tell you before. I tried, but I couldn't. It was in Douglas—of a fever—in a lodging—alone—unattended——"

"Hould hard, sir! Give me time," said Pete. "I'd a gunshot wound at Kimberley, and since then I've a stitch in my side at whiles and sometimes a bit of a catch in my breathing."

He staggered to the porch door and threw it open, then came back panting—"Dead! dead! Kate is dead!"

Nancy came from the kitchen at the moment, and hearing what he was saying, she lifted both hands and uttered a piercing shriek. He took her by the shoulders and turned her back, shut the door behind her, and said, holding his right hand hard at his side, "Women are brave, sir, but when the storm breaks on a man——" He broke off and muttered again, "Dead! Kirry is dead!"

The child, awakened by Nancy's cry, was now whimpering fretfully. Pete went to the cradle and rocked it with one foot, crooning in a quavering treble, "Hush-a-bye! hush-a-bye!"

Philip's breathing was oppressed. He felt like a man at the edge of a precipice, with an impulse to throw himself over. "God forgive me," he said. "I could kill myself. I've broken your heart;——"

"No fear of me, sir," said Pete. "I'm an ould hulk that's seen weather. I'll not go to pieces from inside at all. Give me time, mate, give me time." And then he went on muttering as before, "Dead! Kirry dead! Hush-a-bye! My Kirry dead!"

The little one slept, and Pete drew back in his chair, nodded into the fire, and said in a weak, childish voice, "I've known her all my life, d'ye know? She's been my lil sweetheart since she was a slip of a girl, and slapped the schoolmaster for bating me wrongeously. Swate lil thing in them days, mate, with her brown feet and tossing hair. And now she's a woman and she's dead! The Lord have mercy upon me!"

He got up and began to walk heavily across the floor, dipping and plunging as if going upstairs. "The bright and happy she was when I started for Kimberley, too; with her pretty face by the aising stones in the morning, all laughter and mischief. Five years I was seeing it in my drames like that, and now it's gone. Kirry is gone! My Kirry! God help me! O God, have mercy upon me!"

He stopped in his unsteady walk, and sat and stared into the fire. His eyes were red; blotches of heart's blood seemed to be rising to them; but there was not the sign of a tear. Philip did not attempt to console him. He felt as if the first syllable would choke in his throat.

"I see how it's been, sir," said Pete. "While I was away her heart was changing her, and when I came back she thought she must keep her word. My poor lamb! She was only a child anyway. But I was a man—I ought to have seen how it was. I'm like a drowning man, too—things are coming back on me. I'm seeing them plain enough now. But it's too late! My poor Kirry! And I thought I was making her so happy!" Then, with a helpless look, "You wouldn't believe it, sir, but I was never once thinking nothing else. No, I wasn't; it's a fact. I was same as a sailor working all the voyage home, making a cage, and painting it goold, for the love-bird he's catcht in the sunny lands somewhere; but when he's putting it in, it's only wanting away, poor thing."

With a sense of grovelling meanness, Philip sat and listened. Then, with eyes wandering across the floor, he said, "You have nothing to reproach yourself with. You did everything a man could do—everything. And she was innocent also. It was the fault of another. He came between you. Perhaps he thought he couldn't help it—perhaps he persuaded himself—God knows what lie he told himself—but she's innocent, Pete; believe me, she's——"

Pete brought his fist down heavily on the table, and the rings that lay on it jumped and tingled. "What's that to me?" he cried hoarsely. "What do I care if she's innocent or guilty? She's dead, isn't she? and that's enough. Curse the man! I don't want to hear of him. She's mine now. What for should he come here between me and my own?"

The torn heart and racked brain could bear no more. Pete dropped his head on the table. Presently his anger ebbed. Without lifting his head, he stretched his hand across the rings to feel for Philip's hand. Philip's hand trembled in his grasp. He took that for sympathy, and became the more ashamed.

"Give me time, mate," he said. "I'll be my own man soon. My head's moithered dreadful—I'm not knowing if I heard you right. In Douglas, you say? By herself, too? Not by herself, surely? Not quite alone neither? She found you out, didn't she? *You'd* be there, Phil? You'd be with her yourself? She'd be wanting for nothing?"

Philip answered huskily, his eyes still wandering. "If it will be any comfort to you... yes, I *was* with her—she wanted for nothing."

"My poor girl!" said Pete. "Did she send—had she any—maybe she said a word or two—at the last, eh?"

Philip clutched at the question. There was something at last that he could say without falsehood. "She sent a prayer for your forgiveness," he said. "She told me to tell you to think of her as little as might be; not to grieve for her too much, and to try to forget her, so that her sin also might be forgotten."

"And the lil one—anything about the lil one?" asked Pete.

"That was the bitterest grief of all," said Philip. "It was so hard that you must think her an unnatural mother. 'My Katherine! My little Katherine! My sweet angel!' It was her cry the whole day long."

"I see, I see," said Pete, nodding at the fire; "she left the lil one for my sake, wanting it with her all the while. Poor thing! You'd comfort her, Philip? You'd let her go aisy?"

"'The child is well and happy,' I told her. 'He's thinking nothing of yourself but what is good and kind,' I said."

"God's peace rest on her! My darling! My wife!" said Pete solemnly. Then suddenly in another tone, "Do you know where she's buried?"

Philip hesitated. He had not foreseen this question. Where had been his head that he had never thought of it? But there was no going back now. He was compelled to go on. He must tell lie on lie. "Yes," he faltered.

"Could you take me to the grave?"

Philip gasped; the sweat broke out on his forehead.

"Don't be freckened, sir," said Pete; "I'm my own man again. Could you take me to my wife's grave?"

"Yes," said Philip. He was in the rapids. He was on the edge of precipitation. He was compelled to go over. He made a blindfold plunge. Lie on lie; lie on lie!

"Then we'll start by the coach to-morrow," said Pete.

Philip rose with rigid limbs. He had meant to tell one lie only, and already he had told many. Truly "a lie is a cripple;" it cannot stand alone. "Good night, Pete; I'll go home. I'm not well to-night."

"We'll stop the coach at your aunt's gate in the morning," said Pete.

They stepped to the door together, and stood for a moment in the dank and lifeless darkness.

"The world's getting wonderful lonely, man, and you're all that's left to me now, Phil—you and the child. I'm not for wailing, though. When I got my gun-shot wound out yonder, I was away over the big veldt, hundreds of miles from anywhere, behind the last bush and the last blade of grass, with the stones and the ashes and the dust—about as far, you'd say, as the world was finished, and never looking to see herself and the ould island and the ould faces no more. I'm not so lonesome as that at all. Good-night, ould fellow, and God bless you!"

The gate opened and closed, Philip went stumbling up the road. He was hating Pete. To hate this open-hearted man who had dragged him into an entanglement of lies was the only resource of his stifled conscience.

163

Pete went back to the house, muttering, "Kirry is dead! Kirry is dead!" He put the catch on the door, said, "Close the shutters, Nancy," and then returned to his chair by the cradle.

XX.

Later the same night Pete carried the news to Sulby. Grannie was in the bar-room, and he broke it to her gently, tenderly, lovingly.

Loud voices came from the kitchen. Cæsar was there in angry contention with Black Tom. An open Bible was between them on their knees. Tom tugged it towards him, bobbed his blunt forefinger down on the page, and cried, "There's the text—that'll pin you—*publicans and sinners.*"

Cæsar leaned back'in his seat, and said with withering scorn, "It's a bad business—I'll give you lave to say that. It's men like you that's making it bad. But whether is it better for a bad business to be in bad hands or in good ones? There's a big local praicher in London, they're telling me, that's hot for joining the public-house to the church, and turning the parsons into the publicans. That's what they all were on the Isle of Man in ould days gone by, and pity they're not so still. Oh, I've been giving it my sarious thoughts, sir. I've been making it a subject for prayer. 'Will I give up my public or hould fast to it to keep it out of worse hands?' And I'm strong to believe the Lord hath spoken. 'It's a little vineyard—a little work in a little vineyard. Stick to it, Cæsar,' and so I will."

Pete stepped into the kitchen and flung his news at Cæsar with a sort of wild melancholy, as who would say, "There, is that enough for you? Are you satisfied now?"

"*Mair yee shoh*—it's the hand of God," said Cæsar.

"A middling bad hand then," said Pete; "I've seen better, anyway."

A high spiritual pride took hold of Cæsar—Black Tom was watching him, and working his big eyebrows vigorously. With mouth firmly shut and head thrown back, Cæsar said in a sepulchral voice, "The Lord gave, and the Lord hath taken away. Blessed be the name of the Lord!"

Pete made a crack of savage laughter.

"Aren't you feeling it, sir?" said Cæsar.

"Not a feel near me," said Pete. "I never did the Lord no harm that I know of, but He's taken my young wife and left my poor innocent lil one motherless."

"Unsearchable the wisdom and justice of God," said Cæsar.

"Unsearchable?" said Pete. "It's all that. But I don't know if you're calling it justice. I'm not myself. It isn't my tally. Blasphemy? I lave it with you. A scoffer, am I? So be it. The Lord's licked me, and I've had enough. But I'm not going down on my knees for it, anyway. The Almighty and me is about quits."

With that word on his lips he strode out of the place, grim, implacable, almost savage, a fierce smile fluttering on his ashy face.

XXI.

Grannie came to Elm Cottage next morning with two duck eggs for Pete's breakfast. She was boiling them in a saucepan when Pete came downstairs.

"Come now," she said coaxingly, as she laid them on the table, with the water smoking off the shells. But Pete could not eat.

"He hasn't destroyed any food these days," said Nancy. A little before she had rolled her apron, slipped out into the street, and brought back a tiny packet screwed up in a bit of newspaper.

"Perhaps he'll ate them on the road," said Grannie. "I'll put them in the hankerchief in his hat anyway."

"My faith, no, woman!" cried Nancy. "He's the mischief for sweating. He'll be mopping his forehead and forgetting the eggs. But here—where's your waistcoat pocket, Pete? Have you room for a hayseed anywhere? There!... It's a quarter of twist, poor boy," she whispered behind her hand to Grannie.

Thus they vied with each other in little attentions to the down-hearted man. Meantime Crow, the driver of the Douglas coach, a merry old sinner with a bulbous nose and short hair, standing erect like the steel pins of an electric brush, was whistling as he put his horses to in the marketplace. Presently he swirled round the corner and drew up at the gate. The women then became suddenly quiet, and put their aprons to their mouths, as if a hearse had stopped at the door; but Pete bustled about and shouted boisterously to cover the emotion of his farewell.

"Good-bye, Grannie; I'll say a word for you when I get there. Good-bye, Nancy; I'll not be forgetting yourself neither. Good bye, lil bogh," dropping on one knee at the side of the cradle. "What right has a man's heart to be going losing him while he has a lil innocent like this to live for? Good-bye!"

There was a throng of women at the gate talking of Kate. "Aw, a civil person, very—a civiller person never was."—"It's me that'll be missing her too. I served her eggs to the day of her death, as you might say. 'Good morning, Christian Anne,' says she—just like that. Welcome, you say? I was at home at the woman's door."—"And the beautiful she came home in the gig with the baby! Only yesterday you might say. And now, Lord-a-massy!"—"Hush! it's himself! I'm fit enough to cry when I look at the man. The cheerful heart is broke at him."—"Hush!"

They dropped their heads so that Pete might avoid their gaze, and held the coach-door open for him, expecting that he would go inside, as to a funeral. But he saluted them with "Good morning all," and leapt to the box-seat with Crow.

The coach stopped to take up the Deemster at the gate of Ballure House. Philip looked thin and emaciated, and walked with a death-like weakness, but also a feverish resolution. Behind him, carrying a rag, came Aunty Nan in her white cap, with little nervous attentions, and a face full of anxiety.

"Drive inside to-day, Philip," she said.

"No, no," he answered, and kissed her, pushed her to the other side of the gate with gentle protestation, and climbed to Pete's side. Then the old lady said—

"Good-morning, Peter. I'm so sorry for your great trouble, and trust... But you'll not let the Deemster ride too long outside if it grows... He's had a sleepless night and——"

"Go on, Crow," said Philip, in a decisive voice.

"I'll see to that, Miss Christian, ma'am," shouted Crow over his shoulder. "His honour's studdying a bit too hard—that's what *he* is. But a gentleman's not much use if his wife's a widow, as the man said—eh? Looking well enough yourself, though, Miss Christian, ma'am. Getting younger every day, in fact. I'll have to be fetching that East Indee capt'n up yet. I will that. Ha! ha! Get on, Boxer!" Then, with a flick of the whip, they were off on their journey.

The day was calm and beautiful. Old Barrule wore his yellow skull-cap of flowering gorse, the birds sang on the trees, and the sea on the shore sang also with the sound of far-off joy-bells. It was a heart-breaking day to Pete, but he tried to bear himself bravely.

He was seated between Philip and the driver. On the farther side of Crow there were two other passengers, a farmer and a fisherman. The farmer, a foul-mouthed fellow with a long staff and two dogs racing and barking on the road, was returning from Midsummer fair, at which he had sold his sheep; the fisherman, a simple creature, was coming home from the mackerel-fishing at Kinsale, with a box of the fish between his legs.

"The wife's been having a lil one since I was laving in March," said the fisherman, laughing all over his bronzed face. "A boy, d'ye say? Aw, another boy, of coorse. Three of them now—all men. Got a letter at Ramsey post-office coming through. She's getting on as nice as nice, and the ould woman's busy doing for her."

"Gee up, Boxer—we'll wet its head at the Hibernian," said Crow.

"I'm not partic'lar at all," said the fisherman cheerily. "The mack'rel's been doing middling this season, anyway."

And then in his simple way he went on to paint home, and the joy of coming back to it, with the new baby, and the mother in child-bed, and the grandmother as housekeeper, and the other children waiting for new frocks and new jackets out of the earnings of the fishing, and himself going round to pay the grocer what had been put on "strap" while he was at Kin-sale, till Pete was melted, and could listen no longer.

"I'm persuaded still she wasn't well when she went away," he whispered, turning his shoulder to the men and his face to Philip. He talked in a low voice, just above the rumble of the wheels, trying to extenuate Kate's fault and to excuse her to Philip.

"It's no use thinking hard of anybody, is it, sir?" he said. "We can't crawl into another person's soul, as the saying is."

After that he asked many questions—about Kate's illness, about the doctor, about the funeral, about everything except the man—of him he asked nothing. Philip was compelled to answer. He was like a prisoner chained at the galleys—he was forced to go on. They crossed the bridge over the top of Ballaglass, which goes down to the mill at Cornaa.

"There's the glen, sir," said Pete. "Aw, the dear ould days! Wading in the water, leaping over the stones, clambering on the trunks—aw, dear! aw, dear! Bareheaded and barefooted in those times, sir; but smart extraordinary, and a terble notion of being dressy, too. Twisting ferns about her lil neck for lace, sticking a mountain thistle, sparkling with dew, on her breast for a diamond, twining a trail of fuchsia round her head for a crown—aw, dear! aw, dear! And now—well, well, to think! to think!"

There was laughter on the other side of the coach.

"What do *you* say, Capt'n Pete?" shouted Crow.

"What's that?" asked Pete.

The fisherman had treated the driver and the farmer at the Hibernian, and was being rewarded with robustious chaff.

"I'm telling Dan Johnny here these childers that's coming when a man's away from home isn't much to trust. Best put a sight up with the lil one to the wise woman of Glen Aldyn, eh? A man doesn't like to bring up a cuckoo in the nest—what d'ye say, Capt'n?"

"I say you're a dirty ould divil, Crow; and I don't want to be chucking you off your seat," said Pete; and with that he turned back to Philip.
*

The driver was affronted, but the farmer pacified him by an appeal to his fear. "He'd be coarse to tackle, the same fellow—I saw him clane out a tent with one hand at Tyn-wald."

"It's a wonder she didn't come home for all," said Pete at Philip's ear—"at the end, you know. Couldn't face it out, I suppose? Nothing to be afraid of, though, if she'd only known. I had kept things middling straight up to then. And I'd have broke the head of the first man that'd wagged a tongue. But maybe it was myself she was freckened of! Freckened of me! Poor thing! poor thing!"

165

Philip was in torment. To witness Pete's simple grief, to hear him breathe a forgiveness for the erring woman, and to be trusted with the thoughts of his heart as a father might be trusted by a young child—it was anguish, it was agony, it was horror. More than once he felt an impulse to cast off his load, to confess, to tell everything. But he reflected that he had no right to do this—that the secret was not his own to give away. His fear restrained him also. He looked into Pete's face, so full of manly sorrow, and shuddered to think of it transformed by rage.

"Sit hard, gentlemen. Breeches' work here," shouted Crow.

They were at the top of the steep descent going down to Laxey. The white town lay sprinkled over the green banks of the glen, and the great water-wheel stood in the depths of the mountain gill behind it.

"She's there! She's yonder! It's herself at the door. She's up. She's looking out for the coach," cried the fisherman, clambering up on to the seat.

"Aisy all," shouted Crow.

"No use, Mr. Crow. Nothing will persuade me but that's herself with the lil one in a blanket at the door."

Before the coach had drawn up at the bridge, the fisherman had leapt to the ground, shouldered his keg, shouted "Good everin' all," and disappeared down an alley of the town.

The driver alighted. A crowd gathered around. There were parcels to take up, parcels to set down, and the horses to water. When the coach was ready to start again, the farmer with his dogs had gone, but there was a passenger for an inside place. It was a girl, a bright young thing, with a comely face and laughing black eyes. She was dressed smartly, after her country fashion, in a hat covered with scarlet poppies, and with a vast brooch at the neck of her bodice. In one hand she carried a huge bunch of sweet-smelling gilvers. A group of girl companions came to see her off, and there was much giggling and chatter and general excitement.

"Are you forgetting the pouch and pipe, Emma?"

"Let me see; am I? No; it's here in my frock."

"Well, you'll be coming together by the coach at nine, it's like?"

"It's like we will, Liza, if the steamer isn't late."

"Now then, ladies, off the step! Any room for a lil calf' in the straw with you, missy? Freckened? Tut! Only a lil calf, as clane as clane—and breath as swate as your own, miss. There you are—it'll be lying quiet enough till we get to Douglas. All ready? Ready we are then. Collar work now, gentlemen. Aise the horse, sir. Thank you! Thank you! Not you, your Honour—sit where you are, Dempster."

XXII.

Pete got down to walk up the hill, but Philip, though he made some show of alighting also, was glad of the excuse to remain in his seat. It relieved him of Pete's company for a while, at all events. He had time to ask himself again why he was there, where he was going to, and what he was going to do. But his brain was a cloudy waste. Only one picture emerged from the maze. It was that of the burial of the nameless waif in the grave at the foot of the wall. If he was conscious of any purpose, it was a vague idea of going to that grave. But it lay ahead of him only as an ultimate goal. He was waiting and watching for an opportunity of escape. If it came, God be praised! If it did not come, God help and forgive him!

Meanwhile Pete walked behind, and caught fragments of a conversation between the girl and Crow.

"So you're going to meet himself coming home, miss, eh?"

"My faith, how d'ye know that? But it's yourself for knowing things, Mr. Crow. Has he been sailing foreign? Yes, sir; and nine months away for a week come Monday. But spoken at Holyhead in Tuesday's paper, and paid off in Liverpool yesterday. That's his 'nitials, if you want to know—J. W. I worked them on the pouch myself. I've spun him a web for a jacket, too. Sweethearting with the miner fellows while Jemmy's been away? Have I, d'ye say? How people *will* be talking!"

"Aw, no offence at all. But sorry you're not keeping another string to your bow, missy. These sailor lads aren't partic'lar, anyway. Bless your heart, no; but getting as tired of one swateheart as a pig of brewer's grain. Constant? Chut! When the like of that sort is away foreign, he lays up of the first girl he comes foul of."

The girl laughed, and shook her head bravely, but the tears were beginning to trickle from her eyes, and the hand that held the flowers was trembling.

"Don't listen to the man, my dear," said Pete. "There's too much comic in these ould bachelor bucks. Your boy is dying to get home to you. Go bail on that, Emma. The packet isn't making half way enough for him, and he's bad dreadful wanting to ship aloft and let out the topsail."

At the crest of the hill Pete climbed back to Philip's side, and said, "The heart's a quare thing, sir. Got its winds and tides same as anything else. The wind blows contrary ways in one day, and it's the same with the heart itself. Changeable? Well, maybe! We shouldn't be too hard on it for all.... If I'd only known now.... She wasn't much better than a child when I left for Kimberley... and then what was I? I was only common stuff anyway... not much fit for the likes of herself, when you think of it, sir.... If I'd only guessed when I came back.... I could have done it, sir—I was loving the woman like life, but if I'd only known, now.... Well, and what's love if it's thinking of nothing but

166

itself? If I'd thought she was loving another man by the time I came home, I could have given her up to him—yes, I could; I'm persuaded I could—-so help me God, I could."

Philip was wasting on that journey like a piece of wax. Pete saw his face melting away till it looked more like a skeleton than the face of à man really alive.

"You mustn't be taking it so bad at all, Phil," said Pete. "She'll be middling right where she's gone to, sir. She'll be right enough yonder," he said, rolling his head sideways to where the sun was going round to its setting. And then softly, as if half afraid she might not be, he muttered into his beard, "God be good to my poor broken-hearted girl, and forgive her sins for Christ's sake."

An elderly gentleman got on the coach at Onchan.

"Helloa, Deemster!" he cried. "You look as sober as an old crow. Sober! Old Crow! Ha, ha!"

He was a facetious person of high descent in the island.

"Crow never goes home without getting off the box once or twice to pick up the moonlight on the road—do you, Crow?"

"That'll do, parson, that'll do!" roared Crow. And then his reverence leaned across the driver and directed the shaft of his wit at Philip.

"And how's the young housekeeper, Deemster?"

Philip shuddered visibly, and made some inarticulate reply—

"Good-looking young woman, they're telling me. Jem-y-Lord's got taste, seemingly. But take care, your Honour; take care! 'Thou shalt not covet thy neighbour's wife, nor his ox, nor his ass'——"

Philip laughed noisily. The miserable man was writhing in his seat.

"Take an old fiddler's advice, Deemster—have nothing to do with the women. When they're young they're kittens to play with you, but when they're old they're cats to scratch you."

Pete twisted his body until the whole breadth of his back blocked the parson from Philip's face.

"A fortnight ago, you were saying, sir?"

"A fortnight," muttered Philip.

"There'll be daisies growing on her grave by this time," said Pete softly.

The parson had put up his nose-glasses. "Who's this fellow, Crow? Captain—what? His honour's cousin? *Cousin?* Oh, of course—yes—I remember—Tynwald—ah—h'm!"

The coach set down its passengers in the market-place. Pete inquired the hour of its return journey, and was told that it started back at six. He helped the girl to alight, and directed her to the pier, where a crowd of people' were awaiting the arrival of the steamer. Then he rejoined Philip, who led the way through the town.

The Deemster was observed by everybody. As he passed along the streets there was much whispering and nudging, and some bowing and lifting of hats. He responded to none of it He recognised no one. He, who was famous for courtesy, renowned for gracious manners, beloved for a smile like sunshine—the brighter and more winsome when it broke as from a cloud—returned no man's salutation that day, and replied to no woman's greeting. His face was set hard like a marble mask. It passed along without appearing to see.

Pete walked one step behind. They did not speak as they went through the town. Not a word or a sign passed between them. Philip turned into a side street, and drew up at an iron gate which opened on to a churchyard. They were at the churchyard of St. George's.

"This is the place," said Philip huskily.

Pete took off his hat.

The gate was partly open. It was Saturday, and the organist was alone in the church practising hymns for Sunday's services. They passed through.

The churchyard was an oblong enclosure within high walls, overlooked on its long sides by rows of houses. One of these rows was Athol Street, and one of the houses was the Deemster's.

It was late afternoon by this time. Long shadows were cast eastward from the tombstones; the horizontal sunlight was making the leaves very light.

Philip walked noisily, jerkily, irregularly, like a man conscious of weakness and determined to conquer it. Pete walked behind, so softly that his foot on the gravel was hardly to be heard. The organist was playing Cowper's familiar hymn—

> "God moves in a mysterious way
>   His wonders to perform."

There was a broad avenue, bordered by railed tombs, leading to the church-door. Philip turned out of this into a narrow path which went through a bare green space, that was dotted with pegs of wood and little unhewn slabs of slate, like an abandoned quoit ground. At the farthest corner of this space he stopped before a mound near to the wall. It was the new-made grave. The scars of the turf were still unhealed, and the glist of the spade was on the grass.

Philip hesitated a moment, and looked round at Pete, as if even then, even there, he would confess. But he saw no escape from the mesh of his own lies, and with a deep, breath of submission he pointed down, turned his head over his shoulder, and said in a strange voice—

"There."

The silence was long and awful. At length Pete said in a broken whisper—

"Lave me, sir, lave me."

Philip turned away, breathing audibly. A moment longer Pete stood where he was, gripping his hat with both hands in front of him. Then he went down on his knees. "Oh, forgive me my hard thoughts of thee," he said. "Jesus, forgive me my hard thoughts of my poor Kirry."

167

Philip heard no more. The organ was very loud and triumphant.

```
"Deep in unfathomable mines
    Of never-failing skill,
He treasures up His bright designs
    And works His sovereign will."
```

A red shaft of sunlight tipped down on Pete's uncovered head from the top of the wall. The blessed tears had come to him. He was sobbing aloud; he was alone with his love at last.

He was alone with her indeed. At that moment Kate was looking down from the window of her room. She saw him kneeling and praying by another's grave.

Philip never knew how he got out of the churchyard. He crawled out—creeping along by the wall, and slinking through the gate—heart-sick and all but heart-dead. When he came to himself, he was standing in Athol Street, and a company of jolly fellows in a jaunting-car, driving out of the golden sunset, were rattling past him with shouts and peals of laughter.

XXIII.

Kate was standing in her room with the door open, beating her hands together in the first helpless stupor of fear, when she saw a man coming up the stairs. His legs seemed to be giving way as he ascended; he was bent and feeble, and had all the look of great age. As he approached he lifted his face, which was old and withered. Then she saw who it was. It was Philip.

She made an involuntary cry, and he smiled upon her—a hard, frozen, terrible smile. "He is lost," she thought. Her scared expression penetrated to his soul. He knew that she had seen everything. At first he tried to speak, but he could utter nothing. Then a mad desire seized him to lay hold of her—by the arms, by the shoulders, by the throat. Conquering this impulse, he stood motionless, passing his hands through his hair. She dropped her eyes and hung her head. Their abasement in each other's eyes was complete. He was ashamed before her, she was ashamed before him. One moment they faced each other thus, in silence, in pitiless and awful silence, and then slowly, very slowly, stupefied and crushed, he turned away and crept out of the house.

"It is the end—the end." What was the use of going farther? He had fallen too low. His degradation was abject. It was hopeless, irreparable, irremediable. "End it all—end it all." The words clamoured in his inmost soul.

Halting down the quay, he made for the ferry steps, where boats were waiting for hire. He had lately hired one of an evening, and pulled round the Head for the sake of the breath and the silence of the sea.

"Going far out this evening, your Honor?" the boatman asked.

"Farther than ever," he answered.

Pull, pull! Away from the terrible past. Away from the horrible present. The steamer had arrived, and had discharged her passengers. She was still pulsing at the end of the red pier like a horse that pants after running a race.

A band was playing a waltz somewhere on the promenade. Pleasure boats were darting about the bay. Sea-birds were sitting on the water where the sewers of the gay little town empty into the sea.

Pull, pull! He was flying from remorse, from despair, from the deep duplicity of a double life, from the lie that had slain the heart of a living man. How low he had fallen! Could he fall lower without falling into crime?

Pull, pull! He would be a criminal next. When a man had been degraded in his own eyes, and in the eyes of her he loved, crime stood beckoning him. He might try, but he could not resist; he must yield, he must fall. It was the only degradation remaining. Better end everything before dropping into that last abyss.

Pull, pull! He was the judge of his island, and he had outraged justice. Holding a false title, living on a false honour, he was safe of no man's respect, secure of no woman's goodwill. Exposure hung over him. He would be disgraced, the law would be disgraced, the island would be disgraced. Pull, pull, pull, before it is too late; out, far out, farther than tide returns, or sea tells stories to the shore.

He had rowed like a slave escaping from his chains, in terror of being overtaken and dragged back. The voices of the harbour were now hushed, the music of the band was deadened, the horses running along the promenade seemed to creep like ants, and the traffic of the streets was no louder than a dull subterranean rumble. He had shot out of the margin of smooth blue water in which the island lay as on a mirror, and out of the shadow of the hill upon the bay. The sea about him now was running green and glistening, and the red sun-? light was coming down on it like smoke. Only the steeples and towers and glass domes of the town reached up into luminous air. He could see the squat tower of St. George's silhouetted against the dying glory of the sky. Seven years he had been its neighbour, and it had witnessed such happy and such cruel hours. All the joy of work, the sweetness of success, the dreams of greatness, the rosy flushes of love, and then—the tortures of conscience, the visions, the horror, the secret shame, the self-abandonment, and, last of all, the twofold existence as of husband with wife, hidden, incomplete, unfulfilled, yet full of tender ties which had seemed like galling bonds so many a time, but were now so sweet when the hour had come to break them.

How distant it all appeared to be! And was he flying from the island like this? The island that had honoured him, that had rewarded him beyond his deserts, and earlier than his dreams, that had suffered no jealousy to impede him, no rivalry to fret him, no disparity of age and service to hold him back—the little island that had seemed to open its arms to him, and to cry, "Philip Christian, son of your father, grandson of your grandfather, first of Manxmen, come up!"

Oh, for what might have been! Useless regrets! Pull, pull, and forget.

But the home of his childhood! Ballure—Auntie Nan—his father's death brightened by one hope—the last, but ah! how vain!—Port Mooar—Pete, "The sea's calling me." Pull, pull! The sea was calling him indeed. Calling him to the deep womb that is death, not birth.

He was far out. The sun had gone, the island was like a bird of ashy grey stretched across the horizon; the great wing of night was coming down from the sky, and up out the mysterious depths of the sea came the profound hum, the mighty voice that is the organ of the world.

He took in the oars, and his tiny shell began to drift At that moment his eye caught something at the bottom of the boat. It was a flower, a broken stem, a torn rose, and a few scattered rose leaves. Only a relic of the last occupants, but it brought back the perfume of love, a sense of tenderness, of bright eyes, of a caress, a kiss. His mind went back to Sulby, to the Melliah, to the glen, to the days so full of tremulous love, when they hovered on the edge of the precipice. They had been hurled over it since then. It was some relief that between love and honour he would not have to struggle any longer.

And Kate? When all was over and word went round, "The Deemster is gone," what would happen to Kate? She would still be at his house in Athol Street. That would be the beginning of evil! She would wait for him, and when hope of his return was lost, she would weep for him. That would be the key of discovery! The truth would become known. Though he might be at the bottom of the sea, yet the cloud that hung over his life would break. It was inevitable. And she would be there to bear the storm alone—alone with the island which had been deceived, alone with Pete, who had been lied to and betrayed. Was that just? Was that brave?

And then—what then? What would become of her? Openly shamed, charged, as she must be, with the whole weight of the crime from whose burden he had fled, accused of his downfall, a Delilah, a Jezebel, what fate should befall her? Where would she go? Down to what depths? He saw her sinking lower than ever man sinks; he heard her appeals, her supplications.

"Oh, what have I done," he cried, "that I can neither live nor die?"

Then in that delirium of anguish in which the order of nature is reversed, and external objects no longer produce sensation, but sensation produces, as it were, external objects, he thought he saw something at the bottom of the boat where the broken rose had been. It was the figure of a man, stretched out, still and lifeless. His eyes went up to the face. The face was his own. It was ashy grey, and it stared up at the grey sky. The brain image was himself, and he was dead. He watched it, and it faded away. There was nothing left but the scattered rose-leaves and the torn flower on the broken stem.

The terrible shadow was gone; he felt that it was gone for ever. It was dead, and it would haunt him no longer. It had lived on an empire of evil-doing, and his evil-doing was at an end. He would "see his soul" no more. The tears gushed to his eyes and blinded him. They were the first he could remember since he was a boy. Alone between the two mirrors of sea and sky, the chain that he had dragged so long fell: away from him. He was a free man again.

"Go back! your place is by her side. Don't sneak out of life, and leave another to pay. Suffering is a grand thing. It is the struggle of the soul to cast off its sin. Accept it, go through with it, come out of it purged. Go back to the island. Your life is not ended yet."

XXIV.

"We were just going sending a lil yawl after you, Dempster, when we were seeing you a bit overside the head yonder coming back. 'He's drifting home on the flowing tide,' says I, and so you were. Must have been a middling stiff pull for all. We were thinking you were lost one while there."

"I *was* almost lost, but I'm here again, thank God," said Philip.

He spoke cheerily, and went away with a light step. It was now full night; the town was lit up, and the musicians of the pavement were twanging their banjos and harps. Philip felt a sort of physical regeneration, a renewal of youth, a new birth of heart and hope. He was like a man coming out of some hideous Gehenna of delirious illness; he though he had never been so light, so buoyant, so happy in his life before. The future was vague. He did not yet know what he would do. It would be something radical, something that would go down to the heart of his condition. Oh, he would be strong, he would be resolute, he would pay the uttermost farthing, he would not wait to count the cost. And she—she would be with him. He could do nothing without her. The partner of his fault would share his redemption also. God bless her!

He let himself into the house and shut the door firmly behind him. The lights were still burning in the hall, so it was not very late. He mounted the stairs with a loud step and swung into his room. The lamp was on the table, and within the circle cast by its blue shade a letter was lying. He took it up with dismay. It was in Kate's handwriting:—

"Forgive me! I am going away. It is all my fault. I have broken the heart of one man, and I am destroying the soul of another. If I stay here any longer you will be ruined and lost. I am only a millstone about your neck. I see it, I feel it. And yet I have loved you so, and wished to be so proud of you. Your heart is brave enough, though I have sunk it down so low. You will live to be strong and good and true, though that can never be while I am with you. I have been far below you from the first. All along I have only been thinking how much I loved you, but you have had so many other things to consider. My life seems to have been one long battle for love. I think it has been a cruel battle too. Anyway, I am beaten, and oh! so tired.

"Do not follow me. I pray of you do not try to find me. It is my last request. Think of me as on a long journey. I may be—the Great God of heaven knows.

"I am taking the little cracked medallion from the bottom of the oak box. It is the only picture I can find, and it will remind me of some one else as well—my little Katherine, my motherless baby.

"I have nothing to leave with you but this (*it was a lock of her hair*). At first I thought of the wedding-ring that you gave me when I came here, but it would not come off, and besides, I could not part with it.

"Good-bye! I ought to have done this long ago. But you will not hate me now? We could never be happy together again. Good-bye!"

PART VI. MAN AND GOD.

I.

The summer had gone, the gorse had dried up, the herring-fishing had ended, and Pete had become poor. His Nickey had done nothing, his last hundred pounds had been spent, and his creditors in scores, quiet as mice until then, were baying about him like bloodhounds. He sold his boat and satisfied everybody, but fell, nevertheless, to the position of a person of no credit and little consequence. On the lips of the people he descended from "Capt'n Pete" to Peter Bridget. When he saluted the rich with "How do!" they replied with a stare, a lift of the chin, and "You've the odds of me, my good man." To this he replied, with a roll of the head and a peal of laughter, "Have I now? But you'll die for all."

Ballajora Chapel had been three months rehearsing a children's cantata entitled "Under the Palms," and building an arbour of palm branches on a platform for Pete's rugged form to figure in; but Cæsar sat there instead.

Still, Pete had his six thousand pounds in mortgage on Ballawhaine. Only three other persons knew anything of that—Cæsar, who had his own reasons for saying nothing; Peter Christian himself, who was hardly likely to tell; and the High Bailiff, who was a bachelor and a miser, and kept all business revelations as sacred as are the secrets of another kind of confessional. When Pete's evil day came and the world showed no pity, Cæsar became afraid.

"I wouldn't sell out, sir," said he. "Hould on till Martinmas, anyway. The first half year's interest is due then. There's no knowing what'll happen before that. What's it saying, 'He shall give His angels charge concerning thee.' The ould man has had a polatic stroke, they're telling me. Aw, the Lord's mercy endureth for ever."

Pete began to sell his furniture. He cleared out the parlour as bare as a vault. "Time for it, too," he said. "I've been wanting the room for a workshop."

Martinmas came, and Cæsar returned in high feather. "No interest," he said. "Give him the month's grace, and hould hard till it's over. The Lord will provide. Isn't it written, 'In the world ye shall have tribulation'? Things are doing wonderful, though. Last night going home from Ballajora, I saw the corpse-lights coming from the big house to Kirk Christ's Churchyard, with the parson psalming in front of them. The ould man's dying—-I've seen his soul. To thy name, O Lord, be all the glory."

Pete sold out a second room, and turned the key on it. "Mortal cosy and small this big, ugly mansion is getting, Nancy," he said.

The month's grace allowed by the deed of mortgage expired, and Cæsar came to Elm Cottage rubbing both hands. "Turn him out, neck and crop, sir. Not a penny left to the man, and six thousand goolden pounds paid into his hands seven months ago. But who's wondering at that? There's Ross back again, carrying half a ton of his friends over the island, and lashing out the silver like dust. *Your* silver, sir, *yours*. And here's yourself, with the world darkening round you terrible. But no fear of you now. The meek shall inherit the earth. Aw, God is opening His word more and more, sir, more and more. There's that Black Tom too. He was talking big a piece back, but this morning he was up before the High Bailiff for charming and cheating, and was put away for the Dempster. Lord keep him from the gallows and hell-fire! Oh, it's a refreshing saison. It was God spaking to me by Providence when I tould you to put money on that mortgage. What's the Scripture saying, 'For brass I bring thee goold'? Turn him out, sir, turn him out."

"Didn't you tell me that ould Ballawhaine had a polatic stroke?" said Pete.

"I did; but he's a big man; let him pay his way," said Cæsar.

"Samson was a strong man, and Solomon was a wise one, but they couldn't pay money when they hadn't got it," said Pete.

"Let him look to his son then," said Cæsar".

"That's just what he's going to do," said Pete. "I'll let him die in his bed, God forgive him."

The winter came, and Pete began to think of buying a Dandie, which being smaller than a Nickey, and of yawl rig, he could sail of himself, and so earn a living by fishing the cod. To do this he had a further clearing of furniture, thereby reducing the size of the house to three rooms. The featherbed left his own bedstead, the watch came out of his pocket, and the walls of the hall-kitchen gaped and yawned in the places where the pictures had been.

"The bog-bane to the rushy curragh, say I, Nancy," said Pete. "Not being used of such grandeur, I was taking it hard. Never could remember to wind that watch. And feathers, bless you! Don't I remember the lil mother, with a sickle and a bag, going cutting the long grass on the steep brews for the cow, and drying a handful for myself for a bed. Sleeping on it? Never slept the like since at all."

The result of Pete's first week's fishing was twenty cod and a gigantic ling. He packed the cod in boxes and sent them by Crow and the steam-packet to the market in Liverpool. The ling he swung on his back over his oilskin jacket and carried it home, the head at his shoulder and the tail dangling at his legs.

"There!" he cried, dropping it on the floor, "split it and salt it, and you've breakfas'es for a month."

When the remittance came from Liverpool it was a postal order for seven-and-sixpence.

"Never mind," said Pete; "we're bating Dan Hommy anyway—the ould muff has only made seven-and-a-penny."

The weather was rough, the fishing was bad, the tackle got broken, and Pete began to extol plain living.

"Gough bless me," he said, "I don't know in the world what's coming to the ould island at all. When I was for a man-servant with Cæsar the farming boys were ateing potatoes and herrings three times a day. But now! butcher's mate every dinner-time, if you plaze. And tay! the girls must be having it reg'lar—and taking no shame with them neither. My sake, I remember when the mother would be whispering, 'Keep an eye on the road, boy, while I'm brewing myself a cup of tay.' Truth enough, Nancy. An ounce a week and a pound of sugar, and people wondering at the woman for that."

The mountains were taken from the people, and they were no longer allowed "to cut turf for fuel; coals were dear, the winter was cold, and Pete began to complain of a loss of appetite.

"My teeth must be getting bad, Nancy," he whined. They were white as milk and faultless as a negro's. "Don't domesticate my food somehow. What's the odds, though I Can't ate suppers at all, and that's some constilation. Nothing like going to bed hungry, Nancy, if you're wanting to get up with an appetite for breakfast. Then the beautiful drames, woman! Gough bless me, the dinners and the feasts and the bankets you're ateing in your sleep! Now, if you filled your skin like a High Bailiff afore going to bed, ten to one you'd have a buggane riding on your breast the night through and drame of dying for a drink of water. Aw, sleep's a reg'lar Radical Good for levelling up, anyway."

Christmas approached, servants boasted of the Christmas boxes they got from their masters, and Pete remembered Nancy.

"Nancy," said he, "they're telling me Liza Billy-ny-Clae is getting twenty pound per year per annum at her new situation in Douglas. She isn't nothing to yourself at cooking. Mustn't let the lil one stand in your way, woman. She's getting a big girl now, and I'll be taking her out in the Dandie with me and tying her down on the low deck there and giving her a pig's bladder, and she'll be playing away as nice as nice. See?"

Nancy looked at him, and he dropped his eyes before her.

"Is it wanting to get done with me, you are, Pete?" she said in a quavering voice. "There's my black—I can sell it for something—it's never been wore at me since I sat through the sarvice with Grannie the Sunday after we got news of Kirry. And I'm not a big eater, Pete—never was—you can clear me of that anyway. A bit of bread and cheese for my dinner when you are out at the fishing, and I'm asking no better——"

"Hould your tongue, woman," cried Pete. "Hould your tongue afore you break my heart I've seen my rich days and I've seen my poor days. I've tried both, and I'm content."

II.

Meantime, Philip in Douglas was going from success to success, from rank to rank, from fame to fame. Everything he put his hand to counted to him for righteousness. When he came to himself after the disappearance of Kate, his heart was a wasted field of volcanic action, with ashes and scoriae of infernal blackness on the surface, but the wholesome soil beneath. In spite of her injunction, he set himself to look for her. More than love, more than pity, more than remorse prompted and supported him. She was necessary to his resurrection, to his new birth. So he scoured every poor quarter of the town, every rookery of old Douglas, and this was set down to an interest in the poor.

An epidemic broke out on the island, and during the scare that followed, wherein some of the wealthy left their homes for England, and many of the poor betook themselves to the mountains, and even certain of the doctors found refuge in flight, Philip won golden opinions for presence of mind and personal courage. He organised a system of registration, regulated quarantine, and caused the examination of everybody coming to the island or leaving it. From day to day he went from house to house, from hospital to hospital, from ward to ward. No dangers terrified him; he seemed to keep his eye on each case. He was only looking for Kate, only assuring himself that she had not fallen victim to the pest, only making certain that she had not come or gone. But the divine madness which seizes upon a crowd when its heart is touched laid hold of the island at the sight of Philip's activities. He was worshipped, he was beloved, he was the idol of the poor, almost everybody else was forgotten in the splendour of his fame; no committee could proceed without him; no list was complete until it included his name.

Philip was ashamed of his glories, but he had no heart to repudiate them. When the epidemic subsided, he had convinced himself that Kate must be gone, that she must be dead. Gone, therefore, was his only hold on life, and dead was his hope of a moral resurrection. He could do nothing without her but go on as he was going. To pretend to a new birth now would be like a death-bed conversion; it would be like renouncing the joys of life after they have renounced the renouncer.

His colleague, the old Deemster, was stricken down by paralysis, and he was required to attend to both their duties. This made it necessary at first that all Deemster's Courts should be held in Castletown, and hence Ramsey saw him rarely. He spent his days in the Court-house of the Castle and his nights at home. His fair hair became prematurely white, and his face grew more than ever like that of a man newly risen from a fever.

"Study," said the world, and it bowed its head the lower.

Yet he was seen to be not only a studious man, but a melancholy one. To defeat curiosity, he began to enter a little into the life of the island, and, as time went on, to engage in some of the social duties of his official position. On Christmas Eve he gave a reception at his house in Athol Street. He had hardly realised how it would tear at the tenderest fibres of memory. The very rooms that had been Kate's were given over to the ladies who were his guests. All afternoon the crush was great, and the host was the attraction. He was a fascinating figure—so young, yet already so high; so silent, yet able to speak so splendidly; and then so handsome with that whitening head, and that smile like vanishing sunshine.

In the midst of the reception, Philip received a letter from Ramsey that was like the cry of a bleeding heart:—

"My lil one is ill theyr sayin shes Diein cum to me for gods. sake.—Peat."

The snow was beginning to fall as the guests departed. When the last of them was gone, the clock on the bureau was striking six, and the night was closing in. By eight o'clock Philip was at Elm Cottage.

III.

Pete was sitting at the foot of the stairs, unwashed, uncombed, with his clothes half buttoned and his shoes unlaced.

"Phil!" he cried, and leaping up he took Philip by both hands and fell to sobbing like a child.

They went upstairs together. The bedroom was dense with steam, and the forms of two women were floating like figures in a fog.

"There she is, the bogh," cried Pete in a pitiful wail.

The child lay outstretched on Grannie's lap, with no sign of consciousness, and hardly any sign of life, except the hollow breathing of bronchitis.

Philip felt a strange emotion come over him. He sat on the end of the bed and looked down. The little face, with its twitching mouth and pinched nostrils, beating with every breath, was the face of Kate. The little head, with its round forehead and the silvery hair brushed back from the temples, was his own head. A mysterious throb surprised him, a great tenderness, a deep yearning, something new to him, and born as it were in his breast at that instant. He had an impulse, never felt before, to go down on his knees where the child lay, to take it in his arms, to draw it to him, to fondle it, to call it his own, and to pour over it the inarticulate babble of pain and love that was bursting from his tongue. But some one was kneeling there already, and in his jealous longing he realised that his passionate sorrow could have no voice.

Pete, at Grannie's lap, was stroking the child's arm and her forehead with the tenderness of a woman.

"The bogh millish! Seems aisier now, doesn't she, Grannie? Quieter, anyway? Not coughing so much, is she?"

The doctor came at the moment, and Cæsar entered the room behind him with a face of funereal resignation.

"See," cried Pete; "there's your lil patient, doctor. She's lying as quiet as quiet, and hasn't coughed to spake of for better than an hour."

"H'm!" said the doctor ominously. He looked at the child, made some inquiries of Grannie, gave certain instructions to Nancy, and then lifted his head with a sigh.

"Well, we've done all we can for her," he said. "If the child lives through the night she may get over it."

The women threw up their hands with "Aw, dear, aw, dear!" Philip gave a low, sharp cry of pain; but Pete, who had been breathing heavily, watching intently, and holding his arms about the little one as if he would save it from disease and death and heaven itself, now lost himself in the immensity of his woe.

"Tut, doctor, what are you saying?" he said. "You were always took for a knowledgable man, doctor; but you're talking nonsense now. Don't you see the child's only sleeping comfortable? And haven't I told you she hasn't coughed anything worth for an hour? Do you think a poor fellow's got no sense at all?"

The doctor was a patient man as well as a wise one—he left the room without a word. But, thinking to pour oil on Pete's wounds, and not minding that his oil was vitriol, Cæsar said—

"If it's the Lord's will, it's His will, sir. The sins of the fathers are visited upon the children—yes, and the mothers, too, God forgive them."

At that Pete leapt to his feet in a flame of wrath.

"You lie! you lie!" he cried. "God doesn't punish the innocent for the guilty. If He does, He's not a good God but a bad one. Why should this child be made to suffer and die for the sin of its mother? Aye, or its father either? Show me the *man* that would make it do the like, and I'll smash his head against the wall. Blaspheming, am I? No, but it's you that's blaspheming. God is good, God is just, God is in heaven, and you are making Him out no God at all, but worse than the blackest devil that's in hell."

Cæsar went off in horror of Pete's profanities. "If the Lord keep not the city," he said, "the watchman waketh in vain."

Pete's loud voice had aroused the child. It made a little cry, and he was all softness in an instant. The women moistened its lips with barley-water, and hushed its fretful whimper.

"Come," said Philip, taking Pete's arm.

"Let me lean on you, Philip," said Pete, and the stalwart fellow went tottering down the stairs.

They sat on opposite sides of the fireplace, and kept the staircase door open that they might hear all that happened in the room above.

"Get thee to bed, Nancy," said the voice of Grannie. "Dear knows how soon you'll be wanted."

"You'll be calling me for twelve, then, Grannie—now, mind, you'll be calling me."

"Poor Pete! He's not so far wrong, though. What's it saying? 'Suffer lil childers'——"

"But Cæsar's right enough this time, Grannie. The bogh is took for death as sure as sure. I saw the crow that was at the wedding going crossing the child's head the very last time she was out of doors." Pete was listening intently. Philip was gazing passively into the fire.

"I couldn't help it, sir—I couldn't really," whispered Pete across the hearth. "When a man's got a child that's ill, they may talk about saving souls, but what's the constilation in that? It's not the soul he's wanting saving at all, it's the child—now, isn't it, now?"

Philip made some confused response.

"Coorse, I can't expect you to understand that, Philip. You're a grand man, and a clever man, and a feeling man, but I can't expect you to understand that—now, is it likely? The greenest gall's egg of a father that isn't half wise has the pull of you there, Phil. 'Deed he has, though. When a man has a child of his own he's knowing what it manes, the Lord help him. Something calls to him—it's like blood calling to blood—it's like... I don't know that I'm understanding it myself, neither—not to say *understand* exactly."

Every word that Pete spoke was like a sword turning both ways. Philip drew his breath heavily.

"You can feel for another, Phil—the Lord forbid you should ever feel for yourself. Books are *your* children, and they're best off that's never having no better. But the lil ones—God help them—to see them fail, and suffer, and sink—and you not able to do nothing—and themselves calling to you—calling still—calling reg'lar—calling out of mercy—the way I am telling of, any way—O God! O God!"

Philip's throat rose. He felt as if he must betray himself the next instant.

"Perhaps the doctor was right for all. Maybe the child isn't willing to stay with us now the mother is gone; maybe it's wanting away, poor thing. And who knows? Wouldn't trust but the mother is waiting for the lil bogh yonder—waiting and waiting on the shore there, and 'ticing and 'ticing—-I've heard of the like, anyway."

Philip groaned. His brain reeled; his legs grew cold as stones. A great awe came over him. It was not Pete alone that he was encountering. In these searchings and rendings of the heart, which uncovered every thought and tore open every wound, he was entering the lists with God himself.

The church bell began to ring.

"What's that?" cried Philip. It had struck upon his ear like a knell.

"*Oiel Verree*," said Pete. The bell was ringing for the old Manx service for the singing of Christmas carols. The fibres of Pete's memory were touched by it. He told of his Christmases abroad—how it was summer instead of winter, and fruits were on the trees instead of snow on the ground—how people who had never spoken to him before would shake hands and wish him a merry Christmas. Then from sheer weariness and a sense of utter desolation, broken by the comfort of Philip's company, he fell asleep in his chair.

The night wore on; the house was quiet; only the husky rasping of the child's hurried breathing came from the floor above.

An evil thought in the guise of a pious one took possession of Philip. "God is wise," he told himself. "God is merciful. He knows what is best for all of us. What are we poor impotent grasshoppers, that we dare pray to Him to change His great purposes? It is idle. It is impious.... While the child lives there will be security for no one. If it dies, there will be peace and rest and the beginning of content. The mother must be gone already, so the dark chapter of our lives will be closed at last God is all wise. God is all good."

The child made a feeble cry, and Philip crept upstairs to look. Grannie had dozed off in her seat, and little Katherine was on the bed. A disregarded doll lay with inverted head on the counterpane. The fire had slid and died down to a lifeless glow, and the kettle had ceased to steam. There was no noise in the room save the child's galloping breathing, which seemed to scrape the walls as with a file. Sometimes there was a cough that came like a voice through a fog.

Philip crept in noiselessly, knelt down by the bed-head, and leaned over the pillow. A candle which burned on the mantelpiece cast its light on the head that lay there. The little face was drawn, the little pinched nostrils were beating like a pulse, the little lip beneath was beaded with perspiration, the beautiful round forehead was damp, and the silken silvery hair was matted.

Philip thought the child must be dying, and his ugly piety gave way. There was a movement on the bed. One little hand that had been clenched hard on the breast came over the counterpane and fell, outstretched and open before him. He took it for an appeal, a dumb and piteous appeal, and the smothered tenderness of the father's heart came uppermost. *Her* child, his child, dying, and he there, yet not daring to claim her!

A new fear took hold of him. He had been wrong—there could be no security in the child's death, no peace, no rest, no content. As surely as the child died he would betray himself. He would blurt it all out; he would tell everything. "My child! my darling! my Kate's Kate!" The cry would burst from him. He could not help it. And to reveal the black secret at the mouth of an open grave would be terrible, it would be horrible, it would be awful, "Spare her, O Lord, spare her!"

In a fear bordering on delirium he went downstairs and shook Pete by the shoulders to awaken him. "Come quickly," he said.

Pete opened his eyes with a bewildered look» "She's better, isn't she?" he asked.

"Courage," said Philip.

"Is she worse?"

173

"It's life or death now. We must try something that I saw when I was away."

"Good Lord, and I've been sleeping! Save her, Philip! You're great; your clever——"

"Be quiet, for God's sake, my good fellow! Quick, a kettle of boiling water—a blanket—some hot towels."

"Oh, you're a friend, you'll save her. The doctors don't know nothing."

Ten minutes afterwards the child made a feeble cry, coughed loosely, threw up phlegm, and came out of the drowsy land which it had inhabited for a week. In ten minutes more it was wrapped in the hot towels and sitting on Pete's knee before a brisk are, opening its little eyes and pursing its little mouth, and making some inarticulate communication.

Then Grannie awoke with a start, and reproached herself for sleeping. "But dear heart alive," she cried, with both hands up, "the bogh villish is mended wonderful."

Nancy came back in her stockings, blinking and yawning. She clapped and crowed at sight of the child's altered face. The clock in the kitchen was striking twelve by this time, the bells had begun to ring again, the carol singers were coming out of the church, there was a sound on the light snow of the street like the running of a shallow river, and the waits were being sung for the dawn of another Christmas.

The doctor looked in on his way home, and congratulated himself on the improved condition. The crisis was passed, the child was safe.

"Ah! better, better," he said cheerily. "I thought we might manage it this time."

"It was the Dempster that done it," cried Pete. He was cooing and blowing at little Katherine over the fringe of her towels. "He couldn't have done more for the lil one if she'd been his own flesh and blood."

Philip dared not speak. He hurried away in a storm of emotion. "Not yet," he thought, "not yet." The time of his discovery was not yet. It was like Death, though—it waited for him somewhere. Somewhere and at some time—some day in the year, some place on the earth. Perhaps his eyes knew the date in the calendar, perhaps his feet knew the spot on the land, yet he knew neither. Somewhere and at some time—God knew where—God knew when—He kept his own secrets.

That night Philip slept at the "Mitre," and next morning he went up to Ballure.

IV.

The Governor could not forget Tynwald. Exaggerating the humiliation of that day, he thought his influence in the island was gone. He sold his horses and carriages, and otherwise behaved like a man who expected to be recalled.

Towards Philip he showed no malice. It was not merely as the author of his shame that Philip had disappointed him.

He had half cherished a hope that Philip would become his son-in-law. But when the rod in his hand had failed him, when it proved too big for a staff and too rough for a crutch, he did not attempt to break it. Either from the instinct of a gentleman, or the pride of a strong man, he continued to shower his favours upon Philip. Going to London with his wife and daughter at the beginning of the new year, he appointed Philip to act as his deputy.

Philip did not abuse his powers. As grandson of the one great Manxman of his century, and himself a man of talents, he was readily accepted by the island. His only drawback was his settled melancholy. This added to his interest if it took from his popularity. The ladies began to whisper that he had fallen in love, and that his heart was "buried in the grave." He did not forget old comrades. It was remembered, in his favour, that one of his friends was a fisherman, a cousin across the bar of bastardy, who had been a fool and gone through his fortune.

On St. Bridget's Day Philip held Deemster's Court in Ramsey. The snow had gone and the earth had the smell of violets. It was almost as if the violets themselves lay close beneath the soil, and their odour had been too long kept under. The sun, which had not been seen for weeks, had burst out that day; the air was warm, and the sky was blue. Inside the Court-house the upper arcs of the windows had been let down; the sun shone on the Deemster as he sat on the dais, and the spring breeze played with his silvery wig. Some^ times, in the pauses of rasping voices, the birds were heard to sing from the trees on the lawn outside.

The trial was a tedious and protracted one. It was the trial of Black Tom. During the epidemic that had visited the island he had developed the character of a witch doctor. His first appearance in Court had been before the High Bailiff, who had committed him to prison. He had been bailed out by Pete, and had forfeited his bail in an attempt at flight. The witnesses were now many, and some came from a long distance. It was desirable to conclude the same day. At five in the evening the Deemster rose and said, "The Court will adjourn for an hour, gentlemen."

Philip took his own refreshments in the Deemster's room—Jem-y-Lord was with him—then put off his wig and gown, and slipped through the prisoners' yard at the back and round the corner to Elm Cottage.

It was now quite dark. The house was lit by the firelight only, which flashed like Will-o'-the-wisp on the hall window. Philip was surprised by unusual sounds. There was laughter within, then singing, and then laughter again. He bad reached the porch and his approach had not been heard. The door stood open and he looked in and listened.

The room was barer than he had ever seen it—a table, three chairs, a cradle, a dresser, and a corner cupboard. Nancy sat by the fire with the child on her lap. Pete was squatting on the floor, which was strewn with rushes, and singing—

    "Come, Bridget, Saint Bridget, come in at my door,
    The crock's on the bink, and the rush is on the floor."

Then getting on to all fours like a great boy, and bobbing his head up and down and making deep growls to imitate the terrors of a wild beast, he made little runs and plunges at the child, who jumped and crowed in Nancy's lap and laughed and squealed till she "kinked."

"Now, stop, you great omathaun, stop," said Nancy. "It isn't good for the lil one—'deed it isn't."

But Pete was too greedy of the child's joy to deny himself the delight of it. Making a great low sweep of the room, he came back hopping on his haunches and barking like a dog. Then the child laughed till the laughter rolled like a marble in her little throat.

Philip's own throat rose at the sight, and his breast began to ache. He felt the same thrill as before—the same, yet different, more painful, more full of jealous longing. This was no place for him. He thought he would go away. But turning on his heel, he was seen by Pete, who was now on his back on the floor, rocking the child up and down like the bellows of an accordion, and to and fro like the sleigh of a loom.

"My faith, the Dempster! Come in, sir, come in," cried Pete, looking over his forehead. Then, giving the child back to Nancy, he leapt to his feet.

Philip entered with a sick yearning and sat down in the chair facing Nancy.

"You're wondering at me, Dempster, I know you are, sir," Said Pete, "'Deed, but I'm wondering at myself as well. I thought I was never going to see a glad day again, and if the sky would ever be blue I would be breaking my heart. But what is the Manx poet saying, sir? 'I have no will but Thine, O God.' That's me, sir, truth enough, and since the lil one has been mending I've never been so happy in my life."

Philip muttered some commonplace, and put his thumb into the baby's hand. It was sucked in by the little fingers as by the soft feelers of the sea-anemone.

Pete drew up the third chair, and then all interest was centred on the child. "She's growing," said Philip huskily.

"And getting wise ter'ble," said Pete. "You wouldn't be-lave it, sir, but that child's got the head of an almanac. She has, though. Listen here, sir—what does the cow say, darling?"

"Moo-o," said the little one.

"Look at that now!" said Pete rapturously.

"She knows what the dog says too," said Nancy. "What does Dempster say, bogh?"

"Bow-wow," said the child.

"Bless me soul!" said Pete, turning to Philip with amazement at the child's supernatural wisdom. "And there's Tom Hommy's boy—and a fine lil fellow enough for all—but six weeks older than this one, and not a word out of him yet."

Hearing himself talked of, the dog had come from under the table. The child gurgled down at it, then made purring noises at its own feet, and wriggled in Nancy's lap.

"Dear heart alive, if it's not like nursing an eel," said Nancy. "Be quiet, will you?" and the little one was shaken back to her seat.

"Aisy all, woman," said Pete. "She's just wanting her lil shoes and stockings off, that's it." Then talking to the child. "Um—am-im—lum—la—loo? Just so! I don't know what that means myself, but she does, you see. Aw, the child is taiching me heaps, sir. Listening to the lil one I'm remembering things. Well, we're only big children, the best of us. That's the way the world's keeping young, and God help it when we're getting so clever there's no child left in us at all."

"Time for young women to be in bed, though," said Nancy, getting up to give the baby her bath.

"Let me have a hould of the rogue first," said Pete, and as Nancy took the child out of the room, he dragged at it and smothered its open mouth with kisses.

"Poor sport for you, sir, watching a foolish ould father playing games with his lil one," said Pete.

Philip's answer was broken and confused. His eyes had begun to fill, and to hide them he turned his head aside. Thinking he was looking at the empty places about the walls, Pete began to enlarge on his prosperity, and to talk as if he were driving all the trade of the island before him.

"Wonderful fishing now, Phil. I'm exporting a power of cod. Gretting postal orders and stamps, and I don't know what. Seven-and-sixpence in a single post from Liverpool—that's nothing, sir, nothing at all."

Nancy brought back the child, whose silvery curls were now damp.

"What! a young lady coming in her night-dress!" cried Pete.

"Work enough! had to get it over her head, too," said Nancy. "She wouldn't, no, she wouldn't. Here, take and dry her hair by the fire while I warm up her supper."

Pete rolled the sleeves of his jersey above his elbows, took the child on his knee, and rubbed her hair between his hands, singing—

> "Come, Bridget, Saint Bridget, come in at my door."

Nancy clattered about in her clogs, filled a saucepan with bread and milk, and brought it to the fire.

"Give it to me, Nancy," said Philip, and he leaned over and held the saucepan above the bar. The child watched him intently.

"Well, did you ever?" said Pete. "The strange she's making of you, Philip? Don't you know the gentleman, darling? Aw, but he's knowing you, though."

The saucepan boiled, and Philip handed it back to Nancy.

"Go to him then—away with you," said Pete. "Gro to your godfather. He'd have been your name-father too if it had been a boy you'd been. Off you go!" and he stretched out his hairy arms until the child touched the floor.

Philip stooped to take the little one, who first pranced and beat the rushes with its feet as with two drumsticks, then trod on its own legs, swirled about to Pete's arms, dropped its lower lip, and set up a terrified outcry.

"Ah! she knows her own father, bless her," cried Pete, plucking the child back to his breast.

175

Philip dropped his head and laughed. A sort of creeping fear had taken possession of him, as if he felt remotely that the child was to be the channel of his retribution.

"Will you feed her yourself, Pete?" said Nancy. She was coming up with a saucer, of which she was tasting the contents. "He's that handy with a child, sir, you wouldn't think 'Deed you wouldn't.'" Then, stooping to the baby as it ate its supper, "But I'm saying, young woman, is there no sleep in your eyes to-night?"

"No, but nodding away here like a wood-thrush in a tree," said Pete. He was ladling the pobs into the child's mouth, and scooping the overflow from her chin. "Sleep's a terrible enemy of this one, sir. She's having a battle with it every night of life, anyway. God help her, she'll have luck better than some of us, or she'll be fighting it the other way about one of these days."

"She's us'ally going off with the spoon in her mouth, sir, for all the world like a lil cherub," said Nancy.

"Too busy looking at her godfather to-night, though," said Pete. "Well, look at him. You owe him your life, you lil sandpiper. And, my sakes, the straight like him you are, too!"

"Isn't she?" said Nancy. "If I wasn't thinking the same myself! Couldn't look straighter like him if she'd been his born child; now, could she? And the curls, too, and the eyes! Well, well!"

"If she'd been a boy, now——" began Pete.

But Philip had risen to return to the Court-house, and Pete said in another tone, "Hould hard a minute, sir—I've something to show you. Here, take the lil one, Nancy."

Pete lit a candle and led the way into the parlour. The room was empty of furniture; but at one end there was a stool, a stone mason's mallet, a few chisels, and a large stone.

The stone was a gravestone.

Pete approached it solemnly, held up the candle in front of it, and said in a low voice, "It's for her. I've been doing it myself, sir, and it's lasted me all winter, dark nights and bad days. I'll be finishing it to-night, though, God willing, and to-morrow, maybe, I'll be taking it to Douglas."

"Is it——" began Philip, but he could not finish.

The stone was a plain slab, rounded at the top, bevelled about the edge, smoothed on the face, and chiselled over the back; but there was no sign or symbol on it, and no lettering or inscription.

"Is there to be no name?" asked Philip at last.

"No," said Pete.

"No?"

"Tell you the truth, sir, I've been reading what it's saying in the ould Book about the Recording Angel calling the dead out of their graves."

"Yes?"

"And I've been thinking the way he'll be doing it will be going to the graveyards and seeing the names on the gravestones, and calling them out loud to rise up to judgment; some, as it's saying, to life eternal, and some to everlasting punishment."

"Well?"

"Well, sir, I've been thinking if he comes to this one and sees no name on it"—Pete's voice sank to a whisper—"maybe he'll pass it by and let the poor sinner sleep on."

Stumbling back to the Court-house through the dark lane Philip thought, "It was a lie *then*, but it's true *now*. It *must* be true. She must be dead." There was a sort of relief in this certainty. It was an end, at all events; a pitiful end, a cowardly end, a kind of sneaking out of Fate's fingers; it was not what he had looked for and intended, but he struggled to reconcile himself to it.

Then he remembered the child and thought, "Why should I disturb it? Why should I disturb Pete? I will watch over it all its life. I will protect it and find a way to provide for it. I will do my duty by it. The child shall never want."

He was offering the key to the lock of the prisoners' yard when some one passed him in the lane, peered into his face, then turned about and spoke.

"Oh, it's you, Deemster Christian?"

"Yes, doctor. Good-night!"

"Have you heard the news from Ballawhaine? The old gentleman had another stroke this morning."

"No, I had not heard it. Another? Dear me, dear me!"

Back in his room, Philip resumed his wig and gown and returned to the Court-house. The place was now lit up by candlelight and densely crowded. Everybody rose to his feet as the Deemster stepped to the dais.

V.

"Come, Bridget, Saint Bridget, come in at my door,

The crock's on the bink and the rush—"

"She's fast," said Nancy. "Rocking this one to sleep is like waiting for the kettle to boil. You may try and try, and blow and blow, but never a sound. And no sooner have you forgotten all about her, but she's singing away as steady as a top."

Nancy put the child into the cradle, tucked her about, twisted the head of the little nest so that the warmth of the fire should enter it, and hung a shawl over the hood to protect the little eyelids from the light. "Will you keep the house till I'm home from Sulby, Pete?"

"I've my work, woman," said Pete from the parlour.

"I'll put a junk on the fire and be off then," said Nancy.

She pulled the door on to the catch behind her and went crunching the gravel to the gate. There was no sound in the house now but the gentle breathing of the sleeping child, soft as an angel's prayer, the chirruping of the mended fire like a cage of birds, the ticking of the clock, and, through the parlour wall, the dull pat-put, pat-put of the wooden mallet and the scrape of the chisel on the stone.

Pete worked steadily for half an hour, and then came back to the hall-kitchen with his tools in his hands. The cob of coal had kindled to a lively flame, which flashed and went out, and the quick black shadows of the chairs and the table and the jugs on the dresser were leaping about the room like elves. With parted lips, just breaking into a smile, Pete went down on one knee by the cradle, put the mallet under his arm, and gently raised the shawl curtain. "God bless my motherless girl," he said, in a voice no louder than a breath. Suddenly, while he knelt there, he was smitten as by an electric shock. His face straightened and he drew back, still holding the shawl at the tips of his fingers.

The child was sleeping peacefully, with one of its little arms over the counterpane. On its face the flickering light of the fire was coming and going, making lines about the baby eyes and throwing up the baby features. It is in such lights that we are startled by resemblances in a child's face. Pete was startled by a resemblance. He had seen it before, but not as he saw it now.

A moment afterwards he was reaching across the cradle again, his arms spread over it, and his face close down at the child's face, scanning every line of it as one scans a map. "'Deed, but she is, though," he murmured. "She's like him enough, anyway."

An awful idea had taken possession of his mind. He rose stiffly to his feet, and the shawl flapped back. The room seemed to be darkening round him. He broke the coal, though it was burning brightly, stepped to the other side of the cradle, and looked at the child again. It was the same from there. The resemblance was ghostly.

He felt something growing hard inside of him, and he returned to his work in the parlour. But the chisel slipped, the mallet fell too heavily, and he stopped. His mind fluctuated among distant things. He could not help thinking of Port Mooar, of the Carasdhoo men, of the day when he and Philip were brought home in the early, morning.

Putting his tools down, he returned to the room. He was holding his breath and walking softly, as if in the presence of an invisible thing. The room was perfectly quiet—he could hear the breath in his nostrils. In a state of stupor he stood for some time with bis back to the fire and watched his shadow on the opposite wall and on the ceiling. The cradle was at his feet. He could not keep his eyes off it. From time to time he looked down across one of his shoulders.

With head thrown back and lips apart, the child was breathing calmly and sleeping the innocent sleep. This angel innocence reproached him.

"My heart must be going bad," he muttered. "Your bad thoughts are blackening the dead. For shame, Pete Quilliam, for shame!"

He was feeling like a man who is in a storm of thunder and lightning at night. Familiar things about him looked strange and awful.

Stooping to the cradle again, he turned back the shawl on to the cradle-head as a girl turns back the shade of her sun-bonnet Then the firelight was full on the child's face, and it moved in its sleep. It moved yet more under his steadfast gaze, and cried a little, as if the terrible thought that was in his mind had penetrated to its own.

He was stooping so when the door was opened and Cæsar entered violently, making asthmatic noises in his throat. Pete looked up at him with a stupefied air. "Peter," he said, "will you sell that mortgage?"

Pete answered with a growl.

"Will you transfer it to me?" said Cæsar.

"The time's not come," said Pete.

"What time?"

"The time foretold by the prophet, when the lion can lie down with the lamb."

Pete laughed bitterly. Cæsar was quivering, his mouth was twitching, and his eyes were wild. "Will you come over to the 'Mitre,' then?"

"What for to the 'Mitre'?"

"Ross Christian is there."

Pete made an impatient gesture. "That stormy petrel again! He's always about when there's bad weather going."

"Will you come and hear what the man's saying?"

"What's he saying?"

"Will you hear for yourself?"

Pete looked hard at Cæsar, looked again, then caught up his cap and went out at the door.

VI.

With two of his cronies the man had spent the day in a room overlooking the harbour, drinking hard and playing billiards. Early in the afternoon a messenger had come from Ballawhaine, saying, "Your father is ill—come home immediately." "By-and-bye," he had said, and gone on with the game.

Later in the afternoon the messenger had come again, saying, "Your father has had a stroke of paralysis, and he is calling for you." "Let me finish the break first," he had replied.

In the evening the messenger had come a third time, saying, "Your father is unconscious." "Where's the hurry, then?" he had answered, and he sang a stave of the "Miller's Daughter"—

> "They married me against my will,
> When I was daughter at the mill."

Finally, Cæsar, who had been remonstrating with the Ballawhaine at the moment of his attack, came to remonstrate with Ross, and to pay off a score of his own as well.

"Honour thy father and thy mother, that thy days——" cried Cæsar, with uplifted arm and the high pitch of the preacher. "But your days will not be long, anyway, and, if you are the death of that foolish ould man, it won't be the first death you're answerable for."

"So you believe it, too?" said Ross, cue in hand. "You believe your daughter is dead, do you, old Jephthah Jeremiah? Would you be surprised to hear, now——" (the cronies giggled) "that she isn't dead at all?——Good shotr-cannon off the cushion. Halloa! Jephthah Jeremiah has seen a ghost seemingly. Saw her myself, man, when I was up in town a month ago. Want to know where she is? Shall I tell you? Oh, you're a beauty! You're a pattern! You know how to train up a child in the way——Pocket off the red——It's you to preach at my father, isn't it? She's on the streets of London—ah, Jeremiah's gone——

> 'They married me against my will '—

There you are, then—good shot—love—twenty-five and nothing left."

Pete pushed through to the billiard-room. Fearing there might be violence, hoping there would be, yet thinking it scarcely proper to lend the scene of it the light of his countenance, Cæsar had stayed outside.

"Halloa! here's Uriah!" cried Ross. "Talk of the devil—just thought as much. Ever read the story of David and Uriah? Should, though. Do you good, mister. David was a great man. Aw" (with a mock imitation of Pete's Manx), "a ter'ble, wonderful, shocking great man. Uriah was his henchman. Ter'ble clavar, too, but that green for all, the ould cow might have ate him. And Uriah had a nice lil wife. The nice now, you wouldn't think. But when Uriah was away David took her, and then—and then" (dropping the Manx) "it doesn't just run on Bible lines neither, but David told Uriah that his wife was dead—ha! ha! ha!——

> 'Who saw her diet
> I said the fly,
> I saw her—'

Stop that—let go—help——You'll choke me—help! help!"

At two strides Pete had come face to face with Ross, put one of his hands at the man's throat and his leg behind him, doubled him back on his knee, and was holding him there in a grip like that of a vice.

"Help!—help!—oo—ugh!" The fellow gasped, and his face grew dark.

"You're not worth it," said Pete. "I meant to choke the life out of your dirty body for lying about the living and blackening the dead, but you're not worth hanging for. You've got the same blood in you, too, and I'm ashamed for you. There! get up."

With a gesture of indescribable loathing, Pete flung the man to the ground, and he fell over his cue and broke it.

The people of the house came thronging into the room, and met Pete going out of it. His face was hard and ugly. At first sight they mistook him for Ross, so disfigured was he by bad passions.

Cæsar was tramping the pavement outside. "Will you let me do it now?" he said in a hot whisper.

"Do as you like," said Pete savagely.

"The wicked is snared in the work of his own hand. Higgaion. Selah," said Cæsar, and they parted by the entrance to the Court-house.

Pete went home, muttering to himself, "The man was lying—she's dead, she's dead!"

At the gate of Elm Cottage the dog came up to him, barking with glee. Then it darted back to the house door, which stood open. "Some one has come," thought Pete. "She's dead. The man lied. She's dead," he muttered, and he stumbled down the path.

VII.

While the Deemster was stepping up to the dais, and the people in the court were rising to receive him, a poor bedraggled wayfarer was toiling through the country towards the town. It was a woman. She must have walked far, her step was so slow and so heavy. From time to time she rested, not sitting, but standing by the gates of the fields as she came to them, and holding by the topmost bar.

When she emerged from the dark lanes into the lamplit streets her pace quickened for a moment; then it slackened, and then it quickened again. She walked close to the houses, as if trying to escape observation. Where there was a short cut through an ill-lighted thoroughfare, she took it. Any one following her would have seen that she was familiar with every corner of the town.

It would be hard to imagine a woman of more miserable appearance. Not that her clothes were so mean, though they were poor and worn, but that an air of humiliation sat upon her, such as a dog has when it is lost and the children are chasing it. Her dress was that of an old woman—the long Manx cloak of blue homespun, fastened by a great hook close under the chin, and having a hood which is drawn over the head. But in spite of this old-fashioned garment, and the uncertainty of her step, she gave the impression of a young woman. Where the white frill of the old countrywoman's cap should have shown itself under the flange of the hood, there was a veil, which seemed to be suspended from a hat.

The oddity and incongruity of her attire attracted attention. Women came out of their houses and crossed to the doors of neighbours to look after her. Even the boys playing at the corners looked up as she went by.

She was not greatly observed for all that. An unusual interest agitated the town. A wave of commotion flowed down the streets. The traffic went in one direction. That direction was the Court-house.

The Court-house square was thronged on three of its sides by people who were gathered both on the pavement and on the green inside the railings. Its fourth side was the dark lane at the back going by the door to the prisoners' yard and the Deemster's entrance. The windows were lit up and partly open. Some of the people had edged to the walls as if to listen, and a few had clambered to the sills as if to see. Around the wide doorway there was a close crowd that seemed to cling to it like a burr.

The woman had reached the first angle of the square when the upper half of the Court-house door broke into light over the heads of the crowd. A man had come out. He surged through the crowd and "came down to the gate with a tail of people trailing after him and asking questions.

"Wonderful!" he was saying. "The Dempster's spaking. Aw, a Daniel come to judgment, sir. Pity for Tom, though—the man'll get time. I'm sorry for an ould friend—but the Lord's will be done! Let not the ties of affection be a snare to our feet—it'll be five years if it's a day, and (D.V.) he'll never live to see the end of it."

It was Cæsar. He crossed the street to the "Mitre." The woman trembled and turned towards the lane at the back. She walked quicker than ever now. But, stumbling over the irregular cobbles of the paved way, she stopped suddenly at the sound of a voice. By this time she was at the door to the prisoners' yard, and it was standing open. The door of the corridor leading by the Deemster's chamber to the Court-house was also ajar, as if it had been opened to relieve the heat of the crowded room within.

"Be just and fear not," said the voice. "Remember, whatever unconscious misrepresentations have been made this day, whatever deliberate false-swearing (and God and the consciences of the guilty ones know well there have been both), truth is mighty, and in the end it will prevail."

The poor bedraggled wayfarer stood in the darkness and trembled. Her hands clutched at the breast of the cloak, her head dropped into her breast, and a half-smothered moan escaped from her. She knew the voice; it had once been very sweet and dear to her; she had heard it at her ear in tones of love. It was the voice of the Deemster. He was speaking from the judge's seat; the people were hanging on his lips.

And he was standing in the shadow of the dark lane under the prisoners' wall.

The woman was Kate. It was true that she had been to London; it was false that she had lived a life of shame there. In six months she had descended to the depths of poverty and privations. One day she had encountered Ross. He was fresh from the Isle of Man, and he told her of the child's illness. The same night she turned her face towards home. It was three weeks since she had returned to the island, and she was then low in health, in heart, and in pocket. The snow was falling. It was a bitter night. Growing dizzy with the drifting whiteness and numb with the piercing cold, she had crept up to a lonely house and asked shelter until the storm should cease.

The house was the home of three old people, two old brothers and an old sister, who had always lived together. In this household Kate had spent three weeks of sickness, and the Manx cloak on her back was a parting gift which the old woman had hung over her thinly-clad shoulders.

Back in the roads Kate had time to tell herself how foolish was her journey. She was like a sailor who has alarming news of home in some foreign port and hears nothing afterwards until he comes to harbour. A month had passed. So many things might have happened. The child might be better; it might be dead and buried. Nevertheless she pushed on.

When she left London she had been full of bitterness towards Philip. It was his fault that she had ever been parted from her baby. She would go back. If she brought shame upon him, let him bear it. On coming near to home this feeling of vengeance died. Nothing was left but a great longing to be with her little one and a sense of her own degradation. Every face she recognised seemed to remind her of the change that had been wrought in herself since she had looked on it last. She dare not ask; she dare not speak; she dare not reveal herself.

While she stood in the shadow of the prisoners' yard listening to Philip's voice, and held by it as by a spell, there was a low hiss and then a sort of white silence, as when a rocket breaks in the air. The Deemster had finished; the people in the court were breathing audibly and moving in their seats.

A minute later she was standing by her old home, hers no longer, and haunted in her mind by many bitter memories. It was dark and cheerless. A candle had been burning in the parlour, but it was now spluttering in the fat at the socket. As she looked into the room, it blinked and went out.

During the last mile of her journey she had made up her mind what she would do. She would creep up to the house and listen for the sound of a child's voice. If she heard it, and the voice was that of a child that was well, she would be content, she would go away. And if she did not hear it, if the child was gone, if there was no longer any child there, if it was in heaven, she would go away just the same—only God knew how, God knew where.

The road was quiet. With trembling fingers she raised the latch of the gate, and stepped two paces into the garden. There was no sound from within. She took two steps more and listened intently. Nothing was audible. Her heart fell yet lower. She told herself that when a child lived in a house the very air breathed of its presence, and its little voice was everywhere. Then she remembered that it was late, that it was night, that even if the child were well it would now be bathed and in bed. "How foolish!" she thought, and she took a few steps more.

She had meant to reach the hall window and look in, butt before she could do so, something came scudding along the path in her direction. It was the dog, and he was barking furiously. All at once he stopped and began to caper about her. Then he broke into barking again, this time with a note of recognition and delight, shot into the house and came back, still barking, and making a circle of joyful salutation in the darkness round her.

Quaking with fear of instant discovery, she crept under the old tree and waited. Nobody came from the house. "There's no one at home," she told herself, and at that thought the certainty that the child was gone fell on her as an oppression of distress.

Nevertheless she stepped up to the porch and listened again. There was no sound within except the ticking of the clock. Making a call on her courage, she pushed the door open with the tips of her fingers. It made a rustle as the bottom brushed over the rushes. At that she uttered a faint cry and crept back trembling. But all was silence again in an instant. The fire gave out a strong red glow which spread over the walls and the ceiling. Her mind took in the impression that the place was almost empty, but she had no time for such observations. With slow and stiff motions she slid into the house.

Then she heard a sleepy whimper and it thrilled her. In an instant she had seen the thing she looked for—the cradle, with its hood towards the door and its foot to the fire. At the next moment she was on her knees beside it, doubled over it and crying softly to the baby, looking so different, smelling of milk and of sleep, "My darling! my darling!"

That was the moment when Pete was coming up the path. The dog was frisking and barking about him. "She's dead," he was saying. "The man lied. She's dead." With that word on his lips he heaved heavily into the house. As he did so he became aware that some one was there already. Before his eye had carried the news to his brain, his ear had told him. He heard a voice which he knew well, though it seemed to be a memory of no waking moment, but to come out of the darkness and the hours of sleep. It was a soft and mellow voice, saying, "My beautiful darling! My beautiful, rosy darling I My darling! My darling!"

He saw a woman kneeling by the cradle, with both arms buried in it as though they encircled the sleeping child. Her hood was thrown back, and her head was bare. The firelight fell on her face, and he knew it. He passed his hand across his eyes as if trying to wipe out the apparition, but it remained. He tried to speak, but his tongue was stiff. He stood motionless and stared. He could not remove his eyes.

Kate heard the door thrown open, and she lifted her head in terror. Pete was before her, with a violent expression on his face. The expression changed, and he looked at her as if she had been a spirit. Then, in a voice of awe, he said, "Who art thou?"

"Don't you know me?" she answered timidly.

It seemed as if he did not hear. "Then it's true," he muttered to himself; "the man did not lie."

She felt her knees trembling under her. "I haven't come to stay," she faltered. "They told me the child was ill, and I couldn't help coming."

Still he did not speak to her. As he looked, his face grew awful. The dew of fear broke out on her forehead.

"Don't you know me, Pete?" she said in a helpless way.

Still he stood looking down at her, fixedly, almost threateningly.

"I am Katherine," she said, with a downcast look.

"Katherine is dead," he answered vacantly.

"Oh! oh!"

"She is in her grave," he said again.

"Oh, that she were in her grave indeed!" said Kate, and she covered her face with her hands.

"She is dead and buried, and gone from this house for ever," said Pete.

He did not intend to cast her off; he was only muttering vague words in the first spasm of his pain; but she mistook them for commands to her to go.

There was a moment's silence, and then she uncovered her face and said, "I understand—yes, I will go away. I oughtn't to have come back at all—I know that. But I will go now. I won't trouble you any more. I will never come again."

She kissed the child passionately. It rubbed its little face with the back of its hand, but it did not awake. She pulled the hood on to her head, and drew the veil over her face. Then she lifted herself feebly to her feet, stood a moment looking about her, made a faint pathetic cry and slid out at the door.

When she was gone, Pete, without uttering a word or a sound, stumbled into a chair before the fire, put one hand on the cradle, and fell to rocking it. After some time he looked over his shoulder, like a man who was coming out of unconsciousness, and said, "Eh?"

The soul has room for only one great emotion at once, and he had begun to say to himself, "She's alive! She's here!" The air of the house seemed to be soft with her presence. Hush!

He got on to his feet. "Kate!" he called softly, very softly, as if she were near and had only just crossed the threshold.

"Kate!" he called again more loudly.

Then he went out at the porch and floundered along the path, crying again and again, in a voice of boundless emotion, "Kate! Kate! Kate!"

But Kate did not hear him. He was tugging at the gate to open it, when something seemed to give way inside his head, and a hoarse groan came from his throat.

"She's better dead," he thought, and then reeled back to the house like a drunken man.

The fire looked black, as if it had gone out. He sat down in the darkness, and put his hand into his teeth to keep himself from crying out.

VIII..

The Deemster in the half-lit Court-house was passing sentence.

"Prisoner," he said, "you have been found guilty by a jury of your countrymen of one of the cruellest of the crimes of imposture. You have deceived the ignorant, betrayed the unwary, lied to the simple, and robbed the poor. You have built your life upon a lie, and in your old age it brings you to confusion. In ruder times than ours your offence would have worn another complexion; it would have been called witchcraft, not imposture, and your doom would have been death. The sentence of the court is that you be committed to the Castle Rushen for the term of one year."

Black Tom, who had stood during the Deemster's sentence with his bald head bent, wiping his eyes on his sleeve and leaving marks on his face, recovered his self-conceit as he was being hustled out of court.

"You're right, Dempster," he cried. "Witchcraft isn't worth nothing now. Religion's the only roguery that's going these days. Your friend Cæsar was wise, sir. Bes' re-spec's to him, Dempster, and may you live up to your own tex' yourself, too."

"If my industry and integrity," said a solemn voice at the door—"and what's it saying in Scripture?—'If any provide not for his own house he is worse than an infidel.' But the Lord is my shield. What for should I defend myself? I am a worm and no man, saith the Psalms."

"The Psalms is about right then, Cæsar," shouted Black Tom from between two constables.

In the commotion that followed on the prisoner's noisy removal, the Clerk of the Court was heard to speak to the Deemster. There was another case just come in—attempted suicide—woman tried to fling herself into the harbour—been prevented—would his Honour take it now, or let it stand over for the High Bailiff's court.

"We'll take it now," said the Deemster. "We may dismiss her in a moment, poor creature."

The woman was brought in. She was less like a human creature than like a heap of half-drenched clothes. A cloak which looked black with the water that soaked it at the hood covered her body and head. Her face seemed to be black also, for a veil which she wore was wet, and clung to her features like a glove. Some of the people in court recognised her figure even in the uncertain candlelight. She was the woman who had been seen to come into the town during the hour of the court's adjournment.

Half helped, half dragged by constables, she entered the prisoner's dock. There she clutched the bar before her as if to keep herself from falling. Her head was bent down between her shrinking shoulders as if she were going through the agony of shame and degradation.

"The woman shouldn't have been brought here like this—quick, be quick," said the Deemster.

The evidence was brief. One of the constables being on duty in the market-place had heard screams from the quay. On reaching the place, he had found the harbour-master carrying a woman up the quay steps. Mr. Quarry, coming out of the harbour office, had seen a woman go by like the wind. A moment afterwards he had heard a cry, and had run to the second steps. The woman had been caught by a boathook in attempting to get into the water. She was struggling to drown herself.

The Deemster watched the prisoner intently. "Is anything known about her?" he asked.

The clerk answered that she appeared to be a stranger, but she would give no information. Then the sergeant of police stepped up to the dock. In emphatic tones the big little person asked the woman various questions. What was her name? No answer. Where did she come from? No answer. What was she doing in Ramsey? Still no answer.

"Your Honour," said the sergeant, "doubtless this is one of the human wrecks that come drifting to our shores in the summer season. The poorest of them are often unable to get away when the season is over, and so wander over the island, a pest and a burden to every place they set foot in."

Then, turning back to the figure crouching in the dock, he said, "Woman, are you a street-walker?"

The woman gave a piteous cry, let go her hold of the bar, sank back to the seat behind her, brushed up the wet black veil, and covered her face with her hands.

"Sit down this instant, Mr. Gawne," said the Deemster hotly, and there was a murmur of approval from behind. "We must not keep this woman a moment longer."

He rose, leaned across to the rail in front, clasped his hands before him, looked down at the woman in the dock, and said in a low tone, that would have been barely loud enough to reach her ears but for the silence, as of a tomb, in the court, "My poor woman, is there anybody who can answer for you?"

The prisoner stooped her head lower and began to cry.

"When a woman is so unhappy as to try to take her life, it sometimes occurs, only too sadly, that another is partly to blame for the condition that tempts her to the crime."

The Deemster's voice was as soft as a caress.

"If there is such a one in this case, we ought to learn it. He ought to stand by your side. It is only right; it is only just. Is there anybody here who knows you?"

The prisoner was now crying piteously.

"Ah! we mean no harm to any one. It is in the nature of woman, however low she may sink, however deep her misfortunes, to shield her dearest enemy. That is the brave impulse of the weakest among women, and all good men respect it. But the law has its duty, and in this instance it is one of mercy."

The woman moaned audibly.

"Don't be afraid, my poor girl. Nobody shall harm you here. Take courage and look around. Is there anybody in court who can speak for you—who can tell us how you came to the place where you are now standing?"

The woman let fall her hands, raised her head, and looked up at the Deemster, face to face and eye to eye.

"Yes," she said, "there is *one*."

The Deemster's countenance became pale, his eyes glistened, his look wandered, his lips trembled—he was biting them, they were bleeding.

"Remove her in custody," he muttered; "let her be well cared for."

There was a tumult in a moment. Everybody had recognised the prisoner as she was being taken out, though shame and privation had so altered her. "Peter Quilliam's wife!"—"Cæsar Cregeen's daughter—where's the man himself?"—"Then it's truth they're telling—it's not dead she is at all, but worse."—"Lor-a-massy!"—"What a trouble for the Dempster!"

When Kate was gone, the court ought to have adjourned instantly, yet the Deemster remained in his seat. There was a mist before his eyes which dazzled him. He had a look at once wild and timid. His limbs pained although they were swelling to enormous size. He felt as if a heavy, invisible hand had been laid on the top of his head.

The clerk caught his eye, and then he rose with an apologetic air, took hold of the rail, and made an effort to cross the dais. At the next moment his servant, Jem-y-Lord, had leapt up to his side, but he made an impatient gesture as if declining help.

There are three steps going down to the floor of the court, and a handrail on one side of them. Coming to these steps, he stumbled, muttered some confused words, and fell forward on to his face. The people were on their feet by this time, and there was a rush to the place.

"Stand back! He has only fainted," cried Jem-y-Lord.

"Worse than that," said the sergeant. "Get him to bed, and send for Dr. Mylechreest instantly."

"Where can we take him?" said somebody.

"They keep a room for him at Elm Cottage," said somebody else.

"No, not there," said Jem-y-Lord.

"It's nearest, and there's no time to lose," said the sergeant.

Then they lifted Philip, and carried him as he lay, in his wig and gown as Deemster, to the house of Pete.

IX.

There is a kind of mental shock which, like an earthquake under a prison, bursts open every cell and lets the inmates escape. After a time, Pete remembered that he was sitting in the dark, and he got up to light a candle. Looking for candlestick and matches, he went from table to dresser, from dresser to table, and from table back to dresser, doing the same thing over and over again, and not perceiving that he was going round and round. When at length the candle was lighted, he took it in his hand and went into the parlour like a sleepwalker. He set it on the mantelpiece, and sat down on the stool. In his blurred vision confused forms floated about him. "Ah! my tools," he thought, and picked up the mallet and two of the chisels. He was sitting with these in his hands when his eyes fell on the other candlestick, the one in which the candle had gone out "I meant to light a candle," he thought, and he got up and took the empty candlestick into the hall. When he came back with another lighted candle, he perceived that there were two. "I'm going stupid," he thought, and he blew out the first one. A moment afterwards he forgot that he had done so, and seeing the second still burning, he blew that out also.

So dull were his senses that he did not realise that anything was amiss. His eyes were seeing objects everywhere about—they were growing to awful size and threatening him. His ears were hearing noises—they were making a fearful tumult inside his head.

The room was not entirely dark. A shaft of bleared moonlight came and went at intervals. The moon was scudding through an angry sky, sometimes appearing, sometimes disappearing. Pete returned to the stool, and then he was in the light, but the nameless stone, leaning against the wall, was in the shade. He took up the mallet and chisels again, intending to work. "Hush!" he said as he began. The clamour in his brain was so loud that he thought some one was making a noise in the house. This task was sacred. He always worked at it in silence.

Pat-put! pat-put! How long he worked he never knew. There are moments which are not to be measured as time. In the uncertain handling of the chisel and the irregular beat of the mallet something gave way. There was a harsh sound like a groan. A crack like a flash of forked lightning had shot across the face of the stone. He had split it in half. Its great pieces fell to the floor on either side of him. Then he remembered that the stone had been useless. "It doesn't matter now," he thought. Nothing mattered.

With the mallet hanging from his hand he continued to sit in the drifting moonlight, feeling as if everything in the world had been shivered to atoms. His two idols had been scattered at one blow—his wife and his friend. The golden threads that had bound him to life were broken. When poverty had come, he had met it without repining; when death had seemed to come, he had borne up against it bravely. But wifeless, friendless, deceived where he had loved, betrayed where he had worshipped, he was bankrupt, he was broken, and a boundless despair took hold of him.

When hope is entirely gone, anguish will sometimes turn a man into a monster. There was a fretful cry from the cradle, and, still in the stupor of his despair, he went out to rock it. The fire, which had only slid and smouldered, was now struggling into flame, and the child looked up at him with Philip's eyes. A knife seemed to enter his heart at that moment. He was more desolate than he had thought. "Hush, my child, hush!" he said, without thinking. *His* child? He had none. That solace was gone.

Anger came to save his reason. Not to have felt anger, he must have been less than a man or more. He remembered what the child had been to him. He remembered what it was when it came, and again when he thought its mother was dead; he remembered what it was when death frowned on it, and what it had been since death passed it by. Flesh of his flesh, blood of his blood, bone of his bone, heart of his heart. Not his merely, but himself.

A lie, a mockery, a delusion, a deception! *She* has practised it. Oh, she had hidden her secret. She had thought it was safe. But the child itself had betrayed it. The secret had spoken from the child's own face.

"Yet I've seen her kneel by the cot and pray, 'God bless my baby, and its father and its mother'——"

Why had he not killed her? A wild vision rose before him of killing Kate, and then going to the Deemster and saying, "Take me; I have murdered her because you have dishonoured her. Condemn me to death; yet remember God lives, and He will condemn you to damnation."

But the pity of it—the pity of it! By a quick revolt of tenderness he recalled Kate as he had just seen her, crouching at the back of the cradle, like a hunted hare with uplifted paws uttering its last pitiful cry. He remembered her altered face, so pale even in the firelight, so thin, so worn, and his anger began to smoke against Philip. The flower that he would have been proud to wear on his breast Philip had buried in the dark. Curse him! Curse him!

She had given up all for that man—husband, child, father, mother, her friends, her good name, the very light of heaven. How she must have loved him! Yet he had been ashamed of her, had hidden her away, had been in fear lest the very air should whisper of her whereabouts. Curse him! Curse him! Curse him!

In the heat of his great anger Pete thought of himself also. Jealousy was far beneath him, but, like all great souls, this simple man had known something of the grandeur of friendship. Two streams running into them and taking heaven into their bosom. But Philip had kept him apart, had banked him off, and yet drained him to the dregs. He had uncovered his nakedness—the nakedness of his soul itself.

Bit by bit Pete pieced together the history of the past months. He remembered the night of Kate's disappearance, when he had gone to Ballure and shouted up at the lighted window, "I've sent her to England," thinking to hide her fault. At that moment Philip had known all—where she was (for it was where he had sent her), why she was gone, and that she was gone for ever. Curse him! Curse him!

Pete recalled the letters—the first one that he had put into Philip's hand, the second that he had read to him, the third that Philip had written to his dictation. The little forgeries' to keep her poor name sweet, the little inventions to make his story plausible, the little lies of love, the little jests of a breaking heart! And then the messages! The presents to the child! The reference to the Deemster himself! And the Deemster had sat there and seen through it all as the sun sees through glass, yet he had given no sign, he had never spoken; he had held a quivering, naked heart in his hand, while his own lay within as cold as a stone. Curse him, O God! Curse him!

Pete remembered the night when Philip came to tell him that Kate was dead, and how he had comforted himself with the thought that he was not altogether alone in his great trouble, because his friend was with him. He remembered the journey to the grave, the grave itself—another's grave-how he knelt at the foot of it, and prayed aloud in Philip's hearing, "Forgive me, my poor girl!"

"How shall I kill him?" thought Pete. Deemster too! First Deemster now, and held high in honour! Worshipped for his justice! Beloved for his mercy! O God! O God!

There are passions so overmastering that they stifle speech, and man sinks back to the animal. With an inarticulate shout Pete went to the parlour and caught up the mallet. A frantic thought had flashed on him of killing Philip as he sat on the bench which he had disgraced, administering the law which he had outraged. The wild justice of this idea made the blood to bubble in his ears. He saw himself holding the Deemster by the throat, and crying aloud to the people, "You think this man is a just judge—he is a whited sepulchre. You think he is as true as the sun—he is as false as the sea. He has robbed me of wife and child; at the very gates of heaven he has lied to me like hell. The hour of justice has struck, and thus I pay him—and thus—and thus."

But the power of words was lost in the drunkenness of his rage. With a dismal roar he flung the mallet away, and it rolled on the ground in narrowing circles. "My hands, my hands," he thought. He would strangle Philip, and then he would kill everybody in his way, merely for the lust of killing. Why not? The fatal line was past. Nothing sacred remained. The world was a howling wilderness of boundless license. With the savage growl of a caged beast this wild man flung himself on the door, tore it open, and bounded on to the path.

Then he stopped suddenly. There was a thunderous noise outside, such as the waves make in a cave. A company of people were coming in at the gate. Some were walking with the heavy step of men who carry a corpse. Others were bearing lanterns, and a few held high over their heads the torches which fishermen use when they are hauling the white nets at night.

"Who's there?" cried Pete, in a voice that was like a howl.

"Your friend," said somebody.

"*My* friend? I have no friend," cried Pete, in a broken roar.

"'Deed he's gone, seemingly," said a voice out of the dark.

Pete did not hear. Seeing the crowd and the lights, but only as darkness veined with fire, he thought Philip was coming again, as he had so often seen him come in his glory, in his greatness, in his triumph.

"Where is he?" he roared. "He's here," they answered.

And then Philip was brought up the path in the arms of four bearers, his head hanging aside and shaking at every step, his face white as the wig above it, and his gown trailing along the earth.

There was a sudden calm, and Pete dropped back in awe and horror. A bolt out of heaven seemed to have fallen at his feet, and he trembled as if lightning had blinded him.

Dead!

His anger had ebbed, his fury had dashed itself against a rock. His towering rage had shrunk to nothing in the face of this awful presence. The Dark Spirit had gone before him and snatched his victim out of his hands. He had come out to kill this man, and here he met him being brought home dead.

Dead? Then his sin was dead also. God forgive him!

God forgive him, where he was gone! Presumptuous man, stand back.

Oh, mighty and merciful Death! Death the liberator, the deliverer, the pardoner, the peace-maker! Even the shadow of thy face can quench the fires of revenge; even the gathering of thy wings can deaden the clamour of madness, and turn hatred into love and curses into prayers.

X.

In that stripped and naked house there was one room still untouched. It was the room that had been kept for the Deemster. Philip lay on the bed, motionless and apparently lifeless. Jem-y-Lord stood beating his hands at the foot. Pete sat on a low stool at the side with his face doubled on to his knees. Nancy, now back from Sulby, was blowing into the bars of the grate to kindle a fire. A little group of men stood huddled like sheep near the door.

Some one said the Deemster's heart was beating. They brought from another room a little ivory hand-glass and held it over the mouth. When they raised it the face of the mirror was faintly blurred.

That little cloud on the glass seemed more bright than the shining tread of an angel on the sea. Jem-y-Lord took a sponge and began to moisten the cold forehead. One by one the people behind produced their old wife's wisdom. Somebody remembered that his grandmother always put salts to the nostrils of a person seemingly dead; somebody else remembered that when, on the very day of old Iron Christian's death, his father had been thrown by a colt and lay twelve hours unconscious, the farrier had bled him and he had opened his eyes instantly.

The doctor had been half an hour gone to Ballaugh, and a man had been put on a horse and sent after him. But it was a twelve-miles' journey; the night was dark; it would be a good hour before he could be back.

They touched Pete on the shoulder and suggested something.

"Eh?" he answered vacantly.

"Dazed," they told themselves. The poor man could not give a wise-like answer. He had had a shock, and there was worse before him. They talked in low voices of Kate and of Ross Christian; they were sorry for Pete; they were still more sorry for the Deemster.

The Deemster's wig had been taken off and tossed on to the dressing-table. It lay mouth upwards like any old woman's night-cap. His hair had dragged after it on the pillow. The black gown had not been removed, but it was torn open at the neck so that the throat might be free. One of Philip's arms had dropped over the side of the bed, and the long, thin hand was cold and green and ethereal as marble.

Pete was crouching on his low stool beside this hand. He needed no softening to touch it now. The chill fingers were in his palm, and his hot tears were falling on them. Remembering the crime that he had so nearly committed, he was holding himself in horror. His friend! His life-long friend! His only friend! The Deemster no longer, but only the man. Not the man either, but the child. The cruel years had rolled back with all their burden of trouble. Forgotten days were come again—days long buried under the *débris* of memory. They were boys together again. A little, sunny fellow in velvet, and a bigger lad in a stocking-cap; the little one talking, always talking; the big one listening, always listening; the little one proposing, the big one agreeing; the little one leading, the big one following; the little one looking up and yet a little down, the big one looking down and yet a little up. Oh, the happy, happy times, before anger and jealousy and rage and the mad impulse of murder had darkened their sun shine!

The memories that brought the tenderest throb to Pete as he sat there fingering the lifeless hand were of the great deeds that he had done for Philip—how he had fought for him, and been licked for him, and taken bloody noses for him, and got thrashed for it by Black Tom. But there were others only less tender. Philip was leaving home for King William's, and Pete was cudgelling his dull head what to give him for a parting gift. Decision was the more difficult because he had nothing to give. At length he had hit on making a whistle—the only thing his clumsy fingers had ever been deft at. With his clasp-knife he had cut a wondrous big one from the bough of a willow; he had pared it; he had turned it; it blew a blast like a fog-horn. The morning was frosty, and his feet were bare, but he didn't mind the cold; he didn't feel it— no, not a ha'p'orth. He was behind the hedge by the gate at Ballure, waiting for the coach that was to take up Philip, and passing the time by polishing the whistle on the leg of his shining breeches, and testing its tone with just one more blow. Then up came Crow, and out came Philip in his new peaked cap and leggings. Whoop! Gee-up! Away! Off they went without ever seeing him, without once looking back, and he was left in the prickly hedge with his blue feet on the frost, a look of dejection about his mouth, and the top of the foolish whistle peeping out of his jacket-pocket.

The thick sob that came of these memories was interrupted by a faint sound from the bed. It was a murmur of delirium, as soft as the hum of bees, yet Pete heard it.

"Cover me up, Pete, cover me up!" said Philip, dreaming aloud.

Philip was a living man! Thank God! Thank God!

A whisper goes farther than a shout. The people behind whispered the news to the passage, the passage to the stairs, the stairs to the hall, and the hall to the garden, where a crowd had gathered in the darkness to look up at the house over which the angel of death was hovering.

184

In a moment the room was croaking like a frog-pond. "Praise the Lord!" cried one. "His mercy endureth for ever," cried another. "What's he saying?" said a third. "Rambling in his head, poor thing," said a fourth.

Pete turned them out—all except Jem-y-Lord, who was still moistening the Deemster's face and opening his hands, which were now twitching and tightening.

"Out of this! Out you go!" cried Pete hoarsely.

"No use taking the anger with him—the man's tried," they muttered, and away they went.

Jemmy was loth to see them go. He was afraid to be left alone with Pete—afraid that the Deemster should be at the mercy of this wild creature with the flaming eyes.

And now that Philip was a living man Pete began to feel afraid of himself. At sight of life in Philip's face, his gnawing misery returned. He thought his hatred had been overcome, but he was wrestling in the throes of forgiveness again. Here was the man who had robbed him of wife and child and home! In another moment he might have held him in the grip of his just wrath.

It is an inscrutable and awful fact, that just at that moment when a man's good angel has conquered, but is spent, his evil angel is sure to get the advantage of chance. Philip's delirium set in strong, and the brute beast in Pete, going through its final struggle, stood over the bed and watched him. In his violence Philip tore at his breast, and dragged something from beneath his shirt. A moment later it fell from his graspless fingers to the floor. It was a lock of dark hair. Pete knew whose hair it was, and he put his foot on it, and that instant the mad impulse came again to take Philip by the throat and choke him. Again and again it came. He had to tread it down even amid his sobs and his tears.

But love cannot be killed in an instant. It does not drop down dead. There was a sort of tenderness in the thought that this was the man for whom Kate had given up all the world. Pete began to feel gently towards Philip because Kate loved him; he began to see something of Kate in Philip's face. This strange softening increased as he caught the words of Philip's delirium. He thought he ought to leave the room, but he could not tear himself away. Crouching down on the stool, he clasped his hands behind his head, and tightened his arms over his ears. It was useless. He could not help but listen. Only disjointed sentences, odd pages torn from the book of life, some of them blurred with tears; but they were like a cool hand on a fevered brow to him that heard him.

"I was a child, Philip——didn't know what love was then——coming home by Ramsey steamer——tell the simple truth, Philip——say we tried to be faithful and loyal and could not, because we loved each other, and there was no help for——tell Kirry——yes, Auntie, I have read father's letters——that picture is cracked——"

This in the voice of one who speaks in his sleep, and then in a hushed, hot whisper, "Haven't I a right to you?——yes, I have a right—— take your topcoat, then, the storm is coming——I'll never let you go——don't you remember?——can you ever forget——my husband!— —my husband!"

Pete lifted his head as he listened. He had been thinking that Philip had robbed him of Kate. Was it he who had robbed Kate of Philip?

"I can't live any longer in this house, Philip——the walls are crushing me; the ceiling is falling on me; the air is stifling me——three o'clock, Pete——yes, three to-morrow, in the Council Chamber at Douglas——I'm not a bad woman, Philip Christian——there is something you have never guessed and I have never told you——is it the child, Kate?——did you say the child?——you are sure——you are not deceiving yourself?"

All this in a tone of deep entreaty, and then, with quick-coming breath, "Jemmy, get the carriage at Shimmin's and drive it yourself——if there is any attempt at Ramsey to take the horse out——drive to the lane between the chapel and the cottage——the moment the lady joins you——you are right, Kate——you cannot live here any longer——this life of deception must end——that's the churring of the night-jar going up to Ballure Glen."

Jem-y-Lord, who was beating out the pillow, dropped it, in his fumbling, half over the Deemster's face, and looked at Pete in terror. Would this cruel delirium never break? Where was the doctor? Would he not come at all?

Pete had risen to his feet, and was gazing down with a look of stupor. He had been thinking that Philip had robbed him of the child. Was it he who had robbed Philip?

"Yes, Pete is telling the same story. He is writing letters to himself——such simple things!——poor old Pete——he means no harm—— he never dreams that every word is burning——Jemmy, leave out more brandy to-night, the decanter is empty——"

Pete leaned over the pillow. All at once he started back. Philip's eyes were open and shining up at him. It was hard to believe that Philip was not speaking to him eye to eye. But there was a veil between them, the veil of the hand of God.

"I know, Philip, *I* know," said the unconscious man in a quick whisper; he was breathing fast and loud. "Tell him I'm dead——yes, yes, that's it, that's it——cruel?——no, but kind——'Poor girl,' he'll say, 'I loved her once, but she's gone'——I'll do it, I'll do it." Then, in tones of fear, "It's madness——to paint faces on the darkness, to hear voices in the air is madness." And then, solemnly, with a chill, thick utterance, "There——there——that one by the wall——"

Big drops of sweat broke out on Pete's forehead. Had he been thinking that Philip had tortured him? It was he who had been torturing Philip. The letters, the messages, the presents, these had been the whips and scorpions in his hand. Every innocent word, every look, every sign, had been as thongs in the instrument of torture. Pete began to feel a great pity for Philip. "He had suffered plenty," thought Pete. "He has carried this cross about far enough."

"Good-night, boatman!——I went too far——yes, I am back again, thank God——"

These words brightly, cheerily, hopefully; then, in the deepest tones, "Good-bye, Philip——it's all my fault——I've broken the heart of one man, and I'm destroying the soul of another——I'm leaving this lock of hair—it is all I have to leave——good-bye!——I ought to have gone long ago——you will not hate me now——"

The last words frayed off, broke in the throat, and stopped. Then quickly, with panting breath, came, "Kate! Kate! Kate!" again and again repeated, beginning in a loud beseeching cry and dying down to a long wail, as if shouted over a gloomy waste wherein the voice was lost.

185

Jem-y-Lord had been beating round towards the door, wringing his white hands like a woman, and praying to God that the Deemster might never come out of his unconsciousness. "He has told him everything," thought Jem. "The man will take his life."

"I came between them," thought Pete. "She was not for me. She was not mine. She was Philip's. It was God's doings."

The bitterness of Pete's heart had passed away. "But I wish——what's the good of wishing, though? God help us all," he muttered, in a breaking voice, and then he crouched down on the stool as before and covered his face with his hands..

Philip had lifted his head and risen on one elbow. He was looking out on the empty air with his glassy eyes, as if a picture stood up before them.

"Yes, no, yes——don't tell me——that Kate?——it's a mistake——that's not Kate——that white face!——those hollow eyes!——that miserable woman!——besides, Kate is dead——she must be dead——what's to do with the lamps?——they are going out——in the dock, too, and before me——she there and I here!——she the prisoner, I the judge!"

All this with violent emotion, and with one arm outstretched over Pete's crouching head.

"If I could hear her voice, though——perhaps her voice now——I'm going to fall——it's Kate, it's Kate! Oh! oh!"

Philip had paused for several seconds, as if trying to listen, and then, with a loud cry of agony, he had closed his eyes and rolled back on to the pillow.

"God has meant me to hear all this," thought Pete. God had intended that for this, the peace of his soul, he should follow the phases of this drama of a naked heart. He was sobbing, but his sobs were like growls.

"What's he doing now?" thought Jem-y-Lord, craning his neck at the door. "Shall I call for somebody?"

Pete had picked up from the floor the lock of hair that had been lying under his foot, and he was putting it back into Philip's breast.

"Nothing but me between them," he thought, "nothing but me."

"Sit down, sir," cried the unconscious man. It was only the last outbreak of Philip's delirium, but Pete trembled and shrank back.

Then Philip groaned and his blue lips quivered. He opened his eyes. They wandered about the room for a moment, and afterwards fixed themselves on Pete in a long and haggard gaze. Pete's own eyes were too full of tears to be full of sight, but he could see that the change had come. He panted with expectation, and looked down at Philip with doglike delight.

There was a moment's silence, and then, in a voice as faint as a breath, Philip murmured. "What's——where's——is it Pete?"

At that Pete uttered a shout of joy. "He's himself! He's himself! Thank God!"

"Eh?" said Philip helplessly.

"Don't you be bothering yourself now," cried Pete. "Lie quiet, boy; you're in your own room, and as nice as nice."

"But," said Philip, "will you not kindly——"

"Not another word, Phil. It's nothing. You're all serene, and about as right as ninepence."

"Your Honour has been delirious," said Jem-y-Lord.

"Chut!" said Pete behind his hand, and then, with another joyful shout, "Is it a beefsteak you'll be having, Phil, or a dish of tay and a herring?"

Philip looked perplexed. "But could you not help me——" he faltered.

"You fainted in the Court-house, sir," said Jem-y-Lord.

"Ah!" It had all come back.

"Hould your whisht, you gawbie," whispered Pete, and he made a furtive kick at Jemmy's shins.

Pete was laughing and crying in one breath. In the joyful reflux from evil passions the great fellow was like a boy. He poked the fire into a blaze, snuffed the candle with his fingers, sang out "My gough!" when he burnt them, and then hopped about the floor and cut as many capers as a swallow after a shower of rain.

Philip looked at him and relapsed into silence. It seemed as if he had been on a journey and something had happened in his absence. The secret which he had struggled so long to confess had somehow been revealed.

Jem-y-Lord was beating out his pillows. "Does he know?" said Philip.— "Yes," whispered Jemmy.

"Everything!"

"Everything. You have been delirious."

"Delirious!" said Philip, with alarm.

Then he struggled to rise. "Help me up. Let me go away. Why did you bring me here?"

"I couldn't help it, sir. I tried to prevent——"

"I cannot face him," said Philip. "I am afraid. Help me, help me."

"You are too weak, sir. Lie still. No one shall harm you. The doctor is coming."

Philip sank back with a look of fear. "Water," he cried feebly.

"Here it is," said Jem-y-Lord, lifting from the dressing-table the jug out of which he had moistened the sponge.

"Tut!" cried Pete, and he tipped the jug so that half the water spilled. "Brandy for a man when he's in bed, you goosey gander. Hould, hard, boy; I've a taste of the rael stuff in the cupboard. Half a minute, mate. A drop will be doing no harm at all," and away he went down the stairs like a flood, almost sweeping over Nancy, who had come creeping up in her stockings at the sound of voices.

The child had awakened in its cradle, and, with one dumpy leg over its little quilt, it was holding quiet converse with its toes.

"Hollo, young cockalorum, is it there you are!" shouted Pete.

At the next moment, with a noggin bottle of brandy in his fist, he was leaping upstairs, three steps at a time.

Meanwhile Jem-y-Lord had edged up to the Deemster and whispered, with looks of fear and mystery, "Don't take it, sir."

"What?" said Philip vacantly.—"The brandy," said Jem.

"Eh?"

"It will——" began Jem, but Pete's step was thundering up the stairs, and with a big opening of the mouth, rather than an audible utterance of the tongue, he added, "poisoned."

Philip could not comprehend, and Pete came shouting—

"Where's your water, now, ould Snuff-the-Wind?"

While Pete was pouring the brandy into a glass and adding the water, Jemmy caught up a scrap of newspaper that was lying about, rummaged for a pencil, wrote some words on the margin, tore the piece off, and smuggled it into the Deemster's hand.

"Afraid of Pete!" thought Philip. "It is monstrous! monstrous!"

At that moment there was the sound of a horse's hoofs on the road.

"The doctor," cried Jem-y-Lord. "The doctor at last. Wait, sir, wait," and he ran downstairs.

"Here you are," cried Pete, coming to the bedside, glass in hand. "Drink it up, boy. It'll stiffen you. My faith, but it's a oner. Aw, God is good, though. He's all that. He's good tremenjous."

Pete was laughing; he was crying; he was tasting a new sweetness—the sweetness of being a good man again.

Philip was holding Jem-y-Lord's paper before his eyes, and trying to read it.

"What's this that Jemmy has given me?" he said. "Read it, Pete. My eyes are dazed."

Pete took the paper in his left hand, still holding the glass in his right. To get the light on to the writing he went down on his knees by the bed-head and leaned over towards the fire. Then, like a school-boy repeating his task, he read in a singsong voice the words that Jem-y-Lord had written:—"Don't drink the brandy. Pete is trying to kill you."

Pete made a grating laugh. "That's a pretty thing now," he began, but he could not finish. His laughter ceased, his eyes opened wide, his tongue seemed to hang out of his mouth, and he turned his head and looked back with an agony of doubt into Philip's face.

Philip struggled up. "Give me the brandy, Pete." He took the glass out of Pete's hand, and without a second thought, with only a smile of faith and confidence, he raised it to his lips and drank. When the doctor entered the room a moment afterwards, Pete was sobbing into the bed-clothes, and Philip's hand was resting on his head.

XI.

Early the next morning Pete visited Kate in prison. He had something to say to her, something to ask; but he intended to keep back his own feelings, to bear himself bravely, to sustain the poor girl's courage. The light was cold and ashen within the prison walls, and as he followed the sergeant into the cell, he could not help but think of Kate as he had first known her, so bright, so merry, so full of life and gaiety. He found her now doubled up on a settle by a newly-kindled fire in the sergeant's own apartment. She lifted her head, with a terrified look, as he entered, and she saw his hollow cheeks and deep eyes and ragged beard.

"I'm not coming to trouble you," he said. "I've forgiven *him*, and I'm forgiving you, too."

"You are very good," she answered nervously.

"Good?" He gave a crack of bitter laughter. "I meant to kill him—that's how good I am. And it's the same as if all the devils out of hell had been at me the night through to do it still. Maybe I hadn't much to forgive. I'm like a bat in the light—I'm not knowing where I am ezactly. Daresay the people will laugh at me when they're getting to know. Wouldn't trust, but they'll think me a poor-spirited cur, anyway. Let them—there's never much pity for the dog that's licked."

His voice shook, although so hard and so husky. "That's not what I came to say, though. You'll be laving this place soon, and I'm wanting to ask—I'm wanting to know——"

She had covered her face, and now she said through her hands, "Do as you like with me, Pete. You are my husband, and I must obey."

He looked down at her for a moment. "But you cannot love me?"

"I have deceived you, and whatever you tell me to do I will do it."

"But you cannot love me?"

"I'll be a good wife for the future* Pete—I will, indeed, indeed I will."

"But you cannot love me?"

She began to cry. "That's enough," he said. "I'll not force you."

"You are very good," she said again.

He laughed more bitterly than before. "Dou yo think I'm wanting your body while another man has your heart? That's a game I've played about long enough, I'm thinking. Good? Not me, missis."

His eyes, which had been fixed on the fire, wandered to his wife, and then his lips quivered and his manner changed.

187

"I'm hard—I'll cut it short. Fact is, I've detarmined to do something, but I've a question to ask first. You've suffered since you left me, Kate. He has dragged you down a dale—but tell me, do you love him still?"

She shuddered and crept closer to the wall.

"Don't be freckened. It's a woman's way to love the man that's done wrong by her. Being good to her is nothing—sarvice is nothing—kindness is nothing. Maybe there's some ones that cry shame on her for that—but not me. Giving herself, body and soul, and thinking nothing what she gets for it—that's the glory of a woman when she cares for anybody. Spake up, Kate—do you love him in spite of all?"

The answer came in a whisper that was like a breath—"Yes."

"That'll do," said Pete.

He pressed his hand against the place of his old wound. "I might have known you could never care for me—I might have known that," he said with difficulty. "But don't think I can't stand my rackups, as the saying is. I know my course now—I know my job."

She was sobbing into her hands, and he was breathing fast and loud.

"One word more—only one—about the child."

"Little Katherine!"

"Have I a right to her?"

She gasped audibly, but did not answer, and he tried a second time.

"Does she belong to me, Kate?"

Her confusion increased. He tried a third time, speaking more gently than before.

"If I should lave the island, Kate, could I—must I—may I take the child along with me?"

At that her fear got the better of her shame, and she cried, "Don't take her away. Oh, don't, don't!"

"Ah!"

He pressed his hand hard at his side again.

"But maybe that's only mother's love, and what mother——"

He broke off and then began once more, in a voice so low that it was scarcely to be heard. "Tell me, when the time comes—and it will come, Kate, have no fear about that——"

He was breaking down, he was struggling hard. "When the time comes for himself and you to be together, will you be afraid to have the little one with you—will it seem wrong, Kate—you two and little Katherine—one household—one family—no?—n—o?"

"No."

"That's enough."

The words seemed to come out of the depths of his throat. "I've nothing more to think about. *He* must think of all the rest."

"And you, Pete?"

"What matter about me? D'ye think there's anything worse coming? D'ye think I'm caring what I ate, and what I drink, and what becomes of me?"

He was laughing again, and her sobs broke out afresh.

"God is good," he said more quietly. "He'll take care of the likes of me."

His motionless eyes were on the crackling fire, and he stood in the light that flashed from it with a face like stone. "I've no child now," he muttered, as though speaking to himself.

She slid to her knees at his feet, took the hand that hung by his side and began to cover it with kisses. "Forgive me," she said; "I have been very weak and very guilty."

"What's the use of talking like that?" he answered. "What's past is past," and he drew his hand away. "No child now, no child now," he muttered again, as though his dispair cried out to God.

He was feeling like a man wrecked in mid-ocean. A spar came floating towards him. It was all he could lay hold of from the foundering ship, in which he had sailed, and sung, and laughed, and slept. He had thought to save his life by it, but another man was clinging to it, and he had to drop it and go down.

She could not look into his face again; she could not touch his hand; she could not ask for his forgiveness. He stood over her for a moment without speaking, and then, with his hollow cheeks, and deep eyes, and ragged heard, he went away in the morning sunlight.

XII.

Phillip fell into a deep sleep. When he awoke, he saw, as in a mirror, a solution to the tumultuous drama of his life. It was a glorious solution, a liberating and redeeming end, an end bringing freedom from the bonds which had beset him. What matter if it was hard; if it was difficult; if it was bitter as Marah and steep as Calvary? He was ready, he was eager. Oh, blessed sleep! Oh, wise and soothing sleep I It had rent the dark cloud of his past and given the flash of light that illumined the path before him.

He opened his eyes and saw Auntie Nan seated by his side, reading a volume of sermons. At the change in his breathing the old dove looked round, dropped the book, and began to flutter about. "Hush, dearest, hush!" she whispered.

There was a heavy, monotonous sound, like the beating of a distant drum or the throb of an engine under the earth.

"Auntie!"—"Yes, dearest."

"What day is it?"

"Sunday. Oh, you've had a long, long sleep, Philip. You slept all day yesterday."

"Is that the church-bell ringing?"

"Yes, dear, and a fine morning, too—so soft and springlike. I'll open the window."

"Then my hearing must be injured."

"Ah! they muffled the bell—that's it. 'The church is so near,' they said, 'it might trouble him.'"

A carriage was coming down the road. It rattled on the paved way; then the rattling ceased, and there was a dull rumble as of a cart sliding on to a wooden bridge. "That horse has fallen," said Philip, trying to rise.

"It's only the straw on the street," said Auntie Nan. "The people brought it from all parts. 'We must deaden the traffic by the house,' they said. Oh, you couldn't think how good they've been. Yesterday was market-day, but there was no business done. Couldn't have been; they were coming and going the whole day long. 'And how's the Deemster now?' 'And how's he now?' It was fit to make you cry. I believe in my heart, Philip, nobody in Ramsey went to bed the first night at all. Everybody waiting and waiting to see if there wasn't something to fetch, and the kettle kept boiling in every kitchen round about. But hush, dearest, hush! Not so much talking all at once. Hush, now!"

"Where is Pete?" asked Philip, his face to the wall.

"Oiling the hinges of the door, dearest. He was laying carpets on the stairs all day yesterday. But never the sound of a hammer. The man's wonderful. He must have hands like iron. His heart's soft enough, though. But then everybody is so kind—everybody, everybody! The doctor, and the vicar, and the newspapers—oh, it's beautiful! It's just as Pete was saying."

"What was Pete saying, Auntie?"

"He was saying the angels must think there's somebody sick in every house in the island."

A sound of singing came through the open window, above the whisper of young leaves and the twitter of birds. It was the psalm that was being sung in church—

       "Blessed is the man that considereth the poor and needy;
        The Lord shall deliver him in time of trouble."

"Listen, Philip. That must be a special psalm. I'm sure they're singing it for you. How sweet of them! But we are talking too much, dear. The doctor will scold. I must leave you now, Philip. Only for a little, though, while I go back to Bal lure, and I'll send up Cottier."

"Yes, send up Cottier," said Philip.

"My darling," said the old soul, looking down as she tied her bonnet strings. "You'll lie quiet now? You're sure you'll lie quiet? Well, good bye! good-bye!"

As Philip lay alone the soar and swell of the psalm filled the room. Oh, the irony of it all! The frantic, hideous, awful irony! He was lying there, he, the guilty one, with the whole island watching at his bedside, pitying him, sorrowing for him, holding its breath until he should breathe, and she, his partner, his victim, his innocent victim, was in jail, in disgrace, in a degradation more deep than death. Still the psalm soared and swelled. He tried to bury his head in the pillows that he might not hear.

Jem-y-Lord came in hurriedly and Philip beckoned him close. "Where is she?" he whispered.

"They removed her to Castle Rushen late last night, your Honour," said Jemmy softly.

"Write immediately to the Clerk of the Bolls," said Philip. "Say she must be lodged on the debtors' side and have patients' diet and every comfort. My Kate! my Kate!" he kept saying, "it shall not be for long, not for long, my love, not for long!"

The convalescence was slow and Philip was impatient. "I feel better to-day, doctor," he would say, "don't you think I may get out of bed?"

"*Traa dy liooar* (time enough), Deemster," the doctor would answer. "Let us see what a few more days will do."

"I have a great task before me, doctor," he would say again. "I must begin immediately."

"You have a life's work before you, Deemster, and you must begin soon, but not just yet."

"I have something particular to do, doctor," he said at last. "I must lose no time."

"You must lose no time indeed, that's why you must stay where you are a little longer."

One morning his impatience overcame him, and he got out of bed. But, being on his feet, his head reeled, his limbs trembled, he clutched at the bed-post, and had to clamber back. "Oh God, bear me witness, this delay is not my fault," he murmured.

Throughout the day he longed for the night, that he might close his eyes in the darkness and think of Kate. He tried to think of her as she used to be—bright, happy, winsome, full of joy, of love, of passion, dangling her feet from the apple-tree, or tripping along the tree-trunk in the glen, teasing him? tempting him. It was impossible. He could only think of her in the gloom of the prison. That filled his mind with terrors. Sometimes in the dark hours his enfeebled body beset his brain with fantastic hallucinations. Calling for paper and pens, he would make show of writing a letter, producing no words or intelligible signs, but only a mass of scrawls and blotches. This he would fold and refold with great elaboration, and give to Jem y-Lord with an air of gravity and mystery, saying in a whisper, "For her!" Thus night brought no solace, and the dawn found him waiting for the day, that he might open his eyes in the sunlight and think, "She is better where she is; God will comfort her."

A fortnight went by and he saw nothing of Pete. At length he made a call on his courage and said, "Auntie, why does Pete never come?"

"He does, dearest. Only when you're asleep, though. He stands there in the doorway in his stockings. I nod to him and he comes in and looks down at you. Then he goes away without a word."

"What is he doing now?"

"Going to Douglas a good deal seemingly. Indeed, they're saying—but then people are so fond of talking."

"What are people saying, Auntie?"

"It's about a divorce, dearest!"

Philip groaned and turned away his face.

He opened his eyes one day from a doze, and saw the plain face of Nancy Joe, framed in a red print handkerchief. The simple creature was talking with Auntie Nan, holding council, and making common cause with the dainty old lady as unmarried women and old maids both of them.

"'Why don't you keep your word true?' says I. 'Wasn't you saying you'd take her back,' says I, 'whatever she'd done and whatever she was, so help you God?' says I. 'Isn't she shamed enough already, poor thing, without you going shaming her more? Have you no bowels at all? Are you only another of the gutted herrings on a stick?' says I. 'Why don't you keep your word true?' 'Because,' says he, 'I want to be even with the other one,' says he, and then away he went wandering down by the tide."

"It's unchristian, Nancy," said Auntie Nan, "but it's human; for although he forgives the woman, he can hardly be expected to forgive the man, and he can't punish one without punishing both."

"Much good it'll do to punish either, say I. What for should he put up his fins now the hook's in his gizzard? But that's the way with the men still. Talking and talking of love and love; but when trouble is coming, no better than a churn of sour cream on a thundery day. We're best off that never had no truck with them—I don't know what you think, Miss Christian, ma'am. They may talk about having no chances— I don't mind if they do—do you? I had chance enough once, though—I don't know what you've had, ma'am. I had one sweetheart, anyway—a sort of a sweetheart, as you might say; but he was sweeter on the money than on me. Always asking how much I had got saved in the stocking. And when he heard I had three new dresses done, 'Nancy,' says he, 'we had better be putting a sight up on the parzon now, before they're all wore out at you.'"

The Governor, who was still in London, wrote a letter full of tender solicitude and graceful compliment. The Clerk of the Rolls had arranged from the first that two telegrams should be sent to him daily, giving accounts of Philip's condition. At last the Clerk came in person, and threw Auntie Nan into tremors of nervousness by his noise and robustious-ness. He roared as he came along the path, roared himself through the hall, up the stairs, and into the bedroom, roared again as he set eyes on Philip, protesting that the sick man was worth five hundred dead men yet, and vowing with an oath (and a tear trickling down his nose) that he would like to give "time" to the fools who frightened good people with bad reports. Then he cleared the room for a private consultation. "Out you go, Cottier. Look slippy, man!"

Auntie Nan fled in terror. When she had summoned resolution to invade afresh the place of the bear that had possession of her lamb, the Clerk of the Rolls was rising from the foot of the bed and saying—

"We'll leave it at that then, Christian. These d—— things *will* happen; but don't you bother your head about it. I'll make it all serene. Besides, it's nothing—nothing in a lifetime. I'll have to send you the summons, though. You needn't trouble about that; just toss it into the fire."

Philip's head was down, his eyes were on the counterpane, and a faint tinge of colour overspread his wasted face.

"Ah! you're back, Miss Christian? I must be going, though. Good-bye, old fellow! Take care of yourself—good men are scarce. Good-bye, Miss Christian! Good-bye, all! Good-bye, Phil! God bless you!"

With that he went roaring down the stairs, but came thunging up again in a moment, put his head round the doorpost, and said—

"Lord bless my soul, if I wasn't forgetting an important bit of news—very important news, too! It hasn't got into the papers yet, but I've had the official wrinkle. What d'ye think?—the Governor has resigned! True as gospel. Sent in his resignation to the Home Office the night before last. I saw it coming. He hasn't been at home since Tynwald. Look sharp and get better now. Good-bye!"

Philip got up for the first time the day following. The weather was soft and full of whispers of spring; the window was open and Philip sat with his face in the direction of the sea. Auntie Nan was knitting by his side and running on with homely gossip. The familiar and genial talk was floating over the surface of his mind as a sea-bird floats over the surface of the sea, sometimes reflected in it, sometimes skimming it, sometimes dipping into it and being lost.

"Poor Pete! The good woman here thinks he's hard. Perhaps he is; but I'm sure he is much to be pitied. Ross has behaved badly and deserves all that can come to him. 'He's the same to me as you are, dear—in blood, I mean—but somehow I can't be sorry.... Ah! you're too tender-hearted, Philip, indeed you are. You'd find excuses for anybody. The doctor says overwork, dearest; but *I* say the shock of seeing that poor creature in that awful position. And what a shock you gave me, too! To tell you the truth, Philip, I thought it was a fate. Never heard of it? No? Never heard that grandfather fainted on the bench? He did, though, and he didn't recover either. How well I remember it! Word broke over the town like a clap of thunder, 'The Deemster has fallen in the Court-house.' Father heard it up at Ballure and ran down bareheaded. Grandfather's carriage was at the Courthouse door, and they brought him up to Ballawhaine. I remember I was coming downstairs when I saw the carriage draw up at the gate. The next minute your father, with his wild eyes and his bare head, was lifting something out of the inside. Poor Tom! He had never set foot in the house since grandfather had driven him out of it. And little did grandfather think in whose arms he was to travel the last stage of his life's journey."

Philip had fallen asleep. Jem-y-Lord entered with a letter. It was in a large envelope and had come by the insular post.

"Shall I open it?" thought Auntie Nan. She had been opening and replying to Philip's letters during the time of his illness, but this one bore an official seal, and so she hesitated. "Shall I?" she thought, with the knitting needle to her lip. "I will. I may save him some worry."

She fixed her glasses and drew out the letter. It was a summons from the Chancery Division of the High Court of Justice—a petition for divorce. The petitioner's name was Peter Quilliam; the respondent——, the co respondent——.

As Philip awoke from his doze, with the salt breath of the sea in his nostrils and the songs of spring in his ears, Auntie Nan was fumbling with the paper to get it back into the envelope. Her hands trembled, and when she spoke her voice quivered. Philip saw in a moment what had happened. She had stumbled into the pit where the secret of his life lay buried.

The doctor came in at that instant. He looked attentively at Auntie Nan, and said significantly, "You have been nursing too long, Miss Christian, you must go home for a while."

"I will go home at once," she faltered, in a feeble inward voice.

Philip's head was on his breast. Such was the first step on the Calvary he intended to ascend. O God, help him! God support him! God bear up his sinking feet that he might not fall from weakness, or fear, or shame.

XIII.

Cæsar visited Kate at Castle Rushen. He found her lodged in a large and light apartment (once the dining-room of the Lords of Man), indulged with every comfort, and short of nothing but her liberty. As the turnkey pulled the door behind him, Cæsar lifted both hands and cried, "The Lord is my refuge and my strength; a very present help in trouble." Then he inquired if Pete had been there before him, and being answered "No," he said, "The children of this world are wiser in their generation than the children of light." After that he fell to the praise of the Deemster, who had not only given Kate these mercies, comfortable to her carnal body, if dangerous to her soul, but had striven to lighten the burden of her people at the time when he had circulated the report of her death, knowing she was dead indeed, dead in trespasses and sins, and choosing rather that they should mourn her as one who was already dead in fact, than feel shame for her as one that was yet alive in iniquity.

Finally, he dropped his handkerchief on to the slate floor,-went down on one knee by the side of his tall hat, and called on her in prayer to cast in her lot afresh with the people of God. "May her lightness be rebuked, O Lord!" he cried. "Give her to know that until she repents she hath no place among Thy children. And, Lord, succour Thy servant in his hour of tribulation. Let him be well girt up with Christian armour. Help him to cry aloud, amid his tears and his lamentations, 'Though my heart and hers should break, Thy name shall not be dishonoured, my Lord and my God!'"

Rising from his knee and dusting it, Cæsar took up his tall hat, and left Kate as he had found her, crouching by the fire inside the wide ingle of the old hall, covering her face and saying nothing.

He was in this mood of spiritual exaltation as he descended the steps into the Keep, and came upon a man in the dress of a prisoner sweeping with a besom. It was Black Tom. Cæsar stopped in front of him, moved his lips, lifted his face to the sky, shut both eyes, then opened them again, and said in a voice of deep sorrow, "Aw, Thomas! Thomas Quilliam! I'm taking grief to see thee, man. An ould friend, whose hand has rested in my hand, and swilling the floor of a prison! Well, I warned thee often. But thou wast ever stony ground, Thomas. And now thou must see for thyself whether was I right that honesty is the better policy. Look at thee, and look at me. The Lord has delivered me, and prospered me even in temporal things. I have lands and I have houses. And what hast thou thyself? Nothing but thy conscience and thy disgrace. Even thy very clothes they have taken away from thee, and they would take thy hair itself if thou had any."

Black Tom stood with feet flatly planted apart, rested himself on the shank of his besom, and said, "Don't be playing cammag (shindy) with me, Mr. Holy Ghoster. It isn't honesty that's making the diff'rance between us at all—it's luck. You've won and I've lost, you've succeeded and I've failed, you're wearing your chapel hat and I'm in this bit of a saucepan lid, but you're only a reg'lar ould Pharisee, anyway."

Cæsar waved his hand. "I can't take the anger with thee, Thomas," he said, backing himself out. "I thought the devil had been chained since our last camp-meeting, but I was wrong seemingly. He goeth about still like a raging lion, seeking whom he may devour."

"Don't be trying to knock me down with your tex'es," said Thomas, shouldering his besom. "Any cock can crow on his own midden."

"You can't help it, Thomas," said Cæsar, edging away. "It isn't my ould friend that's blaspheming at all. It's the devil that has entered into his heart and is rending him. But cast the devil out, man, or hell will be thy portion."

"I was there last night in my dreams, Cæsar," said Black Tom, following him up. "'Oh, Lord Devil, let me in,' says I. 'Where d'ye come from?' says he. 'The Isle of Man,' says I. 'I'm not taking any more from there till my Bishop comes,' says he. 'Who's that?' says I. 'Bishop Cæsar, the publican—who else?' says he."

"I marvel at thee, Thomas," said Cæsar, half through the small door of the portcullis, "but the sons of Belial have to fight hard for his throne. I'll pray for thee, though, that it be not remembered against thee when(D.V.) there will be weeping and wailing and gnashing of teeth."

That night Cæsar visited the Deemster at Elm Cottage. His eyes glittered, and there was a look of frenzy in his face. He was still in his mood of spiritual pride, and when he spoke it was always with the thees and the thous and in the high pitch of the preacher.

"The Ballawhaine is dead, your Honour," he cried, "They wouldn't have me tell thee before because of thy body's weakness, but now they suffer it. Groanings and moanings and 'stericks of torment! Ter'ble sir, ter'ble! Took a notion he would have water poured out for him at the last. It couldn't wash him clane, though. And shouting with his dying voice, 'I've sinned, O God, I've sinned!' Oh, I delivered my soul, sir; he can clear me of that, anyway. 'Lay hould of a free salvation,' says I. 'I've not lived a right life,' says he. 'Truth enough,' says I; 'you've lived a life of carnal freedom, but now is the appointed time. Say, "Lord, I belaive; help thou my unbelaife."' 'Too late, Mr. Cregeen, too late,' says he, and the word was scarce out of his mouth when he was key-cold in a minute, and gone into the night of all flesh that's lost.

191

Well, it was his own son that killed him, sir; robbed him of every silver sixpence and ruined him. The last mortgage he raised was to keep the young man out of prison for forgery. Bad, sir, bad! To indulge a child to its own damnation is bad. A human infirmity, though; and I'm feeling for the poor sinner myself being tempted—that is to say inclining—but thank the Lord for his strengthening arm———"

"Is he buried?" asked Philip.

"Buried enough, and a poor funeral too, sir," said Cæsar, walking the room with a proud step, the legs straightened, the toes conspicuously turned out. "Driving rain and sleet, sir, the wind in the trees, the grass wet to your calf, and the parson in his white smock under the umbrella. Nobody there to spake of, neither; only myself and the tenants mostly."

"Where was Ross?"

"Gone, sir, without waiting to see his foolish ould father pushed under the sod. Well, there was not much to wait for neither. The young man has been a besom of fire and burnt up everything. Not so much left as would buy a rope to hang him. And Ballawhaine is mine, sir; mine in a way of spak-ing—my son-in-law's, anyway—and he has given me the right to have and to hould it. Aw, a Sabbath time, sir; a Sabbath time. I made up my mind to have it the night the man struck me in my own house in Sulby. He betrayed my daughter at last, sir, and took her from her home, and then her husband lent six thousand pounds on mortgage. 'Do what you like with it,' said he, and I said to myself, 'The man shall starve; he shall be a beggar; he shall have neither bread to eat, nor water to drink, nor a roof to cover him.' And the moment the breath was out of the ould man's body I foreclosed."

Philip was trembling from head to foot. "Do you mean," he faltered, "that that was your reason?"

"It is the Lord's hand on a rascal," said Cæsar, "and proud am I to be the instrument of his vengeance. 'God moves in a mysterious way,' sir. Oh, the Lord is opening His word more and more. And I have more to tell thee, too. Balla-whaine would belong to thyself, sir, if every one had his rights. It was thy grandfather's inheritance, and it should have been thy father's, and it ought to be thine. Take it, sir, take it on thy own terms; it is worth a matter of twelve thousand, but thou shalt have it for nine, and pay for it when the Lord gives thee substance. Thou hast been good to me and to mine, and especially to the poor lost lamb who lies in the Castle to-night in her shame and disgrace. Little did I think I should ever repay thee, though. But it is the Lord's doings. It is marvellous in our eyes. 'Deep in unfathomable mines'———"

Cæsar was pacing the room and speaking in tones of rapture. Philip, who was sitting at the table, rose from it with a look of fear.

"Frightful! frightful!" he muttered. "A mistake! a mistake!"

"The Lord God makes no mistakes, sir," cried Cæsar.

"But what if it was not Ross——" began Philip. Cæsar paid no heed.

"What if it was not Ross——" Cæsar glanced over his shoulder.

"What if it was some one else——" said Philip. Cæsar stopped in front of him.

"Some one you have never thought of—some one you have respected and even held in honour———"

"Who, then?" said Cæsar huskily.

"Mr. Cregeen," said Philip, "it is hard for me to speak. I had not intended to speak yet; but I should hold myself in horror if I were silent now. You have been living in awful error. Whatever the cost, whatever the consequences, you must not remain in that error a moment longer. It was not Ross who took away your daughter."

"Who was it?" cried Cæsar. His voice had the sound of a cracked bell.

Philip struggled hard. He tried to confess. His eyes wandered about the walls. "As you have cherished a mistaken resentment," he faltered, "so you have nourished a mistaken gratitude."

"Who? who?" cried Cæsar, looking fixedly into Philip's face.

Philip's rigid fingers were crawling over the papers on the table like the claws of crabs. They touched the summons from the Chancery Court, and he picked it up.

"Read this," he said, and held it out to Cæsar.

Cæsar took it, but continued to look at Philip with eyes that were threatening in their wildness. Philip felt that in a moment their positions had been changed. He was the judge no longer, but only a criminal at the bar of this old man, this grim fanatic, half-mad already with religious mania.

"The Lord of Hosts is mighty," muttered Cæsar; and then Philip heard the paper crinkle in his hand.

Cæsar was feeling for his spectacles. When he had liberated them from the sheath, he put them on the bridge of his nose upside down. With the two glasses against the wrinkles of his forehead and his eyes still uncovered, he held the paper at arm's length and tried to read it. Then he took out his red print handkerchief to dust the spectacles. Fumbling spectacles and sheath and handkerchief and paper in his trembling hands together, he muttered again in a quavering voice, as if to fortify himself against what he was to see, "The Lord of Hosts is mighty."

He read the paper at length, and there was no mistaking it. "Quilliam v. Quilliam and Christian (Philip)."

He laid the summons on the table, and returned his spectacles to their sheath. His breathing made noises in his nostrils. "*Ugh cha nee!*" (woe is me), he muttered. "*Ugh cha nee! Ugh cha nee!*"

Then he looked helplessly around and said, "Depart from me, for I am a sinful man, O Lord."

The vengeance that he had built up day by day had fallen in a moment into ruins. His hypocrisy was stripped naked. "I see how it is," he said in a hoarse voice. "The Lord has de-ceaved me to punish me. It is the public-house. Ye cannot serve God and mammon. What's gained on the devil's back is lost under his belly. I thought I was a child of God, but the deceitfulness of riches has choked the word. *Ugh cha nee! Ugh cha nee!* My prosperity has been like the quails, only given with the intent of choking me. *Ugh cha nee!*"

His spiritual pride was broken down. The Almighty had refused to be made a tool of. He took up his hat and rolled his arm over it the wrong way of the nap. Half-way to the door he paused. "Well, I'll be laving you; good-day, sir," he said, nodding his head slowly. "The Lord's been knowing what you were all the time seemingly. But what's the use of His knowing—He never tells on nobody. And I've been calling on sinners to flee from the wrath, and He's been letting the devils make a mock at myself! *Ugh cha nee! Ugh cha nee!*"

Philip had slipped back in his chair, and his head had fallen forward' on the table. He heard the old man go out; he heard his heavy step drop slowly down the stairs; he heard his foot dragging on the path outside. "*Ugh cha nee! Ugh cha nee!*" The word rang in his heart like a knell.

Jem-y-Lord, who had been out in the town, came back in great excitement.

"Such news, your Honour! Such splendid news!"

"What is it?" said Philip, without lifting his head.

"They're signing petitions all over the island, asking the Queen to make you Governor."

"God in heaven!" said Philip; "that would be frightful."

XIV.

When Philip was fit to go out, they brought up a carriage and drove him round the bay. The town had awakened from its winter sleep, and the harbour was a busy and cheerful scene. More than a hundred men had come from their crofts in the country, and were making their boats ready for the mackerel-fishing at Kinsale. There was a forest of masts where the flat hulls had been, the taffrails and companions were touched up with paint, and the newly-barked nets were being hauled over the quay.

"Good morning, Dempster," cried the men.

They all saluted him, and some of them, after their Manx fashion, drew up at the carriage-door, lifted their caps with their tarry hands, and said—

"Taking joy to see you out again, Dempster. When a man's getting over an attack like that, it's middling clear the Lord's got work for him."

Philip answered with smiles and bows and cheerful words, but the kindness oppressed him. He was thinking of Kate. She was the victim of his success. For all that he received she had paid the penalty. He thought of her dreams, her golden dreams, her dreams of going up side by side and hand in hand with the man she loved. "Oh, my love, my love!" he murmured. "Only a little longer."

The doctor was waiting for him when he reached home.

"I have something to say to you, Deemster," he said, with averted face. "It's about your aunt."

"Is she ill?" said Philip.—"Very ill."

"But I've inquired daily."

"By her express desire the truth has been kept back from you."

"The carriage is still at the door——" began Philip.

"I've never seen any one sink so rapidly. She's all nerve. No doubt the nursing exhausted her."

"It's not that—I'll go up immediately."

"She was to expect you at five."

"I cannot wait," said Philip, and in a moment he was on the road. "O God!" he thought, "how steep is the path I have to tread."

On getting to Ballure, he pushed through the hall and stepped upstairs. At the door of Auntie Nan's bedroom he was met by Martha, the housemaid, now the nurse. She looked surprised, and made some nervous show of shutting him out. Before she could de so he was already in the room. The air was heavy with the smell of medicines and vinegar and the odours of sick life.

"Hush!" said Martha, with a movement of lips and eyebrows.

Auntie Nan was asleep in a half-sitting position on the bed. It was a shock to see the change in her. The beautiful old face was white and drawn with pain; the chin was hanging heavily; the eyes were half open; there was no cap on her head; her hair was straggling loosely and was dull as tow.

"She must be very ill," said Philip under his breath.

"Very," said Martha. "She wasn't expecting you until five, sir."

"Has the doctor told her? Does she know?"

"Yes, sir; but she doesn't mind that. She knows she's dying, and is quite resigned—quite—and quite cheerful—but she fears if you knew—hush!"

There was a movement on the bed.

"She'll be shocked if she—and she's not ready to receive—in here, sir," whispered Martha, and she motioned to the back of a screen that stood between the door and the bed.

There was a deep sigh, a sound as of the moistening of dry lips, and then the voice of Auntie Nan—not her own familiar voice, but a sort of vanishing echo of it. "What is the time, Martha?"

"Twenty minutes wanting five, ma'am."

"So late! It wasn't nice of you to let me sleep so long, Martha. I'm expecting the Governor at five. What a mercy he hasn't come earlier. It wouldn't be right to keep him waiting, and then—bring me the sponge, girl. Moisten it first. Now the towel. The comb next. That's better. How lifeless my hair is, though. Oil, you say? I wonder! I've never used it in my life: but at a time like this—well, just a little, then—there, that will do. Bring me a cap—the one with the pink bow in it. My face is so pale—it will give me a little colour. That will do. You couldn't tell I had been ill, could you? Not very ill, anyway? Now side everything away. The medicines too—put them in the cupboard. So many bottles. 'How ill she must have been!' he would say. And now open the drawer on the left, Martha, the one with the key in it, and bring me the paper on the top. Yes, the white paper. The folded one with the endorsement. Endorsement means writing on the back, Martha. Ah! I've lived all my life among lawyers. Lay it on the counterpane. The keys? Lay them beside it. No, put them behind my pillow, just at my back. Yes, there—lower, though, deeper still—that's right. Now set a chair, so that he can sit beside me. This side of the bed—no, this side. Then the light will be on him, and I will be able to see his face—my eyes are not so good as they were, you know. A little farther back—not quite so much, neither—that will do. Ah!"

There was a long breath of satisfaction, and then Auntie Nan said—

"I suppose it's——what time is it now, Martha?"

"Ten minutes wanting five, ma'am."

"Did you tell Jane about the cutlets? He likes them with bread-crumbs, you know. I hope she won't forget to say 'Your Excellency.' I shall hear his voice the moment he comes into the hall. My ears are no worse, if my eyes are. Perhaps he won't speak, though, 'She's been so ill,' he'll think. Martha, I think you had better open the door. Jane is so forgetful. She might say things, too. If he asks, 'How is she to-day, Martha' you must answer quite brightly, 'Better to-day, your Excellency.'"

There was an exclamation of pain.

"Oh! Ugh—Oo! Oh, blessed Lord Jesus!"

"Are you sure you are well enough, ma'am? Hadn't I better tell him——"

"No, I'll be worse to-morrow, and the next day worse still. Give me a dose of medicine, Martha—the morning medicine—the one that makes me cheerful. Thank you, Martha. If I feel the pain when he is here, I'll bear it as long as I can, and then I'll say, 'I'm finding myself drowsy, Philip; you had better go and lie down.' Will you understand that, Martha?"

"Yes, ma'am," said Martha.

"I'm afraid we must be a little deceitful, Martha. But we can't help that, can we? You see he has to be installed yet, and that is always a great excitement. If he thought I was very ill, now—*very*, very ill, you know—yes, I really think he would wish to postpone it, and I wouldn't have that for worlds and worlds. He has always been so fond of his old auntie. Well, it's the way with these boys. I daresay people wonder why he has never married, being so great and so prosperous. That was for my sake. He knew I should——"

Philip was breathing heavily. Auntie Nan listened. "I'm sure there's somebody in the hall, Martha. Is it——? Yes, it's——; Go down to him quick——"

"Yes, ma'am," said Martha, making a noise with the screen to cover Philip's escape on tiptoe. Then she came to him on the landing, wiping her eyes with her apron, and pretended to lead Philip back to the room.

"My boy! my boy!" cried Auntie Nan, and she folded him in her arms.

The transformation was wonderful. She had a look of youth now, almost a look of gaiety. "I've heard the great, great news," she whispered, taking his hand.

"That's only a rumour, Auntie," said Philip. "Are you better?"

"Oh, but it will come true. Yes, yes, I'm better. I'm sure it will come true. And, dear heart, what a triumph! I dreamt it all the night before I heard of it. You were on the top of the Tynwald, and there was a great crowd. But come and sit down and tell me everything. So you are better yourself? Quite strong again, dear? Oh, yes, any where, Philip-sit anywhere. Here, this chair will do—this one by my side. Ah! How well you look!"

She was carried away by her own gaiety. Leaning back on the pillow, but still keeping his hand in hers, she said, "Do you know, Philip Christian, who is the happiest person in the world? I'm sure you don't, for all you're so clever. So I'll tell you. Perhaps you think it's a beautiful young wife just married to a husband who worships her. Well, you're quite, quite wrong, sir. It's an old, old lady, very, very old, and very feeble, just tottering on, and not expecting to live a great while longer, but with her sons about her, grown up, and big, and strong, and having all the world before them. That's the happiest person on earth. And I'm the next thing to it, for my boy—my own boy's boy——"

She broke off, and then, with a far-off look, she said, "I wonder will he think I've done my duty!"

"Who?" asked Philip.

"Your father," she answered.

Then she turned to the maid and said, quite gaily, "You needn't wait, Martha. His Excellency will call you when I want my medicine. Won't you, your Excellency?"

Philip could not find it in his heart to correct her again. The girl left the room. Auntie Nan glanced at the closing door, then reached over to Philip with an air of great mystery, and whispered—

"You mustn't be shocked, Philip, or surprised, or fancy I'm very ill, or that I'm going to die; but what do you think I've done?"

"Nay, what?"

"I've made my will! Is that very terrible?"

194

"You've done right, Auntie," said Philip.

"Yes, the High Bailiff has been up and everything is in order, every little thing. See," and she lifted the paper that the maid had laid on the counterpane. "Let me tell you." She nodded her head as she ran over the items. "Some little legacies first, you know. There's Martha, such a good girl—I've left her my silk dresses. Then old Mary, the housemaid at Ballawhaine. Poor old thing! she's been down with rheumatism three years, and flock beds get so lumpy—I've left her my feather one. I thought at first I should like you to have my little income. Do you know, your old auntie is quite an old miser. I've grown so fond of my little money. And it seemed so sweet to think—but then you don't want it now, Philip. It would be nothing to you, would it? I've been thinking, though—now, what do you think I've been thinking of doing with my little fortune?"

Philip stroked the wrinkled fingers with his other hand.

"What's right, I'm sure, Auntie. What is it?"

"You would never guess."—"No?"

"I've been thinking," with sudden gravity. "Philip, there's nobody in the world so unhappy as a poor gentlewoman who has slipped and fallen. Then this one's father, he has turned his back on her, they're telling me, and of course she can't expect anything from her husband. I've been thinking, now——"

"Yes?" said Philip, with his eyes down.

"To tell you the truth, I've been thinking it would be so nice——"

And then, nervously, faltering, in a quavering voice, with many excuses, out came the great secret, the mighty strategy. Auntie Nan had willed her fortune to Kate.

"You're an angel, Auntie," said Philip in a thick voice.

But he saw through her artifice. She was talking of Kate, but she was thinking of himself. She was trying to relieve him of an embarrassment; to remove an impediment that lay in his path; to liberate his conscience; to cover up his fault; to conceal everything.

"And then this house, dear," said Auntie Nan. "It's yours, but you'll never want it. It's been a dear little harbour of refuge, but the storm is over now. Would you—do you see any objection—perhaps you might—could you not let the poor soul come and live here with her little one, after I—when all is over, I mean—and she is—eh?"

Philip could not speak. He took the wrinkled hand and drew it up to his lips.

The old soul was beside herself with joy. "Then you're sure I've done right? Quite sure? Lock it up in the drawer again, dearest The top one on the left. Oh, the keys? Dear me, yes; where are the keys? How tiresome! I remember now. They're at the back of my pillow. Will you call Martha? Or perhaps you would yourself—will you?" (very artfully)—"you don't mind then? Yes, that's it; more this way, though, a little more—ah! My boy! my boy!"

The old dove's second strategy had succeeded also. In fumbling behind her pillow for the keys, Philip had to put his arms about her again, and she was kissing him on the forehead and on the cheeks.

Then came a spasm of pain. It dragged at her features, but her smile struggled through it. She fetched a difficult breath, and said—

"And now—dear—I'm finding myself—a little drowsy—how selfish of me—your cutlets—browned—nicely browned—breadcrumbs, you know——"

Philip fled from the room and summoned Martha. He wandered aimlessly about the house for hours that night. At one moment he found himself in the blue room, Auntie Nan's workroom, so full of her familiar things—the spinning-wheel, the frame of the sampler, the old-fashioned piano, the scent of lavender—all the little evidences of her presence, so dainty, so orderly, so sweet A lamp was burning for the convenience of the doctor, but there was no fire.

The doctor came again towards ten o'clock. There was nothing to be done; nothing to be hoped; still she might live until morning, if——

At midnight Philip crept noiselessly to the bedroom. The condition was unaltered. He was going to lie down, but wished to be awakened if there was any change.

It was long before he dropped off, and he seemed to have slept only a moment when there was a knocking at his door. He heard it while he was still sleeping. The dawn had broken, the streamers of the sun were rising out of the sea. A sparrow in the garden was hacking the air with its monotonous chirp.

Auntie Nan was far spent, yet the dragging expression of pain was gone, and a serenity almost angelic overspread her face. When she recognised Philip she felt for his hand, guided it to her heart, and kept it there. Only a few words did she speak, for her breath was short. She commended her soul to God. Then, with a look of pallid sunshine, she beckoned to Philip. He stooped his ear to her lips, and she whispered, "Hush, dearest! Never tell any one, for nobody ever knew—ever dreamt—but I loved your father—and—*God gave him to me in you.*"

The dear old dove had delivered herself of her last great secret. Philip put his lips to her cheek, iced already over the damps and chills of death. Then the eyes closed, the sweet old head slid back, the lips changed their colour, but still lay open as with a smile. Thus died Auntie Nan, peacefully, hopefully, trustfully, almost joyfully, in the fulness of her love and of her pride.

"O God," thought Philip, "let me go on with my task. Give me strength to withstand the temptation of love like this."

Her love had tempted him all his life His father had been twenty years dead, but she had kept his spirit alive—his aims, his ambitions, his fears, and the lessons of his life. There lay the beginnings of his ruin, his degradation, and the first cause of his deep duplicity. He had recovered everything that had been lost; he had gained all that his little world could give; and what was the worth of it? What was the price he had paid for it? "What shall it profit a man if he gain the whole world and lose his own soul?"

Philip put his lips to the cold forehead. "Sweet soul, forgive me! God strengthen me! Let me not fail at this last moment."

XV.

Philip did not go back to Elm Cottage. He buried Auntie Nan at the foot of his father's grave. There was no room at either side, his mother's sunken grave being on the left and the railed tomb of his grandfather on the right. They had to remove a willow two feet nearer to the path.

When all was over he returned home alone, and spent the afternoon in gathering up Auntie Nan's personal belongings, labelling some of them and locking them up in the blue room. The weather had been troubled for some days. Spots had been seen on the sun. There were magnetic disturbances, and on the night before the aurora had pulsed in the northern sky. When the sun was near to sinking there was a brilliant lower sky to the west, with a bank of rolling cloud above it like a thick thatch roof, and a shaft of golden light dipping down into the sea, as if an angel had opened a door in heaven. After the sun had gone a fiery red bar stretched across the sky, and there were low rumblings of thunder.

Pausing in his work to look out on the beach, Philip saw a man riding hard on horseback. It was a messenger from Government Offices. He drew up at the gate. A moment later the messenger was in Philip's room handing him a letter.

If anybody had seen the Deemster as he took that letter he must have thought it his death-warrant. A deadly pallor came to his face when he broke the seal of the envelope and drew out the contents. It was a commission from the Home Office. Philip was appointed Governor of the Isle of Man. "My punishment, my punishment!" he thought. The higher he rose, the lower he had to fall. It was a cruel kindness, a painful distinction, an awful penalty. Truly the steps of this Calvary were steep. Would he ever ascend it?

The messenger was bowing and smirking before him. "Thousand congratulations, your Excellency!"

"Thank you, my lad. Go downstairs. They'll give you something to eat."

A moment later Jem-y-Lord came into the room on some pretence and hopped about like a bird. "Yes, your Excellency—No, your Excellency—Quite so, your Excellency."

Martha came next, and met Philip on the landing with a courageous smile and a courtesy. And the whole house, lately so dark and sad, seemed to lighten and to laugh, as when, after a sleepless night, you look, and lo! the daylight is on the blind; you listen and the birds are twittering in their cages below the stairs.

"*She* will hear it too," thought Philip.

He wrote her two lines of a letter, the first that he had penned since his illness—

"Keep up heart, dear; I will be with you soon."

This, without signature or superscription, he put into an envelope, and addressed. Then he went out and posted it himself.

There was lightning as he returned. He felt as if he would like to wander away in it down to Port Mooar, and round by the caves, and under the cliffs, where the sea-birds scream.

XVI.

The night had fallen, and he was sitting in his room, when there was a clamour of loud voices in the hall. Some one was calling for the Deemster. It was Nancy Joe. She was newly returned from Sulby. Something had happened to Cæsar, and nobody could control him.

"Go to him, your Honour," she cried from the doorway. "It's only yourself that has power with him, and we don't know in the world what's doing on the man. He's got a ram's horn at him, and is going blowing round the house like the mischief, calling on the Lord to bring it down, and saying it's the walls of Jericho."

Philip sent for a carriage, and set off for Sulby immediately. The storm had increased by this time. Loud peals of thunder echoed in the hills. Forks of lightning licked the trunks of the trees and ran like serpents along the branches. As they were going by the church at Lezayre, the coachman reached over from the box, and said, "There's something going doing over yonder, sir. See?"

A bright gleam lit up the dark sky in the direction they were taking. At the turn of the road by the "Ginger," somebody passed them running.

"What's yonder?" called the coachman.

And a voice out of the darkness answered him, "The 'Fairy' is struck by lightning, and Cæsar's gone mad."

It was the fact. While Cæsar in his mania had been blowing his ram's horn around his public-house under the delusion that it was Jericho, the lightning had struck it. The fire was past all hope of subduing. A great hole had been burnt into the roof, and the flames were leaping through it as through a funnel. All Sulby seemed to be on the spot. Some were dragging furniture out of the burning house; others were running with buckets to the river and throwing water on the blazing thatch.

But encircling everything was the figure of a man going round and round with great plunging strides, over the road, across the river, and through the mill-pond behind, blowing a horn in fierce, unearthly blasts, and crying in a voice of triumph and mockery, first to this worker and then to that, "No use, I tell thee. Thou can never put it out. It's fire from heaven. Didn't I say I'd bring it down?"

It was Cæsar. His eyes glittered, his mouth worked convulsively, and his cheeks were as black with the flying soot as the "colley" of the pot.

When he saw Philip, he came up to him with a terrible smile on his fierce black face, and, pointing to the house, he cried above the babel of voices, the roar of the thunder, and crackle of the fire, "An unclean spirit lived in it, sir. It has been tormenting me these ten years."

He seemed to listen and to hear something. "That's it roaring," he cried, and then he laughed with wild delight.

"Compose yourself, Mr. Cregeen," said Philip, and he tried to take him by the arm.

But Cæsar broke away, blew a terrific blast on his ram's horn, and went striding round the house again. When he came back the next time there was a deep roll of thunder in the air, and he said, "It's the Ballawhaine. He had the stone five years, and he used to groan so."

Again Philip entreated him to compose himself. It was useless. Round and round the burning house he went, blowing his horn, and calling on the workers to stop their ungodly labour, for the Lord had told him to blow down the walls of Jericho, and he had burnt them down instead.

The people began to be afraid of his frenzy. "They'll have to put the man in the Castle," said one. "Or have him chained up in an outhouse," said another. "They kept the Kirk Maug-hold lunatic fifteen years on the straw in the gable loft, and his children in the house grew up to be men and women." "It's the girl that's doing on Cæsar. Shame on the daughters that bring ruin to their old fathers!"

Still Cæsar went careering round the fire, blowing his ram's horn and crying, "No use! It's the Lord God!"

The more the fire blazed, the more it resisted the efforts of the people to subdue it, the more fierce and unearthly were Cæsar's blasts and the more triumphant his cries.

At last Grannie stepped out and stopped him. "Come home, father," she whimpered. He looked at her with bewildered eyes, then he looked at the burning house, and he seemed to recover himself in a moment.

"Come home, bogh," said Grannie tenderly.

"I've got no home," said Cæsar in a helpless way. "And I've got no money. The fire has taken all."

"No matter, father," said Grannie. "We had nothing when we began; we'll begin again."

Then Cæsar fell to mumbling texts of Scripture, and Grannie to soothing him after her simple fashion.

"'My soul is passing through deep waters. I am feeble and sore broken. Save me, O God, for the waters are come in unto my soul. I sink in deep mire, where there is no standing.'"

"Aw, no Cæsar, we're on the road now. It's dry enough here, anyway."

"'Many bulls have compassed me; great bulls of Bashan have beset me round. Save me from the lion's mouth; for Thou hast heard me from the horns of the unicorn.'"

"Never mind the lion and the unicorn, father, but come and we'll change thy wet trousers."

"'Purge me with hyssop, and I shall be clean; wash me, and I shall be whiter than snow.'"

"Aw, yes, we'll wash thee enough when we get to Ramsey. Come, then, bogh."

He had dropped his ram's horn somewhere, and she took him by the hand. Then he suffered himself to be led away, and the two old children went off into the darkness.

XVII.

There was a letter waiting for Philip at home. It was from the Clerk of the Rolls. Only a few lines scribbled on the back of a draft deposition, telling him the petition for divorce had been heard that day within closed doors. The application had been granted, and all was settled and comfortable.

"I don't want to hurt your already much wounded feelings, Christian," wrote the Clerk of the Rolls, "or to add anything to your responsibility when you come to make provision for the woman, but I must say she has given up for your sake a deuced good honest fellow."

"I know it," said Philip aloud.

"When I told him that all was over, and that his erring wife would trouble him no more, I thought he was going to burst out crying."

But Philip had no time yet to think of Pete. All his heart was with Kate. She would receive the official intimation of the divorce, and it would fall on her in her prison like a blow. She would think of herself, with all the world against her, and of him with all the world at his feet. He wanted to run to her, to pluck her up in his arms, to kiss her on the lips, and say, "Mine, mine at last!" His wife—her husband—all forgiven—all forgotten!

Philip spent the rest of the night in writing a letter to Kate. He told her he could not live without her; that now for the first time she was his, and he was hers, and they were one; that their love was re-born, and that he would spend the future in atoning for the wrongs he had inflicted upon her in the past. Then he dropped to the sheer babble of affection and poured out his heart to her—all the babydom of love,

197

the foolish prattle, the tender nonsense. What matter that he was Governor now, and the first man in the island? He forgot all about it. What matter that he was writing to a fallen woman in prison? He only remembered it to forget himself the more.

"Just a little longer, my love, just a little longer. I am coming to you, I am coming. Older, perhaps, perhaps sadder, and a boy no more, but hopeful still, and ready to face whatever fate befall, with her I love beside me."

Next day Jem-y-Lord took this letter to Castle Rushen and brought back an answer. It was one line only—"My darling! At last! At last! Oh, Philip! Philip! *But what about our child?*"

XVIII.

The proclamation of Philip's appointment as Governor of the Isle of Man had been read in the churches, and nailed up on the doors of the Court-houses, and the Clerk of the Rolls was pushing on the arrangements for the installation.

"Let it be on the Tuesday of Easter week," he wrote, "and of course at Castle Rushen. The retiring Governor is ready to return for that day to deliver up his seals of office and to receive your commission."

"P. S.—Private. And if you think that soft-voiced girl has been long enough 'At Her Majesty's pleasure,' I will release her. Not that she is taking any harm at all, but we had better get these little accounts squared off before your great day comes. Meantime you may wish to provide for her future. Be liberal, Christian; you can afford to treat her liberally. But what am I saying? Don't I know that you will be ridiculously over-generous?"

Philip answered this letter promptly. "The Tuesday of Easter week will do as well as any other day. As to the lady, let her stay where she is until the morning of the ceremony, when I will myself settle everything."

Philip's correspondence was now plentiful, and he had enough work to cope with it The four towns of the island vied with each other in efforts to show him honour. Douglas, as the scene of his career, wished to entertain him at a banquet; Ramsey, as his birthplace, wanted to follow him in procession. He declined all invitations.

"I am in mourning," he wrote. "And besides, I am not well."

"Ah! no," he thought, "nobody shall reproach me when the times comes."

There was no pause, no pity, no relenting rest in the world's kindness. It began to take shapes of almost fiendish cruelty in his mind, as if the devil's own laughter was behind it.

He inquired about Pete. Hardly anybody knew anything; hardly anybody cared. The spendthrift had come down to his last shilling, and sold up the remainder of his furniture. The broker was to empty the house on Easter Tuesday. That was all. Not a word about the divorce. The poor neglected victim, forgotten in the turmoil of his wrongdoer's glory, had that last strength of a strong man—the strength to be silent and to forgive.

Philip asked about the child. She was still at Elm Cottage in the care of the woman with the upturned nose and the shrill voice. Every night he devised plans for getting possession of Kate's little one, and every morning he abandoned them, as difficult or cruel or likely to be spurned.

On Easter Monday he was busy in his room at Ballure, with a mounted messenger riding constantly between his gate and Government offices. He had spent the morning on two important letters. Both were to the Home Secretary. One was sealed with his seal as Deemster; the other was written on the official paper of Government House. He was instructing the messenger to register these letters when, through the open door, he heard a formidable voice in the hall. It was Pete's voice. A moment afterwards Jem-y-Lord came up with a startled face.

"He's here himself, your Excellency. Whatever *am* I to do with him?"

"Bring him up," said Philip.

Jem began to stammer. "But—but—and then the Bishop may be here any minute."

"Ask the Bishop to wait in the room below."

Pete was heard coming upstairs. "Aisy all, aisy! Stoop your lil head, bogh. That's the ticket!"

Philip had not spoken to Pete since the night of the drinking of the brandy and water in the bedroom. He could not help it—his hand shook. There would be a painful scene.

"Stoop again, darling. There you are."

And then Pete was in the room. He was carrying the child on one shoulder; they were both in their best clothes. Pete looked older and somewhat thinner; the tan of his cheeks was fretted out in pale patches under the eyes, which were nevertheless bright. He had the face of a man who had fought a brave fight with life and been beaten, yet bore the world no grudge. Jem-y-Lord and the messenger were gone from the room in a moment, and the door was closed.

"What d'ye think of that, Phil? Isn't she a lil beauty?"

Pete was dancing the child on his knee and looking sideways down at it with eyes of rapture.

"She's as sweet as an angel," said Philip in a low tone.

"Isn't she now?" said Pete, and then he rattled on as if he were the happiest man alive. "You've been wanting something like this yourself this long time, Phil. 'Deed you have, though. It would be diverting you wonderful. Ter'ble fun there is in babies. Talk about playactorers! They're only funeral mutes where babies come. Bittending this and bittending that—it's mortal amusing they are. You'd be getting up from your books, tired shocking, and ready for a bit of fun, and going to the stair-head and shouting down, 'Where's my lil woman?' Then up she'd be coming, step by step, houlding on to the bannisters, dot and carry one. And my gracious, the dust there'd be here in the study! You down on the carpet on all fours, and the lil one straddled across your back and slipping down to your neck. Same for all the world as the man in the picture with the world atop of his shoulders. And your own lil world would be up there, too, laughing and crowing mortal. And then at night, Phil, at night—getting up from your summonses and your warrantees, and going creeping to the lil one's room tippie-toe, tippie-toe, and 'Is she sleeping comfor'bly?' thinks you; and listening at the crack of the door, and hearing her breathing, and slipping in to look, and everything quiet, and the red fire on her lil face, and 'Grod bless her, the darling!' says you, and then back to your desk content. Aw, you'll have to be having a lil one of your own one of these days, Phil."

"He has come to say something," thought Philip.

The child wriggled off Pete's knee and began to creep about the floor. Philip tried to command himself and to talk easily.

"And how have you been yourself, Pete?" he asked.

"Well," said Pete, meddling with his hair, "only middling, somehow." He looked down at the carpet, and faltered, "You'll be wondering at me, Phil, but, you see "—he hesitated—"not to tell you a word of a lie——" then, with a rush, "I'm going foreign again; that's the fact."

"Again?"

"Well, I am," said Pete, looking ashamed. "Yes, truth enough, that's what I'm thinking of doing. You see," with a persuasive air, "when a man's bitten by travel it's like the hydrophobia ezactly, he can't rest no time in one bed at all. Must be running here and running there—and running reg'lar. It's the way with me, anyway. Used to think the ould island would be big enough for the rest of my days. But, no! I'm longing shocking for the mines again, and the compound, and the niggers, and the wild life out yonder. 'The sea's calling me,' you know." And then he laughed.

Philip understood him—Pete meant to take himself out of the way. "Shall you stay long?" he faltered.

"Well, yes, I was thinking so," said Pete. "You see, the stuff isn't panning out now same as it used to, and fortunes aren't made as fast as they were in my time. Not that I'm wanting a fortune, neither—is it likely now? But, still and for all—well, I'll be away a good spell, anyway."

Philip tried to ask if he intended to go soon.

"To-morrow, sir, by the packet to Liverpool, for the sailing on Wednesday. I've been going the rounds saying 'goodbye' to the ould chums—Jonaique, and John the Widow, and Niplightly, and Kelly the postman. Not much heart at some of them; just a bit of a something stowed away in their giblets; but it isn't right to be expecting too much at all. This is the only one that doesn't seem willing to part with me."

Pete's dog had followed him into the room, and was sitting soberly by the side of his chair. "There's no shaking him off, poor ould chap."

The dog got up and wagged his stump.

"Well, we've tramped the world together, haven't we, Dempster? He doesn't seem tired of me yet neither." Pete's face lengthened. "But there's Grannie, now. The ould angel is going about like a bit of a thunder-cloud, and doesn't know in the world whether to burst on me or not. Thinks I've been cruel, seemingly. I can't be explaining to her neither. Maybe you'll set it right for me when I'm gone, sir. It's you for a job like that, you know. Don't want her to be thinking hard of me, poor ould thing."

Pete whistled at the child, and halloed to it, and then, in a lower tone, he continued, "Not been to Castletown, sir. Got as far as Ballasalla, and saw the castle tower. Then my heart was losing me, and I turned back. You'll say good-bye for me, Phil Tell her I forgave—no, not that, though. Say I left her my love—that won't do neither. *You'll* know best what to say when the time comes, Phil, so I lave it with you. Maybe you'll tell her I went away cheerful and content, and, well, happy—why not? No harm in saying that at all. Not breaking my heart, anyway, for when a man's a man—H'm!" clearing his throat, "I'm bad dreadful these days wanting a smook in the mornings. May I smook here? I may? You're good, too."

He cut his tobacco with his discoloured knife, rolled it, charged his pipe, and lit it.

"Sorry to be going away just before your own great day, Phil. I'll get the skipper to fire a round as we're steaming by Castletown, and if there's a band aboord I'll tip them a trifle to play 'Myle Charaine.' That'll spake to you like the blackbird's whistle, as the saying is. Looks like deserting you, though. But, chut! it would be no surprise to me at all. I've seen it coming these years and years. 'You'll be the first Manxman living,' says I the day I sailed before. You've not deceaved me neither. D'ye remember the morning on the quay, and the oath between the pair of us? Me swearing you same as a high bailiff—nothing and nobody to come between us—d'ye mind it, Phil? And nothing has, and nothing shall."

He puffed at his pipe, and said significantly, "You'll be getting married soon. Aw, you will, I know you will, I'm sarten sure you will."

Philip could not look into his face. He felt little and mean.

"You're a wise man, sir, and a great man, but if a plain common chap may give you a bit of advice—aw, but you'll be losing no time, though, I'll not be here myself to see it. I'll be on the water, maybe, with the waves washing agen the gun'ale, and the wind rattling in the rigging, and the ship burrowing into the darkness of the sea. But I'll be knowing it's morning at home, and the sun shining, and a sort of a warm quietness everywhere, and you and her at the ould church together."

The pipe was puffing audibly.

"Tell her I lave her my blessing. Tell her—but the way I'm smooking, it's shocking. Your curtains will be smelling thick twist for a century."

Philip's moist eyes were following the child along the floor.

"What about the little one?" he asked with difficulty.

199

"Ah I tell you the truth, Phil, that's the for I came. Well, mostly, anyway. You see, a child isn't fit for a compound ezactly. Not but they're thinking diamonds of a lil thing out there, specially if it's a girl. But still and for all, with niggers about and chaps as rough as a thornbush and no manners to spake of——"

Philip interrupted eagerly—"Will you leave her with Grannie!"

"Well, no, that wasn't what I was thinking. Grannie's a bit ould getting and she's had her whack. Wanting aisement in her ould days, anyway. Then she'll be knocking under before the lil one's up—that's only to be expected. No, I was thinking—what d'ye think I was thinking now?"

"What?" said Philip with quick-coming breath. He did not raise his head.

"I was thinking—well, yes, I was, then—it's a fact, though—I was thinking maybe yourself, now——"

"Pete!"

Philip had started up and grasped Pete by the hand, but he could say no more, he felt crushed by Pete's magnanimity. And Pete went on as if he were asking a great favour. "'She's been your heart's blood to you, Pete,' thinks I to my-. self, 'and there isn't nobody but himself you could trust her with—nobody else you would give her up to. He'll love her,'. thinks I; 'he'll cherish her; he'll rear her as if she was his own; he'll be same thing as a father itself to her'——"

Philip was struggling to keep up.

"I've been laving something for her too," said Pete.

"No, no!"

"Yes, though, one of the first Manx estates going. Cæsar had the deeds, but I've been taking them to the High Bailiff, and doing everything regular. When I'm gone, sir——"

Philip tried to protest.

"Aw, but a man can lave what he likes to his own, sir, can't he?"

Philip was silent. He could say nothing. The make-believe was to be kept up to the last tragic moment.

"And out yonder, lying on my hunk in the sheds—good mattresses and thick blankets, Phil, nothing to complain of at all—I'll be watching her growing up, year by year, same as if she was under my eye constant. 'She's in pinafores now' thinks I. 'Now she's in long frocks, and is doing up her hair.' 'She's as straight as an osier now, and red as a rose, and the best looking girl in the island, and the spitting picture of what her mother used to be.' Aw, I'll be seeing her in my mind's eye, sir, plainer nor any potegraph."

Pete puffed furiously at his pipe. "And the mother, I'll be seeing herself, too. A woman every inch of her, God bless her. Wherever there's a poor girl lying in her shame she'll be there, I'll go bail on that. And yourself—I'll be seeing yourself, sir, whiter, maybe, and the sun going down on you, but strong for all. And when any poor fellow has had a knock-down blow, and the world is darkening round him, he'll be coming to you for light and for strength, and you'll be houlding out the right hand to him, because you're knowing yourself what it is to fall and get up again, and because you're a man, and Grod has made friends with you."

Pete rammed his thumb into his pipe, and stuffed it, still smoking, into his waistcoat pocket. "Chut!" he said huskily. "The talk a man'll be putting out when he's going away foreign! All for poethry then, or something of that spacious. H'm! h'm!" clearing his throat, "must be giving up the pipe, though. Not much worth for the voice at all."

Philip could not speak. The strength and grandeur of the man overwhelmed him. It cut him to the heart that Pete could never see, could never hear, how he would wash away his shame.

The child had crawled across the room to an open cabinet that stood in one corner, and there possessed herself of a shell, which she was making show of holding to her ear.

"Well, did you ever?" cried Pete. "Look at that child now. She's knowing it's a shell. 'Deed she is, though. Aw, crawling reg'lar, sir, morning to night. Would you like to see the prettiest sight in the world, Phil?" He went down on his knees and held out his arms. "Come here, you lil sandpiper. Fix that chair a piece nearer, sir—that's the ticket. Good thing Nancy isn't here. She'd be on to us like the mischief. Wonderful handy with babies, though, and if anybody was wanting a nurse now—a stepmother's breath is cold—but Nancy! My gough, you daren't look over the hedge at her lammie but she's shouting fit for an earth wake. Stand nice, now, Kitty, stand nice, bogh! The woman's about right, too—the lil one's legs are like bits of qualebone. 'Come, now, bogh, come?"

Pete put the child to stand with its back to the chair, and then leaned towards it with his arms outspread. The child staggered a step in the sea of one yard's space that lay between, looked back at the irrecoverable chair, looked down on the distant ground, and then plunged forward with a nervous laugh, and fell into Pete's arms.

"Bravo! Wasn't that nice, Phil? Ever see anything prettier than a child's first step? Again, Kitty, bogh! But go to your *new* father this time. Aisy, now, aisy!" (in a thick voice). "Grive me a kiss first!" (with a choking gurgle). "One more, darling!" (with a broken laugh). "Now face the *other* way. One—two—are you ready, Phil?"

Phil held out his long white trembling hands.

"Yes," with a smothered sob.

"Three—four—and away!"

The child's fingers slipped into Philip's palm; there was another halt, another plunge, another nervous laugh, and then the child was in Philip's arms, his head was over it, and he was clasping it to his heart.

After a moment, Philip, without raising his eyes, said, "Pete!"

But Pete had stolen softly from the room.

"Pete! where are you?"

Where was he? He was on the road outside, crying like a boy—no, like a man—at thought of the happiness he had left upstairs.

XIX.

The town of Peel was in a great commotion that night. It was the night of St. Patrick's Day, and the mackerel fleet were leaving for Kinsale. A hundred and fifty boats lay in the harbour, each with a light in its binnacle, a fire in its cabin, smoke coming from its stove-pipe, and its sails half-set. The sea was fresh; there was a smart breeze from the northwest, and the air was full of the brine. At the turn of the tide the boats began to drop down the harbour. Then there was a rush of women and children and old men to the end of the pier. Mothers were seeing their sons off, women their husbands, children their fathers, girls their boys—all full of fun and laughter and joyful cries.

One of the girls remembered that the men were leaving the island before the installation of the new Governor. Straightway they started a game of make-believe—the make-believe of electing the Governor for themselves.

"Who are you voting for, Mr. Quayle?"—"Aw, Dempster Christian, of coorse."—"Throw us your rope, then, and we'll give you a pull."—"Heave oh, girls." And the rope would be whipped round a mooring-post on the quay, twenty girls would seize it, and the boat would go slipping past the pier, round the castle rocks, and then away before the north-wester like a gull.

"Good luck, Harry!"—"Whips of money coming home, Jem!"—"Write us a letter—mind you write, now Î "—"Goodnight, father!"

No crying yet, no sign of tears—nothing but fresh young faces, bright eyes, and peals of laughter, as one by one the boats slid out into the fresh, green water of the bay, and the wind took them, and they shot into the night. Even the dogs on the quay frisked about, and barked as if they were going crazy with delight.

In the midst of this happy scene, a man, wearing a monkey-jacket and a wide-brimmed soft hat, came up to the harbour with a little misshapen dog at his heels. He stood for a moment as if bewildered by the strange midnight spectacle before him. Then he walked through the throng of young people, and listened awhile to their talk and laughter. No one spoke to him, and he spoke to no one. His dog followed with its nose at his ankles. If some other dog, in youthful frolic, frisked and barked about it, it snarled and snapped, and then croodled down at his master's feet and looked ashamed.

"Dempster, Dempster, getting a bit ould, eh?" said the man.

After a little while he went quietly away. Nobody missed him; nobody had observed him. He had gone back to the town. At a baker's shop, which was still open for the convenience of the departing fleet, he bought a seaman's biscuit. With this he returned to the harbour by way of the shore. At the slip by the Rocket House he went down to the beach and searched among the shingle until he found a stone like a dumb-bell, large at the ends and narrow in the middle. Then he went back to the quay. The dog followed him and watched him.

The last of the boats was out in the bay by this time. She could be seen quite plainly in the moonlight, with the green blade of a wave breaking on her quarter. Somebody was carrying a light on her deck, and the giant shadow of a man's figure was cast up on the new lugsail. There were shouts and answers across the splashing water. Then a fresh young voice on the boat began to sing "Lovely Mona, fare thee well." The women took it up, and the two companies sang it in turns, verse by verse, the women on the quay and the men on the boat, with the sea growing wider between them.

An old fisherman on the skirts of the crowd had a little girl on his shoulder.

"You'll not be going to Kinsale this time, mate?" said a voice behind him.

"Aw, no, sir. I've seen the day, though. Thirty years I was going, and better. But I'm done now."

"Well, that's the way, you see. It's the turn of the young ones now. Let them sing, God bless them! We're not going to fret, though, are we? There's one thing we can always do—we can always remember, and that's some constilation, isn't it."

"I'm doing it reg'lar." said the old fisherman.

"After all, it's been a good thing to live, and when a man's time comes it'll not be such a darned bad thing to die neither. Don't you hould with me there, mate?"

"I do, sir, I do."

The last boat had rounded the castle rock, and its topsail had diminished and disappeared. On the quay the song had ended, and the women and children were turning their faces with a shade of sadness towards the town.

"Well," with a deep universal inspiration, "wasn't it beautiful?"— "Wasn't it?"—"Then what are you crying about?"

The girls laughed at each other with wet eyes, and went off with springless steps. The mothers picked up their children and carried them home whimpering; and the old men went a way with drooping heads and shambling feet.

When all was gone, and the harbour-master had taken his last look round, the man with the dog went to the end of the empty quay, and sat on the mooring post that had served for the running of the ropes. All was quiet enough now. The voices, the singing, the laughter were lost. There was no sound but the gurgle of the ebbing tide, which was racing out with the river's flow between the pier and the castle rock.

The man looked at his dog, stooped to it, gave it the biscuit, and petted it and stroked it while it munched its supper. "Dempster, bogh! Dempster! Getting ould, eh? Travelled far together, haven't we? Tired a bit, aren't you? Couldn't go through another rough journey, anyway. Hard to part, though, Machree! Machree!"

He took the stone out of his pocket, tied it to one end of the string, made a noose on the ether end, slipped it about the dog's neck, and without warning, picked up the dog and stone at once, and dropped them over the pier. The old creature gave a piteous cry as it descended; there was a splash, and then—the racing of the water past the pier.

The man had turned away quickly, and was going heavily along the quay.

XX.

It had been a night of pain to Philip. All the world seemed to be conspiring to hold him back from what he had to do. "Thou shalt not" was the legend that appeared to be written everywhere. Four persons had learnt his secret, and all four seemed to call upon him to hide it. First, the Clerk of the Rolls, who had heard the divorce proceedings within closed doors; next Pete, who might have clamoured the scandal on all hands, and plucked him down from his place, but had chosen to be silent and to slip away unseen; then Cæsar, whose awful self-deception was an assurance of his secrecy; and, finally. Auntie Nan, whose provision for Kate's material welfare had been intended to prevent the necessity for revelation. All these had seemed to say to him, whether from affection or from fear, "Hold your peace. Say nothing. The past is the past; it is dead; it does not exist. Go on with your career. It is only beginning. What right have you to break it up? The island looks to you, waits for you. Step forward and be strong."

Thank God, it was too late to be moved by that temptation. Too late to be bought by that bribe. Already he had taken the irrevocable course, he had made the irrevocable step. He could not now go back.

But the awful penalty of the island's undeceiving! The pain of that moment when everybody would learn that he had deceived the whole world! He was a sham—a whited sepulchre. Every step he had gone up in his quick ascent had been over the body of some one who had loved him too well. First Kate, who had been the victim of the Deemstership, and now Pete, who was paying the price that made him Governor.

He could see the darkened looks of the proud; he could hear the execration of the disappointed; he could feel the tears of the true-hearted at the downfall of a life that had looked so fair. In the frenzy of that last hour of trial, it seemed as if he was contending, not with man and the world, but with the devil, who was using both to make this bitter irony of his position—who was bribing him with worldly glory that he might damn his soul forever.

And therein lay a temptation that sat closer at his side—the temptation to turn his face and fly away. It was midnight. The moon was shining on the boundless plain of the sea. He was in the slack water of the soul, when the ebb is spent, before the tide has begun to flow. Oh, to leave everything behind—the shame and the glory together!

It was the moment when the girls on Peel Quay were pulling the rope for the men on the boats who were ready to vote for Christian.

The pains of sleep were yet greater. He thought he was in Castletown, skulking under the walls of the castle. With a look up towards Parliament House and down to the harbour, he fumbled his private key into the lock of the side entrance to the council chamber. The old caretaker heard him creep-down the long corridor, and she came clattering out with a candle, shaded behind her hand. "Something I've forgotten," he said. "Pardon, your Honour," and then a deep courtesy.

He opened noiselessly the little door leading from the council chamber to the keep, but in the dark shadow of the steps the turnkey challenged him. "Who's there? Stop!"—"Hush!"—"The Deemster! Beg your Honour's pardon."—"Show me the female wards."—"This way your Honour."—"Her cell." "Here, your Honour."—"The key; your lantern. Now go back to the guard-room." He was with Kate. "My love, my love!"—"My darling!"—"Come, let us fly away from the island. I cannot face it. I thought I could, but I cannot. I've got the child too. Come!" And then Kate—"I would go anywhere with you, Philip, anywhere, anywhere. I only want your love. But is this worthy of a man like you? Leave me. We have fallen too low to drop into a pit like that. Away with you! Go!" And he slunk out of the cell, before the wrathful love that would save him from himself. He, the Deemster, the Governor, had slunk out like a dog.

It was only a dream. When he awoke, the birds were singing and the day was blue over the sea. The temptation was past; it was under his feet. He could hesitate no longer; his cup was brimming over; he would drink it to the dregs.

Jem-y-Lord came with his mouth full of news. The town was decorated with bunting. There was to be a general holiday. A grand stand had been erected on the green in front of the Court-house. The people were not going to be deterred by the Deemster's refusals. He who shrank from honours was the more worthy of being honoured. They intended to present their new Governor with an address.

"Let them—let them," said Philip.

Jem looked up inquiringly. His master's face had a strange expression.

"Shall I drive you to-day, your Excellency?"

"Yes, my lad. It may be for the last time, Jemmy."

What was amiss with the Governor? Had the excitement proved too much for him?

XXI.

It was a perfect morning, soft and fresh, and sweet with the odours and the colours of spring. New gorse flashed from the hedges, the violets peeped from the banks; over the freshening green of the fields the young lambs sported, and the lark sang in the thin blue air.

The town, as they dipped into it, was full of life. At the turn of the Court-house the crowd was densest. A policeman raised his hand in front of the horses and Jem-y-Lord drew up. Then the High Bailiff stepped to the gate and read an address. It mentioned Iron Christian, calling him "The Great Deemster"; the town took pride to itself that the first Manx Governor of Man was born in Ramsey.

Philip answered briefly, confining himself to an expression of thanks; there was great cheering and then the carriage moved on. The journey thereafter was one long triumphal passage. At Sulby Street, and at Ballaugh Street, there were flags and throngs of people. From time to time other carriages joined them, falling into line behind. The Bishop was waiting at Bishop's Court, and place was made for his carriage immediately after the carriage of the Governor.

At Tynwald there was a sweet and beautiful spectacle. The children of St. John's were seated on the four rounds of the mount, boys and girls in alternate rows, and from that spot, sacred to the memory of their forefathers for a thousand years, they sang the National Anthem as Philip passed on the road.

The unhappy man lay back in his seat. His eyes filled, his throat rose. "Oh, for what might have been!"

Under Harry Delany's tree a company of fishermen were waiting with a letter. It was from their mates at Kinsale. They could not be at home that day, but their hearts were there. Every boat would fly her flag at the masthead, and at twelve o'clock noon every Manx fisherman on Irish waters would raise a cheer. If the Irishmen asked them what they meant by that, they would answer and say, "It's for the fisherman's friend, Governor Philip Christian."

The unhappy man was no longer in pain. His agony was beyond that. A sort of divine madness had taken possession of him. He was putting the world and the prince of the world behind his back. All this worldly glory and human gratitude was but the temptation of Satan. With God's help he would not succumb. He would resist. He would triumph over everything.

Jem-y-Lord twisted on the box-seat. "See, your Excellency! Listen!"

The flags of Castletown were visible on the Eagle Tower of the castle. Then there was a multitudinous murmur. Finally a great shout. "Now, boys! Three times three! Hip, hip, hurrah!"

At the entrance to the town an evergreen arch had been erected. It bore an inscription in Manx: "*Dooiney Vannin, lhiat myr hoilloo*"— "Man of Man, success as thou deservest."

The carriage had slacked down to a walk.

"Drive quicker," cried Philip.

"The streets are crowded, your Excellency," said Jem-y-Lord.

Flags were flying from every window, from every roof, from every lamp-post. The people ran by the carriage cheering. Their shout was a deafening uproar.

Philip could not respond. "*She* will hear it," he thought. His head dropped. He was picturing Kate in her cell with the clamour of his welcome coming muffled through the walls.

They took the road by the harbour. Suddenly the carriage stopped. The men were taking the horses out of the shafts. "No, no," cried Philip.

He had an impulse to alight, but the carriage was moving again in a moment. "It is the last of my punishment," he thought, and again fell back. Then the shouting and the laughter ran along the quay with the crackle and roar of a fire.

A regiment of soldiers lined the way from the drawbridge to the portcullis. As the carriage drew up, they presented arms in royal salute. At the same moment the band of the regiment inside the Keep played "God save the Queen."

The High Bailiff of the town opened the carriage-door and presented an address. It welcomed the new Governor to the ancient castle wherein his predecessors had been installed, and took fresh assurance of devotion to the Crown from the circumstance that one of their own countrymen had been thought worthy to represent it. No Manxman had ever been so honoured in that island before since the days of the new Governor's own great kinsman, familiarly and affectionately known to all Manxmen through two centuries as Illiam Dhone (Brown William).

Philip replied in few words, the cheering broke out afresh, the band played again, and they entered the castle by the long corridor that led to the council chamber.

In an anteroom the officials were waiting. They were all elderly men and old men, who had seen long and honourable service, but they showed no jealousy. The Clerk of the Rolls received his former pupil with a shout wherein personal pride struggled with respect, and affection with humility. Then the Attorney-General welcomed him in the name of the Bar, as head of the Judicature, as well as head of the Legislature, taking joy in the fact that one of their own profession had been elevated to the highest office in the Isle of Man; glancing at his descent from an historic Manx line, at his brief but distinguished career as judge, which had revived the best traditions of judicial wisdom and eloquence, and finally wishing him long life and strength for the fulfilment of the noble promise of his young and spotless manhood.

"Mr. Attorney-General," said Philip, "I will not accept your congratulations, much as it would rejoice my heart to do so. It would only be another grief to me if you were to repent, as too soon you may, the generous warmth of your reception."

There were puzzled looks, but the sage counsellors could not receive the right impression; they could only understand the reply in the sense that agreed with their present feelings. "It is beautiful," they whispered, "when a young man of real gifts is genuinely modest."

"Excuse me, gentlemen," said Philip, "I must go into my room."

The Clerk of the Rolls followed him, saying—

"Ah! poor Tom Christian would have been a proud man this day—prouder than if the honour had been his own—ten thousand thousand times."

"Have mercy, have mercy, and leave me alone," said Philip.

"I didn't mean to offend you, Christian," said the Clerk.

Philip put one hand affectionately on his shoulder. The eyes of the robustious fellow began to blink, and he returned to his colleagues.

There was a confused murmur beyond the farther wall of the room. It was the room kept for the Deemster when he held court in the council chamber. One of its two doors communicated with the bench. As usual, a constable kept this door. The man loosened his chain and removed his helmet. His head was grey.

"Is the Court-house full?" asked Philip.

The constable put his eye to the eye-hole. "Crowded, your Excellency."

"Keep the passages clear."—"Yes, your Excellency."

"Is the Clerk of the Court present?"—"He is, your Excellency."

"And the jailor?"—"Downstairs, your Excellency."

"Tell both they will be wanted."

The constable turned the key of the door and left the room. Jem-y-Lord came puffing and perspiring.

"The ex-Governor is coming over by the green, sir. He'll be here in a moment."

"My wig and gown, Jemmy," said Philip.

"Deemster's wig, your Excellency?"—"Yes."

"Last time you'll wear it, sir."

"The last, indeed, my lad."

There was a clash of steel outside, followed by the beat of drum.

"He's here," said Jem-y-Lord.

Philip listened. The rattling noise came to him through opening doors and reverberating corridors like the trampling of a wave to a man imprisoned in a cave.

"She'll hear it, too." That thought was with him constantly. In his mind's eye he was seeing Kate, crouching in the fire-seat of the palace room that was now her prison, and covering her ears to deaden the joyous sounds that broke the usual silence of the gloomy walls.

Jem-y-Lord was at the eye-hole of the door. "He's coming on to the bench, sir. The gentlemen of the council are following him, and the Court-house is full of ladies."

Philip was pacing to and fro like a man in violent agitation. At the other side of the wall the confused murmur had risen to a sharp crackle of many voices.

The constable came back with the Clerk of the Court and the jailor.

"Everything ready, your Excellency," said the Clerk of the Court.

The constable turned the key of the door, and laid his hand on the knob.

"One moment—give me a moment," said Philip.

He was going through the last throes of his temptation. Something was asking him, as if in tones of indignation, what right he had to bring people there to make fools of them. And something was laughing as if in mockery at the theatrical device he had chosen for gathering together the people of rank and station, and then dismissing them like naughty school-children.

This idea clamoured loud in wild derision, telling him that he was posing, that he was making a market of his misfortune, that he was an actor, and that whatever the effect of the scene he was about to perform, it was unnecessary and must be contemptible. "You talk of your shame and humiliation—no atonement can wipe it out. You came here prating to yourself of blotting out the past—no act of man can do so. Vain, vain, and idle as well as vain! Mere mummery and display, and a blow to the dignity of justice!"

Under the weight of such torment the thought came to him that he should go through the ceremony after all, that he should do as the people expected, that he should accept the Governorship, and then defy the social ostracism of the island by making Kate his wife. "It's not yet too late," said the tempter.

Philip stopped in his walk and remembered the two letters of yesterday. "Thank God! it *is* too late," he said.

He had spoken the words aloud, and the officers in attendance glanced up at him. Jem-y-Lord was behind, trembling and biting his lip.

It was indeed too late for that temptation. And then the vanity of it, the cruelty and insufficiency of it! He had been a servant of the world long enough. From this day forth he meant to be its master. No matter if all the devils of hell should laugh at him! He was going through with his purpose. There was only one condition on which he could live in the world—that he should renounce it. There was only one way of renouncing the world—to return its wages and strip off its livery. His sin was not only against Kate, against Pete; it was against the island, and the island must set him free.

Philip approached the door, slackened his pace with an air of uncertainty; at one step from the constable he stopped. He was breathing noisily. If the officers had observed him at that moment they must have thought he looked like a man going to execution. But the constable gazed before him with a sombre expression, held his helmet in one hand, and the knob of the door in the other.

"Now," said Philip, with a long inspiration.

There was a flash of faces, a waft of perfume, a flutter of pocket-handkerchiefs, and a deafening reverberation. Philip was in the Court-house.

XXII.

It was remarked that his face was fearfully worn, and that it looked the whiter for the white wig above it and the black gown beneath. His large eyes flamed as with fire. "The sword too keen for the scabbard," whispered somebody.

There is a kind of aloofness in strong men at great moments. Nobody approaches them. They move onward of themselves, and stand or fall alone. Everybody in court rose as Philip entered, but no one offered his hand. Even the ex-Governor only bowed from the Governor's seat under the canopy.

Philip took his customary place as Deemster. He was then at the right of the Governor, the Bishop being on the left. Behind the bishop sat the Attorney-General, and behind Philip the Clerk of the Rolls. The cheers that had greeted Philip on his entrance ended with the clapping of hands, and died off like a wave falling back from the shingle. Then he rose and turned to the Governor.

"I do not know if you are aware, your Excellency, that this is Deemster's Court-day?"

The Governor smiled, and a titter went round the court. "We will dispense with that," he said. "We have better business this morning." 34

"Excuse me, your Excellency," said Philip; "I am still Deemster. With your leave we will do everything according to rule."

There was a slight pause, a questioning look, then a cold answer. "Of course, if you wish it; but your sense of duty——"

The ladies in the galleries bad ceased to flutter their fans, and the members of the House of Keys were shifting in their seats in the well below.

The Clerk of the Deemster's Court pushed through to the space beneath the bench. "There is only one case, your Honour," he whispered up.

"Speak out, sir," said Philip. "What case is it?"

The Clerk gave an informal answer. It was the case of the young woman who had attempted her life at Ramsey, and had been kept at Her Majesty's pleasure.

"How long has she been in prison?"—"Seven weeks, your Honour."

"Give me the book and I will sign the order for her release."

The book was handed to the bench. Philip signed it, handed it back to the Clerk, and said with his face to the jailor—

"But keep her until somebody comes to fetch her."

There had been a cold silence during these proceedings. When they were over, the ladies breathed freely. "You remember the case—left her husband and little child—divorced since, I'm told—a worthless person."—"Ah! yes, wasn't she first tried the day the Deemster fell ill in court?"—"Men are too tender with such creatures."

Philip had risen again. "Your Excellency, I have done the last of my duties as Deemster." His voice had hoarsened. He was a worn and stricken figure.

The ex Governor's warmth had been somewhat cooled by the unexpected interruption. Nevertheless, the pock-marks smoothed out of his forehead, and he rose with a smile. At the same moment the Clerk of the Rolls stepped up and laid two books on the desk before him—a New Testament in a tattered leather binding, and the *Liber Juramentorum*, the Book of Oaths.

"The regret I feel," said the ex-Governor, "and feel increasingly, day by day, at the severance of the ties which have bound me to this beautiful island is tempered by the satisfaction I experience that the choice of my successor has fallen upon one whom I know to be a gentleman of powerful intellect and stainless honour. He will preserve that autonomous independence which has come down to you from a remote antiquity, at the same time that he will uphold the fidelity of a people who have always been loyal to the Crown. I pray that the blessing of Almighty God may attend his administration, and that, if the time ever comes when he too shall stand in the position I occupy to-day, he may have recollections as lively of the support and kindness he has met with, and regrets as deep at his separation from the little Manx nation which he leaves behind."

Then the Governor took the staff of office, and gave the signal for rising. Everybody rose. "And now, sir," he said, turning to Philip with a smile, "to do everything, as you say, according to rule, let us first take Her Majesty's commission of your appointment."

There was a moment's pause, and then Philip said in a cold clear voice—

"Your Excellency, I have no commission. The commission which I received I have returned. I have, therefore, no right to be installed as Governor. Also, I have resigned my office as Deemster, and, though my resignation has not yet been accepted, I am, in reality, no longer in the service of the State."

The people looked at the speaker with eyes that were full of the stupefaction of surprise. Somebody bad risen at the back of the bench. It was the Clerk of the Rolls. He stretched out his hand as if to touch Philip on the shoulder. Then he hesitated and sat down again.

"Gentlemen of the Council and of the Keys," continued Philip, "you will think you have assembled to see a man take a leap into an abyss more dark than death. That is as it may be. You have a right to an explanation, and I am here to make it. What I have done has been at the compulsion of conscience. I am not worthy of the office I hold, still less of the office that is offered me."

There was a half-articulate interruption from behind Philip's chair.

"Ah! do not think, old friend, that I am dealing in vague self depreciation. I should have preferred not to speak more exactly, but what must be, must be. Your Excellency has spoken of my honour as spotless. Would to God it were so; but it is deeply stained with sin."

He stopped, made an effort to begin afresh, and stopped again. Then, in a low tone, with measured utterance, amid breathless silence, he said— "I have lived a double life. Beneath the life that you have seen there has been another—God only knows how full of wrongdoing and disgrace and shame. It is no part of my duty to involve others in this confession. Let it be enough that my career has been built on falsehood and robbery, that I have deceived the woman who loved me with her heart of hearts, and robbed the man who would have trusted me with his soul."

The people began to breathe audibly. There was the scraping of a chair behind the speaker. The Clerk of the Rolls had risen. His florid face was violently agitated.

"May it please your Excellency," he began, faltering and stammering, in a husky voice, "it will be within your Excellency's knowledge, and the knowledge of every one on the island, that his Honour has only just risen from a long and serious illness, brought on by overwork, by too zealous attention to his duties, and that—in fact, that—well, not to blink the plain truth, that——"

A sigh of immense relief had passed over the court, and the Governor, grown very pale, was nodding in assent. But Philip only smiled sadly and shook his head.

"I have been ill indeed," he said, "but not from the cause you speak of. The just judgment of God has overtaken me."

The Clerk of the Rolls sank back into his seat.

"The moment came when I had to sit in judgment on my own sin, the moment when she who had lost her honour in trusting to mine stood in the dock before me. I, who had been the first cause of her misfortunes, sat on the bench as her judge. She is now in prison and I am here. The same law which has punished her failing with infamy has advanced me to power."

There was an icy quiet in the court, such as comes with the first gleam of the dawn. By that quick instinct which takes possession of a crowd at great moments, the people understood everything—the impurity of the character that had seemed so pure, the nullity of the life that had seemed so noble.

"When I asked myself what there was left to me to do, I could see but one thing. It was impossible to go on administering justice, being myself unjust, and remembering that higher bar before which I too was yet to stand. I must cease to be Deemster. But that was only my protection against the future, not my punishment for the past. I could not surrender myself to any earthly court, because I was guilty of no crime against earthly law. The law cannot take a man into the court of the conscience. He must take himself there."

He stopped again, and then said quietly, "My sentence is this open confession of my sin, and renunciation of the worldly advantages which have been bought by the suffering of others."

It was no longer possible to doubt him. He had sinned, and he had reaped the reward of his sin. Those rewards were great and splendid, but he had come to renounce them all. The dreams of ambition were fulfilled, the miracle of life was realised, the world was conquered and at his feet, yet he was there to give up all. The quiet of the court had warmed to a hush of awe. He turned to the bench, but every face was down. Then his own eyes fell.

"Gentlemen of the Council, you who have served the island so long and so honourably, perhaps you blame me for permitting you to come together for the hearing of this confession. But if you knew the temptation I was under to fly away without making it, to turn my back on my past, to shuffle, my fault on to Fate, to lay the blame on Life, to persuade myself that I could not have acted differently, you would believe it was not lightly, and God knows, not vainly, that I suffered you to come here to see me mount my scaffold."

He turned back to the body of the court.

"My countrymen and countrywomen, you who have been so much more kind to me than my character justified or my conduct merited. I say good-bye; but not as one who is going away. In conquering the impulse to go without confessing, I conquered the desire to go at all. Here, where my old life has fallen to ruin, my new life must be built up. That is the only security. It is also the only justice. On this island, where my fall is known, my uprising may come—as is most right—only with bitter struggle and sorrow and tears. But when it comes, it will come securely. It may be in years, in many years, but I am willing to wait—I am ready to labour. And, meantime, she who was worthy of my highest honour will share my lowest degradation. That is the way of all women—God love and keep them!"

The exaltation of his tones infected everybody.

"It may be that you think I am to be pitied. There have been hours of my life when I have been deserving of pity. But they have been the hours, the dark hours, when, in the prodigality of your gratitude, you have loaded me with distinctions, and a shadow has haunted me, saying, 'Philip Christian, they think you a just judge—you are not a just judge; they think you an upright man—you are not an upright man.' Do not pity me now, when the dark hours are passed, when the new life has begun, when I am listening at length to the voice of my heart, which has all along been the voice of God."

His eyes shone, his mouth was smiling.

"If you think how narrowly I escaped the danger of letting things go on as they were going, of covering up my fault, of concealing my true character, of living as a sham and dying as a hypocrite, you will consider me worthy of envy instead. Good-bye! good-bye! God bless you!"

Before any one appeared to be aware that his voice had ceased he was gone from the bench, and the Deemster's chair stood empty. Then the people turned and looked into each other's stricken faces. They were still standing, for nobody had thought of sitting down.

There was no further speaking that day. Without a word or a sign the Governor descended from his seat and the proceedings came to an end. Every one moved towards the door. "A great price to pay for it, though," thought the men. "How he must have loved her, after all," thought the women.

At that moment the big Queen Elizabeth clock of the Castle was striking twelve, and the fishermen on Irish waters were raising a cheer for their friend at home. A loud detonation rang out over the town. It was the report of a gun. There was another, and then a third. The shots were from a steamer that was passing the bay.

Philip remembered—it was Pete's last farewell.

XXIII.

Half an hour later the Keep, the courtyard, and the passage to the portcullis were filled with an immense crowd. Ladies thronged the two flights of external steps to the prisoners' chapel and the council chamber. Men had climbed as high as to the battlements, and were looking down over the beetle-browed walls. All eyes were on the door to the debtors' side of the prison, and a path from it was being kept clear. The door opened and Philip and Kate came out. There was no other exit, and they must have taken it. He was holding her firmly by the hand, and half-leading, half-drawing her along. Under the weight of so many eyes, her head was held down, but those who were near enough to see her face knew that her shame was swallowed up in happiness and her fear in love. Philip was like a man transfigured. The extreme pallor of his cheeks was gone, his step was firm, and his face was radiant. It was the common remark that never before had he looked so strong, so buoyant, so noble. This was the hour of his triumph, not that within the walls; this, when his sin was confessed, when conscience had no power to appal him, when the world and the pride of the world were beneath his feet, and he was going forth from a prison cell, hand in hand with the fallen woman by his side, to face the future with their bankrupt lives.

And she? She was sharing his fiery ordeal. Before her outraged sisters and all the world she was walking with him in the depth of his humiliation, at the height of his conquest, at the climax of his shame and glory.

Once for a moment she halted and stumbled as if under the hot breath that was beating upon her head. But he put his arm about her, and in a moment she was strong. The sun dipped down from the great tower on to his upturned face, and his eyes were glistening through their tears.

THE END.

36241088R00113

The Manxman

by Sir Hall Caine

Copyright © 7/6/2015
Jefferson Publication

ISBN-13: 978-1514862315

Printed in the United States of America